"SHE'S DONE IT AGAIN!
Linda Lay Shuler's second novel,
Voice of the Eagle, proves that
she is the best of those writing about
America's prehistory. Her skillful
weaving of research material and story
makes the fabric of the lives of
the Anasazi woman Kwani—the one
called *She Who Remembers*—and
her people become reality. Shuler has
clothed the shards of pottery and
the bare stones of ancient dwellings
with a rich imagination to give them
the texture of life. This is a beguiling,
moving story of a time long forgotten."
—Jean Auel

TIME OF REMEMBERING AND LOVING

Kwani sat up beside Tolonqua and put her hand on his shoulder where the bear-paw tattoo proclaimed his hunting skills. "You are the honored Hunting Chief, long respected. This is your home. Mine also now." Her voice quavered. "We are who we are. Time will prove the truth of our words."

"Then why do they question my word? Why?" He sounded bitter. So unlike him.

Kwani looked at him, at the intentness of his face. *What was he thinking?* she wondered. She loved him, but did she really know his secret heart? The depths that lay concealed?

She drew him close and the grimness on Tolonqua's face softened. He lay beside her, pulling her down to him, and nestled his face against her hair—Kwani, a woman of serene powers. She Who Remembers.

VOICE OF THE EAGLE

▲▼▲▼▲▼▲▼▲▼▲▼▲▼▲▼▲▼▲▼

Linda Lay Shuler

A SIGNET BOOK

Signet
Published by the Penguin Group
Penguin Books USA Inc., 375 Hudson Street,
New York, New York 10014, U.S.A.
Penguin Books Ltd, 27 Wrights Lane,
London W8 5TZ, England
Penguin Books Australia Ltd, Ringwood,
Victoria, Australia
Penguin Books Canada Ltd, 10 Alcorn Avenue,
Toronto, Ontario, Canada M4V 3B2
Penguin Books (N.Z.) Ltd, 182-190 Wairau Road,
Auckland 10, New Zealand

Penguin Books Ltd, Registered Offices:
Harmondsworth, Middlesex, England

Published by Signet, an imprint of New American Library, a division of Penguin Books USA Inc. This is an authorized reprint of a hardcover edition published by William Morrow and Company, Inc.

First Signet Printing, September, 1993
10 9

For my sons

"It is true, Iquehuac. When mortal danger confronts thee, heed to the ancients in thy blood. Hear the voice of the eagle."

Zaviar Ramón Corte,
Tenochtitlán

▲ Acknowledgments ▼

This is a book of fiction recreating an ancient past where no written record exists. Therefore, I had to rely on the work of many people—historians, anthropologists, archaeologists, and others—to provide a base for the imagination to build upon. Their books are included in the Bibliography, but five were of special help.

I am greatly indebted to the University of Nebraska Press for permission to quote from *Zuñi, Selected Writings of Frank Hamilton Cushing*, an anthropologist sent to New Mexico by the Smithsonian Institution in 1879 to learn about the Zuñis; his book is a fascinating firsthand account. Also invaluable was the work of the great Alfred Vincent Kidder, especially *Pecos, New Mexico: Archaeological Notes*, published by the Phillips Academy in 1958. Such insight that man had!

My thanks to Loretta A. Barrett for sending me a copy of *The Mystic Warriors of the Plains*, a massive, gorgeously illustrated volume by Thomas E. Mails published by Doubleday in 1972, to which I referred often. Also indispensable was *Sun Chief, The Autobiography of a Hopi Indian*, published by Yale University Press in 1942, and *The Anasazi*, by J. Richard Ambler, published by the Museum of Northern Arizona in 1977.

To my peerless agent, Jean V. Naggar, and inimitable editor, Liza Dawson, my admiration and sincere gratitude.

Thanks to Dr. A. Michael Schultz, and to Kenneth W. Taylor, Fire Chief of Brownwood, Texas, for professional advice. Thanks also to Curtis Schaafsma and Laura Holt, of the Laboratory of Anthropology in Santa Fe, for research assistance. I am indebted to Wes Phillips for a personally conducted tour of the Alibates flint quarries in the Texas Panhandle, and for the loan of his personal copy of *The Pawnee Indians* by George E. Hyde, an excellent reference.

They say writing is a lonely business, and so it is. Encouragement and helpful critiques from colleagues ease the isolation. Herewith my special thanks to M. K. Wren, Joe and Naomi Stokes, and to the Circuit Writers of Brownwood, especially Charlotte Laughlin and Helen Perrin.

Above all, my heartfelt gratitude to my family, especially my husband, Bob, who *listened*, and who applied his logical IQ to problems of plotting—and made lunch when I was too busy. Our daughter Linda, the drama teacher, reviewed the entire manuscript; her fine dramatic hand is evident throughout. Suzi, the EMT expert, advised me on medical matters. Son John, the Alaskan university instructor, spent endless hours teaching me the magic of a computer and WordPerfect. Ed, the electronics whiz, cheered me on.

Bless you all!

The "Towas" of this story were of the *Paequiu* (or *Paequiula*) tribe, known today as "The People of Pecos Pueblo" (Cicuye). However, they spoke Towa and are identified as such in this book.

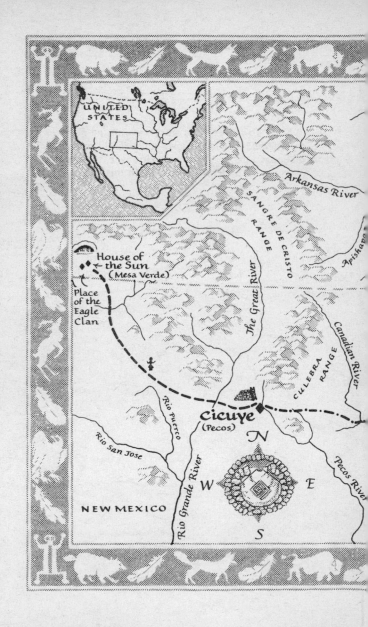

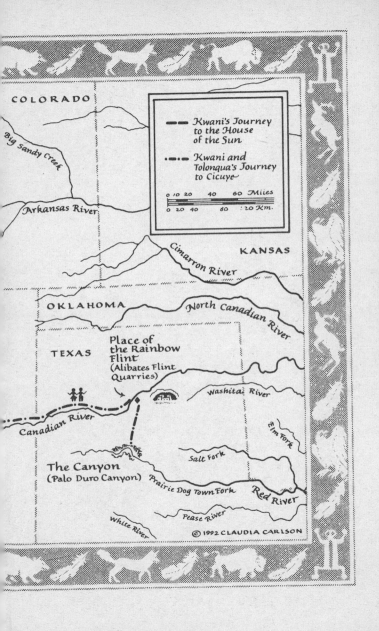

COLORADO

Big Sandy Creek

Arkansas River

Kwani's Journey
to the House
of the Sun

Kwani and
Tolonqua's Journey
to Cicuye

0 10 20   40   60 Miles

0 20 40   80   120 Km.

Cimarron River

KANSAS

North Canadian River

OKLAHOMA

TEXAS

Place of
the Rainbow
Flint
(Alibates Flint
Quarries)

Washita River

Canadian River

Elm Fork

The Canyon
(Palo Duro Canyon)

Salt Fork

Prairie Dog Town Fork

Red River

White River

Pease River

© 1992 CLAUDIA CARLSON

▲ Prologue ▼

The light in the Chief's kiva was dim; only bits of sky showed around the edges of the woven yucca mat covering the entrance overhead. Coals in the fire pit cast a faint glow upon the solemn faces of Chiefs and Elders gathered in conference. They sat in a semicircle facing the fire pit and the altar upon which were prayer sticks, a small bowl of corn pollen—the substance most sacred—and other objects of powerful medicine.

In this circular ceremonial room, dug into Earthmother's domain, chosen men of the clan communed with gods, beseeched the spirits, and discussed important matters among themselves. Above, their proud stone city rose terrace upon terrace, the finest of all the great cave cities built high into cliffs soaring from the canyon floor. Only eagles shared these impregnable heights. Yet the people, proud as their noble city, confronted overwhelming disaster.

Huzipat, the aged Clan and Elder Chief, sat in silent concentration, communing with the spirits of the sacred objects, and wondering how he could say what he must. Sounds of the city, shouts and laughter, snatches of song and the shrill notes of a bone flute, filtered down into the kiva, contrasting with the air of foreboding that hung like invisible smoke. The old Chief folded his hands upon his crossed legs, and bent his chin to his chest. From under shaggy brows he glanced at the others who sat cross-legged, eyes downcast.

All but Zashue.

The young Medicine Chief, whose ragged scar from ear to mouth lifted his lips to a permanent snarl, sat stiffly, gazing stonily ahead. Plotting vengeance, Huzipat knew. Ever since Kwani, who called herself She Who Remembers, had ravaged Zashue's face with her spear and escaped unpunished and unharmed, taking the sacred necklace with her, Zashue lived only for revenge.

Huzipat sighed. Moons had waxed and waned since Kwani

had left with Kokopelli, he of the sacred seed and magical charms, he who played the flute and commanded animals. Huzipat frowned and stared down at his clasped hands so he would not have to look at Zashue whose hatred gnawed at him endlessly, corroding his inner being. How could Zashue be truly a Medicine Chief, healing his people and communing with gods, if his spirit rotted like a decomposing corpse?

At last, he raised his hand in gesture-before-speaking. His voice was calm. "We have fasted, we have sought visions, we have prayed and made sacrifices, yet punishments affect us still. The gods are not appeased." His voice faltered. "We must leave this place."

"No!" It was a cry of despair from them all. All but Zashue whose snarl widened as he said, "Yes! Yes, we go to find the witch who brought death and sickness and who drove away the Cloud People so no rain falls!"

The old Chief rose with dignified authority. "Four moons have passed since Kokopelli took Kwani away. We go to continue our migrations as Masau'u instructed our grandfathers. To honor our Creator. This you know, all of you. Perhaps the gods punish us because we have lingered here too long. It is time, past time, to depart."

Heads bowed in agonized acceptance. Only Zashue held his head high. "The witch has taken the sacred necklace of She Who Remembers. It belongs to us, to our clan, to those who came before us and to those who will come after. It is *ours*." His voice shook with intensity. "We shall go, and we shall find her."

Huzipat speared him with a glance. "No! We are informed that she and Kokopelli have gone east. We must go south where others have gone, to join pueblos along the river. We shall have water again, much water, and we shall grow fine crops again. We go south. I have spoken."

Zashue did not reply. He gazed grimly into space, touching his hand to his scarred face.

Far to the east, a moon's journey away, another kiva fire burned low in the Towa village of Cicuye. Chiefs and Elders had talked long into the night. Now they sat gazing into smoldering coals as Two Elk, Chief of the Towa, spoke again.

"Why do you murmur against me because I allowed our Hunting Chief to serve as guide for Kokopelli and his mate on their journey eastward through the plains? It was my duty to do so.''

"But he has been gone much too long!" an elder said. "He should have returned before now."

"Aye." The Medicine Chief peered at Two Elk solemnly. "I fear for Tolonqua. Something bad has happened to him." There was a moment of strained silence as the Chiefs and Elders considered this. Shadows danced eerily on the kiva walls. Far away, wolves howled in the night.

Finally, a young Chief cleared his throat tentatively. "You have been granted a vision?"

"A dream. I saw our Hunting Chief in great danger. I saw a struggle, and blood. Much blood. Enemies. . . ."

"What of his mate?"

"Danger." He shook his head. "That is all I know."

"Maybe Tolonqua has followed Kokopelli to his home beyond the Great River of the South. Maybe—"

"No!" the Crier Chief said. "Tolonqua would not desert his people."

Heads nodded. Tolonqua was the best Hunting Chief the Towa ever had and intensely loyal. Never would he desert his people!

"It was I who had a vision," the Sun Chief said quietly. "I saw our village abandoned, all of us gone—"

There were shocked murmurs.

"Why?"

"The gods are displeased. That is why something has happened to our Hunting Chief. We are being punished."

An aged elder shook a bony finger at Two Elk. "Surely they are displeased that you allowed Tolonqua to serve as guide and protector to Kokopelli, the Toltec, and She Who Remembers, the Anasazi. We are *Towa* and protectors of our own."

Again there was silence. Ever since Kokopelli, the trader and magician, he of the sacred seed, arrived in Cicuye with Kwani, the blue-eyed Anasazi woman, Tolonqua had shown unseemly interest in Kokopelli's mate. The woman was eight moons pregnant, but beautiful nonetheless, and Tolonqua was not the only man in Cicuye who desired her. Two moons had passed since they left with Tolonqua to guide them to where Kokopelli would obtain a boat and sail with his mate to his distant homeland.

Tolonqua's infatuation with She Who Remembers was obvious. Had he followed them?

Had he been killed?

The Chiefs and Elders stared grimly at their folded hands.

What happened to the Hunting Chief?

Where was he?

PART 1

▲▼▲▼▲▼▲▼▲▼▲▼▲▼▲▼▲▼

CICUYE
A.D. 1272

▲ 1 ▼

Cautiously, Tolonqua followed the bank around a bend, ignoring the footprints his buffalo-hide moccasins left upon the sand.

What he desperately sought was not there.

The canyon was narrow, twisting, thick with brush. On either side, jagged sandstone cliffs—red, green, gray, brown—soared in tortuous formations to an awakening sky. A small river, little more than a stream, ran noisily over rocks and around boulders. Its voice was the only sound in this remote place.

Or was it?

He paused by the stream, listening, alert and motionless, scanning shadows among the boulders, the bushes, the trees. There was no motion but the wind, no sound but the river.

Tall, and lean as a jackrabbit, he walked slowly, searching the bank. Twenty-three winters had hardened his body and the summers had bronzed his red-brown skin. His face, with its high cheekbones and aquiline noise, bore an expression of accustomed authority. An ornately woven cotton band across his forehead held an upright eagle feather fastened in the back and notched in a manner to proclaim his status as Hunting Chief of the Towa. Eyes black as obsidian gazed intently ahead to where the stream rounded another bend. Perhaps what he searched for was farther down. He inspected every eddy, every small cove.

It was not there.

His fresh footprints contrasted with those of the Querecho he had killed nine days ago. Were others of the tribe waiting in ambush?

Tolonqua paused again, watching for a sudden flight of birds or other sign that would betray a hidden enemy. The Querechos of this canyon were implacable killers, expert in ambush. They could be hiding anywhere in the twists and turns, among the trees or the bushes, or behind boulders along the banks. For nine days Tolonqua had searched these

banks, searched the river, but what he sought and must find
was missing. Gone.

He glanced uneasily about. He was at a disadvantage, a
stranger here, a Towa from the village of Cicuye, a moon's
journey away.

Was that a sound? He paused, listening tensely.

These canyon Querechos knew every rock, every tree,
every hiding place. The one who attacked had watched, hidden, and knew when Kwani was giving birth in a cave by
the riverbank. The attack was sudden, silent, and savage.

A movement among the trees? He froze in sudden alarm.
Perhaps other Querechos knew he had killed their kinsman!
Perhaps they knew he had left Kwani and the baby alone,
unprotected!

Thinking of them vulnerable to attack back there in the
cave by the river made his heart jerk. The body of the man
he had killed lay in a hidden place, but if Querechos found
what he had been searching for they would know an enemy
was in their domain. Pursuit and terrible revenge would
surely follow.

The canyon lay in the shadow of early morning; the stream
was noisy, but peaceful. *Deceptive!* All hunters of these
southwestern plains knew how this stream could become a
raging animal clawing at the banks, digging itself deeper.
Tolonqua glanced at the sky where dark clouds formed. It
would storm soon, and the rising river would wash his footprints away.

A few drops of rain fell. A swollen river could climb to
the cave where Kwani and the baby waited. He must return!
Swiftly, he rounded a bend, leaping over brush and rocks
that littered the canyon floor. Slopes mingled with steep
cliffs. Low shrubs and scraggly bushes grew everywhere; in
many places there was not a single level spot. The canyon
rim was the horizon below which the land—crumpled, jagged, tortured—twisted convulsively.

The wind turned cool and heavy black clouds hung low.
The brilliant colors of the cliff walls grew dim. A hawk
swooped over the water. Tolonqua ran faster. He must reach
the cave before the river rose.

Suddenly he stopped. Ahead, a tall cottonwood tree
leaned over the stream. This was a holy place; a miracle
had occurred here. He gestured in reverence and approached with bowed head. Beneath the tree, a dark stain
on the rocky soil marked the sacred spot. He stood solemnly, gazing at it, then up into the leafy branches. This

tree had absorbed the life blood of the White Buffalo, Chief of all buffalo, a Spirit Being.

As a boy, Tolonqua had gone into the wilderness to seek his manhood vision—a vision that would reveal what his talisman and protecting spirit would be. The White Buffalo had appeared to him! It promised that they would meet again.

As he grew to manhood, Tolonqua waited, knowing that if he proved worthy, one day the robe of the White Buffalo would be his. Possessing such a robe would endow him, his clan, his sons and their sons with good fortune and enormous prestige to be handed down, generation after generation, for as long as the sacred robe endured. He, Tolonqua, would be the first Towa to be so honored since his people emerged from the three underworlds to enter this, the Fourth World.

Years passed. At last the promise was fulfilled.

Here, nine days ago, under this tree, Tolonqua encountered the White Buffalo! It had faced him, waiting, offering to be taken.

A miracle!

The great, proud Being had stood in dappled shadow under the cottonwood tree. Tolonqua stopped in his tracks, staring in awe. As he stood there, the White Buffalo approached in grandeur, great head lowered, and gazed at Tolonqua with hypnotic pink eyes. Tolonqua returned the gaze with a strange awareness; it was as if the Spirit Being spoke. "I await the arrow."

Humbly and with exaltation, Tolonqua raised his bow and sped the arrow true.

Now, as he looked down at the dark stain beneath the tree, gratitude welled up in Tolonqua's heart. Murmuring a prayer of homage and of thankfulness, he reached into a pouch at his side, removed a small handful of cornmeal, and sprinkled it upon the stain. The spirits of the tree and of the White Buffalo were united now. Again, he gazed into the leafy branches; the leaves shivered as the wind passed. He gestured a sign of thanks and blessing, and hurried on to where Kwani and the baby waited alone with the sacred hide and flesh of the Spirit Being in their keeping.

The skin of the White Buffalo lay stretched upon the ground, held securely by pegs around the edges. Kwani bent over it, scraping away fat and gristle with her flint scraping stone. She worked carefully, blue eyes intent—blue eyes that marked her, set her apart from normal, brown-eyed people. Her long, dark hair and her necklace with the scallop-shell pendant fell free, swinging back and forth as she worked. Now and again she glanced nervously up and down the canyon, pausing to listen and to search for a sign of something or someone approaching.

Where was Tolonqua? She glanced uneasily downstream. He had hurried away without telling her why.

Beside her in a cradle board, her newborn son, Acoya, seemed to watch her solemnly with his round, dark eyes. How beautiful was her child! His fuzz of black hair, soft as eagle down, stirred in the breeze. He, too, was marked, but gloriously.

Nine days ago, before Acoya's birth and before Tolonqua encountered the White Buffalo, it had come to her in the stream. Kwani remembered her astonished wonder as the Spirit Being appeared on the opposite bank and waded the river, gazing at her. It was as though he spoke without words, telling her the child would be born, it would be a son, and that he, the White Buffalo, would be the boy's guardian spirit. Now Acoya bore proof—an outline of a buffalo head on the sole of his tiny right foot! A miracle too wonderful to believe.

Kwani placed both hands upon the skin stretched on the ground, and murmured a prayer of gratitude.

But she wished she felt differently. Since Acoya's birth, a strange sadness nagged at her spirit. She didn't sing anymore.

If only she did not have to travel the long distance back to Cicuye; if only she could be sure she would be welcome there as Tolonqua's mate! When she and Kokopelli passed through there before, she was Kokopelli's mate. Now that Kokopelli was gone, would they accept her, an Anasazi, as mate of a Towa Hunting Chief?

All her life Kwani had longed for a home and people of her own. But because she was different she could never belong. Because her eyes were blue.

Kwani sighed. Since the baby was born, depression enveloped her like a heavy, dark mantle. She wished she had paid more attention to birthings, but it was her mother, not she, who helped babies to be born and understood how women felt afterward. Kwani sat back on her heels, thinking how happy her mother would be to know she was safe. She was in Sipapu now, where ancestors dwelled, but sometimes she came to Kwani in dreams.

Kwani glanced behind her at the cave where Acoya was born. When her time was due, Tolonqua had brought them here. Kwani remembered how Kokopelli helped her, using his healing skills, as always. But when she woke, he was gone. Because she was Anasazi, a Pueblo, and he, a Toltec nobleman. He realized she would never want her son raised as a Toltec in a faraway place.

He left gifts. And memories.

A cold breeze carried the smell of rain. Kwani glanced at dark clouds pressing low; it would storm soon. Where was Tolonqua?

Always, Kwani had known that Tolonqua loved her. Now Tolonqua was her mate and she loved him. But differently than she had loved Kokopelli. Kokopelli seemed magical, somehow; almost a god. Tolonqua was real, a Pueblo like herself. Their spirits touched.

Thunder growled in the distance.

Surely, Tolonqua would return soon. He could not be hunting; already they had more meat than they could carry home, even with the travois he had fashioned—two parallel poles drawn close together at one end with three crosswise wooden braces. It would carry a heavy load but would be hard to pull. Tolonqua would grasp a pole at the wide end in each hand and drag the load behind him. How could he do it in this rocky canyon with brush and boulders and humps and hollows and steep banks? But he must. The hide of the White Buffalo was infinitely valuable; it could not be abandoned here.

Before Kokopelli departed, he left fine blankets, baskets, bowls, mugs, shells from distant seas, flint knives, bone needles, salt, and many lengths of strong yucca twine. And his heavy golden necklace for Acoya to wear when he became a man. They were wealthy! Dogs were needed to carry it all. But they had only themselves.

The breeze hinted at approaching autumn. She tucked Acoya's covering more snugly around his neck, laid him beside her, and pulled her robe closely about her. Made of cotton, ornamented with shell beads, it tied in a knot over her right shoulder, leaving the other shoulder bare. She pushed her hair back with both hands. Usually she wore it in the traditional squash-blossom style, a roll high over each ear, but the brushing and arranging took much time, time that could not be spared. The priceless skin of the White Buffalo required immediate attention. Already the meat, cut into strips, dried on poles suspended by forked sticks. Jerky would not spoil and would be easier to carry.

Again, she inspected the sky; clouds pressed lower. The jerky should be moved into the cave. What they could not carry would have to be stored until they could return for it.

Across the stream a flock of squawking crows flew up and away. Something had disturbed them. Tolonqua? She slid down the bank and peered uneasily upstream, but saw no one. Could it be Querechos hiding, knowing she was alone? A spasm of fear shook her, remembering.

. . . in the cave, nine days ago . . .

. . . clutching the rocky wall, bracing herself against the pain.

A child's body struggling to emerge from her own. Shouts outside the cave.

Sudden silence.

Howls. An attack! They were being attacked! What was happening to Tolonqua and Kokopelli?

Pain. Her voice like an animal's.

The head. A child's body pushing between her thighs.

Screams. Her own?

Savage yells. Closer.

Her own voice shrieking, calling. "Kokopelli!"

Now Kokopelli was gone. Where was Tolonqua? Were Querechos out there, waiting to attack again?

She ran outside, snatched the baby, and darted back into the cave. She pushed the cradle board into a corner, jerked a blanket from the sleeping mat, and tossed it over the baby, concealing him. He whimpered.

"Hush! Go to sleep!" she whispered.

Frantically, she rummaged in Tolonqua's pack and found his hunting knife, a sharp flint blade fastened to a bone handle. Grasping it in both hands, she inched to the cave's entrance and peered outside.

She saw it. A coyote! Drinking at the stream.

Relief flooded her. "Ho, Brother Coyote!" she called.

He lifted his nose and trotted away.

Kwani laughed and tossed the knife aside. How foolish were her fears! She lifted the blanket from the cradle board. Again, the baby whimpered.

"You are hungry?"

She unlaced the deerskin wrapping on the front of the board and lifted the baby out. He waved his arms and legs in freedom. She sat down and held him to her breast, crooning as he nursed. How fortunate she was to have this beautiful child! To be depressed made no sense at all.

A quick step outside! She muffled a cry.

Tolonqua entered and bent over her, smiling. "I greet you," he said, using the Anasazi phrase that Kwani had taught him.

"My heart rejoices." The customary response, and so true now. "Why did you go? We have meat—"

He sat beside her. "I did not tell you before, but when Kokopelli and I battled the Querecho, I did this with Kokopelli's sword." He drew his finger quickly across his throat. "The head rolled down the bank to the stream."

Kwani gasped. *"The head?"*

Tolonqua nodded, remembering the grimacing face and bleeding neck as the severed head tumbled down the bank leaving the headless body sprawled on the ground.

"I tried to find the head, to bury it so it would not be found. It is gone."

"Oh!" She glanced nervously at the cave entrance. "What if—"

Beheading without burial was a terrible thing, even for an enemy. The spirit would wander restlessly, searching for the head so that the spirit could escape through the opening at the top to enter Sipapu.

Was the canyon haunted now?

"Do not be afraid," Tolonqua said. "We will leave before it rains. Soon we will be out of the canyon and on the plain."

The plain offered few hiding places; enemies could be detected. Not like here, in the canyon, where an entire clan could hide in the twists and gullies. Kwani looked up at her mate, at the lean young face with strong lines, at the black eyes that warmed as her gaze met his, and she was reassured.

Thunder boomed close.

Kwani tucked Acoya back in the cradle board, and she and Tolonqua hurried outside. Tolonqua yanked up the stakes holding the buffalo skin while Kwani pulled armloads of jerky from the drying racks.

He sat on his heels, thinking. It would be no easy task to carry a large pack and haul the travois as well. Scraping had made the hide weigh less, but it was still much too heavy to carry. Then there was the jerky, and all the valuables Kokopelli had left and Kwani's personal belongings, and his own.

And the baby.

He and Kwani would have to lighten their packs. He dumped everything out, and tools and utensils and clothing and the valuables left by Kokopelli tumbled to the floor.

Kwani looked at all their belongings scattered about. "Why do you do this?" she cried.

Surely, he did not think she would leave those things behind. "They are mine—"

"Of course. But it is too much to carry. We must leave some behind and return for it later."

"I must have my medicine arrow with me. The Medicine Chief shot his arrow to kill witches at me but it refused to find me. It protects me! And I shall need diapering. And the brush for my hair . . ."

How like a woman! he thought. We have to get out of this canyon fast and she wants a hairbrush! But he said, "Very well. But first we must get the buffalo hide onto the travois."

They lay the travois on the ground and pulled the hide onto it, hair side up. Tolonqua spread it flat.

"Now the meat."

They piled jerky on top of the hide, and Tolonqua folded the four sides of the hide over the meat to make a bundle and tied it securely to each pole with yucca twine rope. He wrapped more jerky in a torn piece of old garment, making a small bundle easy to open at mealtimes, and fastened it to the travois.

Kwani looked at the load doubtfully. "You can pull that through the canyon?"

"I must."

True, Kwani knew. The skin of the White Buffalo was a priceless treasure. And the meat would give spiritual powers to all who partook of it.

Inside the cave they looked at all their other valuables scattered on the floor. Tolonqua said, "Take only what you can carry along with the baby. I will carry the rest." He began to stuff his pack.

She made her selections and regarded the remainder. His own pack bulged with turquoise and the golden necklace and other treasures left by Kokopelli. Much of the jerky still remained.

Kwani said, "We must store the rest of the meat until we can come back for it."

"There is no time. It will rain soon." He stepped to the cave entrance. The river was rising. They had to get out of there. "We must hurry!" He lifted her pack, hefting it uncertainly. "You put too much in here; it is too heavy."

Why did he think she couldn't carry a heavy pack when she had been doing just that ever since they left Cicuye? Now that they were returning was she suddenly a small girl unable to carry a woman's load? Ha!

"Let me try."

He lifted the pack to her back and she adjusted the carrying thong across her forehead. It was, indeed, much too heavy but she would never admit it.

"I will carry it. And Acoya, also."

"You can do this?" He looked doubtful.

"Yes."

"We must go!"

Jerky still hung outside on the drying racks.

"The meat—"

"We can carry no more. We must leave the rest." He tried to curb his impatience. They must hurry!

"No! It is not for ravens, for wolves, for animals that wander by. It is the meat of the White Buffalo!"

"It is dangerous to linger here!" Why was she being so unreasonable? "We must go. Now!"

Kwani was embarrassed to find her eyes shiny with unwanted tears. She was being a small girl after all. "At least carry it into the cave to be protected from rain." Her voice was soft and pleading. "Please!"

He looked into her blue eyes and his heart melted. Without a word he strode to the racks, removed the rest of the drying strips, an armload full, and carried them into the cave. After a while, he returned.

"I put the meat on a ledge. Animals cannot reach it."

She smiled. "Thank you."

It was hard to resist her smile, and he smiled back. He hoisted his heavy pack onto his back and stepped between the two poles of the travois. Grasping a pole with each hand, he dragged the load along the ground. Kwani saw the muscles bulge on his arms and back as he bent forward, straining. She followed, bent under her own heavy load, holding the cradle board with Acoya in both arms. She felt the pressure of it against the scallop shell of her necklace, and was comforted. It was the necklace of She Who Remembers, the talisman of all those before her.

That is who I am, she thought. *I am one with the Ancient Ones, all who were She Who Remembers before me.*

Her load seemed lighter now, and her spirit lifted. She

was on her way to Cicuye, Tolonqua's home that would now be hers. Not since her people drove her away to die alone had she had a home of her own. Or a child of her own. Or security. How fortunate she was! All her yearning dreams would be fulfilled.

She followed Tolonqua over the rocky terrain. She struggled to use both arms to carry the cradle board and the baby and could not brush away hanging branches or thorny bushes that clutched at her.

They paused to rest. The stream rushed more noisily over its rocky bed; otherwise there was no sound but the wind. On either side, the cliffs soared to the plain, their brilliant colors dimmed by shadow. The air tasted of rain. A few drops fell, then more.

With great effort, Tolonqua dragged the travois higher along the bank. Kwani struggled after him, panting. The carrying thong of her pack cut into her forehead, and the cradle board with her sleeping baby grew heavier.

Thunder boomed; lightning cracked and hissed. Acoya began to cry. Suddenly rain fell as if a huge sky bowl of water overturned, dumping its contents into the canyon. Kwani, drenched, tried to stumble on, carrying the cradle board and her heavy pack.

"Up there!"

Tolonqua pointed up the slope where an overhang from the cliff jutted outward, forming a small shelter underneath. He tried to drag the travois up the rocky slope, but the heavy travois dug into the wet soil and slid this way and that.

"I will help." Kwani took a pole in one hand and the two of them dug their feet into the muddy, rocky soil. They fought the travois up the slope to the shelter as rain pounded down.

They huddled against the cliff with the travois beside them. The wind blew in some rain, but they were protected from the force of the downpour.

The baby cried louder. Kwani rocked him in her arms, crooning to him. Thunder boomed repeatedly and lightning lit the canyon with an eerie glow.

"We must reach the trail to the plain!" Tolonqua pulled a blanket from his pack. "Here. It will keep some of the rain off. Put the baby inside it; I will carry the cradle board."

Kwani tucked Acoya in the blanket and he snuggled against her chest. Fumbling in haste, Tolonqua tied the cradle board to his pack with yucca twine.

"Now we go." Tolonqua shouldered his pack, gripped the poles of the travois, and stepped outside, bending and panting under his load. Kwani followed.

The river was rising swiftly. Kwani saw it churning where the canyon narrowed; the water boiled around a bend choked with boulders. She felt a stab of alarm. The canyon that had once seemed peaceful was peaceful no longer.

As they tried to climb higher on the slope, the heavy load of the travois dug into the ground and slid erratically back and forth to Tolonqua's muttered curses. Rocks, loosened by the downpour, tumbled down. Kwani dodged one. She slipped and fell, clutching the baby.

"Tolonqua!"

He whirled, let go of the travois, and slid after her, digging his heels into the ground and grabbing brush to steady himself. "Don't move!" he shouted. "I'm coming!"

Kwani tried to remain motionless, but she felt herself sliding headfirst to the river. Pebbles dug into her back and scraped her legs. Thorny brush scratched and tore. Sliding mud pushed her down and down.

Was this the dead Querecho's revenge? To drown her and the baby in the ravenous river?

Kwani tried to stop sliding and snatched desperately at brush, but the river roared in her ears. Helplessly, she dug her heels into the mud but water lapped at her hair, tugging her to be swept away. The baby screamed and she clutched him closer. She saw Tolonqua climbing down to her and the travois sliding crazily after him.

Desperately, she prayed to the Ancient Ones. "Help us!"

Tolonqua lost his footing and began to slide down sidewise. The travois careened past and tipped over at the water's edge. The small bundle of jerky fell out and disappeared in the river.

Kwani's cooking pot, two mugs, and a bowl broke loose from her pack, tumbled to the water's edge, and lay nearby. She flung out an arm for them.

"Stop!" Tolonqua grabbed a branch of a small juniper tree, steadied himself, slid cautiously the rest of the way down, grabbed Kwani's arm, and dragged her back up.

She scrambled to her feet. "Get the travois!"

He pulled the travois from the water's edge. Kwani's cooking pot and the mugs and bowl were swallowed by the river, which grew more ravenous as it grew in strength. He dragged the travois to where Kwani, streaked with mud, clutched the screaming baby. Pouring rain beat down. She stared at the river, watching her prized belongings career around the bend. The jerky had disappeared. What gods were these to transform a peaceful stream into this? She shivered.

"Let's go back to the shelter." Anything to get the baby out of this downpour.

"No. The trail is ahead, up there. We have to reach it. We will be safe then."

Together they dragged the travois up the treacherous slope, pausing now and then to brace themselves against the roots of scraggly shrubs. Above, cliff walls rose steeply in jagged formation. Below, the swollen river surged wildly around the bend where the canyon narrowed, obliterating the bank. The trail leading up to the plain lay ahead. They were nearly there.

He glanced at Kwani struggling under her too-heavy load. Women were accustomed to heavy loads, he knew, but perhaps it had been a mistake to allow her to carry so much.

He looked at her again. In the pouring rain she bent under her load with the carrying thong pressed deeply against her forehead. Her face strained with weariness as she plodded beside him. Her mouth, usually sweet with soft curves, was grim with effort. He felt a surge of tenderness and concern. When they reached the plain and were free from danger, he would make camp and she could rest. Perhaps, rested, she would be more like the person she had been before the baby came. Maybe she would want to sing again. And make love again . . .

"I can pull the travois alone now. Give me the pole."

Kwani nodded, relieved, and plodded after him.

The gods threw lightning spears with terrifying power, shouting so all might fear their might. Their voices boomed through the canyon, echoing and reechoing. The cliff walls, the ground, even the air seemed to shudder.

Raindrops bounced on boulders, dug small trenches on the banks, and ran down to the river rising to meet them. Kwani struggled after Tolonqua, blanket pulled low over her bent head to keep out some of the downpour. Water poured from the blanket in rivulets. Acoya sobbed no longer; he whimpered like a puppy wanting in from the rain.

"Be courageous!" Kwani whispered to him. But she thought, It is I who must be courageous. She remembered the words of the Old One who was She Who Remembers before her. *"We who are She Who Remembers are not of one clan, one people. We are of all womankind and must endure much. It is struggle that strengthens and makes us aware, that tempers the spirit and opens the mind's eye.''*

Strength flowed into her. She stood straight and let the rain wash her face. She looked down at the river and was not afraid. The trail to the plain lay ahead. Soon they would be there.

"Tolonqua!" she called.

He turned, his face drawn with strain.

She smiled at him. "We are nearly there!"

Her buoyant voice, her smile, the way she stood, warmed his blood. His pack seemed lighter and the travois easier to pull. "Yes! It's just around the bend."

The rain stopped as suddenly as it had begun. Kwani pulled the dripping blanket back from her head and from Acoya. "See?" she told him. "The rain has gone away."

Tolonqua pointed. "There's the trail!"

As they rounded the bend, the canyon widened. The trail, worn deep by countless buffalo, wound upward to the plain. The going was easier now. Soon they reached the trail. As they climbed higher, they looked back and could see beyond the bend.

Tolonqua stopped, staring intently into the canyon. Something moved down there.

"What is it?" Kwani asked.

"I am not sure." He continued to gaze.

"Who?"

He turned away and did not reply. But Kwani had seen them.

Two men.

The severed head wobbled as it swept downstream. The eyes, open and staring, seemed to search for what had been left behind. Black hair squirmed in the water; no sound came from the gaping mouth. Small fish followed and nibbled at bits and pieces of the neck while the head bumped into rocks, whirled crazily in the water's eddy, and bobbed away, appearing and disappearing in the river.

▲ 2 ▼

Kwani trudged after Tolonqua as he pulled the travois with its heavy load over the uneven terrain of the plains. It was the second day since they had left the canyon and Sunfather's hot breath had dried the ground and the grasses. Prairie dogs darted into their holes, barking tiny alarms as the intruders approached. Tolonqua tried to avoid them but sometimes the colonies were enormous and it was necessary to go around them. Now and again, the travois bumped over rocks hidden in the dun-colored grass; once, it nearly turned over, to Tolonqua's muttered curses.

He stopped and wiped perspiration from his face. "I need dogs to pull this load."

"And mine." She slipped the carrying thong from her forehead and let her pack fall to the ground. She sat on it and looked up at him. "Let's rest awhile."

He reached for the baby. "Give him to me. I'll hold him now."

She handed Acoya to him gratefully and sat on the ground to use her pack as a backrest. In every direction the plains swept to an unbroken horizon, empty, endless. All her life she had been surrounded by mountains and by sheltering cliffs. Here there was nothing to lean the eyes against, nothing to offer protection. She felt totally exposed and vulnerable, pierced with homesickness for the canyons and cliffs she knew. Yet it was from there she had been driven away. She must face the present, forget the past.

"Where will we get dogs?"

"At the Place of the Rainbow Flint if we do not encounter hunters with dogs before then." He shaded his eyes with his hand and peered into the distance. "Hunters come for buffalo."

Kwani had heard of the place where the valuable colored flint was found, but she was anxious to reach journey's end at Cicuye. To begin her new life as She Who Remembers for the Towa, teaching the young girls all they should know.

And to be the honored mate of Cicuye's Hunting Chief. And to be home.

She gazed into the empty horizon. "Do you think hunters will come this way?"

He shrugged. "Possibly."

She glanced about uneasily. No one had followed them from the canyon; she was certain of that. And the Querechos of the Plains had befriended them when they passed this way before. So why this foreboding?

"What tribes come, other than the Plains Querechos?"

"Many from distant places. Pawnees. Kiowas. Wichitas. Apaches—"

"Apaches?" Kwani gasped. She feared those wandering marauders above all others. "Apaches can see in the dark like cougars! They kill like cougars."

He sighed. How like a woman! But he saw her fear and came to kneel beside her. "The plains are wide. We may see no hunters at all. If we do, they will have dogs with travois, and we have much to trade."

We do have much, Kwani thought. Too much. All the valuable gifts left by Kokopelli. The priceless hide of the White Buffalo and its meat to give spiritual powers to those who partake of it. She thought of the severed head in the stream, and of the men she had seen in the canyon. Were they of the Querecho clan whose man attacked while Acoya was being born? A cold finger poked at her spine.

"If we get dogs from hunters, can we go directly to Cicuye? I am tired—"

"We can rest at the Place of the Rainbow Flint, the village there—"

"I want to rest at our home."

He sat back on his heels and looked at her, frowning. No Towa woman would be so obstinate about obtaining valuable flint to trade for dogs. But she was Anasazi; he must remember that.

"We may not encounter hunters. With dogs or otherwise." He handed Acoya to her and rose. "We must be on our way." He lifted her pack and was abashed; even without the cooking pot and other things lost to the river, it was still too heavy. He set it back down, opened it, and began taking things out.

"No!" Kwani cried. "What are you doing? I need—"

He turned away his face to hide his feelings. A Towa was never abashed. "You need to remember I am your mate and I am Towa. You will do what I tell you to do."

"I am not a slave or a dog or a child to be ordered about!" she said hotly. "I am your mate, indeed. And I wish to be treated as such." Her voice shook.

He paid no attention and continued to remove things from her pack and toss them to the ground. When he removed her medicine arrow she snatched it from him.

"This is the arrow the Medicine Chief tried to kill me with, but it refused. It protects me! I—"

She stopped. He had removed his own pack and was stuffing some of her things into it. It was difficult, but by taking Kwani's feather blanket to cover the travois he managed to get it all in.

"Your pack will be lighter now," he said matter-of-factly. "You may keep your medicine arrow."

How bossy he was! But she was embarrassed about being angry; he was only trying to make this difficult journey easier for her. She held the arrow in her hand, remembering how it saved her. Now she had Tolonqua, the mate she had always longed for. And a son who would have a people and a clan of his own—because Tolonqua wanted her son to be his, also. What more could she ask?

She looked up at him, her eyes eloquent. "Thank you!"

He glanced at her with pleased and puzzled surprise. He was not inexperienced with women; he thought he understood them, understood Kwani. But she surprised him continually. Who could understand fury at one moment and the look she was giving him now?

He swept her in his arms, kissed her soft mouth, her eyes, her throat. "Tonight . . ."

Tolonqua had stopped to make camp in late afternoon. They had seen no one, nor smoke from cooking fires. Kwani sat in the grass, nursing her child. She caressed the downy head at her breast and reveled in the beauty of him. Again, she inspected the birthmark on the sole of his tiny right foot—the head of the White Buffalo. Her son was a Chosen One. He would be a great Chief someday. How fortunate she was! She sighed happily. When they reached Cicuye all her dreams of a home of her own, a people of her own, would be fulfilled. And in Cicuye would she not be She Who Remembers again?

She fingered her necklace with its scallop-shell pendant inlaid with turquoise in a mystical design, a necklace worn only by those who had been She Who Remembers for generations. For a moment she thought of the clan to whom it belonged. But they had given her the necklace long before they drove her away. It was her duty to keep it until she chose and trained a successor.

Tolonqua looked up as he fanned the cooking fire. "You are happy?"

"Yes."

He came and knelt beside her. "I am happy, also." His obsidian eyes seemed to ignite. "Tonight I will show you."

He leaned to caress her but stopped abruptly. He raised his head, listening.

"What is it?" Kwani asked.

He did not answer but rose to a crouch, searching the horizon. Kwani looked also, but saw nothing.

He gestured. "Listen!"

Kwani strained to hear, but there was only a small wind in the grasses. "What do you hear?"

He shook his head. "I do not hear it now. It was strange. Like nothing I have heard before."

He bent to the fire, added dried buffalo chips to the blaze, and cleared away more grass from around it. He felt a prick of unease. That was no ordinary sound he had heard. It was like something from the underworld, a spirit call. What did it portend? He glanced at Kwani still nursing the baby, and his heart constricted. This was the woman for whom he had waited a lifetime. He had won her from the invincible Toltec. Was Kokopelli planning revenge? That sound . . .

Kwani replaced the diapering of shredded cedar bark in the cradle board, and snuggled the sleeping boy into it. She laced up the soft deerskin covering, admiring the beauty of it again. It was embroidered with bits of bright shell and turquoise beads and painted with happy colors, the most beautiful cradle board she had ever seen. Tolonqua's gift before Acoya was born.

"Where did you find this?" she asked.

"I traded salt and turquoise for it."

Kwani smiled. It was costly gift, indeed, and she prized it. Her cooking pot was gone, so she scooped out a small hole in the ground, lined it with a piece of tough hide, poured in water, and waited for the fire to heat rocks hot enough to make water boil. Tolonqua added more buffalo chips to the fire and it burned hot. When the rocks were heated enough, she took two forked cooking sticks from her pack and added the stones to the water. There was a loud hissing and puff of steam. As the water warmed, more stones were added until the water boiled. Then Kwani added a handful of pemmican, sat back, and enjoyed the aroma.

Pemmican was dried buffalo meat pounded into a pulp and sealed with tallow into a buffalo-skin bag. When cooked, it would swell to three times its size and become a hearty and delicious meal. A bag of pemmican would keep for as long as fifteen or twenty years, an invaluable commodity against starvation that threatened always.

Kwani and Tolonqua ate their meal by the fire, watching the smoldering coals, listening to the quiet of approaching twilight.

She began to sing softly a remembered melody.

> *"Does one live forever on earth?*
> *Not forever on earth, only a short time here.*
> *My melodies shall not die, nor my songs perish.*
> *They spread, they scatter."*

Tolonqua's rich voice joined hers and the song floated into the night. Kwani loved Tolonqua's singing with her. It was another kind of mating.

Darkness enfolded them like a soft blanket while the distant campfires of ancestors burned brightly in the night sky.

Sunfather reached his afternoon path, burning down at Kwani and Tolonqua trudging through brown grass. Kwani peered at the sun. They were going north. Cicuye was west.

"Why do we go north?"

"That's where the rainbow flint is. Near the river."

Kwani had heard much of the flint of many colors. Beautiful, and extremely hard. Valuable in trading. They needed no more valuables; they had more than they could carry now. But they did need dogs.

Tolonqua seemed to read her thoughts. He said, "We will trade the heavier things for flint. And people there will have dogs and travois." He did not add that he had always wanted to visit the rainbow flint mines. Women did not understand such things.

Kwani stopped to wipe her sweaty face. Empty plains surrounded them in every direction.

"Where are the buffalo?"

"Everywhere. Farther than we can see." He dropped the poles of the travois, removed his pack, and squatted to rest.

She sat beside him and laid the baby upon the grass. He was listless in the heat and she shaded him with her feather blanket. Long ago she and her mother had made the blanket from turkey feathers woven with yucca fiber thread. Kwani prized it; the blanket held her mother's spirit.

She looked at Tolonqua resting in the brown grass, and feeling welled up in her.

Tolonqua watched her. "What are you thinking?"

How could she explain? Finally, she said, "I am happy that you wish to be the father of my son."

Tolonqua nodded. "He shall have a naming ceremony when we get there." The ceremony should have been held the fourth day after birth, but better late than never.

"When will that be?"

"Less than a moon. It depends upon how long we stay at the flint mines and how many dogs we obtain. If we get dogs from hunters before we reach the mines, we shall go faster."

Kwani looked again into the lonely horizon. "There are no hunters."

"There will be." He stood and shaded his eyes with his hand. Instantly, he became alert. "Look!"

A band of antelope drifted like a cloud shadow across the landscape. Suddenly they leaped high in unison as though to a mysterious signal, then stopped. Simultaneously, they quivered their hides, flashing white hairs and the shades of buff on their coats in spectacular display. Then they vanished, dun-colored bodies blending into dun-colored grassland.

"Ah!" Kwani sighed. She had never seen that.

Tolonqua gazed after them with a hunter's yearning. "If we needed meat I would follow them."

"But they run swiftly!"

"Yes. For a long time. But then they are tired, very tired, and can run no more. That is when my arrows find them." He lifted the poles of the travois and prepared to pull. "Come."

Reluctantly, Kwani rose. "Couldn't we camp here and wait for hunters to come with dogs?"

He looked into her blue eyes ringed with shadows. Without a word, he took Kwani's feather blanket, laid one end on the loaded travois, and held it there with rocks. The other end he stretched at an angle to the ground, holding it securely with more rocks. It formed a little shelter underneath.

"Give me your pack." He lifted it from her. "You and the baby rest now."

''Thank you.'' She carried the baby with her as she crawled under the blanket. It was a relief to be shaded from the hot sun. ''You will rest beside me when stars are shining.''

He laughed. ''Maybe I cannot wait until then.''

Tolonqua lay on the grass, shading his face with his arm. High above, vultures circled in a hot blue sky. Hoping he might be dead soon?

As indeed he might. Kwani and the baby, too; they were easy prey to any roaming band. He wondered about those men he had seen back in the canyon. Had they found the severed head? Were they tracking him? And what of the Querecho he had killed? A roaming spirit had no need of rest, no travois to pull. It rode the wind.

He turned to his stomach and crept through the grass to a shallow gully a short distance from where Kwani lay. For some time he lay there, concealed. Then, very cautiously, he raised his head to search the horizon.

Nothing.

The day passed. Sunfather descended to the underworld to begin his trip to his eastern home. It grew cooler and Kwani left the baby sleeping as she crawled out from under the blanket. She had slept, too, and looked refreshed.

Tolonqua sat on his haunches, watching the sky change from turquoise to gold, to purple. A breeze ran across the plain, bending the grasses, stirring a strand of Kwani's hair as she bent to the cooking fire. As always, she moved with unconscious grace. It made him want to make love to her. But last night when he had tried, she did not respond with her usual passionate abandon. She was passive, even tender. But that was not what he wanted and needed from her. He wanted the Kwani who used to be. Was it too soon after the birthing?

He would wait. Remembering other times, other nights, he would wait.

He looked up into the purple sky. No vultures were there. Discouraged when he did not die, no doubt. Tolonqua knew that when Sipapu called he must go, but that could not be until the new city stood high on the ridge. The safety of his clan, his people, depended on it. How could he achieve this without making it seem he was setting himself above the others as a leader—a fatal error for a Towa to make? A man should never assume leadership and should decline it if offered. He was one of the clan, the tribe, a part of the whole; he must work with others as hands and feet and head and arms work on a man's body. Of what good is a foot detached from the leg?

Yet, the city *must* be built. Cicuye stood at the head of a pass, a strategic spot, the last Pueblo village before the Great Plains spread eastward to the buffalo ranges. Tribes from the plains and Pueblos from the west came to Cicuye to trade for things they could not obtain otherwise. The village was growing, becoming wealthy. *It would be attacked again.* Could the warriors of Cicuye—farmers, hunters, weavers— defeat a large and determined war party from one of the marauding bands that prowled these plains and the mountains and canyons like starving wolves?

More and more unknown tribes from distant places roamed this vast hunting ground. How could his people be persuaded to build another city in a safer place?

Worry was heavy upon him.

The baby woke and Kwani lifted him from under the blanket and bathed his little bottom with a bit of water from the water bag. Tolonqua admired the Pueblo mark-of-birth, the small, gray spot at the base of the spine that would fade away when he was six. A proud heritage of a people long upon this Fourth World, whose migrations from the ice barrier of the north to the edge of the world at the south, and from the Sunrise Sea of the distant east to the Sunset Sea of the distant west, were recorded on stone and related by those who passed the sacred knowledge from generation to generation.

On the horizon, a wavering line appeared. Buffalo. Hunters would follow tomorrow; perhaps they would have dogs to trade. He glanced at their bulging packs. They had much with which to bargain—gifts left by Kokopelli because he could not carry it all to his homeland: medicine pipes, fine mugs, fine bowls, bone scrapers, arrow straighteners, rabbit-skin blankets, tools of bone and flint, salt, yards of yucca twine, cotton cloth, turquoise, pinon nuts, juniper seeds, and the valuable claws of a large grizzly bear. The turquoise he would not trade, nor the heavy, golden necklace Kokopelli left for Acoya; these things he carried in his pack with other belongings. The buffalo skin, the most valuable possession of all, must be protected at any cost. Tolonqua knew well what that cost could be. One man and a woman with a baby could be disposed of easily and their bodies left to scavengers.

He shifted anxiously. They were vulnerable prey. How could they protect themselves?

Darkness fell. Only starlight illumined the plain reaching beyond and beyond.

Kwani tucked Acoya into the cradle board. "Shall we keep the fire burning?"

"No."

"But animals—"

"I will watch."

Tolonqua did not want to build another fire to betray their presence, but they were hungry. He unwrapped the buffalo hide. It was skin side out and could be the hide of any buffalo—as long as it remained rolled up. He removed the jerky, gave some to Kwani, and rewrapped the hide, fastening it securely once more. He spread the rest of the jerky over the hide to conceal it, and covered the entire bundle with a blanket.

They ate their evening meal in silence, washing the jerky down sparingly with water. They huddled together, comforting each other in their aloneness under the vast dome of sky.

Kwani slept, and woke with a start. It was not yet dawn but she heard something. A strange wailing in the distance. It came again, and Tolonqua jerked upright.

Kwani wrapped the blanket closely around her. "What is that?"

He peered into the predawn darkness. "I do not know, but I have heard it before."

Kwani shivered. "It sounds like something hurting." She felt a stab of dread, but she would not let him know. "It is far away," she said, making her voice matter-of-fact. "I am hungry already. Let's eat and be on our way." Maybe they could escape whatever it was.

Kwani nursed Acoya as they ate meat of the buffalo. She hoped the sacred food would give them mystical powers. She clasped the shell of her necklace to her, seeking reassurance, and was comforted.

The sky paled as they left. The strange sound did not come again, but Tolonqua was tensely alert, scanning the horizon. Buffalo drifted in the distance but no hunters appeared.

The eastern sky glowed as Sunfather arrived from his night's journey and rose in splendor. Tolonqua stopped to sing his morning chant to the sun. Kwani heard it every morning but she never tired of hearing it again. He stood with bowl in hand, facing east, bathed in golden light.

He sang.

> *"Now this day,*
> *My sun father,*
> *Now that you have come out standing*
>   *in your sacred place,*
> *Prayer meal,*
> *Here I give you."*

He tossed a handful of cornmeal toward the sun. Kwani's spirit soared and she sang with him.

> *"Your long life,*
> *Your old age,*
> *Your waters,*
> *Your seeds,*
> *Your riches,*
> *Your power,*
> *Your strong spirit,*
> *All these to me may you grant."*

As if in response, from the east appeared a hunting group. Kwani asked, "Who are they?"

Tolonqua shaded his eyes with his hand and stood silently, gazing.

"Who?" Kwani asked again.

He tucked the bowl in his pack. "I am not sure. I don't think I've seen them before when my hunters and I were around here."

"Will they . . . are they friendly?"

"Who knows? Maybe they will trade." He looked down into her troubled eyes. "Do not be afraid. I will protect you."

As he stood there, straight and tall, with his face set in strong resolve, Kwani knew that he would. He and their protecting spirits. Confidence surged in her and she began to sing a wordless song, her clear voice sounding in the wind. She strode beside him, her head high, her gaze fixed upon the approaching hunters as she sang.

Tolonqua glanced at her. This was the Kwani he knew; she lit a flame inside him. He began to sing, too, and the weight of the travois became less. Together they approached the dogs and the hunters. There were seven men and twelve shaggy dogs with travois; some of the travois were empty.

Kwani and Tolonqua stopped singing and stood watching. As the men grew closer, Kwani saw they were short and squat. Their black hair was shiny with bear grease, parted in the center, and braided into three thick braids tied at the ends with buckskin thongs dyed red. One man had a short braid dangling between his eyes, fastened with a turquoise bead that bumped back and forth as he walked. Chunks of turquoise hung from each ear, and their faces were painted in red, yellow, and black designs. Similar designs embellished both arms. A thin sliver of bone pierced each nostril like a long whisker. Another sliver pierced the lower lip and hung down to the bottom of the chin. Shaggy black eyebrows shaded deep-set black eyes that stared at them without expression.

Tolonqua and Kwani stood silently, facing them. Tolonqua did not draw his bow although some of the men were doing so. He stood in stoic dignity, making the sign for "friend" and for "Towa."

The man with the braid dangling between his eyes stepped forward. He reached inside a pouch at his side and removed a giant shell, round at one end and tapering to a point at the other. Along the length a raised lip shone inside with a rosy glow. He lifted the pointed end to his mouth and blew.

There was a long, wailing, compelling howl, a sound to linger in the air and freeze the blood. The sound continued as the man approached, followed by the hunters and by snarling dogs.

The shell's sound called from the depths of Sipapu. Kwani wanted to turn and run but she stood motionless, facing them, hoping her trembling did not reveal her fear.

The shell silenced, and was replaced in the pouch. The men stepped forward and called the dogs to retreat; they crouched, still growling. The men still had bows in hand, but arrows remained in quivers. Again, Tolonqua made the sign of "Towa" and of "friend." He signed that he wanted to trade.

The hunters glanced at one another, grinning, and stared at Kwani and at Tolonqua's travois, their small black eyes gleaming. The leader with the braid between his eyes strode to the travois, jerked off the blanket, and stared down at an ordinary bundle of jerky. He guffawed and tossed the blanket to the hunters.

"My feather blanket!" Kwani cried.

They ignored her.

The leader signed, "You think we need to trade for jerky? We, the greatest hunters of the Plains?" He gestured to several travois piled with tanned hides, and thrust out his chest, posturing. "It is an insult!" He raised his bow, arrow in hand. "Show us what is in the packs."

Tolonqua looked him calmly in the eye. He signed, "I will trade the blanket for dogs."

"No!" Kwani cried. How could he trade her treasured blanket that held her dead mother's spirit? "It is mine!"

Tolonqua did not take his eyes from the hunter who stood with drawn bow. He whispered, "Your medicine arrow. Now!"

Swiftly, Kwani removed the painted arrow that she carried in a small case at her side; it had saved her life. Once before, in a time of mortal danger, she had summoned from some mysterious inner source a sound that was not a cry, not a song, but an eerie combination of both. Now it came again, a shrill, fierce sound that lanced the air as she held the arrow, the arrow to kill witches, in both hands and thrust it toward the hunters.

They stared in astonishment at the small woman whose strange eyes burned with blue fire and whose voice summoned ancestors in the blood. The arrow was a medicine arrow with supernatural powers. Hers was powerful medicine! The leader hesitated, then slowly lowered his bow. The others followed.

Again, Tolonqua signed. "I will trade the blanket for dogs."

The leader glanced at Kwani who still held the arrow. This was no ordinary woman. Perhaps she, herself, was a witch! Fear flickered in his eyes and was immediately concealed. He turned to the others and they conversed in an unknown tongue, gesticulating, glancing at Kwani and Tolonqua who stood calmly, watching.

The men examined the blanket. It was like none they had seen before, made of fine turkey feathers woven closely with yucca twine. Obviously, it was a thing of unusual value and would endow the owner with important prestige.

The leader removed his necklace and offered it. It was of bird bones cut into small beads and finely polished. Bear claws dangled in front.

Tolonqua stepped closer. Imperiously, he pointed to the pouch containing the shell horn.

"No!" The hunters scowled and made threatening gestures. Again, the leader raised his bow, arrow ready.

Kwani had been standing with her medicine arrow in her lowered hands. Now she stepped forward and thrust the arrow at the leader. She flung back her head. Again came the fierce, singing sound as she stood like a Spirit Being, eyes closed, while the terrible cry summoned those unseen.

As if in response, a flock of ravens swooped low, circling, their loud cries mingling with hers.

The men gaped in superstitious awe. Slowly, the shell horn in its pouch was offered to Tolonqua. Only then did the singing cry cease and the ravens fly away.

Tolonqua accepted the shell and Kwani lowered the arrow. The hunters strode swiftly away, clutching the blanket, glancing fearfully behind them.

Tolonqua stared at Kwani. Never had he heard such a sound as she had made. More compelling than the sound of the shell!

Kwani stared back at him. "My blanket . . ." Her voice shook. "My mother's spirit—"

"Perhaps it was she who summoned the ravens."

Could it be? Did her mother assume a raven's form and gather the flock to protect them? Kwani gazed into the distance, seeking sight of the birds, but they were gone.

▲ 3 ▼

Huzipat, aged Chief of the Eagle Clan, stood with his people on the mesa, gazing across the wide ravine at the cliff city they were leaving forever. The great, arched cave stared back like a dying eye. The Chief turned abruptly away.

Beside him was young Zashue, he of the torn and jagged face, Medicine Chief since his father died—killed by a cougar, the latest of overwhelming disasters. Zashue's scarred lips twisted in a scowl.

"It is the witch. But for her we could remain."

The Chief did not bother to reply. He had long since given up hope of making Zashue accept the fact that he and others brought disasters upon themselves and upon the clan by not protecting Kwani as Kokopelli demanded. Kokopelli had warned that disasters would befall if they did not protect his mate. Instead, they accused her of witchcraft and drove her away. Disasters, indeed, had haunted them since. Their beloved Sun Chief was dead. As were Woshee, his mate, and Okalake, their son. The Old One, who was She Who Remembers before Kwani and who had appointed Kwani as her successor, was also in Sipapu. The Medicine Chief had died horribly, ripped apart by the cougar's claws. There was no rain; Earthmother refused to give birth. No trees were left on the mesas; too many had been cut for fuel and for timber. The Wolf Clan and other clans among the mesas threatened attack for they, too, were hungry.

Now it was time to leave this place, to continue migrations as the gods decreed. The old Chief bowed his head; the burden of sorrows and of years weighed heavily upon him.

He gestured, and the people turned away to begin their journey southward to the banks of the Great River where other Pueblo tribes dwelled. Women could not contain their tears. The Place of the Eagle Clan was the most beautiful city of all, built by their grandfathers, added to and cared for lovingly over the generations. It held memories. It was where spirits of those in Sipapu came to them in dreams. It was home.

Yatosha, the Hunting Chief, led the way, for he and his hunters knew the trails. The people followed, two hundred fifty of them. Even children were laden with burdens. Women carried babies in cradle boards, and toddlers were carried by older sisters or brothers or aunts. An aged drummer beat a small cottonwood drum to lighten the heart and soon chants echoed among the mesas, beseeching Masau'u and Motsni, his divine bird, for a safe journey.

Tiopi, mate of Yatosha, led the group of women. Not only was she mate of the Hunting Chief, but she had established herself as She Who Remembers since Kwani escaped. The witch had taken the necklace with her—the sacred necklace with the scallop shell, treasured by the Eagle Clan since time began. Resentment and hatred boiled up again as Tiopi visualized Kwani wearing the necklace that was rightfully Tiopi's now. She fingered the shell bracelets given to her by Kokopelli at their last mating. The bracelets hung as pendants upon a necklace of burned and polished juniper seeds. Beautiful, of course, but a far cry from the true necklace of She Who Remembers, the necklace belonging to the Eagle Clan, and to her.

She shifted the cradle board on her back. At least she had Kokopelli's son, the result of their last mating. That was more than Kwani had even though Kokopelli chose Kwani as his mate. Ha! She wondered how Kwani liked the idea of Kokopelli mating with a woman from every village he visited. Only she, Tiopi, had been chosen not once, but twice, to receive the hallowed seed that would assure the clan of good fortune . . .

Good fortune? Her thoughts veered away.

But it was she who bore Chomoc, the son of Kokopelli. One day this boy would be a man, strong and powerful. She reached behind her back to touch his head in the cradle board. "You will learn from Chiefs and become a Chief," she whispered. "You, Chomoc, will avenge your people and me. The knowledge of this you drink from my breast."

She joined in the chanting. Chomoc, son of Kokopelli, would find and destroy Kwani, the witch—if she were not found and destroyed already.

▲ 4 ▼

Kwani watched Tolonqua dragging the travois up a small hill. "Why didn't you trade for dogs instead of the shell horn?"

"We can get dogs at the flint quarries. The shell has powers no dogs possess. Every hunter has dogs. How many possess a shell that shouts?" He turned to look at her. "We are nearly there. You shall have many dogs." He smiled.

Kwani did not reply. The way she felt, bent under her burden, she would have preferred a dog now to any number of shell horns later. But maybe the horn did have powers. . . .

They paused at the top of the hill and looked with interest at the landscape that was different from where they had come. It rolled up and down and around in gentle hills and sudden gullies, some of which were unexpectedly deep.

Tolonqua pointed to where the trail leveled between two hills in the distance. "The going will be easier there."

He stood relaxed, with one foot resting on top of the travois and an arm on the raised knee. Kwani looked at him with admiration. As he leaned forward, his necklace with the carved bone talisman of a Towa Hunting Chief hung loose, swinging a little. His lean face with high cheekbones and aquiline nose was enhanced by the ornate band he wore across his forehead holding his shoulder-length black hair in place. The feather was notched in a manner to indicate his Chief status. Red feathers hung from each ear, and a bear paw tattoo, symbol of power, embellished his right shoulder. How handsome he was! Somehow, her weariness vanished, and she experienced an emotion she had not felt since Acoya was born.

He sensed her gaze and turned to look at her. Black eyes, sharp with intelligence, warmed. "What are you thinking, small one?"

She felt her cheeks flushing. "That I want to lie with you."

"Here?"

"Yes."

"Now?"

"Yes."

He laughed. "Why not?"

He took the baby, removed the blanket, and laid both upon the soft turf beside the trail. He pulled her dusty garment over her head and stood a moment, gazing down at her lovely nakedness. Lifting her in his arms, he kissed both breasts, caressing each nipple with a demanding tongue. He carried her a short distance away to a little gully and laid her down. She reached both arms for him and he sank into the warmth and softness of her, growling with pleasure and desire.

Later, she lay cradled against his chest, listening to the voice of his heart. She said, "What you told me is true."

"What?"

"That you would teach me how a Towa loves."

He propped on an elbow to look down at her. "Is my way different?" He wanted to say "different from Kokopelli," the renowned lover. . . .

She smiled. "You love with your heart as well as with your body."

He laughed. "I teach you again!" He pulled her to him. She held him close.

Birds wheeled and watched, and white clouds passed, but it was as if time and constellations ceased to be.

At last the village came into distant view, and Kwani stood staring. So many dwellings! They were different from any she had seen before. They were two stories, built of stone and adobe with a roof of sod. Single pole ladders leaned against walls; entrance was from the roof. And there were so many people! As Tolonqua and Kwani approached, heads popped up from the entrances like prairie dogs.

Tipis of different tribes clustered on the outskirts of the village. There were fields of corn and squash and beans where women worked, bent to their tasks. Children ran everywhere and dogs followed, yapping. The sound of their commotion rode the breeze.

Kwani swallowed nervously. She and Tolonqua were both dusty, exhausted, and travel-worn; she wanted to look nice when she entered the village. As they grew closer, a crowd gathered, pointing. Would they welcome her and Tolonqua? She swallowed again.

"Who are they?" she asked.

"The Flint People."

"Do you think they are . . . friendly?"

"We shall see. But we will not display what we have."

He removed his blanket from his pack and covered the travois. He drew the shell horn from its pouch, took a long, deep breath, and blew hard. There was an eerie, moaning cry. He blew again, and this time a great wailing sounded across the plain, lingering.

Immediately, there was a reaction. More people gathered. Men, women, and countless children ran from tipis and from the fields to join the others. They stood in excited groups, gesticulating.

Kwani laughed. "Look at them! They heard!"

He nodded, replacing the shell in its pouch. "Now we wait."

"Will they invite us to come to the village?"

"Perhaps. If not, we shall go there anyway." He lifted his pack. "We must have gifts ready." He removed a shell and turquoise necklace from his pack, one of Kokopelli's luxurious gifts, and slipped it around his neck. It glittered in the sunlight.

Kwani sighed. "It is beautiful. Every man will want that. And every woman, too."

A procession seemed to be forming. A group of men lined up, walking two abreast behind their leader, accompanied by a tall, muscular man beating time with a heavy drum. The sound seemed to come from Earthmother's belly. *BOOM! BOOM! BOOM!*

Kwani glanced at Tolonqua with alarm. "Isn't that a war drum?"

"Yes."

"Will they attack?"

"No. They are traders. So many warriors are not needed to dispose of us. The drum is their answer to my horn."

But as they grew closer, Kwani was not reassured. The hair on the left side was cut unevenly above the ear, but had been allowed to grow long on the other side. Some of the men had looped the long hair into a bundle and tied it, but the leader's hair flowed to his knees and was ornamented with feathers and clumps of shells. The exposed ears on the left were pierced in many places from the top down, and displayed ornamental hoops of white shell. Brief aprons of buffalo hide hung before and behind, and buffalo-hide footwear reached above the ankles. They wore necklaces of polished bone and animal claws; the leader also wore arm and leg bands of bear claws. A wide stripe of red paint reached from side to side over and around the eyes so that the eyes peered from within a red enclosure, giving them a sinister, animal-like expression. As they walked in time to the beat of the drum, they brandished buffalo-hide shields, handsomely painted and adorned with feathers that fluttered impressively.

The group stopped a short distance away. The leader stepped forward, carrying a tall staff adorned with hawk and eagle plumes. He signed, "Who are you?"

"Towa."

The man's eyes peered maliciously at Kwani, and the painted red band seemed to glow. "Who is she?"

"My mate. She Who Remembers."

The man swung his staff with a threatening gesture. "Leave this place!"

One of the men stepped forward with a sharp exclamation. He spoke to the leader. Others gathered around, and there was heated discussion in their strange guttural language. Now and then they turned to stare at Tolonqua and at the small woman with blue eyes who returned their stare with those eyes. Blue!

"What do they say?"

"I do not know."

The loud talk stopped suddenly. The leader strode to Kwani, looked her over, and grunted. He turned to Tolonqua. He signed, "My Hunting Chief says he knows of you. You hunt buffalo with men of the Plains."

Tolonqua nodded, face expressionless.

The leader continued, "He says you have good medicine."

"Yes."

"This woman"—his eyes darted at Kwani—"it is said this woman is a witch."

Tolonqua's black eyes ignited. "A lie by enemies who seek to repudiate her powers."

"What powers?"

"She is a Caller," Tolonqua signed. "She called a deer for the people of Puname. She is a Storyteller. She is She Who Remembers."

The leader turned again to his men and there was more discussion. Finally, he turned back to Tolonqua.

"She called a deer?"

"Yes."

"The deer came?"

"Yes."

"Can she call also the buffalo?"

"Of course."

He jerked his staff up and down, making the feathers flutter, and stared coldly at Tolonqua who stared back. "What proof?"

Tolonqua swept the blanket from the travois to reveal a pile of jerky. He signed, "Behold the meat of the White Buffalo!"

The leader snatched the meat, smelled it, licked it, took a bite, spit it out, and tossed the remainder to the dogs.

"This could be the meat of any buffalo. Show me the hide."

Tolonqua stood stiffly, staring at the leader with contempt. "I do not desecrate the sacred object. It will be displayed before those who are worthy. In a kiva, only."

He replaced the blanket on the travois while the leader and his men watched every move. Again, Tolonqua removed the shell and lifted it to his lips. Again came the wailing howl to freeze the blood and call the unseen.

The big drum answered with a BOOM that made Kwani's backbone vibrate. The leader signed, "What do you want?"

"To trade for flint and for dogs." He removed the necklace and stepped forward, offering it to the leader. He signed, "A token of my respect."

The leader accepted the necklace impassively, looped it over his wrist, and allowed his men to inspect it. The turquoise pendant glowed in splendor. His eyes slid to the travois and at the packs carried by Tolonqua and Kwani. There was no hide, obviously. Who did this man think he was bluffing? "What have you to trade?"

Tolonqua hesitated. It would be dangerous to disclose his wealth here. He signed, "I trade my hunting skills known to all. And the powers of my mate, She Who Remembers, the Caller."

Kwani tried to follow the conversation, but the signing was too rapid for her to get it all. But she did realize that her skills as a Caller were being bartered. Without her permission! Her powers were sacred, and hers alone to call upon when she, and she alone, felt the need to do so. Tolonqua had no right!

Again, the leader and his men grouped for loud discussion. Agreement was reached, and the leader turned to To-

lonqua. "Your mate will call the buffalo, and you will go
with us when we hunt." He brandished his staff. "Come!"

He turned, and Kwani and Tolonqua followed him with
the men behind them keeping pace to the drum. Kwani was
acutely conscious of stares from expressionless eyes and the
threatening proximity of bodies smelling of rancid bear
grease.

She tugged at Tolonqua's arm. "I do not like this. Where
are we going?"

"We go to trade."

"These people are not friendly."

"Remember that we are few and they are many. But do
not be afraid. They will fear and respect your powers."

She stopped to stare up at him, and the entire procession
came to a halt. She said, "My powers are bestowed by the
Ancient Ones, all who were She Who Remembers before
me. They are sacred and not for barter."

He tugged at her arm but she refused to budge.

"You traded my feather blanket, the blanket with my
mother's spirit. You will not presume to trade my powers!"

The men snickered at this unseemly confrontation, and
Tolonqua stood in frozen embarrassment. His black eyes,
usually so warm as he gazed at her, were cold.

"I bartered your blanket to save our lives. I am bartering
my hunting skills and your powers to save your life, and
mine, and Acoya's. Or perhaps you would prefer that we
forget the bargaining and be taken as slaves?"

Kwani knew the fate of slaves. Women slaves killed their
newborn girl babies rather than have them suffer a similar
fate. She glanced at the men pressing close, and at their
eyes peering from within their red hiding places, and her
heart jerked with alarm. But she was protected by the Ancient Ones. She clasped the necklace to her.

"I will *not* call the buffalo!" she whispered fiercely. He
would learn her powers were not his to manipulate as he
saw fit.

As if in response there was another great BOOM of the
drum, followed by marching time in double rhythm. Kwani
had to trot to keep up with Tolonqua who strode wearily,
his face impassive. The cradle board fastened to his heavy
pack bounced up and down a little as he leaned forward,
pulling the travois. The sight of that cradle board, which
she cherished and which he had given her, made her
ashamed she had embarrassed him before these warriors.
He was her mate and she loved him.

She touched his arm. "I am sorry. I will call the buffalo."

He gave her a quick glance and she was surprised to see a smile tug at his mouth. "It will not be necessary. I have a plan."

Again, the rhythm of the beat quickened, and Kwani had to trot faster while the men watched Tolonqua from the corners of their eyes to see if he could keep the pace as he pulled the travois. His muscles bulged, and perspiration beaded his body, but he did not miss a beat.

Acoya whimpered and Kwani shifted his position where he was fastened in a sling arrangement in her blanket. She wished she and Tolonqua were in Cicuye among his people who would be her people now. Hers and Acoya's. All her life she had been different, never quite belonging. An outcast. Now she and her son would have what she had always sought and longed for: a home, a clan, and people of her own. At last. Of course she would.

Yellow Bird, ancient matriarch of Cicuye, squatted in her dwelling and glared at her grandson, City Chief Two Elk. From under shaggy white brows her eyes, nearly hidden in withered folds, flashed with outrage. She shook a bony finger under Two Elk's nose.

"You heard what they said, those traders. Tolonqua and Kwani were seen going to the Place of the Flint. And without Kokopelli!"

She shook her head so that her hair, still black but for a few white streaks, flapped around her craggy old face. "Why is your Hunting Chief squandering time when he is needed here, where he belongs? And where is Kokopelli, I ask you?"

Two Elk shrugged. "This is not known, Honored One." He crossed his arms in resignation. Obviously, this was to be another of his grandmother's tirades. The older she got, the meaner she became. He said, "Perhaps he wants the flint for arrows for his hunters. The flint—"

"We have flint!" Yellow Bird snorted. "We need meat. Your hunters bring little. And I want to know what happened to Kokopelli. The traders think Kwani is mate of Tolonqua now. What have you to say to that?"

Two Elk concealed a smile. If Tolonqua were responsible for Kokopelli's disappearance, it would ruin forever Tolonqua's chances of usurping the power of himself, Two Elk, the best Clan Chief Cicuye had ever had. There would be no more whispers about Tolonqua becoming Clan Chief one day. And Tolonqua's unwise insistence upon building a fortified city up there on the ridge would be ignored. A fact that would certainly gratify Yellow Bird who bitterly opposed the idea.

He bowed his head respectfully. "You ask me what I have to say about Tolonqua taking Kwani as mate, and about Kokopelli's disappearance. I say I find these things unworthy of a Hunting Chief, or any Chief, for that matter. But typical of one who talks of uprooting our city for another up there." He jerked his thumb to the flat-topped ridge soaring beyond the cornfield. "He is a disrupting influence. As for Kwani—"

"A foreigner, I remind you. An Anasazi from the Eagle Clan of the west who came here as mate of Kokopelli. Now that Kokopelli has disappeared, what right has she to be among us?" Again she waggled a bony finger. "I want you to send someone to find out what has happened, and I want that person to report to me."

"It shall be done, Honored One."

Two Elk did not bother to conceal his smile.

▲ 5 ▼

Tolonqua stood in the ceremonial lodge, facing the men gathered in a semicircle before him. A small fire in the fire pit was the only light; it cast weird shadows on the walls and carved dark faces into masks. It was late night. Dogs howled at the moon and a baby cried fretfully.

The ceremonial pipe had been passed, introductory comments given, and now the men stared at Tolonqua in silence, waiting. The hide of the White Buffalo, skin side out and tightly rolled, lay beside him. He would unroll the hide at the proper time. First, he would tell of the White Buffalo.

"Long ago," he signed, "when I sought my manhood vision, the White Buffalo came to me and told me that one day I would find him and the robe of the White Buffalo would be mine. The Spirit Being also appeared to my mate, She Who Remembers, in dreams. He told her to come to him. We sought him together."

He paused and looked down into expressionless eyes. "In the nearby canyon of many colors, he came to us."

There were murmurs, and the men glanced at one another. Tolonqua continued, "He came first to my mate, She Who Remembers, and told her that her child would then be born, it would be a man child, and the White Buffalo would be his guardian spirit."

An old shaman rose, signing, "What proof of these statements?"

"I have proof," Tolonqua signed. "But first—"

"Let us see this proof."

"Very well. Send for the child."

The old shaman gestured, and sat down. A man left the lodge, and Tolonqua continued, "As I walked by the river, I saw the Spirit Being waiting for me under the big cottonwood tree that leans over the water where the river bends."

A flicker of acknowledgment appeared in some of the eyes. They knew the place. Tolonqua continued, "The White

Buffalo gave himself, as he promised. Here is the sacred hide.''

He untied the hide and unrolled it with a flourish. ''Behold the Spirit Being!''

There were more murmurs. Some of the men reached to examine it but Tolonqua jerked it back. ''It is for me to touch, and for my clan and my family only.''

The old shaman rose, bracing himself on his staff. ''It is the hide of the White Buffalo,'' he signed. ''But where is proof that what you have said is true? How do we not know someone else obtained this hide and you stole it from him?''

The sound of a crying baby reached them before the man entered carrying Acoya who thrashed his little arms and legs, bellowing outrage.

Tolonqua took the child and spoke softly to him. At the sound of his father's voice, the sobbing diminished. Tolonqua lifted one tiny foot and stepped forward for the men to examine the outline of a buffalo head on the sole. ''The White Buffalo marked him as his own.''

The men gaped in awe, and babbled excitedly. Again, the shaman rose. He signed, ''Your son is a Chosen One. Your ownership of the hide of the White Buffalo is acknowledged. We are honored that you are here.'' He sat down.

The War Chief, the leader who had met Tolonqua and Kwani on the trail and brought them to the village, signaled that he would speak. He signed, ''You say you wish to barter your hunting skills and the skills of your mate for flint and for dogs. It is agreed. Your mate will tell us where the buffalo are and you will go with us on the hunt. Is this not so?''

Tolonqua nodded.

The War Chief continued, ''Inform your mate the calling ceremony will take place this night on the dancing plaza.''

''No. She Who Remembers chooses to commune with the spirits of the buffalo in secrecy and in privacy. She will do so in the dwelling to which you have assigned us.'' He turned to go.

The shaman jerked his staff in agitation. ''I must be present during the ceremony!''

''I regret that it is not possible.''

''I insist!''

''One cannot command the spirits,'' Tolonqua signed respectfully. ''It is their wish that She Who Remembers communicate with them in a secret ceremony.'' He paused, swinging the heavy hide over his shoulder in preparation to leave. "If the hunting is to be successful, the spirits must be obeyed." He shifted the baby to his other arm, and stalked out.

After he had gone, there was heated discussion. Finally, the old shaman said, "I shall speak," and the men quieted. "Never have I seen a mark of the White Buffalo. It is an omen. Gods are among us."

The men glanced at one another uneasily, and around the room as though gods might be revealed. A hunter said, "Hunting will be better than ever before."

All knew that hunting had not been good for more moons than they would admit. In devoting much time and effort to slave trading, controlling the flint quarries, and trading flint for buffalo meat and hides, they had neglected their hunting skills. They needed more meat than trading provided.

The War Chief rose, draped his long hair over one arm, and stood in the firelight, his shrewd eyes gleaming. "Perhaps all the Towa tells is true. Perhaps his woman *is* a Caller and will speak with the spirits of the buffalo to tell us where they may be found. This we shall know when we are on the hunt." He folded his arms and sat down, grunting in satisfaction as the men nodded solemnly.

Kwani huddled in the small room, staring up at the only door, a hatchway in the roof reached by a one-pole ladder with unevenly spaced cross rungs. A warrior had climbed down that ladder, snatched the baby from her arms, and climbed up again. She had followed, screaming, and watched helplessly as he carried Acoya into the medicine lodge.

What were they doing to her child?

She wrapped her arms around herself and rocked to and fro, trying to calm her frantic heart. Sounds of the village, chatter, laughter, dogs barking, and shrill shouts of children playing drifted in with the smell of smoke from cooking fires. Occasionally, a boy or girl would run across the roofs and stop to peer down into her room. Sometimes, they would speak, but she could not understand what they said. They would stare at her, bright eyes alive with curiosity, giggle, and run away.

What was happening to Tolonqua?

She looked about her, seeking something to occupy her attention and ease her fear. The room was nearly bare. There were sleeping mats, a water jar, and a blanket neatly folded. An oval-shaped metate and mano were in a corner, and a basket of corn sat beside them. Two empty baskets awaited, so she put pemmican in one and jerky in the other. Her pack and Tolonqua's had been dumped upon the floor for sorting and were covered with a blanket to conceal their wealth from curious eyes peering down the hatch.

Kwani saw that part of the blanket was ripped. She would mend it. Watching the hatch, Kwani lifted a corner of the blanket to search for her sewing things. She found her small packet of bone needles and a length of yucca twine thread.

It would be awkward to try to repair the rip while it covered their treasures; she wanted to hold the blanket in her lap. But that would expose their wealth and these people were strangers.

Overhead, quick footsteps approached, hesitated, and passed.

Kwani glanced at the folded blanket upon the floor, placed there for her use. That would do it! Quickly, she shook open the blanket, snatched the ripped one away, and replaced it. She draped the torn blanket over her lap, threaded her bone needle, and began to repair the rip.

Keeping her hands busy helped. But her mind had a will of its own. *What are they doing to my son? Tolonqua should be back by now. Is he telling them I will call the buffalo? I have called a deer, but never a buffalo. . . .*

The needle paused in the blanket. She fingered the scallop shell of her necklace, seeking communication with the Ancient Ones. *Tell me what to do!*

A shadow appeared at the hatchway and a woman's face peered down. She signed for permission to enter. Kwani nodded, and the woman climbed down the ladder and squatted next to Kwani. She was old, perhaps forty years or more, and her face, round as Moonwoman's, beamed kindly. From inside her robe she brought a small bundle of corn cakes and offered it with a gap-toothed smile.

Kwani realized she was hungry. She accepted the cakes with thanks, and offered the woman a strip of jerky. She signed, "The meat of the White Buffalo. It gives spiritual powers."

The woman held it reverently. She signed her thanks, and gazed with unabashed curiosity at the pile on the floor covered with a blanket. Kwani continued her mending and pretended not to notice as the woman inched closer to the pile. She thought, I cannot let her see under the blanket! I must distract her.

Impulsively, she dumped the torn blanket on the woman's

lap. She signed, "I do not sew well enough to repair this. Can you help me?"

The woman stared at Kwani in astonishment, took a bite of the meat, chewed, and nodded. The bone needed appeared and disappeared in the blanket with amazing rapidity. Kwani watched, signed complimentary remarks, and ate corn cakes as the woman worked. Now and then the woman would take another bite of meat, chew vigorously with what teeth she had left, and place her hand over her heart and to her forehead, signing that already she felt the spiritual powers.

Again, the hatchway darkened, and Tolonqua descended, carrying Acoya and the buffalo hide. "I greet you!"

"My heart rejoices," Kwani said with feeling, and took the baby. "As you see, this woman is repairing our blanket that was damaged."

Tolonqua signed a greeting to the woman, took the blanket from her, handed her another piece of buffalo meat with warm thanks, and indicated that she could go now.

Smiling and nodding, the woman accepted the meat with profuse gestures of thanks, climbed the ladder, and disappeared.

Kwani held Acoya close, satisfied he was unharmed. "Why did that warrior take my baby? What happened?" Her blue eyes demanded answers.

He looked down at her, with her long black hair falling free and her soft mouth firm against its trembling, and he thought, she grows more beautiful each day. He said, "We will have a buffalo calling ceremony here, and then I go with the hunters for buffalo." He smiled. "The mark of the White Buffalo convinced them."

"Is that why he took Acoya? To see the mark?"

"Yes. They know he is a Chosen One."

"So he is." She paused. How could she say what she must? "It is because I am She Who Remembers that I cannot allow anyone to barter powers given to me by the Ancient Ones. That is why I refused to agree to call the buffalo. I—"

"I understand. You will not have to. So what we shall do is give a convincing performance only. Now. They are waiting." He climbed the ladder and closed the hatchway. "I told them it must be private and in secrecy. What you must do is to chant loudly. I will blow the horn and together we will make a suitable impression." He chuckled.

"But what about the buffalo?"

"Remember the buffalo we saw in the distance late yesterday?"

"Yes, but—"

"I saw the direction in which they were going, and I think I know where they will be tomorrow. I will tell the hunters that is where you said the buffalo will be. After communing with the spirits of the buffalo during the ceremony, of course."

"But what if the buffalo are not there?"

"I will say they have moved since their spirits communicated with yours."

"Ah. And what if they do not believe?"

"We must take that chance." He struck a pose. "Let the ceremony begin!"

Kwani tucked Acoya into his cradle board, and paced around the small room, preparing herself. To make the ceremony convincing she must feel that she really was calling the buffalo; she must feel it inside. She began a low chant.

> *"You of the distant places,*
> *you of the prairies,*
> *you of the distant hills,*
> *come closer, come this way."*

Tolonqua took the conch-shell horn and blew a low, wailing cry.

> *"Come closer, come this way,*
> *tell us where you are.*
> *The White Buffalo,*
> *Chief of all buffalo,*
> *commands you."*

The horn gave a great shout, curdling the air, lingering in eerie echo. Outside, people had gathered, listening. They cringed, and covered their ears at the sound, and glanced at one another fearfully.

For hours Kwani continued the chant until her throat was sore and she could chant no more. The horn bellowed again and again in emphasis, and finally quieted.

Kwani whispered, "I know where the buffalo are."

"To the southwest?"

"Yes. In a deep, narrow valley with two hills on either side."

"How do you know?"

"They told me."

He stared at her. This small woman, this mate of his, continually astounded him. "You mean you really did communicate?"

"They listened to me, and told me." She brushed the hair away from her face with both hands, and sat down. "I am tired. I must rest now."

During all the commotion, Acoya had not made a sound. It was as though he understood what was happening, as though the buffalo were speaking to him, too. Now he whimpered that he was hungry. Kwani cradled him in her arms and nursed him while Tolonqua watched, still marveling.

He said, "I will tell the hunters."

When he opened the hatch, he was greeted by a crowd. The old shaman was in the forefront, holding his staff. Beside him stood the War Chief with his long hair draped over one arm. Hunters and villagers crowded close, babbling inquiries.

Tolonqua stood silently, looking over the crowd. He went to the shaman, bowed his head respectfully, and signed, "She Who Remembers has communed with the spirits of the buffalo. They are nearby in the southwest. They await us."

There was a shout from the hunters and excited discussion. The Hunting Chief stepped forward. He was young, squat, barrel-chested, broad-shouldered, with bear claws encircling spindly legs. He smiled broadly, eyes sparkling. "We hunt tomorrow!"

Tolonqua nodded assent. "She Who Remembers needs rest," he signed, and waved the people away. They departed reluctantly, looking back, talking and gesticulating to one another. Only the old shaman remained.

He signed, "The gods have brought you here. We invite you to remain."

Tolonqua bowed his thanks. "My clan awaits me; I must return home after the hunt. After the trading."

The shaman did not reply. He turned and walked slowly away, leaning upon his staff with plumes of eagle and hawk fluttering in captivity.

Tolonqua stood looking after him, trying to ignore a feeling of unease. Every tribe had its own way of hunting and he had never hunted with these people before. It was unlikely any of them disguised themselves with a wolf skin and crawled on hands and knees to approach a herd—a method he used often and with great success. These people were traders and warriors; they obtained what they wanted by barter and by raid. Their hunting skills would not be those of a Towa. How would they handle a large buffalo herd?

What if the hunting was unsuccessful?

He and Kwani would be discredited. They and Acoya would be in danger, trapped like game in a deadfall.

▲ 6 ▼

Kwani sat on a rooftop in pre-dawn light, watching Tolonqua and other hunters preparing to leave. The usual four days of preliminary ceremonies and preparations for a hunt were deemed unnecessary since She Who Remembers had communed with the spirits of the buffalo that now awaited them. The Medicine Chief and others of the Medicine Society were not pleased; their powers and importance were ignored. They prophesied dire happenings, but the hunters were eager to go.

There was an air of excited festivity as men conversed loudly over the shouts of small boys who ran about in a frenzy, exciting the dogs, and who were, in turn, shouted at by women trying to load the animals. They held the heads of the dogs between their legs as they fastened the collars of travois to shaggy necks, securing the poles of the travois firmly to hold big loads of meat to come. Some fitted the dogs with saddles to carry food that might be needed before hunting began, and whatever other things the Hunting Chief decided were necessary.

The War Chief strode about impatiently giving orders; women barked commands at dogs who barked back, and an aged drummer thumped his drum in an ecstasy of longing to be a hunter again, going for buffalo.

At last, the dogs were loaded and the hunters formed a group with Tolonqua and the Hunting Chief in front. The Medicine Chief chanted a final prayer, women shouted good-byes that were, of course, ignored by the hunters who considered good-byes to be an implication that they might not return in triumph. With a final thump of the drum, the group strode away, accompanied by dogs that trotted in formation, obviously pleased to be on the move again.

Kwani watched until Tolonqua was beyond the hills and could be seen no more. Villagers who stayed behind, and those from villages nearby, drifted away. From the roof where she stood, Kwani could see many dwellings clustered here and there in the distance, and the tipis of visitors come to trade. She wondered where the flint quarries were.

As she stood gazing, the old woman to whom she had given the buffalo meat approached, followed by a group of other women who stared at Kwani and chatted among themselves. The old woman stopped. From within her robe she removed the buffalo meat Tolonqua had given her, and waved it back and forth excitedly, proclaiming its wonders. The women listened avidly, glancing at Kwani. Finally, she tucked the meat back into her robe and climbed the ladder to the roof where Kwani stood. The woman was flushed and her eyes bright. She signed, "I wish to speak."

Kwani smiled. "Speak."

"I have told how the meat of the White Buffalo gives spiritual powers. I have eaten the meat and now I have these powers." She raised both arms overhead, chanting words Kwani could not understand.

Kwani stood in silence, not certain of what to do. She knew that meat had powers, but she and Tolonqua had eaten it and it didn't affect them this way.

The woman finished her chant and pointed to the group below that had grown larger as more women arrived. She signed, "They wish to trade for the meat of the White Buffalo." She tugged at Kwani's arm. "Come."

"Yes," Kwani signed, "but not now. When the hunters return we shall trade for dogs."

The woman went to the edge of the roof, leaned over, and called to the group below who glanced at one another and called back. The woman turned to Kwani. "They want to trade now. They have salt and turquoise and other valuables. Now!"

Kwani shook her head. "My mate is Hunting Chief of the Towa. It is he to whom the White Buffalo came. Therefore, it is he and only he who will trade the meat of the White Buffalo. We must wait for his return."

Again the woman called to those below. There was ominous muttering.

I must do something, Kwani thought. She signed, "I cannot trade, but I would be honored if you would allow me to give each of you a small sample of the meat that gives spiritual powers. Please wait."

Excited exclamations followed as she climbed down the ladder to her room, closing the hatch after her. She had to get her flint knife from the things that had been in Tolonqua's pack and she was not about to display the contents to curious eyes. She found the knife, selected a large piece of meat, cut it into bite-sized portions, poured it into a basket, and balanced it neatly upon her head. She thought, I hope there's enough for everybody. Acoya slept soundly in his cradle board, so Kwani climbed back up the ladder and pushed back the door of the hatch.

Women jammed the rooftop, jostling one another for standing room, while more women climbed the ladder from below. They stared avidly. One tried to snatch the basket. Kwani gripped it with both hands, then realized she needed one hand to sign. "I am honored that you come. But there is not enough room here. We shall go to the plaza."

The women reluctantly agreed, and motioned Kwani to descend the ladder first. But Kwani realized if she climbed down, the contents of the basket would be easily accessible to those climbing from above and behind her. Women could grab handfuls and there would not be enough to go around. She signed, "Allow me to get my baby first. You go to the plaza; I shall meet you there."

The women looked at one another, and nodded. When they had gone, Kwani returned to her room and fastened the cradle board to her back with the strap that went around her shoulders. Acoya still slept as she replaced the basket on her head and left for the plaza.

They saw her coming and hurried to meet her, led by the old woman waving her arms, chanting. A crowd of babbling children followed.

How shall I handle this? Kwani wondered. She was a stranger here, an alien, whose mate and protector was far away by now. These women could turn hostile in an instant. She clasped the shell of her necklace, pleading for wisdom.

The old woman reached Kwani and faced her, still chanting and flinging her arms about. Kwani took a deep breath, raised her own arms, and began to chant even more loudly. This gave the old woman pause. She quieted and stepped back while the other woman stared at Kwani without expression.

Kwani finished chanting, lowered her arms, and gazed searchingly at the crowd. She turned to the old woman and signed, "You are the one with spiritual powers. It must be you who gives the meat of the White Buffalo."

She handed the basket to the old woman who accepted it with pleased surprise, then walked among the women, handing each a piece of the meat. The women chewed vigorously; some exclaimed that already they felt the powers!

When everyone had some, there were still a few pieces left. The old woman signed to Kwani, "Who shall have these?"

Kwani thought for only a moment. "The Medicine Chief."

The women nodded. It was a wise decision. A boy was instructed to summon the Medicine Chief who appeared from his lodge so quickly that Kwani suspected he had been waiting. With enormous dignity, the old woman approached the Chief and offered the basket. There was a brief conversation. The Chief glanced at Kwani, accepted the basket, and disappeared into his lodge.

Kwani turned to go, but a woman grasped her arm. "We wish to make you welcome. Come."

She led Kwani through the village, followed by the rest of the women and excited children who ran ahead to tell everyone that the buffalo Caller was coming! More women came from tipis of other tribes who were there for the trading, and women in the fields put down their hoes of buffalo bone and their rakes of antler horns and hurried to learn the cause of the commotion.

Acoya was lifted from his cradle board and was much admired and exclaimed over as he was handed from woman to woman. They inspected the mark on his foot with awe. He took it in good nature, staring at them solemnly with his round, dark eyes.

Two men and a woman were building an addition to a dwelling, and Kwani stopped to watch. The new room being added had a double foundation of large stone slabs that the men placed vertically in a parallel row with the space between the rows filled with rubble and adobe applied by the woman. Now the men were adding unshaped stones horizontally, held together with adobe mortar expertly applied. Four large posts were already in place to support a roof of logs over which brush would be laid, packed down, and covered with adobe.

How unusual! Kwani thought. She had seen many villages on her journeys, but never construction like this.

She was curious about the two men; they seemed in no way to be related. The older resembled the others she had seen here, but the younger was taller, with aquiline features, and hair had been shaved from both sides of his head leaving a crest standing upright from forehead to the back of his neck. Obviously, he was of another tribe.

"Who is he?" Kwani signed.

"A slave. From the east." The woman lifted her chin proudly. "We are wealthy."

Kwani knew that slaves were valuable and widely traded, but she knew also what it was like to be captive. She turned away. "Please. We go now."

She wanted to see the flint quarries, but instead they took her from house to house where she was invited inside. Usually, they climbed the ladder to the roof and entered through the hatchway, but sometimes they entered through a low tunnel, what seemed to be a ventilating shaft at ground level, and had to crawl in on hands and knees. Rooms were much the same as the one where she and Tolonqua stayed, with floors and walls of smooth adobe. Adjoining storerooms were reached by low tunnels, and new rooms had been added as needed. Bowls, baskets, and other furnishings were shoved aside to make room for the women crowding inside.

Kwani sat facing the women who regarded her with curiosity, awe, and expectancy. Their round faces had no paint, but some had neat tattooed designs on forehead and chin. Their hair was in two braids wrapped with strips of deerskin in bright colors. Necklaces of bone, seed, and carved mussel shells rested between bare breasts, and garments of buffalo hide, embroidered and painted, hung from waist to knee. They looked at her in silence, and seemed to be waiting. Kwani wondered what she was supposed to do.

Finally, a woman signed, "We want to hear you sing."

"Ah." What shall I sing? she wondered. She remembered a song from her childhood, listening to people sing in springtime to make things grow. She signed the words as she sang.

> *"Yellow butterflies over the blossoming corn,*
> *With pollen-painted faces*
> *Chase one another.*
> *Blue butterflies over the blossoming virgin*
> *beans*
> *With pollen-painted faces*
> *Chase one another."*

The women listened raptly. The one who held Acoya rocked to and fro as though to a lullaby.

> *"Over the blossoming corn, over the virgin beans,*
> *Wild bees hum.*
> *Over the blossoming beans, over the virgin beans,*

Wild bees hum.
Over the field of growing corn
All day shall hang the thundercloud.
Over the field of growing corn
All day shall come the rushing rain."

When she had finished, they sat for a moment in silence. Then they signed, "Sing it again!"

Kwani sang it again, knowing, as she looked into eager and responsive faces, that she and her son and her mate would be safe. *If the buffalo hunt was successful.*

Kwani woke in the darkness, acutely conscious of Tolonqua's absence. Acoya slept by her side; his soft breathing in quick rhythm was comforting. There was no other sound; the village slept. Where was Tolonqua now?

Moonwoman's light shone through edges of the closed hatchway. Kwani climbed the ladder and pushed back the door to let the night and the moonlight inside. She climbed to the roof and stood for a moment looking over the village. These people had welcomed her, feasted her. But they had not shown her the Place of the Rainbow Flint. Why? Kwani wondered. Were the mines too valuable to be shown to outsiders? Tolonqua had brought her a long way to this place because of these mines and Kwani expected to see them. She considered going to find them while Moonwoman showed the way, but if she was seen wandering alone at night people might think she was a witch, planning evil deeds.

I'll wait until morning.

The village was already stirring when Acoya woke her, wanting to be fed. She nursed him and tucked him into his cradle board.

"Today we shall find the rainbow flint."

As she climbed down the outside ladder, there was the sound of children waking and of the mano stone on metate as women ground corn for the morning gruel. The breeze swept in from the plains bringing the fragrance of drying grasses and windswept places. It was a good smell, and Kwani breathed deeply.

Sunfather rose beyond the mountain, and a golden eagle soared majestically in a sky of vibrant blue. A day to savor!

The village was built on a hill leading to a terrace overlooking the river below. As Kwani wandered toward the river, men passed her hurriedly, with curious glances. Some men seemed to be from different tribes. Slaves, going to work at the quarries?

Curious, Kwani turned to follow them. A narrow, rocky trail climbed a hill thick with brush. The land spread before, behind, and all around like a crumpled blanket, with hills and hollows reaching to distant mountains shouldering white clouds. The wind blew more vigorously here, bending the grasses, tugging at her hair and her garments. "Why are you here?" it seemed to ask.

A pebble lodged in her sandal and Kwani sat to remove it. She looked closely at the shrubs and bushes around her. Some she knew, but others she had not seen before.

This was a foreign place.

Again the wind said, "Why are you here?"

For a moment Kwani hesitated. Maybe she should turn back. But no, she wanted to see what was up there.

The sound of men's voices and of loud pounding drew her on. Then she was there at the top of a crumpled hill. Men worked everywhere, some in ditches so deep only their arms showed as they heaved up baskets of rocks. Others struggled to wrest pieces of rock from a boulder jutting upward from deep within Earthmother's domain.

Kwani stood watching in fascination. Men in small groups worked in a wide area over low hills separated from one another by small gullies. Two men with a long pole tried to pry a chunk loose from a rocky outcrop. The pole was poked into a crevice in the rock, and both men leaned on the pole, grunting and straining, until at last a chunk broke loose. As the stone rolled on its side, Kwani saw that underneath the outer crust the stone was streaked with beautiful colors: red, white, brown, gray, green!

The men called, and a man (a slave?) hurried over, heaved the chunk to his shoulder, and strode away. Elsewhere, men stood at the edge of pits, heaved big rocks down into them, then jumped into the pits and emerged with loaded baskets.

As Kwani continued to watch, she was astonished to see a tall, muscular woman with small breasts stride over, lift the heavy basket to her head, and stride away, her robe flapping around muscular legs.

Suddenly, someone touched Kwani's shoulder. She turned, startled. It was the woman who had come to her dwelling. The woman signed, "It is forbidden for you to be here." She tugged at Kwani's arm.

"Why is it forbidden?"

"This is the Place of the Rainbow Flint. Only men come."

Kwani saw that men glanced at them, scowling. Again, the woman tugged at her arm. "We must go! Now."

Kwani nodded, and followed her back down the trail.

"I saw a woman there. A big woman with small breasts—"

"A *berdache*. A man who lives as a woman. He is strong and carries big loads. A slave."

"But—"

"He has no man parts. All cut off. He is flat here." She pointed to herself.

Kwani was shocked. What a terrible thing for a man to have no man parts! Not to make love or make babies. "How does he urinate?"

"Like this." The woman squatted. "Same as us."

Kwani was suffused with compassion. How demeaning for him! "Do men despise him and make fun of him?"

The woman stopped and looked at Kwani with disdain. "No. They use him as a woman. Fight over him sometimes."

"But . . ." Kwani frowned in puzzlement. "How—"

"They use him here." She pointed.

Kwani shook her head. "How can he enjoy that?"

"He wants to please them. He is a slave."

Kwani walked the rest of the way back in silence.

It was the third day since Tolonqua and the hunters had gone. There was no word of them. Kwani was tense with anxiety. If the buffalo were where she said they would be, the hunters should be on the way home by now. Maybe they would arrive tomorrow.

She bent over the hide of the White Buffalo staked to the ground for tanning. Women and children gathered to watch respectfully as she worked. Some offered to help, but were refused with thanks. No one must touch it but she and Tolonqua. And Acoya, when he was old enough. And maybe other children to come . . .

A boy pounded a cheerful rhythm on a small cottonwood drum with a clear musical voice. Kwani kept time with the mano stone, smooth and oval-shaped, used to rub the tanning solution into the hide. The skin was already scraped of flesh and fat that remained after Tolonqua's hasty skinning. Now she used a paste of fat, cooked brains, and liver, given by one of the women, and worked the greasy substance into the scraped hide. When it was thoroughly oiled she would let it dry in the sun. Later, she would saturate it with warm water and roll it into a bundle to soak overnight in preparation for stripping, followed by the graining and limbering of the leather. She would do that tomorrow. Now she rubbed the mano stone forward and back in time to the pulsing beat of the drum. Her necklace with the scallop-shell pendant swung to and fro as she worked. She had braided her hair as the women did here, in two braids tied at the end with buckskin thongs to which brightly colored beads of stone or bone or turquoise had been added; her braids with their turquoise beads swung, too.

Acoya was propped nearby in his cradle board. He was not yet one moon old, but it seemed that her spirit and his were united, somehow. She smiled at him. It was a beautiful day, blue and bright, and she was surrounded by people who respected and admired her, and she was working on the hide of the fabled White Buffalo belonging to her mate and to her son . . . and his sons to come. She was happy.

Or would be if she knew Tolonqua had found the buffalo. She wondered how soon he would return. She wondered if these people would be as welcoming if the hunters returned empty-handed. She worked carefully, pressing the tanning grease clear to the edges, rubbing hard. She remembered seeing the White Buffalo in the stream, and saw again in her imagination how the Spirit Being approached her, how he commanded her with his mystical pink eyes, and how he spoke without speaking. Again she felt the wonder.

She paused in the rubbing and placed both hands upon the hide, communing with the sacred spirit within it, and murmured a prayer.

"I thank you," she whispered. "I shall treasure you all of my life."

The people saw her praying, and quieted reverently. Some began to chant.

> "Spirit Being,
> Spirit Being,
> Behold us here!
> We honor you!"

Again the drum spoke, softly at first and then more loudly as others took up the chant, swaying.

Kwani knelt upon the hide as she worked, surrounded by chanting, swaying, gesticulating people paying homage to the spirit of the White Buffalo.

The fervor grew in crescendo. Suddenly it stopped.

A young brave from another tribe staggered into the group, panting. They greeted him with astonishment; they had been so intent upon their chanting they had not seen him coming.

A painted buckskin band above his right elbow bore a runner's insignia; he brought news. He wore only a brief apron before and behind, and ragged sandals. Perspiration glistened on his bronze body and he wiped his face with the back of his hand. He spoke rapidly in the language Kwani did not understand.

The people listened intently, glancing now and then at Kwani. They talked rapidly among themselves, and Kwani felt the sting of their eyes.

"What has happened?" she signed.

No one replied.

▲ 7 ▼

"**T**ell me!" Kwani signed.

She was ignored in a tumult of talk. Kwani shouldered her way to the runner, and faced him. She stared up at him, her blue eyes burning into his. "What happened?"

"Who are you?"

"I am She Who Remembers, mate of Tolonqua, Hunting Chief of the Towa."

His glance was scornful. "I went to where you said the buffalo were. No buffalo. No hunters." He smiled grimly. "Maybe you tell us now where they are."

Kwani stared at him without expression. "They were there when I said they were there. Do buffalo remain always in one place?" She turned to the women. "He takes us for fools."

She snatched Acoya from the woman who held him, turned her back, and marched to her dwelling, ignoring a babble of voices. Inside her room she slumped to the floor.

What had happened?

What if no buffalo were found?

Three more days passed and the hunters did not return. Kwani sensed distrust and resentment that hurt more than the sting of their eyes. She busied herself with the buffalo hide, trying to pretend that she was glad that no one was with her now. She was ignored.

The hide had been soaked. Now she wrung out the surplus moisture, stretched the hide onto a frame she had found stored in her room, and with a flat, smooth bone rod she pressed hard against the hide, drawing the rod steadily from top to bottom. A ripple of water oozed out each time. When she had removed as much water as she could, she left the hide on the frame to dry and bleach until it was ready for graining. Working made it easier to endure the shame of ostracism and the agony of suspense. Where was Tolonqua?

Another day passed. No word of the hunters. The Medicine Chief and those of the Medicine Society were loud in their reminders that proper preparations for the hunt had not taken place. They had warned of disasters. What else could be expected?

Again, she busied herself with the hide, pretending not to see the hostile glances, nor to hear the sarcastic tone of voice in remarks to one another. When small boys threw rocks at her, she threw them back with an accuracy that brought surprised howls but no more rocks. She hid her tears.

Using a sharp, globular piece of bone sliced to expose its spongy inner texture, she rubbed the hide to remove what fibers remained. Satisfied with the smoothness and uniformity, she carried the hide down to the river where willows and cottonwood trees grew. She stretched a piece of Tolonqua's yucca fiber rope between two willows and draped the hide over it. Grasping an end in each hand, she seesawed the hide back and forth over the rope so that the heat of friction would finish drying and limbering the hide. It was soft now, ready to be fashioned into a robe, the sacred robe of the White Buffalo, for Tolonqua.

Where was he?

Another day passed. Kwani remained in her room, subsisting only upon the meat of the buffalo, and water brought from the river. She waited to see when no other women went for water, then climbed down the steep bank to the river to fill her water jar. Returning, she walked proudly, the jar upon her head, and looked straight ahead, ignoring those who ignored her, and felt a weight in her heart heavier than the weight of the water jar.

Once she saw the berdache who glanced at her as he strode past with a big basket of flint on his head. She wanted to follow and see the knappers working the flint, but she did not. Not now.

Very early in the morning on the tenth unendurable day, Kwani woke to a distant sound. She jerked upright from her sleeping mat. Could it be? She listened intently. It came again, faintly, from a distance.

The conch-shell horn!

With a cry of joy, Kwani climbed to the roof. Others heard and gathered on rooftops and in the plaza. Again came the haunting wail, lingering in the air. Kwani strained to see in the predawn light. At last, the hunters appeared, walking slowly, bent under burdens. Dogs plodded along, struggling with huge loads.

A shout arose. "They come! They come!"

Men ran to meet them and women hurried to prepare for the feasting, Kwani remained on the roof, watching. She felt every pore had eyes searching for Tolonqua. At last he appeared, marching side by side with the Hunting Chief at the head of the procession.

"Tolonqua!" she called as though he could hear.

She must prepare to welcome him! Hastily she climbed back down and splashed water upon herself from the water jar. She smoothed the water over her body, thinking of Tolonqua's caress, and her senses stirred, waiting for him. She dried herself with a corner of a blanket, brushed her hair, and wrapped her robe around her waist, leaving her full breasts bare with the scallop shell nestling between. She climbed back to the roof to watch for him, realizing how much she had missed him and how much she wanted him. Right now.

There were shouts as the hunters and dogs staggered into view, loaded with buffalo. Obviously, they could have used twice as many dogs; the burdens carried by the hunters were enormous. Dogs crouched wearily as women hastened to unload them, and hunters gladly relinquished loads to men and boys who dragged the meat to the preparation area. Already, big pots were suspended over fires or placed directly upon coals. Women exclaimed over the huge bundles of hides, jostling one another to look. The War Chief strode about in an effort to obtain order from chaos, while the Medicine Chief chanted loudly, thanking the gods for granting his personal request for a successful hunt, thereby turning a potential catastrophe into a triumph.

In the hubbub of commotion, Tolonqua stood indifferent to congratulations and accolades, searching for sight of Kwani. He saw her standing there, aloof, like a goddess upon a sacred mountain, aglow in dawn light. He elbowed his way through the throng and climbed up to her. Instantly she was in his arms.

"Come!" she whispered, leading him to the hatchway. He followed her down the ladder, tossed her robe aside, and laid her down on the sleeping mat. He bent over her, caressing her breasts, her thighs, her woman part.

"Beautiful! Beautiful! Beautiful!"

She held him close, pulling him closer, crying out. Then the delirium of crescendo, the warm flooding, the joy and peace afterward. She lay close to his heart again, listening to its voice. How she had missed him!

Finally, she said, "What happened? The runner—"

"He went to the wrong place. The buffalo were where you said they would be. A huge herd! So big that the Hunting Chief wanted to get as much meat as possible—more than if we took what we could with arrows. The herd was drifting west toward a place of steep cliffs, so we followed, waiting until they got close enough—"

"To drive them over the cliff?"

"Yes. But then they began to go in another direction. We had to drive them to the right way."

"How?"

He raised his head to smile down to her. "Can you guess?"

"No. Tell me!"

"The shell horn. The hunters positioned themselves to head the herd toward the cliff. Then I blew the horn. The buffalo ran! Right over the cliff! More men, many more men and dogs will be needed to bring back even a part of what is left."

She gazed at him solemnly. "You will go with them again?"

"No. We trade for dogs and for flint, and return to Cicuye."

"Good." She kissed him and listened to the pounding of his heart as he pulled her to him again.

Evening fires burned high and feasting was under way. Kwani and Tolonqua sat in a place of honor beside the Hunting Chief who stood in the firelight, repeating the story of the hunt, telling how his wisdom in driving the herd over a cliff provided his people with this feasting—and the feasting to come, as well as the hides, the bones, the sinews, the skulls, and all the parts of the buffalo that were now theirs. With more awaiting at the bottom of the cliff.

Slaves scurried about, hauling baskets of buffalo chips for the fires, jars of water for the pots, and big hunks of meat to be roasted or boiled in stews with corn and delicious seeds or tubers. Cakes from dried and pounded mesquite beans flavored with herbs were dipped into the stew and devoured with appropriate lip smacking and polite belches afterward.

The berdache, dressed elaborately in womanly finery and with many necklaces, ear ornaments, and bracelets, unloaded the heaviest burdens with a flourish, and with frequent glances at Tolonqua.

Kwani whispered, "Do you know who that is?"

"A berdache."

"Yes. He notices you." She kept her voice matter-of-fact.

"Us. He notices us, and why not? We are honored here."

Kwani wanted to say more, but she did not. Feasting continued, stories were told and retold about the hunt and about the buffalo Caller who made it possible. One would never know, thought Kwani, that she had been ostracized and scorned and had rocks thrown at her all those days before. Women who had eaten the meat of the White Buffalo told of their visions and new powers, and exulted that now they could trade for more of the sacred food, thanks to the wonderful powers of She Who Remembers and the mystical persuasion of the shell horn.

Kwani looked about her, at the men with their red eye paint, at the women who had belittled her, and she wanted to leave this place. When it was over and they were back in their room at last, Kwani said, "When may we go from here?"

"Tomorrow. After the trading."

Kwani remembered the hovering slave whose glances at Tolonqua had grown more frequent and intimate.

"I do not like the berdache."

"Why?"

"He looks at you as if—"

"Yes. He knows I am interested in him."

Kwani was shocked into silence.

Tolonqua continued, "I will trade for him. He is strong. He will be useful to us on the way back to Cicuye."

"But I do not like him!"

Tolonqua shrugged. How typically female she was! "It does not matter whether or not you like him. He will protect you and Acoya. He is strong, and a good worker. He will care for the dogs and their loads, and carry a heavy load himself on the way back. And if we are attacked . . ." He paused, and shrugged again. "We shall not be, but if we are, he will be helpful. I am told he is an excellent bowman. He is a good investment, valuable for trade."

Kwani remained silent, for what could she say? Remembering the slave's narrow face with eyebrows all plucked out; remembering the sardonic twist of thin lips and the hooded stare of glinting eyes, she knew instinctively that here was a rival. And a potential enemy.

▲ 8 ▼

Trading was under way. Because people came from distant tribes for the prized flint, it was a logical place to gather for trading. Tipis crowded the hills around the village and along the riverbanks. On a comparatively level area between the town and the river, wares were spread upon the ground and on blankets for display. There was a babble of talk, a frenzy of signing, and a jumble of color in costume and in face and body paint. The enticement of delicious odors from cooking pots and the exhilaration of cool breeze and warm sun enhanced the excitement of successful bargaining.

People wandered from one display to another, and squatted to examine wares. There were fine skins of mountain sheep, beaver, elk, mountain lion, deer, and buffalo. There were live eagles in cages, tallow, pemmican, shells, corn, salt, pigments, baskets, cooking pots, mugs, beautiful carved pipes of stone and of bone, smooth pipes of clay, and other objects of bone and of wood for ceremonial uses, flutes and drums, rattles and whistles, bows and arrows, blankets, gambling pieces, jewelry—everything to be desired was there. Including, of course, the most valuable trade item of all, the slaves. Kwani was gratified to see that the berdache was not among them.

They stood in a small group: men, women, and several children carefully supervised by an elder of the Warrior Society while potential buyers examined the wares. Men and women were felt for muscles in legs, arms, and back. The children, three young boys and a small girl, were hefted for weight and examined in the mouth. When the little girl cried she was hushed sharply. The boys stood like men, staring straight ahead without expression.

Kwani sat with Tolonqua who wore, as a mantle over his shoulders, the handsome robe Kwani had made for him from the tanned hide of the White Buffalo. Spread before him was what was left of the buffalo meat; most had been traded for six husky dogs and their equipment, and for a selection of choice flint. Also displayed were several handsome (and heavy) bowls of the Anasazi, greatly prized. Beside him, his bulging pack contained items not yet offered for trade, as well as turquoise and other valuables obtained in trading so far. An eager crowd squatted around the blanket, bargaining vigorously in sign language. Tolonqua would bargain with one, then another, and soon the traders would be bidding against one another, offering more turquoise, or tools of flint and of bone, or other valuables.

Kwani watched as Tolonqua sat with legs crossed, the sacred mantle folded about him, and his face intent and eyes alert as his hands spoke so swiftly she could not always read the words. Then agreement would be reached, objects would change hands, and Tolonqua would hand Kwani another treasure to stuff in the pack.

She thought, We are wealthy beyond belief. But it is yet a moon's journey to reach Cicuye. It is dangerous; much can happen. . . .

A sudden boom of the drum commanded attention. The Warrior Chief stood by the group of slaves and raised his right hand for silence. When it was reasonably quiet, he signed, "Now is the opportunity to trade for slaves. You have seen them, examined them, and judged their value. Trading shall now begin."

He stepped aside, and the Clan Chief strode forward. He was taller than most, and magnificently adorned in a buckskin breechcloth embroidered with dyed porcupine quills from the east, shell beads from the Sunset Sea, and turquoise from the mountains of the west. He wore a headdress of buffalo horns and eagle plumes, and his red eye paint was enhanced with vertical black lines from eye to chin. Scarlet feathers at both ears stirred dramatically with each movement. There was a murmur of admiration, another boom of the drum, and at last he spoke, signing simultaneously.

"You have seen, you have examined, these slaves. They are young, healthy, and strong, and will give many moons of excellent service." He turned to gaze approvingly at the small group who ignored him. He continued, "As you know, my people have the reputation of trading only the best. Therefore, we accept only the best. Trading may now begin."

There was a flurry of signing. One slave left the group, and then another, while valuables changed hands. Finally, the little girl stood alone, sucking her thumb.

"I want her!" Kwani whispered.

"No. It is too far to Cicuye."

"But—"

A woman from a distant tribe had already stepped forward. She offered the Clan Chief a blanket of woven buffalo hair, soft and warm. The Chief inspected it carefully, inch by inch, on both sides. Satisfied, he shoved the girl toward the woman who lifted the child in her arms and carried her away, smiling, holding her close.

Kwani thought, She had no girl child, but now she does. The child will be her daughter. Loved. But why must she buy a slave for a daughter? Kwani wondered. Among the Anasazi, if she had no daughter and yearned for one, her sister or another clan member would share a daughter with her; the child would have two mothers.

I want a daughter. . . .

For a moment there were no traders at their blanket, and Tolonqua rose. "Stay here with these things. Watch them carefully."

"Where are you going?"

He did not reply, but took two grizzly bear paws with long claws from his pack. Kwani watched as he approached the Clan Chief who stood with a group of other Chiefs. Tolonqua greeted the Chiefs who acknowledged him. Kwani could not see the signing, but she could see the reaction of the Clan Chief as Tolonqua presented him with the bear paws. He was pleased and impressed. There was more signing, and Tolonqua returned and picked up his pack. "I shall trade with the Chiefs now."

"For what?" she asked as he walked away. He did not reply, but she knew.

The berdache.

Tolonqua sat in the lodge of the Clan Chief, legs crossed, hands on knees in suitable dignity. The white mantle over his shoulders shone palely in the light from the fire pit and the hatchway overhead. Also present were the Medicine Chief, the Warrior Chief, and other Chiefs of various societies. The ceremonial pipe had made two rounds and was returned to the Clan Chief who puffed it, coughed, puffed again, and laid the ornate clay pipe upon the altar where other sacred objects rested.

After the proper period of silence, the Clan Chief spoke, signing as he did so for Tolonqua's benefit.

"You have a matter of importance to discuss?"

"I do."

"I wait to hear it."

"Tomorrow, my mate, my son, and I leave here to return to Cicuye. As you know, it is a journey of one moon. Unknown tribes come now to the plains, tribes we have not met before. It will be dangerous. I request protection."

"A war party to accompany you? It is not—"

"No. I wish only for a good bowman. A slave to protect my wife and my son if I am killed. I offer to trade for the berdache."

There was a shocked silence. A Chief spoke. "The slave belongs to me. He is not for barter."

Tolonqua nodded respectfully. "I understand. However . . ." He opened his pack and removed a necklace even more lavish than the one the Warrior Chief had received and which now rested in splendor upon his bare chest. He offered it to the slave's owner who eyed it covetously, but shook his head. Tolonqua spread the necklace upon the floor before him, and rummaged in his pack. He removed a handsome belt woven of dog and of human hair in mystical design, and with a long, luxurious fringe. He passed the belt to the Chief beside him, indicating that it should be passed around for examination. The belt went slowly from hand to hand as the men admired the fine workmanship and design. When it reached the slave's owner, he examined it carefully, hesitated, swallowed, and shook his head.

The belt was handed back to Tolonqua who laid it beside the necklace. Again, his pack yielded a treasure, a small bag made from the skin of a young rabbit, embellished with tiny shell beads and adorned with multicolored feathers. He opened it and spilled the contents upon the floor. Peyote. The sun plant for communication with gods. The plant most sacred.

There was a gasp. The men looked to the Clan Chief. Such an offer must be considered seriously!

The Medicine Chief spoke, signing, "I have partaken of the meat of the White Buffalo. Its spirit speaks to me. The sun plant is for our people." He gazed sternly at the slave's owner.

Once more, Tolonqua reached in his pack. There was a tiny tinkling sound. Slowly, glancing at the slave's owner, he removed an ear ornament of shiny white shell from which dangled a little copper bell, a rare prize from the distant south. He held it up, shaking it gently, and the bell sang enticingly.

There were excited murmurs, and hands reached to examine it, but he laid it on the floor with the necklace, the belt, and the peyote.

He signed, "All this for the berdache."

The Clan Chief signaled, and a Chief rose and climbed through the hatch. The slave's owner looked down at his clasped hands. There was a twitch in the corner of one eye, and his mouth was set in a grim line. But he glanced at the objects offered for barter and did not shake his head.

There were footsteps overhead. The Clan Chief signed, "The berdache comes."

The Chief descended the ladder, followed by the slave who seemed to know at once what had transpired. He looked at Tolonqua, eyes gleaming in his narrow face. The Clan Chief spoke, and the slave went to Tolonqua and knelt with bowed head.

Tolonqua replaced the peyote in its bag, and drew the drawstring. He gathered up the necklace, the belt, and the jingling ear ornament and handed all to the slave, signing to whom it should be given. The slave took them to his former owner, and a look passed between them. The Chief leaned forward and looped the ear ornament over the slave's ear, speaking softly. The slave touched his forehead to the floor, whispering. Then he returned to sit behind Tolonqua.

Tolonqua tried not to reveal his satisfaction. His objectives were accomplished. Now they could return home.

It was the second day since Kwani, Tolonqua, and the slave left the Place of the Rainbow Flint. Kwani carried Acoya in a sling tied inside her blanket. She carried no pack nor even the cradle board; all were loaded on the dogs that trotted obediently under the slave's expert direction. Kwani walked easily, swinging her arms, and Tolonqua strode beside her.

He said, "It is good to be relieved of burdens, is it not?"

She thought, He wants me to admit he was right about buying the slave. So she nodded, but made no comment. The slave had loaded and unloaded the dogs and fed them each day. He spoke to the animals in confidential terms as though they were people, and the dogs understood what he said. Kwani had to admit he was useful—indispensable, in fact—but there seemed to be an unspoken communication between him and Tolonqua that excluded her. She thought, Well, they are both men and that's how men are with each other. But it rankled.

She watched the slave walking ahead of them. His hair was in two long braids, tied with strips of red buckskin, and was shiny and clean as a woman's. He wore a woman's robe from the waist down, and necklaces dangled between pudgy breasts. Women's moccasins of buffalo hide reached to his ankles and were elaborately embroidered with porcupine quills dyed red, green, blue, and black. Bracelets of bone, shell, and turquoise encircled both big wrists. Many ornaments dangled from one ear; the other held only the white shell with the little bell that swung and tinkled as he walked.

As though he sensed her gaze, he turned to glance at her. There was something about his face. . . . Maybe it was the light brown eyes with dark flecks, eyes that seemed to seek escape from the confines of a narrow face and cheekbones humped high on either side of a narrow nose. His eyebrows were plucked out, giving his forehead an austere appearance. He had a way of flicking his tongue as though to taste the air as a snake does. He did this now, as he glanced at her, and licked his lips afterward. He turned to Tolonqua.

"The dogs want water," he said in Towa.

Kwani had been surprised to learn he spoke several languages. She wondered if he had been traded frequently. She watched as he removed a bowl from one of the packs, poured water into it from a buffalo-stomach water bag, and placed the bowl on the ground for the dogs to drink.

Tolonqua turned to Kwani. "Rest now."

She sat on the tawny grass to nurse the baby, and Tolonqua sat beside her, smiling at Acoya who sucked vigorously. "Are you thirsty?" he asked Kwani.

"I'm always thirsty." She laughed. "He drinks me dry."

He handed her his water bag and she drank deeply, allowing the blanket over her shoulders to slip down so that her full breasts and the nursing baby were exposed to the slave's gaze.

Let him see what he can never have, never do.

If the slave noticed, he gave no sign but busied himself with the dogs. When they had licked the water bowl dry, he returned it to the pack.

Tolonqua lay on his back, his hands clasped behind his head, looking up at the sky. It was a clear turquoise-blue, bare of clouds or even of birds. Kwani sat beside him, watching his chest rise and fall with his breathing. She wanted to lay her head there again and listen to his heart. If the slave were not present, she would.

Tolonqua turned his face to the slave. "What is your name?"

The gleaming eyes showed surprise. "I am slave."

Tolonqua frowned. "Everyone is given names. Tell me yours."

He shrugged. "Call me what you will."

"Call him Lapu," Kwani blurted, and was immediately ashamed. Lapu was cedar bark, used for diapering and for holding menstrual flow. It was the ultimate insult, and the slave had not deserved it. Why was she reacting like this? She said, "I apologize. I shall call you Owa, because you are strong." Owa meant "rock."

"A good name," Tolonqua said, but his glance at Kwani was puzzled. Something was troubling her, but what? He shook his head. Never would he understand women, even this remarkable mate of his. But her beauty—the round face with its small nose and great blue eyes over which dark brows hovered—did not need to be understood, only loved.

Before resuming their journey, Kwani had to relieve herself. There was no place offering privacy, so she simply turned her back, and squatted. Owa came to squat beside her, and Kwani muffled a gasp. Where his man parts had been was a hideous scar, wrinkled and red, from which the urine trickled.

Owa saw her horrified glance. "You see?" he whispered. "I am but a slave."

It was Kwani's turn to flush crimson. "You are Owa," she said.

▲ 9 ▼

The Querechos padded quietly through the canyon in the shadow of early morning. There were five of them, quiet and alert, following the stream. The leader, short, squat, and young for his responsibility, raised his hand to halt. They stood silently, peering upstream. There was no sound but the river; nothing moved but the wind.

The leader spoke. "We know the White Buffalo was here before the river rose. We have not seen his tracks since." He turned to the others with a gesture that rattled his bracelets of bone and claws. "Can it be that the meat we discovered in the cave was that of the White Buffalo?"

The men glanced at one another. That would be why buffalo meat in this canyon of plenty was carefully saved until the hunters could return for it. Only barbarians from the plains would kill the White Buffalo.

The leader continued, "Perhaps our kinsman tried to prevent it and that is why they killed him."

The hunters nodded, scowling. The severed head of their Chief—what was left of it—had been found on the bank when the river receded. The body had not been found. A double disaster. That, and the murder of the sacred White Buffalo, bringer of good fortune and good hunting, were the ultimate desecration.

"We shall be ready when the hunters return." The leader raised his bow with a war whoop. "Revenge!"

The others joined until war cries echoed and reechoed in the canyon, sending squirrels up the trees, rabbits to their burrows, and deer swiftly to higher ground.

Days passed, but the hunters did not return. Some of the Querechos wanted to abandon the ambush, but the leader persisted. "They will return for the meat of the White Buffalo."

Sentries were posted to observe the trails into the canyon, and at last they were rewarded. Three men were seen. Immediately, the sentry reported to the War Chief, and a war party was formed. A scout was sent to investigate and to report. He did so, and returned with news.

"These are not men of the Plains. They are from the west."

The Chief nodded. "That is why it took so long for them to return. What else did you discover?"

"Their heads are flat in back."

"Ah. Flatheads! They are Anasazi!"

"Two are hunters. The other has a big scar like this"— he ran a finger from ear to mouth—"that pulls up the corner of his mouth like this." He grimaced. "Maybe he is a shaman."

"Of course. That is why he returns for meat of the White Buffalo."

"Aye!" The men nodded so that their ear ornaments jingled. One, whose face was that of a killer who relished his profession, said, "We shall capture the shaman and see if his magic will prevent the kind of death we shall give him!"

"Kill the others also!"

"And give their heads to the river!"

"Aye!" The cry was unanimous.

Zashue, young Medicine Chief of the Eagle Clan of the Anasazi, and two of the clan's hunters made their way carefully down the trail to the canyon floor. It was rocky and steep, and none of them had been there before.

"Are you sure they came this way?" asked young Soyap. He had never before been so far from home and he wished he were back there right now. This canyon was not a place for strangers. Too many places for enemies to hide.

"Of course!" Zashue turned to him impatiently. "Kokopelli and the witch were seen headed this way. They would come here for water and shelter." He flicked his eyes to Naua, the grizzled tracker who had brought them this far. "Do you question my decision?" His small eyes sparked defiance.

Naua gazed intently into the canyon and did not reply. He raised a hand for silence, listening. It was perfectly still. He shook his head and rubbed his chin with a gnarled hand.

"It is too quiet." He turned quickly to Zashue who was about to protest in outrage. "They would come here, you are right. But—"

"But what?" Zashue's snarl widened with impatience. "Maybe they are still here. With the necklace. *Our* necklace." Once the necklace was returned to his clan and to

Tiopi who regarded herself as She Who Remembers now, Zashue's triumph would be complete. He could establish a clan of his own. No longer would he be ordered about by Huzipat, aged Chief of the Eagle Clan. He would be respected and feared, a great Chief in his own right!

Naua rubbed his chin again and tried not to reveal his impatience with this young Medicine Chief whose inner scars were deeper and more ugly than those which were visible.

"Perhaps others are here now who will not welcome us. They could be hiding, watching us right now."

The men stared uneasily into the canyon. They were hot and very thirsty and the cool green and the silvery water looked wonderfully inviting. But anyone could hide down there in the twists and turns among the trees and the boulders. Maybe an entire clan!

"It is too quiet," Naua said again.

Zashue snorted. "Of course it is quiet. They see us coming. And here we stand like rabbits. Scared rabbits. We have come all this way and now that we are here what do we do? Just stand here?"

"We would be wise to hide," Naua said.

"Very well. We shall hide. Down there!"

Zashue pushed ahead, sliding and stumbling down the steep trail, not bothering to glance behind to see if his companions followed. He would do it alone if he had to. He would obtain the necklace and return it to his people! He would be a Chief to remember! And one that Kwani, the witch, would yearn to forget. He touched his scarred face. What a pleasure to rip her face from mouth to ear as she had torn his with her spear! He fingered the flint knife at his waist.

It grew cooler as they descended. The breeze swept through, sweet with the taste of the stream. The men reached the bank and knelt eagerly to drink, gulping the clear, cold water from their hands.

There was a sudden *thunk*. Zashue froze with hands mid-air. Soyap fell face down into the stream with an arrow protruding from his back. He gurgled and did not rise.

"Hide!" Naua hissed, and rose to dart among the trees. An arrow pierced him between his shoulder blades and all the way through his body so that the arrowhead's point thrust from his chest. He threw both hands in the air and fell sprawling.

Zashue scrambled up the bank, panting in terror. A large

boulder squatted between two scraggly junipers; Zashue ran for it. He crouched, trembling, beneath a small overhang. He fitted an arrow in his bow, and waited.

Waited for what? Kokopelli carried no weapons. Whose arrows found Soyap and Naua?

He listened, straining to hear. Nothing. Then a faint scraping sound. Footsteps?

With drawn bow he inched around the side of the boulder. Arrows flew from among the trees, bouncing off the stone. Zashue darted back, his heart thumping. He was ambushed!

Another sound. From the right. He turned, bracing himself. His hands, slick with sweat, gripped the bow more tightly.

A sound from the left! He whirled. Nothing.

Slowly, very carefully, he eased far enough to the left to peer around the boulder. He did not see the Querecho who leaped from the right and struck Zashue a blow that threw him to the ground in a crumpled heap. Instantly, the Querecho was upon him, wrenching the bow from his grasp and the flint knife from his belt.

Whooping in satisfaction, four more Querechos ran from behind the trees. They jerked Zashue to his feet and tore the ornaments from his ears, leaving them bleeding. They snatched the necklaces from his neck and yanked off his bracelets and his handsome belt and quiver. His breechcloth was ripped away with derisive hoots at the meagerness of the man parts revealed.

When they had stripped him naked but for his sandals, which were much worn and not worth removing, they signed, "You are a shaman. Let us see how your magical powers protect your brothers."

Zashue fought to be free as they dragged him to the stream where Naua lay sprawled on the bank and young Soyap lay face down in the water, his head wobbling in the current. Four men held Zashue as the fifth took Zashue's sharp flint knife, lifted Naua's grizzled head by the hair, slashed the neck, let the blood gush, then sawed through the backbone. He held the head by the hair and swung it around over his head.

"You did this to our kinsman. Now we do it to yours."

He released the head and it flew through the air, landing in the stream with a splash. He pulled the necklaces from the gaping neck and tossed them to the others who grabbed for them. Zashue jerked an arm free.

He signed. "You kill wrong men! None of us have been

here before.'' How dare these barbarians ambush and murder Anasazis! How dare they attack him, Medicine Chief of the Eagle Clan!

Again, he signed, ''We were not here. You kill wrong men!''

The Querecho ignored him and grabbed Soyap's feet to pull him from the water. Soyap had seen but fourteen summers; his manhood vision had directed him to follow his Medicine Chief to noble deeds. Zashue growled in rage and struggled harder but the men held him fast.

As Soyap's head emerged from the water, Zashue saw that a piece of the nose was missing; something had taken a bite from it. The Querecho lifted the head and pointed to the mutilated nose.

''Ha!'' he chortled. ''The river is hungry!'' He reached for the knife.

Zashue turned his head away but he heard the slashing, the grinding. One of the men forced Zashue's head to turn back.

''Look! Look! You did this to our kinsman. We do it to yours!''

''No!''

The head flew through the air, splashed into the water, and bobbed grotesquely downstream.

''No!'' Zashue cried again. How could this be happening? He touched the tiny scar between his ribs. This was where the secret of his power lay—a bit of crystal no larger than a seed. He had removed it from the side of his dead father and inserted it into himself, a Medicine Chief's secret, passed from one to the other. He pressed it and felt the tiny lump under his skin. His power!

He faced the Querecho and signed arrogantly, ''I am Medicine Chief of the Eagle Clan. Anasazi. I come for the necklace.''

''What necklace?''

''Stolen from us by the witch who calls herself She Who Remembers. It is ours. I demand to have it. Where is she?''

The Querecho regarded him with amused contempt. ''You lie!'' He gestured briefly. Zashue was thrown to the ground and the Querecho straddled him, grinning.

Zashue tried to cry out once more, but no cry came. Again, there was the sound of slashing and of grinding, but Zashue did not hear it.

* * *

Valuables from the bodies had been accumulated and the headless dead left for scavengers. Now the Querechos sat in the cave where the buffalo meat was stored. They had been in consultation for some time.

One said, "I wonder about the necklace."

"I, also," another replied. "And about the witch. Those things she left. Odds and ends—"

"Worth little."

"Why would an Anasazi woman come here? A moon's distance—"

"To escape, perhaps? A witch . . ."

The men glanced at one another. What if the shaman was telling the truth after all?

The leader said, "The necklace has powerful medicine or they would not come so far to get it." He paused, fingering necklaces recently acquired, and looked at each in turn. "Our sentries watch the trails; they will see intruders and take suitable action. The woman was not alone; two men were with her. That we know. Heavy rains washed away tracks but some will be found. We shall follow and get that necklace. Powerful medicine will be ours!"

"Aye! And the hide of the White Buffalo!"

There were jubilant shouts. "Follow!"

▲ 10 ▼

Yellow Bird, aged grandmother of Two Elk, Clan Chief of Cicuye, lay miserably upon her buffalo robes and soft matting. Sleep would not come. From the kiva came the pulse of drums and the cadence of chanting voices, but Tolonqua's voice was not among them.

Where was he? It had been too long since he departed with Kokopelli to find that foreign woman, Kwani, who disappeared. Yellow Bird hoped secretly that Kwani had died, but no. Runners said she and Tolonqua were returning but no one knew where Kokopelli was. It was rumored that he was dead. Did Tolonqua kill the Toltec to obtain his mate?

Yellow Bird stirred uneasily on her bed that seemed to grow more uncomfortable with passing seasons. She needed more buffalo robes, robes that Tolonqua, the Hunting Chief, provided. But evil forces were at work, she was certain of this. Witches, no doubt. Maybe they would encourage Tolonqua to force the building of a new city on the *mesilla*, the flat-topped ridge, as Tolonqua wanted to do. Deserting this fine pueblo at the base of the ridge, the pueblo where she and her ancestors had lived all these long years! This pueblo was where her spirit, and theirs, would enter Sipapu, not up there on that ridge where cold winds probed the bones.

What would happen if everyone left this old Cicuye for the new? She would be alone.

She sat up abruptly, looking about her. "No!" she said aloud. "No! I shall not allow it! I will find the witch responsible and that witch shall die!"

She lay back down, feeling better. At least she, Yellow Bird, had authority. And she would use it, yes indeed.

In an adjoining room Two Elk lay with his wife. He, too, found that sleep eluded him. While Tolonqua was gone there had been no mention of a new city on the ridge, and communal harmony was restored. Tolonqua, as great a hunter as he might be, was dangerous to the tribe. Clan survival depended upon all working together as one. Under one lead-ership—his. The Hunting Chief was becoming too individ-ualistic. He stood out from the others and endangered them all by doing so. Something must be done, but what?

He had to relieve himself and stepped outside to urinate against a wall. There was no moon. The sentries posted nearby would be unable to see enemy movement at a dis-tance. He thought briefly of the wall Tolonqua wanted to build around a new city on the ridge. . . . He pushed the thought from his mind. This pueblo had survived all these years and would continue to do so.

A coyote called, and another. Two Elk listened intently. Animal, or human calls signaling? He glanced up at a sentry on a roof, barely visible against starlight. ''What do you hear?''

''Coyotes.''

Coyotes were tricksters. Sometimes, witches took coyote form. ''If they come closer, get the War Chief.''

''I will get him.''

''And the Medicine Chief.''

The sentry did not reply for a moment. ''I will,'' he said respectfully.

''Very well.''

Two Elk nodded and returned to his sleeping mat. One could not be too careful about witches.

When he had gone, the sentry snickered quietly. Calling the War Chief and the Medicine Chief for coyotes! The old Clan Chief's years were betraying him. The sentry squatted on the roof, looked up at the stars, and wondered when Tolonqua would come home.

Kwani sat in the light of the campfire, watching Tolonqua and Owa preparing camp for the night. They worked well together, each helping the other. The dogs had been un-loaded and a blanket was spread for her and Tolonqua to sleep upon. Owa refused a blanket and slept on the dry grass of the bare ground where they spent the night.

A pot of water with pemmican bubbled upon the coals, emitting an enticing aroma. She had fed Acoya and now she tucked him in his cradle board. He objected. He did not take to a cradle board contentedly as most babies did. He wanted freedom to kick his arms and legs. She smiled into his round little eyes. ''Very well, small one. You shall sleep on a blanket tonight.''

As she spread another blanket and lay beside him, she looked up at the stars, brilliant in the obsidian sky.

"See?" she whispered to Acoya. "Your father's campfire is up there."

Okalake. Son of the Sun Chief of the Eagle Clan, who was to be Sun Chief himself one day. No, she would not think of that, not now. It all happened long ago. Or so it seemed; much had happened since.

The journey. The long, hard journey to the canyon where Acoya was born. Now the return journey was nearly ended. Soon they would be back in Cicuye with Tolonqua's people. She would have a home, a clan, and people of her own.

At last.

She gazed up into the great obsidian bowl of stars.

"Did you send the ravens?" she whispered.

There was no reply. The plains lay in vast silence. No wolves howled, no buffalo bellowed into the night. There were only the quiet voices of Tolonqua and Owa busy with their tasks, and the sounds of the dogs settling down. Darkness enfolded them, bringing them close together against the terrible solitude.

I am weary deep inside, Kwani thought. Once I am in Cicuye I shall never leave it. I have gone too far and left my spirit behind. I must wait for it to catch up. When we are in Cicuye, all will be well.

But nagging unease squatted on her chest and poked at her heart. No longer was she the mate of Kokopelli. Would the Towa accept her, an Anasazi, as mate of their Hunting Chief? Would they allow her to be She Who Remembers and teach young girls all they should know, women's secrets handed down from generation to generation? To teach this was her destiny, a sacred responsibility bequeathed by the Old One, She Who Remembers before her.

She clasped the scallop shell of her necklace, seeking reassurance. She closed her eyes, visualizing the House of the Sun, the sacred temple on the mesa where the Old One chose her as successor. She saw in memory the altar stone in the Room of Remembering where she knelt to learn the secrets. Her mother's spirit and the spirit of the Old One had come to guide and to comfort her.

"Take me there again!" she beseeched the Ancient Ones.

She was there. In the silent room open to Sunfather's eye and the sweep of constellations. At the end of the room the altar waited, a waist-high stone worn smooth by centuries. Reverently, Kwani approached and knelt, stretching both arms upon it. She lay her cheek upon the cool surface, waiting for the powers of the stone to rise and envelope her, to give her knowledge and wisdom once more.

From some mysterious depth it came, a sense of *knowing*. As before, layers of consciousness dissolved one by one until knowledge was exposed like a deep and shining pool.

Time is a great circle; there is no beginning, no end. All returns again and again, forever.

Kwani felt herself enfolded with serene power. She summoned the ancient past. *She remembered.*

When the people entered the Fourth World into Sunfather's holy radiance, women were weak. Men were bigger and stronger. Many women died when hunters could find but little meat and there was enough but for a few, those few who were strongest. Women suffered the most during late pregnancy when they were awkward and heavy, or when they had small children to feed and to protect.

It was as though the Old One were speaking, telling it all to her again.

Earthmother taught women to survive. She taught them to recognize plants and roots and seeds that were good food. When hunting was scarce, it was women who sustained the tribe with food gathering.

Women grew stronger and wiser; they learned guile. They bartered their women's bodies and their gathered food for protection for themselves and their children, and for meat. They developed a special instinct. Unconsciously, they remembered wisdom stored in ancestral memory generation after generation, and no man, however strong, could best a woman skilled in remembering.

The great sky circle turned many times. Women forgot they knew how to remember. Knowledge lay hidden in a secret place, waiting to be summoned. Even when the knowledge was used, women did not know they had used it; the precious gift lay neglected and ignored.

Teachers were needed to instruct young girls so they would not forget, but there were none who could teach. Earthmother grieved. She said, "I will make a teacher." She took a grain of corn and made it grow strong. The ear became a head, the silk became hair, the leaves became arms, and the stalk divided at the bottom and became legs. The legs pulled themselves from the earth and walked, and She Who Remembers was created.

Earthmother said, "You must teach another and she must teach another, forever. You are to wear a symbol of your status, for you are one apart, a chosen person. This symbol will help you remember, so guard it well. You must choose a successor who is Of The Gods. If you fail, if there is none to follow you, I shall refuse to accept your body into my keeping and your spirit will roam homeless, seeking haven in Sipapu, never to enter. Women will forget they can remember, and the gifts I bestow will be as seeds drifting aimlessly in the wind.''

Time is a great circle; there is no beginning, no end. All returns again and again, forever.

"Kwani."

She awoke as from a dream. But she knew it was more than a dream. Her quest was heard; she had been granted a vision.

Tolonqua bent over her, smiling. "You must eat, my love. To give you strength." He beckoned her to the fire.

Still under the spell of the dreamlike vision, she went to sit by the fire where Owa had placed a stack of corn cakes beside the steaming pot of pemmican. They took turns dipping corn cakes into the pot and scooping up the pemmican.

Tolonqua and Owa conversed briefly between bites, but Kwani did not hear what they said. It was as though she were in a separate place. As if she were surrounded by those she could not see but could only sense their serene and powerful presence. The weariness of her long journey and the anxieties about Cicuye were gone. She felt whole. As if her spirit had found her again.

Tolonqua said, "You look rested. You slept. That is good."

She said solemnly, "I did not sleep. I was at the House of the Sun."

"Ah." Tolonqua met her gaze. She had slept, after all, and her spirit took her there. "What did you see?"

"It is a secret. For women."

Tolonqua laughed, and Owa's eyes gleamed in the firelight. He said, "Where is the House of the Sun?"

Kwani did not reply. Because he had no man parts did not make him a woman. Why should he know?

Tolonqua said, "It is an Anasazi temple on the mesa near the Place of the Eagle Clan where the cliff cities are."

"For women only?"

"No. For holy men of the clans and for She Who Remembers."

The lion-colored eyes turned to Kwani. "You are She Who Remembers?"

"Yes."

"I have heard . . ."

He did not finish, but lifted his head in a sudden gesture and peered into the darkness. In the far distance a coyote called, and another. There was a stirring among the dogs.

In an instant Tolonqua was on his feet, drawn bow in hand. "What is it?" he whispered to Owa.

"I go to see." He took his bow and quiver and melted into the night.

Kwani hurried to the blanket where Acoya slept, and scooped him in her arms. She felt no terror, but every nerve was alert.

"We are followed?"

"Perhaps. Those were not coyotes."

"How can you tell?"

"Hunters know." He doused the fire.

Acoya whimpered and Kwani cuddled him close, hushing him. She peered into the darkness. There was no sound, no motion.

Owa walked carefully, feeling the pressure of the grass against his feet, easing each foot down. He made no sound; there was only the tiny tinkle of the bell at his ear. It was a small sound, but he removed the ornament and tucked it into the belt at his waist. He must be part of the darkness itself, totally silent. Now and again, he stopped to listen, straining to penetrate the secrets of the night.

The coyote cry did not come again. Whoever, whatever, had called might be closer now. He grasped his bow; as always, it gave him a feeling of security. It was a good bow and he was a good bowman. He had saved the lives of two of his former owners, and he would allow no harm to come to Tolonqua. Kwani was another matter. He had learned well, very well, what women could be and he had excellent reason to despise them. Eventually, he must find a way to save Tolonqua. All women were evil but one with the powers of She Who Remembers could be infinitely more so. *Dangerous.*

He glanced back toward the camp. The fire was out; only Tolonqua's head and shoulders were outlined faintly against the stars as he sat beside Kwani and the baby who lay beside him. Owa's foot felt the indentation of a wallow; he slid down into it.

The baby. A beautiful man child. He would protect him also. He remembered how Kwani flaunted her woman's breasts, nursing, and he clenched his teeth. True, he had no such breasts. True, he could not bear a child. He was not a woman, not a man. He was something . . . unnatural. Like a fawn he had seen once, born with two heads. Something to be laughed at, to turn the face from . . . He muffled a groan.

Was that a sound? He raised his head, scanning the starlit horizon. A movement? He couldn't be sure. What if it was Pawnees? He was Pawnee, born Pawnee, captured as a baby by Kiowas, and raised as a slave. He would not kill a kinsman. But what if Tolonqua was attacked by Pawnees? He would have to let instinct tell him what to do.

There was no sound and his senses detected no movement. But he did not relax his grip on the bow.

At last the moon rose, flooding the plain with cool light. The buffalo wallow where he lay was not the only one scooped into the plain. And there were shallow gullies where enemies could lay concealed and rush to attack without warning. If they were in hiding now, they would probably wait for early dawn.

He was weary, but he would not allow himself to sleep. He lay on his stomach, raising his head high enough now and then to search the horizon. He could see Tolonqua and Kwani faintly in the distance.

They were making love.

He tried to muffle a groan, but there was a small choking sound.

Almost, he wished he were really a woman.

But no! Not after what he experienced at the hands of the Kiowa's feared Bear Women Society. He did not want to remember it, not again, but it forced itself into his mind.

It was Red Cloud, the short, squat, dark Kiowa chief who seduced him when he was but a boy, and who, thereafter, used him almost exclusively, thereby arousing the furious jealousy and implacable enmity of Pula-ka, his mate. Pula-ka went to the old women of the secret—and dreaded—Bear Women Society, demanding revenge. Never would he forget.

It was early in the morning. He had gone outside to relieve himself against a tree. It had rained the night before and the tree was already wet, he remembered that. And the eerie sound of muffled footsteps. He turned, his man parts exposed, to see the Bear Women rushing toward him, howling. Each carried a short stick lance. Some threw, and most missed, but one pierced him in the groin.

He doubled over with a cry as the screaming old women were upon him. One yanked out the lance.

"A-a-a-yee!" she yelled, pointing to his torn and bleeding man part. "Let's see how that can pleasure Red Cloud now!"

"Remove it!" another woman hollered.

"Yes!"

"Cut it off!"

"All of it!"

He struggled in terror and pain, but the women stomped him, sat on him, and held him down as another brandished a flint skinning knife and slashed at his groin. His spirit left his body then and did not return until the Bear Woman waved something dripping with blood in front of his face.

"See! Look at what you will never use again!"

She threw it to dogs nearby who snatched at it eagerly.

His spirit left his body again. When it returned he was in excruciating pain, lying in the lodge of the Medicine Chief who was applying a poultice to where his man parts were. Had been.

The Chief, ancient and vastly experienced in medical lore, glanced at him.

"It is painful, is it not?"

"Ah, yes."

"You will heal. But you must be brave."

"Why did they not kill me? I would rather—"

"Because you are a slave. Too valuable to kill."

Remembering, Owa turned on his side to ease the scarred place. It had healed, but it had never stopped hurting entirely. He had been traded, and traded again. And lived the life of those whom he hated—women—doing women's work, being used by men who had no women or by those who regarded a berdache as an exotic rarity to be enjoyed. But he was still a man, a Pawnee, a warrior, an expert bowman. He would show Tolonqua what that meant!

Perhaps he dozed, but a sound nearby jerked him awake. Cautiously, he raised his head and peered through the grasses. In predawn light the plain was barely visible. There was no wind, but grasses moved between his hiding place and Tolonqua's camp.

An animal? He inched to the edge of the wallow and raised on one knee to see the camp. There was no movement there; they were still sleeping. As Owa watched, a head emerged from the grasses, and another and another. Querechos! Five of them, stalking the camp.

Swiftly, Owa drew his bow. It released the arrow with a *twang* and a Querecho fell without a sound. Instantly, another rose, aiming in Owa's direction, but before he could spot the hiding place, he gave a cry and fell with an arrow in his chest.

With a yell, the three remaining Querechos ran toward him. Owa was about to shoot again when the one he was aiming at stopped, spun around, and fell with an arrow in his back. Tolonqua ran and dived for cover in the grass.

The two remaining Querechos shouted "Ambush!" and raced like antelope with arrows at their heels. As they disappeared, Owa and Tolonqua faced one another.

"You are, indeed, a good bowman, Owa."

"You, also."

They grinned. Tolonqua said, "They run better than they fight."

They laughed together. Owa said, "They may return. With others."

"We shall be at Cicuye tomorrow. Good warriors are there. Towas." He caught a look in Owa's eyes, and added, "But no bowman better than you."

Owa tossed his braids, smiling.

Kwani watched as the two men approached in an obvious glow of triumph and camaraderie. When Owa tossed his braids in that womanly gesture, it was too much. But tomorrow they would be in Cicuye and Owa would be needed no longer.

She would bide her time.

▲ 11 ▼

Anitzal, elder sister of Tolonqua, sat on the roof of her dwelling and dangled her feet over the edge. Although she had lived long—over fifty years—her face was young and the two braids of her graying hair were entwined with brightly colored strips of buckskin and bits of red and yellow cotton fabric. In her lap was the latest of her famed pottery creations, a large storage jar, which she balanced while she dipped a yucca fiber paintbrush into pigment in a paint pot.

Her face was intent as she bent to her work. She would adorn her jar with an ornate black design; hers would be the best, as always.

Beyond, near the base of the ridge, another of the *yaya,* the elder mothers of Cicuye, fed hot blazes in preparation for firing the pottery being made by those who were not required to harvest and husk the corn. Some, blanket in hand, screened their blazes from the wind or poked fires until columns of pungent black smoke billowed around them, hiding them from view.

In the courtyard and around the village women sat in busy groups surrounded by piles of golden husks up to their heads. Shouting children jumped in and out of piles, followed by yapping dogs, and were shooed out of the way by mothers and aunts and sisters carrying piles of corn in blankets. The women climbed ladders to the roofs and spread multicolored ears to dry in the sun. Some sliced squashes into spirals to be suspended to dry from exposed beams in adobe walls.

From time to time, Anitzal turned to gaze beyond the valley to where it opened to the plains. Tolonqua should be returning; he had been gone too long. As an esteemed yaya and sister of Cicuye's Hunting Chief, Anitzal enjoyed a position of honor in the clan. But this rumor about Kokopelli's mate being Tolonqua's now . . . The paintbrush paused midair.

What had happened to Kokopelli? And who was the big woman returning with them? A runner had said the woman managed the dogs and carried big loads. A slave? Anitzal shook her head. Tolonqua was not given to foolish extravagance. One did not need slaves here where many willing hands did all that was necessary. What was needed was more meat, buffalo and deer and elk that Tolonqua's hunters provided. The men had provided game, but not as much as when Tolonqua was with them, not enough to feed them all.

Kwani. Was she actually Tolonqua's mate now? Those blue eyes . . . Anitzal frowned. Kwani was Anasazi, from the Eagle Clan to the west. She should be with them, not here. But if she were there, Tolonqua would be there, too, and he was needed among his own people.

"Ho! Anitzal!"

It was Lumu, so much younger than Anitzal that she seemed to be more child than sister. Their mother had long since joined ancestors in Sipapu; Anitzal and their aunts had raised Tolonqua and little Lumu whose happy laugh brightened everything.

"I greet you, Lumu."

"Here. Help me with this."

Lumu climbed the ladder and heaved a huge load of corn to the roof. "Spread this and I will go for more. A good crop. *Tuh!* It is heavy!" She opened the blanket and dumped the ears.

Anitzal smiled at Lumu's exuberance, and continued painting. "I must finish this for the firing. See?" She turned the jar around, displaying the design. "The fires are ready. You spread the corn while I finish this."

Lumu glanced at the jar and tossed her head. Since she had found a mate, a young flint knapper of the Turquoise Clan, Lumu felt she was of equal importance to her sister even though Anitzal was of the yaya.

"Very well. You make the jar and I bring what goes in it." Her black eyes flashed and for a moment she resembled her brother, Tolonqua. "Of what good is an empty jar?" Then, of its own accord, her laugh bubbled and she climbed down the ladder and was gone.

Anitzal looked after the slender figure with long braids swinging, and suddenly she was acutely aware of having outlived most women of her generation. She would forget being a senior yaya if only she could be young again. . . . Her own mate was dead, killed by Utes on a raid, and her two children were called to Sipapu before they could walk.

Tolonqua and Lumu and cousins and aunts and uncles were her family now. She sighed. If only her babies had lived . . .

Children ran everywhere, up and down ladders, in and out of dwellings, across the courtyard and into the fields, shrieking joyfully. Little boys with bows and arrows and sticks and stones chased dogs in wild hunting games; canine yelps sounded throughout the village. It was a comfortable pandemonium. Anitzal inspected the design on her jar and was about to take it to the fire when a head emerged from the roof entrance of an adjoining dwelling. It was Shumatl, another of the yaya.

"Ho!" Shumatl called. She climbed to the roof, carrying a jar. "See my new jar!" Her wrinkled face beamed.

Anitzal admired it dutifully, refraining from comparing it with her own. "Let's take these to the fire."

They made their way carefully through ears of corn spread on the roofs and past the groups below surrounded by piles of husks, avoiding the rushing onslaught of children and dogs. As they approached the fires, a woman called, "Here! This fire is ready!"

Another called, "So is this one! Bring your jars here!"

Anitzal and Shumatl went to the nearest fire and set their jars among the coals, poking the flames until smoke billowed. It was midafternoon. As the pottery was fired, Anitzal and Shumatl joined a group of women sitting against the wall on the shady side of the village. Some were scraping corn from the cobs onto blankets spread upon the ground. Others polished pottery creations with a smooth stone, rubbing and rubbing. Babies were nursed and changed and tucked into cradle boards while those of the yaya watched approvingly and joined in the gossip.

"Could it be true that Tolonqua has taken Kwani as mate?"

They cast significant glances at one another. One said, "She is beautiful."

"She has powers," another said.

"Powers can be dangerous."

There was silence for a moment.

Anitzal said, "Tolonqua is no fool, as we all know. He has good reasons for what he does."

"His baby-maker has the best reasons, maybe."

There were snickers. Anitzal rose. "Tolonqua has powers of his own, hunting powers upon which we all depend. It would be wise to control your tongues."

She was about to leave when Aka-ti, mate of Two Elk, approached. As wife of the Clan Chief, Aka-ti was the most important and honored yaya of Cicuye—next to Yellow Bird, of course. The women greeted her respectfully.

Aka-ti acknowledged their greeting and glanced sharply at Anitzal whose flushed cheeks and angry eyes belied her regal composure. "I have word of Tolonqua."

"Aye-e-e-e!" the woman cried. "Tell us!"

"He comes." She pointed east. "That way. He and Kwani and a big woman. With dogs and travois!"

Jars and corn and cradle boards were ignored as women clambered up the ridge to see into the distance.

"Look! So many dogs!"

"What do they carry?"

"Kwani has a baby!"

"Who is that big woman?"

"She walks like a man."

"Where is Kokopelli?"

They watched, curious, as Tolonqua stopped, removed something from a pouch at his waist, and lifted it to his lips. There was a long wailing cry.

"Aye-e-e-e!"

"What is that?"

More people clambered up the ridge to look. Women snatched their children and ran to their dwellings. Such a sound could only mean that evil spirits were about.

Two Elk, the Clan and City Chief, gritted his teeth. He had been first on the ridge, watching Tolonqua approach. With dogs and loaded travois and that female creature who walked like a man. A slave? Could it be? And that sound! What sort of instrument produced a noise to summon listeners to Sipapu? He turned away, gripping the handsome buffalo-hide shield, symbol of his authority. When he heard that Tolonqua approached, he had planned to greet him with a reminder of who Two Elk was. Now he returned to the kiva and seated himself at his usual place by the altar. Let Tolonqua come to him!

Tolonqua replaced the shell horn in its pouch. He turned to Kwani. "They know we come."

She nodded, but did not reply. Where was the welcoming party? She suppressed a small stab of unease. The welcoming group would be on the other side of the ridge, of course.

Owa said, "Do they have slaves?"

Tolonqua smiled. "You would be the only one. But you

have brought us safely home. I give you your freedom. You are slave no more."

Owa stared. "But I am berdache." He flushed. "I want to be berdache for you."

"Tolonqua does not need a berdache," Kwani said, keeping her voice gentle. "He has me."

The flush reached the lion-colored eyes and flamed the ears. "I am good bowman—"

"Indeed you are," Kwani said, holding the gleaming gaze. "You will be safe returning to your people." Almost, her voice shook. "You are free. Go."

"No, not yet." Tolonqua gestured beyond the ridge. "We must get the dogs and travois to the village. Many valuables—"

"Of course," Kwani said. Her voice was calm but she was not calm inside. What was wrong with her? It was as though she were gripped with an illness. This man who was not a man, not a woman—this berdache—did she fear him? Was that what hurt and burned in her stomach? But she had been afraid before, often, and it was not like this. Nor was it hatred. How could one hate a pathetic creature, a man with no man parts? Perhaps, when she could see behind his eyes to the secret place where his spirit dwelled, she would understand why he made her feel as she did. She held her head high and strode behind Tolonqua and Owa who walked side by side with the dogs and their burdens.

As they rounded the ridge, the dogs in the village set up a fierce clamor. There were shouts and cries, and men and boys ran to meet them with dogs racing ahead. As the village dogs encountered the dogs with travois, they attacked. There was a wild melee, a blur of shaggy bodies, snarls, slashing teeth, and overturned travois with contents scattered.

Shouting men wrestled the dogs apart. Some of the dogs bled from torn ears and jagged wounds, and a few of the men were wounded, also. When the dogs were finally separated and subdued, the men of the village stood gawking at the contents of the travois that lay in a jumbled, scattered heap. They stared at Tolonqua as though he were a stranger, this man with the robe of the White Buffalo slung over his shoulders! And at Owa who commanded the dogs and who was gathering turquoise and pouches of salt and fine tools and other treasures from the ground. And at Kwani who returned their stares with those mystical blue eyes. And at her baby.

But most of all, they stared in awe at Tolonqua. The robe of the White Buffalo! There were murmurs.

Tolonqua laughed. "Ho, friends! What welcome is this for one who has been gone long? I greet you!" He lifted the conch-shell horn to his lips and blew hard.

"Aye-e-e-e!" Hunters and boys gathered around, touching the buffalo robe, examining the horn, exclaiming over the contents of the travois, and glancing curiously at Owa who stood silently to one side. Kwani was ignored. This was a man's reunion.

Tolonqua noticed the glances at Owa and beckoned him to come forward. He did so, face expressionless, eyes downcast. He stood beside Tolonqua, head bowed.

"This is Owa, a slave who is a slave no more. A fine bowman. A berdache."

"Ah!" A sigh like a small wind rose.

A boy said loudly, "What is a berdache?"

"A man who lives as a woman."

He gawked. "Why?"

There were embarrassed whispers and the boy was hushed.

Owa smiled. "I show you." He pulled his garment aside. "See?"

The men gasped, and the boy's face screwed into an expression of shock and distaste.

Owa smiled. "Not man, not woman. Berdache."

The boy stepped close and touched the scar. "Does it hurt?"

"Sometimes." He covered himself.

A hunter spoke. "Two Elk waits for you, Tolonqua."

"We go."

They became a procession: Tolonqua, Kwani, and Owa with dogs and reloaded travois, followed by men and boys chattering excitedly. Now and then the men glanced at Owa with speculation, and at Kwani with curiosity and distrust.

Where was Kokopelli?

Yellow Bird sat on the roof of her dwelling, watching the procession. Others of the yaya, the old mothers, sat with her.

"A strong-looking woman, that big one," one said.

"She walks like a man."

Yellow Bird snorted. "That *is* a man."

"No. She wears women's clothing, and the hair—"

"A man, I tell you. Look at those legs, those arms. Look

how he walks. A woman that big would have these.'' She used both hands to indicate big breasts. ''I have heard of such. It is a man who lives as a woman. A berdache.''

The old women looked at one another. One said, ''That is not good. The men—''

They glanced at one another again.

''He is a slave.''

They watched in silence as Tolonqua spoke quietly to Kwani, then approached the kiva while hunters stood respectfully aside. Owa stayed with the dogs and travois, while Kwani stood uncertainly alone. Immediately, she was surrounded by women and girls who exclaimed over Acoya and handed him from one to the other, smiling and bouncing him and talking baby talk, while Acoya regarded them solemnly with his round, dark eyes.

Kwani watched, smiling. She was in Cicuye once more. She was home!

''Bring her to me,'' Yellow Bird said.

Kwani stood before Yellow Bird who squatted in her dwelling and peered up at Kwani with a beady stare. Kwani's heart beat hard. She had expected a warm welcome. Instead, an air of suspicion enveloped her like smoke; she felt choked with it.

''Where is Kokopelli?'' Yellow Bird asked again.

''I have told you,'' Kwani answered, keeping her voice steady. ''I slept, and when I woke Kokopelli was gone. I think he returned to his homeland.''

''Why did he leave you?''

Kwani could not keep the tears from her voice. ''Because he knew I would not be happy in his distant homeland. Because I would not want my son raised as a Toltec.'' She swallowed. ''Maybe because he decided I would not be a suitable mate for him there. But he left many gifts—''

Black eyes flashed in the craggy old face. ''There is no proof. It is believed that Tolonqua killed Kokopelli to have you as mate and to acquire Kokopelli's wealth. What have you to say to that, eh?''

''I say it is a lie! An evil lie!''

Kwani knelt before the old woman and leaned close so that Yellow Bird could see the necklace. ''See this? The shell pendant with the secret design? This is the necklace of She Who Remembers, the Ancient Ones, all of those who were She Who Remembers before me. They speak to me through it. I cannot, I will not, defame them nor myself

with lies.'' She rose straight, head high. "I am She Who
Remembers, mate of Tolonqua who does not lie as you know
well. I am mother of Acoya, son of Okalake, and now son
of Tolonqua, your Hunting Chief. My son and I are honored
to be among you and we expect to be honored in return.''

For a moment Yellow Bird gazed up at Kwani without
expression. She said dryly, ''You speak rashly for one who
expects to be honored.'' She gestured with a bony hand.
''Go!''

Kwani did not bow in respectful acknowledgment. She
turned and climbed up the ladder without good-bye.

Two Elk sat in his honored and accustomed place before
the altar upon which were a bowl of water from the sacred
spring, a small bowl of corn pollen, the substance most
sacred, a reddish stone shaped like a buffalo that Earthmother had given him when he was a boy, and other objects
of powerful medicine. To one side were his buffalo-hide
shield elaborately painted and adorned with hawk and eagle
feathers, and a long, round, buffalo-hide pouch containing
handsome bows and arrows. On the other side, closest to
the fire pit, was his sleeping mat of thick buffalo hides upon
a mat of reeds for those times he chose to sleep in the kiva.
He leaned against a woven backrest, waiting for Tolonqua
to be brought before him.

He heard the sounds of excitement outside, growing
closer, and he felt a constriction in his stomach. He was
growing old. No longer did he count the seasons; there were
too many. His authority was challenged by a hunter who
was half, less than half, his age. One who now possessed
the robe of the White Buffalo. He was sure of it. He had
seen it only at a distance, but there could be no mistake.
The White Buffalo!

And that sound! What magical device had Tolonqua acquired?

Two Elk wrapped a braid around his forefinger; it helped
him to think. He tugged at the braid as though to open a
place in his head for wisdom to leak out.

The answer came, as he knew it would.

He sat straight against the backrest as Tolonqua descended, followed by several other Chiefs of the clan. Tolonqua smiled a glad greeting and bowed respectfully.

''I greet you, Two Elk.'' He removed the robe with a
flourish and spread it before the Chief. ''I bring this to my
clan.'' The smile faded as Two Elk regarded him coldly.

"Where is Kokopelli?"

"He is gone."

"I see that he is gone. Gone where?"

"I do not know. I went to bury the Querecho, and when I returned, he was gone."

There were murmurs. Two Elk tugged at his braid. "What Querecho? Where?"

"In the canyon near the Place of the Rainbow Flint. He attacked while Kwani gave birth. He tried to kill Kokopelli and I did this"—he drew a finger across his throat—"with Kokopelli's sword. The head rolled down the bank to the river. I dragged the body away and buried it in the cliff. When I returned to Kwani, Kokopelli was gone—"

"Ah!" Two Elk leaned back, smiling grimly. "It was his head in the river, perhaps?"

Tolonqua's face flushed, then paled. "I do not lie."

"I know only that Kokopelli has disappeared and that his mate is now yours." Two Elk squinted, and he smiled the same smile. "I suppose Kwani saw this happening and will say you speak truthfully?"

"No. She was giving birth. She did not see it."

"I think I understand." Two Elk was enjoying himself. "We know, all of us know, how Kokopelli commanded animals. It was he who took the White Buffalo, and it was his robe you stole after you killed him. Is that not so?"

Tolonqua lanced the Chief with a glance. "The Spirit Being appeared to me in my manhood vision. He said he would come to me again, and he did. Under the big cottonwood tree where the stream bends. He was there. Waiting for me."

Tolonqua bent, scooped up the robe, and held it before Two Elk. "I took the White Buffalo, I bring the sacred robe to you, to my clan, to my people. And you accuse me of lies, of theft." His voice shook in outrage. "The White Buffalo gave himself to *me*. Who here is equally worthy? Not one. Because you are not, and never will be, you accuse me of speaking with two tongues." He dangled the robe before each Chief in turn. "Tell the Spirit Being he offered himself to one who lies. Tell him!"

Two Elk turned to a young Chief-in-training. "Summon the Medicine Chief."

While they waited, Tolonqua slung the robe over his shoulders and stared down at the assembled Chiefs with contempt. "Perhaps one day a rabbit may come to you and offer to be taken. If any of you are worthy by then."

Two Elk rose, flaming with fury. "You dare to insult us? You, who killed Kokopelli so you may have his mate and his riches?"

There was a bedlam of talk. The hiss of a spirit rattle announced the arrival of the Medicine Chief who descended the ladder with the young Chief-in-training following. There was a strained silence as the old Chief stood regarding them.

He had seen perhaps fifty winters that had grayed his hair and plowed crevices on his face. His hair hung in two braids, and his totem, a stuffed chickadee, was fastened to the braid behind his left ear. An arrow had taken one eye in his youth, and he wore an eye patch of thin and polished wood inlaid with a turquoise and obsidian eye in a permanent transfixing stare. The other eye, small and dark and sharp, surveyed the scene.

The rattle hissed again. "Why am I summoned?"

Two Elk gestured to Tolonqua. "Repeat your words."

"I shall." He flung open the robe and held it before the Medicine Chief. "Behold the robe of the White Buffalo!"

The Chief stared. He stepped close, examined it, and gestured a blessing. "It is the sacred one."

"Yes. But these here"—he jerked his head at the group—"say I killed Kokopelli, stole the robe from him, stole his mate, stole his riches. They say this because the White Buffalo has never come to any of them and they do not wish to believe it has come to me."

"He insults us!" Two Elk snarled. "He said—"

"It is I who am insulted!" Tolonqua shouted.

"Enough!" The Medicine Chief strode forward, swinging his rattle overhead. The eerie sound rang in a room suddenly quiet. The Medicine Chief turned to Two Elk. "Bring the Truth Pipe."

Smoking that pipe was the most solemn oath of truth a man could make. To refuse it implied a lie.

Tolonqua stared coldly at the Medicine Chief and at each of the others in turn. He shook with controlled fury.

"You, all of you, have known me since birth. I do not lie. This you know. I bring the robe of the White Buffalo to you, to my clan, my people, the first Towa to be so honored. And now the Truth Pipe must speak for me?" His voice was ice, cracking.

Again, he flung the robe over his shoulders. "I shall not listen more!" He climbed the ladder and disappeared.

A babble of talk quieted under the baleful stare of the turquoise and obsidian eye, and the rattle's insistent voice.

The Medicine Chief said, "It is true that Tolonqua does not lie. Is that not so?"

Two Elk scowled. "Why did he refuse the Truth Pipe? Where is Kokopelli? Why would he disappear, leaving his mate and his riches for Tolonqua?"

Lopat, the Warrior Chief, said, "Maybe he discovered his mate was a witch."

There were shocked murmurs. A Chief said, "She called the deer at Puname. A witch could not do that."

"Nor do witches bear children."

"She is She Who Remembers."

"Aye."

But they shifted uncomfortably. Those blue eyes . . .

And Tolonqua had refused the pipe.

▲ 12 ▼

Kwani and Tolonqua lay on their sleeping mat. It was the time of *pulatla*, when Sunfather flings a golden mantle across the horizon before his appearance, but they had slept little, talking most of the night. How could they prove the truth of their words?

"No proof should be necessary," Kwani said again. "All know you do not lie."

"Then why do they question my word? Why?"

She turned to look at him. In the dim light she could see his face and the grimness there, and the bitterness, so unlike him.

"Perhaps it is because of me. Maybe they think I have changed you."

He sat up and wrapped both arms around his knees. For a time he did not speak. Finally, he said, "I must decide what to do."

The village still slept; the only sound was the call of a night bird from somewhere on the ridge. Kwani looked up at the beamed ceiling. Owa was on the roof; he had slept up there. Was he listening?

She sat up beside Tolonqua and put her hand on his shoulder where the bear-paw tattoo proclaimed his hunting skills. "You are the honored Hunting Chief, long respected. This is your home. Mine also now, and Acoya's . . ." Her voice quavered, but she had not shed a tear all this time and she would not do so now. "We are who we are. Time will prove the truth of our words."

The night bird called again and Tolonqua raised his head, listening. Was the bird telling him something? Calling him to the ridge?

Kwani looked at him, at the intentness of his face. What was he thinking? she wondered. She loved him, but did she really know his secret heart? The depths that lay concealed?

There was a tinkling sound, the little bell on Owa's ear ornament. He was eavesdropping, Kwani knew.

She said softly, "Owa is up there. Whisper in my ear."

The grimness on Tolonqua's face softened. He lay beside her, pulling her down to him, and nestled his face against her hair. "Shall we give him something to listen to?"

Kwani laughed and drew him close.

Owa turned away; he could not bear to listen more. He had loved before, but not with the intensity of this feeling he had for Tolonqua. When he saw the Hunting Chief sitting in the kiva, enshrined with the splendor of the White Buffalo, his heart leaped. It still did, remembering.

Now Tolonqua lay with another. *A woman.*

Kwani. Who flaunted her breasts, her baby. A woman. With dangerous powers. She Who Remembers.

He clenched both fists.

Sunfather returned from his underworld journey and rose with his usual dramatic display of scarlet and gold. Farmers whose fields were distant had long departed, taking corn cake and piki bread and venison with them; they worked first and ate later in the day. Boys splashed noisily in the cold stream, bathing. Even in winter they did this to "harden the meat." Hardship would make them strong.

After bathing, those boys who practiced for the ceremonial races ran like antelope into the valley and disappeared. Meanwhile, women rolled up the blankets and buffalo robes that were their sleeping mats, and swept the floors with yucca fiber brooms. Naked toddlers were given a bit of corn cake and sent outside to play. Young girls carried chamber pots to the dumping place, while older girls helped their mothers with household chores.

Old men gathered with their cronies to sit in the sun and discuss the weather and the wonderful crops of long ago, while old women watched their daughters and granddaughters and nieces making the morning gruel and wondered aloud why gruel didn't taste the way it used to when she was a girl. The old ones who had lost their teeth slurped their gruel and smacked their lips in appreciation as courtesy required, wishing they could do as they used to and tear succulent meat from bone with strong teeth, especially the rich meat of the bear or mountain sheep.

The morning dragged by. Tolonqua had gone without saying where, and Kwani was left alone. For a while she busied herself with Acoya and with sorting through their belongings. She would have to make baskets to hold it all; she must go to the river to find reeds.

She hesitated. She wasn't sure where reeds grew here, but that was not the real reason she hesitated. She was reluctant to face the people who questioned her word and who regarded her with suspicion. What if they confronted her as Yellow Bird had done?

She closed her eyes to look within herself, and clasped her necklace, pressing the scallop shell to her, seeking reassurance and wisdom. She strained to communicate with the Ancient Ones.

"Tell me what to do!" she prayed.

There was no answer.

Kwani rocked to and fro in despair. She had been so sure that her lifelong dream was realized—her longing for security, for a mate and a child, for people and a clan of her own. She had Tolonqua and Acoya, but could they continue to live here, accused?

Again, she clasped the shell to her. "Tell me!"

For a time there was no answer. Then it seemed that silent voices murmured within the room. It was as though the Old One spoke.

"You are She Who Remembers, as we are, as you will always be. You must be strong. It is struggle that strengthens and makes us aware, that tempers the spirit and opens the mind's eye. . . . ." The murmuring faded and was gone.

"Wait!" Kwani cried. "Don't go!"

But the room was silent once more.

Acoya whimpered his hunger. Kwani lifted him and held him in her arms. His small mouth searched for her breast and she gave it to him, watching as he nursed. Did he drink from her spirit, also?

What would be his path of life? Where would it lead him?

"Be strong!" she crooned.

The roof entry darkened and Tolonqua climbed down. The grimness in his face was less, but something lingered in the eyes.

"I greet you!" His voice was determinedly casual, and he came to squat beside her. "I have been up on the ridge. I know what I must do."

"What?"

"I shall seek a vision."

"Ah." She nodded. "When?"

"Tomorrow. But I must purify myself first. I go to the sweat lodge now." He gestured farewell and was gone.

She was alone again. In the dim room with the sound of the city outside.

She rose. She would hide no longer. She would face the people and make them realize she belonged here.

There was a sound from above. A tiny tinkle. Kwani felt a prick of unease and of anger. Why was he there?

"Owa!" she called.

His head appeared at the roof door. "I am here."

"Why?"

"Tolonqua wishes it. To protect you."

"It is not necessary. Go."

"I stay." His head was withdrawn.

Kwani fumed. Was protection necessary here, in Tolonqua's home, among his people? Perhaps it was. The thought was not comforting.

She lifted the cradle board to her back, slipped her arms through the shoulder straps, climbed the ladder, and entered the village with Owa following close behind.

The sweat lodge was a small, round hut with a low ceiling. Tolonqua removed his clothes, offered cornmeal and prayers to the spirit of the lodge, and bent low to enter. The ceiling of arched willow poles covered with earth and adobe was too low for him to stand upright. He squatted to build a fire in the fire pit to heap the stones over which water would be poured to make steam. Pungent smoke filled the room before escaping through a small hole in the roof. He reached for the loosely woven bag of yucca fiber containing fresh grass, bit down, and breathed through it until the smoke dissipated; the grass tasted clean and filtered the smoke.

While the stones heated, Tolonqua chanted prayers for wisdom, knowing that his prayers would rise with the smoke to the Above Beings. Perhaps they would grant him a vision when he went on his quest.

The stones grew hot and Tolonqua flicked water upon them. The water sizzled and vanished; it was time. He poured a ladle of water over the heated stones; immediately there was a crackling sound and a loud hissing as steam billowed. He hunched forward, head between his knees, as steam enveloped him. The purification was beginning.

He forced his mind to empty itself, to be cleansed of resentment and bitterness. Only a clean mind made purity of heart possible, and a vision would come only to one whose heart was pure.

The heat increased. Sweat poured from him, mingling with the wetness of the steam. Enervated, he stepped outside to the cool of the morning. The lodge sat by itself in a spot overlooking the stream. He watched boys playing and splashing themselves and one another, and he remembered how he used to do that. He had been happy then.

Why was his word not believed? Why was he degraded? He, who possessed the robe of the White Buffalo?

Again, bitterness seeped into his soul. He reentered the lodge and added water to the stones several times. The heat decreased to a damp, comforting warmth, and his bitterness faded. He felt renewed.

He offered meal to the spirits of the lodge, took his clothes, and went to a remote spot in the stream to bathe. He would eat nothing that day, take an emetic that night, bathe again in the morning, then go alone to a distant, solitary place to commune with gods.

Kwani stood with other women in the river, washing Tolonqua's garments and her own. Sunfather shone on the water, making it sparkle and shine, and children shouted and splashed. The air was fresh and smelled good, and the cold water tingled on her arms and legs. Anitzal and Lumu, Tolonqua's sisters, were there and greeted her when she came, but Kwani sensed reservations. Until the truth was proven it would be that way, no matter how long it took. She slapped the garments upon a large, smooth stone, squeezing, rinsing, and slapping again until the garments were clean. The harder she slapped, the better it made her feel.

Owa sat on the bank nearby. His own garments were spotless and cords of brilliant colors were entwined in each braid. He sat with ankles crossed, displaying fine foot coverings of soft deerskin embroidered with porcupine quills in an ornate pattern of red, blue, yellow, and green. Many bracelets adorned each arm, and necklaces glittered in the sun. The breeze played with the tiny bell at one ear and tugged at the feather ornaments in the other. He was quite a splendid sight, and the knowledge of it gratified him.

Women glanced at him furtively, some with obvious hostility, but he was accustomed to that. He returned their glances with acute dislike. He was there only because Tolonqua wanted him to stay with Kwani, and whatever Tolonqua wanted him to do, he would do. He watched Kwani, wishing she would drown in the river.

A group of small boys ran by, and stopped. They approached him tentatively. One stepped forward.

"May we see the scar?"

"Why?"

The boy shuffled his feet. "We heard—"

"What you heard is true. I have a scar. But it is not for display." He gestured. "Go!"

The boy made a face. "Bare-dot-chay! Bare-dot-chay!" he chanted. The others joined, "Bare-dot-chay!"

Owa jumped up. "Go!" he shouted. The boys scurried away.

Kwani felt a sudden pang of compassion. She turned to him. "Children are children. One cannot take them seriously."

Pale eyes under hairless brows regarded her without expression, and he did not reply.

Kwani gathered her wet garments and spread them upon bushes to dry. Some she took home and hung them from exposed beams on the roof. She hummed as she worked. It had not been difficult to face the people. They had been reserved, but not unfriendly. Tomorrow she would go for reeds.

Owa sat silently, dangling his feet over the edge of the roof, his back to her. Kwani glanced at him, thinking she would like to push him off to fall to the ground below. What was it about him that antagonized her so?

"Ho!"

A man's head emerged from the door of an adjoining roof. He was munching a corn cake. He was of average height, lean and brown, and his broad face with prominent cheekbones bore the crevices of years although he was not yet thirty. Several teeth were missing in front, and a scar from an old injury creased his left cheek.

"Ho!" he said again, and stepped to the roof. For a moment he and Owa regarded each other in silence.

The man said, "I am Talasi of the Warrior Society." He gestured a sign of greeting. "Welcome!"

Owa returned the sign. "I thank you."

Kwani thought, He should welcome me, also, but she did not speak.

Talasi took another bite of corn cake and offered Owa the rest. "This is good. My sister makes it for me. I have no mate."

Owa accepted the remainder of the cake and ate it with obvious relish as was expected. Talasi gestured to his dwelling. "I have more. Come and I will share with you." He paused. "I am alone."

Owa considered. He was a slave no longer; he could pick and choose. Members of the Warrior Society patrolled the village, settled disputes, and wielded power. A member would be useful to him.

He nodded, and the two men descended the ladder to Talasi's dwelling.

Tolonqua walked swiftly through the narrow valley where he had run as a boy and where he often went to trade with other villagers. Behind him was the ridge. To the east, where the mountains leveled, the Great Plains lay. Ahead and to his left, the sacred mountain that would be known one day as the Blood of Christ soared against an awakening sky. He breathed deeply of the sweet morning breeze, allowing it to wash him inside. He wore only a breechcloth and moccasins and the robe of the White Buffalo. No proud eagle feather adorned his head; one approached the gods in humility.

He bypassed a number of villages and avoided runners practicing for the races. It was necessary for him to be alone with his inner self. He paused at a shrine, a small pile of rocks, and added one to the pile, praying for the success of his quest. Sunfather rose beyond the mountain, and Tolonqua sang his morning chant, offering meal from the pouch at his waist.

The mountain was thick with juniper and pine and brush, and sloped steeply to the valley. As Tolonqua began to climb, he remembered the steep bank in the canyon where the river raged. Instinctively, he glanced behind into the distance, wondering if he might be followed by those two Querechos who escaped his arrows. Were they forming a war party for revenge? For a moment Tolonqua was concerned for his village and his people. And for Kwani and Acoya. But Owa was with them. . . .

He shook his head to clear it; he must think only of his quest. His mind and his spirit must be one with Masau'u and the spirits of rock and tree, and of birds and animals and insects—all that Masau'u created. And with Earthmother upon whose body he trod.

He stopped, knelt, placed both hands upon the ground, and bent to touch his forehead to the earth.

"Accept me in your holy place," he prayed.

Above, the mountain rose in rugged grandeur. Somewhere on those heights he would find the place he sought.

He resumed his climb around boulders and brush. From time to time, he had to use low-hanging branches to pull himself upward. He encountered prints of cougar and elk, glimpsed rabbits, saw a coyote grinning at him from a narrow ledge, and watched a squirrel climbing a tall spruce. Squirrels carried messages to the gods.

"I seek a vision!" he called.

The squirrel darted higher and disappeared in the branches. Did the Above Beings receive his message?

Higher and higher he climbed. It grew cool, even in Sunfather's warmth. Tolonqua had not eaten since the previous day, and he had taken an emetic to cleanse himself internally the night before, but he was not hungry. Rather, he felt an exaltation, a lightness, as though a part of his physical being had dissolved so that his spiritual self might emerge.

At a high ledge he stopped to gaze around him. Below, the valley spread in majesty. Beyond the opposite mountain lay the vast, open emptiness of the Great Plains where white clouds billowed in splendor. Overhead, the sky was sharply, brilliantly blue. Two hawks circled there, dipping and soaring with the wind. Behind and above him the mountain hovered, brooding and beautiful, concealing holy mysteries.

This was the place.

He must purify himself once more. He built a small fire of spruce boughs, and stood so that the smoke enveloped him. He prayed.

"Masau'u, Great Spirit, you have been always, and before you no one has been. Everything has been made by you. The heavens you have made and finished. All creatures on earth you have made, all things that grow you have made. Lean close to this place, I pray, that you may hear my voice."

"Thunder Beings, behold me! You of the Great Winds, behold me! You, whence comes the morning star and the day, behold me! You where the summer lives, behold me! You in the depths of the heavens, an eagle of power, behold! And you, Earthmother, who are merciful to your children, accept me here!"

"Great Spirit, I pray for a vision. Give me a sign. Show me how to prove the truth of my words that my people may believe me again. Grant me a vision, I pray!"

The small flames flickered and died. Gradually, the smoke grew less and blew away, carrying his prayer.

Now he must wait for a vision.

Three days and nights passed. He ate nothing, and drank but a few drops from his water bag. At night he lay upon the ledge facing the stars. By day he stood gazing into the distance and up at the secret mountain, chanting supplications. No vision came.

Another day passed. On the fourth night, when Moon-woman was directly overhead, her light began to waver. Tolonqua rose, staring in awe as trees and rocks wavered also and began to throw off green sparks. Blue deer ran down the mountain and out into space, soaring like birds.

Upon the ledge before him a white mist rose. It swirled, changed colors to red, green, blue, then back to white, and began to change form. The White Buffalo!

"Ah!" Tolonqua gasped.

The Spirit Being gazed at him with eyes of green fire. "I have come," it said.

Tolonqua collapsed to his knees, trembling. He tried to speak, but no words came.

The White Buffalo spoke, and his voice was like a storm wind. "You refused the Truth Pipe. Why?"

Tolonqua searched his soul and could not answer.

The White Buffalo came closer, and the green fire of his eyes burned into Tolonqua's innermost self. Again he spoke, and his voice was like a waterfall thundering.

"You insulted your people. Why?"

"I was proud," Tolonqua cried from the depths of his heart. "I was proud."

"Yes." The White Buffalo turned away.

"What must I do?" Tolonqua called as the vision receded.

"Truth will be revealed."

The White Buffalo dissolved into mist once more, and was gone.

Tolonqua's spirit left him and did not return until the time of pulatla, when Sunfather flings a golden mantle across the horizon.

▲ 13 ▼

Yellow Bird stood by the ladder, looking up through the hatchway to the night sky. Moonwoman would not appear until nearly dawn; only stars could be seen, and some of those were hidden in drifting clouds. She could hear people singing and talking in the plaza; they would be gathered long around the community fire. Now she could do what she must.

The ridge humped against the sky, a foreboding, evil presence. She stared at the black bulk, surely an abode of witches. Never would she forsake the place where she was born, where her ancestors were born, and where she would join them in Sipapu!

Never would a new city be built up there!

Never. No matter what Tolonqua said. She would not allow it.

It was cool; the community fire blazed high. People clustered around it, singing, laughing, telling stories. Yellow Bird knew they would talk long about the announcement made that day by the Crier Chief. He had circled the village four times announcing that Tolonqua requested the Truth Pipe. The Truth Pipe! She must act tonight; the ceremony would take place at sundown tomorrow. Such momentous news would be discussed excitely until the fire burned low. They would not notice her, a small figure clad in black, blending with the shadows.

But she must be careful. She crawled on hands and knees to the outside ladder and painfully climbed down, rung by rung, looking to see if anyone watched. Bending over and shuffling as quickly as her old legs allowed, she reached the kiva of the Medicine Chief and huddled in the shadows. Had she been seen?

Nobody noticed.

The following day, all of Cicuye's Chiefs and Elders sat in solemn assembly in the medicine lodge, an oblong adobe building that stood alone on the eastern side of the village to face Sunfather's morning house. The inner walls were plastered white, with niches holding the Medicine Chief's bowls, jars, and baskets of herbs, roots, bark, and other substances of healing and spiritual potency. Clusters of dried pods and tubers hung from the rafters; their surfaces, wrinkled and brown, reflected light from the small blaze in the fire pit. Fourteen men, seated on ledges around the walls, breathed the fragrance of sacred spruce smoke, drying plants, and the acrid odor of healing substances in bowls and baskets, as if to inhale the essence of wisdom and curing powers. Each man had removed his moccasins, sung suitable chants, and offered prayers. Now they sat in silence contemplating the altar, a sanctified space on the floor behind the fire pit, freshly adorned for this decisive occasion.

The altar stood against the wall behind the fire pit. It was a low stone ledge before which stood a row of narrow, knee-high wooden slats carved and painted in sacred colors and designs representing deities. On the floor before these were four *pahos,* or prayer sticks, a small bowl of corn pollen, a *tiponi*—four perfect ears of corn tied in a bundle with shells and eagle plumes—and a pouch of tobacco. The Truth Pipe, a bowl of scarlet pigment, and a paintbrush of yucca fibers lay upon a reed mat. Moments before, Sunfather had departed for his underworld journey to his eastern home. It was time.

Tolonqua sat cross-legged before the altar, head bowed. It was a great effort to swallow resentment, but he kept his vision in mind. Whatever appeared in a vision became a man's totem, protecting him and determining his destiny. The White Buffalo was the most powerful totem of all. Truth would be revealed; the White Buffalo had said it.

The Medicine Chief sat beside the altar, a prayer mat spread before him. He raised his hand in gesture-before-speaking and cleared his throat to prepare it for the proper tone of solemn authority.

"Tolonqua, he who possesses the robe of the White Buffalo, says the Spirit Being awaited him and offered to be taken. He brings the robe to his family and to us. He says he killed a Querecho in self-defense, went to bury the body, and when he returned, Kokopelli was gone leaving many gifts. He requests that he be given the Truth Pipe to prove the truth of his words."

The Chief paused, and the turquoise and obsidian eye stared at each man in turn while the other eye probed for

signs of objection. For some time the eye dwelled on Two
Elk, the Clan Chief, who scowled but said nothing. Finally,
the Medicine Chief said, "If any man here wishes to speak,
speak."

Tolonqua gazed tensely at his folded hands. No one
spoke.

The Chief took the pipe from the altar. Chanting, he
pointed the stem toward the Six Sacred Directions: north,
east, south, west, above, and below, then laid it upon the
prayer mat before him. He did the same with the bowl of
red pigment, placing it beside the pipe. Carefully, with incantations, he painted the stem to where two eagle feathers
were attached at the base of the bowl, and laid the pipe upon
the stone ledge of the altar.

He then reached for his medicine bag suspended by cords
from the ceiling to avoid contamination. This was an
envelope-shaped pouch of finest deerskin, elaborately
fringed and embroidered, a prize captured from a Pawnee
shaman. Reverently, he opened it and removed a forked
stick, the shaft of which was painted red and adorned with
hummingbird feathers. He offered this to the Six Sacred Directions, and placed it beside the pipe.

Raising both hands, he addressed the Above Beings with
the Truth Pipe Song, one of many long and elaborate chants
a Medicine Chief knew word for word and recited with impressive gestures and dramatic intonations. To be remiss in
a single word or gesture would render the prayer useless.
Not only would the entire ceremony and all the prayers have
to be repeated, but the four days of fasting and purification
before the ceremony would again be required.

He finished with both arms crossed overhead, palms facing the Above Beings.

"May one who lies—he with two hearts, the heart of an
animal and the heart of a man—be stricken dead if he
smokes this pipe. May truth be revealed."

Prayer completed, he lifted the Truth Pipe and pointed
the stem again to the Above Beings. Next, he pointed it
to Earthmother and then to the Four Winds, and turned it
toward Tolonqua.

"This pipe unites you with the Above Beings and with
Masau'u and all that Masau'u has created. If your words
are straight, long life will be yours. If you have two hearts
and speak with two tongues, your life will be short. Are you
prepared to accept the pipe?"

Tolonqua's voice was steady. "I am ready."

Solemnly, the Chief stuffed tobacco in the pipe and handed it to Tolonqua who accepted it with the proper gesture of turning the bowl to the Chief. With rhythmic incantation, the Chief used the forked stick to remove a coal from the fire pit and light the pipe.

"Let truth be known."

Tolonqua smoked, blowing the sacred essence toward the Above Beings. The assembled Chiefs sat stiffly, faces expressionless, as custom required.

As he held the stem of the pipe in his hand, Tolonqua luxuriated in the smoothness of it. The smoke warmed his mouth and throat like a blessing, proclaiming his truth.

Suddenly, without warning, the bowl broke from the stem, tumbled to his lap, and rolled to the floor.

There were gasps and shocked exclamations. Tolonqua held the stem in his hand, gazing unbelievingly down at the bowl from which a thin wisp escaped.

"An omen!" the Medicine Chief said hoarsely.

Two Elk jabbed an accusing finger. "The pipe refused to be smoked!"

The men looked at one another; there were murmurs.

Slowly, Tolonqua lifted the bowl. He fitted it to the stem where eagle feathers fluttered. "Why?" he asked the pipe. "Why?"

Two Elk said again, "The pipe refused to be smoked. I also ask why."

Again, the Medicine Chief raised his hand. To Tolonqua he said, "This must be discussed without your presence. Leave us."

"Wait." Tolonqua held the pipe so all might see. "Look. The bowl was cut from the stem, leaving but a thin portion attached. See where the cut place was concealed by the cord that fastened the feathers to the stem. Someone killed the Truth Pipe so truth would not be revealed." Anger choked his voice. *"Who did this?"*

The Medicine Chief reached for the pipe, and Tolonqua handed him the pieces. He peered at them with his one eye and handed them to the Chiefs to be passed around.

Tolonqua said, "You ask me to leave. I leave." He climbed the ladder and stomped away.

Never, in all the years of his experience, had the Medicine Chief encountered such a thing, and he was at a loss to explain it. To desecrate a sacred object was unthinkable. Assuming, of course, that the bowl had been deliberately cut from the stem.

There was heated discussion. Some said Tolonqua was right, and the bowl had been cut. Others insisted the bowl detached itself because it refused to verify the truth of Tolonqua's words. One or two went so far as to say the pipe was very old, from the time of their grandfathers, and it had to break sometime. It meant only that the pipe should be replaced.

"Let us remember that our Hunting Chief has always spoken truth," the Medicine Chief said. "And he did ask to smoke the Truth Pipe."

"But only after a vision told him to," Two Elk said.

Another spoke. "The vision was of the White Buffalo."

"The totem most powerful!" the Medicine Chief reminded them.

The men lowered their eyes and did not reply.

The Medicine Chief said, "I shall commune with the Above Beings and seek their wisdom. Tonight, at the evening fire, I will announce their decision."

Word passed quickly through the village, and there was loud discussion, whispered comments, and tense expectation.

Kwani sat with Tolonqua in their dwelling with the woven door mat covering the entrance. Kwani hugged her knees, rocking miserably back and forth.

"What does it mean?" she asked again. "I am afraid—"

His voice was hard. "It means I have an enemy."

"Who?"

He shrugged. "It does not matter. Truth will be revealed. The White Buffalo said it."

"Shall we be at the fire tonight?"

"Of course." His voice softened as he looked at her. "You and Acoya and I will be there, and I will announce Acoya's birthing ceremony."

For a moment Kwani gazed at him wordlessly, her heart overflowing. He knew how much she wanted Acoya to be presented to Sunfather, and how she regretted the child was born where the ceremony could not take place. "But it is so late! It should have been within four days—"

"It will be a naming ceremony, but it will be for the birthing, as well. He must be presented to Sunfather so that his path of life may be blessed."

For a man to give the birthing ceremony was an official declaration that he was the father of the child, even though it might be sired by another. Kwani flung both arms around him.

"I love you, Towa!"

Smoke from the evening fire in the plaza drifted fragrantly as people gathered as usual for news, songs, discussion of the crops and weather, and community matters. They were eager for word of the Medicine Chief about Tolonqua and the Truth Pipe. People talked of little else.

"He asked to smoke the pipe."

"But it broke in his hand! Surely that means—"

"Yes. The pipe refused to say he spoke truth."

"But they say the stem was cut. Who—"

"He wants to build a new city. Who can believe the truth of his reasons?"

"Tolonqua brings us the robe of the White Buffalo."

"Our Hunting Chief does not lie."

"But—"

Kwani and Tolonqua were among the first to arrive at the fire. She carried Acoya in her arms; he resisted the cradle board more and more. He was growing fast and acquiring a personality. Kwani thought he would become a strong-willed, serious little boy. With the White Buffalo as his protector, his path of life should be straight and beautiful.

Anitzal and Lumu came to sit beside her. They took Acoya and talked baby talk to him, and passed him from hand to hand so that all might marvel again at the mark of the White Buffalo. As sisters of Tolonqua, they were staunch in their defense of him in gossip sessions. Lumu, especially, was outraged that her brother's word was questioned. Anitzal, as an esteemed yaya, was listened to respectfully as she reminded them of Tolonqua's virtues.

"From childhood he has not lied. He is loyal to us. He is honorable, strong, and a hunter upon whom we all depend. He participates in all the dances, sings all the songs, attends to all his sacred duties. When his first mate died in childbirth, he grieved long. He seeks to build a new city on the ridge because he wishes for us, his people, to be safe. He is all a Towa should be, and those who presume to question his word should seek within themselves why this is so."

Yellow Bird and all the yaya were at the fire, as was every member of the village, waiting for the Medicine Chief to emerge from the kiva with word of the decision of the Above Beings. The cool evening breeze swept from the mountains, stirring the hair on Kwani's cheek. Owa sat with Talasi, conversing intimately, and glanced now and then at Kwani who returned his hostile looks with some of her own.

Twilight deepened to evening, but the Medicine Chief did not appear. His loud chants for wisdom rose and fell in cadence with his spirit-talker, a gourd rattle with pebbles inside and with elaborate ornamentation of painted symbols, dangling shells, and a scarlet macaw feather.

Children grew restless, babies cried and slept, boys wrestled one another noisily, men discussed the crops and the weather, and women talked behind their hands about Kwani.

"She is beautiful. No wonder Tolonqua—"

"I wonder what she did to send Kokopelli away."

"If he was sent away."

"That necklace! I've never seen such!"

"It is the necklace of She Who Remembers."

"Will she be teaching our girls?"

"Only if she speaks truth."

"She is beautiful."

"Yes, but—"

At last the Medicine Chief emerged from the kiva, spirit-talker in one hand and the broken parts of the Truth Pipe in the other. He strode to the fire, faced the people, and swung the rattle overhead in a wide arc, making it hiss and sing. The people quieted, waiting tensely. Kwani reached for Tolonqua's hand, and clutched it as if to keep from falling.

The spirit-talker quieted. The Chief gazed silently at the people, commanding their total attention. In the firelight, the turquoise and obsidian eye seemed omnipotent, the eye of an unknown and fearsome god. He held the broken pipe in his outstretched hand.

"Behold the Truth Pipe. It is dead."

Murmurs.

"It died in the hand of our Hunting Chief."

More murmurs, and sharp glances at Tolonqua.

"Why did it die? I did not know and sought an answer from the Above Beings and from the spirit of the pipe itself."

Again, the spirit-talker spoke, and quieted.

"It required many sacrifices, many prayers, to learn the answer." He paused, turning from side to side so he might see all gathered there, and they could see him. "The pipe itself has spoken to me. It says it was wounded before Tolonqua held it. When it knew it must die, it chose to die in the hand of one who spoke truth."

"Ah-h-h!" the people sighed as with a single voice.

The Chief strode to Tolonqua, holding the broken pieces in his outstretched hand. "I give the pipe to you. It is yours. Do with it as you wish." He turned to face the people who gazed at him and at Tolonqua with astonished reverence. "Our Hunting Chief speaks truth. The White Buffalo came to him and offered to be taken. He, his son, his son's sons, and our clan possess the sacred robe, the first of our people to be so honored. Tolonqua is a Chosen One. This the Truth Pipe knew and that is why it chose to die in Tolonqua's hand." He turned to Two Elk. "It is your privilege to appoint a craftsman to create another pipe to replace the one that is no more."

With a final flourish of the spirit-talker, the Medicine Chief disappeared into the kiva.

There was an explosion of talk. A hunter jumped up, shouting, "Our Hunting Chief is a Chosen One and we are Chosen People!"

People clustered around Tolonqua, asking to see the broken pieces. There were mutterings.

"How did the pipe become wounded?"

"See that mark on the bowl!"

"Not a natural break."

"Was it cut?"

"Who would do such a thing?"

"It was old. Very old. Perhaps—"

"Yes. It was old."

All knew well how age brought death.

Kwani hugged herself with relief and with pride. No longer would they be questioned. Tolonqua was a Chosen One. As was Acoya. As was she.

Tolonqua rose and stood in the firelight with the white robe shining and the broken pipe in his hand. As he stood tall and erect with firelight flickering on the planes of his face with its high cheekbones and strong jaw, it seemed that the spirit of the White Buffalo was within him as well as within the robe. He cupped the pieces of the pipe in both hands as he spoke.

"I honor this pipe that died in my hand. One day I shall know who wounded it, who wanted to make it seem that I lie. *I will know because the pipe will tell me.*"

He stood looking over the people seated around the fire. Some glanced at one another. Those who had questioned him sat with bowed heads; others regarded him with profound respect. Two Elk gazed down at his folded hands, his face impassive. Yellow Bird was shaking. The wind was cold; Aka-ti removed the blanket from her own shoulders and draped it around Yellow Bird to ease the chill.

Owa said loudly, "We honor you, Tolonqua!"

"Aye!" the hunters cried.

"Thank you." He smiled at the hunters. "We must plan a hunt to have much meat for feasting." He turned to the Crier Chief, a young man whose booming voice earned him the honor. "I shall ask you to announce the time of the naming ceremony for my son. And a marriage celebration for Kwani and me. When we return from the hunt."

There were more smiles and nods of approval. People settled comfortably for a pleasant evening. A grandfather said, "I will tell a story. How the rabbit lost his long tail. . . ."

Moonwoman rose in splendor, and a sweet night wind swept from distant places, from mountains and valleys unexplored.

"Come!" it whispered.

A group of young men began to chant in strong, clear voices:

"Hay-nah en-neh hay-nah."

Far away, a coyote called. Kwani lifted her head, listening. Again the call came, rising, falling, drifting with the wind.

Was it Brother Coyote? Telling her something?

What if it were not a coyote at all?

▲ 14 ▼

Night was pulled back like a bowstring, Sunfather appeared, and Acoya's Day-Before-Naming began. Tolonqua and the hunters had returned with elk and deer; there was an abundance. Already, the fragrance of roasting meat and steaming pots greeted the morning.

Kwani sat in the plaza with Anitzal grinding multicolored corn for cakes and stews and dumplings. Acoya lay upon a blanket beside her, kicking his feet and making happy noises. Two perfect ears of corn, his Corn Mothers, lay beside him, auguries of life and plenty. He would treasure these for a lifetime, she knew. They would be in his medicine bundle when he was a man, and would be with him when he joined his ancestors in Sipapu. The Corn Mothers should have been given to him immediately after birth, but surely the gods understood there was no corn available in that remote place. They had blessed him through the White Buffalo. Her son was robustly healthy and content.

Other women brought metates and manos to the plaza to grind more corn and to enjoy one another's company while they watched preparations for tomorrow's celebration.

The Crier Chief appeared, dressed in his finest breechcloth of cotton adorned with porcupine quills dyed red and black, and with a handsomely fringed belt dangling to his knees. He was short and squat with powerful shoulders and spindly legs. His good-humored, round face flashed a missing tooth like an open window when he smiled, which was often. He carried the Crier Chief Shield, symbol of his authority, which proclaimed important ceremonial announcements. Bright feathers and cotton streamers fluttered impressively from the shield with each step.

Two musicians strode in front of the Crier Chief, a drummer and a young boy with a shrill flute fashioned from the leg bone of a turkey. Each time the Crier Chief paused for breath during his announcement, the small cottonwood drum could punctuate with a loud staccato flurry and the flute would echo with a triumphant trill.

It was an impressive performance, dramatically enhanced with the Crier Chief's booming, melodious voice.

"Know all people this is the Day-Before-Naming! The day we prepare for the naming ceremony of the son of She Who Remembers!"

Drum flurry. Shrill flute.

"Tomorrow, our Hunting Chief will present the son of Kwani to Sunfather so that the child's path of life might be blessed."

Drum and flute in loud emphasis.

"Tomorrow, Tolonqua takes Kwani's son as his own. We shall celebrate also that She Who Remembers, mate of Tolonqua, is now one of us!"

Drum flurry. Flute trill.

"Prepare the feasting, prepare the elk, the deer, the stews, the cakes!"

Drum and flute in hearty emphasis.

"Make ready for visitors from other villages, other clans, and distant places. Prepare the celebration!" His rich voice soared, and he raised the shield overhead to indicate the announcement was over.

A final, rousing drum flurry was accompanied by a prolonged, passionate trill of the flute as the Crier Chief and the musicians circled the plaza. The people applauded. Their young Crier Chief and his assistants did things right!

Kwani bent over her sandstone metate that was worn nearly smooth. She needed a sharp-edged stone tool to hammer the surface, roughing it again, but now was not the time. She pushed the mano stone back and forth, letting her necklace swing free. Her hair was braided in Towa fashion with red and yellow cords entwined, and the part of her hair was painted red.

She looked at the women gathered about her, bent to their tasks. They had washed their hair in yucca suds and shaken dust from their garments as was customary before grinding corn. The sun was warm in the plaza and women still wore their summer garments of a short cotton skirt fastened at the waist with a belt of woven human and dog hair in intricate design, with a luxurious, long fringe into which turquoise or shell beads were sometimes entwined. Necklaces dangled between bare breasts. Those unfortunates who were experiencing the moon flow that day were, of course, isolated in the women's hut so that their presence would not contaminate others or the food to be consumed. All knew how a bleeding woman endangered all about her and could antagonize the spirits of game animals, causing them to forsake hunting grounds.

"Kwani, look!"

It was Lumu, pointing. Owa approached, carrying a large, very heavy metate on his head, and an oblong, two-hand mano and a tall jar of corn in his arms. He swaggered to the group with his man gait, placed his burdens on the ground, and squatted with an air of benevolent authority.

He tossed his braids. "I shall grind corn with you."

There were muffled giggles. Anitzal said, "You took game with the hunters. Why are you not with them now?"

He gave her a condescending glance. "I am berdache."

"Yes," Kwani said. "Your dwelling adjoins ours. I hear you with Talasi."

More giggles. Owa speared her with a look of pure hatred, poured corn into the metate, slammed the heavy mano stone upon it, and bent to grinding with a force that made grains dance to the rim.

Visitors began to arrive, bringing piki bread, paper-thin and baked on a hot stone slab; blue corn cake sweetened with saliva and mixed with ashes; and delicious little blue corn dumplings cooked in boiling water. They brought flutes, whistles, rattles, drums, gambling pieces, trade items, their mates, their children, and dogs. There was an uproar of greetings, shouting, laughter, and dog fights.

Two Elk was in the kiva, smoking the hospitality pipe with visiting dignitaries. Tolonqua was in the plaza with his hunters and those from other clans, retelling the story of how he took the White Buffalo. Never did they tire of hearing it and they asked for it again. Young men played shooting-at-moving-targets game while they eyed the girls who pretended not to notice and eyed them back. Trading was already under way with much bargaining, and valuables changed hands.

Women clustered around Acoya, exclaiming in awe at the mark on the sole of his foot, while he kicked and cooed and waved his arms.

"He is a Chosen One!" they whispered.

Kwani smiled without reply. She felt that Acoya must be weary of crowds and of strangers, but it would be rude to deny them the pleasure of seeing the boy they had heard so much about. However, when they wanted to hold him and hand him around, Kwani said tactfully, "I must nurse him and put him in his cradle board. Will someone take my place at the metate?''

There were immediate volunteers. Kwani took Acoya to the dim quiet and solitude of their dwelling; she needed it as much as he did. She laid Acoya on a blanket and lay beside him, looking up at the patch of blue sky showing through the hatchway. Tomorrow, her son would be given many names from which he could choose when he was older. Tomorrow, at sunrise, he would be presented to Sunfather in a ceremony to assure long life, good health, and happiness. He would become a Towa, a son of Tolonqua, a member-to-be of the Turquoise Clan with his father. No longer would he be Anasazi; only his blood would remember. No longer would he be hers alone.

The realization gave her mixed feelings. He was hers, born of her body, nourished by her spirit, a physical and spiritual part of her, an extension of herself. Acoya needed a father to give him a clan, a people, and a place of his own. To teach him all he must know.

"You shall have a father," she crooned.

Her son would have all she never possessed. Until now. All she had longed for was hers: love, a mate, a child, a home, security. Then why this hidden feeling, this secret, unexplained sadness? She had not acknowledged it before but it was there, perched like a crow pecking at her heart. Pretending it was not there would not make it go away.

She held the necklace to her, seeking communication with the Ancient Ones. Where was the wisdom they promised her? What more must she learn?

She closed her eyes, praying. "Sacred Ones, there is a grieving inside me I do not understand. Tell me what it is."

She strained to hear the silent voices. None came.

"I plead for wisdom!"

Then, like an echo of her own voice, the answer came.

"You are one of us. The blood remembers."

Her Anasazi blood. In a Towa world.

And always she would be the Chosen One, one apart, of no single clan or people, but of all womankind.

Alone. Lonely.

More visitors arrived. Tipis sprouted like weeds around the village. Kwani tucked Acoya in his cradle board (over his objections) and returned to the plaza to continue with the grinding. She saw with alarm that a number of the newly arrived tipis were Querecho. Were they of the friendly Plains tribe, or the treacherous tribe of the south? The shields displayed by the tipi door flaps identified the owners, but she could not be sure about the clans. And they smelled so bad! Towas were meticulous about bathing in the river but these Plains tribes seemed to never bathe at all. That, and the bear grease they used lavishly. . . . She kept her distance.

She looked for Tolonqua. He was still with his hunters, and Owa was with him, hovering close.

She bit her lips. *Owa must go!*

Anitzal still worked at the metate, grinding vigorously, pausing now and then for emphasis as she told avid listeners again how her brother, Tolonqua, obtained the robe, and how the White Buffalo marked her nephew, Acoya. The women exclaimed in fascinated awe as if they had not heard it all before.

When the story was finally ended, Kwani pointed to the tipis. "Can you tell me what Querechos they are? Where they come from?"

Anitzal stood to look, shading her eyes with her hand. Some of the others joined her. Anitzal said, "I am not sure."

Another said, "I don't think I have seen them before."

"Many new tribes are on the plains now. Hunting buffalo. They come for trading," a woman said.

Anitzal said, "They come to eat. They have heard—"

"What do they bring to the feast?"

They looked at one another and shook their heads.

Anitzal frowned. It was an inviolate law of hospitality that visitors be fed. But there were so many; there might not be enough for everyone. Discussion was in order.

"I shall confer with Yellow Bird."

Others said, "We shall join you."

They left, and Kwani was at the metate alone but for another group grinding corn nearby. They motioned for her to join them, but she smiled her thanks and said, "I wait for Anitzal to return."

They nodded. It was proper for Kwani to be with the sister of Tolonqua, especially since Anitzal was of the esteemed yaya.

Kwani watched as Anitzal and the others climbed the ladder to Yellow Bird's roof. The old matriarch was not sitting at her usual place on the roof, and after a moment the group climbed down into Yellow Bird's dwelling. Finally, they reappeared and returned.

''She is not feeling well today, but she sends for the Warrior Chief,'' Anitzal said.

A boy scurried to the kiva and called down, ''Yellow Bird summons the Warrior Chief!''

The Warrior Chief and those of his Society were responsible for the security of the village. They made it a point always to know who was in the vicinity, and why. The Warrior Chief, an austere and regal personage, emerged from the kiva. He made his way to the conference with Yellow Bird, after which he approached Anitzal and the group who pretended they were not agog for the news.

Anitzal glanced up at him casually. ''We welcome you,'' she said politely, as was expected.

He nodded briefly, and intoned, ''Yellow Bird wishes me to inform you about the Querechos.'' He gestured to the tipis. ''They are of the Plains, but they are not those who have been here before. They come for trading. From another area.'' He turned to go.

''Wait!'' Kwani said. ''From what area?''

He frowned. It was not her place to speak, and he did not reply.

''From where?'' Anitzal asked sharply.

He gestured vaguely and strode back to the kiva.

Kwani said, ''I don't think he knows. What if—''

Anitzal gave her an understanding glance, and her face crinkled in a reassuring smile. ''Many friends are here, and many warriors. Do not be afraid. We are safe.''

''Aye!'' the other said, nodding in sympathy. All had experienced attacks upon the village by one tribe or another, but Cicuye's brave warriors always drove the attackers away.

Kwani bent again to her grinding, but she thought of the night recently when she and Tolonqua and Owa were stalked and attacked on the plain. By Querechos.

Where were the two who escaped?

She shook her head. This was not time for such thoughts. It was time to rejoice, to be happy. A time for celebration! She would sing; that always lightened her heart.

She threw back her head and began to sing the Corn Grinding Song that women sang to make corn grow tall. Her clear voice soared.

> *''How-hay-he, yow-ow-ah,*
> *Hay yow, yoo-oo*
> *Is it not beautiful?*
> *Is it not truly?''*

Anitzal and the other women joined her, rubbing the mano stones in time to the rhythm.

> *"On every side They are,*
> *The Trues, the rain-commanders.*
> *Do you not hear their thunder drum?"*

They began to harmonize, smiling at one another as they sang.

> *"Because of that you will see*
> *This year the vapor floating;*
> *Because of that you will see*
> *This year the drizzling rain.*
> *Is it not beautiful?*
> *Is it not truly?"*

Several young men ran to their tipis for rattles and flutes. Somebody produced a drum. Soon there was music to accompany the singers, and people gathered to enjoy the performance.

> *"In all the fields the corn upspringing.*
> *Like the young pine it comes up;*
> *Like the green aspen;*
> *In all the fields the corn upspringing,*
> *Tall like the tail of the thrush;*
> *Tall like the roadrunner's tail.*
> *Is it not beautiful?"*

The musicians and some of the bystanders joined in the final words of the song.

> *"Yay yay yay yay! Yow how how how!"*

It was such fun they decided to do it again.

Tolonqua stood to one side, unable to conceal his pride. Kwani's voice was like a bird soaring, and as she leaned to and fro at the metate, the shell swung back and forth upon her lovely bare breasts, caressing. Now and then she flung back her head as if to release the words of the song, and her round, red-brown face glowed, and her eyes—those blue, blue eyes—sparkled. There were a number of women in the group, but people saw only Kwani. She had more than beauty; she had something inside that enveloped her like an aura.

Owa was beside him, and Tolonqua turned with a smile to share his pride.

"Your mate sings well," Owa said dutifully, and his face was smooth and hard as stone.

Excitement grew as the day passed. More visitors arrived, more tipis sprouted, and trading was brisk. Evening fires brought the first night of feasting and of stories, singing, gossip, and news. It was said that the Eagle Clan had abandoned their home in the cliff and had joined another clan along the Great River. Lack of rain caused many Anasazi and others to seek new lands near water. It was said also that Zashue, young Medicine Chief of the Eagle Clan, he of the scarred face, had gone with two warriors on a secret mission and had not returned.

There was speculation about Kokopelli. Was he dead? Whispers about possible involvement by Tolonqua and Kwani were met with scowls by the people of Cicuye who told of the Truth Pipe Ceremony in great detail. Tolonqua and his robe were displayed with pride, and the story of how the White Buffalo offered to be taken was repeated over and over. Owa sat next to Tolonqua, eagerly telling how they killed three of five Querechos who attacked from ambush. Never had Cicuye basked in such renown!

Moonwoman rose and stars walked their celestial paths. Couples disappeared into the shadows. Fires burned low and families drifted to sleeping mats to await pulatla. Night birds called, wolves and coyotes sang to the moon, and the breeze carried the rich aroma of coals burned low and food awaiting tomorrow's feasting.

Kwani lay with Tolonqua on the sleeping mat, and Acoya slept soundly nearby with his Corn Mother on either side. Overhead, stars shone through the hatchway. One day, Tolonqua's campfire would be among them. So would hers be. She rejected the thought; she wanted to be with him here, always.

In the darkness he seemed to read her mind. He leaned over her, and she smelled the man scent of him, a scent she could not identify but could only respond to.

He said, "Tomorrow we celebrate." He laughed softly. "Shall we begin now?"

"Yes. Oh, yes!"

Lips and hands caressed her, igniting inner fires. She felt

the male strength of him, the hardness, the eagerness. She pulled him closer, deeper. And deeper still.

"Kwani . . . Ah, Kwani . . ."

Inner fires exploded to conflagration. She cried out as in a delirium.

On the roof above them, concealed in shadows, Owa crouched, listening. He turned away and stuffed a fist in his mouth to stifle wrenching sobs.

▲ 15 ▼

It was the time when Earthmother wakens and birds announce pulatla. Tolonqua was at the river, cleansing himself for Acoya's naming ceremony. The water was clean and cold and felt good, and so did he.

The buffalo robe hung from a low branch of a tree by the river. Soon the sacred robe would become a medicine bundle to be unrolled and displayed for ceremonial uses only. Until then, he would wear it to assure his rightful place as the one to whom the White Buffalo appeared, offering to be taken. No other person in memory of his clan had experienced this; emphasis was suitable and expected.

Owa sat beneath the tree, watching him. Although he was a slave no longer, he insisted upon acting like one, and was Tolonqua's constant companion and protector. True, he lived with Talasi, and no doubt served him well, but it was obvious where Owa's devotion lay. For an instant Tolonqua wondered how Owa would serve him more if allowed to do so.

"Come in the water!" he called, splashing like a boy.

Owa shook his head. He disliked rivers.

Tolonqua swam downstream, allowing the current to sweep him along. As he neared a bend, he swam to the bank and clambered out, surprising a bear who lumbered away.

A bear! A good omen!

Returning to the bank he encountered Owa who had followed him, the robe in one hand and a bow in the other. He handed the robe to Tolonqua, and together they returned to the village.

Tolonqua did not mention the bear. Owa was Pawnee, no privy to Towa ceremonial secrets. The tattoo of a bear's paw mark on Tolonqua's left shoulder, symbol of power, had been given to him by the Medicine Chief when the bear appeared to Tolonqua in a dream during his boyhood initiation ceremony into the Turquoise Clan. How long ago that seemed!

At the village, Kwani was dressing Acoya in the little squirrel-skin robe given to her by the Clan Chief's mate at Puname after she killed the deer. Remembering the old woman's kindness and motherly concern gave Kwani a pang of nostalgia, so she pushed the thought from her mind and concentrated on Acoya. He had grown much in two moons. It seemed to Kwani that he understood all she told him, and she felt a closeness to him she had never experienced with anyone.

the hatchway darkened as Tolonqua appeared.

"Come. It is time." He saw that Acoya was dressed, and he frowned impatiently. "He must be unclothed so that Sunfather's rays enfold him all over. Remove the robe."

"But—"

"Remove it!"

Kwani heard a small tinkle as Tolonqua abruptly withdrew. Owa was with him again. Anger surged in her and she jerked off the robe in a way that made Acoya whimper.

She cradled the little body in her arms. "I am sorry. It is Owa who makes me act so."

She carried him naked outside where people thronged the plaza, waiting. The horizon glowed red-gold; it was nearly time for Sunfather to appear. Yellow Bird stood with Two Elk, Anitzal, Lumu, and the Medicine Chief, watching as Kwani entered the plaza.

"Bring the child to me," Yellow Bird said. She seemed more feeble than usual, and braced herself with a staff.

Anitzal took Acoya from Kwani's arms and carried him to Yellow Bird. Kwani followed, thinking it was she who should carry her son, but Anitzal was of the yaya and she was not. Anitzal knelt before Yellow Bird so that the old woman could see the boy easily. Yellow Bird looked at him for some moments. She squinted. "He does not look Towa."

Kwani pointed to the mark on Acoya's foot. "He is a Chosen One, Anasazi born," she said proudly, but with an edge to her voice. "Now he will become Towa."

Tolonqua appeared, carrying a small, carved stone bowl. He handed it to Anitzal. "The sacred pollen."

Kwani watched as Tolonqua's sister performed the duty expected of her—to rub corn pollen over the body of her brother's infant child. The Medicine Chief mumbled hurried incantations, for Sunfather's gleaming rim was nearly seen. Musicians stood by, ready with rattles, whistles, and flutes to accompany the Birthing Song.

"Now!" Tolonqua said.

Anitzal handed Acoya to Tolonqua who strode to the easternmost edge of the plaza. Sunfather was the giver of life, so life must be presented to him in turn. He lifted Acoya toward Sunfather as the holy radiance appeared. A rhythmic cadence soared with Tolonqua's rich voice in the Birthing Song.

> *"Now this day*
> *Our child*
> *Into the daylight*
> *You will go standing.*
>
> *"Our fathers,*
> *Dawn priests,*
> *Have come out standing to their sacred place.*
> *Our sun father,*
> *Having come out standing to his sacred place,*
> *Our child,*
> *It is your day.*
>
> *"This day*
> *The flesh of white corn,*
> *Prayer meal,*
> *To our sun father,*
> *This prayer meal we offer."*

The Medicine Chief stepped forward and tossed a handful of meal to the sun. Then the people joined in Tolonqua's song, singing with him in rhythm with the flute and whistle, and the mystic emphasis of the rattle.

> *"May your road be fulfilled,*
> *Reaching to the road of your sun father*
> *When your road is fulfilled.*
> *In your thoughts may we live,*
> *May we be the ones whom your thoughts will embrace.*
> *For this, on this day,*
> *To our sun father*
> *We offer prayer meal."*

Chanting, the Medicine Chief tossed another handful of meal to Sunfather, then turned to Tolonqua.

"May his path be straight." He gestured a blessing.

"Aye!" the people cried.

"Your son is ready for his naming," the Medicine Chief said.

At that moment Sunfather finished his emergence in total glory. The music swelled triumphantly.

Holding the boy in outstretched arms, Tolonqua sang,

> *"My sun father,*
> *I bring this child, my son,*
> *To receive your blessing.*
> *Bestow on him your powers,*
> *Your long life,*
> *Your old age,*
> *Your waters,*
> *Your seeds,*
> *Your riches,*
> *Your strong spirit.*
> *May his life be straight.*
> *May his life be beautiful."*

Again, the Medicine Chief tossed prayer meal. The people sang, "May his life be straight. May his life be beautiful."

The music ceased, and there was solemn silence. Tolonqua held the boy before him and gazed into his face.

"I name you Acoya."

Kwani stood proudly as Anitzal stepped forward. As the baby's senior aunt, Anitzal was the first of his other relatives to give him a name that he might choose to keep when he was older. She held one of the Corn Mothers adorned for the occasion with an eagle feather to impart spiritual power. She touched the corn to Acoya's face and neck, then waved it back and forth over his head as she prayed.

"May you live many years. May you have good crops of corn. May you have good health and many sons. I name you Buffalo Walker."

Lumu, the youngest aunt, stepped forward, her pert face grave. She took the Corn Mother and repeated Anitzal's gestures and prayer. Then she said, "I name you Running Antelope."

Yellow Bird was next. She named him Rain On The Mountain. Others followed, each giving a name. When all the names were bestowed, the Medicine Chief flourished his spirit-talker rattle.

"The son of Tolonqua is coming to his home!"

"Let him come!" the people cried happily.

Tolonqua handed Acoya to Kwani. "Our son comes home."

The ceremony was complete. People crowded around Kwani and Tolonqua, welcoming the child with gifts of clothing, jewelry, blankets, toys, and objects of sacred power. Kwani thanked them all, her face aglow, her eyes misty.

Only one person gave no gift.

Owa.

Feasting was under way. Sunfather walked higher on his sky trail and more tipis rose beyond the village, their poles pointing like fingers at an eagle circling in turquoise sky. Those who had come from the plains to trade and who had remained in the background during the ceremony gathered now around the cooking pots, dipping corn cakes into stews, and slicing big chunks from elk and buffalo roasts sizzling over fires. They would sink their teeth into the meat, then use a sharp flint knife to cut off a big piece.

Girls who had experienced the moon flow and were eligible for mates and young braves from other clans found ways to meet and to talk and make evening plans. There was laughter, conversation, much singing, and the usual shouts of children running about, yelps from dogs, and occasional noisy dog fights with owners intervening. Over all floated the delicious aromas and the fragrance of wind from mountain and plain.

Kwani sat with Tolonqua and his sisters and other relatives: cousins, sisters of grandmothers who were also called grandmother, and a brother of Tolonqua's grandfather who was also called grandfather. Both of the original grandparents were in Sipapu so substitute grandparenting was welcome. All gathered around Acoya, smiling as he waved his arms and kicked strong little legs as he lay upon a blanket beside his mother.

Kwani was overwhelmed. She wasn't sure how to cope with so many of a family!

Word has passed swiftly among the visitors that Tolonqua's mate was She Who Remembers of the Eagle Clan of the west, she who called the deer at Puname, the buffalo at the Place of the Rainbow Flint, and who was also a Storyteller. People glanced at her with respect tinged with awe.

A little girl came timidly to Kwani and stood twisting a finger in her long hair. Kwani smiled at her and the girl ducked her head shyly, but she did not go away.

"What is your name?" Kwani asked.

For a moment the girl did not answer. Then she peeked up through her hair.

"I am Bird That Runs."

"Come sit with us."

She shook her head but still stood there. Finally she said, "Will you tell a story?"

Kwani smiled. "You want a story?"

She nodded.

Tolonqua said, "Where is your mother?"

The girl pointed at one of the tipis. She was Querecho.

Tolonqua and Kwani glanced at each other. The child wore no clothing; she could have been from any tribe.

Tolonqua said, "There will be stories tonight. And songs, and riddles. We will look for you there."

"You will sit by me," Kwani said.

The girl nodded and ran away, the wind tossing her hair.

There was a tense silence. Anitzal said, "She is Querecho. From the plains."

Kwani nodded. "I know."

Lumu said, "But you invited her to sit with us! It is not—"

"To sit with *me*."

Anitzal shook her head. "You are one of us now." Pause. "Are you not?"

I wonder, Kwani thought.

Tolonqua spoke sharply. "She is. And she is She Who Remembers who teaches young girls and who tells them stories. It is suitable that they come to her."

"Not Querechos. Of the plains or otherwise," one of the old grandmothers spoke up. "They may come with their families to the evening fire, but they may not join our group. They are Querechos."

"Children are children," Kwani said hotly.

"And Querechos are Querechos," Anitzal said.

"Friends." Tolonqua gestured to close the subject. "I hunt with them. They welcome me to their hunting ground and to their tipis. We welcome them here."

He had spoken. There was a resentful silence as Tolonqua's sisters and cousins and grandmothers glanced at once another and at others nearby who heard but pretended they had not.

Across the plaza, Owa stood alone, ignoring curious stares and tentative approaches. The naming ceremony, the gift giving, the adulation of Kwani and her son burned like coals in his stomach. But worse was the presence of Quer-echos whose numbers steadily increased. Tolonqua had said these were the Querechos of the Plains, steadfast friends, but Owa noticed that Tolonqua did not know many of them and had not seen them before.

Owa could smell and taste danger; he felt it crawling along his spine. Should he warn Tolonqua? No, there was no proof yet. And Tolonqua sat close to Kwani who would hear, and he did not want Kwani to know. What happened to her did not matter.

He would warn Talasi. The Warrior Society should be informed and prepared. Just in case.

Feasting was nearly over and trading was under way. Owa made his way past displays of hides, pemmican, tallow, bowls, jars, jewelry, mats, baskets, blankets and belts, bows, arrows, arrow straighteners, and tools of every de-scription. The sun was high now, warming the accumulation of feces by dogs and people, creating an accustomed stench that mingled with the odor of dying fires and smoke and rancid bear grease that the Plains people used on their hair.

Owa found Talasi bargaining vigorously for yucca fiber rope. The owner squatted with coils of rope before him, protesting the meager quantity of buckskin offered for trade. Owa, his ear ornament jingling, strode purposefully to Tal-asi.

"I must speak with you."

Talasi ignored him. Bargaining was at a critical point.

Owa stood in silence, waiting for the trade to be consum-mated. When Talasi had acquired the amount of rope he desired, he turned to Owa.

"Do not interrupt when I am trading!"

Owa looked at him calmly, concealing his distaste for the man who had taken him as berdache—and who would be replaced one day by Tolonqua. "It is important that we go where none can hear us speak."

Talasi hefted his armload of rope. "I go to put this in my dwelling. We can speak there."

The roofs were crowded with women, mostly of the yaya, who busied themselves with womanly tasks while they gos-siped and watched the activity below. As Talasi and Owa passed, they glanced at one another and made remarks be-hind their hands.

Talasi and Owa climbed down into their dwelling, and Talasi covered the hatchway. Owa watched patiently as Talasi stacked the rope in precise coils. Finally, Owa said, "Many Querechos are here."

"Of course. They come to eat. And to trade."

"You have seen them all before?"

Talasi shrugged. "There are many."

"Tolonqua has not seen them all before. He told me." Owa scowled. "I do not like it. It is dangerous."

"They are friendly. We trade."

"You trade, yes." Owa leaned forward, his eyes sharp under the hairless brows, his narrow face tense. "I am Pawnee. Of the Plains. I know Querechos. Some good. Some not. These not."

Talasi shifted uncomfortably. "How do you know?"

Owa thumped his chest with a big fist. "I know here." He slapped his brow. "And here." He glanced up at the hatchway and lowered his voice. "We must be ready."

Talasi frowned. "But many warriors are here. Ours, and from other clans. From other villages. Why would Querechos attack?"

"Because there is much wealth here. Things they want."

"We trade—"

"Yes. And they want it all back. And more. They want women, too. And slaves."

"Would they attack so many of us?"

"Maybe. Or maybe they wait until visitors go." He tossed his braids. "I could learn more from one of their warriors. If you wish." His thin lips parted in a bland smile.

Talasi scowled, and was silent for some time. From above came the soft voices of women and distant sounds from the plaza. He stood and reached for his staff of authority, a handsomely adorned rod of many colors and buckskin fringe.

"Come. We shall confer with the Warrior Chief."

It was evening, Kwani sat with Tolonqua by the community fire. Moonwoman had not yet appeared; only campfires of ancestors burned in a black sky. A crowd of visitors from the plains and from other villages sat with the people of Cicuye around the warm blaze, watching sparks float upward and die in the darkness. Songs had been sung, riddles told, and now an aged chief from another village was finishing a story. Firelight flickered on his regal old face as he continued.

"The people put up the medicine lodge, painted their bodies in a sacred manner, and sang songs to Earthmother from whose body life is reborn. The children made clay figures of buffalo, antelope, and elk, and brought them into the lodge as a symbol of life's renewal. Since then, whenever the little figures are placed inside the medicine lodge during the dance, some of these animals will come near and gaze upon the sacred tipi, and some of their animal power will linger on.''

There was the satisfied sigh of having heard a story well told. Kwani had listened with interest for she had not heard the story before. But she noticed that Owa and the members of the Warrior Society sat on the outer edges of the circle and were not paying attention to the stories being told. They conferred in whispers, glancing about. Kwani thought, I wonder why they do that, and she felt a prick of unease. Acoya slept beside her in his cradle board and she lifted it to hold him in her arms.

She turned to Tolonqua. He sat with legs folded, arms across his chest, face expressionless. What is he thinking? she wondered. Lately, he seemed, sometimes, to be in a distant place, leaving her alone.

"Aliksai!"

Another story was to be told. Here, a Storyteller always began with *Aliksai*! This time, it was a young Pueblo trader from another village.

"Ho! I tell of days long past, when Earthmother was young and all crows were white as snow. . . .''

The people settled happily, waiting to hear a favorite tale again. Kwani did not listen; her thoughts were with Tolonqua. In the firelight, with the sacred white robe about him, it seemed that the Spirit Being had assumed man form. She looked at his profile—the proud nose, the strong jaw, the high line of cheek sloping to a resolute chin, and the wide brow encircled by the ornate band holding eagle feathers in back, and her heart melted, as always.

He sensed her gaze and turned to her. His eyes, black as the night, warmed as they looked into hers. He leaned close.

"You do not like the story?" A smile tugged at his mouth.

How did he always know when she desired him? She smiled. "What story?"

He laughed softly and put an arm around her.

Beyond the fire, in the shadows, Owa watched, eyes in his narrow face reflecting light like a cougar's.

The storyteller finished, ". . . and the big crow managed to fly out of the fire. But he was badly singed, and some of his feathers were charred and he was no longer white. 'Caw,

caw, caw,' he cried, and flew away.'' The storyteller flapped his arms like wings, and people laughed. ''. . . And the crow escaped. But ever since, all crows have been black.''

It was a good story, and people sighed with pleasure. The hour was late, but no one wanted to go home. Moonwoman rose as if to music unheard. The night wind touched the fire and sparks soared, danced, and died. On the outer edge of the circle there was a stirring as a few warriors slipped away.

''Where are they going?'' Kwani whispered.

''They are sentries. They go to watch.''

Kwani glanced nervously at the forest of tipis clustered on the outskirts of the village. The buffalo-hide coverings were translucent; only a few glowed faintly from small fires inside where aged ones had retired for sleep.

There was a faint sound far away. A coyote?

''Kwani, we wish to hear your story!'' the Crier Chief said.

''Yes! Tell us a story!'' the people cried as if no stories had been told that night.

Kwani lay Acoya beside her. He slept soundly, lashes dark against his cheeks. She was reluctant to tell a story because to do so her spirit must be happy. Hers was uneasy. But a glance from Tolonqua reassured her. She fingered her necklace, seeking inspiration. It must be the right story—to bring her closer to Tolonqua's people. She prayed silently to the Old Ones. ''Help me!''

Unease lessened, faded away.

Aliksai!

''Ho! I tell of Earthmother and when people and animals were created.''

The little Querecho girl, Bird That Runs, stood up and took a tentative step toward Kwani. Kwani held out her arms.

''Come and sit on my lap while I tell a story.''

There were glances and disapproving whispers behind Towa hands, but Tolonqua spoke up. ''Yes, little one. Come.''

The girl ran to Kwani and snuggled in her lap. Kwani began her story.

''The earth was once a person, like us. A woman. The Great Spirit said, 'You will be the mother of all people.' Earth is still alive, but she has changed. The soil is her flesh, the rocks are her bones, the wind is her breath, trees and grass are her hair. She lives spread out, and we live upon her, our earth mother. When she moves, the earth shakes and quivers.''

People looked at one another, and nodded. It was true.

"After changing the woman to Earthmother, the Great Spirit gathered some of her flesh.'' Kwani scooped up a handful of soil. "The Great Spirit rolled this into balls as we do with clay. He made the first group of these balls into the ancient creatures, the beings of the early world.''

Kwani let the soil drift down through her fingers as people watched, visualizing.

"Some of the creatures were like people, and some were like animals. Some could fly like birds; others could swim like fishes. All could speak at that time, and talk to one another. But deer were never among the ancient beings; they were always animals, even as they are today.''

"Aye,'' an old hunter said. "It is so.''

"After the Great Spirit made the ancient creatures, he made real people, like us. He took the last balls of Earthmother's flesh and shaped them like us, and blew on them to make us live.''

The night wind came again, touching each one.

"We are alive. Yes.'' Kwani looked at the people around her. "We are all from the flesh of Earthmother. We are one.''

There was silence. The fire burned low, and Moonwoman's glow was a benediction.

"We are one,'' Kwani said again.

There was a sigh.

"Aye,'' a man said.

People glanced at one another, strangeness falling away. "Aye.''

"We are one.''

From a distance a sound came, rising, falling, fading away.

Coyotes?

▲ 16 ▼

Moonwoman was high; the hour was late. Visitors from nearby villages were gone, but those from the plains stayed to spend the night and depart in the morning. Few sentries were on the roofs where moonlight would make them sharply visible; only one or two crouched motionless. Others lurked in shadows in the fields and around the village.

It was unusually silent.

Within the kiva, coals still smoldered, fed now and then for light and warmth for those gathered in long consultation. The Warrior Chief, Talasi, and all others of the Warrior Society, Two Elk, and other Chiefs and Elders had talked at length; now they listened to Owa.

"I am Pawnee, Of the Plains. I know Plains warriors. They steal under cover of darkness, but they do not like to attack at night. Nor do they bring women and children with them on war raids."

"Then what is the danger?" Two Elk asked. He was weary and his stomach hurt from too much feasting; he wanted his sleeping mat. This berdache, brought to Cicuye by Tolonqua, caused the Warrior Society and all of them needless concern.

Owa was speaking again. "The danger is the wealth here. Things the Querechos want. And women and children—for slaves. They may go, but a war party will return. Silently, in darkness. Then, in early morning—" He shot an imaginary arrow, flung an imaginary lance, and stabbed an imaginary foe with a realism that was all the more horrifying in his woman's array.

"We must be ready," the Warrior Chief, Lopat, said.

"Aye!"

Two Elk shook his head. "We have traded with Querechos for many moons, many seasons. They are friends. If they harm us, they harm those upon whom they depend the most for trading. It makes no sense." He gestured in disgust. "Let us think as men, not as females."

Tolonqua said, "What harm to be prepared?"

The Warrior Chief nodded. "Better to be prepared needlessly than to be caught unprepared and suffer the consequences."

"Aye!"

Two Elk kept his dignity. "I am Chief," he said solemnly. "The welfare of Cicuye and its people is my primary responsibility. I shall confer with the Above Beings to obtain their assistance and protection."

"That is good," said the Medicine Chief, and nodded so that his totem, the stuffed chickadee on the braid behind his ear, nodded also. "I shall do so as well."

"Now we plan," Owa said.

They talked far into the night.

By dawn, remaining visitors from other Pueblo villages had departed, and the women of the Querecho camp were dismantling their tipis swiftly. The ornately painted buffalo-hide covers were removed and the poles dismantled and formed into a travois. Tipi covers were rolled into a bundle and loaded on the travois along with personal belongings, food and water for the trail, objects obtained in trading, and small children. It was all done swiftly and quietly, with little talk. Travois were fitted to dogs that whined in eagerness to be on the move. Final speeches were made, farewells spoken, gifts exchanged, and they were gone.

Kwani and Tolonqua stood on the roof and watched the thin cloud of dust following the Querechos' departure.

"I am glad they are gone," Kwani said. She felt as if some mysterious threat were fading away.

"Yes. But—"

"But what?"

He looked down at her, his black eyes intent. "I want you and Acoya to go to a hiding place. There is a small cave—"

"But why?" Kwani cried. "I do not want—"

"Owa says some of the warriors may return on a raid. For valuables, and for women and children to take as slaves."

Kwani stared up at him. "*Owa* says?"

"Yes. He is Pawnee, of the Plains. He knows—"

"So. I am to take Acoya and run away and hide in a cave because of something Owa says?"

"Yes."

Outrage, long suppressed, exploded. "You send me and my son—our son—away to cower in a cave somewhere because Owa wants to get me out of the way so he can have you all to himself. And you agree to this!" Her eyes blazed blue fire and she shook with fury. "I shall not go. No! Not now, not ever!" She took a step toward Talasi's dwelling that adjoined theirs. She shouted, "It is Owa who will go! Let him hear! Let everybody hear!"

Tolonqua flushed from chin to brow. He swept her up in his arms and she fought to be free, but his was a bear-trap grip. He carried her down the ladder, closing the hatchway after them, and set her on her feet none too gently. He glared down at her with eyes like flint knives.

"My concern is for your safety. Yours and Acoya's. And you presume to humiliate me before my people, before the entire village!"

"Owa—"

"Pawnee, I tell you! He knows Querechos and he says those who were here are dangerous. They may come back—"

"Owa pretends to be a woman. Will he run to hide somewhere also?"

"No. He stays to fight. He is a bowman—"

"He is berdache. He wants me gone so he can have you!"

"Enough." His voice was icy. "I give you a choice. Stay here with Acoya, take the chance I will not be killed and you and Acoya will not be taken as slaves—if you live, that is. Or protect yourself and him by taking refuge in a safe place." He thrust his face close to hers. "Never again are you to speak to me in public. You speak here, only." The black knives of his eyes thrust deep. "Remember that."

He whirled, climbed the ladder, and was gone.

Kwani stared after him, shaken and numb.

Daybreak.

Already, farmers had shouldered their buffalo-bone hoes and elk-horn rakes and left for distant fields, as usual. Those families responsible for maintaining the irrigation system and repairing the dams, and those whose duty it was to clean the springs, departed. Women carried baskets of laundry on their heads and went to the river. A group of small boys, playing hunter, left for a rabbit hunt with loud good wishes from Tolonqua and other hunters. Mothers with young children were nowhere to be seen; it was rumored they had left in darkness for a visit to another village. Yellow Bird, and others of the yaya who were too old to travel to distant villages, remained in their dwellings. Old grandfathers squatted on rooftops, busied themselves with making arrow shafts or other duties, and watched village activity, taking advantage of their rooftop vantage point to scan the horizon and the area surrounding the town. Their conversation was hushed.

"Did the women take weapons with them when they left during the night?"

"Yes. Bows, arrows, lances. They hid them where Tolonqua told them to."

"The women going to the river—"

"Arrows are in the baskets with the clothes. Bows are fastened to their legs under the robes. They will hide them along the river."

"The farmers . . . I saw no weapons."

"They know where the women hid them during the night. They will find them all."

"Ah."

"The young hunters, the boys. Were they warned not to go to the ridge?"

"Aye. Danger up there. Querechos, watching."

They glanced up at the ridge, pretending to scan the sky. "I see nothing."

"The boys will watch. They go over there." A wrinkled thumb jerked to a rise opposite the ridge. "They pretended to hunt, but always they watch."

"What if no attack comes?"

"But what if it does? Owa says—"

"Aye. If Querechos attack, we shall be ready. Because Owa warned us."

Some paused in their work, wondering what their ancestors would think of Cicuye being saved by a Pawnee berdache. Some shook their heads. Others frowned. One ventured to comment that perhaps Tolonqua was right about building a new city on the ridge. Defending a city would be easier up there.

A toothless ancient spit at a fly on his bare leg, and hit it squarely. "It is not seemly," he said.

All knew he was right. Tolonqua's setting himself up and apart as a leader was an affront to the tribe. A man should be part of a whole, putting the interest and welfare of the tribe above personal ambition. Total unity was essential to survival. Individual ambition endangered unity and was, therefore, an attribute of witchcraft.

Piko, an aged brother of Tolonqua's long-dead grandfather, whom Tolonqua also called Grandfather, removed a shaft from a grooved arrow-straightening stone and held the shaft up to his one good eye, sighting it. "If the matter of a new city were discussed properly in council, perhaps Tolonqua would not feel alone in his responsibility for our safety." He returned the shaft to the groove, turning the shaft as he pushed it back and forth. "Perhaps his concern for our welfare is greater than concern for his own."

There was a thoughtful silence.

In the kiva, Owa, Tolonqua, Two Elk, and other Chiefs spoke in low tones.

Owa said, "All is ready. When they come—"

"If they come," Two Elk interjected.

"They will come. Maybe not today. But they will come."

There was the sound of running footsteps stopping at the hatchway. A boy's face peered down, surrounded by others.

"We saw Querechos. On the ridge."

"Do they know you saw?"

"No. We hunt. See?" He dangled a limp rabbit by the ears.

"Good!" Tolonqua said. "You are fine hunters. Now do what the Warrior Chief said. Run to your mothers in the next village."

"We pretend to hunt more!" The boy's eyes sparkled with adventure and excitement. "Maybe we get another rabbit!"

"Run!" the Warrior Chief said.

As footsteps faded, Two Elk looked down at his folded hands. "Perhaps they come to trade more," he said lamely.

"An arrow for a life," Owa replied.

Kwani huddled miserably in the dimness of her dwelling. Coals burned in her stomach and in her chest, and she fought a surge of nausea. The knives in Tolonqua's obsidian eyes had cut so very deeply she felt as if she were bleeding inside.

She rocked to and fro, moaning. She clutched the shell of her necklace, holding it tightly in both hands. "Help me!"

There was no answer.

Outside, it was suddenly very quiet. No children shouted. There were no city sounds, no women's voices, no chanting, no singing. Silence.

Premonition and sudden fear pierced her. What was happening? Could it be that Owa was right, after all? She snatched Acoya in her arms and climbed up the ladder to peek outside. The rooftops were deserted but for a few old men who usually sat on the ground in a shady place. Why were they on a roof? Where was everyone else?

Dogs were behaving strangely. They grouped together, forming a pack. Heads were hunched low and there was a growling like the sound of rushing water. Something threatened them. What?

As Kwani watched, Two Elk, Tolonqua, Owa, and others emerged from the kiva and strolled casually (too casually?) toward their dwellings. Kwani noticed that Tolonqua glanced several times up at the ridge. She climbed a little higher and turned to look. She gasped. Querecho warriors appeared, one by one, silhouetted against the sky.

An attack!

Hastily, she withdrew, her heart pounding. She tucked Acoya into his cradle board. Her hands trembled and she could hardly sling the board to her back and fasten the carrying strap across her shoulders. Why had she not listened to Tolonqua? Why had she not taken Acoya and fled to safety?

Escape! She must find a way!

Tolonqua's horn gave a long, shrill call and pandemonium erupted. The dogs barked fierce warnings. Again, Kwani peeked outside. Querechos—a large band!—swooped down from the ridge, howling a war cry, and the dogs rushed to attack.

Kwani watched, choked with terror, as dog after dog fell writhing with arrows protruding and blood gushing. Now Querechos were nearly at the village. Kwani could see their fearsome war paint; her heart froze with the howling of their blood lust.

Suddenly heads appeared through roof hatchways, Towas with drawn bows in hand! Again, the shell horn sounded.

Arrows flew in both directions. The Querechos reached the plaza. Some fell and were ignored by the others who ran toward the dwellings.

Now, the Towa farmers and warriors who had disappeared reappeared like ghosts summoned by the shell horn. Querechos fought savagely to prevent being surrounded. There were howls, cries, moans, screaming, and arrows flying everywhere. One landed with a sharp thud on the roof near Kwani.

Fingers fumbling, she closed the hatch and slid down the ladder.

Escape was impossible.

She slumped weakly to the floor and leaned against the wall. Acoya was sobbing in terror but she could hear only the howls and screams, the shouts and the moans, and footsteps running crazily overhead.

For a moment her spirit departed. When it returned, she was totally calm, as though fear had departed with her spirit and refused to return. She could see better, hear better. It was as though another person, another part of herself, had taken possession.

Swiftly she removed the cradle board; it fell to the floor. Acoya still cried, and she cradled him close.

"Hush, little one. All will be well."

The blood-lust howls were louder. Close.

I must protect Acoya.

But how? Where?

Her eyes darted in every corner, seeking a hiding place. There was but one possibility, the cubbyhole storage space covered by a buffalo-hide curtain. Could she and Acoya squeeze in there?

Footsteps on the roof. They stopped. Someone fumbled with the hatch.

Swiftly Kwani lifted the cubbyhole curtain. The space was packed full with sacks of pemmican and valuables they had accumulated. But she had to get in there!

Someone was lifting the door of the hatch.

Strength surged into her. With a mighty heave, Kwani pushed and made room among the sacks. She squeezed inside, huddled into a tight ball, and barely managed to make room for the curtain to fall naturally. Acoya's crying had diminished but he still whimpered.

"Hush!" she whispered frantically, and gave him her breast. He quieted.

There was the scraping sound of footsteps descending the ladder.

She *must* have a weapon! Her skinning knife! It was there, tucked into a little crevice where she had stored it! She grasped it tightly in one hand, held Acoya with the other, and waited. Listening.

A sound. Someone had bumped into the cradle board. Soft footsteps. *A tinkling!*

Carefully, she removed Acoya from her breast and laid him behind her. He snuggled down to sleep.

The tinkling came closer.

She tried not to breathe, to make no sound, no movement. She was a rabbit about to be snared in its dark hole.

Footsteps close.

The curtain was ripped aside and Owa grinned down at her. He squatted to grab her. She slashed at his face, cutting him across his cheek and nose. Blood spurted, and he leaned back, wiping blood from his eyes.

She darted out and ran for the ladder. He stumbled after her, snarling in fury and pain.

She reached the ladder. Her breath came in wheezing gasps and she began to climb. She was halfway up. He grabbed her. Jerked her down. Skin scraped from her hands as she clutched the ladder poles, but she felt no pain.

She swung at him again with the knife. He wrested it from her hand and ripped off her robe so that she stood naked. With one big fist he pushed her against the wall, and brandished the skinning knife with the other. Wolf's eyes glittered at her. He smiled.

"You like your woman's breasts, yes? Ha! You have them no more."

He swung his arm back to lunge with the knife, and gave a choked cry. His head was jerked backward by the braids, and he was thrown to the floor. Tolonqua stood over him, lance in hand. His shoulder was bloody and blood oozed from a wound on his leg, but he seemed not to feel it. He stomped Owa back down when he tried to rise, wiping blood from his eyes.

"Tolonqua! Tolonqua!" Owa cried. He grabbed Tolonqua's foot and clung to it. "I am your berdache!"

Tolonqua raised the lance, preparing to strike.

"No! No! I love you! I love—"

The words became a moaning gurgle as the lance pierced his heart through.

▲ 17 ▼

Kwani stood on the roof, gazing in shock and horror. The plaza was strewn with the dead. Querecho and Towa warriors lay where they had fallen; some still twitched in grotesque agonies. Dying dogs tried to rise or to walk, and fell, glazed eyes staring. Screams and heartbroken cries mingled with the moans of the wounded as women returned from hiding places to find dead and bleeding sons, fathers, uncles, friends. Above all was the smell of blood, of bodies spilling their contents. The smell of death.

A Querecho sprawled on the roof beside Kwani, an arrow protruding from one eye. He had lived perhaps fourteen years. Kwani looked down at him. So young, so young.

But he was there to kill. Straining with effort, she dragged him to the edge of the roof and shoved him over. He would not kill again.

Tolonqua had dragged Owa up to the roof and he and Talasi had carried the body away while Talasi babbled brokenly, "You killed him! You killed him!" Kwani tried to see where they had gone, but they had disappeared.

In the plaza, Kwani heard Lumu's voice soaring above the others. She was bent over her mate, trying to stanch a gush of blood from his throat.

"Help me!" she screamed, looking around wildly. "Help me!"

Anitzal ran to her, making her way among those, both women and men, who stripped valuables from dead Querechos and from some who were not yet dead but who still struggled to fight until a knife or a lance let them struggle no more.

Lumu pressed both hands to her mate's throat but blood spurted through her fingers. Anitzal pressed her hands upon Lumu's, trying to help stanch the flow. Kwani could see that it was useless. She turned away; she could watch no longer.

Acoya was crying and she climbed down to him. Her hands were sore where she had scraped them on the poles of the ladder; she must prepare a healing ointment for them.

Acoya still lay in the cubbyhole where she had put him when she heard Owa's bell. She lifted him out and held him close.

"You are safe!"

And so was she, thanks to Tolonqua. Did he mean it when he told her never to speak to him in public again? He was furious. But he had saved her from the one who caused the trouble between them. Kwani remembered the look in Owa's eyes as he raised his arm to slash at her. She swallowed convulsively and put both hands on her breasts, still whole.

"Thank you!" she prayed to her protecting spirits. "Thank you for sending Tolonqua to save me!"

But other mothers had lost their sons. She could not remain here and do nothing. She tucked Acoya into his cradle board, lifted him to her back, and began the climb to the roof.

She stopped. She had never seen so many dead or bleeding. She knew little about healing wounds, and her own hands were hurt. But she had to try. Were not these people her people now?

She remembered Tolonqua's bleeding shoulder and the blood on his leg. He was wounded, too. Where had he gone? Resolutely, she climbed to the roof; she ignored the red trail where Owa had been dragged, ignored the darkening stain from the young Querecho's pierced eye, and headed for the plaza.

Talasi and Tolonqua heaved Owa's body to the burial platform they had prepared for him far from the village on a rise overlooking the plains. A Pawnee was not given to Earthmother, but to Sunfather and Moonwoman and the constellations. A scaffold was built high enough to be out of the reach of animals. When the body decayed and the bones were exposed, the skull would be removed and placed in a sacred spot. This was the Pawnee way.

Talasi arranged Owa's body carefully, folding the arms and adjusting the garments. The long braids were tenderly placed on either side of the dead face. The ear ornaments, all of Owa's jewelry, were left with him. When only bones remained, the jewelry would be retrieved by the Medicine Chief, cleansed by prayer and ceremony, and used or dispensed with as the Chief saw fit. Until then, the jewelry would not be touched; it held the spirit of Pawnee dead.

Talasi stood staring at Owa's face. He stroked the cheek, rearranged the braids.

"You killed him!"

"Yes."

"It was he who saved us! He warned us! But for him our homes, our people, all would be gone!"

With a choked cry, Talasi yanked the hunting knife from his belt and brandished it wildly. "It was you he loved! Now you join him!" He lunged blindly at Tolonqua.

Tolonqua caught Talasi's arm and jerked the knife from his hand. He held both of Talasi's arms in a viselike grip while Talasi struggled, babbling.

"You will listen!" Tolonqua said in a voice that commanded obedience. "Owa tried to kill my mate. It is only because he warned my people that I am allowing him to enter Sipapu as a Pawnee. Otherwise I would leave him alone on the plain for wolves and vultures to feed."

Tolonqua released his grip and Talasi crumpled to the ground. Never would a Towa disgrace himself by weeping like a woman. But Talasi bent his head between his knees and sobbed.

It was the fourth day since the Querechos' attack, the day when the spirits of the dead left to enter Sipapu. The bodies of the Querechos had been burned and those of the Towa buried. Now the dead and their spirits were gone and it was necessary to pursue daily activities as usual. The names of the dead were not to be mentioned; their spirits might be lured back to haunt the living.

The bereaved grieved in silence and solitude—all but Lumu, who threw herself upon the grave of her mate and screamed his name, and who poured ashes upon herself and wandered aimlessly about the village, ignoring Anitzal's pleas and Tolonqua's orders to forsake the spirit of the dead.

Kwani sat with Tolonqua in their dwelling while she inspected his wounds; they were healing, and so were her hands, thanks to the cleansing and poultices she had applied—learned from working with others who tended the injuries of the wounded. Tolonqua sat quietly, smiling his thanks. Tension between them because of Owa had disappeared with his death; it was as though it had never been.

Kwani said, "Your wounds will soon be well." She squatted beside him. "There were too many hurt, too many dead. Maybe Two Elk and Yellow Bird and the others who objected to a new city on the ridge will think differently now."

"Perhaps." He lifted his foot, inspecting a bruise on the outside edge just below the instep.

Kwani had noticed that he was limping, but bruises were like that; they hurt for a while but gradually healed.

"Is it getting better?"

"No."

"Let me see."

She held the foot in her lap and bent to look at it closely. It appeared to be an ordinary stone bruise except that it seemed to be more swollen.

"How did it happen?"

"I don't know. During the battle."

"It hurts more?"

He shrugged.

"We will watch it."

He nodded. "I go to the kiva of Two Elk. There may be talk about a new city."

"Good!"

When he had gone, Kwani nursed Acoya, sang to him, and laid him on a blanket beside her so he could kick and wave his arms as he liked to do. She poured corn into her metate, and bent to work. The rhythm of pushing the mano stone back and forth helped her to think, to understand her feelings.

Tending the wounded, remembering the Querecho boy on her roof with the arrow through his eye, remembering all the dead and bleeding and dying, had changed her, made her see herself inside. When she had made herself go to help the wounded, she found that when she sang, pain was eased. Her voice helped the healing.

It was a power she had not had before. Or did she have it and not know it until now? A gift from the Ancient Ones?

As she worked and lived among the Towa, a realization had sprouted within her like a mushroom. No matter how much she wanted Tolonqua's people to be hers, they could not be. It was as though something inside her was determined that she should know this. She tried to deny it, remembering how Tolonqua's people welcomed Acoya at the naming ceremony, and how they made her one of their own.

"Why?" she asked herself. Her own people, the Anasazi, had abandoned her and driven her away to die. Tolonqua's people were all she had. And all she had wanted—before now.

Was it because the Towa were so different from the Anasazi? Kwani thought about that. Because Cicuye was far from the eastern Pueblo villages, and close to the plains, perhaps that was why Cicuye was different; the people absorbed some of the ways of the plains. Here, men owned the houses. Imagine! And they did not honor the dead with a sacred charcoal path from the grave to the village, nor did they pay homage to the spirits of a dwelling when they entered or left. They did not honor others by breathing upon the hand of another to bestow the breath of life. Their pottery was ugly. They could not make waterproof baskets, and nowhere were there turkeys. Their garments, their jewelry, everything was inferior. But worst of all was the wretched women's hut where women had to isolate themselves during the time of their moon flow. A bleeding woman was regarded as unclean, a threat to protecting spirits and to game. She was an outcast. It was degrading.

Kwani poured more corn into her metate, but she did not grind it. She sat back on her heels, thinking, forcing herself to be logical.

Tolonqua's people are all I have. I must accept this. Although Tolonqua is Towa, he is superior in every way. And he has taken my son as his own. Acoya will have a good life here. How fortunate we are!

Then why this unease in my spirit, this secret grieving?

She had never admitted it before, but perhaps she had expected too much of Cicuye. When her own people cast her away, and during the long journey afterward, she had dreamed and hoped for a home, a people, a clan of her own. People who would revere her as She Who Remembers. Who would give her the security and love she had never known.

The people of Cicuye had been kind, even welcoming most of the time (all except Yellow Bird), even though she was not Towa. But Kwani sensed reservations. She was different. Her eyes were blue. She was not Towa. She was trying to be, but she was Anasazi.

The blood remembers.

She bent again to her grinding, pushing the mano stone back and forth, back and forth.

She stopped. She clasped the necklace to her and closed her eyes, yearning to be once more at the House of the Sun, to feel its spiritual power, and to communicate with those who were She Who Remembers before her, those who were like herself.

"Tell me what I must do!" she cried.

It took a long time, but the answer came. It was the silent voice of the Old One.

"You are not of one clan, one people. You are of all womankind. You are She Who Remembers."

"How can I be, here among the Towa?"

"You are She Who Remembers."

The voice faded away.

"Wait!" Kwani cried. "Don't go! Tell me . . ."

The voice was gone.

Kwani opened her eyes. She looked up at the open hatchway; a bird flew across blue sky. Was that the spirit of the Old One who answered her call?

Again, she bent to the metate. Her heart was heavy. She had pleaded for help, but was told only what she had been told before and what she already knew, that she was She Who Remembers.

She was different.

There was a sound from Acoya, a soft cooing. He looked at her and cooed again, a comforting sound. She picked him up and held him close. The child of her blood, of her body.

Her responsibility.

Responsibility! With a flash of insight, she understood what the Old One was telling her. That she must *assume* responsibility as She Who Remembers, and teach women's secrets to girls of any tribe, any clan. Because she was of all womankind.

It was another revelation. Come to her through Acoya.

She looked down at the small face, so much like her own, and for a moment she glimpsed the unimaginable. She saw him as a man, a shaman in a faraway place, a stranger in a strange land.

"No!" she cried. He would stay here, in Cicuye, and become a great Chief. With a clan, a people, of his own. He would have no secret yearning; this would be his home, the place where his heart would be at rest.

Tolonqua sat with other Chiefs and Elders in the kiva of Two Elk. For some time they had discussed everything but what was most on their minds. The counsel pipe made another round. Finally, Talasi spoke, his face expressionless.

"Owa saved us."

Heads nodded. "That is so." No one looked at Tolonqua.

Tolonqua said, "I saved my mate."

Two Elk was not unaware that his Hunting Chief had been having problems with Kwani because of the berdache. But one does not kill a man because one's mate dislikes him. He smiled inwardly. "Tell what happened."

"I saw Owa entering our dwelling. I knew Kwani and the baby were there alone. I followed." He paused and looked at the men seated in a semicircle before the altar; they stared down at their hands. "Owa had stripped her naked and pushed her against the wall. He was about to kill her with a skinning knife; I save her just in time."

"Tolonqua killed him," Talasi said dully.

The Warrior Chief looked up sharply. "A skinning knife?"

Two Elk said, "The berdache was a bowman. What would he be doing with a skinning knife when he was fighting Querechos?"

"Fighting to save us all!" Talasi said more loudly than necessary.

Tolonqua said, "It was Kwani's knife. She was trying to protect herself and Acoya. She cut Owa here." He pointed. "He jerked the knife from her hand—"

"Of course!" Talasi interjected. "Would not you do the same?"

"Had I not killed him, it would be Kwani who died. My mate. She Who Remembers." He looked at each man in turn. "The berdache did warn us. That is why, and only why, he entered Sipapu as Pawnee." He rose to leave, and turned, smiling grimly. "I go now so you may talk of how the Querechos attacked from the ridge." He limped to the ladder and left.

There was an uncomfortable silence.

The Medicine Chief raised his hand. He had made no comment, but now he would speak. The turquoise and obsidian eye stared solemnly, and the stuffed bird behind his ear bobbed a little as the Chief turned his head, looking from one man to the other.

"We must reason as men. Perhaps the berdache was not what he seemed. Perhaps he was sent by our protecting spirits to warn us of more than Querechos. New tribes come from the plains; there could be more such raids. Many more. And worse. Owa may have been warning us of them, also."

The men glanced at one another.

Two Elk said, "There have been raids before. There will be again. But our warriors—"

"Those who have not been killed, you mean," the Warrior Chief said sharply. "We lost too many, more than ever before. We cannot allow this to happen again."

Once more the Medicine Chief raised his hand. "I shall purify myself, fast, and commune with the gods to determine what must be done. Until then, it would be well to consider the advantages of a city on the ridge, and the problems involved in building it.'' He rose. ''I have spoken.''

There were murmurs of acknowledgment. Only Talasi was silent. If the one who killed Owa wanted a city on the ridge, he, Talasi, would use every means to prevent it.

No matter what it took.

▲ 18 ▼

Tolonqua sat on the flat-topped ridge that overlooked Cicuye on one side, and meadows spreading to a river and to distant plains on the other. This is where his city would be. High and secure and beautiful.

He shifted position to ease the weight on his foot. He had hardly been able to put on his moccasin this morning; the swelling had increased and the dark bruise was spreading. Climbing the ridge made it hurt more. It throbbed. Perhaps he should discuss it with the Medicine Chief. He would do so when he climbed back down, but he would rest awhile first.

A sharp pain jabbed his foot and shot up his leg. He sat down on a small boulder. Tolonqua did not remember bruising his foot during the battle. It was as though the bruise appeared by itself afterward. It took magic to overcome magic; he must talk to the Medicine Chief.

He rose, and sat back down abruptly. If he waited awhile longer, perhaps the pain would subside.

Kwani had asked about his foot this morning, but he did not want her to see it. To be in this condition was humiliating. Kwani had strengths and powers equal, even superior, to his. The mate of such a woman as She Who Remembers could not acknowledge weakness, physical or otherwise.

Visualizing Kwani's face, her lovely, ardent body, his heart constricted. He loved her. More each day. But something in her eyes, in her spirit, disturbed him. It was as though she were turning inward, turning away from him.

The most serious crimes a Towa could commit were to kill someone except in self-defense, to steal the mate of another, and to lie. He had killed Owa to defend Kwani, he had stolen Kokopelli's mate, and he had been accused of lying—unjustly, and later exonerated—but did the gods know that? Was it they who were punishing him?

He looked down at his throbbing foot. Cursed by a witch? If so, who could it be? Who wanted him harmed?

I must confer with the Medicine Chief.

He rose, more painfully than before, and made his way down the ridge, pausing often.

Several days passed but the pain in Tolonqua's foot increased.

"You must go to the Medicine Chief," Kwani urged, and at last he agreed. Another day passed while Tolonqua remained in the kiva with the Medicine Chief. That night, Tolonqua returned to their dwelling. He limped painfully, and his face was pale. "It is decided."

Kwani listened with dread as he told her what must be done.

Now she sat in the medicine lodge with Tolonqua's head in her lap. Flames burned in the fire pit; ashes would be needed during treatment. The Medicine Chief and all the Elder Priests of the Medicine Society were gathered for grave discussion. They spoke calmly, glancing now and then at Tolonqua who lay to one side on a woven mat. His face was blanched and drawn, but expressionless. He wore only a breechcloth. The injured foot was exposed, swollen and ugly nearly to the knee, and covered with yellow powder made from pollen and a bitter root with which the injury had been dressed.

Kwani tried not to listen to the medicine men; what they were saying was horrifying. The violence of an injury had so weakened his foot and leg that they were either infested with maggots or the flesh was dead and becoming maggots. The worms must be removed or Tolonqua would die.

The Medicine Chief did not wear his eye patch; it might have a disturbing influence on the wound. His empty eye socket emphasized the authority of the other eye as he said, "It may be that seeds of maggots are in the bone. If so, they must be removed also."

The old priests nodded. It was well known that good, fresh red blood was the source of new flesh; when it became thinned and black it was weakened and spoiled and must be removed and replaced with fresh blood. Just as blood was the source of new flesh, so water was the first source of new blood, of life itself, because nothing could live without water. Since the willow tree always lived near water it contained within its roots the very essence, the very source of life. Therefore, an infusion of its roots and bark became brightly red, and a source of new life blood to renew decaying flesh. The infusion, red and clear, was ready in a small bowl at Tolonqua's side. A cane sucking-tube rested in the bowl.

"We begin," the Medicine Chief said, and gestured.

A priest gently lifted Tolonqua's leg and bathed away the astringent powder. One by one, the priests knelt to examine the foot and leg closely, touching nose to the flesh to smell it, pressing the swollen flesh lightly, examining the toes. Examination completed, they compared notes. It was agreed that certain muscles in the foot had died or were dying from the violence done them, and were *wi-wi-yo-a*, becoming wormy, in the depths of the foot. Therefore, an inverted T-shaped incision would be made so that the skin could be lifted up in two flaps, the dead flesh removed, the decayed black blood fully extracted, and the maggots and their seeds found and removed.

Kwani put both hands on Tolonqua's cheeks. She leaned over him and whispered, "The White Buffalo is your talisman. All will be well." She told this to herself as well as to him. His skin was hot to her touch and his face was strained and totally without expression. He was commanding his spirit to take him elsewhere.

The Medicine Chief reached in his buckskin medicine bag and removed three pieces of obsidian, several neat splints of cedar, and masses of freshly gathered, clean yellow pinyon gum. With a blunt knife he tapped off several thin, sharp flakes from the obsidian. Six of these were selected and mounted, each in the cleft end of one of the cedar splints; some as to form straight lancets and others at right angles to the splint handles, one or two of which were wrapped with sinew near the point of insertion in the splint so that only a small portion of the tip protruded.

These surgical instruments were laid in a row upon the floor. A quantity of shredded cedar bark, buckskin scrapings, and a large bowl of water were added. All was in readiness.

The Chief and his priests covered their mouths with their hands and breathed upon them as they prayed for strength of breath for their patient.

The Chief chanted, "By the power of the Above Beings may our Hunting Chief's will be strengthened and may he quieted be. May our methods be straight; may they be successful."

Kwani prayed, too. Silently, to the Ancient Ones. "Protect him! Heal him! Heal him!"

The Medicine Chief bent over Tolonqua. His one good

eye was compassionate. "Things are as they must be. You will endure for you are Hunting Chief, and a Towa."

He patted Tolonqua's arm kindly and turned to his assistants. One said gently to Tolonqua, "Stay yourself," while another took the foot with both hands and turned it up, stretching the skin by pressure. Tolonqua did not flinch, but Kwani sensed his pain as the Chief grasped one of the obsidian lancets and deliberately and deftly slashed down from the ankle toward the little toe. Quickly he made another slash from the instep straight down to the middle of the first cut. Taking one of the other lancets, he deepened both incisions, avoiding with utmost skill the crooked vein descending over this portion of the foot and the tendon lying over the tarsal and metatarsal bones.

The priest holding the foot squeezed it hard. Kwani gasped and turned her head as stinking pus gushed forth. Wads of cedar bark soaked up the pus, and water was poured into the wound to cleanse it. Scraped buckskin stanched the flow of blood.

Tolonqua lay motionless, expressionless, his face ashen. Perspiration beaded his forehead. Again, Kwani bent over him.

"All will be well."

He looked up at her and she saw the shadow of death in his eyes.

From unknown depths within her, Kwani summoned a determination that *Tolonqua would live.* She clasped the scallop shell of her necklace in both hands, willing the power of the Ancient Ones to save Tolonqua. Almost of its own accord, a soft, singing chant welled from her throat, willing him to be healed.

The priests glanced up in surprise and understanding, and continued their work. They took up one after another of the straight lancets and dissected away the proud flesh and other diseased tissue, removing it cleanly, without severing vein or artery or tendon, until the bone was exposed.

"Ah!" they murmured in unison.

A swollen and diseased tendon was exposed. Ruthlessly, they cut it out and examined it critically, stuffing cedar bark into the wound. They laid their lancets down and leisurely discussed the question as to whether the diseased bit of tendon was already a maggot or only becoming one.

Tolonqua's breath came in short, wheezing gasps. Kwani's soft singing continued as she soothingly held his face with both hands and tried not to let her voice quaver.

It was decided that the maggot, or becoming-maggot, was not the chief cause of the disease, and the bit of tendon was laid carefully aside on ashes that had been put in a hollow potsherd. No maggot could escape from ashes. The cedar bark was removed and more water was poured into the wound until the bone was cleanly exposed. The membrane of connective tissue was inflamed and discolored.

"That is where the seed worms are!" the Medicine Chief exclaimed. The obvious source of the disease.

With pleased satisfaction, they scraped until every particle of the discoloration was removed and placed in the ashes. The Chief removed a small medicine stone from his pouch, and with chanting that mingled with Kwani's, he laid it in the wound as a sponge of mystical power to absorb the disease. Then he removed the stone, triumphantly raised it overhead as he finished his chant, and placed the stone in the ashes to be cleansed.

Two priests held the incision open while the Medicine Chief, using the tube in the red liquid, sucked the liquid in his mouth and repeatedly sprayed the open wound. All dissected surfaces were then washed and dried and sprayed again with the red fluid. The openings were stuffed with the pinon gum softened by warmth of the breath and in the hands that were constantly kept wet with the red fluid. More gum was spread on narrow strips of buckskin, more of the yellow powder was thickly dusted on the wound, and the foot and leg were bandaged with the buckskin strips.

It was finished. Everything was done that could be done.

▲ 19 ▼

"**E**arthmother grants permission. Proceed."

The Medicine Chief gestured to the five priests of the Medicine Society, and each one poured a basket of riverbank sand upon the floor of the medicine lodge. They smoothed the sand with their hands, pressed it down with bare feet, and smoothed it again.

For four days the Medicine Chief had fasted and purified himself, beseeching Earthmother to allow herself to be re-created in a sand painting so that her healing powers could enter their Hunting Chief, his foot would be strengthened, and he could walk upon her body without pain.

On the night following the fourth day, the Medicine Chief dreamed. His totem, a chickadee, appeared to him with a small pebble in its beak. Earthmother offered herself! The Medicine Chief awoke, rejoicing.

Now Earthmother's re-creation could begin. Chanting sacred songs in unison, the priests and the Medicine Chief knelt in a circle. Before them lay bowls of fine sand colored with pigments made from pulverized stone of different colors, charcoal from a tree struck by lightning, corn pollen, sacred ash from the kiva fire pit, and pigments from sources known only to them to provide the necessary colors—red, green, white, yellow, black, blue, brown.

To one side, against the wall, Tolonqua sat upon the robe of the White Buffalo with a crutch beside him. He wore nothing but a small pouch on a cord around his neck containing sacred objects to thwart evil influences. His foot still refused to carry him and he felt but half a man, a helpless hunter, hobbling about on a crutch. A Hunting Chief should stride mountains and plains, lead his men to deer, elk, antelope. Go for buffalo.

He watched reverently as the holy men bent to their work. A sand painting was powerful medicine, a supplication to holy beings to heal body and spirit. This painting would recreate Earthmother as she lay in splendor upon her back with arms and legs extended and the organs of her body exposed.

The Medicine Chief began. He took a small handful from the bowl of sand colored green. Trickling the sand between his thumb and forefinger, he drew a straight line to form a cornstalk representing earth and food.

"Your spinal column is created," he sang.

Now each priest dipped a hand into a bowl and worked together with the Medicine Chief to enclose the spinal column with an outline of the torso, an oval pointed at each end. Then they drew the legs and arms, and the head with its mystical horn headdress. The yellow part of the horns symbolized pollen, or everlasting life. Blue tips on the horns represented turquoise, worldly wealth. A blue disc between the horns was Sunfather, with rays extending upward. White dawn, black darkness, blue haze, and yellow twilight formed colored bars across Earthmother's face; red afterglow and dark night extended downward on either side. Red wind and blue sky adorned her throat.

Tolonqua leaned forward, watching intently. As colored sand trickled expertly from red-brown fingers, forming perfect lines and figures, his spirit reached for them, seeking their healing powers. He prayed silently, "Enter me!"

Earthmother's arms from shoulder to elbow became the yellow of vegetables; blue vegetation grew from elbows to hands. Blue and red blossoms bloomed on her elbows, and each hand held a vessel containing seeds of all food plants and medicines.

The cornstalk grew leaves and a tassel; the silk became lungs.

"Your lungs are created," sang the Medicine Chief.

Beside it, a green circle became the Sacred Mountain.

"Your heart is created," the Chief sang.

Another mountain grew on the right side.

"Your liver is created."

A small circle became the gall bladder. Peaks of another mountain became kidneys, and a mountain at the base of the cornstalk became the bladder. Within the torso, black veins flowed—water, Earthmother's blood. A black circle beneath the corn tassel contained the little winds, Earthmother's breath. A small black square at the base of the cornstalk was Sunfather's house. Above the house, a black triangle became a cloud. Below the house, Moonwoman's white face glowed. From Earthmother's womb emerged red and gray dotted lines for rainbows, clouds, and fogs. The feet were clouds; rainbows striped the knees. On either side, great rainbows arched from hand to foot, encircling the torso.

Earthmother was created in all her glory.

Many hours had passed. Tolonqua bowed in reverence as the Medicine Chief and the priests sang chants to the Being they had created. The Medicine Chief motioned him to the painting.

"Sit. Receive Earthmother's healing power."

Carefully, so as not to disturb the lines of the painting, Tolonqua sat upon Earthmother's body.

Spirit-talker rattles spoke as the priests summoned the spirits of Bear and Badger, healers of the animal kingdom, to bestow their powers. The Medicine Chief sprinkled water from the sacred spring on Tolonqua's head, being careful to sanctify the top from which the spirit emerged at death.

"Receive Earthmother's healing blood," he chanted.

Again the rattles spoke.

"Bear and Badger impart their strength," sang the priests.

Tolonqua sat motionless, his face impassive. Smoke from sacred spruce blended with the fragrances of dried plants and medicinal substances stored in niches in the walls. A benediction.

Closing his eyes, Tolonqua sang the Healing Song and opened his inner self to allow the healing to enter.

All day they had waited. Now Kwani and all of Tolonqua's relatives and clan brothers were gathered outside the medicine lodge, waiting for Tolonqua. Always, a sand painting was destroyed at sundown. Now that Sunfather had departed, small portions of sand from the painting would be sought because of its curative powers.

Kwani waited anxiously. The sound of the spirit-talkers, the chants, and Tolonqua's voice singing the Healing Song drifted from the lodge with mystic potency.

"Heal him!" she prayed.

Tolonqua's relatives and clan brothers had provided this special ceremony for Tolonqua. A sand painting required participants of great skill and dedication and was, therefore, a costly procedure. The fee of turquoise, salt, and other valuables had been paid to the Medicine Chief and his priests, with feasting to be provided afterward. Now fragrances from cooking fires permeated the air grown cooler with sundown.

At last the singing ceased and the Medicine Chief and the

priests emerged from the lodge. Tolonqua stepped out, leaning on his crutch, wrapped in the robe of the White Buffalo.

Kwani was first to greet him. She questioned him with her eyes.

"I am healing." Tolonqua smiled down at her.

She looked deeply into the face she knew and loved so well.

Almost, she believed him.

Several weeks passed, but Tolonqua still could not walk upon rugged terrain for any distance.

Kwani sat with Tolonqua on the floor of their dwelling, gazing at the pieces of the broken Truth Pipe Tolonqua held in both hands. His face was grim. For weeks he had said, "Earthmother forsakes me." What evil was at work? Who was the witch?

From outside came laughter and shouts of children at play, dogs barking, women's voices—the usual sounds of a busy pueblo. But here in this room Tolonqua's brooding bitterness was a silent, poisonous presence.

He fingered the broken pieces. "Who do you think did this?" he asked again.

She shook her head. "I do not know. But what does it matter now? It was proven you spoke truth."

"It does not matter that I have an enemy?" he scowled.

"Your enemy was defeated." She put both arms around him. "You are Cicuye's famed Hunting Chief—"

"Who can hunt no more."

"Any hunter can hunt. You are Chief, with a Chief's responsibilities. The success of the hunting depends upon ceremonies only you can provide. Your hunters wait for you to plan a hunt, to call the spirits of the game. To be Chief again."

He did not reply, but fingered the broken pipe.

She continued, "You cannot walk to distant places, but you have a Hunting Chief's power. Use it. Demonstrate it to your hunters so that they may feel power, also." She put both hands on his cheeks and turned his face to hers. "If you cannot walk far with your hunters, it does not matter if you give them power and your spirit walks with them. They need to feel the spirit of their Chief."

His black eyes clouded as they looked into hers. "I have displeased the gods; they take revenge. Such a Chief is not worthy of his hunters." He turned away.

She felt a sudden flush of anger. "You whimper like a

child, a boy. You are a man, a Chief. Act like one! A man! Whose spirit does not crumble because of a weak foot!''

Kwani snatched Acoya, stomped to the ladder, and disappeared through the hatchway.

Tolonqua stared after her, surprised and abashed. He gazed down at the broken pipe, turning it in his hands, over and over.

It was true. He behaved as if his spirit were broken like the pipe. Whoever broke the pipe did so to destroy his spirit. Would he allow it?

"No!" he cried.

He laid down the pipe, and rose. He would inform the Crier Chief to announce a meeting to prepare for a hunt. And he would go to the compound where working dogs were kept to inspect his own.

He would need them when he hunted again.

Kwani walked alone on the ridge. She had accused Tolonqua of evading his responsibilities—while evading her own as She Who Remembers. She had feared objections, even ridicule from these people who knew nothing of the Ancient Ones. When the Crier Chief announced Tolonqua's meeting, she was ashamed of her cowardice.

"I request an announcement also," she told him. "Say that She Who Remembers will teach young girls the women's secrets handed down from generation to generation. Tomorrow, on the ridge."

This was the day.

It was customary for one who was She Who Remembers to have her own sacred place to teach, but until such a place became available, this spot up here on the ridge, high above the village and closer to the Above Beings, would suffice.

The village spread below, serene in morning light. Tolonqua was in the kiva, conducting a ceremony for his hunters, Kwani knew, and Acoya was with his doting aunts. She was alone with Earthmother and the spirits of bush and tree, beetles and mice and rabbits—all living things here on the ridge. Beyond, into the distance, the valley spread in sublime peace. But Kwani felt no peace. She was from another clan and another tribe; she did not know these young girls well. Would they accept her as a teacher? Never before in Cicuye had there been one who was She Who Remembers. Did they realize the importance of what she was about to teach?

What if the girls took it lightly as a social event such as

their mothers enjoyed—gossiping, playing games, and gambling? Or what if they laughed about it in the village, treating the whole thing as a joke?

Again, Kwani gazed down at the pueblo—hers and Acoya's now. She was accepted there as mate of the Hunting Chief and mother of Acoya, a Chosen One. They knew Kwani was She Who Remembers, but they did not really understand what that meant. Only when the girls returned from their lessons and spread the word in the village would her position as She Who Remembers be understood. Subsequently, her status would be evaluated. Her future, and that of Acoya and Tolonqua, would be influenced strongly by what these young girls said about her.

She felt a sudden pang of homesickness for the Place of the Eagle Clan and the girls she taught there in the cliff city: Miko, Ki-ki-ki, and all the others. Were they still there? Or, as some said, had all the people of the cliff cities left to join other pueblos along the Great River of the South?

Who prayed now at the House of the Sun?

Or was it deserted, empty but for spirits lingering?

Kwani wished she was there; she needed to be. To kneel again at the altar and feel its mystical power rising within her like water in a spring too long dry.

Voices on the trail! The girls were coming. Kwani pressed her necklace to her with both hands, calling the Ancient Ones. "Speak for me!"

They arrived a few at a time, and stood shyly to one side, whispering, peeking at her, and giggling behind their hands. There were fourteen of them; some had known as many as twelve winters, others but four. Kwani assumed the regal posture expected of She Who Remembers. She beckoned.

"Come. Sit before me here."

Hesitantly, they sat in a semicircle, facing her. The youngest ones still giggled; the older girls hushed them and sat them down, but not without a few giggles of their own. A few looked afraid, and hung back.

"Come," Kwani said again.

Hesitantly, they sat with the others, all except the youngest who looked as if she were about to cry.

Kwani went to her and leaned close. The girl backed away, chin trembling.

"What is the matter?" Kwani asked softly.

The girl burst into tears and turned to run away. An older girl grabbed her and pulled her into the group.

"She is afraid of you."

"Why?"

"Your blue eyes."

"Ah." Kwani nodded. "That is because she does not know that one with sky eyes belongs to the Sky People." Kwani did not know why she said that; the words just came.

"Aye-e-e-e!" The girls stared in awe.

Kwani settled herself on a ledge protruding from a large boulder. The littlest girl sat on the lap of the older one; she had stopped crying but she still sniffled a bit. Kwani looked at the girls clustered around her, their faces like cups up-turned, waiting to be filled.

How should she begin? She touched the shell of her neck-lace.

"I am She Who Remembers. Do you know why I am called that?"

"Of course," an older girl said. "You think we know nothing?" She flipped her braids, smiling at titters from the other girls.

Kwani looked at her calmly. Here was one who liked to show off. "Very well," she said, smiling. "Tell us."

"Because you don't forget things." She glanced around, smirking.

"Very good. There *are* things I do not forget. Now tell me, what is your name?"

"Chosovi."

"Bluebird. A good name." Kwani removed her necklace and held it in outstretched hands. "Chosovi, do you know the story of this necklace?"

The girl shook her head, pretending disinterest.

Kwani fingered the polished stone beads of many colors. "Each bead holds the spirit of an Ancient One, those who were She Who Remembers before me." She touched the scallop-shell pendant with its turquoise inlay in sacred de-sign; the pendant swung slightly as though Kwani's touch stirred it to life. "This is a shell from the Sunset Sea, many moons away. And this"—pointing to the inlay—"holds a se-cret." She paused for emphasis. "When I press the shell to me—like this—it enables me to speak with the Ancient Ones, those who have been She Who Remembers since Earthmother created the first one."

The girls leaned close to see. Some rose and came for-ward, reaching for it. They had never seen a scallop shell before, and this one had sacred powers!

Kwani drew back. "It is forbidden. Only She Who Re-members may touch it." She slipped the necklace back over her head and the girls sat down again, whispering to one another.

Chosovi said, "If you are of the clan of Sky People, and if you speak with Ancient Ones, will you do it for us?" She glanced at the others triumphantly. She would put this outsider in her place!

For a moment Kwani did not reply. Now was not the time for sacred communication. But these girls must know and be convinced of who and what she was.

"Yes. I will."

Kwani rose from the boulder where she sat and climbed to the top. She stood silently, regally, holding the shell to her as she gazed into the turquoise sky.

She began to sing; songs carried power. Her voice soared.

> *"You who dwell in the sky world,*
> *You who walk on Sunfather's trail,*
> *You whose campfires glow in Moonwoman's light,*
> *You who were She Who Remembers before me,*
> *See us here. Send a sign, I pray."*

A breeze came, and from a distance a jay called. Nothing more.

"Send a sign!" Kwani pleaded.

No answer.

The girls glanced at one another.

"Perhaps you have lost your rabbit," Chosovi said. An insulting remark, implying incompetence.

Kwani ignored the snickers. Both arms outstretched, she gazed up into the sky. "Send a sign, Holy Ones! Show that you hear my prayer." Her voice soared higher, flooding the ridge, ringing over the valley.

Nothing. Only the voice of the wind.

Chosovi whispered behind her hands. The others giggled.

"Hear me, Holy Beings!" Kwani sang. With all her spiritual strength she sought response. "I pray for a sign!"

"Look!" a little girl pointed.

From high, high above, a hawk swooped down. Like a fire spear it dived, disappeared into brush nearby, then darted up, clutching a squirming rabbit. The hawk flew over them, so close they heard the sound of its wings. When it was directly above Kwani, the rabbit fell, tumbled to the boulder where Kwani stood, and froze there, trembling. The hawk flew away.

Kwani stood, staring down at the rabbit. The girls gasped, transfixed. Kwani bent low.

"Go!" she whispered.

The rabbit slid down the boulder and hopped away. Kwani stood and sang joyously.

"Thank you, Above Beings! Thank you, Sky People!"

The girls sat in silent awe.

Kwani looked at them as they gazed up at her. Now she could teach.

Time passed. How much, Kwani did not know for the girls listened eagerly as she told what happened when women entered this, the Fourth World. And how Earthmother created the first She Who Remembers from a cornstalk whose leaves became arms and whose roots became legs and pulled themselves from the earth to walk. The older girls understood all of it, Kwani knew, but what about the younger ones?

"I will ask some questions now. See if you can answer." She smiled. "You have been told how women were weak when they entered this, the Fourth World. Do you remember what happened?"

"Yes!" a little girl said. "Men were bigger and stronger and they ate most of the meat. Women got only what was left."

"If there was any," another said.

"That is correct. And when women were big with babies it was harder because they couldn't run fast from enemies or predators—"

"Like bears?"

"Yes. Sometimes the men protected themselves only and left the women to do as best they could by themselves. Do you remember what happened then?"

"Yes. Earthmother taught them."

"Taught them what?"

"To know which plants and roots and seeds were good to eat so when the men ate all the meat, the women would still have food."

An older girl tossed her head. "I know how to do that, and Earthmother didn't teach me. My mother did, and my mother's sister, and—"

"Yes, because Earthmother taught these things to women long ago, and they taught their daughters who grew up and taught other girls. One day you will teach your daughters these things. That is how it has been always since the first woman was taught by Earthmother."

The girls smiled, visualizing the time when they would have children. And mates.

Kwani continued, "When women learned how to find food that grew, they became stronger. Sometimes men returned from hunts with no game, and only women had food. So women saw a way to get protection for themselves and their children. They traded themselves and their food to men for protection and for meat. When there was some. And they learned something else. Do you know what it was?"

"Not to give men their food?" a little girl asked.

"That's stupid! A big, strong man could take the food any time he wanted!" another said.

Kwani interrupted, "Women learned to *remember* what their mothers and grandmothers knew, and their grandmothers before them. This is called intuition and it is with you when you are born and stays within you until you die. It is a secret knowledge only women possess. Like a little voice inside you."

A small girl said, "I don't hear any voices."

Kwani smiled. "It isn't really a voice. It's more like a *knowing*, as though your ancestors are telling you something. It will come to you often as you grow older. So no matter how big and how strong a man may be, if you know how to remember, your secret knowledge will guide you."

The girls sat in silence for a moment, listening to their inner selves. An autumn breeze blew, touching each one, carrying the sounds of the village below. A bird called, and another.

Kwani said, "It is important to remember that for a clan or a people to exist, babies must be born, and only we can have babies. If all the men died but one, that one man could still seed many women and the tribe would survive. But if all the women died but one, she could not have babies fast enough to keep the tribe alive, and it would disappear. So we are more important to the tribe than men are. Men know this, but they don't like to admit it because it is their nature to want to be best at everything."

"Boys are like that, too," a girl said, and the others nodded wisely.

"Of course. They are men growing up. Just as you are growing to be women. We need men to protect us and to love us and give us babies, but always we know men are bigger and stronger than we are and can do us harm. So we use the knowledge given us to keep men happy and content so they will protect and not harm us. It is Earthmother's secret power that only we possess. There is something else men don't know that we know.''

The girls gazed up at her eagerly.

''It is said that in every man is a bit of his mother, absorbed from her womb. So he has a bit of woman in him. But a man's nature is to be a hunter and warrior, to achieve goals he sets for himself, and to possess what he desires. So he fears the mother part of him because he thinks it weakens him. But that is the part which makes him a man rather than merely a predator. We must encourage him not to be afraid of the bit of woman inside him. A man who is gentle proves he is strong enough to afford gentleness. A strong man, a warrior, a hunter, cannot have babies but he can create beautiful things. And he can protect us and make us love him.''

She looked at the young faces alight with understanding, and her heart went out to them. What would be their paths of life?

''That is all the lesson for today. There will be more next time.''

She watched as they made their way down the path in solemn conversation, walking proudly.

▲ 20 ▼

Coals smoldered in the kiva; the hour was late. Discussion about the advisability of a new city had continued long. Talasi looked around the kiva with satisfaction. He, a mere captain of the Warrior Society, had been invited by the Warrior Chief to be the only non-chief present during an important discussion about the possibility of a new city on the ridge. Since the Querecho attack, people were uneasy about Cicuye's vulnerability. No one blamed the Warrior Society for Cicuye's losses during the attack, at least not openly. But the Warrior Chief and his men were responsible for the safety of the city and its people.

Talasi, as captain, was second in authority to the Warrior Chief. If the Chief died or if his position as Chief were taken from him because of incompetence or some other reason, Talasi would inherit his place. He, Talasi, would become the esteemed Warrior Chief. The thought gave him a powerful thrill and he glanced at the breechcloth between his folded legs to see if the erection showed.

Tolonqua spoke. "I say again that we should inspect the ridge and consider all possibilities. And if a city should be built there, we must decide where the kiva will be." The kiva would be the heart; the city would be built around it.

Talasi gazed at the one who had killed the berdache. Tolonqua desperately wanted a new city. Never would he have it! Owa would be avenged; his killer would be destroyed. How, Talasi did not yet know, but Owa's spirit would tell him.

Two Elk spoke. He sat leaning against a backrest of reeds woven in an ornate pattern appropriate to his importance as City Chief. He turned impatiently to Tolonqua.

"You speak of a new city as though building it would be a simple matter. Cicuye was here before you were born; you have never experienced the building of a city. You do not know what is involved." He turned to Piko, an old weaver who had lived long and remembered much; as an honorary chief he was revered for his wisdom. "Tell what would be necessary to build a city on the ridge."

"Well . . ." Piko rubbed a blind eye as if to make it see the past. "I was but a small boy when I helped my clan build a new city on the mountain slope—" He pointed northwest. "Tall trees grew there. Aye." He paused, visualizing. "Fine beams they made." He paused again. "Aye."

Tolonqua spoke impatiently. "Many trees are on the mountain. We can take what we need."

Piko nodded. "It is true, and our stone axes are strong. But it takes many suns to cut enough trees, remove the bark and branches, shape the beams. Then the logs must be carried across the valley and up the ridge, smoothed, fitted in place—"

"We have beams already," Tolonqua interrupted. "Here. We can use what we already have." He pointed to the heavy beams holding up the roof and to the roof beams overhead.

"No!" The Medicine Chief shook his head so that the stuffed chickadee fastened behind his left ear nearly fell off. "If the beams are removed, all will collapse. Spirits abide within this kiva, these dwellings." He gazed around as if seeing the invisible, and the turquoise and obsidian eye gleamed balefully. "If we destroy their living places, the spirits will take revenge. Revenge!"

There was silence as the men contemplated this fearsome possibility. Talasi smiled inwardly. Tolonqua would find that his plan of a new city would not be accepted as easily as he thought.

Piko fingered one of his long braids, still dark but for a few gray streaks. His creased old face was intent as he continued, "After the beams are carried to the building place, stones must be carried there, also. And shaped to fit one another—"

The Crier Chief snorted. "Accumulating stones will be no problem. Earthmother has them in abundance up there, as we know."

Piko nodded. "Many. But not all of the right size and shape. It is easier to find and to carry the right stones than to chip and smooth those that are too large and shaped wrong." He regarded his folded hands, seeing the past. "Aye."

Talasi watched Tolonqua trying to curb his impatience. Even the White Buffalo could not help the Hunting Chief if he could not control his arrogance. Talasi waited hopefully for Tolonqua to blunder, but the Hunting Chief sat silently.

The Warrior Chief said, "All of us came to Cicuye when we took mates who lived here. This pueblo was already built; we of the Warrior Society did not choose the location." He paused significantly. "It is my opinion that we should at least inspect the ridge to consider the wisdom of building a city in a location more easily defended."

There were murmurs. "Aye."

Two Elk's expression did not change, but Talasi was surprised and disconcerted to see a flick of satisfaction in his eyes. Two Elk had always objected to a new city before. Had he changed his mind?

Two Elk said, "Tomorrow. At pulatla."

Early morning.

Aka-ti, mate of Two Elk, emerged from the hatchway of her dwelling with a steaming bowl of porridge resting upon the carrying pad on top of her head. She was a little sparrow of a woman whose small-boned frame belied her strength and indomitable will. She lifted the bowl carefully and set it on the roof. "Your porridge, Grandmother."

Yellow Bird had insisted on climbing the ladder to the roof to watch village activity rather than eating her morning meal as usual by the comfort of the fire pit. Aka-ti waited as Yellow Bird slurped the porridge, crouching over the hot bowl, lifting it gingerly with crooked, bony fingers to her toothless mouth.

Yellow Bird was Two Elk's grandmother, and was, therefore, hers also. But Aka-ti wished the old woman would do what she should have done long ago and join her ancestors. It was a chore to feed and to care for this cantankerous old female always complaining about building a new city and finding fault with everything and everybody, even Tolonqua. Yellow Bird blamed Tolonqua for the Querecho attack. He and the berdache. Had they not killed Querechos on the way from the flint mines to Cicuye, there would have been no assault on the city, she said. Even though Tolonqua and Kwani had repeatedly told how the Querechos attacked them.

Secretly, Aka-ti admired Tolonqua's vision and courage for proposing the new city even though Two Elk said another city was unnecessary. The word of a village Chief was indisputable, but Tolonqua persevered. Since the Querecho attack, more people agreed with Tolonqua—a matter that displeased Two Elk considerably and infuriated his grandmother, the senior yaya.

Yes, Aka-ti thought, you are displeased, old woman, but the time may come when your displeasure will mean nothing. I have talked with Two Elk and told him how a new city would glorify his name long after Sipapu calls. He is considering it. If he and the men of Cicuye decide they want the city, good reasons will be found to build it whether or not the senior yaya approves. Ha! I hope I live to see that day.

Yellow Bird finished the porridge and handed it to Aka-ti without thanks. Aka-ti took it and descended the ladder to her dwelling. *She never thanks me for anything.*

Yellow Bird watched her go. Of course Aka-ti realized what a privilege it was to serve the elder yaya, but why did she do it so grudgingly? I shall talk to Two Elk about that. Where was he?

She wiped her mouth with the back of her hand and watched for him in the plaza that bustled with usual morning activities. Young boys returned from their cold baths in the river, shivering. Naked toddlers munched corn cake, tried to keep it from dogs who snatched at it, and yelped with distress when the dogs won. Girls carried night pots to the emptying place. Yellow Bird remembered how she used to do that, hating it, waiting for the time when she would be old enough to make the porridge and somebody else would empty the pots.

But one grew old too soon.

She rubbed her hands together. The warm porridge bowl had eased the pain a bit, but her hands still hurt. She ached all over, a price one paid for defeating death so long. She sighed. Sometimes she thought she would will herself to enter Sipapu, but no, she could not do that. Not yet. Cicuye needed her wisdom. Especially now with all the talk of building a new city on the ridge. That would never happen; she would not allow it. Could not! To be forced to leave her comfortable home and move up there would be like tearing a corn plant from its roots. It would wither and die. As would she.

Looking over the plaza and the city where she was born, Yellow Bird saw it all as it used to be. The handsome chief from a distant pueblo who saw her dancing; his flute sang to her that same night. He came to her, over there, where another dwelling is now. They lived there, their babies were born there . . . until it burned down. Gone, now. Like her mate, her babies . . . buried beside the east wall of that dwelling where others live now who did not know the flute player, or the two beautiful babies who lie nearby.

She no longer wept.

"I will not leave you," she whispered.

She saw Tolonqua limping up the ridge. Something must be done to defeat his idea of a city up there. The Truth Pipe . . . She had risked everything to discredit Tolonqua and his determined efforts to build the city. She had failed, and the knowledge of it burned in her stomach. But she would not give up. There had to be a way to prevent that city from being built, and she would find it. Somehow.

She watched a young girl returning home with an empty night pot. The girl stopped and stared up at the top of the ridge. Another girl joined her, and the two talked excitedly.

Yellow Bird turned to look.

Two Elk was there! And the Warrior Chief and the Medicine Chief and other notables, striding around, obviously looking the place over!

Could it be that . . . but no. Querechos had been up there and the Chiefs were looking for something. Obviously.

She continued to watch. There could be no mistake. Those fools planned a city up there! She clasped both gnarled hands in grim determination. Something must be done.

She sat for some time, staring thoughtfully at the plaza without seeing it.

"It is decided." Two Elk regarded the Chiefs and Elders seated before him in the kiva. "We have inspected the ridge and I have conferred with the Medicine Chief, and with each of you. A new city will be built there." A new Cicuye would carry his fame far. Long after he was in Sipapu, his name would be spoken and his remarkable achievements sung at evening fires.

Talasi spoke. "It is true; you did confer with the Chiefs and Elders, but not with the captains, those of us who are second in command." Small eyes above prominent cheekbones flashed angrily. "Is our opinion of no importance here? We who carry as much responsibility as many of you?"

Two Elk regarded him with distaste. A relationship between a berdache and a captain of the Warrior Society had been unsuitable. A warrior should seed women and produce babies. He said, "I conferred with your Chief. Is that not enough for you?"

Talasi crossed his arms and assumed an expression of superior authority. He intoned, "I have had a vision. My totem speaks warnings. Evil spirits abide on the ridge. They will not welcome us."

There were uneasy murmurs; a vision was a serious matter.

The Medicine Chief turned sharply to Talasi. "You did not tell this before. When did this vision appear?"

"Last night."

The turquoise and obsidian eye stared coldly. "You were gambling at a neighboring village last night. You won two arrow-straighteners."

Talasi looked away; a small scar on his left cheek twitched. He had shown off those arrow-straighteners when he returned; he had forgotten about that.

"I had the vision later. Before pulatla."

Two Elk raised his hand. "We must consider this."

"Aye." It was unanimous. Only Tolonqua remained silent.

The morning dawned clear and cool, and fragrant with the breath of distant mountains swept by the breeze. This was the season of rabbit drives, seed gathering, hunting, courting, and women's dances. Preparation was under way for Butterfly Dances, the favorites—social dances rather than sacred ceremonies. Rehearsals would take place tomorrow in a kiva set aside for the purpose, but now the women sat together in the morning sunshine, making fancy headdresses and moccasins and fringed belts and jewelry and other pretty things to adorn themselves and the children who would participate in the dances. Delicious bits of food to be tossed to spectators during the dances had been prepared and were stored in baskets.

Kwani sat with a group of women in the plaza—on the western side, as usual; the men's place was the eastern side, the area claimed by Sunfather. Anitzal and Lumu sat with Kwani, surrounded by most of the women of the village. Unobtrusively, Kwani watched Lumu. Since her mate was killed during the attack by Querechos, Lumu had openly grieved even though it was known that grieving might cause the spirit of the dead to return and haunt the village. Only lately had Lumu seemed more like her former self.

There was much talk and laughter and gossip.

"Has there been any word of Kokopelli?" a woman asked.

Another said, "It is said he was seen in the east."

Kwani looked up eagerly. "I did not hear that. Where in the east?"

"I don't know. Someone from the plains who was here for the feast and the trading said it was heard that Kokopelli had passed that way. Bestowing his seed, as usual."

"Such a baby-maker he has!" one said.

There were glances at Kwani, and smiles behind hands.

Lumu said, "Tell us what he was like."

"Yes! How hungry was his baby-maker?"

"Yes! How many times?"

Kwani paused a moment, remembering. She was not offended; it was natural for women to be curious about a man's performance. Finally, she said, "It was not just his man part. It was his voice, his eyes, his hands, his mouth. . . ." She touched her breasts. "He growled like an animal. . . ."

"Ah!"

"Yes. He made me burn inside. He . . ."

She stopped, pierced with a pang that surprised her. She had loved Kokopelli once.

She said, "He cast magic spells. . . ."

"Why did he leave you?" Anitzal asked. She knew, they all knew, but they liked to hear it again. How the mate of the esteemed She Who Remembers abandoned her.

"Because I was Anasazi, a Pueblo. He was Toltec from far beyond the Great River of the South. I could not go so far away from my people and take my son to become Toltec. Acoya is Pueblo. Towa now." She smiled. "Kokopelli left his necklace for Acoya to wear when he becomes a man."

"Ah!"

Kwani looked at the women gathered around her. Her sisters now. Her future, her welfare, could be good or bad depending upon how these women felt about her and Acoya. Since she had begun teaching the girls, Kwani's proud status as She Who Remembers seemed secure. Almost, Kwani felt she belonged. But the old yearning for the House of the Sun was a thorn in her heart, isolating her from these Towa women. She must be careful.

She said, "I am happy to be here."

Lumu said, "We are happy, also, that you are here. Look." She held up a pair of moccasins she had made from deerskin, embroidered with tiny beads of bone and of juniper seeds burned shiny black and polished. Everyone recognized the handiwork of a renowned bead maker in a neighboring pueblo. His beads commanded much in trade.

"See my design! It will make me dance!" Her pert face was animated. "I shall never tire!"

There were nods and comments of approval.

"Show us your headdress, Kwani," Anitzal asked.

She was weaving slender, flexible stems of the rabbit bush into a frame to fit on the head. Fastened to this would be bright streamers and brilliant feathers and whatever else she could devise. She passed the frame around so all could see and try it on. It was unusual; most headdress frames were made of hide of one kind or another. This would be light-weight and easy to fasten things to.

Lumu popped it on her head, jumped up, and began a Butterfly Dance step in clown fashion, a caricature.

Applause and laughter were interrupted by the arrival of Sikawa and Micho, the two swiftest runners of Cicuye, returning from a practice race. They would compete with runners from other villages during the Butterfly Dance ceremonies. They trotted by, muscular and sleek as elk, panting, heading for the community water jar in the eastern side of the plaza.

Kwani noticed a lingering glance between Lumu and Micho as he passed, his muscular body gleaming. She said, "A fine runner he is. Handsome, too."

Lumu's cheeks turned pink.

Anitzal said, "He plays the flute well, also. He does not come to our dwelling. Where do you meet him?"

"Yes, tell us so we may hide and watch!" a woman said.

"Tell us about the races of his baby-maker!"

Lumu tossed her head. "He is Badger Clan. Not as important as our Turquoise Clan. But—" She paused.

"But his man part is strong and digs deep, like a badger?"

"Ha!" The women laughed, nudging one another.

Lumu ignored them, pretending not to mind the laughter since it was a sign of camaraderie and tolerant affection.

Kwani said, "Our runners will win. Nobody can beat Sikawa and Micho! They will have many blankets!"

All agreed. They knew that one hair from the big toe of either of these runners was worth a blanket. The hair would be carried in the little pouch that a racer wore on a cord around his neck, enabling him to run faster than ever before—but not faster than the racer with the valuable hair on his toe. Rewards for winning were lavish, but best of all was the prestige. Winning a ceremonial race gave a man honor. He could adorn his shield with a footprint to commemorate his achievement, and talk about it at evening fires when he was old.

Kwani watched the runners lope across the plaza. Tolonqua was one of the swiftest. Or used to be. She looked at him across the plaza, watching Sikawa and Micho at the water jar surrounded by admirers wishing them well. Tolonqua stood alone. Her heart went out to him—an eagle with a broken wing. But he still expected to hunt again, and he polished his hunting bow and made fine new arrows, and walked about with his hunting dogs, speaking to them in words they seemed to understand. He had conducted the first hunting ceremony since his foot was wounded in the battle.

Now his hunters roamed the hills for deer and elk. Without him. But since she had challenged him, he hid his grief and bitterness. He limped about, maintaining his dignity, telling himself and telling her he would hunt again.

Kwani concealed her fears. Maybe building a new city would be enough to make him happy again . . . if the city was to be built.

She pressed the scallop shell to her with both hands.

Yellow Bird sat on her roof in the early morning chill, waiting for her porridge. With all the activity and preparation for the Butterfly Dances, she didn't want to miss anything that might require her suggestions and advice. She wrapped her blanket more closely around her. Already there was snow on the mountain peaks, and their noble flanks glowed with colors celebrating the autumn season. The undulating hills of the valley floor were tawny with summer gone.

Yellow Bird breathed deeply of their fragrance. She sighed. For a long lifetime she had loved this valley, these hills, the embracing mountains lavish with trees, and the little river threading the valley. The village, snuggled at the base of the ridge, was on a small rise of its own, and from her rooftop Yellow Bird could see the fields and the gentle hills spreading into the valley. It was the perfect village site. How could anyone want to leave it to build up there on that rocky, exposed place?

It would not happen. No.

Cicuye was awake and busy. Women and girls hurried to the kiva for dance practice, and a group of boys left for a rabbit hunt with loud good wishes from all. The fragrance of smoke from the cooking fires and the aroma of porridge bubbling in clay pots made her hungry.

"Aka-ti!" she called down the hatchway.

"I am busy now."

"I want my porridge." The insolence!

"It is not yet ready."

Two Elk emerged from the hatchway. "I greet you, Grandmother," he said without enthusiasm.

"Where is my porridge? What kind of mate have you, eh?"

Two Elk ignored her remark. "The porridge is cooking." He climbed down the outside ladder and headed for the plaza without explanation or farewell.

Yellow Bird watched him go. People today had no manners. When she was his age . . . She shrugged. Leave them to their laziness and poor judgment. When she was no longer here they would regret not partaking of her wisdom. Two Elk and all the others would wish for her advice but it would be too late. She smiled; the thought was comforting.

From the kiva came voices of women and children singing the songs of the Butterfly Dances. Tomorrow they would dance in the plaza as she had done so often years ago.

Thinking of the women in the village, of the children, and of her own in Earthmother's arms, she suddenly knew what she must do to save them and herself from the ridge.

She hugged her knees in exultation.

▲ 21 ▼

The village was crowded with visitors; young men from half a day's journey away were already racing. There were wagers on who would arrive at Cicuye first. It was a fine morning and the dances were under way. Children danced first, groups from each clan, dressed in their finest ceremonial adornments. Back and forth, around and around they stepped in time to a whistle and the drum, singing the Butterfly Song while a flute echoed the melody.

Kwani stood on the sidelines with the other women waiting to dance. Dancers were barefooted, and Kwani had painted her feet and ankles yellow. Anklets of deerskin thongs held pretty seed pods painted in bright colors so that she seemed to be wearing fancy yellow moccasins. Her best cotton robe, embroidered with tiny shell beads, was tied in a knot at her right shoulder, as usual, leaving the left shoulder bare. Necklaces, bracelets, and ear ornaments added a blaze of color, and the headdress, lavish with red cotton streamers and bright feathers, was the most dazzling of all.

The air of festivity banished her worries about Tolonqua, and she felt like a girl, eager to see and to do everything.

Tolonqua relished the excitement, too. All morning he had laughed and talked and visited with friends from other pueblos. It was a fine day.

Now Tolonqua was on a rooftop with his Turquoise Clan brothers. Kwani saw them looking at her and laughing the way men do when they talk of women. She was too far away to hear what they said.

"How beautiful she is!"

"My baby-maker agrees."

"Ha!"

"See how she moves."

"Like water."

"How does she move on the sleeping mat, Tolonqua?"

"You will never know, brother."

"Those eyes! Blue fire!"

"That body. So . . ."

"Dangerous."

"Yes."

"How beautiful she is!"

Applause announced that the children had finished dancing. They were rewarded with praise and tasty tidbits. Now was the women's turn. Those of the yaya who wished to dance would be first, followed by those of the various clans, each displaying their costumes and expertise.

The yaya danced with surprising vigor to loud cheers. Now it was time for those of the Turquoise Clan, Tolonqua's people. Kwani adjusted her headdress, tossed a smile to Tolonqua who smiled back, and answered the call of the drums. Her bare feet glided on the hard-packed ground, her anklets clicked in rhythm, and the streamers from her headdress fluttered in the breeze. As she sang with the flute and the whistle and the voice of the drum, her heart sang, too.

Sunfather rose higher, more visitors arrived, more musicians joined in the accompaniment, and more cooking fires wafted enticing aromas. There were flirtations, dog fights, squalling babies, and dance after dance. As each dance was completed, women tossed delicious tidbits to the spectators who devoured them on the spot, shouted thanks and compliments, and yelled for more.

Up on the ridge, watchers waited for smoke signals to relay the approach of Micho, Sikawa, and the other racers. A boom of the thunder drum announced they were sighted. There was a hubbub as dances ceased and the plaza was cleared. Two Elk drew a finish line on the ground with a stick, and the Clan Chiefs gathered to judge the finish. Spectators ringed the plaza two and three deep and gathered on ladders and rooftops. Tolonqua joined the other officials who stood by the finishing mark, waiting for the racers to appear.

A shout. "They come! They come!"

Two runners appeared, followed by three more. Like antelope they ran, faces taut with effort, eyes straining to sight the finish mark. As they drew closer, a cry went up.

"Sikawa! Sikawa leads!"

Closely following Sikawa was a runner from another village. Micho trailed in third place.

"Micho!" the people shouted.

"Faster, Micho!"

"Sikawa! Sikawa!"

With a final furious effort, Micho overcame the runner

behind Sikawa and followed the leader over the finish line.
Cheering men lifted Micho and Sikawa to their shoulders
and marched triumphantly around the plaza while the other
racers staggered across the line.

Tolonqua watched as Micho was carried past, strong
young body glistening, muscular arms raised, young face
triumphant. He flashed Lumu a cocky smile.

Tolonqua cheered with the others, but there was no cheering in his heart. Watching Micho, suddenly he felt old. He
glanced down at his foot with its red scars.

He knew, he knew he would never race again.

Dances were completed on the third day. Now was the
time of feasting, trading, gambling, courting. Several braves
from other pueblos approached Lumu with gifts, and their
lovesick flutes sounded throughout the night. It was whispered that one or another had been welcomed. But now she
sat on a roof with Kwani and other women of Cicuye who
nursed their babies (while still in cradle boards), gossiped,
and watched activities below.

"The dances were good this year."

"Yes. Better than ever before."

Kwani said, "I don't see Yellow Bird. Where is she?"

"Over there," Lumu answered. "Look, she's coming!"

Kwani watched the bent old figure making its slow and
painful way across the roofs, assisted dutifully by Aka-ti.
Although roofs joined one another, some were a little lower
or higher than the others, and Yellow Bird leaned heavily
on her staff. She jerked her arm away from Aka-ti, then
found she needed help to cross from one roof to another
and grudgingly allowed her grandson's mate to assist her.

As she approached, Lumu said, "I wonder what she
wants."

"Hush! She will hear you!" Anitzal whispered.

When Yellow Bird reached the roof where the women sat,
they greeted her respectfully and made a place for her to sit
with her back to the sun. Aka-ti eased the bony old body
down, and Yellow Bird hunched in her blanket, peering from
one to another. Seasons too many to recall had cut deep
grooves in her face, but her hair was still dark but for a few
gray wisps. From under bushy brows surprisingly white, her
small eyes, piercingly alert, regarded the group in silence.

The group waited uncomfortably. It would be discourte-
ous to the senior yaya to speak before she did. Acoya slept
at Kwani's breast where he had fallen asleep in the cradle

board, still nursing. She removed him and he woke, whimpering.

"Feed him!" Yellow Bird demanded.

Kwani offered him the breast again, but he refused.

"I think he wants to be changed," Kwani said.

"Then do so!"

As Kwani unlaced the cradle board to lift Acoya out, Yellow Bird turned to the others.

"There is a matter of importance to discuss. However, you are not to mention this to any man. *Any* man!" She looked pointedly at Kwani and Aka-ti.

Kwani swallowed resentment. Who was this imperious old woman to dictate to whom she could speak? But she remained silent.

Yellow Bird continued, "It is about the ridge. It is true. Evil spirits abound in that place!" She pointed a bony finger at the ridge. "But those who wish to build up there refuse to acknowledge this truth. Evil spirits blind them to danger."

"What danger?" Kwani asked.

Eyes sharp as a crow's darted at her. "How can you ask when your mate, our Hunting Chief, will hunt no more? When—"

"He is healing! He—"

"No. Witches took the power from his foot. Witches brought the Querechos to their abode"—again she jerked a finger at the ridge—"and now our warriors are in Sipapu. Witches!"

There were gasps. Witches were feared above all.

"The Truth Pipe!" one said. "Witches killed the pipe—"

"Because Tolonqua wants to build—"

"Aye!" Yellow Bird nodded. "Witches do not want us up there."

She grimaced in what Kwani felt sure was satisfaction. She peered at the wrinkled face under the scraggly thatch of hair, remembering what Tolonqua had told her. Yellow Bird did not want to move to the ridge because she did not want to leave the home where she had lived all her life. This old one was devious. Could it be that . . .

Kwani said, "I have been on the ridge. It is beautiful up there. A good place—"

Yellow Bird waggled her finger. "An evil place!"

Aka-ti spoke with an obvious effort to make her voice respectful. "Perhaps you will tell us how you know witches are up there."

Yellow Bird scowled so that her eyes nearly disappeared in their wrinkled folds. "You question *me*?" She turned to the women, peering at each one. "My granddaughter chooses to question me. How can this be? You know, you all know that Talasi was given a vision. He saw evil on that ridge!"

Kwani said, "He saw an opportunity to discredit one who killed Owa."

There was shocked silence. Kwani challenged the senior yaya!

Yellow Bird sat straight in frigid dignity. She glared coldly at Kwani who had placed Acoya on his stomach with his bare little bottom exposed to the sun, and was pretending she didn't notice the senior yaya's outrage.

"You dare to accuse Talasi of lying about a vision?" Her voice cracked. *"You who presume to be Towa?"*

Kwani looked at Yellow Bird who returned her gaze with unconcealed, poisonous hatred.

Kwani felt stabbed, bleeding invisibly. From deep within herself she summoned the power to see behind Yellow Bird's eyes to the place where her spirit dwelled.

She looked, and *saw*.

The revelation stunned her.

She swallowed. "Perhaps Talasi should smoke the Truth Pipe." Unswervingly, she held Yellow Bird's gaze. "Perhaps this time the Truth Pipe will not be cut by one who does not want the new city to be built."

There were stunned whispers.

Yellow Bird looked as if she had been struck. She withdrew into her blanket like a tortoise into its shell. Her face was impassive as she made a great effort to rise to her feet. Aka-ti reached to help her and was brushed aside. It was Lumu who was permitted to grasp both withered arms and pull Yellow Bird to her feet.

Yellow Bird acknowledged the help with stony dignity, and faced the group. "I have told you. Witches abide up there. You may choose to question this to your sorrow."

She turned to leave. Again, Aka-ti tried to assist her, and again she was brushed aside. It was Lumu who helped Yellow Bird across the roofs and down into her dwelling.

Kwani lay with Tolonqua on their sleeping mat. Stars shining down through the hatchway had walked their celestial pathways; the hour was late. Kwani and Tolonqua had talked for a long time.

"Are you sure it was Yellow Bird who cut the pipe?"

"I am sure. I saw the place behind her eyes—"

He turned on his side to look at her. The dim starlight was reflected on her face. He touched her forehead. "Here?"

"No. Behind the eyes. I can see—" She stopped. How could she explain? It was like being at the House of the Sun; knowledge welled up inside her. She said, "When my own spirit seeks the spirit of another, I look into the secret place behind the eyes. *Knowing* comes." She shook her head. "I do not understand how this is so. Perhaps it is the wish of the Ancient Ones."

He sat up, wrapped both arms around his knees, and stared silently into the darkness. "Yellow Bird is an honored one, the senior yaya. But she is old and her spirit lives in the past." He paused, searching his memory. "At one time she feared we would destroy her home along with others to take the beams for new dwellings."

"But the new city would be close—"

"Yes. But here is where she was born, and here is where she is determined to stay. Because she is the senior yaya she believes she can have her own way. I think she will do anything she can to prevent a new city . . . up there. . . ." He gazed up through the hatchway as though he could see the ridge beyond. "I do not do battle with women, but I will not allow her to defeat my purpose. The future of Cicuye is at stake. Yours, Acoya's, mine, all of us here." He rose and strode around the room, ignoring his limp. "All who come to Cicuye to trade or for ceremonies can see our wealth. *And the vulnerability of our location here.* Word travels far. We shall be attacked again and again and again."

"No," Kwani said calmly. "We shall not. The city will be built. A strong city, because you will be the builder."

He stopped pacing and looked at her for a long moment. "I am Hunting Chief."

Kwani knew he braced himself for a reminder that he could not hunt. But she said, "You are. The best Cicuye has ever had, and ever will have. But the concept of a new Cicuye was born in you. Who could build it better?"

He gazed down at her, his obsidian eyes warming in the way she knew well. He sat beside her, smiling. "You really believe I could get that city built, don't you?"

He leaned close and she smelled the scent of him, the man scent.

"I do, yes."

He caressed her cheek. "And you do not fear that the senior yaya is my enemy?" His hand slid to her bare shoulder.

"I trust your totem. And you, Towa."

He leaned closer, sliding his hand beneath her robe to her warm breast, kissing the nipple with his fingers. "I will ask the White Buffalo to hide the secret place behind my eyes."

"Why?"

"Because already you are too wise. And too beautiful . . ."

He laid her down and stretched himself upon her, caressing her body with his own. She felt the strength of him, the hardness, the passion. Her own passion surged in a wild flood and she rose to him.

Stars walked far on their sky paths before Kwani and Tolonqua drifted into sleep.

Yellow Bird could not sleep. She lay upon her sleeping mat, staring at the ceiling. Two Elk had closed the hatchway as usual; no sky, no stars, could be seen. Heavy ceiling beams hung above her—beams she felt would fall and crush her unless she held them up by the power of her will.

Kwani knows.

But she could not. Nobody saw. Nobody. I made sure. . . .

She knows.

But how? I must find a way to overcome this.

The ceiling beams seemed lower. It took all her will to keep them in place, to keep from being crushed like a beetle.

I must find someone to help me, someone who also opposes the new city.

She turned restlessly on the mat to ease herself, but her bones ached, protesting.

I must find someone. Who?

The answer came at last. Why hadn't she thought of it before?

Talasi.

▲ 22 ▼

Talasi was taking his morning swim in the river. Sun-father had not yet topped the mountain and the water ran cold and dark. He shivered. Cold hardened a man's meat, but it was not a pleasure. He turned to swim on his back and look up at the sky where a small cloud drifted. More clouds were needed; rain clouds. The usual sacrifices had been made, and clans and societies held the usual ceremonies, but no rain came. It was said around evening fires that refugees from drought-stricken western pueblos were migrating south and eastward, seeking to join other pueblos near water. As yet, no refugees had appeared at Cicuye, but it was only a matter of time. Cicuye was the easternmost pueblo, the last before the Great Plains opened to immensity. Where nomadic tribes followed the buffalo. Eventually, Pueblo refugees would arrive in Cicuye. It would become a large city.

A rich city.

Open to attack.

If only it had been someone other than Tolonqua who originated the idea of a city on the ridge . . .

"Talasi!"

It was a boy running along the bank.

"Talasi!"

"You see I am here."

"Yellow Bird wants to speak with you."

"Now?"

"Yes. In her dwelling."

Talasi sloshed to the bank. What did the old crow want? "I come."

He dried himself with a tattered bit of robe that could use a bathing of its own, and made his way, still naked, to his dwelling. As he dressed, he stared at the wall separating his dwelling from Tolonqua's as though he could see through it to the other side. Where Owa was killed. Grief and hatred rose like bile in his throat.

Owa, on the scaffold out there on the plain. Alone. But for birds cleansing the bones . . .

His face twisted in pain. Never would he forget.

Yellow Bird sat propped up against her backrest of woven reeds. She wore her best robe, and had asked—no, told—Aka-ti to leave her alone to discuss a matter of importance with Talasi. Aka-ti grudgingly agreed, and Two Elk had gone to his kiva. Now she was alone and ready.

Footsteps approached on the roof, and Talasi appeared at the hatchway.

"I am here."

"You may enter," Yellow Bird said in her most welcoming voice. A captain of the Warrior Society was accustomed to respect. She must persuade, not antagonize.

Talasi climbed down and stood before her respectfully. "I greet you, Honored One."

Yellow Bird nodded in acknowledgment. She gestured. "Sit."

When he was seated cross-legged on the floor, she allowed him to wait in silence for a time. It was well to let him know who was the important one here. Finally, she said, "It seems there are those who do not believe witches abide on the ridge."

Talasi seemed surprised, but only momentarily. He smiled. "There are always those who refuse to see truth."

"Exactly. That is why I have summoned you."

"I am honored to be here."

"Of course." She scratched her head; the lice were more vigorous than usual. "It is our duty to help those ignorant ones accept what is true."

"Ah." Talasi clasped his hands. Carefully, he said, "How may I assist?"

Yellow Bird had not missed the quick flick of pleasure in his eyes. She gloated inwardly. He was impaled like a field mouse on a stick. She said, "You will assist the Medicine Chief in convincing those who do not want a new city that the city should, indeed, be built."

He squirmed. "But—"

"It is customary for Medicine Chiefs of other villages to be invited for consultation, and to conduct ceremonies, is it not?"

"Sometimes. However—"

"You will, of course, confer with them privately in advance. Persuade them to conduct their ceremonies as usual, but then they must determine and announce that the city should *not* be built under any circumstances.''

He squinted. ''They may not agree. They may feel that a fortified city on the ridge will make their own pueblos more secure.''

''You will persuade them.''

''How?''

''There are those here who are eager for the city to be built. They will be pleased to present suitable rich gifts to visiting medicine men to come and conduct ceremonies—to communicate with the gods and prove the wisdom of building a city on the ridge.'' She paused. ''Of course you will take the gifts with you when you go to see them. Explain that the gifts are expressions of appreciation in advance for finding the ridge unsuitable because of witches and evil spirits abiding up there.''

He squirmed again. ''And if they refuse?''

''The value of the gifts must assure that they do not. You will convince the givers of the importance of being generous.'' Surely this dolt understood the usefulness of a bribe.

Talasi hesitated, but his eyes had a shrewd gleam. ''They will not be pleased when the Medicine Chiefs announce their decisions. The gifts—''

She shrugged. ''You cannot be blamed if Tolonqua is defeated. You tried to help.'' She watched that sink in, then added, ''Unfortunately, it will cause our Hunting Chief much embarrassment. It could ruin him. But we must consider the alternative.''

''Yes.'' *It could ruin him.* He smiled. ''We must plan.''

In the plaza, the evening fire blazed high, chasing shadows. Sparks flew upward, glowed, and died. Moonwoman displayed her curved, thin self, occasionally hidden briefly by a drift of fragrant smoke. Everyone in Cicuye was gathered around the fire, including Yellow Bird who huddled in her blanket. Kwani and Tolonqua sat with Acoya in his cradle board across Kwani's lap. She sensed tension in the air, but could not identify the source.

She whispered to Tolonqua, ''Is something going to happen?''

''Perhaps. There is talk about Talasi and Yellow Bird. Yesterday they were alone in her dwelling for a long time.''

That was not good news; Kwani was uneasy.

The Crier Chief was finishing his announcements. ''Tomorrow is the day of gathering pinyon nuts. Many birds flock in the pinyon trees this year. It is a big crop, so carry large baskets. We depart at pulatla.'' He sat down to pleased comments.

Two Elk rose. He stood in self-conscious dignity, raising his hand for silence. When all was quiet, he said, "As you know, the Chiefs and Elders have decided that a new city will be built on the ridge. The Medicine Chief and I conferred with the Above Beings, and we agree. However, Talasi has warned us of a vision. He tells that evil spirits abound up there."

There were shocked murmurs. Two Elk turned to Talasi who sat nearby. "You will speak." He wrapped his blanket around himself with a flourish, and sat down.

Talasi rose slowly. He stood for a moment, looking at the fire as though to gain inspiration from it. Finally, he said, "It is true. A vision told me of evil spirits on the ridge. However . . ." He swallowed. "However, I did not understand this because our wise Chiefs and Elders said the city should be built. I wondered if witches had given me the vision to defeat us. I prayed long, and I dreamed." For a time he was silent, gazing at the people around him who gazed back, faces expressionless. He swallowed again.

"I dreamed. My totem, the fox, came to me. My totem said that witches feared for a city to be on the ridge because up there the city would be closer to the Above Beings and would have power. More power . . . To fight evil."

There was excited comment. Talasi signaled for silence. He seemed sure of himself now. He continued, "My totem said to invite the best Medicine Chiefs from other villages to conduct a ceremony on the ridge to prove that no evil spirits abound there. And that the new city should be built. I was told also to seek the help of a woman of wisdom." He paused dramatically. "I sought our senior yaya. She said to discuss this with you here, and to rely upon your judgment. I have spoken." He sat down.

There was a babble of talk. Yellow Bird raised her hand, and there was immediate silence. She said, "Talasi speaks truth." She withdrew into her blanket. Kwani noticed how the blanket quivered.

Two Elk stood. "Tomorrow morning all Chiefs and Elders will assemble in the kiva to discuss whether or not the Medicine Chiefs of other pueblos should assist us. This is a matter of grave importance. Talasi, you will attend also." He turned to go. "Tonight I shall seek wisdom." He strode away.

Kwani saw Talasi glance furtively at Yellow Bird who pretended not to see him. He smiled.

"I don't understand it," Kwani said again to Tolonqua.

They spoke quietly in their dwelling with the hatchway closed, and sat across from the wall that adjoined Talasi's to avoid the chance of being overheard. The evening fire was over and people stood in groups and sat upon roofs, discussing the extraordinary situation. Kwani and Tolonqua had hurried back to talk in privacy.

"It doesn't sound true," Kwani said. "Something is not right."

Tolonqua nodded. "I agree." He sat rubbing his foot with both hands. "Talasi is hiding something. But what?" He continued rubbing the scarred places, and his ankle and toes.

"Let me." Kwani tucked his foot between her knees and bent over it, kneading with her strong fingers. "Do you think Medicine Chiefs from other pueblos will want to help?"

"Yes. Especially if they are suitably rewarded."

"Talasi has never shown interest in the new city. And Yellow Bird has always objected to it. Bitterly." She shook her head. "I saw the way Talasi looked at Yellow Bird. Something is hidden; you are right." She sat back on her heels, thinking. "Everyone knows how Yellow Bird feels about a city on the ridge. Yet, he went to her for advice about how to prove the city should be built. It makes no sense."

Tolonqua stretched his leg, flexing his toes. "That feels good. Stronger, I think."

She kneaded his leg to the knee. "Has it been easier to walk today?"

"I think so. Maybe a little." He stood and walked around the room. He still limped, but it seemed to be not as much as before. "Soon I shall hunt again." He sat down, facing Kwani. "I shall confer with my own totem, and perhaps you should speak with the Ancient Ones. I do not trust Talasi's dream."

"Not Talasi."

They looked at each other in solemn agreement.

Kwani was wakened by the voice of the Crier Chief making his morning announcements from a rooftop.

"All people, arise! Be vigorous and strong! Rejoice in

Sunfather's coming!'' The strong, deep voice reverberated through the village. "This day, after porridge, Elders and Chiefs will meet to decide whether or not the Medicine Chiefs of other villages shall be invited to conduct ceremonies on the ridge. To determine whether or not witches and evil spirits abide there, and if the new city should be built. I shall make known their decision.'' He glanced at the knotted cord he carried to remind him of things to be said; each knot was an announcement. "Today is also the first day of pinyon nut gathering. Birds flock in the trees; nuts must be gathered quickly. Take the large baskets and fill them all!'' He flashed a good-humored smile and fingered another knot. "Piko, honored grandfather of our Hunting Chief, has finished making a new Truth Pipe. It will be in the medicine lodge this day to receive our gifts and homage. We of Cicuye have a new Truth Pipe!'' His voice soared in climax. "Sunfather comes! Rejoice!''

Tolonqua stood on the roof, waiting to sing his morning chant. Acoya was already awake. Kwani knew he was hungry, but he did not cry. He waited for her. His round eyes watched as she came to him and lifted him to her breast. He smiled. She looked down at him, at his small, round mouth drinking eagerly, and love overflowed like water in a jar too full.

Tolonqua sang to Sunfather, his rich voice repeating words Kwani knew so well.

> *"Your seeds,*
> *Your riches,*
> *Your strong spirit . . ."*

She touched Acoya's cheek. "All these to you may he grant.''

Tolonqua returned with the bowl of sacred meal and placed it upon their family altar, a flat-topped stone near the fire pit. The altar held objects of spiritual power including Kwani's necklace and the small, round shell with a spiral inside, given to her by Earthmother when she was a child. She had found it and knew it was for her. Above the altar, Tolonqua's medicine bundle held the two Corn Mothers from his birthing ceremony and enclosed the sacred robe worn now only for ceremonies. It would be Acoya's one day.

Tolonqua squatted beside Kwani and watched Acoya nursing. He smiled fondly. "A fine man cub he is!''

"Yes, isn't he?''

"I must choose his ceremonial father. To teach him the sacred things. I cannot decide. . . ."

"You will know when it is time to know."

He looked at her, at the dark hair tumbled around her face and the sky eyes. "You are wise." He bent close. "And beautiful, beautiful." He cupped her face in both hands and kissed her deeply.

She caught her breath. "You know what happens when you do that."

He laughed. "Later. I must go now to the kiva."

She watched him climb the ladder. His foot seemed stronger, and hope surged in her. Maybe he would hunt again. . . .

When he had gone, she replaced the shredded cedar bark in the cradle board with fresh, and bathed Acoya quickly with cold water. He did not like that, and screamed objections.

"It will make you strong." She laughed.

The hatchway darkened, and Lumu and Anitzal peered down.

"We come."

"Enter and welcome!" Kwani handed Acoya to Anitzal who cuddled and warmed him while Lumu talked baby talk and made him smile.

Hospitality demanded that whenever a visitor entered, food was to be offered immediately. If a matter of importance was to be discussed, it would not be until after eating. Kwani tossed pemmican into a pot of water simmering upon coals in the fire pit. While it cooked she spread a blanket on the floor and lay out her finest eating bowls and a basket tray for corn cakes. Cakes left over from yesterday were already stacked in a bowl by the fire; Tolonqua would have some when he returned from the kiva.

Kwani lay Acoya beside her near the fire pit so his bare little body would bask in the warmth. He cooed and kicked and waved his arms and watched Kwani arranging cakes on the basket tray.

Kwani gestured. "Sit and eat."

Lumu ate eagerly, her mouth busy in her smooth, round face. Her black hair was neatly braided and arranged to conceal the too-short places where she had slashed at her hair in grieving for her mate. Her delicate hands, not yet gnarled from years of labor, took a thin, flat cake, scooped up some pemmican, folded the cake, and popped it into her mouth. As she chewed, she took another.

"Good!" she said. "Tolonqua spoke truly; you cook well!"

"I wish to please him. And his family—my family now," Kwani said truthfully. To become part of a family, an extended family with close ties binding generations, would give her and Acoya security. He would have strength for his path of life.

Anitzal held a cake on her palm, inspecting it closely. She tore it in two slowly, and nodded. "It is of good texture, not too hard, not too easily broken. And the meal was properly ground." She scooped up some pemmican and ate with a flattering smack of her lips. "We of the Turquoise Clan are known for our cooking. Not like women of some clans here whose cakes fight the stomach. And their pemmican!" She held her nose. "To give a dog distemper." She chortled, nodding her head vigorously. Her gray braids, entwined with blue and red feathers proclaiming wealth and status, nodded with her. Laughter brightened the agelessness and unforgotten sorrows creasing her face. The loss of her mate and her only child left crevices around her mouth and eyes—sharp eyes that softened when she looked at Acoya.

As though he acknowledged the admiration, Acoya sprayed a fine arc that hit the fire in an odorous sizzle. Uproarious laughter seemed to puzzle him, which made them laugh more.

Lumu said, "He wishes to show he is a man."

Anitzal wiped her eyes with both hands. Laughter and good food eased the heart. She belched politely and patted her stomach. "I am content."

"I, also," Lumu added.

It was the signal that discussion could now begin. Kwani removed the bowls, set the basket aside, and sat crosslegged, waiting.

Anitzal said, "The yaya wonder if the spirit of Yellow Bird strays. She is not as she was before."

"She grows older," Lumu said. "A door shuts inside, maybe." She patted her temple with a forefinger.

"Aye, she is old," Anitzal said. "But wise."

"Except about a city on the ridge," Lumu said. "She does not want to be up there."

Kwani nodded. "Old ones want to stay where they are. Like old trees. She does not want her roots cut away. I think she is afraid."

"Of what?"

''That if she moves, her spirit will be left behind.''

''Then why does she say now that Talasi speaks truth when he says the city should be built?'' Anitzal shook her head. ''It does not fit.''

Lumu glanced up at the hatchway and leaned forward, speaking softly. ''Talasi and Owa . . . Tolonqua killed the berdache—''

''So Talasi hates Tolonqua. Who first thought of a city up there,'' Anitzal said. ''Talasi is not known for generosity or a forgiving spirit. Why does he now say Tolonqua is right and the city should be built?''

''He is of the Warrior Society. Even he can see that a city on the ridge offers protection,'' Kwani said carefully.

Lumu snorted and tossed a braid. ''A warrior who takes a berdache is a *warrior*? Ha!''

''He has no mate—''

''He is ugly!'' She screwed her face in a grimace. ''Even when he smiles.'' She arranged her mouth in excruciating imitation.

Kwani giggled. ''That is Talasi!''

Anitzal said firmly, ''Our talk is wandering. Let us bring it back.'' She settled herself like a turkey hen. ''It is strange that Yellow Bird who did not want the new city, and Talasi who hates our brother, now say they want what Tolonqua wants. Very strange, is it not?''

''They plan something!'' Lumu said.

Footsteps approached on the roof, and passed.

Anitzal leaned forward, whispering. ''They plan. You must warn Tolonqua!''

Kwani nodded. ''I shall. Indeed, I shall.''

▲ 23 ▼

The kiva, round as Sunfather and Moonwoman, lay in Earthmother's domain. Smooth, white-plastered walls held built-in niches for ceremonial paraphernalia and other sacred objects. A ledge all the way around served as a bench upon which Chiefs and Elders were now seated. Light through the hatchway slanted down upon Two Elk standing in the Chief's place-to-speak by the fire pit. He gestured emphatically, looking from one to another.

"Decisions must be made. We have talked long. We must agree if Medicine Chiefs of other pueblos are to be invited to conduct their ceremonies on the ridge. If so, we must decide who is to invite them. Who." He paused, assuming a posture of modest authority.

Tolonqua said, "I suggest yourself, the Medicine Chief, the Warrior Chief, and the Elder Chief."

Talasi frowned and opened his mouth to speak, but the Elder Chief was already speaking. He was short, but straight and strong for one so old—over fifty winters—and respected for his wisdom.

"No. I must refuse." He spoke quietly, but his eyes, deeply recessed in his weathered face, were angry. "I shall agree to invite them if it is the wish of all here. However, as I said before, as I say again, I do not think it is wise. Or necessary."

The Medicine Chief said calmly, "Perhaps not. But there are those in Cicuye who still doubt that the new city should be built. What harm could come from ceremonies proving the wisdom of our decision?"

"What if the ceremonies prove otherwise?"

Talasi said sharply, "You question the decision of our Elders and Chiefs? You question their knowledge?" He glanced at the others with a tight-lipped smile, then realized he had spoken out of turn. The smile faded.

The Elder Chief cast him a scornful glance. "I do not question their knowledge. I do question their wisdom."

Angry voices spoke at once. The Elder Chief raised a hand, and continued, "We of Cicuye know well that our village is envied by those of other pueblos. Ours is the biggest, the richest, the most powerful of all. Is it not possible that others might fear our becoming stronger? Could they not use the ceremonies to defeat us and benefit themselves?"

Talasi shifted uneasily. The discussion was getting uncomfortable. He raised a hand; he must observe protocol this time. He was not an Elder or Chief and to be rude would defeat his purpose.

"I wish to speak."

Two Elk gestured permission.

"It is true they could do this. But they will not if they are properly approached."

"How?"

"With gifts. Suitable gifts."

Tolonqua said, "Gifts will make them willing for Cicuye to become stronger?"

"You do not understand," Talasi said smoothly. "We will be offering homage for their renowned skills." He smiled sardonically. "They know well that our Medicine Chief, all our Elders and Chiefs, are widely honored for their powers. They will be anxious to prove their own. If our ceremonies and decisions conflict with theirs, whose will be believed? They would lose face!"

There was a thoughtful silence. For a Medicine Chief to lose face would destroy him. He would go into the wilderness alone to die.

For a time no one spoke. Sounds of the city drifted down. Children played and shouted, dogs yapped, and footsteps ran across the roof. From nearby came women's voices singing the Corn Grinding Song; Tolonqua heard Kwani's voice above them all. His mate. His son. His people. They must be protected—by a city on the ridge. But not everyone agreed. Perhaps Talasi was right.

He said, "I will contribute a gift."

"I, also," another said.

"And I."

The Warrior Chief said, "The safety of our city and our people are at stake here. I will give two gifts."

Soon many gifts had been offered. Talasi smiled proudly.

Two Elk nodded. "It is agreed. Now we decide who takes the gifts to all the pueblos and invites the Medicine Chiefs."

Tolonqua said, "I have made my suggestion. You, our

Medicine Chief, and our Warrior Chief. Our Elder Chief declines,'' he added respectfully.

Again, Talasi raised his hand.

"Speak."

"Our Chiefs are needed here. Especially since the Querecho attack.''

"Aye!" the Warrior Chief said.

Talasi continued, "If our Chiefs make the journey they must be protected. By warriors. This will make a sizable party. As you know, new people come to the valley, people who do not know us. They might see such a group as a war party. Possessing objects of value.'' He shook his head. "We cannot take that chance. Whoever goes should be alone. A single traveler on his way to a pueblo. No threat, no riches.''

"There is more to consider,'' the Warrior Chief said. "If these small pueblos are approached by a group from a larger, richer city, they may believe we think we can make them do whatever we want by offering gifts. An insult to their own importance. And their manhood. No. We must approach as a cougar approaches. Quietly, carefully. And alone.''

"Aye, alone,'' said the Medicine Chief. He had no wish to undertake such a perilous journey. At one time, perhaps, when he was younger . . .

"Alone,'' others agreed.

Talasi could barely conceal his triumph. How easy it had been!

"Very well,'' Two Elk said. "Who?''

"I would be proud to,'' Talasi said, hoping he had not spoken too quickly. "For our people and our city.'' He bowed his head humbly. "If that is your wish.''

"Aye!''

All agreed but the Elder Chief who remained silent. Tolonqua yearned to be the one, but he knew his foot would refuse the distance. A knot tightened in his stomach.

Yellow Bird sat on her roof, basking in the sun. She had seen Talasi enter the kiva with the others, and she waited tensely for them to come out.

Sunfather walked higher. The men did not appear.

Could Talasi convince them? He was shrewd, but not adroit. Women disliked him, but men, in their blindness, did not. Perhaps they would believe him.

When, at last, the men emerged, one by one, Yellow Bird waited for Talasi to appear. He climbed out last, and she knew instantly he had been successful. He bore himself with an air of importance, barely concealing a swagger.

"Ah!" she sighed. She looked over the pueblo where she had been born. How it had grown! And was still growing. At the eastern edge, preparation was under way for a new building. Women had gathered a large pile of twigs and sedge grass and set it afire; smoke billowed upward and swept over the valley. When the fire became half coals and half ashes they would throw clay and water on it and mix it all together; charcoal provided temper. A few pebbles would be added to give more strength. Fine adobe walls would begin to rise, a little at a time, smoothed and patted by the hands of the women who imparted their own strength into the adobe. It would be beautiful.

Yellow Bird sighed again. No one would be building a new dwelling if another city were to be up there on that accursed place. She was safe. This is where she was born. This is where her spirit would enter Sipapu. Never would she have to abandon it, to wrench lifelong roots from the deep places of her heart.

Her spirit was at ease.

"You will give a gift?" Kwani was shocked. "Do you not realize what is happening?" She paused in the kneading of Tolonqua's foot. It was still weak. Had the weakness invaded his wisdom?

Tolonqua rested an arm on the upturned knee of his other leg, and frowned. It was not seemly for a woman to question a decision of her mate. Not even Kwani. "All Chiefs and Elders offer gifts. We will be asking the Medicine Chiefs of other pueblos to come here and intercede with the gods on our behalf. To do so without offering suitable gifts is not our way. Not Towa."

Kwani sat back on her heels and looked at him. "It is true. You are generous—as are all of the Towa. Could this be used against you?"

"How?"

"Consider. You killed Owa. How does Talasi feel about that? You know; he is an enemy. Does he want you to be successful at whatever you undertake? No. He tried to defeat your idea of the new city by a so-called vision, and went about telling everybody the city should not be built because evil spirits were up there. Now he says he had a dream and the city must be built. Why?"

"He is of the Warrior Society—"

"He was when he insisted the city should *not* be built. And what about Yellow Bird? Why has she changed her mind? All this time she has—"

"The Querecho attack. That changed her mind."

"Why? Has Cicuye not been attacked before?"

"Many times." He looked away, thinking.

"Talasi was with Yellow Bird a long time. Talking. They plan something."

She bent again to his foot, working her fingers into the muscles and tendons, willing them to be strong, to be as they used to be. He watched her as she worked, her necklace swinging back and forth as she bent to and fro.

"Have you spoken with the Ancient Ones?"

"I tried to." She looked up at him. "While you were in the kiva."

"Ah. And what did they say?"

"Danger . . ."

"From what? Who?"

She shook her head. "I do not know. Only that there is danger. But don't you see? Talasi and Yellow Bird plan something. That is where the danger is."

"Hm-m-m." He sat watching her small, square hands demanding strength from his foot. It was not strong yet, but it would get better. Of course. "I shall confer with my totem." He reached for his medicine bundle, removed the robe, and flung it about him. "I go to the medicine lodge."

Acoya lay on his stomach, making swimming motions on the blanket. Tolonqua patted his bare little bottom. "One day my son shall go to the lodge with me."

Kwani watched him climb the ladder and she heard his footsteps across the roof. She clasped the necklace to her and felt the scalloped ridges pressing her skin. It was the spirit touch of those who had gone before, all who were She Who Remembers.

"Protect him!" she prayed.

A sound from Acoya made Kwani glance at him. He had turned himself over. It was the first time he had done that.

"My big, strong son!" She laughed, bending over him.

He smiled and kicked his legs, waving the mark of the White Buffalo on his foot like a banner. She scooped him into her arms, rocked him back and forth, and looked down into his face. What was he thinking? She searched the place behind his eyes but it was still new and unformed.

What would be his path of life?

She began to sing a melody rising from within her, beseeching the spirit of the White Buffalo to protect her son and make his path beautiful. And to be with Tolonqua in the dangerous days ahead.

"Protect them!" she sang, and her voice floated up through the hatchway to be caught by a bird and carried to the Above Beings.

▲ 24 ▼

"When do you think Talasi will return?"

Tolonqua was with the Medicine Chief in his lodge, making pahos—prayer sticks—to be placed on the ridge to sanctify it before the ceremonies, and to favorably influence cloud deities.

The old Chief shrugged. "When the gods send him."

They worked carefully, fastening strong eagle plumes to the painted willow sticks wrapped with yucca fiber cords dyed blue. Then each paho was sprinkled with corn pollen and topped with the downy white eagle breast feathers that brought clouds. Deities dwelled in clouds, and the intercession of deities would be needed during the coming ceremonies on the ridge.

Tolonqua worked silently. It had been nearly a moon since Talasi left. Twice, runners had mentioned hearing of his visits to pueblos, but they had not seen him. Much, too much, depended upon the success of Talasi's journey. Was he safe? He had worn his plainest robe and carried a modest pack tightly filled with shell and turquoise, other objects of great value, and pemmican for his journey; pemmican was of light weight and took little room. His water bag was small since water would be available from the river threading the valley. He had been properly prepared for his journey and all should be well.

Where was he now?

Tolonqua fastened a fluffy white feather, a cloud token, to his paho, weaving it into the wrapping cord, but his mind was on the ridge. Too many people still believed evil spirits were there. Even though Talasi changed his mind after a dream and wanted the city to be built. Or so he said.

Tolonqua paused in his work. Uneasiness tugged at his mind. In his eagerness for the city to be built, had he allowed himself to be deceived? His totem had told him to beware a snare. Kwani was right. Something about Talasi's plan was not straight. A knot to be untangled. He frowned, trying to concentrate upon his work, but Kwani's words echoed in his mind. *"Talasi and Yellow Bird plan . . . "*

The Medicine Chief finished the last paho and laid it upon the altar. There were four of them, four being the sacred number. He sat back and looked at Tolonqua whose pahos were as good as his own. He had invited Tolonqua to the medicine lodge to make pahos with him—a rare honor. Now the obsidian and turquoise eye shone palely in the kiva's dim light while the other eye, small and sharp and dark, regarded Tolonqua solemnly.

"How many days since you brought the robe of the White Buffalo here to commune with your totem?"

"It was three days before Talasi left."

"Ah. Nearly a moon. Has your totem spoken since?"

"No."

The old Chief was silent for a time, watching the coals smoldering in the fire pit. Then he began a low chant, beseeching the Above Beings for wisdom.

Tolonqua sat in respectful silence. He knew the Medicine Chief wanted to know what Tolonqua's totem revealed, but knowledge bestowed by one's totem was sacred and not to be shared.

The Medicine Chief finished his chant and lifted the long-stemmed medicine pipe from the altar. He stuffed the bowl with tobacco, lit it, blew smoke to the Six Sacred Directions, and offered the pipe to Tolonqua.

"It is you to whom the spirits first bestowed the thought of a new city. Pray now for wisdom."

Tolonqua accepted the pipe and held it reverently before him. "I have prayed. Many times. But still I seek wisdom."

The Medicine Chief watched as Tolonqua acknowledged the Six Sacred Directions and smoked quietly. Sounds of the city drifted in with the voice of a drum and chanting in preparation for the ceremonies.

Tolonqua finished smoking and handed the pipe to the Medicine Chief who returned it to its place on the altar. Tolonqua said, "It is time for a hunt. I must attend to the prehunt ceremonies." If he stayed longer, he might reveal the warning of his totem. Had he indeed been snared? If so, he would rather no one know, especially the Medicine Chief.

The Chief gestured dismissal. Tolonqua rose and bid respectful farewell.

The old Chief watched him go, then sat for some time, pondering. Tolonqua refused to tell what his totem had revealed. So be it. But all was not as it should be; he knew this instinctively. He sighed, and watched the coals burning with an inner light; he wished that light were in his spirit.

Foreboding lay upon him.

More days passed. Sunfather rose, walked his sky path, and descended to the underworld to travel again to his eastern house. Corn ears were removed, inspected, blessed with prayer songs and returned to neat stacks in their dwelling places. Women worked long at metates, and small girls made tiny clay pots and bowls and played with their little people—pretty stones from the river, easily imagined as a man and a woman and children. Boys practiced throwing their curved rabbit sticks at dogs whose yelps proclaimed a successful aim, or sat with old Piko as he instructed them in the proper straightening of an arrow or the softening and bending of wood for a bow.

Life went on. But not as usual. Under and over all was the tension of divided opinion, of anxiety about the arrival of important visitors and the ceremonies for which much preparation must be made. Drums and chants sounded far into the night, and an additional dwelling was being built for the visiting Chiefs to have their own sleeping place and storage for their belongings.

Kwani walked alone on the ridge. She had left Acoya with Anitzal and Lumu, both of whom regarded him as their own. She felt the need to be alone, to be on the ridge where she had been with Tolonqua before Acoya was born. How long ago that seemed!

She found the three boulders that looked to have been tossed there by playful gods, and sat upon one of them. It was smooth and warm, reflecting Sunfather's eye. This is where she had sat with Tolonqua when Kokopelli brought her to Cicuye during their journey. She remembered watching a hawk swoop low for a field mouse and soar away; she had visualized that mouse as herself, captured by Tolonqua, swept into the sky by a wild bird. . . .

Hers now. Her wild bird. Tolonqua.

She gazed at the ridge sloping upward, rocky and dotted with green and gray brush. She breathed deeply, letting the fragrance of brush and grasses, of earth and air, cleanse her deep inside. Tolonqua's foot was not stronger. Instinctively, Kwani knew he would never hunt again. What of his dream of the new city? What of her own longing—to be once more at the House of the Sun? Now, more than ever before, she felt the need to kneel at the altar stone, to feel the power of it rising from within the stone's mystical depths to give her wisdom and courage, and unite her with the Ancient Ones once more.

She needed courage now. And wisdom, yes. What would happen to Tolonqua's spirit and to his prestige if the plan for a new city were defeated? If he were humbled, she and Acoya would be humbled, also. Then could She Who Remembers teach as before?

Below, the pueblo basked in warm autumn air and the sweet breath of the valley. She heard the faint throb of a drum—the heartbeat of Earthmother herself. A breeze carried chanting and the song of a flute, and the sound of children at play. It was a good sound. From a good pueblo. But *Towa*. If only . . .

There was a rustle behind her. She whirled. The sound came again from behind a rabbit bush nearby. Remembering the Querecho attack, Kwani's heart jerked. She clutched her necklace to her, and prepared to slide from the boulder and run wildly down the ridge. The rabbit bush quivered and a tawny head appeared, followed by a furry body.

Kwani gasped in surprise. "Brother Coyote!"

For an amazing instant the coyote sat looking at her.

He is telling me something.

He lifted his nose as though he were about to sing his coyote song, then trotted away, disappearing among the rocks and bushes.

Kwani sat entranced, gazing after him. Was he really Brother Coyote—who had befriended her long ago? Or was it a Spirit Being in coyote form? As she watched him disappear, her attention was caught by a puff of smoke. It rose in the distance, a small puff dissolving to a thin wisp floating high. As she looked, the smoke stopped, then came again, and stopped.

A signal!

She watched intently, listening with her eyes to what the signals said. With a cry, she slid from the boulder and scrambled down the ridge, running as fast as her legs would take her.

Tolonqua squatted on the roof, knapping a piece of rainbow flint. It was hard flint, but beautiful, and responded to his skill with the shaping stone. He smiled in satisfaction and held it up to admire it again. A commotion rose suddenly at the edge of the city, and he stood to see what was happening.

It was Kwani, running and calling. Word swept through the village.

"They come! Talasi brings the Medicine Chiefs! They come!"

Excited people crowded the plaza and surrounded Kwani. Tolonqua climbed down and hurried toward her as quickly as he could. Two Elk was already there.

"Begin preparations!" Two Elk shouted over the babble. "To the cooking pots! To the kivas! Do not delay! Begin!"

Tolonqua elbowed his way to Kwani. "What happened?"

"I saw Talasi's smoke signal. All the Chiefs come." She looked for Anitzal and Acoya, but did not see them. "I must find Acoya; he will be hungry now," she told those crowding close. She tugged Tolonqua's arm so he would follow.

The Warrior Chief had taken command and already cooking fires smoked. Tolonqua and Kwani climbed to their dwelling, closed the hatchway, and sat close together, whispering.

"I was on the ridge," Kwani said, "and Brother Coyote came to me. At least I think it was Brother Coyote. He sat and looked at me; he was telling me something. . . ."

Tolonqua gazed at her. She never ceased to astonish him. "Brother Coyote?"

"Yes. And then I saw the smoke signals." She leaned closer. "I am afraid."

"Why?"

"I do not know. It is only a feeling." She fingered her necklace and looked up at him. "There are many of them! A large party!"

That was not good news, but he would not reveal his concern. He put both arms around her and held her close. "Do not be afraid; I will protect you. And so will the Ancient Ones. You are safe. Show no fear when you meet the visitors." He pulled her to her feet. "Come, we must go to the plaza to welcome them properly."

The plaza was cleared and people encircled it, waiting eagerly. The Crier Chief stood with Two Elk on a roof, calling news to those below even though they could see the group approaching in the valley spread before them.

"It is a large party, with banners. And musicians!"

"Aye-e-e! They bring their own musicians!"

The musicians of Cicuye brandished their fine rattles and

whistles and flutes and rasps and drums. No musicians were better than they!

"A large party!" the Crier Chief called again, and a note was in his voice not there before. "Many warriors!"

The Warrior Chief had been supervising events on the plaza; now he clambered up to the roof so that he might give orders when the visitors neared the village. The party was still far up the valley but keen eyes were accustomed to scanning distances.

"Talasi marches in front!" the Crier Chief called as though no one else had seen. "Medicine Chiefs march with him, and musicians. Warriors follow."

There was excited talk.

"Why so many warriors?"

"To protect the Chiefs."

"Protect them from whom?"

"Strangers in the valley, perhaps."

"Look at their shields!"

"All warriors carry shields."

"We don't want all those warriors here!"

"Nor their weapons."

"We invited the Chiefs only. Talasi—"

"Talasi is a captain in our Warrior Society. He invited the warriors, maybe."

"The Chiefs must be protected on their journey."

"Aye."

Two Elk called to the principal drummer. "Those musicians will be playing as they arrive. We are to greet them with music louder and better. Understand?"

"Of course."

Women returned to the cooking pots and men readied the kivas. Sleeping mats and night jars were placed in the new dwelling and members of the Medicine Society took the pahos to the ridge and placed them in strategic places, chanting prayers. A welcoming signal fire flamed high. Villagers donned their finest ceremonial garments; Cicuye's wealth and prestige would be suitably displayed. Evident, but not so obvious, would be the bows and arrows and lances and shields casually carried by the warriors during the welcoming ceremony.

Excitement mounted as the party grew near, marching in time to drums and flutes. Kwani stood in the plaza with Lumu and Anitzal who still carried Acoya in his cradle board as she loved to do. His bright eyes shone with interest at the sounds and activity.

Lumu turned to Kwani and pointed at the ridge. "Look!"

Tolonqua stood on the ridge. The robe of the White Buffalo was over his shoulders. In one hand he carried a staff embellished with bright streamers; his other hand held his ceremonial shield, a powerful one of buffalo hide, painted with the likeness of his totem and adorned with hawk and eagle feathers. The Hunting Chief feather was in his headband, and the shell horn in a pouch at his waist. His breechcloth was one Kwani had made of softest deerskin embroidered with shell beads taken from a garment of her own. Necklaces of shell and turquoise shone upon his bare chest and bright feathers were at his ears. He was a handsome, impressive personage and there were murmurs of admiration.

Kwani could not hide her pride. She said to Acoya, "See your father up there! One day you, too, shall wear the robe of the White Buffalo! See him!"

The sound of flutes and drums drew close and the Medicine Chiefs and warriors marched briskly, banners waving in the breeze, while Talasi marched before them in a stride that was almost a swagger. The Chiefs wore headdresses identifying their clans—buffalo horns, bear claws, antlers of antelope and deer, fox tails, and others. Warriors wore face and body paint in fierce designs. As the party was about to enter the edge of the city, their drums gave a shout, and as if by signal the warriors raised their shields and began a loud chant.

Involuntarily, the people of Cicuye moved back. Mothers and aunts and grandmothers grabbed children, and men clutched their weapons.

Chanting more loudly, and with drums booming, the party entered the city with an arrogant air—as though taking possession.

A sound stopped them in their tracks.

BOOM! BOOM! BOOM! The great thunder drum—answered by a piercing, wailing cry from the ridge, swelling as from the depths of Sipapu, calling the unseen, freezing the blood.

A moment of dead silence.

A long hiss of rattles and rasps from Cicuye's musicians. Then shrill cries of whistles and flutes in overwhelming, triumphant crescendo.

As the visiting party stood in stunned silence, Talasi stepped forward to be met by Two Elk and Cicuye's Chiefs and Elders. Talasi gestured greeting. "As you see, they have come."

Two Elk nodded. "We see, indeed."

Talasi smiled and motioned for the visiting Chiefs to approach. As they did so, the people of Cicuye inspected them minutely, whispering behind their hands. The fine headdresses of the Chiefs were much worn. Their garments were painfully shabby. Sandals and moccasins were meagerly adorned. Only their jewelry was of outstanding value—gifts donated by the people of Cicuye. The elaborate ear ornaments, bracelets, and necklaces seemed oddly out of place.

Two Elk spoke in sign language, a courteous formality.

"We of Cicuye are proud to welcome you. A dwelling is prepared for the Medicine Chiefs; tipis will be prepared for the others. We invite you to feast with us and to join us tonight at evening fire." He gestured. "Come, sit, eat."

One of the Medicine Chiefs stepped forward. He was of indeterminate age, thin, bony, and arrow-straight. Above prominent cheekbones, large dark eyes regarded Two Elk with quiet assurance.

He spoke in Towa. "I am Man Who Runs. Raven Clan. We thank you for your gifts and for your welcome. We are honored to be among you." He glanced up at the ridge. "We are prepared to commune with gods." He reached into a pouch at his waist and brought out a small object that he held in his closed hand. "I bring medicine." He opened his hand and extended it to Two Elk. Upon the open palm lay a quartz crystal, clear and shining.

"Ah!" It was a collective sigh. Such a crystal held powerful magic. A worthy gift!

Two Elk accepted it with courteous expressions of appreciation. Formalities were over.

Kwani whispered to Anitzal, "What do you think?"

Anitzal said, "I am not sure. Man Who Runs is not as I expected."

"Nor I. And the others?"

"Watch how they look at Talasi."

Kwani whispered, "I did. And I saw."

A look of intimate conspiracy.

▲ 25 ▼

It was not yet dawn. Talasi walked alone on the plain, alone but for those unseen. Ceremonies would commence with Sunfather's appearance, but there was something he must do first.

Moonwoman had departed but stars still glimmered. A cold autumn wind carried the fragrance of brush and grasses and of Earthmother's preparation for winter's rest. Behind him, Cicuye slept on its slope beside the ridge; before him, the plain spread endlessly under dimming stars.

It was silent but for the footsteps of the wind.

I must do it.

Slowly, Talasi approached the burial platform that rose in ghostly silhouette against the stars. He stood beside it with bowed head. After a time, he reached up for the hand at the platform's edge, and moaned softly at the touch.

"This is the day, my berdache. This day. I pledge my life. You will be avenged."

Only the wind heard.

Yellow Bird sat on the roof in the predawn chill and pulled her blanket more closely about her. Soon it would be pulatla; the day would begin. She wanted to see it all, savor it all. From this day, never would she be forced to leave the place where she was born and where her spirit would enter Sipapu. Never.

Her plan to defeat Tolonqua with the Truth Pipe had failed. But now success was assured. *There would be no city on the ridge.* Thanks to her and to Talasi. She hugged herself in triumph.

Aka-ti emerged from the hatchway with two bowls of porridge. She handed one to Yellow Bird and squatted beside her. They ate in silence, cupping the warm bowls in their hands.

Yellow Bird was glad they were alone. Two Elk was in the kiva where he had been for the last three days and nights,

praying, making sacrifices to the Above Beings, pleading
for success of the ceremonies. All very well, of course, but
as senior yaya, she was entitled to more personal attention
than Two Elk chose to give her lately. Instead, he expected
his mate to attend to all the wishes of his esteemed grandmother. She shook her head. How ungrateful he was!

Aka-ti pointed to the visiting Medicine Chiefs gathered
on the ridge. "They await Sunfather."

Yellow Bird peered, trying to see. "How many are
there?"

Aka-ti counted. "Six. No, seven." She swallowed a
mouthful of porridge and licked the rim of the bowl. "I
wonder what they are going to do up there. Nobody else is
allowed to be with them."

"Not even our Medicine Chief?"

"No."

Yellow Bird was relieved; without interference from the
local Chief it would be easier for the visiting Chiefs to do
what she and Talasi expected of them.

Near the fields at the edge of the city, firelight glimmered
through the translucent buffalo-hide coverings of tipis
erected for the visiting warriors. It had been a busy place
with singing, visiting, gambling, and loud discussions far
into the night. And many of Cicuye's girls had been enticed
with flute serenades to welcome an ardent suitor to her
dwelling or to a secret trysting place.

Now several warriors emerged from their tipis. Some urinated; others headed for the river.

Yellow Bird snorted. "They go to wash their man parts."

Aka-ti laughed. "Yes. They worked hard."

Yellow Bird slurped the last bit of porridge from the bowl
and wiped her mouth with the back of her hand. "It is good
that more of our girls will now have mates. More men to
work in the fields. More babies in the spring."

"Except from men who were with Talasi. If Talasi could
have babies, Cicuye would grow fast. But who would wish
for many little Talasis?" She spat in disgust.

For once, Yellow Bird held her tongue.

Kwani watched Tolonqua preparing for his morning chant
to Sunfather. The light of pulatla shone down through the
hatchway upon him as he knelt at their family altar and
removed the small bowl of meal that had been sanctified by
water from the sacred spring. He offered the bowl to the Six
Sacred Directions.

"You who are born of Earthmother, you who are fed by sky waters and embraced by gods of the wind, I give you now to Sunfather."

He rose. It was time.

Kwani took Acoya and followed Tolonqua up the ladder. Roofs were crowded with villagers and visitors facing east, bowls in hand. Because this was an important ceremonial day, musicians would accompany the singers in their salute to Sunfather.

The sky was bare; Cloud People had not come. But Sunfather's golden mantle glowed in splendor, growing brighter as he prepared to appear. When at last his rim was seen, drums and flutes and eagle-bone whistles shouted a glad accompaniment to the many voices singing, some in one language, some another.

Kwani looked at Tolonqua, splendid in his ceremonial garments and the robe of the White Buffalo. He sang to Sunfather as though for the first time, offering homage. Her heart swelled, and her voice joined his until the song was ended.

There was a sound from Acoya. He gazed at the golden sky, making sounds he had not made before. Kwani held him up to Tolonqua. "Your son sings also."

Tolonqua laughed and lifted Acoya high.

"See!" he called. "A boy who wishes to be Sun Chief!"

With laughter and talk, people gathered around the fires for porridge and corn cake. Girls who had found those they wanted as mates showed them off proudly while the men they had chosen looked with proprietary interest at the village—the fine dwellings and obvious luxuries—knowing that the people of Cicuye would now be theirs. With them they would share responsibility for the welfare of all.

Until now the visiting Medicine Chiefs had remained in the kiva performing final rites before confronting the gods on the ridge. Or so it was assumed. Food had been taken to them and handed down through the hatchway, the cover of which was lifted only enough for the bowls to be passed through. A stick with a strip of cotton cloth dyed red, thrust into the ground beside the hatchway, indicated that sacred rituals were in progress and entrance was forbidden. Now the kiva was empty but for the spirits. The Medicine Chiefs stood in a group on the ridge, conferring secretly.

Cicuye's Medicine Chief remained in his medicine lodge. The visiting Chiefs had been invited to conduct their ceremonies as Cicuye's guests; they were free to do so without intrusion. Cicuye's holy man prayed long to the Above Beings, beseeching them to bestow wisdom upon the visiting Chiefs and making their decisions true.

Upon the ridge, Man Who Runs gazed at the Chiefs gathered around him; his deep-set eyes illuminated the bony planes of his face as he spoke. "We know our responsibility—to determine if witches or evil spirits are here and whether or not a new city should be built." He fingered his several costly turquoise necklaces, ear ornaments, and bracelets. "We are adorned with gifts from the people of Cicuye who have much wealth; it is proper for them to give us objects of value in exchange for our services. As all of us know, Talasi, captain of Cicuye's Warrior Society, requests that we announce this place to be cursed by evil spirits so that Cicuye will not build another city here."

The men fingered their own ornaments with meaningful smiles.

Man Who Runs continued, "We of other pueblos know well that Cicuye is larger than ours, with more warriors to defend it. Many tribes come here for trade, some who covet riches and who ponder attack. A city here on this high place"—he swept his arm to encompass the view—"will grow stronger. And the stronger it becomes, the weaker we shall seem in comparison. Easy prey."

"Aye!"

Man Who Runs stood straighter and his face was stern. "However, it may be that only good spirits are here and will welcome a new city. Or perhaps evil spirits do dwell on this ridge. Our responsibility is to discover truth."

"Evil spirits abound!" a young Chief said, laughing and assuming a posture of ludicrous terror. His was the most lavish jewelry of all.

Man Who Runs speared him with a glance. "Let us remember who we are. Those who commune with the Above Beings. Holy men."

"And poor," the young Chief said.

Deep-set eyes regarded him with contempt. "We are rich in qualities of worth. Or do those of your village believe such qualities to be of no value?"

The young Chief scowled in angry embarrassment.

Man Who Runs said, "Talasi asked me to find this ridge haunted by evil ones, but I said only that I would determine whether or not evil spirits are, indeed, here." He paused and stared coldly at the young Chief and at the others. "Did any of you agree to find this ridge haunted regardless of whether or not it is? Because of valuables given?''

There was stony silence.

Man Who Runs reached into his medicine bundle and removed an owl—skin, feathers, and head intact. He slipped it over his hand and held it in lifelike pose. The eyes, carved yellow stones, stared hypnotically as the head turned from side to side.

The Chiefs murmured in awe and stepped back.

''My totem,'' Man Who Runs said. ''It speaks to me. It says I must speak truth. *This I shall do.*''

He returned the owl to his medicine bundle and stood silently, gazing into the distance at the sacred mountain where a cloud rose to touch the mountain's crest. His lips moved in silent communication with the unseen. Then he removed a long-stemmed pipe and a lump of polished crystal from his bundle and held the crystal in his outstretched hand. It reflected Sunfather's eye in brilliant sparkle.

''It may be that evil spirits *are* here. If so, Sunfather will tell us. Now we begin.''

Chanting, he pointed the long stem of his pipe to the Six Sacred Directions.

In the plaza, the Warrior Society gathered to dance. Talasi of the Warrior Society was in charge and strode about with pompous authority.

Kwani watched, frowning. He was not always so self-assured. Why was he now? She turned to search for Yellow Bird and saw her sitting with Aka-ti on the roof. The old woman spoke with happy animation. This was not usual, either.

Something is going to happen.

She wanted to be with Tolonqua, to feel the assurance of his presence, but he was busy with ceremonial duties. On the ridge, the Medicine Chiefs dispersed, each to a different area. What would they find?

She turned to Anitzal and Lumu sitting beside her. ''I can't help but feel that—''

''That something is wrong,'' Anitzal interjected. ''I feel the same way.''

''And I,'' Lumu said. ''But maybe we are wrong.''

''Maybe not,'' Kwani answered.

Hours passed, and the Medicine Chiefs remained on the ridge. In the plaza, dance after dance took place as various societies performed, but tension grew. What was happening up there?

The small cloud grew larger, rising over the mountain. A good omen!

Tolonqua stood on a roof with one of his hunters, Long See, renowned for keen eyesight. He was young and scrawny with thin hair, but with braids so thick it was suspected he padded them with buffalo hair as was done sometimes by those as unfortunate as he. Long See shaded his eyes with his hand as he peered long at the ridge.

"What do you see?"

"A flash of light. And another."

"Crystals?"

"I think so. And smoke. They smoke their pipes."

Tolonqua nodded. Smoke from sacred pipes sanctified and drove away evil spirits. "What else?"

Long See studied a Chief who stood outlined on a rise. He turned to Tolonqua with shocked surprise.

"An owl! An owl perches on his hand!"

Tolonqua stared. "Are you sure?"

"Look!" Long See pointed. "See his arm outstretched?"

Tolonqua shaded his eyes. "Yes, I see the arm. Something on his hand . . ." He remembered the macaw Kokopelli carried. "How do you know it is an owl?" Owls were supernatural beings, used by witches. Surely a Medicine Chief would not use an owl. "Perhaps it is a young eagle, or—"

"No. It is an owl."

"We saw no owl when the visitors arrived."

"Look at the head, the ears. An owl."

Tolonqua stared hard, but he could not see it clearly enough to know what bird it might be.

The two men glanced at each other uneasily. Tolonqua felt a knot in his stomach. Too much depended upon the decision of the Medicine Chiefs. What if they decided the city should not be built? His dream of a new city would be swept away like a straw in a flooding river. Even though the robe of the White Buffalo was his, his prestige and that of his family would be devastated.

He would not let himself think of it. His totem might be offended and would protect him no longer. But the knot grew tighter as shadows lengthened.

The dances ended and people stood on the roofs, staring up at the ridge, trying to see what was happening. Talasi, surrounded by admirers, told again of his journey to the pueblos, his meetings with the Medicine Chiefs, his pleas to help Cicuye, and the resulting agreement of each Chief to help Cicuye's people. He accepted congratulations modestly.

Yellow Bird watched from her vantage point on the roof. She saw the tiny flashes of light on the ridge and knew that crystals were at work. Crystals always told the truth. What if the crystals proved the ridge to be safe? Would the Chiefs say otherwise? Would they dare to lie?

A flicker of doubt touched her heart.

She looked at Tolonqua standing on a roof with Long See. They had been watching Talasi and talking with each other. Could it be that the Hunting Chief suspected? But no, that was impossible. There was no way Tolonqua could know what she and Talasi had planned. A masterful strategy!

Again, a tiny flash. What did the crystals reveal?

She swallowed, and clasped her hands nervously. Would Medicine Chiefs lie in return for rich gifts? Greed was a powerful persuader.

What would happen if they said it would be safe to build up there? What if it became known what she and Talasi had done?

Unthinkable.

She clasped her hands more tightly and murmured a prayer.

Kwani lay on her sleeping mat, Acoya beside her. She had come here to nurse him and to escape the crowd and the noise and the increasing tension. But tension still gripped her. She looked at Acoya, sound asleep, dark lashes against his round little cheeks. His future, too, was being decided. She sat up and hugged her knees. She wanted to be with Tolonqua, but he was with his men as a Hunting Chief should be. How would they regard him if his plan for a new city was defeated? He would lose face. She, Acoya, all the family would lose face. There would be no new city; Tolonqua's dream would die.

She rocked back and forth, moaning softly.

The cloud drifted over the mountain, arching into the blue. Man Who Runs inspected it with a seer's eye. Did Cloud People listen when he commanded witches and evil spirits to make themselves known and depart? Were his pleas for wisdom heard?

He and the other Medicine Chiefs had been long on the ridge. Now Man Who Runs called them together for conference. They stood on a high spot swept by winds, surrounded by mountains enclosing the narrow valley where the stream curved and glistened. Overhead, a golden eagle soared, dipping and circling with the wind. Below, the village waited. Man Who Runs saw Tolonqua standing on a roof; the white of his sacred robe was sharply visible. It was he who dreamed of the new city, a strange dream for a Hunting Chief. Did the White Buffalo inspire his desire?

He faced the Chiefs before him. One of them spoke. "I searched the southwest corner, over there." He waved an arm. "My crystal inspected every rock and bush. I communed with Earthmother. Prayers rose with the smoke of my pipe, but nothing answered, nothing spoke to me. I found neither good nor evil. As if this place were unborn."

"And you?" Man Who Runs asked another.

"I found a place where three large rocks sit together. My crystal clouded; something bad happened there, I think. I am not sure—"

"Yes!" the youngest Medicine Chief said loudly. "My crystal clouded also. Evil spirits are here!" He darted glances at the others. "Did you not find them?"

"Show me the place," Man Who Runs said. He removed his crystal and held it in readiness. He turned to the others. "Bring yours, also. We must be certain."

The young Chief flushed scarlet. "You question the powers of my crystal? You question my word?"

"Yes."

"You dare to insult *me*? Medicine Chief of the finest pueblo in the valley? You, of the poorest?" He stepped close, thrusting his face at Man Who Runs. "My people shall hear of this!"

Man Who Runs said coldly, "Your people are not as poor as mine, but they are poor." He flicked a glance at the rich necklaces heaving on the young man's chest. "Valuables will buy food but they will not buy honor." He turned away.

The young Chief lunged after him, but others grabbed him. He struggled to be free. "He insults me, my people, my village!"

Crowfeather, an older Chief with a scarred lip, released his grip on the arm of the young Chief and gave it a shove. "Man Who Runs speaks truth; we must remember who we are. Maybe no evil exists where Man Who Runs searched. But it could exist elsewhere. Take us to where your crystal clouded so that we may verify your discovery. The Medicine Chief of Cicuye—all the people there—expect us to speak of what we see with our own eyes." The scarred lip stretched in a mild smile.

"That is true." Man Who Runs stepped forward. "Some of you have not yet told of your discoveries. Tell us now."

"My crystal found a witch," one said. "Markings on a stone."

"Evil spirits hide in a small cave on the other side of the ridge. The crystal trembled in my hand," said another.

"You hear?" the young Chief shouted. "Evil is in this place!"

Crowfeather raised his hand to silence angry voices. "I found no witch, no evil spirits." He glanced at sullen faces confronting him. His scarred lip affected his speech but he spoke with dignity. "Good spirits are here."

The young Chief turned to confront the others. With obvious effort he restrained his anger enough to speak without shouting.

"We came here from our own pueblos as the people of Cicuye requested. We have labored long. We have done as we agreed. Now we shall tell what we have found here. We have earned these!" He removed his necklaces and shook them at Man Who Runs. "These buy corn, pemmican, food for my children, my family."

"Aye!" some cried.

"The welfare of our own people, our own pueblos, comes first. Do we want Cicuye to build a new city here so they may grow stronger?"

"No!" others shouted.

"We cannot lie. We are medicine men," Crowfeather said.

"You agreed to Talasi's request, did you not?" The young Chief's voice oozed derision.

"Yes. I thought he *knew* evil spirits were here and wanted the truth known to protect his people. I—"

He retreated to murmurs and snorts of disdain.

Argument followed, growing louder. Those who agreed with the young Chief were the loudest.

Man Who Runs frowned with concern. Perhaps evil spirits were here, after all, to cause holy men to behave this way. He stepped forward, speaking calmly.

"Let us discuss this as medicine men."

They ignored him.

When blows seemed about to be struck, a great sound

rose from the village, the chilling voice of the shell horn. Had something happened? The medicine men hurried to the edge of the ridge and stared down. People jostled one another, pointing to the sky. They shouted.

"Look! Look!"

Above the ridge where the medicine men stood, Cloud People gathered in majesty. Against a turquoise sky, misty and white, appeared an immense cloud figure.

The White Buffalo!

The men gasped and murmured in awe. The Spirit Being moved slowly; a dark eye gazed down. Commanding.

"Ah-h-h!"

"Aye-e-e!"

"You shall have your city!" Man Who Runs cried to the White Buffalo. "Here, on this place!" He raised both arms and began a sacred chant.

One by one, the others joined. Their voices rose to the golden eagle who received them on the wind and carried them to the Spirit Being and those who dwell among gods.

Shadows were long when the Medicine Chiefs returned, each with his sacred medicine bundle under the left arm. They descended the ridge in single file, led by Man Who Runs. People surged into the plaza, waiting eagerly. Cicuye's Medicine Chief with Two Elk, Talasi, Tolonqua, and the other Chiefs and the Elders stood in the center of the plaza, ready to receive them. They approached solemnly. A drummer began a throbbing beat as they lined up before Two Elk.

There was a pause, a moment of silence, pierced by the hiss of a spirit-talker rattle.

Man Who Runs spoke. "We have searched the mesa. We have spoken with Earthmother and with the Above Beings. We have conferred long with one another." He stood arrow-straight in his ceremonial garment that seemed to have lost its shabbiness. Deep-set eyes gazed at the people before him and at those crowding the plaza. It was suddenly quiet; even children were silenced by that gaze, that presence.

He continued, "By our sacred medicine we have spoken with the spirits of the ridge. We have communed with the White Buffalo."

There was a hushed murmur and people crowded closer. Man Who Runs gazed at Talasi who shrank back as though from a hot fire.

"It is true that our pueblos are small. It is true we have

few riches. But our medicine is good. It is powerful, and shall be obeyed."

Slowly he removed his new necklaces, bracelets, and ear ornaments and held them in his outstretched hand.

"I am humbled. I cannot accept these gifts as payment for a lie. We are shamed to admit that some of us agreed to say that evil spirits exist on the ridge so that we might receive these. It is not true; only good spirits are there. They welcome you. We are shamed. I return these riches given by Talasi in exchange for a lie."

He stepped forward and handed them to Two Elk who stood in stunned shock. Slowly, other Medicine Chiefs removed their jewelry, gave it to Two Elk, and stood with bowed heads. One by one, the rest followed. Some glanced bitterly at Talasi.

There was a muted growl like the sound of distant thunder, then an explosion of outrage as people turned to Talasi, encircling him like wolves.

Over the babble came the shout of the visiting warriors. "Build the new city!"

Cicuye's Warrior Chief elbowed his way through the crowd surrounding Talasi. Talasi cowered as from a hail of stones while people shouted in fury, "You gave our riches to make them lie! You lied to us! You lie! Two hearts! Witch!"

Talasi ran frantically to where Yellow Bird sat on her roof. "Tell them!" he cried. "Tell them I did your bidding!"

Yellow Bird gave a piercing cry. She bent her head between her knees, covered herself with both arms, and huddled in a tight ball as though returning to the womb.

The Warrior Chief strode to Talasi and confronted him with withering contempt. "You are captain no more. You dwell here no longer. Go!"

"Go!" the crowd shouted, shoving him. He fell and was kicked. He staggered to his feet and stumbled away with a crowd chasing him like dogs after a rabbit.

Only when he fled the city did they abandon him.

The plaza rang with happy cries. "A new city! A new city on the ridge! The spirits welcome us!"

Shouts of homage. "Tolonqua!"

Again came Yellow Bird's high, piercing cry.

The ceremonies were over, the visitors gone. A warrior with a prospective mate in Cicuye would weave a marriage robe for his bride, and return to help with the building of a new Cicuye. It would be a great city, beautiful, powerful, renowned, embracing forever the spirits of all whose hands created it.

Tolonqua and Kwani basked in triumph; already plans for building were under way.

Discussion about Talasi was endless. He had disappeared. Where was he now? No one knew.

Yellow Bird, also, was gone. Her body remained, but her spirit was in Sipapu. She was found upon her sleeping mat, her face turned to the wall. She was old, they said, and had willed herself to die. The broken Truth Pipe lay with her in her grave.

No one grieved.

It was some time before Talasi was discovered. Circling vultures marked the place. He lay beside Owa upon the burial platform, still wearing what was left of his ceremonial garments. The skeletal mouth gaped open in a silent scream; no eyes remained to stare at hovering birds.

One arm dangled over the platform's edge. The wrist had been slashed and the blood given to Earthmother.

▲ 26 ▼

Tolonqua limped up the trail to the ridge. It was cloudy and cold, not yet dawn. He walked carefully, leaning on his staff. First snow covered the trail; a chilling wind penetrated his blanket and probed his bones.

At the top of the ridge he stood in the semidarkness beside a pile of stones accumulated for building. They had been carried there by strong arms, or hauled by dogs and travois. To one side lay several large logs felled from the mountain and carried across the valley and up the trail by teams of strong young men. Some of the logs were already stripped of bark and smoothed, awaiting construction when it was finally decided what the plan of the new city should be. There had been much discussion, some of it heated, but no decision.

He had carried few stones and no logs. Two moons had passed since the sand painting, but his foot was no stronger.

The wind gusted cold, but no colder than the bitterness of his heart. He faced the truth at last. His foot would be weak always. A cripple he would remain until Sipapu called.

No challenging the horizons, no striding the plains for antelope and buffalo.

No exploring mountains for deer and elk and mountain sheep.

No running, running, running after game until the animal collapsed in exhaustion and he, triumphant, sped the arrow.

No dancing wild and free.

Never, ever, another race.

A cripple.

Forever.

He gripped the staff with both hands and pounded it upon Earthmother. "Why did you not heal me?" He pounded harder, jabbing his staff into the earth.

"Why?"

From the depths of his innermost self surged a fierce,

despairing cry that echoed over the ridge and across the valley.

"Why?"

Again, he jabbed his staff as though to pierce Earthmother's heart, then fell kneeling, and touched his forehead to the ground.

"Forgive me!"

He stretched at full length, pressing his face to the earth. He did not know how long he lay there, every part of him beseeching Earthmother.

"You withhold your healing power. You have a reason. Tell me what it is. Tell me, Sacred One!"

He opened his inner self, listening, seeking Earthmother's response with every pore. He did not know how long he lay there, but slowly, quietly, softly as first snow came the silent voice.

"Cloud People have spoken. The White Buffalo has spoken. Why do you not listen?"

He raised his head to gaze into the sky. A tiny cloud drifted along toward the Morning Star that burned with Sunfather's fire and Moonwoman's beauty.

"Behold!" the silent voice said.

The star's glow pulsed, descended, illumined the ridge. Before him, as in a dream, Tolonqua saw the new Cicuye as it would be—a fortress of stone, three and four stories high, encircling a vast courtyard. Solid outside walls with no openings faced a low wall surrounding the city—a boundary to be breached at an invader's peril. Mystical music, heartbeat of drums, chants of many voices, rose like invisible smoke to the Above Beings.

Tolonqua stared, spellbound with awe, entranced by beauty.

Again the silent voice spoke. "This is the city you will plan, the city you will build. To honor me, the White Buffalo, and the gods. People will work eagerly, for you are Building Chief of the new Cicuye. Share your dream."

The voice, the vision, faded and were gone. The Morning Star still glowed as Sunfather cast his mantle across the horizon.

Tolonqua rose, facing east. His spirit soared free, taking away bitterness and sorrow like an eagle carrying prey to its lofty nest.

He gazed at the Morning Star and a song surged within him. He flung his arms wide, singing.

"*A new city shall rise here.*
A new city will be born.
To honor you, O Holy Ones,
To honor you.
I will plan it, I will build it, Holy Ones!
Building Chief has promised.
Building Chief has spoken."

▲ 27 ▼

Huzipat, Clan Chief of the Eagle Clan, sat on his roof-top in the pueblo overlooking the Great River of the South. This is where he had brought his people four years ago when they abandoned their cliff city to join other pueblos where water would be assured always. This was a good pueblo with friendly villagers and fertile soil; crops were abundant and his people were happy here.

All but one. Tiopi.

Tiopi, mate of Yatosha, Hunting Chief of the Eagle Clan, still loudly proclaimed she was the rightful She Who Remembers. Never had she ceased demanding that the Eagle Clan send a party to obtain the sacred necklace now possessed by Kwani, the witch. And not a day passed but what she beseeched her mate to take her to Cicuye where it was known that She Who Remembers lived.

"Have you no pride?" she would say to Yatosha, poking his chest with her finger. "You allow that outsider, that witch, to possess the necklace belonging to us, to the Eagle Clan, and to me? Must I wait until my son—*my* son by Kokopelli—is a man to do what you will not nor cannot do?

Huzipat sighed and tugged at his ear as he was wont to do when worry was upon him. He was old. His young assistant was eager to become Chief. Too eager, maybe, but perhaps the time had come. Also there was the matter of Yatosha and the private conversation they had just this morning.

"Tiopi wants to migrate again. To Cicuye." Yatosha had looked down at his clasped hands, face expressionless, but Huzipat knew how unhappy and embarrassed he was.

"To obtain the necklace?"

"Yes. But more than that. She wants to confront Cicuye with proof—what she thinks is proof—that Kwani is a witch. She wants to destroy her and take her place as She Who Remembers." He clenched his folded hands. "She has been talking to the mates of my hunters, telling them what a fine place Cicuye is, and now some of my men want to migrate again, too.'' He shook his head. ''Why can't she be satisfied? A good place, good people—''

''Good people who become restive at Tiopi's constant agitation. I regret to say this, but it is true.''

Yatosha bowed his head. ''Yes. I should leave her. But . . .''

''But she is beautiful and has many fine qualities.'' Huzipat did not add that although Tiopi's beauty was fading and her fine qualities were few, Yatosha loved her helplessly.

''Then perhaps—'' The Hunting Chief glanced at Huzipat with something like relief. ''For the welfare of the Eagle Clan and the people who have welcomed us here, maybe it would be best if we go. I could take the hunters and their families with me who want to come; the others could remain here.''

''I shall go with you,'' Huzipat said.

''No! It is not necessary. You—''

''My assistant wishes to take my place. He has waited four years; it is time. I shall go.''

Remembering Kwani, Huzipat experienced affectionate concern. She would need him more than did the Eagle Clan when Tiopi unleashed her hatred. He tugged at his ear; unease lay heavily upon him.

Dangerous days awaited.

PART 2

▲▼▲▼▲▼▲▼▲▼▲▼▲▼▲▼▲▼▲▼

THE
POLLEN
OF DAWN

▲ 28 ▼

Tiopi huddled close to the night fire. All were gathered close—Yatosha and those of his hunters and their families who had chosen to make the journey to Cicuye; Huzipat, the old Chief of the Eagle Clan, weary with the journey, and Chomoc, asleep in his blanket—Kokopelli's son, four years old now. Around them, immense darkness of the empty plain closed in; above, a great black dome of moonless sky, glittering with stars, bent to an endless horizon. The night silence was breached now and again by the howl of distant wolves, or the call of coyotes, or the whine and whistle of the wind.

Tiopi shuddered. This was a foreign, evil place. No sheltering cliffs or caves, no sacred mountain. But Kwani had endured this journey and so would she. Tiopi wrapped both arms around her knees and inched closer to the fire. When they reached Cicuye, the necklace would be hers. At last. Tiopi smiled, grim lines sharp in the oval, aging face once so beautiful. She gazed into the fire, watching sparks drift upward in the darkness. If Kwani refused to relinquish the necklace, Yatosha and his hunters would change her mind. Yes. Not that Yatosha had agreed; that had not been discussed. It would happen when she, Tiopi, found it necessary to persuade her willing mate to do what must be done to achieve justice.

She looked at Yatosha sitting beside her on one side, and Chomoc asleep on the other. Years had not been kind to her mate; already he seemed old. It was Chomoc who gave her joy. At age four he was Kokopelli reborn. The same sloping brow, lion-colored eyes, and the promise of a fine hawk nose when he was a man. His little man part, too, would be fine and commanding one day. Like his father's . . .

Where was Kokopelli now?

It had been four years and nine moons since last he embraced her, hands and arms and lips and voice caressing.

Remembering, Tiopi felt a sudden moisture between her thighs.

But it was Kwani he had chosen as mate. Tiopi bit her lips.

Now Kokopelli was gone. Disappeared; no one knew where. Runners said Kwani had another mate now, the Building Chief of Cicuye. They saw the city on the ridge and told of its marvels.

A sudden thought jerked Tiopi upright. Did Kwani know they were coming? Did she realize the necklace—and the position and power that went with it—would be hers no longer? If so, she and the people of Cicuye might be prepared to defend—

She turned to Yatosha. "Does Kwani know we are coming?"

He shrugged. "Many people come. More are of little consequence."

"But does she know *I* am coming? I and Chomoc?"

For a moment he did not reply. Then he turned and surprised Tiopi with a burning glance.

"Look at the people here," he whispered, bending his head close. "Twenty-three of us seeking a new home, a better life, more forgiving gods. If Kwani and her people know you come, and why, permission may not be granted for us to join them, or even to enter the city. What then?" He bent his head closer. "Forget the necklace. It—"

"Never!" Tiopi hissed.

Four winters, four summers had come and gone, and with them Kwani's dream of the House of the Sun. She lived each day, each moon, each passing season as She Who Remembers, mother of Acoya, and mate of Cicuye's renowned Building Chief. Her own standing as She Who Remembers was now secure; she was respected and admired. But the old secret yearning for her own people, even though it was they who turned against her and cast her away, still lurked within her.

The blood remembers.

But she was Anasazi no longer. Towa now.

Today she sat in the inner courtyard of the new city, grinding corn with a group of other women, some recently arrived from remote villages where drought and Pawnee raids had driven them away. Kwani looked around her at the city enclosing them with strong stone arms. How beautiful it was!

Dwelling units were joined side by side, forming a vast oblong so that the rear wall of each unit formed one massive exterior stone wall with no openings. The only entrance to the city was by a gate with a heavily barred door protected by guard-houses on either side. A number of ladders led up the outer walls to the roof of the first story; the ladders were strong but light in weight and could be pulled up in an instant.

The courtyard formed a plaza faced by two- and three-story dwellings fronted by a continuous walkway all the way around on each story. Dwellings on the second and third stories were set back to allow room in front for the walk-way; the buildings formed giant steps. Roof overhangs offered protection from snow and rain or blistering sun, and provided a shady, breezy place underneath—to work, and to hang corn and squash to dry, or to sit with friends and gossip and watch activity in the plaza below. Ladders connected the stories; more reached down to the plaza where three circular kivas, dug into Earthmother's domain, poked ladders through roof openings, fingers pointing at the sky.

In years to come, newcomers would marvel at the city's defensive construction; villagers could go anywhere inside the city without leaving the outer wall formed by the ad-joining stone dwellings. Anyone standing on the top roof on that high ridge had a sweeping view in every direction.

What a fine city Tolonqua had built! Kwani thought. Her heart filled and she began to sing.

"Is it not beautiful? Is it not truly?"

Other women joined in the Corn Grinding Song, pushing the mano stones back and forth on the metates in time to the rhythm. It was a fine day in early spring. It had rained the night before and the air was redolent with the earthy smell of stone walls secured with adobe mortar, and the fragrance of Earthmother's breath from mountains where snow still clung to the peaks. The homey smell of pinyon smoke from cooking fires and the tantalizing odors from simmering pots floated over the city that stood proud and beautiful on the ridge. Children ran and shouted, chasing one another. Kwani looked for Acoya but he was not among them. At age four he was eager to learn and was probably with Tolonqua or the weavers, or flint knappers, or the Medicine Chief, or the Sun Chief, asking endless questions.

How beautiful our city is! Kwani thought again. She

warmed with pride at Tolonqua's achievement, and her eyes searched for him where more second-story dwellings were being built. He was nowhere to be seen.

She turned to Lumu who sat nearby, pushing a mano stone back and forth with effort. Lumu was pregnant and rejoicing; already her belly swelled. Micho, her adoring mate, said the child was a boy with long legs for running—like his father—and those legs took up much room.

Kwani swallowed her envy. She wanted to give Tolonqua many children, but these last years had been fruitless. Often Kwani wondered if she would ever have the daughter she longed for. Lumu already had two small girls.

"Lumu, do you know where Tolonqua is?" Kwani asked.

Lumu looked up from the metate and Kwani noticed again the dark circles under her eyes and the drawn look about her face. Not all was well with Lumu, Kwani knew, and she felt a pang of concern; she had become fond of Tolonqua's pert little sister.

There was a sound of pounding, stone hammer on wooden beam. Lumu smiled. "There is your answer."

It was true. Wherever building was in progress, Tolonqua was there, supervising and helping. Kwani sighed. Tolonqua had brought honor to his people, his city, and to her and Acoya. Yet his spirit seemed shadowed. Why did he not laugh and sing and joke with the hunters as he used to do? True, Long See was Hunting Chief now, but although Tolonqua was no longer Chief he was invited to conduct pre-hunting ceremonials as he had always done, an honor bestowed because of his powerful totem and the robe of the White Buffalo. Ceremonies completed, the hunters would depart, bidding Tolonqua farewell.

How difficult it must be for him! Kwani thought. Men are brothers to cougars and to all predators. Born to hunt, to kill for food. When the tribe's best hunter is left always behind . . . But he is Building Chief now. The first.

Kwani scooped her ground corn into a basket, placed the basket upon the metate with its mano stone, and rose. "He will be hungry soon." She lifted the heavy metate to her head in one graceful motion and strode toward their dwelling.

Lumu watched her go. She thought, I wonder if Kwani knows.

Tolonqua stood on a second-story roof inspecting a new stone wall being built by one of Anitzal's nephews recently arrived from a distant village. The boy was a thin, taciturn youth who spoke seldom, but he knew mortar and stone. It would be a good wall.

Tolonqua looked down at the city he had created. It was still growing as refugees continued to seek admission and escape from drought and Pawnee raids. As newcomers arrived, a few at a time from different places, different clans, they were absorbed into the Turquoise Clan, Tolonqua's own, or the Cottonwood Clan. Both these ancient clans originated in the old village, deserted now but still standing at the base of the ridge. Many of its strong timbers were enshrined in dwellings in the new Cicuye.

Tolonqua climbed a ladder down to the roof of the first story where he sat and dangled his legs over the edge. Yes, it was a good city. The fame of Cicuye and its Building Chief had spread; some traveled for many moons to see it. The city would continue to grow with more immigrants, more clans, greater wealth as newcomers brought more skills.

But Tolonqua was not content; a feeling of dissatisfaction nagged at him. Cicuye was not yet the city revealed to him by the Morning Star. Memory of the vision haunted him, tugging at his consciousness, returning in dreams. His city should be taller, longer, wider, with a low wall encircling the entire outer edge of the ridge to mark Cicuye's boundary—a boundary to be breached at a trespasser's peril. The White Buffalo and the Above Beings had decreed it.

It must be done. For four years he had planned, organized, supervised every aspect of construction, driving his men to labor through winter's cold and summer's blazing heat, but no matter how much was accomplished, unfinished work remained and his dream was unfulfilled.

In the courtyard below, boys played hunting games with dogs and with one another; their shouts and the yips of dogs rang clearly in the morning air. Tolonqua remembered how he played as a boy, how he grew to become master hunter, esteemed Hunting Chief, challenging the horizon in long hunting trips for buffalo.

The great sweep of sky and plain, the camaraderie among his hunters, the nights at the campfire, the rising at pulatla for another fulfilling day, and then, at last, the great brown herd of massive animals against whom he and his men pitted their skill and courage—as their grandfathers had done before them for countless generations.

The stalk, the cunning approach, the masterful kill. The triumphant rejoicing in the blood!

The return home, laden . . .

He swallowed. That was long ago. He was Building Chief now.

"Father!"

It was Acoya, climbing a ladder to Tolonqua. The boy's sturdy legs brought him swiftly to the roof. He was tall and strong for a four-year-old Towa. But of course he was Anasazi. It was hard to remember that. Acoya was born of Kwani, but the boy belonged to him and to his people. Always, he had longed for more sons. But—

"I greet you, Father."

"My heart rejoices," Tolonqua replied in what he knew was an Anasazi manner, but courtesy was courtesy regardless of tribe and valuable for his son to know. He looked down at the round face aglow with exuberance, and dark eyes sparkling, and smiled as he always did.

"Father, it is time!"

"For what?"

"See?" He opened a small fist to show a crushed flower, a mallow rosy as sunset. "It is spring!"

"Ah. So it is. The first flower."

"Yes!" Acoya bounced with excitement. "You said I would be old enough for a bow and arrows when spring came. Remember?" Again he held up the flower. "It is time!"

Tolonqua concealed his surprise. He had been so involved with making his city grow and with latest news from a runner—news he had concealed from Kwani—that he had almost forgotten that Acoya was growing fast. He was four years old; now his education should begin. He must master the bow and rabbit stick, learn how to make and use snares, how to track, to hunt, to survive under all conditions. He must learn to plant and make crops grow; to build, knap flint, make weapons, weave; to master all manly skills. He must understand the tribe's political structure: the individual clans consisting of an extended family and those adopted into it; the secret societies, the various Chiefs and their responsibilities to all the clans, and the City Chief, the head of all, leader of all. And he must learn tribal history, customs, chants and ceremonials, and his responsibilities to family, clan, city, and tribe. Above all, he must thoroughly learn his sacred, all-important obligations to the gods.

Tolonqua put his hand on the boy's shoulder. How small and vulnerable it seemed!

"Come. We shall begin."

Kwani knelt at the spring to fill her water jar. Lumu was there with her two little girls helping since she was big and heavy with child. Kwani tried to ignore envy of Lumu's daughters but it was difficult. She wanted a little girl so badly—like Lumu's beautiful youngest who was as pert as her mother and who promised to be as athletic as her father, the racer Micho.

Kwani lowered her water jar into the spring by a net fastened to a rawhide rope. The filled jar was heavy and Kwani strained to pull it back up.

"I will help," Lumu said.

"No! Let me!" the girls cried in unison.

"Thank you, but I can do it," Kwani said. Then seeing their disappointment, she smiled. "But it would be nice to have help."

The girls grabbed the rope with Kwani and the three of them pulled up the jar with much little-girl squealing.

Lumu laughed. "It makes them feel grown-up."

Kwani lifted the heavy jar to her head. "Thank you," she told the girls, and started up the worn and rocky path to the ridge. The path was steep, but Kwani's sandaled feet knew it intimately. Occasionally, she reached up to balance the jar more securely, but her small body knew the path also and commanded each muscle to carry her in regal erectness, jar and all.

"Ho, Kwani!"

Two girls approached with water jars. They were former students whose first moon flow proclaimed their marriageable status. They were on the way to the spring where young braves might be waiting; it was a good place to meet away from watchful eyes. Many a girl had found a mate there.

"I greet you," Kwani said. As the girls grew closer, she added, "Lumu and her daughters are down there but they will be finished soon."

The girls blushed and giggled. One said lamely, "We go for water."

"Of course." Kwani smiled as they passed. They were so young. What would be their paths of life?

As she neared the top of the ridge, the city sounds, the smells, the looming stone walls with ladders reaching up, the sounds of pounding, of men working, were comforting in their assurance of invincibility. Kwani stopped to gaze as she often did, and again her heart overflowed with pride at what Tolonqua had accomplished, and was still accomplishing as more people came and the population grew. This morning the Crier Chief had announced that more new arrivals were on the way. More newcomers would require even more dwellings and hard work for Tolonqua who felt his responsibility keenly.

She rounded the steep path to the city exterior. Two logs lay where four young men straddled them, scraping off the bark with flint tools. Others climbed ladders to the roofs with bulging baskets of stones on their backs while boys gathered small stones and pebbles to be used in mortar. There were loud grunts of effort, snatches of talk, and quick bursts of laughter. More building was under way for the new arrivals. Who would they be?

Usually, Tolonqua would be standing by, helping and supervising, but he was not there. She spoke to one of the young men, little more than a boy, a refugee recently arrived. He straddled a log and bent over it, scraping.

"Where is the Building Chief?"

He pointed to a roof. "I saw him up there with his son." He bent again to his work, intent upon proving his worthiness to be accepted in Cicuye. Kwani saw that he had cut the back of his hand and it bled a little as he pushed the flint scraping tool back and forth.

"You have hurt your hand. Come with me and I will apply a poultice."

He shook his head, scowling.

Kwani understood. He did not want to abandon a man's job because of a little cut and be treated for it like a child. It would diminish his manhood.

Kwani left him and followed the wall to the ladder leading to the roof of their dwelling. Bracing the water jar with one hand, she climbed the ladder and set the jar down on the roof walkway that extended all the way around. It was a busy place with women sitting outside their doors in the fresh morning air to repair winter garments or to make new sandals or pretty ceremonial things; some women had carried out their metates and manos and sat in a group, grinding corn and gossiping. Others freshened the walls of their dwellings with new white plaster. Naked toddlers wandered about, puppies yipped and tumbled, little girls sat with their mothers to do what their mothers did, or played down in the courtyard, running, shouting at games with the boys. From the kivas came chants and drums in preparation for Ceremonies Before Planting.

Across the courtyard on the opposite walkway from where Kwani stood, a stone wall was being built for another third-story dwelling, and a group of old men stood around offering advice. Tolonqua and Acoya were not with them.

"Ho, Kwani!" Anitzal called. She sat with friends outside the door of her dwelling, stringing stone beads. "Come join us. We have news!"

"Yes. When I put this away."

Kwani carried the water jar to the door of her second-floor dwelling that opened to the walkway. In front of each door was a short little wall extending into the walkway to mark an area belonging to whoever lived there. Kwani stepped over hers (would there ever be a crawling baby protected there?) and the sandstone sill, and entered her luxurious home. The floor, which was the roof of the story below, was built of cedar shakes across which were laid twigs of willow and wild cherry, then topped with adobe the thickness of a man's hand from wrist to tip of the middle finger. The surface was nicely finished to form a smooth, hard floor for the second story, and felt good under bare feet. Kwani set the jar down, slipped off her sandals, and wiggled her toes. How refreshing was the caress of cool adobe after the climb from the spring!

A hatchway in the corner led to the first-story room below. This was special, a wonderfully convenient and safe storage place especially good for corn. The floor was sandstone slabs to protect against burrowing animals and to prevent moisture from seeping up. Sometimes, Kwani stored her water jar there, but today she set the jar by the fire pit in the corner of the second-story room—her cooking and working room—and went into the adjoining sleeping room to tidy up before joining Anitzal. Anitzal, the senior yaya since Yellow Bird died, always looked nice and Kwani felt self-conscious if she didn't look as presentable as She Who Remembers should.

She stood in the sleeping room—Imagine! A room only for sleeping and for storing clothing and ceremonial things!—and brushed her hair with a bundle of twigs fastened tightly at one end. She shook a bit of dust from her cotton garment, rearranged her necklace, and added another of bird-bone beads finely polished. She wondered idly what the news might be; there was always something going on of one kind or another.

"Come!" It was Tookah, one of the women with Anitzal, standing outside the door. "We have important news!" Her round, plump face quivered with excitement and effort to restrain herself from blurting what was the senior yaya's privilege—being first to tell.

Kwani smiled. Tookah relished gossip as a dog loved bones. "I'm coming."

The women seated with Anitzal moved over to make room for Kwani and Tookah as they came. The group sat on the short little wall in front of Anitzal's door, so she was the hostess and had provided a bowl of pinyon nuts and another of buffalo jerky that were passed around and dipped into. Most women were busy mending or making something so hands would not be idle as they visited.

"I greet you," Anitzal said, using the Anasazi welcome for Kwani.

"My heart rejoices." Kwani sat down with Tookah and helped herself to the nuts. "What's the news?"

"Ah." Anitzal beamed at Kwani, her aged face aglow. "More people come."

"Yes, I know." Kwani hid her disappointment. This was little news; people came all the time to trade or to visit. "The Crier Chief announced this morning—"

"But he did not say who these people are." Anitzal selected several beads from a small bowl and held them in her hand as she spoke. "You may know them." She popped the beads in her mouth to be removed one at a time to be strung, relishing Kwani's avid interest. "They are Anasazi."

Kwani gasped. Her own people! "From where?"

"The runner did not say. But Long See saw smoke signals," Anitzal answered carefully, ejecting a bead from her mouth. "He says they are come from the Eagle Clan. They are going to ask permission to live here."

Tookah said, "From the Eagle Clan!" She lay her handwork down and leaned forward, peering at Kwani with sharp little eyes. "Aren't they the ones who claimed you were a witch?"

Anitzal spit beads into her hand with a force that sent some flying. "Everyone knows about that, Tookah. One with the powers of She Who Remembers will have enemies. Enemies who will lie in an effort to destroy her. I will not allow these lies to be repeated."

Anitzal glared at Tookah who ducked her head like a prairie dog diving into its hole. The other women became very busy with what they were doing and did not look up.

Kwani's heart jerked. What if it was Tiopi? But she spoke calmly. "They may be the ones; not all accused me."

There was a strained silence.

Finally, Kwani asked, "Was there a woman with a boy about the age of Acoya?"

Anitzal gave Kwani an understanding glance. "Women and children are among them. Families. Migrating." She paused, and added, "This is your home; we are your people now." Softly, "Have no fear."

Kwani pressed the scallop shell of her necklace to her to still her jerking heart. Tiopi was coming. She knew that with certainty.

With Tiopi came trouble; that was certain, too.

▲ 29 ▼

"**W**hy didn't you tell me?"

They sat by the fire pit, Kwani and Tolonqua and Acoya, scooping pemmican stew into corn cakes Kwani baked on a slab built-in for the purpose. Kwani flipped a corn cake and handed it to Tolonqua. "You *knew* they were Anasazi. You knew—"

"I was afraid your old enemies might be among them, but I could not be sure." He scooped up the stew with the corn cake and took a big bite. "I saw no reason to tell you what I did not know to be true. To concern you needlessly." Another bite. "Delicious!"

"Delicious!" Acoya echoed in excellent imitation, with juices running down his chin.

Kwani sat back on her heels with exasperation. "Instead, you let me learn from Anitzal in front of Tookah, that old gossip, and all the others." She brushed damp hair from her forehead with both hands. "I was humiliated."

"What is hum—" Acoya tried to say the word.

"It means I am very angry with your father."

"I apologize," Tolonqua said, smiling. He rose, swept Kwani into his arms, and held her tightly. "I shall make amends." He kissed her hard several times and set her back down.

Kwani was not appeased. "They may be here by tomorrow. I must prepare myself, seek a vision. Tiopi—"

Remembering, it was like yesterday. How Zashue and Tiopi conspired to have her accused of witchcraft by finding owl feathers in her dwelling—feathers they had concealed. She had escaped in the darkness, stumbling blindly through the canyon, seeking a hiding place where none existed while Yatosha and his hunters tracked her with baying dogs. She remembered how she clawed her way up a cliff and climbed a tree to be surrounded by dogs and by hunters with drawn bows as if she were an animal. . . . Had Kokopelli not arrived when he did, she would be in Sipapu now.

Instinctively, Kwani held her necklace to her with both hands. She was protected by the Ancient Ones. But Tiopi . . .

For a moment Tolonqua sat looking at her, understanding warming his gaze. There was no banter in his eyes or his voice as he said, "You are my mate. My people are your people. We, all of us, will protect you from enemies, no matter who they are. Don't you realize that?"

Kwani looked up at him, at the lean, bronze body bare but for a breechcloth, and the strong face with black eyes burning—eyes that melted her anger like sun on snow. She saw the ardor in him, the strength. The old sweet fire in her flamed again.

Tolonqua saw her glance and responded with his own. He crouched behind her, encircling her with both arms, kissing her neck, her cheeks, murmuring soft words. He slipped his hands inside her garment and cupped both breasts, teasing, caressing. He felt their warm response.

"Now?" he whispered.

"Yes!"

He picked up Acoya and carried him to the door. "Go to Lumu. She will feed you also."

"But—"

"Go!" Tolonqua said firmly. He picked up a new little bow he had made for Acoya. "Here, show them your new weapon."

Acoya took the bow and ran down the walkway. When his footsteps died away Kwani was already naked on the sleeping mat, her legs parted in invitation. With a growl of pleasure and desire, Tolonqua tossed his own garment aside and threw himself beside her, caressing, murmuring, caressing, until she could wait no longer and pulled him close. *Closer.*

As he thrust deeper and deeper still, Kwani cried out in wild delirium. It was as though they had never mated before.

This time, surely, Tolonqua's seed would grow.

Tiopi stood with her group, staring up at the remarkable city on the ridge aglow in midmorning sunlight. On either side of the ridge, steep rocky slopes, bare of trees and brush, defied concealed approach. As they watched, ladders that had leaned against blank exterior stone walls were pulled up, and warriors with bows and arrows appeared on rooftops.

"They take no chances," Yatosha said with unconcealed admiration. "We must ask for admission."

"Yes." Huzipat stepped forward. The long journey had taken its toll; he leaned heavily upon a staff. "I will signal." Holding his staff in both hands, he raised it overhead and down several times. He turned to Yatosha. "Now the arrow."

From his quiver Yatosha lifted an arrow with a red feather where the flint head should be. Aiming carefully, he shot the arrow high and true so that it landed on the roof where warriors stood.

Tiopi watched tensely. If the red feather were returned, permission for an emissary to approach would be granted. Otherwise, any approach would be an act of war.

For some time a discussion took place on the roof. Then the arrow arched high, returning, and landed a distance away. Chomoc ran to pick it up and brought it to Yatosha. The red feather remained on the tip. Permission was granted.

"I will go," Huzipat said.

"I will go, too!" Chomoc announced to the amusement of everyone but Tiopi. She looked down at her small son, so like Kokopelli with that arrogant, four-year-old stance.

"Someday you shall."

"I want to! Now!"

"No." Yatosha's voice was firm. This boy was becoming a problem. More Toltec than Anasazi.

Chomoc tilted his head to look down his nose at Yatosha. "Someday I shall."

"We shall see," Yatosha said.

Huzipat took Yatosha aside. "I think Chomoc should come with me."

Yatosha flushed angrily. "Why?"

"Because Kwani is there."

Tiopi overheard and shot Huzipat a sharp glance. The old Chief was growing feeble. Chomoc was son of Kokopelli, Kwani's former mate. The boy she should have had. To flaunt Chomoc under Kwani's nose now was hardly wise if they wanted acceptance, especially if Kwani were in a position of authority—as She Who Remembers certainly should be. And would be when she, Tiopi, had the necklace and position that were rightfully hers.

"Chomoc should stay here with me."

But he was already gone, striding manfully beside Huzipat as slowly they climbed the steep path to the ridge.

Tiopi watched as a ladder appeared and was lowered. Three men descended and stood waiting for Huzipat and the boy. On the roof beside the ladder stood a woman, and Tiopi knew at once who it was. The way she stood and held herself was unmistakable.

"Kwani!" she said, and clenched both fists.

Kwani watched them coming, the bent old man and the boy.

The group at the base of the ridge huddled together like deer encircled by hunters. Kwani strained to see them. Were they really Eagle Clan? Was Tiopi among them?

Knowledge pierced her like an arrow. She felt, more than she saw, Tiopi. There was no mistake; the animosity Kwani sensed was tangible. *Never would that woman enter the city!* Kwani climbed down the ladder, ignoring shocked comments from those gathered to watch, and joined Two Elk, Tolonqua, and the Warrior Chief who stood waiting for the old man and the boy.

Two Elk scowled. "You should not be here."

"They are Eagle Clan and do not speak Towa. I will translate for you," Kwani said graciously. She had become fluent in Towa during these past years.

Tolonqua cast her a quizzical glance. He could translate, also, and sign language was understood by all. But he stood silently with Two Elk and the Warrior Chief as the old man made his laborious way up the path with the boy at his side.

"Oh!" Kwani gasped.

Tolonqua turned to her. "What—"

"Huzipat!"

She ran to meet him. He saw her coming and stood, arms outstretched, waiting. She flung her arms around him.

"Huzipat!"

How good to see him! But how aged he had become! She hugged him again, savoring the smell of his garment and of him. Anasazi.

Finally, she said, "I greet you." She did not feel the tear on her cheek.

"My heart rejoices," the old Chief said brokenly, and wiped away a tear of his own. He gestured for the boy to come forward. "This is Chomoc, son of Tiopi."

Kwani looked down at the boy who returned her gaze with one so like Kokopelli's that Kwani was momentarily undone. That brow, the downward turn of those lips, the eyes, that stance . . . But this was Tiopi's child.

"I greet you, Chomoc."

"My heart rejoices," he replied dutifully, and pointed to the ladder. "I shall climb up there."

"You shall stay with me and be silent," Huzipat said. He leaned forward and whispered to Kwani, "They wait for us."

Kwani saw that Tolonqua, Two Elk, and the Warrior Chief were waiting with obvious impatience and embarrassment. Her impulsive action had been improper; that she knew. Regaining her composure, she led Huzipat and Chomoc to Two Elk.

"This is my friend, Clan Chief Huzipat of the Eagle Clan, and Chomoc, son of Tiopi, mate of Yatosha, the Hunting Chief."

Turning to Huzipat, she said in Anasazi, "This is Clan Chief of the Towa, Two Elk. And the Warrior Chief. And my mate, Tolonqua, Building Chief of Cicuye."

Huzipat and Chomoc took the hands of Two Elk and the other two and breathed upon them as Anasazi custom required. Breath was the essence of life and to bestow it was a gesture of respect.

Introductions completed, Two Elk regarded Huzipat and Shimak with pompous authority. He looked at the group waiting at the base of the ridge, glanced at Tolonqua and the Warrior Chief, and back at Huzipat. Ignoring Kwani, he said in sign language, "Why have you come?"

"We seek admission to your city." Huzipat was fluent in sign language and his gestures were graceful, though slow.

Two Elk turned to the Warrior Chief and said in Towa, "Shall we invite him to discuss it?" Usually, such an invitation was routine, but Kwani's action in greeting Huzipat first had usurped his authority and he was not pleased.

The Warrior Chief looked at Tolonqua. Tolonqua looked at Kwani. It would be her decision. She swallowed, and fingered her necklace, silently beseeching the Ancient Ones.

"Help me!"

Huzipat stood in stolid dignity, gaze averted politely. Chomoc tried to imitate Huzipat, but his four-year-old curiosity made him stare avidly at everything. Below, the group waited. Kwani knew their weariness; she had made that journey. But she sensed Tiopi's bitter malice like a poisonous essence.

Again she looked at Huzipat. He returned her gaze, and she saw the appeal in his eyes, the desperate weariness. She remembered his kindness when she needed it most. She looked at Chomoc and the amber eyes, Kokopelli's eyes, looked back.

She turned to Two Elk. "A discussion will allow you to reach a decision," she said in Towa. "It might be wise to invite Huzipat and the boy into the city for that purpose while the others wait where they are."

"I agree," said the Warrior Chief.

Tolonqua nodded. "And I."

"Very well." Two Elk motioned Huzipat to the ladder, and Chomoc followed eagerly.

Observers on the roof parted to make way for Huzipat and the odd-looking boy. Two Elk led them down another ladder to the courtyard.

"We shall confer in the kiva."

Women were not allowed in kivas except by special invitation. Kwani waited to be invited, but Two Elk still smarted under her breach of etiquette that he felt had demeaned him.

Tolonqua said, "Since these are Eagle Clan, I think Kwani should be present during the discussion."

"Yes. She knows them, knows how they think," the Warrior Chief added. "That is a large group out there."

Two Elk frowned. But Kwani was She Who Remembers.

"Very well," he said grudgingly, and Kwani followed them down the ladder.

It was cool and dim and smelled of mountain tobacco. The Medicine Chief was already there. The stuffed chickadee he used to wear had finally come apart, but another was firmly in place behind his left ear, and the obsidian and turquoise eye was baleful as ever. He rose in greeting.

Introductions over, they sat on mats provided, and Two Elk took his position of honor by the fire pit. Kwani sat beside Tolonqua who leaned to whisper, "You did well."

Two Elk took a pinch of cornmeal from a bowl by the fire pit, offered it to the Six Sacred Directions, and tossed it into the coals smoldering there. Deities dutifully honored, he cleared his throat and assumed a position of suitable dignity.

He spoke in sign language. "You have said that you of the Eagle Clan wish to join us in our city here. Why?"

Huzipat rose slowly. Kwani could almost feel the pain in his joints. He signed, "We are migrating as the gods decree. As our fathers did, and their fathers. We have come far. We respectfully request permission to stay."

The Medicine Chief's good eye shot a penetrating glance.

"You passed other cities on the way here. Why did you not stop there?"

"They are poor."

It was an honest statement, and understood.

"Ah. You wish to be here because Cicuye is rich?"

Huzipat hesitated only a moment. "Yes. Because we can make it richer."

"How?" Two Elk asked quickly.

"Our Hunting Chief is famed for his skills, as are his hunters. Our women are fine potters, our men good weavers, good farmers." He paused, and added, "Our warriors are among the best."

Two Elk frowned at the subtle warning. "All those we already have. A poor pueblo needs you more than do we." He paused. "Reveal to us the real reason you wish to settle here."

Huzipat was not intimidated. He signed, "I have told you. We obey our gods. Can you use more strong young men to help with the building? Can you use more hunters, more potters, more weavers and makers of fine things? More brave warriors? These we offer in trade for what your city offers us."

Kwani smiled. Two Elk was no match for the old Anasazi Chief when it came to negotiation. Of course Cicuye needed what was offered. Needed it badly.

Tolonqua raised his hand in gesture-before-speaking. "I suggest that the matter be brought before the Chiefs and Elders for consideration, and that the Eagle Clan people be invited into our city for rest and for food until a decision is made."

"Provided their weapons are left at the wall," the Warrior Chief said.

It was agreed.

Kwani struggled with mixed feelings. She was glad for Huzipat, glad for Chomoc who had behaved well during the discussion, sitting silently and respectfully. But Tiopi . . .

▲ 30 ▼

Kwani stood on the roof, watching the approach of the Eagle Clan people. They were a ragged, travel-worn group, and her heart went out to them. Then she reminded herself that these were the ones who had wanted to kill her and who had driven her away to die alone in the wilderness. But children were among them, dirty and thin, and there were babies in cradle boards. She knew others lay in Earthmother's arms between here and the cliffs of home.

Yatosha walked in front, Tiopi beside him. As Tiopi came closer, Kwani saw how the bitterness in her face had aged her. But a measure of her great beauty remained, a fact not lost upon men watching on the roof. There were comments.

"Look at that one."

"I wonder who she is."

"Too old for me."

"Not for me. I like them ripe."

"I wonder who she is."

As Tiopi reached the ladder, she looked up at Kwani. It was as though a spear were thrown. From deep inside herself Kwani summoned calm indifference and returned the gaze coldly. Flushing, Tiopi averted her eyes, climbed the ladder, and passed Kwani by. The others followed: young men with bows and arrows, shields and spears and heavy burdens; their mates with packs and cradle boards and children. No aged people were among them; only Huzipat had endured the journey.

As they reached the roof, they were welcomed. Men were asked to leave their weapons, and were reluctant to do so, but savory cooking smells enticed, and they agreed.

Eagerly, Kwani sought faces she knew. It had been nearly five years; the men were from other clans who had joined the Eagle Clan when they took mates; none she knew.

"Kwani!"

It was Ki-ki-ki, a young woman of fifteen now, with a

mate and a baby. Kwani hugged her and they babbled news until Ki-ki-ki's mate intervened.

"Food is ready. Come, I'm hungry!"

All were led to the courtyard where pots hung over fires and bowls and baskets of food awaited. Chomoc was there with Huzipat, seated by a cooking fire, gnawing a juicy hunk of venison. He saw Tiopi and Yatosha and ran to them, meat in hand.

"Look! Here, have some."

They declined with dignity. They were starving, but it would not be seemly to admit it by sampling their son's food.

Kwani watched as the group observed the usual preliminaries—tossing a bit of food into the fire as an offering to the gods before eating. Then they impaled a large piece of meat on whatever they had that was sharp enough, bit into it, sliced a piece off, chewed with gusto, then bit into the meat again and sliced off another piece.

The Warrior Chief strode about giving orders while he looked the men over secretly, making sure no weapons remained.

Tolonqua saw Kwani and came to meet her, limping as usual.

"Did you see anyone else you know?"

"Only one, Ki-ki-ki, who was a child then. She has a mate and a baby now." Kwani laughed. "It makes me feel like an old yaya."

He glanced to where Tiopi sat with Chomoc and Yatosha. "What about her?"

"I think she still wants to be She Who Remembers instead of me. She wants the necklace. I think that is why she came." Kwani's voice was steady but Tolonqua sensed the tension.

"If she tries to make trouble they will not be allowed to stay. You know that."

"When will the meeting take place to decide whether or not they can live here?"

"Tomorrow."

Kwani touched her necklace. Tiopi had nearly destroyed her once. Could she do it again?

Preliminaries were over: the solemn incantations, the offering of meal to the gods, the smoking of the Medicine Chief's pipe and his prayers to the Above Beings. Now Two

Elk faced the Chiefs and Elders gathered before him; they sat in the courtyard so that all might hear the discussion.

In front were Huzipat and other men of the Eagle Clan. Behind them women and children sat close together as if for mutual support. Only Tiopi was aloof, gazing stonily ahead with Chomoc at her side. The courtyard and roofs were crowded with people of Cicuye and some from neighboring pueblos who came to trade and to relish the proceedings; open meetings on such a matter were rare and not to be missed. Whispered rumors claimed that enemies of She Who Remembers were among the visitors—incredible news! There was an undercurrent of excited expectation.

It was a sharply cool morning in late spring. In the valley below, and to the west and the south, spring had come weeks before, but in these highlands, open to winds sweeping from the plains, spring came late. A frost the night before lingered in the air to chill bare arms, and Kwani pulled a blanket closer around her shoulders. Tolonqua, splendid in the robe of the White Buffalo, sat with the other Chiefs; Acoya was with a group of boys, whispering and giggling and shoving one another about until quieted by stern reprimands.

A murmur of anticipation quieted as Two Elk cleared his throat to begin.

"We of Cicuye welcome those of the Eagle Clan who honor us with their presence," he intoned grandly, signing the words simultaneously. "We hope your hunger is satisfied and that your sleeping mats will be comfortable this night."

He paused, looking over the visitors who murmured in appreciation, and continued, "All weapons are in the safekeeping of our Warrior Society and will be returned when the decision of our Chiefs and Elders is known as to whether or not our visitors may remain. If they are to stay, the weapons will be given to them at once. If not, weapons will be returned after our honored visitors are outside of the city."

The visitors looked at one another; there were uneasy comments.

Two Elk continued, signing, "Cicuye's Chiefs and Elders will now discuss whether or not Eagle Clan people may live among us."

The Medicine Chief rose. He regarded the visitors solemnly, turning his head from side to side so that the stuffed chickadee bobbed in lifelike fashion. His remarkable obsidian and turquoise eyes was admired by all.

"I have conferred with my totem and with the gods," he signed. "They urge caution." He sat down.

Now the Sun Chief rose. He was tall and thin, with deep-set eyes surrounded by a mass of wrinkles. The austere planes of his bony face, and the way he stood, proud and straight, gave him profound dignity.

"I am Sun Chief of the Towa," he signed. "I mark the years, the seasons, the days. Sunfather's path, Moonwoman's journey, the passage of stars, are in my keeping. As you know." He inclined his head courteously. "Time, like constellations, moves in a circle; there is no beginning, no end. All returns. All." He paused for emphasis. "Therefore, let us consider what has happened in the past so that we may plan the future with wisdom." He gestured to Tolonqua. "I respectfully ask our Building Chief, mate of She Who Remembers, to relate the past as it involves us of the Towa and those of the Eagle Clan."

He sat down. There was silence for a long moment. Finally, Tolonqua rose, limped to the front, and faced the people. Whispers quieted as he stood there. In the sharp sunlight, with the wind tugging at his sacred robe and blowing the hair from his forehead so that his black eyes pierced like lances, he commanded respect.

"It is true. I am mate of She Who Remembers, formerly of the Eagle Clan, formerly mate of Kokopelli. It was Kokopelli who rescued her from the Eagle Clan."

Kwani was surprised; this was a frontal attack. There were uneasy glances, whispers, murmurs.

Tolonqua continued, "It is not for me to tell what happened to She Who Remembers. She is here. She will tell you herself." He sat down.

Kwani was shaken. Why hadn't he prepared her for this? Instinctively, she grasped her necklace and sat motionless for a moment. Then she rose.

"The Eagle Clan has a noble heritage," she began, trying to keep her voice steady and calm. "I am proud of that heritage for although I am Towa now, I am Anasazi by birth." She looked at Huzipat. "Some of the Eagle Clan welcomed me and treated me kindly when Kokopelli brought me to their city. I thank them for that." Huzipat smiled, and Kwani continued, "But others did not want me there and conspired to accuse me of witchcraft." Kwani gazed pointedly at Tiopi for a long moment, ignoring shocked murmurs growing louder.

"Accusations proven true!" Tiopi shouted.

"Never!" Tolonqua cried. He rose to stand by Kwani, facing them. "Again and again, jealous enemies"—he looked pointedly at Tiopi who glared furiously—"have tried to prove witchcraft, and always they have been proven to be wrong, proven to be what they are. Jealous. Envious. Two-tongued. Unworthy to empty the night pot of She Who Remembers, let alone assume her place."

Yatosha jumped up. "I demand an apology! I—"

Shouts from the people of Cicuye drowned him out.

Slowly, Huzipat stood, raising his hand for silence and for gesture-before-speaking. His age and his dignity, his calm assurance, quieted the crowd.

When it was totally silent, he said, "It is true that we of the Eagle Clan did not honor She Who Remembers as we should. That we regret—"

"No!" Tiopi cried.

"That we regret," Huzipat continued quietly. "But that is past, swept away, a broken pot on a flooding river. It is past." He gazed a moment into the distance as though the past swept by. "Now we are here, offering ourselves, our skills, our good intentions—"

"Not enough," Tolonqua interrupted. "You of the Eagle Clan drove Kwani away to die. You chased her with hunters and dogs and tried to kill her. All returns, as our Sun Chief has said. How can we know that you of the Eagle Clan, and Tiopi, she who sits there"—he pointed—"will not again try to destroy my mate and seek the powers of She Who Remembers, giving the necklace once more to the Eagle Clan?"

"The necklace is ours!" Yatosha waved a hand at his people.

"Aye!" they shouted.

"Given to us by Earthmother," Tiopi cried.

"Aye!"

"No," Kwani said. "Earthmother gave it to the first one she chose to be She Who Remembers. It belongs to no clan, only to she to whom it is given. We who are She Who Remembers are not of one clan, one people. We are of all womankind."

"Chosen by the gods," Tolonqua said. "This you know."

"It is ours!" Tiopi shouted.

"Aye!"

"They have what is ours!" Tiopi jumped to her feet, her face flushed, her eyes wild. "Take it!"

A sound like distant thunder filled the courtyard. Some

of the Eagle Clan men rose. Immediately, Cicuye warriors surrounded Kwani, bows drawn.

"Send them away!" the people of Cicuye shouted.

"Now!"

"Aye! Now! Now!"

In the hubbub that followed, Cicuye's warriors whipped arrows from quivers; drawn bows pointed at men of the Eagle Clan who stood in furious helplessness with no weapons, and closed in by hostile bystanders.

Again, Huzipat rose. Again, he signaled for silence, but a rumble remained.

"It is not necessary to threaten us," Huzipat said. "You have our weapons."

The Warrior Chief signaled, and slowly the bows were lowered. Only then was it silent once more.

Huzipat turned to gaze at the people thronging the courtyard and crowding the roofs. Kwani saw his weariness, his bitter defeat, heard the despair in his voice as he continued.

"We shall depart. We have no wish to be among those who threaten us, who do not want us here."

"Go!"

"Yes, go. Now!"

Kwani looked long at Ki-ki-ki and her baby, at the exhausted women and thin children. She saw their defeat and fear.

"Wait!" She faced the people of Cicuye with raised hand. "I wish to speak."

It took some time for silence, but when at last it came, Kwani spoke loudly and clearly so that all might hear. Signing simultaneously, she said, "I cannot allow the skills these people bring to be lost to us because of what has happened in the past. It would not be good nor wise. Surely you, all of you"—she indicated the men in particular—"will not ignore our needs and best interests because of the foolish, long-past actions of a woman."

The sarcasm in her voice was not lost on the warriors of both sides. They squirmed. Tiopi's efforts to shout again were muffled by Yatosha's hand clapped to her mouth.

Kwani continued, "These are Anasazi, people of my blood. I do not fear them. Nor do I fear that woman, Tiopi," she added, and looked at the Cicuye men with a glance that implied "Do you?"

Sardonic chuckles, whispers, glances.

"Let us consider the advantages to us all. Anasazis are fine craftsmen, good farmers, successful hunters, obedient to the gods. They are peaceable. They work hard. They have good medicine, good dances. Their pottery brings much in trade.''

There were nods of grudging agreement. Anasazi pottery was famous, much superior to that of the Towa, and was traded over vast distances. Unquestionably a valuable resource.

Kwani noted the response. They were listening.

''They come to trade themselves and their skills for what our city provides. How wise would we be to refuse?'' She turned to Two Elk. ''I respectfully request that the people of the Eagle Clan be allowed to stay.''

There was stunned silence, followed by a sound like wind in the grasses. People whispered among themselves, gazing at Kwani, and at Tiopi who sat in stony-faced silence.

Tolonqua turned to Two Elk and to the other Chiefs. ''If She Who Remembers agrees, should we refuse?''

Two Elk sat in silence, pondering. He gestured, and the Chiefs and the Elders grouped together for quiet conference.

There was uneasy silence as people waited. Babies cried and were hushed; children squirmed impatiently. The Eagle Clan people showed no emotion; their faces were blank as an adobe wall. But Kwani sensed their tense anxiety.

Two Elk rose and motioned for Huzipat to join them. The old Chief did so, bracing himself on his staff.

Again there was quiet conference, uneasy waiting.

At last, Two Elk rose. ''I invite Huzipat of the Eagle Clan to speak.''

Huzipat faced his people. No hesitancy was in his voice as he said, ''The Chiefs and Elders of Cicuye ask us to remain. I have accepted. From this moment we and the Towa are brothers.''

''And sisters,'' Kwani added.

''Not I!'' Tiopi said under her breath. But nobody heard her in the din of surprise and welcome.

▲ 31 ▼

Kwani walked alone on the ridge. She wanted to be away from the city, to be by herself awhile. To think.

A moon had passed since the Eagle Clan people came. They were eager to be incorporated into the life of Cicuye and outdid themselves in making things and helping with the building of their dwellings; even the women worked with the building, carrying stones and bringing pebbles from the river to be used in mortar. Kwani saw Tiopi seldom; Tiopi avoided her. Ki-ki-ki made friends with others her age and sat often at their doors, sewing or grinding corn or playing games or just visiting. Huzipat was regarded with respect by the Chiefs and various clans, and spent much time in the kivas.

It was good to have Anasazis there, even those she had not known, but Kwani was surprised to discover it was not as she had expected. For four years she had lived with Plains culture blended with Pueblo—the Towa of Cicuye. And although this was her home, her life now, her spirit was not at ease. It was as if her spirit felt it did not really belong here. Yet when she was with the Eagle Clan, Kwani did not feel as she thought she would, that they were truly of her blood.

The northern part of the flat ridge was higher than the rest, rocky and barren. Kwani climbed to the highest edge and sat on a small boulder overlooking Cicuye surrounded by its mountains, and at the valley with its little river running through. It was pleasantly warm and sublimely peaceful there, under blue, blue sky with floating clouds and surrounded by rugged terrain where lizards and rabbits and mice and other small creatures concealed themselves.

As Kwani watched, a rattlesnake slithered around a rock and saw her. It did not coil and rattle to threaten her; rather, it paused and looked at her, its handsome markings shining in the sun.

"I greet you, Honored One," Kwani said respectfully. Serpents were Spirit Beings; they brought rain.

For a moment the snake was motionless, looking at her. Its tongue flicked. Was it telling her something? Then it slid gracefully away, disappearing among the rocks.

For some time Kwani sat there, allowing the peacefulness to seep into her and clear her mind.

How fortunate I am to have all I ever wanted—a home, a mate, a child, and people who regard me as their own.

Then why this haunting spiritual unease?

She clasped her necklace in both hands and closed her eyes, straining for communication with the Ancient Ones and with the Above Beings. Lately they seemed more inaccessible; it was harder to reach them. She prayed earnestly.

I am Anasazi, but not one of them. I am Towa, but not Towa. My spirit seeks what I do not know. I am blessed with all my heart ever yearned for, yet I am somehow alone. This I do not understand. . . .

A mockingbird swooped by, trilling. The notes trailed like bright ribbons in the breeze.

Tell me who I am!

There was no response. But the answer was already known, lingering in her consciousness to be heard once more. *You are not of one clan, one people. You are of all womankind. . . .*

One of many who had gone before. Loved, admired. But alone.

Alone.

It was the price one paid for being She Who Remembers.

Again the mockingbird flew by, singing. *"Beautiful, beautiful, all, all, all!"* it rejoiced.

Is this what the Ancient Ones wanted to tell her? All was beautiful, all was well? Birds carried messages to and from the Above Beings. Her heart eased.

She rose and started the walk back to the city. Her mind was clear; the dark cloud within was blown away as if by the wind. True, she was alone in spirit. But she was loved, she had Tolonqua, she had Acoya, the child of her blood and her body. Someday, perhaps, she would have another. A daughter.

Cicuye glowed in the morning light. It was a beautiful day; she would return the long way around. The city faced east; she would go by the western side where cloud shadows made patterns on the mountains across the valley.

She ignored a small shadow within. Response from the Ancient Ones came seldom now. Was it because the Ancient Ones felt they were needed less?

Yes, that was it. Of course.

Acoya walked along the edge of the ridge. He was naked as he enjoyed being, and although the wind was cold, Sunfather's morning light was pleasantly warm. He chewed on a handful of jerky as he looked down at the cluster of tipis spread below. The newcomers lived there until his father had more homes built for them inside the city. It looked like an interesting place but he was forbidden to go there.

He wondered where that boy was. The one with the long nose and funny-colored eyes. He had seen him with his mother, the woman called Tiopi, but she had not let him play on the ridge.

The ridge was fun to play on, especially the west side where everything that nobody wanted was tossed over the edge. There was a pile reaching halfway down to the bottom. He looked at it, trying to see what had been thrown away. Broken pots, a worn-out sandal, lots of corn husks, bones, all sorts of things. He wanted to slide down to the pile and poke around, but the side of the ridge was too steep. Besides, Tolonqua had told him to stay away.

"Ho!"

It was the boy with the long nose. He stood a distance away, looking at Acoya in a way that made Acoya feel he might want to be friends, but wasn't sure.

Acoya gestured and pointed to the pile. "Look."

The boy came and stood looking. He was naked also but for a short breechcloth that he pulled aside to urinate into the pile. That seemed a good idea, so Acoya urinated, too.

The boy spoke in a language Acoya did not understand, so Acoya shook his head.

The boy pointed to himself. "Chomoc."

"Acoya." He attempted sign language. "Can you play up here now?"

Chomoc understood. He signed, "No. But I do."

He looked at the bit of jerky left in Acoya's hand. Acoya offered it and Chomoc accepted it matter-of-factly, chewing with relish.

They sat companionably, dangling legs over the edge of the ridge.

Acoya signed, "Your eyes are funny."

"Kokopelli." Chomoc spoke proudly, looking down his

nose. He signed. "I am like my father." Again, he said, "Kokopelli."

Acoya was impressed. He didn't know who Koko-somebody was, but he must be important for Chomoc to talk that way. A Chief, maybe. "My father is Building Chief."

"I know." Chomoc chewed the last bit of jerky and swallowed. "Your mother is a witch."

"She is not!"

"She is! That's why she has blue eyes."

"She is not!"

"She is! My mother told me."

Acoya gave Chomoc a shove. "She is not!"

Chomoc shoved back. "Yes she is!"

Acoya shoved harder and Chomoc shoved harder still. A shoving match followed. Acoya tumbled over the edge of the ridge, sliding, clutching at rocks that came loose and slid with him. He landed in the smelly pile of refuse, scratched, bruised, and outraged. "Look what you did!"

Chomoc tried to laugh, but he was scared; he wasn't supposed to be on the ridge at all. How was he going to get Acoya back up? People came here all the time to dump trash; somebody would see them and tell Yatosha. Or worse, they would tell the witch!

"Get me out of here!" Acoya shouted.

Chomoc did not understand the Towa words, but there was no mistaking the meaning. He pondered the situation. Of course he could run home and pretend he knew nothing about it and let somebody else find him and get him out. But he couldn't leave the witch's son in such a predicament; she would do something terrible to him and maybe his whole family. No. He had to get Acoya out himself before anybody came.

He looked around for something to hand down for Acoya to grab on to and be pulled up. Nothing.

"Get me out!" Acoya shouted again. "Get my father!"

Chomoc judged the distance to where Acoya was. It was a long way, but maybe he could ease himself down, carefully so as not to slide, and then reach down to hand Acoya something to pull him back up with. But what?

His breechcloth! It would do. He pulled it off, held it in his teeth, and inched over the edge of the ridge. His toes dug into the rocky soil for a footing. Some rocks broke loose and rolled down.

"Ow!" Acoya yelled. "That hit me!"

Chomoc clutched the soil and scrabbled with his feet for footing, but more rocks broke loose and he began to slide. Helpless to stop, he tumbled down and landed beside Acoya.

They looked at each other. Acoya sat on his rump in stinking rubbish, and Chomoc had landed at an angle so that one arm and leg were covered with something gooey and the other leg stuck up in the air. The breechcloth was still in Chomoc's mouth, and he looked ridiculous. Acoya giggled, and Chomoc yanked the breechcloth from his mouth with his free hand, scowling furiously. Rubbish on the slope, loosened, tumbled down and landed on Acoya's head leaving a crown of debris with a corn husk dangling in front of his nose.

Chomoc laughed. Acoya jerked the corn husk away and laughed, too. They laughed together—so hard they did not notice the one who stood on the ridge, staring down at them unbelievingly.

"Acoya!" Kwani shouted.

"Get me out!"

"Don't move! Stay as still as you can. I'll get help."

Kwani hurried toward the city. Acoya and Chomoc, laughing down there in the rubbish pile! Laughing when they could tumble down to the rocky bottom of the ridge at any moment! She had to find Tolonqua. He had forbidden Acoya to play there; he would be angry! How did those boys get down there, anyway? How would Tolonqua get them back up?

The sound of pounding led her to Tolonqua on a second story. It was he who did the pounding, inching a heavy beam in place.

"Tolonqua! Come!"

He looked up, startled. "What is it?"

"Acoya and Chomoc are in the rubbish pile. Get them out before they fall all the way down!"

Workers heard and gathered in disbelief. "In the rubbish pile? How?"

"Who knows? Get them out!"

Tolonqua grabbed a rope used for hauling up a basket from below. Others snatched whatever was handy that might be useful, and ran. Kwani followed. Word spread fast, and soon a crowd headed for the dumping place. They gathered at the edge of the ridge and looked down at two scared four-year-olds who were no longer laughing.

Kwani called again, "Don't move!"

"I won't."

Chomoc said nothing, staring up into blue eyes.

Swearing under his breath, Tolonqua tied a large knot at one end of the rope. "I told him to stay away from here." He leaned over the edge. "I'm going to throw down a rope. Hold it tight in both hands and I'll pull you back up. Use your feet to help push yourself up the slope."

He tossed the rope down and Chomoc caught it. Kwani thought he would want to be the first to come up, but he gave her an odd glance and handed the rope to Acoya.

"No," Acoya said. "You first."

But Chomoc pushed the rope at Acoya, insisting.

Acoya took it, grasped it firmly above the knot, and used both feet to push his way up as Tolonqua pulled. Rocky soil loosened and fell, tumbling to rocks far below.

Kwani bit her lips. Acoya's face was taut with effort, his eyes screwed almost shut. For an instant Kwani remembered how she swung high over rocks below when she was lowered by ropes to the Place of the Eagle Clan; how frightened she was.

But Acoya was protected by the White Buffalo. She must remember that.

"You are safe," she called to him. "Don't be afraid."

Another long tug and Acoya was on the ridge. Kwani enfolded him in her arms. He smelled bad and he was filthy, but she couldn't hold him close enough.

Acoya released himself and looked at her.

"I wasn't afraid," he lied. "But—" He looked at Tolonqua, straining on the rope as he pulled up Chomoc.

"I know. You disobeyed." She wanted to reassure him, to tell him he would not be punished, but he had to learn to be a man. Instead, she held her nose. "You smell awful. Go bathe in the river."

But Acoya stood with Tolonqua, watching while Chomoc was pulled up. When he reached the top, they faced each other, grinning.

Acoya signed, "We stink. Let's go to the river."

As they ran off, Kwani felt someone staring at her from behind. It was Tiopi. She shot Kwani a dark glance and disappeared in the crowd.

The show was over, so the crowd dispersed, laughing at the remembered sight of two small, very dirty boys in the rubbish pile. But Tolonqua was not amused.

"He must learn that when he is forbidden to do something, it is for his safety," he told Kwani. "They could have fallen—"

"You are right, of course. But do you remember how you were when you were his age? Were you adventurous, too?"

He smiled suddenly. "Yes, as a matter of fact. But I learned discipline. So must he."

Kwani nodded. Discipline was necessary. But . . .

At the river Chomoc and Acoya wallowed and splashed, laughing and bragging about how they pulled themselves up with the rope. But secretly each worried about what awaited in the punishment certain to be forthcoming and didn't want the other to know he was scared.

They did not have to wait long. Tolonqua and Yatosha appeared on the bank.

"Come out now," they ordered.

When the boys stood dripping before them, Tolonqua said, "What happened?"

The boys glanced at each other, hung their heads, and did not reply.

"Speak!" Tolonqua ordered.

"I fell," Acoya said.

Yatosha had learned some Towa during hunting trips. He said, "What made you fall?" and repeated the question to Chomoc in Anasazi.

Acoya did not reply. Chomoc squirmed. "He fell, so I tried to pull him out—"

"With what?"

"My breechcloth."

Yatosha and Tolonqua glanced at each other. Tolonqua's lips twitched. He signed, "And you fell in, too?"

Chomoc nodded.

Yatosha looked sternly at Acoya. "What made you fall?"

Acoya hesitated. "We were playing—"

Yatosha turned to Chomoc. "What made Acoya fall?" he demanded sternly.

Chomoc looked away as though he had not heard.

"I slipped," Acoya said.

Again Tolonqua and Yatosha exchanged glances.

Tolonqua said, "You were forbidden to go there, you know that. And now you know why; it is dangerous. Both of you could have fallen to the rocks below and been squashed like beetles. You disobeyed. You must be punished."

Yatosha said the same thing to Chomoc. The boys stood in stolid silence, water dripping, heads bowed, waiting to learn their doom.

Tolonqua said, "You must empty our night pot every morning for an entire moon."

Acoya was stunned. A girl's job! And a nasty one, at that! He flushed red and stared stonily ahead.

Yatosha suppressed a chuckle with great effort. He could not impose a similar punishment because they used no night pots in tipis; they stepped outside. Instead, he said, "For an entire moon you shall have no bow, no arrows, no rabbit stick. Nor are you to use those of any other."

Chomoc swallowed. His rabbit stick and bow and arrows were his greatest joy. To be deprived for an entire moon was forever. But Acoya had shown no emotion, and neither would he.

As the boys stood in stolid silence, the men looked at each other with unconcealed pride. Each boy refused to implicate the other and they accepted their punishment without protest.

They would be men to reckon with one day.

▲ 32 ▼

Another moon passed, and with it, the sixth moon of Lumu's pregnancy. Labor had begun and stopped. Now, in the seventh moon, it began again.

Kwani and Anitzal sat with Lumu in her dwelling. Kwani was much concerned; Lumu did not look as she should. Her face was drawn and feverish, and dark shadows lay under both eyes. Her ankles and legs looked strange. Puffy.

Anitzal bent over Lumu who lay on her sleeping mat although Sunfather was high on his path.

"Here, drink this." Anitzal handed Lumu a mug of hot brew made from the boiled roots and leaves of a mountain plant that would stop labor. Lumu swallowed it and promptly vomited.

"It won't stay down."

"You must try again," Anitzal said anxiously.

"Here, let me help," Kwani said. She poured the rest of the brew into the mug. "I will sing it down."

Remembering how her singing helped to ease pain on the battlefield, Kwani began a soft, sweet, wordless song and handed the mug to Lumu.

"Drink it slowly," Anitzal said, her face tight with concern.

The brew stayed down, but Lumu groaned. "It hurts. Sing some more."

Words began to form in Kwani's song.

> *"Wait, baby, little one.*
> *Wait. It is not yet time."*

Micho, Lumu's mate, appeared at the door. He stood in worried silence, watching. Finally, he said, "The Medicine Chief and his helpers will come." His face screwed itself into a pretense of his old cocky smile. "You won't have to go to the medicine lodge. I have paid them already. . . ."

His voice trailed off as Lumu groaned again, turning her face away.

Kwani thought, We need the midwife, not the medicine men, but the midwife was in a distant village attending to a relative. She sang to the unborn child.

> *"Wait, little one.*
> *It is not yet time."*

Footsteps approached. Kwani thought it was the Medicine Chief and she stopped singing, but Tiopi paused at the door. Kwani gaped in surprise; since the meeting in the courtyard, Tiopi kept to herself.

Tiopi saw Lumu and an expression flickered in her eyes and was gone. Without a word she walked away.

Anitzal and Kwani looked at each other.

Kwani said, "I wonder why—"

"Curious, perhaps." Anitzal turned to Micho. "Is the sand ready? If the baby comes it will be needed."

"Sand is here."

Two of Tolonqua's aunts eased through the door carrying a pile of sand on an old blanket. They placed it on the floor beside Lumu's sleeping mat. This is where she would squat if the water broke and the baby was ready to be born; the sand would absorb the blood and the afterbirth.

The sound of whistles and a flute announced the coming of the Medicine Chief and three helpers. The Chief chanted as he came, tossing meal to the gods. He paused at Lumu's door.

"I command evil spirits to leave this place." He waved an eagle feather over the doorway and entered the room followed by the helpers, all chanting and offering meal to the spirits of the dwelling.

The small room was crowded now, so Kwani squeezed into a corner. The air was too warm—heavy with the odor of the bitter roots smoldering in the fire pit, and the smell of the medicine men and the ointments and paints on their sweating bodies.

The Medicine Chief bent over Lumu and his good eye inspected her carefully. He felt her abdomen, laid his ear to it and listened, and pressed, massaging.

The water broke, brownish green, and gushed with a foul smell, a stench. It made Kwani's flesh crawl.

Could it be the odor of death?

She had to get outside! She slipped along the wall and

stepped out to the walkway. Relatives were there—aunts and cousins and clan brothers—waiting to know if the baby had come. Lumu's two little girls approached Kwani eagerly.

"Do we have our baby now?"

"Not yet." Kwani tried to sound reassuring, but death was in that room. She felt it.

The youngest said, "We want to go in there."

Kwani shook her head. "The medicine men are busy; they do not like children to be present when they are bringing babies. It is harmful to the mother."

"Oh." She looked wistful. "I want to see my mother."

"You may. Later."

An agonized scream pierced the air, and another and another.

"Mama!"

The people on the walkway crowded the door to look inside. One said, "The baby is coming now. But not the head—"

They talked in hushed, frightened voices. Another scream trailed to muffled silence.

"Mama!" the little girl cried, sobbing.

Micho stumbled out the door, leaned over the walkway, and gagged wretchedly. Then, ashamed of displaying weakness, he hurried away.

Another scream. Moaning. Silence.

The Medicine Chief emerged. His face and body paint were streaked with sweat. The obsidian and turquoise eye was pushed up to his forehead where it stared in terrible intensity at the people pressing close. His one good eye searched among those who waited breathlessly.

"Where is Micho?"

"He left. He was sick—"

"Bring him back!"

A cousin, a young boy, ran after him.

There was a gasp as Anitzal emerged with a bloody little bundle wrapped in rags. Tears streamed and her voice choked with sobs.

"Dead. Covered with blisters, rotting." Tears gushed, and she held up the little bundle. "A boy. Dead." She could say no more and returned inside where the tiny body would be buried under the floor so that its spirit would return to be reborn.

A heartbroken cry arose. Kwani pushed herself through the grieving group and looked in at the door. One medicine priest held Lumu in a crouching position over the sand; she hung limply in his grasp. Another helper pushed down on her back while the Medicine Chief pushed down on her abdomen to expel the afterbirth. The other priest chanted supplications to the gods while the aunts who had carried in the sand huddled against the wall.

"She bleeds too much!" one cried.

Softly, Kwani began to sing her wordless song. Her voice blended with the chanted supplications, pleading for Lumu's life. On and on she sang, but the afterbirth did not come.

"Stop!" Lumu gasped weakly. "Let me rest."

Another gush of blood stained the sand already crimson. The Medicine Chief gestured, and they laid Lumu upon her mat.

Still Kwani sang, pleading, but the mat turned red, and redder still.

Lumu's eyes closed, and she was still.

The Medicine Chief rose wearily. "I can do no more. It is the will of the gods."

Micho burst through the door. He saw, and threw himself beside her. Her face, serene at last, seemed touched with a smile.

"Lumu!" he whispered. "It is I, your Micho."

Only her spirit heard.

Lumu was buried outside a corner wall of her dwelling, wrapped in the finest blanket the Turquoise Clan could provide. Grieving was allowed for four days until Lumu and her baby were safely in Sipapu. After that, no mention would be made of the dead; the spirit might return to haunt the living.

But the heart holds its secret sorrow; Lumu was loved. Tears were shed where none could know.

Kwani sat alone in her dwelling with the door closed. She hugged her knees, moaning as she rocked back and forth.

I tried to save them. I prayed, I sang. . . .

Sounds of the city drifted in. Footsteps ran across the roof and a dog followed, barking. Somewhere a woman laughed.

I called to the gods. They refused to hear me.

Kwani clutched her necklace with both hands, pressing it to her. She closed her eyes, commanding her spirit to find the Ancient Ones.

You who were She Who Remembers before me, come!

She strained to hear the words unspoken, to feel the comforting presence.

Nothing.

A cold finger poked Kwani's heart. Were her powers fading?

Three weeks passed.

Early one morning Kwani sat on the small boulder where she came sometimes to be alone and close to Earthmother. She removed her sandals and pressed her feet to the ground. Small pebbles in the rocky soil kissed her feet.

"I greet you, Sacred One," Kwani said respectfully. She wiggled her toes and her feet, acknowledging Earthmother's welcome.

For a time she sat there, gazing at the distant mountains aglow in Sunfather's early light. She breathed deeply of the cool, sweet air, cleansing herself inside, refreshing her spirit. Cleansed and renewed, perhaps her spirit could reach the Ancient Ones again.

A beetle crawled over her foot, tickling with his tiny legs. "Ho, little brother!"

It scurried away among the pebbles, leaving no trace.

Kwani clasped her necklace and closed her eyes, straining to find the Ancient Ones.

Earthmother greets me, your little beetle comes to me. Why do you not hear me?

For a long time Kwani waited, pressing the necklace close. There was no reply.

Somehow, she had offended the gods and the Ancient Ones! She was being punished. Despair enveloped her.

"Forgive me! Come to me!"

There was no reply, but slowly Kwani's mind quieted like a pool whose ripples reach the shore.

A sudden realization made her gasp; her moon flow was long past due. Tolonqua's seed was growing!

She was pregnant!

▲ 33 ▼

Tiopi, Yatosha, and Chomoc sat in their tipi eating the last meal of the day. It was piki bread, thin and delicious, with rabbit stew and roasted squash seeds; a feast. Tiopi watched Chomoc and Yatosha with satisfaction as they ate with loud enjoyment, smacking their lips and belching in appreciation. Never would they find one who cooked better than she! When they finished and were content would be the time to say what she was waiting to say.

Yatosha wiped his mouth with the back of his hand and gave a final comfortable belch. Chomoc wiped his mouth in the same way, but couldn't manage another belch. They sat back on their heels.

Yatosha said, "That was good."

"Good!" Chomoc echoed.

Now was the time.

Tiopi said, "I keep wondering about that baby. Born dead with all those blisters. So unnatural."

Yatosha nodded without reply.

Tiopi offered more squash seeds, and Yatosha took a handful, giving some to Chomoc.

Chomoc said, "The baby smelled bad."

"It was dead—killed inside its mother." She turned to Yatosha. "Why would Kwani do such a thing?"

"What do you mean? Kwani—"

"That little baby was killed by a witch."

Yatosha spat in disgust. "You weary me with your accusations. Kwani is She Who Remembers and will remain so until Sipapu calls—or until she chooses a successor. You may be sure she will not choose you. Remember, also, we are newcomers here and she is mate of the powerful Building Chief. You endanger us—"

"I saw her standing right there when that poor woman was dying. I saw with my own eyes!" Tiopi leaned forward, jabbing her finger at Yatosha's chest. "And then she sang!

They told me. Everybody knows a witch can sing the Death Song, calling the spirit away."

Yatosha scowled. "That is enough! Say no more!"

Chomoc shook his head. "I told Acoya his mother was a witch and that's why her eyes are blue. But he says—"

Tiopi gave him a glance of warm approval. "You were right, of course."

Chomoc still looked doubtful. "But—"

Yatosha said sharply, "Men do not argue with each other about the mothers of their friends. That is not important—"

Tiopi felt her anger surge in a hot flood. Her voice rose. "A mother is not important? *I* am not important? Is that what you tell our son—*my* son—that his mother—your mate, I remind you—is of no importance?" Her voice shook.

Chomoc jumped up. "My father does not say that!"

Yatosha said, "It makes no difference. Your mother will believe what she chooses. True or not."

Tiopi sat looking at them in silence to allow her anger to cool.

I must retain control.

She busied herself with removing the bowls and baskets from the blanket on the floor where the food had been served. When she could make her voice casual, she said, "Perhaps you are right, Yatosha."

Yatosha shot her an astonished glance.

She continued, "Chomoc, you may continue to play with Acoya and to be with him in his home. Observe his mother. Acoya will know if his mother has owl feathers, for example. Hidden perhaps." Only witches had owl feathers.

Yatosha said hotly, "I will not allow Chomoc to spy—"

Tiopi made her voice mild. "I am suggesting only that he verify the truth of your words, that Kwani is not a witch. Surely you will allow Chomoc to prove you are right?"

"I will watch," Chomoc said with such an air of importance that Yatosha had to restrain a smile. "Very well. She Who Remembers is not a witch; she is an esteemed person. Therefore, I will permit you to go with Acoya to his home, but only if he invites you. And you are to remember your manners."

Tiopi smiled. Her son, so much like Kokopelli, would feel responsible to discover truth. Kwani, with her blue eyes, her incantations, her Towa ways, would seem suspicious to a four-year-old looking for something unusual and, therefore, suspect. Chomoc would watch Kwani's every move, ready to accuse, eager to prove his young manhood. He would be believed more easily than would she.

Chomoc would succeed where she had failed.

Again she smiled and touched the place between her breasts where the scallop-shell pendant of the necklace would rest when justice was done. Kwani may have stolen Kokopelli—after he had chosen her, Tiopi, not once but twice for mating!—but Kwani would learn she could not steal the necklace, too. And the powers and prestige of being She Who Remembers that belonged to the Eagle Clan. And to her.

She hoped Kokopelli would hear that it was his son who avenged her, who enabled his mother to overcome the shame, the bitter humiliation of being twice chosen and then discarded for another! And that it was she, Tiopi, who was She Who Remembers now since Kwani was proven to be a witch. At last.

Ha!

Tookah sat in the first floor of her dwelling that served as a storage area for corn and other necessities. In addition, it was nearly filled with debris that would have to be piled in baskets and taken to the dumping place one of these days. With her was Hopua, a woman of the Cottonwood Clan, whose tight little mouth squeezed smaller as she listened avidly while Tookah related recent events. Hopua had just returned from visiting in another pueblo and had come immediately to Tookah to learn the news. Not only would Tookah tell everything, but she had a way of making it especially interesting. They were in the storage room to be sure they would not be overheard.

Tookah made more room for herself among a pile of corn husks and settled comfortably, her round face aquiver with pleasure. It was a privilege to talk to one who appreciated her insight and thoughtful opinions.

"And there she was!" Tookah said. "That woman Tiopi of the Eagle Clan. You know, the one who wants to be She Who Remembers." Tookah snickered and leaned close to Hopua, whispering dramatically, "I will tell you. Something is very strange about that woman Tiopi. Very. I suspect—"

Tookah shook her head as though reluctant to reveal her suspicions.

Hopua leaned closer. "You suspect what?"

Tookah relished Hopua's interest. It was good to have a

friend she could tell things to. But not everything, of course. There was no point in relating how that woman Tiopi had made every man in Cicuye notice her, especially Tookah's mate, Beaver Paw, who followed that woman down to the spring one day. It was said he carried Tiopi's water jar. Imagine!

"As I was saying, there Tiopi was, standing at the edge of the ridge, looking down at that son of hers—what is his name? Cho-something?—and I tell you she was surprised! Because that was not what she expected, you see? Maybe she *knew* Acoya would be down there in the rubbish pile. Maybe she wanted him to fall all the way down and be killed. He is Kwani's son, you know. But she was surprised to see Cho—what's his name?—down there, too." Tookah leaned back, regarding Hopua with a knowing look. "Now, why, I ask you. Why?"

Hopua shook her head, agog with interest.

"There is more. When Lumu—" She caught herself. The name of the dead must never be mentioned. "When Micho's mate was having her baby, Tiopi came. Why? She hardly knew Lu—the woman. Then you know what happened." She shook her head. "Terrible! Terrible!"

Hopua's jaw dropped so that her mouth formed a perfect little O. It was known that such details could be caused by witches. "You mean—"

Tookah's plump face assumed a righteous expression. "These things happened. I do not accuse anyone of anything. You must draw your own conclusions."

Hopua rose, her face flushed with excitement. "I must go now." She babbled excuses and left.

Tookah smiled in grim satisfaction. The seed was planted. That woman Tiopi could find somebody else to carry her water jar.

It was the time of the Planting Moon when softest sandals were worn because Earthmother was pregnant. As I am! Kwani thought, rejoicing. She pressed both hands over the place where Tolonqua's seed grew. At first it had been hard to believe. She had wondered if maybe her moon flow was delayed and she would have to retreat to the woman's hut again—as bleeding women did to protect the city and its people from contamination. Kwani had lived at Cicuye for over four years but she was not yet resigned to this. So when she knew beyond doubt she was pregnant and there would be no hut for moons to come, her joy was boundless.

She sat on the walkway outside her door, making a tiny winter robe of rabbit skin. The wind was soft, carrying the fragrance of new leaves and the calls of birds returning to their summer home. It was a day to be outside, savoring the season, but Acoya was indoors in the kiva with other boys his age, waiting for his education to begin.

How fast he was growing! Soon he would be a man, to hunt, to build, to plant, to take a mate and depart to live with the people of his mate's clan. He would be gone. The bone needle in the rabbit skin lay idle for a moment. Again Kwani pressed both hands to her stomach.

"Be a girl!" she whispered.

Below in the courtyard a group of girls played with a new crop of puppies, pretending the pups were babies. They held them to their chests, trying to make them suck at little nipples. The puppies squirmed and yipped until the girls set them down.

Kwani smiled. One's children could be too independent. She remembered Acoya down there in the rubbish pile. He could have fallen to the rocks below. . . . But his totem, the White Buffalo, protected him. What would protect the child within her?

She tried not to think again of Lumu and the bloody little bundle. That would not happen to her. No.

Nor would she think about the Ancient Ones. Their refusal to hear her might be only temporary until the baby came. Kwani touched her necklace. As long as she was She Who Remembers, the Ancient Ones would not abandon her.

A sudden thought. Could it be that her powers were being transferred to the child within her?

Could it be?

"Kwani!"

On the walkway across the courtyard, a group of women sat with heads together, gossiping, looking to be sure they were not overheard. They called again for Kwani to come, but she smiled and shook her head. Kwani liked to sit by herself sometimes, to be alone with her thoughts. But the women persisted, so Kwani gathered up her sewing and joined them.

"—and then, when the baby was born, poor thing"—the woman held her nose—"Tiopi was there. I saw her. Strange, is it not?"

It was Running Bird speaking. Two fat, shiny braids framed her pudgy face. Several missing teeth gaped as she spoke. Again, she said, "Strange. Is it not?"

Kwani wasn't sure where the conversation led since she had just arrived. "What is strange?"

There was a moment of surprised silence.

Running Bird leaned forward. "Tiopi made Acoya fall, you know. Then Chomoc tried to reach him, and fell, too; that was an accident. The baby . . . A witch did that."

For a moment Kwani froze, thinking she was suspected of witchcraft again. Chomoc had been acting strange lately, watching her intently, poking around. Did they think that— But no, they were accusing Tiopi! She sat silently in stunned astonishment.

Running Bird glanced over her shoulder to be sure nobody overheard, then leaned forward again, whispering loudly. "I saw Tookah's mate—you know, old Beaver Paw— following her to the spring. They say he carried her water jar!"

The women nodded in unison; they had heard that, too.

Another woman said, "The way she looks at the men—"

"You mean the way they look at her!"

"Aye." They glanced at one another.

A brief, potent silence.

Running Bird said, "A witch endangers every one of us."

Kwani opened her mouth to speak, but the words refused to come. She knew too well what it meant to be accused of witchcraft, and Tiopi was no witch. She should say so now, and emphatically. But she looked down at her hands and said nothing.

It was the first time Acoya and the other boys his age had been allowed in a kiva and Acoya stared in awe. The round room, dug into Earthmother's domain, held sacred mysteries. Each clan had its own kiva, and this, of the Turquoise Clan, was surely the most sacred and splendid of all. Acoya gazed at the ceremonial masks, the pipes, the flutes and whistles and drums, all the objects stored in niches in the surrounding walls. How mysterious and beautiful they were!

The altar, against the wall behind the fire pit, held the clan fetish, a wondrous rock shaped like a bear the size of a man's palm. Tied to its back by a cord around its middle were gifts of shell and of turquoise. On the altar around it were offerings of corn pollen, the substance most sacred, with which the fetish was fed each day. Suspended from the beamed ceiling above the altar was a parfleche, a case of fine buckskin, brilliantly painted in ornate designs, which was almost as long as Acoya was tall. This, he knew, held the robe of the White Buffalo. Acoya stared in reverence. Someday it would be his.

Acoya admired his father standing by the fire pit, looking down at the boys seated before him. Tolonqua wore a handsome breechcloth embroidered with shell beads and adorned with beautiful painted designs in bright colors. An eagle feather, notched to show his position as Building Chief, stood upright behind his head in the band that crossed his forehead and was fastened in back. He wore a necklace of bear claws proclaiming his achievements as a master hunter, and another of turquoise to identify his clan. How wonderful was his father!

"Greetings, young warriors," Tolonqua said solemnly. The Anasazi boys and others who did not know Towa had picked up the language amazingly fast—enough so that Tolonqua did not have to sign. "Today you begin to learn. I am Building Chief, as you know. But before that I was Hunting Chief. For many rains, many snows, many seasons." He glanced away, as though glimpsing the past. "So I shall be your teacher of hunting."

The boys squirmed in happy anticipation. "When do we go hunting?" one asked eagerly. "This moon?"

"No. Perhaps you may go when you are ten or eleven. If you have learned what you must by then."

"Ah-h-h-h!" A sigh of incredulous disappointment.

Acoya counted on his fingers. He was four. That meant six more years! Another lifetime!

Tolonqua smiled. "I felt as you do when my father told me what I have told you. There is much to learn, so now we begin.

"First, you must remember always that all things that live are our relatives. All of us were made by He of the Above Beings, the Great Spirit. So birds and animals are our brothers to be regarded always with respect. We learn much from them for each has abilities that we do not. To acquire these abilities for yourself you must study each animal, each bird, until you learn what they know and what they will do. I shall tell you what I have learned, but it is the animals and the birds that will teach you what you must know to be a hunter.

"Many songs you will learn because songs have spiritual power to call animals. Deer, elk, antelope—all game, even rabbits—want to come to us and we sing to show them the way. On a hunt, we sing to locate game. A deer, for instance. There are songs to sing while tracking wounded deer, and while skinning it, while cutting it up, and another song while carrying the deer home. Songs speak to animal spirits to make game want to come to us, to forgive us for taking their lives for food, and to make more game grow. Songs have power.''

The boys gazed at Tolonqua, their faces soaking up knowledge as dry earth drinks rain.

Tolonqua continued, ''A hunter must see and hear like an animal so it is necessary to learn to see and hear everything about you. Each day you are to go outside of the city and look carefully at everything, and listen for every sound, no matter how small. When you return, I shall ask you what you have seen and heard.

''This is your first lesson. Go now.''

The boys scrambled up the ladder, but Acoya remained behind. He approached Tolonqua shyly.

''I thank you, Father.''

Tolonqua placed a hand on the boy's shoulder. ''You will learn quickly and become a good hunter.''

''I want to sing the way you do.''

Tolonqua smiled. ''I will teach you.''

As they looked into each other's eyes, Acoya felt that Tolonqua had reached out and embraced him.

''Let's see what's underneath,'' Acoya said.

He and Chomoc squatted by a rock embedded near the river. It was a large, strange-looking stone with colored pockmarks on the surface. The boys tried to lift it, but it was too heavy.

''We have to do it the way they do at the flint mines. My father showed me.'' Acoya pointed to a broken branch on the ground nearby. ''We need that. And a rock to push against.''

They found a large, smooth stone by the riverbank and placed it in front of the big rock.

''Now lay the branch on top of the little rock and poke it under the big one,'' Acoya said.

The boys shoved the branch under the big rock as far as they could, then the two of them pushed down hard, leaning on the branch. The big rock shook, then rolled over.

Acoya gasped. A rattlesnake nest was exposed! A large snake coiled instantly, rattling its tail, flicking its tongue, its black eyes fixed intently upon him. Acoya jumped back. But Chomoc sat motionless, staring.

''Get away!'' Acoya shouted.

Chomoc did not move. The snake turned its head to Chomoc, flicking its forked tongue, tasting Chomoc's presence.

Acoya wanted to grab Chomoc away, but he was afraid the snake would strike. "Get away!" he shouted again.

But the rattle ceased. The snake uncoiled itself and settled back down, its small black eyes watchful.

Chomoc turned to Acoya. "We have to put the rock back. I said we would."

"You didn't say anything."

"Yes I did. I told him."

"But—"

"I talked to him in my mind. He said to hurry and put the rock back."

Acoya stared, speechless.

"Come on!" Chomoc said impatiently. He reached for the branch. "Move the small stone over on the other side."

The snake lay motionless, eyes intent, as the boys heaved the big rock back. For the first time they noticed the small hole by the side of the rock where the snakes entered, and were careful to leave it exposed.

When the rock was safely in place, Acoya squatted on his heels and stared at Chomoc. He had grown accustomed to his friend's strange appearance—the cougar-colored eyes, the beak nose, the sloping forehead—but now Chomoc seemed a stranger again. Talking to snakes in his mind!

Chomoc returned Acoya's gaze matter-of-factly. "What did the snake say to you?"

"Nothing."

Chomoc seemed surprised. "I thought he did."

"I didn't hear anything." Chomoc looked puzzled, and Acoya blurted, "I don't know how to do that. Show me how."

For a moment Chomoc fixed Acoya with an expressionless gaze. Then he looked down his nose.

"Maybe." He glanced at the sun. "It's time to eat and I'm hungry. Let's ask your mother to feed us."

Acoya wondered why Chomoc never suggested they go to his dwelling to eat, but no matter; Kwani seemed to enjoy having Chomoc around.

The boys clambered up the bank and climbed the ladder at the city wall. Acoya couldn't wait to tell his mother how Chomoc talked to the snake and how the snake understood.

When Kwani heard she looked at Chomoc with an odd expression as though she were not very surprised. Acoya was disappointed; he wanted her to be as astonished as he was.

But he was hungry, too, and ate in silence, wondering. Could Chomoc talk to animals and birds, too?

▲ 34 ▼

Now that Acoya was four, he was old enough to have his own sleeping mat. And his own bowl and mug, and a ceremonial garment that he was expected to care for; it hung on a peg at the foot of his mat. Acoya liked to look at the soft deerskin shirt and leggings embroidered with dyed porcupine quills. There were painted designs, too. It was a beautiful garment—nicer than Chomoc's—and Acoya was proud that his mother made such fine things, and that it was his.

But his most prized possessions were the bow Tolonqua made for him, and the arrows in a little quiver with fringe. They were with him all day and lay beside him at night as he dreamed of wonderful exploits as Hunting Chief. He was getting better with his aim; he had killed a small squirrel. Kwani tanned the skin and it was now a little pouch to hold treasures: pretty rocks from the river, a blue feather, a bit of rainbow flint Tolonqua had given him, and a tiny bird's claw he found on a bush as though the bird had flown away, leaving it there. The best was a little piece of dead wood shaped like the buffalo-head mark on his foot; he had found it under a cottonwood tree by the river. Tolonqua said this was a gift from the White Buffalo so it had special powers. Kwani would make a medicine pouch for it so he could wear it around his neck. Acoya smiled, thinking of it. He would feel very grown-up to wear a medicine pouch as the men did.

It was not yet pulatla but Acoya was too excited to sleep. He woke early because this was the Planting Moon and to-day boys would go with their fathers to family fields to help with the first corn planting. This was a ceremony using special seed. Then four days later they would do the regular planting and put things in the field to scare away hungry ravens. He and Chomoc would make these—the first time they would be allowed to do so. They had planned for a long time how they would manage to obtain what they needed: old rags, pieces of dog and coyote skins, streamers of moss or of anything that would move in the wind, wrinkled rawhide, something to make a rattle with, corn husks—all sorts of useful things.

It would not be easy to get the rags. Kwani and Tiopi, like all women, used every scrap. If a garment was too ragged to be worn it was stored in the wanting-time basket and used on sleeping mats for children who wet at night, or was stuffed into cracks around doors or hatchway mats, or made into holders of hot things, or used in other ways that women knew. But fathers told them how necessary rags were in a cornfield and mothers wanted the corn, so rags were grudgingly provided.

During the Planting Moon, even some Chiefs became farmers, working in far distant fields and those nearby to give Earthmother her seed to make it grow and provide food. Tolonqua's field was nearby in the valley. Acoya visualized himself in the field with his father, scaring ravens away. How proud his father would be! When he and Chomoc were older, they could go with relatives to fields far away and spend the night there in brush shelters. How exciting!

Acoya sighed happily, ignoring for a moment the sounds coming from the adjoining room where his parents slept. The noises continued and Acoya sat up, alarmed. His mother sounded as if she were hurting! He crept to the door and peeked in. They were struggling! Terrified, Acoya crawled back to his sleeping mat and pulled the blanket over his head. It couldn't be! Never would his father hurt Kwani! But why was she making those noises?

Acoya huddled under the blanket until the noises stopped. Was she dead? But then she was laughing! She came in and leaned over him.

"Get up! It's pulatla and today you plant corn!"

Acoya sat up, enormously relieved. They had been playing!

From outside came the voice of the Crier Chief calling from the tallest roof in Cicuye.

"Arise! It is pulatla! Soon Sunfather comes!" He began a mournful chant handed down over so many generations that some of its meaning was lost. Then his voice rose clearly. "The Sun Chief declares today is the best day of Planting Moon. The Medicine Chief has completed the prayers and sacrifices. Rejoice! This day, first corn will be planted. Arise! Sunfather comes! Let all be glad!"

Acoya could hardly wait for the morning meal to be over

and for the Morning Song to Sunfather to be completed. Kwani took her water jar and left for the spring; he and his father were alone. Acoya fidgeted while Tolonqua took the Grandfather planting stick from a shelf and squatted to sharpen the point against one of the stones surrounding the fire pit. The stick was as long as Acoya's arm, made from a straight-grained juniper sapling. Near the pointed end a small branch protruded, long enough for the foot to push down on it. Even Tolonqua did not know which of his grandfathers had made it, and it glistened from generations of use.

When the point was sharp enough, Tolonqua turned to Acoya.

"Get for me my feather pot."

The feather pot! Never before had he been allowed to touch it! Reverently, Acoya stood on tiptoe to reach it in its niche. It was a beautiful black and white pot made by his mother, and it had a lid. Carefully, Acoya handed the pot to Tolonqua who set it beside him, and reached for his paint pots.

"Watch carefully," Tolonqua said. "You must learn to make pahos. There are many kinds; this is a simple one for planting."

Acoya nodded eagerly. He wondered if Chomoc was learning how to make pahos. Usually, boys had to be older to learn this.

From the shelf where the Grandfather stick was kept, Tolonqua removed a red-willow stick as long as Acoya's elbow to fingertips. To it he attached an eagle feather from the feather pot.

"You must know that when our people emerged from the three underworlds to enter this, the Fourth World, they met an eagle and asked his permission to live here. The eagle made them pass some tests—you will learn about those when you are older—and when the people passed the tests, the eagle said, 'When you want to send a message to the Above Beings, you may use my feather, for I conquer the air and master heights. I can deliver your prayers.'"

Acoya gazed at the eagle feather with its powerful cloud colors of white and gray. "Where do you get the feathers?"

"In trade. From those who raise eagles."

Acoya visualized eagles of his own. He would have his own eagle feathers! And use some in trade. Think of all the fine things his feathers would buy!

"I want to raise eagles."

Tolonqua paused in his work and looked at Acoya. For a while he said nothing. Then he nodded. "Yes, I think you should. We shall discuss that when you are older."

"I want to now!"

Tolonqua did not reply, but took a paintbrush made of a yucca stalk frayed at one end. He dipped this into the pot of turquoise-blue, and painted the stick from top to bottom.

"Observe. This is the color for sky and for waters that come from the sky."

"Where eagles are," Acoya said. "I want—"

"I know what you want," Tolonqua said sternly. "Pay attention."

Chastised, Acoya watched silently as Tolonqua reached for a spotted fawn-skin bag hanging from an antler hook. The fawn looked almost alive as it hung head down, its body stuffed with specially prepared and sanctified corn of all colors. From it Tolonqua selected six kernels of corn, each of a different color, wrapped them in a corn husk with the paho, stuffed all in a carrying pouch, and slung the pouch over his shoulder. He tucked the Grandfather digging stick under his arm.

"Come."

Acoya followed his father outside and down the walkway. Anitzal was waiting and she scurried after them with a bowl of cold water. She splashed Tolonqua lavishly—symbolic of rain—a traditional gesture for one who departs for the first planting.

"Go!" she shouted, laughing. "You and the corn. Go!" She splashed him again.

Thoroughly drenched, Tolonqua limped down the steep path to the valley and to his field near the slope of the ridge. Acoya followed. He knew this field had belonged to his grandfathers; now it was Tolonqua's, one of the best fields the people possessed. Someday it would be his if he cared for it well.

When they reached the field, Tolonqua stood for a moment in a spot in the center. Acoya looked at him standing there, tall and proud in his field, surrounded by the stubble of last year's fine crop. How wonderful was his father! Acoya watched closely as Tolonqua stepped to four nearby points equally distant from the center, pressed the sharp point of the planting stick into the soil, and pushed it down with his foot, turning the stick around and around, digging a deep hole each time.

"Observe," Tolonqua said. "The first hole is to the

north, the second to the west, the third to the south, and the fourth to the east. Now I shall dig a hole for the Above.''

He dug to the left side of the hole of the north.

''Now for the below.''

He dug a hole to the right of the hole of the south.

Acoya watched intently. ''Someday I shall do that.''

Tolonqua did not answer, but stepped again to the center spot and knelt facing east. From his pouch he removed a little bag of cornmeal and ran it through his fingers to make a cross on the ground.

Acoya stood at a respectful distance, watching. ''What is that for?''

''The four cardinal points, and for the stars that watch the field at night. Do not disturb me now. Observe, and listen.''

Taking the paho, he planted it in the center of the cross and sprinkled it with meal. From the fawn-skin pouch he selected three grains of each of the six colors—yellow, blue, red, white, speckled, and black—and placed them with the grains that had been wrapped in the shuck with the paho. Kneeling, he faced the hole of the north, held the four grains of yellow color in his left hand, dropped them into the hole as he chanted in a monotone:

> ''U—ai—o-a—ho—o
> U—ai—o-a—ho—o
> U—ai—o-a—ho—o
> *Off over yonder,*
> *Toward the north-land,*
> *I pray that my yellow corn grains*
> *Shall grow and bear fruit. This I sing.*
> U—ai—o-a—ho-o''

Acoya watched in awe. His father knew powerful medicine!

As Tolonqua sang the last refrain, he shifted about to face westward. Without a pause in the chant, he took the four blue grains and repeated as before except that he sang to the ''westland'' and of the ''blue corn grains'' as he dropped them into the hole. He continued until all the grains were dropped into the holes: red into the southern, white into the eastern, speckled into the upper, and black into the lower.

The ceremony was now complete.

Tolonqua turned to Acoya. ''Now we plant the rest of first corn. You may help by covering the holes.''

Following the four lines of the cornmeal cross, Tolonqua planted rows far out into the field until the corn in the fawn-skin pouch was exhausted. Acoya followed eagerly, covering the holes with soil and stamping it down. From time to time, Tolonqua turned to watch, and nodded approval.

"You do well."

Acoya beamed with pride. Such crops he would grow one day! He wondered if Chomoc was permitted to help Yatosha. Because they were newcomers they had to go far to find good farming land that was not yet claimed. Acoya wondered where they went.

Four days must pass during which planters of first corn would fast, chant prayers to Sunfather, and remain in their kivas away from their mates. The main planting would begin on the fifth day.

On the fourth day while Tolonqua and Yatosha remained in their kivas, Chomoc sat with Acoya in Kwani's dwelling, eating corn cakes and dried squash stew. Kwani was putting the finishing touches on Acoya's little squirrel-skin bag for his treasures, and Chomoc sat close to her, watching in admiration.

"I wish my mother would make one for me."

"Bring me something to make one with and I will make it for you."

Chomoc looked up at Kwani with unabashed adoration. It had been plain for a long time that Chomoc loved Kwani and she was fond of him. No wonder Chomoc was there all the time! Acoya felt a pang of jealousy as Kwani put her arm around Chomoc and gave him a hug. Kwani seemed to notice how Acoya felt because she hugged him, too. That made him feel better.

Kwani said, "Tomorrow is planting day. Do you have everything you need to keep ravens away?"

Acoya nodded.

Chomoc said, "My father gives permission for me to go with Acoya and help him."

Acoya glanced at Chomoc with surprise. Chomoc had said nothing to him about this, and Acoya wasn't at all sure he wanted anyone else along; he wanted to be with Tolonqua by himself, helping him man to man.

Acoya looked away and was silent.

Kwani said, "Chomoc wishes to help you, Acoya."

"I don't need help."

Chomoc's lion-colored eyes regarded him. He said, "The coyote skins. I have them. And rags. And old shoulder-blade bones to make a rattle, and the wrinkled piece of rawhide for the face.''

It was true. Acoya looked at Chomoc who returned his gaze with unconcealed triumph. These things were needed to make what Acoya had to make, and there was no way to get more before tomorrow.

Kwani said to Chomoc, ''Who will keep ravens away from your father's field?''

''He is sharing a field with a hunter from home. The hunter will do it.''

Kwani said to Acoya, ''Two workers can do more than one. Tolonqua needs you. Maybe you can use help, too.''

Put that way, it seemed different. As though he were the Chief and Chomoc the helper.

''All right,'' Acoya said grudgingly. ''But I will make the scarecrow.''

''I will make the scarecrow's bone rattle.''

''But—''

Chomoc looked down his nose. ''They are *my* bones.''

Kwani said quickly, ''The two of you will make a fine team. Every raven for miles around will be terrified.''

The boys glanced at each other.

Kwani said, ''Those ravens will tell each other about that scarecrow and that rattle and all the rest, and say that Acoya and Chomoc have dangerous medicine.''

''Yes!'' Chomoc and Acoya said simultaneously.

They looked at each other and grinned.

Kwani stood at the edge of the ridge looking down at the cornfield beyond the old village. The corn had been planted and now Tolonqua and the boys worked at setting up waist-high cedar poles all over the field, each pole topped with a little bunch of its own or other prickly leaves so ravens could not light there. They worked well together, her mate, her son, and Kokopelli's son who should have been hers. . . .

No, she would not think of that. Chomoc was Tiopi's child. But sometimes he looked so much like his father it made her heart turn over.

She had seen little of Tiopi lately. It seemed that Tiopi avoided everyone—which was unlike her, or at least the way she used to be, always at the front of everything, accustomed to being admired. She was older now, but some beauty remained, enough to make men want her. It was whispered that men who had no mates, and some who did, visited her tipi when Yatosha was away on a hunt. Gossip was never in short supply.

Below, Tolonqua and the boys strung cords of split yucca leaves from pole to pole. Kwani watched as tattered rags, pieces of dog and coyote skins, streamers of moss and anything that would move in the wind were looped over the cords so that the field was alive with motion in every breeze. A few ravens flew by squawking in alarm, and Chomoc and Acoya shouted at them, laughing.

They worked well together, the tall man and the two small boys trying hard to be men—as they would be too soon. Acoya stopped work to say something to Tolonqua who stood listening, then put his hand on Acoya's shoulder in an affectionate gesture.

She would have her son but a little time longer. Boys struggled to be men as birds forced themselves from the shell. Soon Acoya would be old enough to be initiated into the Turquoise Clan and would spend most of his time in the kiva or outdoors. Some children nursed until another baby came—up to five or six years, but Acoya weaned himself at age three, and Kwani missed that. She loved the closeness of her small son when he drank from her. But another child would be at her breast in six moons.

A daughter.

Kwani glanced at the sun; it was nearly overhead. Tolonqua and the boys would be hungry and waiting for her to bring corn cake and jerky. She turned back to the city.

It took all day, but finally the scarecrow was finished. Acoya and Chomoc stood back and admired their handiwork. "Does it look real enough?" Acoya asked Tolonqua.

Tolonqua regarded it gravely. It was a stuffed old woman with a basket on her back and arms outstretched. In her hand was a stick-and-bone rattle that hissed as the wind blew. She had streaks of long moss hair, a black rawhide face with eyes of husk balls popping out of her yellow painted face, and evil-looking cornstalk teeth in her open mouth where a great red tongue hung out and lolled from side to side with every breeze.

Tolonqua nodded. "If I were a raven I would stay very far away. In fact, I, myself, would not care to encounter that old woman on a dark night."

"It does look scary," Acoya said, beaming.

"It is my magic," Chomoc said matter-of-factly.

Tolonqua looked down into amber eyes that returned his gaze with amazing aplomb for a four-year-old. For a moment Tolonqua was swept into the past with Kokopelli.

Or was it into the future?

▲ 35 ▼

Tiopi stood outside the tipi, glancing uneasily at the sky; it had a strange yellowish cast and the sun was hazy. She inhaled deeply. Dust! An angry wind god was about to blow grit from his mighty lungs! Hunters or men in distant fields would have to cope as best they could, but children needed protection; they should be inside. Where was Chomoc?

She shaded her eyes with her hand to ease the harsh yellow light and stared up at the ridge. Sometimes Acoya and Chomoc were on the roof and she could see them, but not today. Were they in the old village? They played there sometimes. She covered her head with a soiled piece of torn blanket to protect herself from the dust when it arrived in force.

Tiopi hurried toward the old village at the base of the ridge where some newcomers lived until their new homes were built. She passed others but they hurried by without acknowledging her greeting. That seemed strange, but no doubt they, too, were worried about the coming dust storm and the wind god's vengeance. She wondered what the Medicine Chief and his helper priests did or did not do to arouse such anger.

As Tiopi neared the village, dogs and children were called indoors, rooftops were cleared of drying meat or clothes or other valuables to be protected, and hatchways were closed. Tiopi climbed to the first dwelling and lifted a corner of the thick mat covering the hatchway.

She called down, "I seek Chomoc. Is he there?"

"No."

"Have you seen him?"

"No."

She tried several others with the same blunt response. These people were not Anasazi; to them she was a stranger. But they could have invited her inside—a common courtesy. Lately it seemed that people looked at her differently and avoided her. Even the men.

The wind gusted, growling. A billow of gritty dust swirled.

I must find Chomoc!

Was he in the city? She would see. Clutching the piece of blanket around her face, she climbed the ridge, bending under the wind that blew harder, grinding dust into her blinking eyes and into her nose as she tried to breathe through the blanket. The men arriving from fields nearby hurried into kivas or retreated to their dwellings. Hunters and farmers in distant fields would hunker down. Birds were silent.

What if Chomoc and Acoya were off somewhere, playing as boys do with no thought to danger or an approaching dust storm to claw at the eyes and choke the breath? There were small caves on the steep slopes of the ridge. If the boys were caught in the storm they might try to find shelter there. And fall . . .

But no. They must be in the city. Probably with Kwani, since Chomoc had been obedient about visiting there. He was faithful in reporting all that Kwani did, but so far he was not suspicious of anything. In fact, he seemed to enjoy being with Kwani. . . .

For a moment Tiopi paused, bracing herself against the wind. A thought pierced like a thorn.

Perhaps I have made a mistake sending Chomoc to Kwani. Maybe she has put a charm on him. He is only a little boy. . . .

I must talk to Chomoc!

She pushed on, coughing. She climbed the outer ladder to the first roof, struggling against the wind. The roofs were bare and deserted; only an old dog cowered at a doorway. Tiopi climbed to the second story and made her way toward Kwani's door. As she approached, she heard Kwani singing the Roadrunner Song.

> *"Roadrunner with the bushy head*
> *Is always crying 'Poi! Poi!'*
> *As he runs around the house.*
> *'Poi! Poi!' around the house."*

Tiopi heard the boys laughing, yelling "Poi! Poi!" She knew how they ran around the room, flapping their arms, being roadrunners.

Enough was enough. She banged on the door. "It is I, Tiopi."

The door opened a crack against the wind, and Kwani peeked through. She stared a moment in surprise, then flung open the door, pulled Tiopi inside, and pushed the door shut. They stood looking at each other.

Kwani gestured automatically. "Sit and eat." She pointed to where Tolonqua and Yatosha sat by the fire pit in comfortable camaraderie, nibbling parched corn as they polished bows and traded hunting stories.

Tiopi glared at Yatosha. She had no idea he spent time here! She thought he was out hunting—as he should be. Their meat supply was low. And here he sat in Kwani's dwelling! And Chomoc and Acoya stood close to Kwani as though seeking her protection. That was too much! Tiopi flushed with anger.

"I come for Chomoc."

Yatosha rose. "Why?"

Tiopi's flush deepened. "I wish to take him home."

"Why?"

"He is my son, and I want him with me. I do not have to give reasons."

Tiopi grabbed Chomoc by the arm and yanked open the door. Yatosha jumped up and slammed the door shut. He pushed Chomoc behind him and scowled down at Tiopi, humiliation and embarrassment at his mate's rudeness staining his cheeks and forehead.

"He stays!"

"No!" Tiopi reached for Chomoc who backed away.

Chomoc tried to scowl as his father did. "I want to stay!"

"You come with me!" Tiopi yelled. She struggled to push Yatosha aside and grab Chomoc, but the boy ran to hide behind Kwani.

Tiopi glared at Kwani. It had been over four years since Kwani left the Eagle Clan; why had she not aged? She was more beautiful than ever in a robe of white cotton embroidered with porcupine quills dyed in bright colors. As usual, it was tied over the right shoulder leaving the other shoulder bare. On Kwani, it was seductive. The necklace with its polished stone beads of many colors glowed against Kwani's throat, and the scallop-shell pendant inlaid with turquoise nestled between lovely breasts. Kwani's hair was not arranged in Anasazi squash-blossom style or even braided in proper Towa fashion, but fell loosely around her shoulders and framed her face. Blue eyes met Tiopi's with maddening inscrutability.

Kwani had a witch's beauty to cast spells. No wonder Yatosha was here! Seduced! And little Chomoc—

Tolonqua came and stood beside Yatosha. Quietly, he said, "When the dust is gone we will send Chomoc home. Meanwhile, won't you stay and eat with us?"

"No," Kwani said. "She does not wish to stay."

This was the ultimate insult! Tiopi trembled with fury. Of course she did not wish to stay, but to be told that was to be invited—no, ordered—to leave.

"I want my son!" Her voice cracked. "Now!"

Tiopi tried to step aside from Yatosha and Tolonqua, but they would not let her pass.

"He stays with me," Yatosha said firmly.

Tiopi backed against the door and looked up at this man who was suddenly a stranger. Never had Yatosha defied her this way! Again she tried to pass but he and Tolonqua were an impenetrable barrier. Behind them Kwani stood in an ocean of calm with Acoya and Chomoc beside her, staring.

A sudden stab of fear penetrated Tiopi's rage. Something unnatural was here! Without another word she jerked open the door. A blast of dust blew in as she left.

Tears made muddy rivulets on Tiopi's cheeks as she stumbled down the path, choking in the dust. When she reached her tipi, she struggled to fasten the door flap securely against the wind, then sat down on the floor that was gray and gritty—as was everything else. She wrapped both arms around her knees and buried her head. Her eyes hurt, her throat hurt, and grit was between her teeth and in every pore. Her heart pounded with anger, frustration, and, yes, fear.

They are against me. Yatosha, Chomoc, everyone is against me. Because of Kwani.

Kwani!

She sobbed, great choking sobs that shook her. Hatred boiled up with poisonous power. The sobs quieted. Slowly she rose and looked around the tipi, searching.

Tiopi was not sure what she searched for, but she would know when she saw it.

The community fire blazed in the courtyard; Moonwoman had not yet appeared and campfires of the Ancients burned holes in a black sky. People crowded the plaza, enjoying the evening. There was much talk of last week's dust storm, the worst many had experienced.

Was a witch responsible? Tookah and Hopua sat with a group of women, heads together. There were furtive remarks about Tiopi. She was not at the fire, but Yatosha was. He and Long See were with Tolonqua and a group of hunters, discussing an antelope hunt. Acoya and Chomoc and other boys sat nearby, listening avidly.

Kwani was with Anitzal whose ravaged face revealed her secret grieving. Lumu's name was never mentioned. Nearby were old Huzipat with Ki-ki-ki's young mate and her baby. They had fit easily into the life of Cicuye and seemed content.

The Crier Chief had made his announcements; it was time for songs and stories. Newcomers were expected to tell their tales, which would be different from those already known and eagerly awaited. Beyond the city, where the ridge rose to the highest point, a group of young men sang, their clear, strong voices carried on the wind.

> *"Where my kindred dwell*
> *There I wander.*
> *The Red Rock House,*
> *There I wander.*
> *With the pollen of dawn upon my trail,*
> *There I wander."*

Kwani sat quietly, listening. It was a Healing Song to ease the heart and refresh the spirit. Smoke drifted upward to the stars. In the far distance, a wolf's call rose, fell, and faded away.

> *"In the house of long life,*
> *There I wander."*

Tolonqua's rich voice soared, joining the song.

> *"In the house of happiness,*
> *There I wander."*

Other voices rose, Kwani's with them. She sang for the wonder and joy of a child growing within her. Her voice, high and sweet, soared with Tolonqua's.

> *"Beauty before me,*
> *With it I wander.*

> *Beauty behind me,*
> *With it I wander.*
> *Beauty below me,*
> *With it I wander.*
> *Beauty above me,*
> *With it I wander.*
> *Beauty all around me,*
> *With it I wander."*

Abruptly Kwani stopped singing. A sharp pain had knifed her. It came again in her back and abdomen. A birthing pain!

She wrapped both arms around herself. She had experienced false labor with Acoya, but this seemed different.

The pain came again. She must have help! She could not bear to lose this child! Where was the Medicine Chief?

Kwani rose, searching. He was with Two Elk and the Crier Chief, seated close to the fire, singing raptly.

> *"In old age traveling,*
> *With it I wander.*
> *On the beautiful trail I am,*
> *With it I wander.*

Anitzal rose to stand beside her. "What is it?"

"Birthing pain!"

The song ended and there was a moment of silence. Anitzal's voice rang out clearly. "She Who Remembers seeks the Medicine Chief!"

The Chief glanced at Kwani as she stood with her arms over her abdomen. He rose and beckoned her to the medicine lodge. Tolonqua hurried to Kwani, his face tense.

"The baby?"

She nodded.

Anitzal said, "Take her to the medicine lodge." To Kwani she said, "Do not be afraid. This child will be born healthy and whole."

They looked into each other's eyes, each knowing what was in the other's mind. *Lumu and the bloody little bundle.*

Anitzal said again, "Do not be afraid."

But Kwani trembled as Tolonqua swept Kwani into his arms and carried her through the murmuring crowd.

Tookah whispered loudly, "The witch does this!"

There were angry voices and a man shouting. Was it Yatosha? But Kwani did not hear. She was carried into the lodge and laid upon a mat covered with the skin of Bear, healer of the animal kingdom.

Tolonqua leaned close. His black eyes burned into hers, forcing the power of his spirit into her. "The Ancient Ones protect you. The Medicine Chief will heal you. All will be well."

The Medicine Chief gestured him aside and bent over Kwani. His one good eye was intent as he examined her eyes and mouth. He probed her breasts and lay his ear to her abdomen. Gently he inspected her woman part for secretions, then lay his ear to her again. Carefully, methodically, he probed her abdomen with both hands as another pain contracted.

"Please. Save this baby!" Kwani pleaded.

"There is more than one. It is twins."

Kwani gasped, and Tolonqua exclaimed, "Two babies! That will be too hard—"

Kwani was overwhelmed. "I don't want two babies!" she cried. "One only!"

The Chief nodded. "Then I will put them together."

A small jar with a lid rested on a pedestal nearby. The Chief removed the lid and scooped up a tiny portion of cornmeal. Chanting, he stepped outside and offered it to the Six Sacred Directions. His voice rose in solemn cadence to the Above Beings.

Another pain. Kwani clutched her stomach. "I'm afraid!"

Tolonqua took her hand and placed it on the scallop shell. "The Ancient Ones. Call them."

Would they hear her? Kwani looked up into his black eyes, warm and reassuring. She pressed the necklace to her with both hands and closed her eyes.

"You who were She Who Remembers before me, listen! Help me, I pray! I am hurting. Two babies are within me. I cannot care for two. Make them one, I pray! A daughter!"

There was no reply. Outside, the voice of the Chief beseeched the gods. Nearby, there was a murmur of voices from people gathered, waiting.

"Ancient Ones, help me!"

Slowly, calm entered Kwani's spirit like cool water, and the pain was gone.

"They heard me!"

The Medicine Chief returned. His face wore the exalted look of one who has communed with gods. From the medicine altar he removed a small figure of a bear carved from obsidian to which mysterious sacred objects were attached. Reverently he held the nose of the figure to his mouth, breathed deeply to inhale the bear's life essence and healing powers, and returned the fetish to its honored place. He did not speak, but stood looking down at Kwani with his one good eye. He nodded. From a niche in the wall he removed a basket, rummaged in it a moment, and pulled out a small bundle of cotton cords of various colors. He selected one white and one black cord, each the length of his arm. From a sheath at his waist he removed a flint knife and cut off a portion of each cord. He twisted them together, then tied them around Kwani's left wrist.

"This will twist the two babies into one. You will speak to them often, telling them to be one." He turned to Tolonqua. "Have intercourse every four days. It is like irrigating a crop; it will make the baby grow. If you stop, the birthing will be difficult."

Tolonqua smiled. "I will not stop."

"Take care to injure no animal; it will hurt the baby. If you cut off the foot of any living creature, the baby may have a club foot or a deformed hand—or no hand at all. Be careful not to loop anything around a creature's neck; it may cause the navel cord to loop itself about the baby's neck." The Chief wrapped his fingers around his throat, indicating suffocation.

Tolonqua nodded. He knew these things, but he listened attentively. This baby, this little man cub, must be safely born.

The Chief squatted beside Kwani and placed both hands on her abdomen as if he were hearing through his hands.

"The pain is gone?"

"Yes."

"Good." He rose. "You must be careful to do all things you should do for a Towa baby. Anitzal will instruct you." For a moment he stood looking down at her solemnly. Then he smiled, his good eye twinkling. "One Anasazi baby and one Towa baby twisted together will make a fine child!"

Kwani looked up at him, at his wrinkled, weathered face with the staring obsidian and turquoise eye, and at the desicated chickadee clinging to stringy braids entwined with wilted wisps of feathers and odd medicinal objects. How kind, how beautiful he was!

"And another thing," Anitzal said. "Do not look at the serpent images displayed during ceremonies. It may turn the

baby into a water snake and raise up its head at birthing
time instead of lying head down seeking a way out.''

Kwani and Anitzal were washing clothes in the river. It
was a fine spring day, sunny and windy, a good day for
clothes to dry. Kwani slapped a wet undergarment on a
smooth rock embedded in the river bottom, and rubbed the
undergarment vigorously. It was important to exercise her
body so that she would be strong for the birthing.

Suddenly she paused, remembering. ''I saw a snake the
other day. On the high place beyond the city.''

''Ah.'' Anitzal frowned. ''Was it coiled?''

''No.''

''Did it look at you?''

''Yes. Then it went away.''

''M-m-m. You must be careful not to let anyone walk in
front of you when you sit; it will make the birthing difficult.'' She sloshed a garment in the water, rinsing out the
yucca root soap.

Downstream, Lumu's two little girls washed small garments, playing more than they worked. Kwani saw Anitzal
watching them fondly; all members of the Turquoise Clan
adopted the girls when Lumu died, but Anitzal was their
mother now. Micho had gone to live with his sister's family
in another village.

''Remember not to hold someone else's child on your lap
or breathe into the face of small children,'' Anitzal said.
''It will make them waste away.''

Kwani nodded. There was so much to be aware of and
dangers to avoid. Sometimes she wondered how Acoya was
born so strong and healthy when she knew none of these
things then. But this would be a Towa baby and she took no
chances. She avoided anything to do with the tanning of
skins, for example. It would spoil the skins and hurt the
baby—or so Anitzal and Rainfeather, the old midwife, said.

Kwani had been startled when she met Rainfeather; she
thought at first it was a child who approached. But it was a
woman the size of a small child, with stubby little arms and
legs and a round face that looked as if the features had been
pushed in and made smaller. Black hair, shiny and neat,
framed the old-young face where squinty black eyes peered
kindly at Kwani when, from time to time, she examined
Kwani's abdomen, feeling it with her palms to determine if
the twins were now one. Satisfied, she would feed Kwani
the raw flesh of a weasel and rub the skin on Kwani's body

so that the baby would be active and come out swiftly, in the way the little animal slips through a hole.

Sunfather walked higher. Kwani slapped more clothes on the rubbing stone. The water was cold and felt good on her feet and legs, and Sunfather's breath was warm on her back. More women arrived with baskets of things to be washed—clothes, bowls, mugs, cooking pots—while children splashed and swam in the river. Ki-ki-ki came with other Anasazis who remained close as a group; there was talk and laughter and gossip. A happy time.

Only a circling hawk saw Tiopi hiding in the bushes, gripping a stone-headed maul in both hands. Only the hawks saw her crouched motionless, watching Kwani.

▲ 36 ▼

Acoya lay on his back, floating on the water. He had left his bow and arrows on the bank and had gone upstream to a favorite spot where the shallow river was deeper; it carried him gently along over slippery rocks, turning him this way and that as he drifted downstream toward the place where women gathered to wash clothes.

Willows and cottonwoods drifted by, leaning over the river. Acoya inspected each one, observing the shape and color of the leaves and how they dangled from the branches. He noted the different colors and formations of the bark and the way the branches grew. Cottonwoods thrust strong branches up and outward, while willows drooped down, trailing leaves like fingers in the water.

A yellow songbird flew by and another appeared on a high branch. These were the birds that brought summer. Acoya listened carefully to their song; he would play it on a flute when he learned how. He wondered if playing the summer bird's song in winter would make the cold go away.

The water grew shallow so Acoya stood and waded close to the bank so he could see everything.

Chomoc was with some other Anasazi boys playing in the river where the women worked. Acoya watched Chomoc climb a boulder in the middle of the river and slide off with a splash. Girls were there, too, playing and swimming and bathing puppies as though the pups were babies. How stupid! Dogs bathed themselves in the river as anybody knew. Anybody but girls, that is. Acoya's own dog, Chuka, usually swam with him but he was off chasing rabbits somewhere.

A chipmunk darted from under a bush and peered at Acoya with shiny little eyes.

"Ho, little brother!" Acoya said, admiring the white stripes on the furry sides and on the face from ears to the pointed nose. The small ears stood upright and were edged with white, too. The chipmunk flicked its long tail and scurried up a tree. A blue jay scolded and dived at him and the chipmunk scurried back down and ran under a bush. The jay followed, perched on the bush, cocked its head, and made raucous noises. Acoya did not understand blue jay language, but he guessed what the bird was saying. He laughed. He would have something to tell when Tolonqua asked what he had seen that day.

His laugh startled a young cottontail rabbit bounding away. Acoya hurried to where his bow and arrows lay on the bank. Maybe he could kill that rabbit and give it to his mother to cook! She had finished washing clothes and was spreading them on bushes to dry. How proud she would be if he brought her a rabbit!

He picked up his bow and the quiver of arrows, and fastened the thong of the quiver around his wet waist. Nearby, a large bush quivered. It was the faintest of quivers, but Acoya saw it. Maybe the rabbit was there! His heart beat hard as he fitted an arrow in his bow. He stood motionless, as hunters should, waiting for the rabbit to appear.

Another quiver. Acoya was about to inch closer when Kwani approached, carrying a wet garment to spread on the bush. Acoya tried to wave her away, but she held the garment up in such a way that she could not see him. He couldn't kill the rabbit if she was in the way.

"Stay back!" he shouted.

With an answering yell, Tiopi leaped from the bush. Acoya froze in terrified astonishment as she lunged at Kwani, swinging a stone-headed maul. Kwani dropped the garment and ran screaming into the river, scrambling to escape among the trees on the opposite bank. Tiopi ran after her, eyes wild, hair streaming, face contorted, swinging the heavy maul as though it weighed nothing.

Children screamed. Women gasped and cried, "Stop! Stop!" Some waded after Tiopi. "Stop!"

Kwani stumbled and fell in the water, floundering as she tried to regain her footing by the boulder where the boys had been playing. Tiopi was nearly upon her.

Instinctively, as though directed by an inner command, Acoya raised his small bow, sighted over his right thumb, and let the little arrow fly. It hit Tiopi squarely in the back, quivered there, and dropped off leaving a red stain.

With a shout, Tiopi jerked around, and slipped. She fell with a splash and hit her head against the boulder. Slowly, she collapsed facedown into the water and lay there. Kwani ran up the opposite bank and disappeared among the trees.

There was a moment of astounded silence, then a babble of voices.

"Acoya!"

"Acoya killed Tiopi!"

"She fell and hit the rock."

"Acoya killed the witch!"

Ki-ki-ki hurried toward Tiopi who still lay motionless, facedown. Women shouted at her.

"Be careful! The maul—"

Chomoc came, half wading, half swimming. He grabbed Tiopi and tried to turn her over.

"Mama!"

Others reached her and pulled her up on the boulder. Tiopi was limp, with a gash on her forehead oozing red and a small wound on her back.

"Dead! She is dead!"

"Mama!" A choked cry.

One of the women reached to the river bottom and pulled up the maul. She held it so all could see.

"This is what Tiopi tried to kill Kwani with."

Chomoc stared at it. With both fists he yanked it from the woman's hand and held it. He looked at it, sobbing great wailing cries that shook his small body. Ki-ki-ki tried to comfort him but he refused to be touched. With all his strength he threw the maul back into the water and floundered to shore, still sobbing.

Acoya ran to him. "I had to do it. I am sorry, but I had to. Kwani—"

"Go away!"

Chomoc ran alone, wet, naked, and sobbing to the tipi he called home.

Two Elk faced the men seated before him in the kiva. Tolonqua knew there were few times when Two Elk did not relish being the principal Chief, but this had to be one of those times. Tension hung in the air.

Cicuye's Chiefs and Elders sat in front. With them was Piko, the old weaver, completely blind now. Behind them and around the kiva walls were Huzipat and other men of the Eagle Clan, the Anasazis. Yatosha was not present.

Two Elk said, "We have heard, and it has been said here, how"—he almost said her name but caught himself in time—"how a woman of Cicuye died. This is regretted by all."

A young man of the Eagle Clan said loudly, "I see no grieving among the Towas."

He had not raised his hand before speaking; it was a rude interruption.

Another said, "How can we really know what happened when we have only the word of women?"

There were murmurs of agreement.

Tolonqua raised his hand in gesture-before-speaking, and stood beside Two Elk. He looked at each man.

"I remind you we have also the word of my son, Acoya. I made the bow and arrow he used; I know what it will do and not do and at what distance. Acoya was on the bank; she was in the river beyond the big boulder and almost to the opposite side. Those of us who saw the small wound the arrow made know it was the blow on the head, that and only that, which could have killed the mate of Yatosha."

The Medicine Chief nodded. "Tolonqua speaks truth."

Tolonqua continued, "If, indeed, my son's little arrow was in any way responsible for what happened, I can only be grateful. It saved She Who Remembers from a blow by a stone-headed maul." He sat down.

"So some *women* say." The voice of the young Anasazi oozed sarcasm.

Huzipat rose. "I wish to speak."

Two Elk nodded. "Speak."

"It is true we have only the word of women and children. But some of those women are Anasazi. They tell the same story." He turned to the men seated in back. "I do not believe our women lie. Nor do I believe others lie. It happened as they say it did; that we must accept, painful though it be. Only the gods know what evil spirit possessed the mate of Yatosha; it was not she who acted as she did. It was the spirit possessing her."

"Aye!" the Medicine Chief said.

Huzipat's creased old face seemed older as he continued. "We grieve for Yatosha who loved his mate as we know well. And for Chomoc who loved both his mother and Kwani. No wonder Chomoc avoids us; his heart is torn asunder. We grieve for Acoya who bears our accusations— a heavy burden for a man, and he is but a small boy. And we grieve for She Who Remembers who feels she is responsible and who fears for her child unborn. . . ." Huzipat shook his head. "It is a sad time. Aye. But we must allow the sorrow to pass. Today, Yatosha takes his mate to her burial place. In three more days she will be in Sipapu where there is no unhappiness and where all is beautiful. She will be at peace. So must we. I have spoken."

Huzipat stood for a moment in silence, then sat down.

Some of the men glanced at one another; others gazed down at their hands. No one spoke. From above came the shouts of children at play and the sound of manos on metates. Ordinary, comforting sounds. But Tolonqua was uneasy; there was an undercurrent of conflict here. As the city grew and outsiders arrived they brought problems with them. Anasazis were Anasazi first and citizens of Cicuye last.

Trouble must be avoided. But how?

Tolonqua brooded about that later at night as he lay sleepless. Beside him, Kwani's even breath indicated she was asleep at last. They had talked far into the night.

"We must do something to help Acoya. Chomoc, too," she had said earnestly. "It is not right for them to lose their friendship for each other." She turned away. "It is because of what happened to me." She put both arms protectingly over her swollen abdomen. "I fear for the baby."

"Has he not been moving?"

"Yes." She turned again to look at him. Tolonqua saw fear in her eyes—fear in remembrance of a bloody little bundle.

He drew her close. "No evil spirit can harm either of you. You are She Who Remembers, protected by the Ancient Ones. Have you forgotten?"

"No." Nor had she forgotten Lumu's agony, or the smell when the water broke, or the rotting blisters. . . . "I have not forgotten."

"Acoya is protected, too. By the White Buffalo. But his spirit bleeds. Chomoc avoids him and goes with Yatosha to their distant field and sleeps there, the two of them alone in their grieving."

"Acoya is not as he used to be. He is too quiet. What can we do?"

"I don't know. I must think about it."

They lay together, man and mate and baby unborn, comforting one another. In the distance a love flute called a girl to rendezvous. The melody crept through the town, pleading and sweet, lingering, teasing, inviting.

Kwani looked at him, her blue eyes pools to drown in, responding to the flute's call. She pulled his face to hers and kissed him deeply. Her breasts, grown fuller with pregnancy, offered their cactus-fruit tips. He tasted hungrily, teasingly, caressing with his tongue, caressing her all over.

Kwani responded as she always did, sweeping him into a vision place.

After a time, Tolonqua patted her abdomen. "We nourish him well."

"Him? It is a girl."

Kwani had laughed but she was serious, Tolonqua knew. She did not believe it was a boy, a son of Tolonqua's blood. At last.

Now she slept. The flute was silent; had a girl obeyed her lover's call? Did they lie somewhere upon the grass, beneath the stars?

Someday Acoya would love a girl.

Acoya.

Tolonqua stared at the ceiling. How could he heal the boy's spirit? He brooded long. An undercurrent of Anasazi animosity still existed; it was not good for Cicuye. Was Chomoc the key? If a way were found to heal Chomoc, if the boys could be friends again, perhaps all would be well between them, and maybe Yatosha's heart would be eased, also. When grief passed, perhaps conflicts would pass also.

Tolonqua brooded long. At last he knew what he must do.

"See! I told you that woman was a witch!" Tookah leaned forward, looking at each of the women grouped around her. They sat on a walkway with their metates in the morning sunshine. "Did you see how she looked when she chased Kwani?" Tookah's plump face twisted itself into a gruesome expression. "Like that. And she waved that heavy maul around overhead—" Tookah waved a plump arm vigorously.

"And then Kwani fell in the water," Hopua interrupted, eager to tell those who were not there even though they had already heard it several times.

"And Acoya shot her with an arrow," Tookah said. "A little arrow. It hit her here." She turned and pointed to her back. "Right there."

"Left a little wound. Not enough to hurt—"

"Not enough to kill a mouse," Tookah added. "But she gave a yelp and—"

"And turned around to see what happened," Hopua said. "And slipped—"

"And hit her head on that boulder—you know, that big one in the middle of the river. That's what did it." Tookah sat back and regarded her listeners with satisfaction. It was a story to be repeated around fires for years. "The way she hid in the bushes and jumped out at Kwani! Ha! I told you that woman was a witch!''

''Who buried her?'' a woman asked.

''Yatosha. Who else?''

''Poor man.'' Hopua pursed her lips and shook her head. ''Have you noticed how he looks?''

''Terrible,'' a woman said.

''Like this.'' Tookah pulled both cheeks down with her palms.

''He avoids everybody.''

''Except those Anasazis.''

''Yes. Those Anasazis.''

The women looked to see who might be listening. One must be careful speaking of Anasazis; for one thing, She Who Remembers was Anasazi born. They bent over their metates for a few minutes, pushing the mano stones on the corn.

''Some say it was Acoya who killed her.''

''Some men, you mean. No men were there, you know.''

''Aye.''

''I wonder what's going to happen.''

''We'll find out soon enough.''

''Maybe.''

''Maybe not. Men don't tell us everything, you know.''

''Aye!''

They bent to their work in silence.

''Come,'' Tolonqua said to Acoya on the following day. ''We go to the village of Man Who Runs.''

Acoya's eyes brightened with a spark of interest. ''Why?''

''You will see. Wear your breechcloth and moccasins; it's a long walk.''

Kwani handed them a pouch of corn cake and a water bag; they would be gone two or three days. Tolonqua had explained his plan and she reluctantly agreed.

''Take one of the dogs.'' She did not add, ''For protection,'' but they both knew why a dog was necessary. To scent an ambush or to frighten away a predator.

''I will take Chuka,'' Acoya said with more animation than he had shown since Tiopi's death. Chuka was large, shaggy, and much given to vociferous barking for no reason. He had been Acoya's pet since babyhood.

Tolonqua and Kwani glanced at each other. Chuka would be more of a hindrance than a help. But Acoya was eager.

''Very well,'' Tolonqua said. ''Go and get him, and bring

Mo as well." Mo was small, fierce, ugly, and afraid of nothing.

Acoya hesitated. "Mo doesn't like me."

"Mo doesn't like anybody but me, but he will be company for Chuka."

Acoya thought that over, and nodded. "Chuka likes company." He hurried outside.

Kwani watched him go. "I think your plan is a good one. He is more like himself already."

Tolonqua nodded and put the food pouch and water bag in his pack with some of the fine turquoise necklaces obtained in trading at the flint mines. He reached for his staff, strapped on his flint knife, slung the case with his quiver and the bow over his shoulder, tied the pouch with the shell horn around his waist, and took Acoya's little bow and arrows from where they had been left since Tiopi died; Acoya had not touched them since.

Footsteps ran down the walkway and Acoya dashed in, Chuka after him, big, smelly, and barking as usual.

"I tied Mo outside. We are ready. Let's go!" He jumped up and down with impatience.

Tolonqua and Kwani looked at each other and smiled.

"We go." He handed Acoya his bow and arrows matter-of-factly, kissed Kwani good-bye, and patted her swollen abdomen. "Take care of him. And yourself."

Acoya saw that Tolonqua carried his bow and arrows, so after thoughtful consideration he strapped the quiver around his waist and carried his bow. He allowed himself to be hugged, and then they were gone.

It was a blue day in early summer, already warm. Tolonqua and Acoya walked through the valley, Mo dashing ahead and Chuka bumbling after. Even though Tolonqua limped, Acoya had to walk fast to keep up with him.

"Why do we go to the village of Man Who Runs?"

Tolonqua was waiting for that question. Up to now, Acoya had been too excited about going away for a few nights that he did not ask why.

"Man Who Runs is the Medicine Chief. But he is also a maker of fine flutes."

Acoya stopped and looked up at Tolonqua with surprise. "Flutes?"

"Yes. To make bird music." Tolonqua knew that would interest Acoya most. "His flutes bring much in trade." He did not add that Man Who Runs made few flutes and traded seldom. His flutes had powers and were given only to those whom Man Who Runs considered to be worthy.

Acoya's eyes sparkled. "Will you trade for a flute for me?"

"Yes." He would find a way. "And one also for Chomoc. Kokopelli played a flute well."

Acoya nodded. "Chomoc told me. What will we trade?"

Tolonqua noted the "we" and smiled inwardly. This was going to work. "A turquoise necklace."

"Will that be enough?"

"I think so."

For a time they walked in silence. Occasionally, a cloud drifted by, its shadow gliding majestically over valley and mountain. Tolonqua noticed how Acoya looked closely at everything, and held his bow in readiness in case a rabbit or a squirrel appeared within arrow range. But Chuka bounded about, sniffing and barking and making a commotion, frightening every creature away.

Tolonqua thought, Maybe old Chuka will be more useful than I expected. Bears were known to inhabit these mountains; they came to the valley for berries. If they had cubs they would be dangerous. Cougars and wolves lived here, too, but avoided people and barking dogs.

It grew warmer. When Sunfather was overhead Tolonqua said, "We rest now. And eat." He did not mention how his foot hurt. "Find a nice tree for us to sit under in the shade."

Acoya nodded seriously, assuming responsibility. He pointed to a tall oak on a slope ahead. But just then Mo raced to the tree, barking his shrill, choppy bark, and clawed the trunk in a furious effort to climb the tree. Chuka followed, stood on his hind legs with his forelegs on the tree trunk, and bayed into the branches.

"Don't move!" Tolonqua whispered. He whipped out an arrow and fitted it into his bow. "It may be a cougar."

Acoya fitted an arrow into his bow, too, and tried not to look scared. "Will it come after us?"

"Not unless it feels cornered. Stay here and *do not move*."

A cougar skin would be a triumph—valuable for trade. Slowly, quietly, Tolonqua approached the excited dogs who barked more loudly than ever. If he could get the animal to jump down and run, it would be an easy target with no danger to himself. He picked up a large stone and threw it into the branches.

The branches quivered, but no animal appeared.

Tolonqua threw another stone. Again, nothing happened. The dogs would keep the animal treed indefinitely; he called them away. Chuka left obediently, but Mo refused, clawing the trunk, jumping, snarling, determined to climb the tree.

Carefully, Tolonqua circled the tree to approach it from the opposite side; the animal would be watching Mo. As he drew closer, Tolonqua saw a flash of brown among the branches. Brown! A cougar's color was a light reddish-tan. This was a bobcat.

Tolonqua turned and motioned Acoya to come. Hesitantly, Acoya approached, Chuka with him.

Tolonqua said, "Look up there!"

It was a handsome animal, brown with dark spots, a light belly, and a pale spot under the tip of its short tail. It crouched in the branches, snarling, twitching its tail. "He will make a fine skin. I think we are close enough so your arrow will kill him. Aim at his chest."

As if the bobcat heard him, it shifted position, snarling again, showing sharp teeth.

"Aim!" Tolonqua said. "He's getting ready to jump."

He was shaking, but Acoya aimed and let the arrow fly. The bobcat tumbled to the ground, the arrow protruding from its chest. Instantly, the dogs were upon it.

Tolonqua dragged them away; Mo had to be kicked before he would obey.

Acoya shouted, "I killed it! I killed it!" He beamed, face aglow.

Tolonqua knew that although the arrow had pierced the animal's chest in a shallow wound, it was the dog, Mo, whose grip on the jugular had finished the bobcat. But he said, "Your aim was good. See how the arrow pierced right here. It will be a beautiful skin and make something fine for you. But we must apologize for taking the animal's life, and allow its spirit to return as another bobcat."

Tolonqua removed the arrow and handed it to Acoya who gazed at the bobcat with awe and joy.

From his pack Tolonqua removed a small pouch of cornmeal. Taking a pinch, he sprinkled it over the furry coat as he chanted the Prayer of Thanks and the Plea for Forgiveness.

"Now we offer meal to the Six Sacred Directions. First, to the north."

Tolonqua was pleased to see that Acoya was accurate in his direction as he faced north, took a pinch of meal from the pouch, and tossed it.

"Now east . . . south . . . west . . . above . . . and below. Good."

Tolonqua lay the bobcat upon the grass nearby. "I am going to skin it now, so keep the dogs away. They can have the carcass later."

It took some hard scuffling, but Acoya managed to keep Mo and Chuka under control as Tolonqua gutted the animal, saved the ears, the teeth, and the paws, and removed the furry hide with the stubby tail intact. He tossed the rest to the dogs who devoured it on the spot.

Tolonqua held up the skin, admiring it. "Beautiful! Your aim was sure. You are ready for a larger bow and stronger arrows," he said proudly.

Acoya was transformed with joy and pride. He wiped the little arrow on his breechcloth to clean the arrowhead, and tucked it into his fringed quiver while Tolonqua rolled up the skin and the parts saved and put them in his pack. Only then did they remember they had not eaten. They sat under the oak tree, ate the corn cake, drank from the water bag, and were soon on their way again.

Acoya seemed tireless, but Tolonqua leaned heavily on his staff. He was relieved when the village appeared.

"We will announce our coming now."

Tolonqua removed the horn and lifted it to his lips. The commanding wail sent a flock of ravens flying. Immediately, a crowd appeared on rooftops and dogs came rushing to confront the newcomers. For Chuka it was an opportunity for canine rejoicing, but Mo immediately became involved in a noisy dogfight, as usual. Tolonqua called him off with the aid of his staff, and the dog sullenly followed Tolonqua and Acoya as they approached the village.

A cluster of two-story adobe dwellings faced a modest plaza where a welcoming group awaited. Tolonqua recognized the tall, lean figure of Man Who Runs and raised his staff in salute.

"Ho!" he called. "I bring news and greetings!"

"Welcome!"

Tolonqua and Acoya were escorted to the dwelling of the village Chief, Little Crow, a stooped man of indeterminate age whose mate gestured for them to sit at the eating blanket where porridge and bowls awaited.

"We thank you," Tolonqua said politely although the porridge did not look inviting. This was a poor village. But he and Acoya ate what was offered while people crowded the room and stood watching.

Tolonqua glanced often at Man Who Runs who returned his gaze calmly. The deep-set eyes lingered on Tolonqua's crippled foot with a Medicine Chief's interest.

"You come for me to treat your foot?"

Acoya glanced up in surprise and was about to speak when Tolonqua said, "Your powers are well known. I shall be grateful."

There was pleased murmuring in the crowded room. Tolonqua, famed Building Chief and former Hunting Chief of rich Cicuye with a renowned Medicine Chief of its own, had come to their village seeking help!

Tolonqua finished the porridge with polite belches. Acoya tried manfully and managed a belch also. The meal was finished; business could now begin.

Chief Little Crow said, "We shall go to the plaza where all may hear news you bring."

Already the plaza was crowded with people seated in a semicircle, waiting. Children squealed, "They come!"

Chief Little Crow led Tolonqua and Acoya to the plaza, facing the crowd. He raised his hand for silence.

"Tolonqua, Building Chief and former Hunting Chief of Cicuye, has come with his son, Acoya. He requests treatment for his foot from our Medicine Chief." He paused for the surprised murmurs. "He brings news. Let all hear."

He sat down, leaving Tolonqua and Acoya standing alone. Acoya started to sit down, too, but Tolonqua gestured for him to remain standing.

"My son and I are honored to be here and we thank you for your hospitality. As Chief Little Crow has said, we bring news. You know of Yatosha, Hunting Chief of the Anasazi."

There were nods. The Anasazis had passed through on their way to Cicuye.

"His mate was possessed by an evil spirit." Tolonqua went on to tell what happened in dramatic detail, and the people listened avidly. What a story to repeat at evening fires! When he had finished, Tolonqua turned to Acoya.

"Show the bow and the arrow you used."

Acoya removed the arrow from its quiver and held it overhead in one hand, and the bow in the other. Tolonqua took them and handed them to Chief Little Crow.

"Perhaps your people may care to examine these."

As the Chief inspected the bow and arrow with feigned interest, Tolonqua removed the bobcat skin from his pack and held it up.

"My son shot this bobcat with that arrow on the way here." He paused. "He is four years old."

There were surprised comments. All small boys played with bows and arrows, but to use what was little more than a toy to kill a bobcat was unusual. The bow and arrow were passed from hand to hand with interest, as Acoya blushed with self-conscious embarrassment and pride.

Tolonqua said to him, "You may sit down now." He went to sit with a group of boys who moved over to make room for him.

Tolonqua continued, "As you see, my foot is weak, but I have walked the distance to come here, not only to be treated by your famed Medicine Chief, but to obtain wood with which to make my son a larger, stronger bow that will be light enough in weight for him to handle easily. This wood we do not have in Cicuye."

The hunters nodded. They knew the tree from which the wood should come. It grew in the mountains of the northwest.

Chief Little Crow turned to the village Hunting Chief. "Did you not obtain some of the wood in trade on your last journey?"

"Aye," he said reluctantly. "But—"

"Observe," Tolonqua said. From his pack he lifted the handsome turquoise and shell necklace the Hunting Chief had been given by Talasi and shamed by Man Who Runs to return. "I offer this in trade."

Tolonqua handed the necklace to the Chief who took it with unconcealed pleasure. He put it on, accepted the admiring comments of bystanders, and nodded.

"I trade with wood for the bow."

"We go now to the medicine lodge," Man Who Runs said. Acoya was the center of an admiring group, so he added, "Your son may remain here."

Tolonqua smiled. "I do not think he objects."

The lodge was small and redolent with the scent of roots and stalks and leaves hanging in bunches from ceiling beams. Jars and baskets leaned against the walls, and an altar held small bowls of sacred substances. The Chief's medicine bundle lay beside the altar. On a shelf in one wall lay two wooden flutes ornately carved and adorned with buckskin fringe. They were beautiful and Tolonqua tried not to stare at them; he did not want the Medicine Chief to guess the real reason he was here.

Man Who Runs unrolled a bearskin beside the fire pit and

motioned for Tolonqua to be seated there. From another shelf the Chief brought a round pottery jar with a narrow opening stopped with a wad of buckskin. Carefully, he placed the jar beside the fire pit. Coals still burned; the Chief added pinecones and chunks of juniper and fanned them to flame. Satisfied, he used two forked sticks to lift a stone from the fire pit and place it upon the flames. As the stone heated, Man Who Runs squatted before Tolonqua and held his crippled foot in both hands.

"It pains?"

"Yes."

"Remove the moccasin."

Tolonqua did so, exposing his scarred foot soiled with dust and perspiration from his journey. The Chief dipped a rag into his water jar and washed the foot, paying special attention to the scars. Then he kneaded the foot with strong fingers, probing the bones and tendons.

He sat back on his heels and gazed at Tolonqua with compassion. "I cannot heal what cannot be healed. But I can make it feel better."

"I shall be grateful for that."

From one of the large baskets the Chief took a wooden block and set it upon the stone rim of the fire pit. "Prop your foot here."

Tolonqua lay his foot on the block above the place where the stone was heating at the edge of the fire pit. The Chief lifted the pottery jar, removed the stopper, and poured a bit of cloudy liquid upon the stone. It sizzled with a strong fragrance of balsam fir. From another basket came a piece of buffalo hide.

"This will enclose the steam."

He poured more liquid on the hot stone, enough to make steam, and covered Tolonqua's foot with the hide. Tolonqua felt the hot steam enveloping his foot; he felt as if the moist heat penetrated to the bone. As the steam subsided, the Chief poured more liquid, and so on, until the jar was empty.

Tolonqua lay on the skin of Bear, feeling its healing power, feeling the steam on his foot, feeling the pain lessen. When the steam was gone, the Chief massaged Tolonqua's foot again.

"Is it better now?"

"It is."

"Good." Man Who Runs sat back and regarded Tolonqua with a searching gaze. "Is there pain elsewhere? In the spirit, perhaps?"

Tolonqua looked into the deep-set eyes in the regal old face. He wondered, How does he know?

"Yes. There is pain in the spirit."

"Ah." Man Who Runs motioned Tolonqua to join him before the altar. They sat, arms and legs folded, in silence to allow their spirits to communicate with each other. Finally, Man Who Runs said, "Tell me now."

"It is because of the death of the Anasazi woman. The one Acoya shot with his arrow. Although the woman was possessed by an evil spirit, and although Acoya shot his arrow to save She Who Remembers, he has been blamed by the Anasazis for the woman's death. He grieves."

From outside came shouts and laughter of boys playing. A voice shouted, "Acoya is next!"

"My son is happy here. He can forget Chomoc for a while."

"Chomoc?"

"Son of the woman who was killed."

"They are friends?"

"They were. Now Chomoc avoids everyone except his father who grieves, also. They go alone to their distant field and sleep there. The Anasazis blame Acoya and She Who Remembers. . . ."

Man Who Runs sat in silence, head bowed, bony hands clasped. Shouts of the boys at play faded into the distance. From nearby came the song of a flute, high and sweet.

Tolonqua had been wondering how to bring up the matter of the flutes. He glanced at the Chief whose head was still bowed in silence. Again, the flute sang.

"It is beautiful," Tolonqua said. "Is that a flute you made?"

Man Who Runs nodded absently, still gazing at his folded hands.

Tolonqua continued, "The flute's song heals the spirit."

The old Chief raised his head and gazed at Tolonqua as though, like Kwani, he could see the secret place behind the eyes. He smiled faintly.

"You wish to obtain one of my flutes." It was not a question but a statement of fact.

"I wish to trade for two. One for Acoya and one for Chomoc."

Again the faint smile. "I may consider trading for one for Acoya. He is worthy. But not for Chomoc."

"May I ask why?"

"You may. He is the son of one possessed of an evil spirit. That does not make him worthy of my flute."

"He is also the son of Kokopelli."

"Ah." Again, Man Who Runs sat in silence.

The flute's song lingered, then faded away. From somewhere a girl's voice sang the melody. It was beauty to wring the heart.

Tolonqua reached in his pack for his most splendid necklace. It was of turquoise and shells with beads of obsidian and polished claws of Bear, the healer—an object of great value. He lay it gleaming upon the stone altar.

"I offer this to you and to your gods."

The Chief looked at it without expression and did not reach to hold it. Finally, he said, "It is worth many flutes. Even mine. Yet you trade it for two. Why?"

"The people of my city are one against another because of the woman's death. My mate, She Who Remembers, grieves and fears for her unborn child. Acoya bears a heavy burden for one so young. And the heart of Chomoc, son of Kokopelli, is torn asunder. Your flutes are needed for healing. Therefore, I trade not for flutes alone, but for their healing powers.

Tolonqua reached in his pack and removed a medicine man's pipe of clay, beautifully made, with a carved figure of Bear walking upon it. He lay this upon the altar, also.

"I offer this for my son."

Slowly, Man Who Runs picked up the pipe. He examined it carefully, turning it over, running his fingers over the finely polished surfaces. He returned the pipe to the altar, picked up the necklace, and fingered each of the curved bear claws. He lay the necklace beside the pipe.

"I accept your offer."

"I am grateful."

"On one condition. That both Acoya and Chomoc take these flutes with them when they seek their manhood vision. They are to play for me then. I shall be in Sipapu for Sipapu calls, but my spirit will answer the flute's song. If Acoya and Chomoc are worthy, my spirit will bring them a vision. If they are not worthy, if they dishonor the gods, my flutes will refuse to sing and no vision will appear."

To be denied a vision would mean they would be doomed to wander aimlessly through life with no protecting spirit or spiritual guidance. They would be less than men. Pitied and ignored in matters of importance.

"I will tell them and make them promise to do as you request. I cannot assume responsibility for Chomoc. But if either of the boys dishonors the gods, I promise the flutes will be returned to you or to your clan."

"It is agreed."

Man Who Runs took the flutes from the shelf and brought them to Tolonqua. Holding them, Tolonqua saw how fine was the handwork, how beautiful the colors of the buckskin fringe. Carefully, he tucked them in his pack and replaced the moccasin on his foot, which felt stronger.

He rose and faced Man Who Runs. "I wish to pay what I owe for the treatment to my foot."

The Chief picked up the pipe and held it in both hands. "Your son has paid."

"Very well." Tolonqua smiled. "I go now for the wood for the bow. We shall spend the night and return to Cicuye in the morning."

They parted friends, each wishing he knew the other better, each knowing they would not meet again.

But neither knew why they would not.

▲ 37 ▼

"**H**old it this way."

Long See, Cicuye's young Hunting Chief, held the flute to Acoya's lips and showed him where the fingers should be placed. Long See was known as the best flutist for miles around, and he had agreed to teach Acoya how to make the flute sing.

Acoya did as he was told.

"Now blow."

Acoya took a deep breath and blew. The flute squawked shrilly.

"Try again, and move the fingers on the holes."

The flute squawked again, but not so shrilly this time.

"Good. You and the flute must become acquainted. Keep practicing until your spirit and the spirit of the flute know each other. Then the flute will sing for you."

Acoya looked at the scrawny young Hunting Chief with the stringy hair and surprisingly fat braids. Long See had magical power to make flutes sing with a sweet voice.

"I will practice."

Acoya wanted to be able to play a melody before he gave Chomoc his gift; it would encourage Chomoc to accept it and they would be friends again. Acoya was self-conscious about trying to play when anyone was around to hear, so every day he took his fine new bow and arrows and his flute to a remote place on the ridge. There he would sit on a big rock, gaze over the valley to the peaks where mountain gods dwelled, and seek the spirit of his flute to make it sing.

One day as his fingers danced on the flute and he gazed into the distance, concentrating, footsteps approached on the rocky soil. Acoya stopped playing and turned around. Chomoc stood there.

The boys looked at each other.

Acoya turned to his flute and played some more. Chomoc came closer and stood by Acoya with such a look of longing that Acoya stopped playing again.

"I greet you," he said politely.

Chomoc did not reply. He just stood there. He looked thin, as though he had been sick. He stared at the flute.

Acoya handed it to him. "Here. You play it."

Chomoc took the flute and held it in both hands, looking at it. He lifted it to his lips. His fingers sought the holes as though they knew where the holes were but had not been there for a long time.

He blew, and the flute spoke. He blew again, and a sweet note trembled in the air.

Chomoc removed the flute from his lips and stared at it. A light came into his face and he smiled and began to play again, tentatively at first, then more confidently as his fingers found their way.

Acoya was surprised. He wondered where Chomoc learned to play like that. Did he already have a flute? Acoya hoped not; he wanted to give Chomoc something he did not have. He wanted to be friends again. He wanted everything to be as it used to be, but Chomoc did not seem to notice he was there. It was just himself and the flute, which sounded different when Chomoc played it.

"See my new bow!"

Acoya offered the bow to Chomoc who glanced at it and stopped playing. Acoya removed an arrow from his new quiver and offered the arrow and the bow to Chomoc.

"Try it."

Chomoc looked at the flute, turned it over in both hands as though he wanted to remember how it looked, then handed it to Acoya and took the bow and arrow.

Acoya said, "I killed a bobcat with my other one so my father made me this. It is strong. Try it."

Chomoc shot an arrow into the sky. It went higher and higher.

"Ah!"

Acoya said, "You may use it whenever you want."

Chomoc nodded, but his gaze was on the flute.

"I have a present for you at my house. Come and I'll give it to you." Acoya jumped up and down, smiling. "Come on."

Chomoc picked up the arrow where it had fallen. He looked at Acoya, and it was as though something cold in his face melted. He smiled again.

"What is the present?"

"Come and see."

They trotted back to the city while Acoya told Chomoc

about the bobcat and the journey to see Man Who Runs. Now and then they stopped to try the bow again. Chomoc kept looking at the flute but Acoya pretended he didn't notice. When they neared Acoya's dwelling they heard Kwani singing.

Chomoc hesitated. "Will she want to see me?"

"Of course. Come on."

The door was open and they went in. Kwani knelt at the metate, singing the Corn Grinding Song as she worked. She looked up and saw them.

"Chomoc!"

Kwani flung both arms wide and Chomoc ran to her. She hugged him, and he buried his face on her shoulder and clung to her.

"It is so good to see you, Chomoc."

Tolonqua entered from the adjoining room. "It is, indeed. Welcome."

Chomoc smiled up at him and Acoya saw that Chomoc's eyes were shiny.

"Give Chomoc his present!"

Kwani said, "You give it, Acoya."

Acoya went to the next room where his things were, and Chomoc followed. Acoya pointed.

A flute lay on a low shelf. It was like Acoya's but with different colors and more beautiful buckskin fringe.

"Take it. It is yours."

Chomoc took the flute and held it a moment, gazing. Slowly, lovingly, he lifted it to his lips and began to play.

In the next room Tolonqua and Kwani listened, astonished. They glanced at one another.

Kokopelli.

▲ 38 ▼

Kwani stood on the walkway outside her door, watching Rainfeather's approach. She thought, I cannot and will not eat another bite of raw weasel! The thought of it made her feel worse than she did already.

Rainfeather's stubby little legs carried her across the courtyard where children ran to greet her. An adult as small as a child never ceased to intrigue them and she was surrounded. She called them by name and patted the dogs as she always did. Finally she reached the walkway where Kwani waited.

"I greet you," Kwani said, "but I hope you bring no weasel this time."

The tiny woman's pushed-in face smiled so that her cheeks bunched up into round balls and her small eyes nearly closed. "I bring the skin only. To rub on you again. Come, we shall see how the twins are doing, eh?"

They entered Kwani's dwelling where she undressed and lay down upon the sleeping mat. Tolonqua was in the kiva with Acoya teaching the boys to be hunters. Kwani felt guilty because she should be teaching the girls; she had neglected her duties as She Who Remembers lately; it seemed that this pregnancy had taken strength from her spirit. She would resume teaching once the baby was born.

Rainfeather squatted beside Kwani and peered into her eyes and inspected her tongue. She felt Kwani's breasts, pinching the nipples gently to see what oozed out. She nodded.

"You will have good milk. I will give you milk medicine so you will have enough for twins."

"But they are twisted into one!" Kwani said. "One baby only."

"Maybe. But that one baby will be twins just the same. You will see."

Rainfeather's strong little hands probed Kwani's abdomen. The baby responded, kicking vigorously.

"They know it is the ninth moon," Rainfeather said, chuckling. "They are turning around to be head down." She nodded. "That is good. They are big." She sat back on her heels and reached in the medicine basket she always carried. "Now we make it easy for them to come out." She produced a smelly, ragged piece of weasel skin and waved it in Kwani's face.

Kwani turned her head away. The odor made her stomach churn. "I don't want any more of that!"

"Maybe you don't like it, but the twins do. You will be glad they had it when you try to push them out."

She rubbed the skin on Kwani's abdomen, hips, and woman part, leaving an odorous residue.

"Enough!" Kwani said. "I shall have no more."

"Very well. I have done my best." Rainfeather picked up her basket and tucked the skin into it. "Remember not to allow anyone to walk in front of you; it will make the birthing difficult. Have you tanned skins?"

"No."

"Have you worked hard to make your body strong?"

"Yes. Until lately. I don't feel like it now."

Rainfeather nodded. "It is nearly time. I shall be ready." She leaned over Kwani's abdomen, patting it. "Good-bye, little ones. I shall return soon." She picked up her basket, bid Kwani farewell, and departed.

Kwani lay there, listening to the short footsteps fading away. Rainfeather's talk of twins made her uneasy. The weasel odor made her stomach churn again and she felt she might vomit. She had eaten enough weasel meat to satisfy a dozen babies; she did not have to put up with this. She dipped a rag into a bowl of water and washed herself, luxuriating in being clean once more.

From the kiva came the sound of a flute, high and sweet. Chomoc. Kwani listened, remembering how Kokopelli's music probed the secret places of the heart. Chomoc would discover that power one day. Since he had the flute, and he and Acoya were close friends once more, Yatosha also seemed more like his former self. He and Chomoc lived with old Huzipat now, and Yatosha helped Long See, the Hunting Chief, in the planning of hunts as well as with the hunting. Since Long See worked with Chomoc, teaching him to play the flute, Yatosha and Long See had become friends.

Tiopi's death was no longer discussed; it was best for it to be forgotten lest her spirit return to haunt the living.

Several days passed and Kwani grew increasingly uneasy. "Rainfeather keeps saying it is twins," she told Tolonqua.

"Twins twisted into one. That is what the Medicine Chief says, and I believe him rather than Rainfeather."

Of course he believed the Medicine Chief; he was a man. But women knew more about babies and birthings than men did. "I don't feel as I did with Acoya. I feel different—"

"This baby is not Acoya; he has different ways."

Kwani's temper flared. "What do you mean, *he*? I want a girl. That is what it will be. A girl! Why do you always say he?"

"We shall see." He must be careful about making Kwani angry; it would harm the baby.

Another day passed. Kwani felt no birthing pains, but she knew instinctively it was her time—as animals knew, preparing. She sent Acoya to the river for sand from the riverbank, and asked Tolonqua for a good supply of juniper wood. The Medicine Chief was alerted, and Rainfeather appeared, beaming.

"It is time, eh?"

"Yes."

"Pain?"

"Not yet."

She nodded. "It will come. I am ready."

Pain did not come until two days later when it struck hard. Tolonqua sent Acoya to stay with Chomoc. Anitzal hurried over, the Medicine Chief came, and Rainfeather appeared with her medicine basket. Immediately, Rainfeather put a large bowl of water to heat on the coals in the fire pit. The Medicine Chief bent over Kwani and pressed both hands on her abdomen, feeling the position of the baby's body.

Kwani groaned as pain grew more severe. She tried not to think of a bloody little bundle, but could not help herself.

"Is anything wrong?" she asked.

His good eye regarded her with compassion. "The baby is large. It will not be easy." He gestured to Tolonqua. "Go now."

"Is it one baby?"

"Yes. Of course."

"Twins," Rainfeather said. "Go."

"I shall be nearby," Tolonqua told Kwani. "I will come if you need me."

Anitzal took Kwani's hand and held it comfortingly. "All

will be well." Kwani knew Anitzal remembered the little bundle, too.

More pain, grinding down.

"Move to the sand."

Kwani pulled herself to the little pile of sand on the birthing blanket and knelt on her hands and knees. When pain struck harder, she raised her head a little and bore down. The water broke. It had a clean, natural smell. Kwani breathed it in, bearing down hard. Pain knifed her with searing force.

The Medicine Chief stood behind Kwani and pressed down on her abdomen, shaking her a little in an effort to force the baby out. It would not come.

Rainfeather had been busy preparing a brew with juniper and other substances from her medicine basket. She lifted a small bowl to Kwani's lips.

"Drink. It will help."

Kwani tried to gulp it down, but spilled half of it as savage pain wrenched her again. She heard herself making animal sounds. Groaning.

Anitzal's voice. "You're opening! I can see—"

Rainfeather: "Get out of the way, Anitzal. Move!"

The Medicine Chief: "The baby needs help to come out. Lay her down."

Kwani felt herself stretched out on the blanket and the damp sand. She knew vaguely that the Medicine Chief bent between her raised knees. She felt pressure, movement. She heard screams. Hers?

"Bear down!" The Medicine Chief ordered.

She was lifted up, held around her waist, shaken.

"Bear down!"

Kwani did not feel the blood running down her legs as membranes stretched to the tearing point and the baby's head and shoulders emerged.

"They come!" Rainfeather cried.

Kwani felt the little body being pulled from her own. A baby's cry! She looked down at the tiny being the Medicine Chief handed to Rainfeather.

A *girl!*

"A girl!" she cried. "A girl!" She wanted to lie down and rest and hold the baby, but they were still joined by the umbilical cord.

Rainfeather cut the cord with a fleshing knife to make the girl a good tanner of hides. Anitzal wrapped her in a blanket and laid her near the fire while Rainfeather folded back the cord and tied it a finger's length from the navel, using strands of Kwani's hair as the tie.

Again the Medicine Chief stood behind Kwani and held her by the waist to help her expel the afterbirth. Anitzal handed Rainfeather the bowl of juniper potion and Rainfeather held it to Kwani's lips.

"Drink. This will give you strength."

The Medicine Chief pressed down on her abdomen, and shook her. The afterbirth did not come.

He pressed against her back and her stomach. "Stick your finger down your throat and make yourself gag."

She poked her finger down her throat as far as she could, and gagged, vomiting. The juniper potion spewed. Rainfeather gently pulled on the dangling cord and the afterbirth slowly emerged.

Kwani panted with weariness. She wanted to lie down with the baby, but Rainfeather shoved a short stool—the birthing stool—under her.

"Sit here so the blood drips on the sand. Now, we shall have a look at the twins."

Anitzal brought the baby and lay her in Kwani's arms as Rainfeather unwrapped the blanket. They examined the baby closely. A large child, large for a girl, beautiful and perfect.

"Look!" Rainfeather pointed to the Pueblo mark-of-birth at the base of the spine, a small mark like a bruise that faded at age six. It was shaped like a tiny penis.

"I told you it was twins!" she crowed. "She is both girl and boy!"

"See this, also." The Medicine Chief pointed to the little head, still wet from the birthing. Instead of the hair curling itself into one little whorl, there were two.

"Twins twisted into one," the Medicine Chief announced with satisfaction. "I have finished. Rainfeather will do the rest." Wearily, he rose to go. The older he became, the more difficult birthings seemed to be. "I shall tell Tolonqua."

While Anitzal bathed the baby in warm water and yucca suds, Rainfeather gave Kwani juniper tea to clear the womb. Gratefully, Kwani lay on her mat while Rainfeather bathed her in the warm suds, wrapped her in a blanket, and laid her on her side before the fire so that the bones could fit back into place. Anitzal laid the baby beside Kwani who gazed and gazed, inspecting each tiny finger and toe. A girl!

Tolonqua entered. He bent over Kwani and the baby, and his face was tender with concern. "You are all right?"

"Yes. Look!"

Kwani showed him the mark of twins. "She is both boy and girl!"

"The Medicine Chief told me." Tolonqua smiled. "I have my son and you have your daughter. What could be better?"

Kwani looked up at him, at the strong, lean face close to hers. Did he mean it? She searched the place behind his eyes, the secret place, and saw bitter disappointment as well as deep love for her.

She drew his face to hers and kissed him. "The boy in her is you. She will be a special child, and make us proud."

Carefully, Rainfeather swept up the bloody sand with a little corn-husk broom and emptied the sand into an old rag. She placed the broom and the afterbirth on the sand and sprinkled the whole with meal. Then she rolled up the rag with its contents and handed it to Tolonqua.

"Put it on the trash pile." This was so no one would step on it and cause his feet to become sore and chapped, his eyes yellow, and his urine thick.

When he had gone, Anitzal said, "I go to bring more water and baby wrappings." She hurried away.

Rainfeather sat beside Kwani, her short legs spread out like a child's. Her round, middle-aged face framed by black braids bore an expression of satisfaction.

"I shall require payment for two," she said. "Twins."

Kwani gave her a look. "The Medicine Chief requires payment for one only."

The small black eyes snapped. "For nine moons I have cared for you. How many moons has the Medicine Chief done so?"

Kwani did not feel like arguing. Not now. "Discuss it with Tolonqua. He is the one who pays."

"I shall do so. Meanwhile, you are to remain here with the door closed, avoiding light, for twenty days. Anitzal will care for you now. I depart." She gathered up her belongings and put them in her basket. "Drink plenty of juniper tea and purify yourself with juniper smoke. If you need me, I will come." She turned to go. "That will cost extra." She nodded briskly, and left.

Kwani looked down at the tiny one beside her and lifted the baby to her breast. The little mouth sucked, pink lips stretched wide over the nipple. Kwani touched the downy head where two whorls grew, and admired the miniature lashes on miniature cheeks. How beautiful was her daughter!

Anitzal entered with cornmeal, two white corn ears, and baby wrappings. She came with a smiling face and a happy heart to bring the baby good luck and to ensure the child would have a happy spirit. But when she saw the baby nursing, her bright face darkened with alarm.

"No! It is too soon! Your milk is not yet ready!"

"But I nursed Acoya this way."

"This is a Towa baby. You must wait for the milk."

Anitzal leaned to take the baby, but Kwani refused to let her go.

"This is my daughter. She will drink from me now and whenever she wishes."

Anitzal yanked the baby from Kwani's arms.

"This is a Towa baby, I tell you. I cannot allow you to harm her."

Kwani watched, fuming, as Anitzal spoke tender baby-talk words and rubbed juniper ashes over the baby's skin to make it smooth. Then she sat, raised her garment, and laid the baby across her bare thighs.

"You are my child of the Turquoise Clan. You will live long and have many children of your own."

"She is *my* child!" Kwani protested.

"Of course," Anitzal said gently. "But she has family and clan. Is this not what you wish for her?"

Kwani was ashamed. "I do wish it. Forgive me."

Anitzal smiled. "You have given me a beautiful child of Tolonqua's blood, which is my blood also. I am grateful. You are tired," she added kindly. "Rest now."

Kwani watched as Anitzal chewed some juniper twigs, spat upon the tiny earlobes, and rubbed them to numbness. With a sharp little bone needle she pierced the ears and passed a thread through to keep the holes open. The baby cried only a short while. Then Anitzal placed the little arms by their sides, wrapped the baby in a warm blanket, and tucked her in the cradle board already stuffed with shredded juniper bark. She set the cradle board beside Kwani and put an ear of corn on either side.

"One is for you and one for your baby," Anitzal said. "I shall come in the morning to make the after-birthing house. Sleep now."

Kwani slept, and dreamed. Her spirit left her body and journeyed to the House of the Sun, the sacred temple that stood on the mesa across the ravine from the Place of the

Eagle Clan. The Old One, She Who Remembers before Kwani, was there, waiting.

Kwani stood in awe. "I greet you, Honored One."

"Come." The Old One gestured to the altar, the waist-high stone in the Place of Remembering.

Kwani approached the stone and knelt there, the Old One beside her.

"Why have you not fulfilled your duties as She Who Remembers?" the Old One asked.

"I have taught."

"Not lately. And you are not training a successor. Do you think Sipapu will never call?" Luminous dark eyes, blind no longer, gazed at Kwani from inside the folds of a feather blanket. "You are chosen of the gods. Now they give you a daughter. Teach her what she must know."

The figure in the feather blanket dissolved and faded away.

"Don't leave me!" Kwani cried. But the Old One was gone.

Kwani woke.

She lay there in the darkness, listening to Tolonqua's quiet breathing. She reached to touch the baby, who stirred. For some time Kwani lay awake, thinking of the dream and remembering the Old One. What am I to teach my daughter? she wondered. Should it be what I teach all young girls? Or do the Ancient Ones want her to be my successor?

Always, She Who Remembers had chosen the one to be She Who Remembers after her, a special and demanding privilege. Did the Old One see the future and fear for Kwani's daughter? Was there something more Kwani should teach her? If so, what?

Kwani pressed the necklace to her, fingering the scallop shell and its mystic turquoise inlay, straining to communicate with the Ancient Ones, those who were She Who Remembers since Earthmother created the first one.

"What must I do?" she whispered.

The answer came, silent words like music unheard. *Danger awaits. Your daughter has powers.*

"What powers? What dangers?"

There was no reply. Kwani lay wondering. It was long before she drifted into exhausted sleep.

Shortly after pulatla, Anitzal appeared with a bowl of finely ground cornmeal.

"Now I shall make your after-birthing house," she announced happily.

Taking the meal, she rubbed five horizontal lines as long

as a man's hand, one above the other, on the four walls of the room. As each day passed it would be her duty to scrape one line off and carry the scrapings to the edge of the mesa, pray for a long life for Kwani's child, and toss the meal to Sunfather.

"Now I have made a house for you. You shall stay here twenty days while we wait for you." She draped a blanket over the door. "Sunfather's light must not enter here until the baby is presented to him."

"Does Acoya know he has a sister?" Tolonqua asked.

"Yes. He tells everyone."

"Good. I'll bring him home today."

"This room must stay dark for twenty days," Anitzal reminded Tolonqua. "And you are not to have intercourse during those days or the twenty days afterward. If you do, a new baby will be started and it will make this little one sick and give her nervous spells and maybe spoil her for life. Remember that."

"We will remember," Kwani said, smiling.

"But it will not be easy," Tolonqua said, looking at Kwani. She lay naked, her lovely stomach flat once more, and her breasts more beautiful than ever with the milk within.

"Go now," Anitzal said. "I have much to do here."

Tolonqua reluctantly departed, and Anitzal lit a fire that was to burn night and day for twenty days. She laid juniper twigs on the fire and sprinkled water upon it.

"Stand over it," Anitzal said when smoke billowed. "It will cleanse you."

Kwani straddled the smoke and felt it enveloping her. When the smoke evaporated, Kwani lay on her mat while Anitzal again bathed the baby in yucca suds and warm water and rubbed juniper ashes on the little body. Then she was tucked back in the cradle board and handed to Kwani, cradle board and all, for nursing. Kwani watched the little mouth drinking. Was the baby drinking from her spirit, also? Did a mother's milk contain a mother's love to be absorbed like food?

When the baby slept, Anitzal laid the cradle board down. "People will be coming soon to see the baby and you. I will bathe you, but first you must drink the juniper tea."

She handed Kwani a mug of hot tea, and Kwani sipped it while Anitzal bathed her with yucca suds and juniper solution.

Anitzal talked as she worked. "We shall have a fine naming ceremony, with feasting and visitors from other pueblos.'' She nodded happily. ''Yes. And singing. Our little girl child will have the finest naming ceremony Cicuye has ever seen, for never before have we named a child who is twins twisted into one.'' She paused, thinking. ''What name will you give her?''

Kwani looked at the sleeping face, all that could be seen of her daughter tucked in the cradle board. ''I have not decided.''

''She will be given many names. I shall call her—'' Anitzal stopped. ''I forgot. I must not say the name until the naming ceremony.''

Again Kwani was wrapped in a blanket and laid on her side by the fire. Visitors arrived, each careful to let in no daylight. They brought piki bread and corn cake and venison jerky and dried squash and pinyon nuts and berries and pretty things for the baby—lavish gifts. Each admired the child, congratulated Kwani, wished them well, and left.

''I will come later to change the baby and prepare food,'' Anitzal said. With kindly pats and crooning sounds, she bade farewell and departed as Tolonqua entered with Acoya.

Acoya marched to the cradle board and stood staring down at it.

''What do you think of your sister?'' Kwani asked.

''She's so little!''

''You were that little once.''

''Babies grow fast,'' Tolonqua said in a man-to-man tone. ''Antelope have twins, you know, and they grow fast, too. They are beautiful. . . .'' He gazed into the distance, remembering.

Acoya touched the baby, running a finger over her downy hair and miniature nose. ''What will her name be?''

''We will not know until the naming ceremony.''

''Give the baby to me,'' Kwani said.

Tolonqua laid the cradle board beside Kwani, and he and Acoya went to the adjoining room on masculine business of one kind or another.

Kwani held the baby close and bent her cheek to the tiny face.

''I know your name,'' she whispered. ''It is Antelope Child.''

PART 3

▲▼▲▼▲▼▲▼▲▼▲▼▲▼▲▼▲▼▲▼▲▼

THE MORNING STAR

▲ 39 ▼

It was a warm summer day with a drift of white cloud. Upstream, at the river's edge, Antelope, Acoya, and Chomoc crouched behind a boulder and watched a young cottontail rabbit darting into its hole. A willow bent low over them, trailing green fingers.

"Now!" Acoya whispered. He flipped shoulder-length hair out of his eyes and reached for the forked stick he had prepared, but Antelope already had it in her brown little hand.

"I want to do it!" she said loudly.

Acoya looked at the round face close to his. It was dirty, as usual, and strands of dark hair dangled over her forehead.

"Be quiet!" he hissed. "You scare everything away."

"The rabbit is already scared," Chomoc said in his high, disdainful voice. "Nothing else is around here."

"See?" Antelope crowed.

Acoya sat back on his heels and looked at his sister, and at Chomoc who was supposed to be his best friend but who sided with Antelope every time.

"It is *my* stick," Acoya said firmly with the authority of a brother four years older. "I made it, so I am going to get the rabbit."

He grabbed the stick to yank it from Antelope's hand, but she hung on to it with both of hers. She was strong for a girl, especially one who was only six. It was because she was twins.

"I want to!" she screeched. "I want to!"

She leaned back on her heels and pulled. The forked end of the stick broke and she fell backward into the water, feet in the air.

The boys laughed uproariously. Antelope stood in the water and glared, but her lips trembled.

"I want that baby rabbit. To keep."

Acoya handed her the stick. "You broke the forked end, see? Go ahead and poke that down the hole and see if it will tangle itself in the rabbit's fur without a fork. Ha!'' He snorted with disgust.

Tears welled up in Antelope's brown eyes and trickled down both cheeks. She stomped her foot in the water with a splash.

"I hate you!" She snatched the stick and tried to hit Acoya with it, but Chomoc grabbed her.

"You shall have the rabbit, foolish one. Without the stick.''

He stood straight. He was not as tall as Acoya, but he was tall enough to make Antelope look up at him as he took the stick away from her. He assumed a lordly stance.

"I shall speak to the rabbit." He looked down his beak nose. "If you will keep quiet while I do."

Antelope's eyes grew big and her mouth was a rosy little O. Then she said, "I will be quiet, Chomoc."

Acoya fumed. Antelope always made Chomoc pay more attention to her than to him. "If you will stay quiet long enough the rabbit will come out by itself." He gave Antelope a shove. "Why don't you just go away for a while?"

She shoved him back. "I don't have to. Chomoc says—"

"I know what Chomoc says." Acoya assumed Chomoc's arrogant pose and looked down his nose. "I will talk to the rabbit," he said in an excellent imitation of Chomoc's high voice. "Ha!"

Chomoc's face turned pink all the way up his sloping brow to the dark brown hair pulled back in a single short braid. "You think I can't, don't you? Watch."

Chomoc lay down on his stomach beside the rabbit hole and put his mouth to the opening. Antelope crouched beside him, motionless and silent for a change. Acoya wanted to crouch beside Chomoc, too, but there wasn't room for the three of them by the boulder where the hole was, and if he pushed Antelope out of the way there would be another yowling commotion. So he climbed the boulder where he could look down at the hole that was covered now by Chomoc's head.

The three of them were silent and motionless for a long time. Finally, Acoya said, "How can the rabbit come out if your head is in the way?"

Antelope put her finger to her mouth. "Sh-h-h-h!"

Imagine Antelope shushing *him*! "I'll talk if I want to!" he shouted.

They glanced at him with surprise. Acoya was usually the calm, soft-spoken one, slow to anger, who thought everything over. It was Chomoc whose temper flared quickly and who acted on impulse.

Nearby, a low bush rustled, and a little rabbit popped out and dashed away.

"My rabbit!" Antelope cried, and ran after it.

Acoya slid down the boulder. "There's another hole beneath that bush over there."

"Maybe it was the same rabbit. You frightened it."

Acoya shook his head. "It can't be the same rabbit."

"Why not?"

"A different hole. What else?"

"A different hole but the same burrow, maybe."

"Ha! A different rabbit, you mean. You bragged to Antelope about talking to a rabbit. Your talk scared it away. But Antelope is gone, so now we can find another rabbit."

He would have Chomoc to himself. Finally. They would make another stick with a sharp little fork at the end, thrust it down the hole and twist it around until the rabbit's fur was caught, then pull the rabbit out. They would go home with something to be cooked for the evening meal. A triumph! "Come on. Let's find another burrow." Chomoc was always ready to do something; he never had to stop and think about everything first.

Chomoc turned to go with Acoya, but sobs and slow footsteps approached. Antelope.

"My rabbit got away." Tears streaked her cheeks and dripped from her small nose. "You scared it, Acoya!" Loud wails. "I want my baby rabbit!"

Chomoc went to her and put his arm around her. "You stay here. I will find your rabbit."

Chomoc strode away, and Acoya followed in frustration. Antelope always got her way. It wasn't fair. Chomoc was *his* friend, and they should be hunting rabbits for a meal and not looking for a pet for some girl even if she was his sister.

But as they searched for tracks, Acoya became as engrossed as Chomoc. It was a small rabbit and tracking was difficult at best. Occasional broken twigs, pebbles moved out of their marked places, tiny rabbit tracks, were often obliterated by Antelope's passage. Soon they lost track altogether.

Chomoc looked at Acoya. "I can't find it." His glance said "What shall I do?" but he did not say that. He did not say anything more but sat down, looking embarrassed.

Acoya understood how he felt. In fact, he would be em-

barrassed, too, if both of them returned to Antelope with
no rabbit to show for their manly hunting abilities. He said,
"We can make another stick and find another burrow. Or
set snares. Come on."

"Yes." Acoya couldn't talk to animals, but he was fun.
He always knew something to do. "Antelope does make a
lot of noise, so we will tell her to stay there and wait for
us."

"Good!" Chomoc made sense at last.

They returned to the boulder through tree shadows on
crunchy leaves. There Antelope sat beneath the willow,
holding a little rabbit close in her arms. She saw the boys
coming, and beamed.

"Look! My rabbit!"

The boys stood gawking.

"Where did you find it?" Acoya asked.

"Right there." She pointed to the rabbit hole. "It sat
right there and I went and picked it up. It likes me!" She
nuzzled the soft fur.

The boys looked at each other. The first rabbit! It had
heard Chomoc and obeyed! In spite of himself Acoya was
overcome with admiration.

"You did it! You made him come out." How wonderful
was his friend!

Chomoc did not reply. He stood looking at Antelope as
she cuddled the little creature and made tender noises. He
smiled.

"Your sister will hold my baby that way someday. Hers
and mine. Then Chomoc and Acoya shall be true brothers."

Acoya was speechless, for what could he say?

Kwani sat on the walkway under the welcoming shade of
the roof overhang. With her were Anitzal and Lumu's two
girls, Weomah and Imka, now eight and nine. The girls
were not beauties, but they had Lumu's sunny ways and
would make good mates for lucky braves one day.

Anitzal watched fondly as the girls mended worn robes,
slim fingers adept with bone needles and sinew thread. Anitzal's hair, nearly white now, framed her creased face that
still smiled a young smile. "You do well," she told the
girls.

Imka returned the smile. She looked up at the roof above
them. "Where is Antelope?"

Antelope often clambered along rooftops like a mountain
goat, but nobody was surprised. She was twins and had

special powers to protect herself. However, no light footsteps were heard today.

Kwani said, "She went rabbit hunting with Acoya and Chomoc."

Anitzal nodded. "Sometimes I think she is more boy than girl."

"I know. Look at these sandals." Kwani held up Antelope's sandals badly in need of repair. "She wears these out as fast as Acoya does. She is wearing new ones today, but they will look like these in no time." She laid the sandals in her lap and looked away for a moment. "It is not easy to be mother of a twin child. She is in an emotional storm of one kind or another half the time. As though the twins are fighting each other. I don't know what to do—"

"Because sometimes she is boy and sometimes girl, is that not so?"

"Yes. But I am not always sure which is which."

"Well, I think she is lucky," Imka said. "She has Acoya and Chomoc, like two brothers."

"To protect her," Weomah added.

Anitzal said, "She is an Antelope child; her spirit protects her."

A commotion in the courtyard below made them lean over the rail to look. Antelope was there, surrounded by curious children and a pack of dogs yapping excitedly.

"What is that?" Weomah asked.

"What?"

"That thing Antelope is holding in her arms. See?"

"It looks like a little rabbit!" Kwani said with surprise.

"A live rabbit. The dogs are after it," Anitzal said worriedly. "They may try to get it and hurt her." She turned to the girls. "Bring her up here right away."

The girls ran down the walkway to the ladder; soon they were pushing their way through children and dogs to Antelope. Imka tried to take the rabbit but Antelope refused to let it go.

"Mine!" she cried. "It is mine!"

A dog lunged at the rabbit and nearly knocked Antelope down. Imka picked up Antelope and carried her, rabbit and all, up the ladder to the walkway and set her on her feet.

"Come here," Kwani said, beckoning.

Antelope came reluctantly, cradling the rabbit protectively. "It is mine. Chomoc got it for me."

"Where?"

"Upstream. By a big rock. Chomoc told it to come out of the hole for me, and it did."

Imka and Weomah glanced at each other and giggled. Anitzal said kindly, "Rabbits don't come out of holes because somebody asks them to. I guess the rabbit didn't know Chomoc was there."

Kwani said, "Kokopelli communicated with animals. I saw him do it." These Towas did not recognize Kokopelli's powers and abilities. Maybe Kokopelli's son had them also. If so, he had better be careful until he was old enough to know how to use them without being suspected of witchcraft.

"I want to keep it for a pet." Antelope's brown eyes searched Kwani's pleadingly. "Isn't it pretty?"

"Yes." Kwani touched the soft fur and felt the animal's trembling. "But your pet will not be safe here. The dogs—"

"I will keep it up here. Away from the dogs."

"Rabbits need their own homes, their soft, dark burrows. They cannot be happy away from Earthmother's arms, or from trees and bushes, and plants they like to eat. You want your pet to be safe and happy, don't you?"

"Yes. But I want to keep it here, with me."

"It will not be happy here, and it will die. But I know how you can keep it as a pet and make it happy, too."

"How?"

"First, we put your marker on it."

Kwani reached in her thread basket and removed a short length of cotton cord dyed bright red. She tied it around the rabbit's neck in a loose knot.

"As your pet grows you must loosen the knot so it isn't too tight. Now, we will take the rabbit back to its home, but every day you can go to play with it, and you will know it is your rabbit because it wears a red bow."

"But what if it isn't there?"

"You will know it is finding something to eat, but it will always come back to its home just as you do. Wait for it."

Antelope's lips trembled. "I want it with me all the time."

"Of course. But you don't want it to die; you want it to be happy and be your friend. Feel how it is trembling now."

"It's cold."

"It is afraid. It wants to go home. Come, I will go with you to keep the dogs away."

Antelope's brown eyes sparked and she stamped her foot. "No! I will keep it with me!"

She turned and ran down the walkway, Kwani after her. When Antelope reached the ladder she scrambled down, holding the rabbit with one hand and the ladder with the other. The rabbit squirmed to be free and fell to the ground. It darted frantically this way and that, the dogs after it.

"Stop!" Antelope screamed. "Stop! Stop!"

But the dogs were upon it, ripping it to bloody bits.

Kwani scooped Antelope in her arms. "Don't watch."

Antelope sobbed wildly. "You wouldn't let me keep it! It's your fault!" She fought to free herself. "Put me down!" she screamed.

Kwani gripped her more tightly and carried her up the ladder. It was not easy; Antelope fought like a bobcat.

"Where is Chomoc?" she asked the girls.

"With the other boys in the kiva. Learning about eagles."

"Get him. Tell him to bring his flute."

"I will go," Anitzal said, and hurried away.

Antelope screamed and fought. It took all of Kwani's strength to hold her. But at last the struggles ceased and Antelope collapsed, clinging to Kwani in limp sobbing.

Kwani brushed the hair from her daughter's wet face and rocked her, crooning. A child such as Antelope faced inevitable heartbreaks in years to come. How can I prepare her? Kwani wondered. The girls sat in silence, not knowing what to do.

Soon Chomoc came running, flute in hand, followed by Anitzal who puffed up the ladder after him.

Chomoc stood looking down at Antelope. "Why do you cry?"

"My rabbit! The dogs got it!" More sobs.

"But they did not get the rabbit's spirit. I will call it to another rabbit. You will have it again."

The sobbing dissolved to shuddering hiccups. "You will? Another rabbit for me?"

"Maybe. But you cannot keep it here. It has to stay in its own home."

"But I want it with me!" Again, tears flooded down.

Chomoc sat and crossed his legs. He held the flute in his hands for a moment, then lifted it to his lips.

There was the music of the river and birds in the willow tree. There was the sweet sound of wind in the grasses and the talk of leaves to one another as the wind passed. And the happy sound of scampering rabbit feet.

"Listen," Kwani whispered. "He calls the rabbit spirit."

Chomoc played on, eyes closed, fingers dancing on the wood, fringe swaying as the flute moved with the dancing. Anitzal and the girls sat entranced, listening to their childhood selves. Kwani heard another flute—in a cave long ago—when Kokopelli, the Toltec trader, found her nearly dead at the foot of a cliff and carried her to a sheltering cave. He healed her with his magic and his flute . . . long ago.

Kwani watched Chomoc. How like his birth father he was! He had Kokopelli's talents. Would he also have his father's wandering moccasins, and his seduction skills—utilized at every opportunity? Kwani wondered how many other little Kokopellis existed between there and Kokopelli's distant homeland. The thought was disquieting.

Antelope climbed down from Kwani's lap and knelt beside Chomoc. She watched his fingers as she listened to the flute's song, her eyes luminous, smiling. When Chomoc finished, she touched the flute.

"Did the rabbit spirit hear?"

"Yes."

"It will come to another rabbit?"

"Yes. If you let it stay in its own home."

"I will!" She flung both arms around him. "I love you!"

Kwani thought, Be careful, my daughter! But she did not speak.

▲ 40 ▼

Acoya stood upon the kiva roof with Chomoc and the other boys waiting for Tolonqua's arrival. He and the others wore their best breechcloths and moccasins because this was a special occasion—the first step toward initiation into their clans and, therefore, their first entry into manhood. They were eager to enter Earthmother's domain and to learn more about hunting and about eagles, but the kiva spirits would be offended if they—uninitiated boys—presumed to invade a spirit place without invitation and escort by a clan member, preferably a Chief.

It was a sunny morning, already hot, and they had been waiting for a long time.

"Where is your father?" one asked Acoya.

"I don't know. He went somewhere after the Morning Song to Sunfather." Often it was not easy to be Tolonqua's son. More was expected of him than of other boys.

Chomoc said, "He purifies himself in the river. I see him sometimes when I go there early."

Acoya flipped the hair from his face and squirmed impatiently; the purification ritual could take a long time with prayers and chants and purging of the stomach.

"Look! He comes!"

Tolonqua approached slowly, leaning on his staff and limping more than usual.

"His foot hurts," Chomoc said in his high voice.

"Of course it does," Acoya answered. "Because the Morning Star wanted him to be Building Chief instead of Hunting Chief and made my father's foot weak. That's why. My father was the best Hunting Chief Cicuye ever had." Acoya knew he bragged, but he could not contain his pride.

"We shall hunt eagles!" a boy said, bouncing with excitement.

"And raise them in cages! I know what I shall buy with all the eagle feathers my birds will give me!"

"You have to catch them first."

"Tolonqua will teach us."

"Stand up. He comes."

The boys rose respectfully as Tolonqua arrived.

"I greet you," he said. "Enter."

He descended the ladder to the kiva, followed by Acoya and the other boys who scrambled to sit close to him as he faced them from beside the altar. After they were seated, Two Elk, the Medicine Chief, Long See, Tolonqua, and Yatosha entered, followed by Popoc, Chief of the Cottonwood Clan, a stocky, middle-aged, taciturn fellow from the west, so dark-skinned that Ute ancestors were suspected. Ordinarily, old Huzipat, Chief of the Eagle Clan, would be there, but he was on a vision quest. The men lined up against the wall.

They all looked more solemn than usual, Acoya thought. Probably because it was an important occasion.

Sunfather's light slanted down through the hatchway and illumined Tolonqua as he stood bracing himself on his staff. He looked searchingly at each boy who straightened up under that gaze.

Acoya watched his father pick up a plume and hold it reverently.

"Today you will learn more about eagles. They are of the sky, the place of the Above Beings. You have watched them fly into the sky and disappear."

"Aye!" The boys nodded.

"They fly up and up"—he raised the plume in spiral fashion high overhead—"and enter the sky hole to Sunfather's house. Then they fly down again, circling." He demonstrated the eagle's graceful soaring. "They mingle with Cloud People and see everything below. That is why Eagle is He of the Above in the Six Sacred Directions, and why his feathers have power."

The boys watched in awe as Tolonqua pointed the feather's stem skyward in the manner of a sacred pipe and his lips moved in silent prayer. He returned the plume to the altar and faced the boys.

"Before we tell you more about eagles, there is something our Medicine Chief wishes to say."

He gestured to the Medicine Chief who stood and regarded the boys with his one good eye.

"I shall tell you at once because you are about to enter manhood and must learn to face whatever comes." He paused, and the boys glanced at one another nervously. "Witches may be among us."

The boys gasped. Witches were feared above all.

Acoya was shocked. No mention of this had been made to him by either of his parents, or by anyone.

Chomoc raised his hand for permission to speak.

"Speak."

"Who are they?"

"It is not yet known. You will remember when an evil spirit entered the mate of Yatosha." The Medicine Chief shook his head sadly. "You remember also the infant who died in its mother's body, and the death of the mother, as well. Now Rainfeather tells that another baby has died immediately after it was born, before its first cry. This is not as it should be. I, myself, have been called to heal many wounds, many sicknesses, much more than usual. All is not well. I fear witches are among us."

Acoya clenched both hands and the boys glanced fearfully around the room. Sometimes witches could be seen, taking the form of an animal or bird or insect. They peeked at one another furtively. Maybe it was even one of them!

The Medicine Chief continued, "I have fasted, purified myself, made sacrifices, and prayed. I requested a vision. It was granted to me. I know what must be done." For a moment he gazed into space and it seemed to Acoya that the turquoise and obsidian eye saw what other eyes did not.

The old Chief bowed his head. "We of Cicuye are to blame. We have no eagles here. We trade for them only with others who are wiser than we and who keep eagles to communicate with the Above Beings and keep witches away. We have considered only the power of their feathers and not of the eagles themselves. This must end. Witches can destroy us. They withhold rain and wither the crops. They cause fevers, deliriums, pains in the head and the body, and sicknesses of the spirit."

The Medicine Chief's dark eyes, nearly hidden under ragged brows, glanced piercingly at each boy.

"You who become Eagle Hunters can help us; the fate of Cicuye is in your hands. I go now to pray. I have spoken."

There was absolute silence as the Medicine Chief climbed the ladder and departed.

Tolonqua wiped his brow with the back of his hand, and Acoya saw that the hand holding the staff was not as steady as it used to be. He said, "Now you know why it is important to become an Eagle Hunter. Eagle has power. Power to communicate with the Above Beings. Power to keep witches and evil spirits away. That is why Pueblos raise eagles, to have their protection and their feathers. We shall do so. To have their protection, and their feathers for ceremonies, for arrows, for healing—many important uses. And to trade with others who need Eagle's power. But first we must obtain the birds.''

He leaned heavily on his staff and looked down at the upturned faces. ''Eagle must be hunted. I hunt no longer, as you know. Therefore, Long See will teach what you must know.''

Tolonqua sat down and Long See took his place. His weathered young face with its deep-set eyes and protruding cheekbones was framed by black braids. Acoya noticed the braids were thicker than usual even though his hair was skimpy. Acoya wondered if Long See added even more buffalo hair to his braids. Long See did not need fat braids to make people like him. It was what was inside of him that people liked.

Long See cleared his throat, scratched his nose, and looked around the room. He was a master hunter, master flutist, but unaccustomed to teaching. He cleared his throat again.

''Eagles must be taken from the nest to be raised in cages when they are very young. This is not easy because they nest in dangerous places. Therefore, you cannot become an Eagle Hunter until you are initiated into your clan and have sought your manhood vision.''

There were disappointed groans. Acoya raised his hand.
''Speak.''
''How old must we be?''
''Ten.''

All the boys were near that age. They babbled excitedly.

Long See gestured for silence. ''You will learn more about that later, but meanwhile you must learn about eagles so you will be ready. As you know, Yatosha was Hunting Chief of the Eagle Clan before he came here. He will tell you about the different kinds of eagles.''

Long See sat down with obvious relief and Yatosha rose. He was not tall, but he was broad of shoulder and lean of hip. His square face, creased and bronzed, contrasted with white streaks in his dark hair—streaks that appeared after Tiopi's death. Brown eyes regarded the boys solemnly, and they returned his gaze with respect.

''As Long See told you, there are different kinds of eagles. Bald Eagle and Golden Eagle are the best. But there is also Red Eagle, which some call the Red-Tail Hawk. And Water Eagle, also known as Osprey who—''

"With a white head and breast," Chomoc said loudly.

Because Chomoc was Yatosha's son, the rude interruption was especially embarrassing. He should have raised his hand for permission to speak. Yatosha shot him a sharply disapproving glance, and continued.

"White feathers, the color of clouds, are necessary for pahos and for ceremonies to bring rain. As you know.''

The boys nodded wisely whether they had known it or not.

"Bald Eagle gets no white feathers until the second year. Tell me what Bald Eagle eats.''

"Rabbits," Acoya said.

"Yes. But that is not what he likes best.''

Chomoc looked around to see if any of the others would answer. Eagles seldom hunted near cities; he had seen them during the journey to Cicuye. Satisfied that he was the only one who knew, he said, "Bald Eagle likes fish, and sometimes he steals it from Water Eagle.'' He sat back and folded his arms.

"That is correct. What does Golden Eagle eat?'' He glanced at Chomoc. "I have taught you this already, so remain silent.'' He searched the upturned faces. "Do you know what Golden Eagle hunts?''

None of the boys ventured a reply. Golden Eagle was so large, so magnificent and formidable, he could probably have anything he wanted.

"Hunters must know what those we hunt like to eat. And where they have their sleeping places. You cannot be a hunter until you know these things. So remember. Golden Eagle eats jackrabbits, squirrels, and prairie dogs. He builds his nest on a high cliff, or sometimes on top of a yellow pine or a cottonwood. Look for him in cottonwood trees far upstream. And remember that when you hunt rabbits he is better at it than you can ever be.''

"Aye!" Long See said. "Watch for him.''

"You will learn how to catch and to raise eagles after your initiation and manhood vision.''

Yatosha sat down and again Tolonqua rose. "You will come tomorrow to begin initiation into your clan. As you know, this is your first step in becoming a man. You are to eat nothing and drink nothing after Sunfather departs this day. Bathe in the river at pulatla and come naked here. I have spoken.''

Acoya glanced at Chomoc and wondered if Chomoc felt the same way he did—proud and a little bit scared at the same time. It was fun to be a boy and do boy's things with few responsibilities. What would it really be like to be a man? And what must he endure to become one?

Chomoc sat impassively, his amber eyes remote.

Acoya thought, Chomoc is a little bit scared, too, but he doesn't want anyone to know. And he is embarrassed about speaking without asking permission first; he doesn't like to ask permission about anything.

Long See and Yatosha bid the spirits of the kiva farewell and departed. Tolonqua gestured for the boys to do likewise. As they lined up quietly to climb the ladder, Acoya remained behind. He wanted to somehow justify his friend's rude interruption, but he didn't know what to say. When Chomoc was gone, Acoya stood awkwardly, looking down at his bare feet.

Finally he said, "Chomoc will not do it again."

Tolonqua nodded gravely. He put his hand on Acoya's shoulder.

"Sometimes it is hard not to tell what we know."

Acoya looked up into his father's face and they smiled at each other in mutual understanding, man to man.

Acoya lay sleepless on his mat, staring into the darkness. Tomorrow he would begin initiation into the Turquoise Clan. Usually children automatically belonged to the clan of their mothers, but he would belong to his father's clan because his case was different. Kwani was Eagle Clan by adoption only, and his birth father was Eagle Clan also. Kwani was Towa now, and since she had no clan of her own, the Turquoise Clan claimed her because she was mate of Tolonqua, and because she was She Who Remembers who would bring them honor.

Acoya wondered how long the initiation would take. He did not want to ask his father because being concerned about that would not be manly. The boys had discussed it among themselves. Some said it would take a few days; others said as long as a moon because nobody knew how long it took to be granted a manhood vision.

Acoya tossed restlessly. What would happen during the initiation? All his life Acoya had heard of the terrible masked figures who whipped boys to drive away bad influences; it was part of the initiation process. Never had he been whipped. Could he endure it in silence, as he was expected to do? Would he bleed?

From a distance came the hoot of an owl. Acoya swallowed and his heart beat hard. An owl's cry meant somebody would die. What if it were Kwani or Tolonqua? Or Antelope? What if it were himself?

He listened intently for sounds from the adjoining room where his parents and Antelope slept. He heard no breathing. Nothing. His heart thumped harder. As quietly as he could, he crawled to the doorway and strained to see the sleeping figures. They were motionless. *Maybe they were dead!*

Swallowing hard, he crawled to the mat where his parents lay; Kwani lay curled against Tolonqua's back. Acoya bent close. She was breathing!

Suddenly Tolonqua jerked upright. He stared at Acoya. "What is it?"

Acoya was embarrassed. How foolish he was!

"What is wrong?" Tolonqua asked.

Kwani woke and lay quietly, listening.

"I—I heard an owl."

"Ah."

Kwani said, "I have heard owls in the night. I was afraid."

Acoya could not imagine his mother being afraid of anything. "Will somebody die?"

Tolonqua shrugged. "This Fourth World is a big place. Somebody is always dying somewhere. Who knows where the spirit is that the owl calls? It may not be a person. It could be a mouse or other small creature, and the owl is hungry." He lay down and motioned Acoya to lie beside him. "Sleep now. You must be ready for initiation tomorrow. The owl calls no more; he has found his meal."

Gratefully, Acoya lay beside his father. Soon his parents were asleep again, but Acoya still gazed into darkness.

Again came the owl's voice, long and low.

Acoya listened fearfully. Would the owl call his name?

Then he remembered the mark on the sole of his foot. He was protected by the White Buffalo; he was a Chosen One.

Chosen for what? Perhaps he would learn the answer during his manhood vision.

Morning. Acoya ran naked to a place upstream where he knew he would be alone. In predawn light the river was sanctified, shiny and dark as an eagle's eye. He plunged in; the water clutched him in icy embrace and Acoya gasped at the cold but he was careful to keep water out of his mouth for he must not drink. He swam to his secret place beyond the bend, a little cove hidden by a boulder and the trailing branches of a willow tree. Parting the branches, he entered the cove and stood in the chest-deep water.

"I greet you," he said to the spirits of the place.

There was no answer, but Acoya sensed their welcome. He waded to the deep place where water reached his chin and stood motionless. Behind him the wall of leafy branches and the big boulder enclosed the cove. Before him, the river's sandy bank sloped steeply up to the forest where another boulder stood on a high spot overlooking the river. A cottonwood rose beside it; thick bushes surrounded the base.

It was quiet and sublimely beautiful, a sacred place.

Acoya gazed reverently up at the boulder high on the bank. Brush at the base of the tall, smooth stone nearly concealed a figure painted upon it—a holy man standing with arms upraised. Who was he? Surrounding him were mystical designs. What did they mean?

As Acoya gazed in silent wonder, ignoring the cold of water up to his chin, the brush at the base of the boulder moved and was pushed aside. A tawny figure emerged, sleek and low. A cougar! She climbed down the bank and crouched at the water's edge to drink. As she lowered her head she saw Acoya. Blue-gray eyes locked into his, holding his gaze with spellbinding intensity as her tongue lapped up the water. She was so close that Acoya could hear the sound of her drinking. Then silently, swiftly, she turned and disappeared into the brush.

An omen! Acoya stood transfixed. Cougars were fierce predators; hunters appealed to the spirit of Cougar for strength and cunning, and a successful hunt. Acoya remembered the power of those blue-gray eyes. What was the cougar telling him?

A flock of ravens rose from the cottonwood, squawking. Something disturbed them, something dangerous.

Suddenly Acoya was afraid. He turned quickly, parted the trailing branches, and swam beyond the bend to the shore. As he ran home he glanced behind him, half expecting to see a tawny figure padding swiftly, silently, after him.

He reached the city as people finished the Morning Song

to Sunfather. Acoya heard Tolonqua's voice soaring above the others.

> *"Your riches,*
> *Your power,*
> *Your strong spirit,"*

Acoya stood naked in Sunfather's golden light and joined the song.

> *"All these to me may you grant."*

He scrambled up the steep path to the city. The ladders had not yet been lowered and Acoya had to reach the single one let down for the boys, some of whom were running for it as he was. A group of girls stood on the roof, giggling. Some carried night pots to be taken to the emptying place. One of the girls tossed the pot's contents at a boy running past, and hit him squarely; he had to run back to the river to bathe again.

Acoya was outraged. He wanted to hit that girl and teach her a lesson, but that would demean him. It was beneath his dignity. He ignored it and made his way with the other boys to the kiva.

Two Elk stood by the hatchway, waiting for the boys to assemble. He wore a ceremonial garment of fox skins and a cotton breechcloth dyed yellow. His face and body paint of yellow and black and his buffalo-horn headdress attested to the importance of the ceremony about to take place.

Acoya looked at the breechcloth with interest, wondering about the man part underneath. It was said that since Akati, Two Elk's mate, entered Sipapu a few years ago, the man part of which he was so proud—the largest and finest in Cicuye—had refused to perform with other women and hung limp and withered. A catastrophe.

In one hand Two Elk held a pole with a red banner to indicate a ceremony would take place in the kiva and only participants could enter; the other hand held his ceremonial shield of buffalo hide adorned with mystical figures and eagle plumes. The boys regarded him with awe. He motioned for them to line up and they did so, uncomfortable in their vulnerable nakedness as people crowded the roofs, watching.

The haunting cry of an eagle-bone whistle, accompanied

by the shout of a cottonwood drum announced the approach of a procession emerging from another kiva. One by one seven men appeared, formidable in mystical designs of body paint and terrible masks. In the right hand of each was a buffalo-hide whip.

The boys tried not to show fear, but it was frozen on their faces. Four times the procession circled the courtyard, the drum beating and whistle lancing the air. Then the men lined up beside Two Elk.

Fearful masked faces confronted the boys who stood shivering in warm sunshine. Four times Two Elk raised the red banner, keeping time to the drum and the whistle that suddenly ceased in a thunderclap of silence.

Two Elk regarded the boys stoically.

"In entering manhood you leave your former selves behind. Bad influences and evil spirits that seek to do you harm must be destroyed. Therefore, our priests of the Medicine Society are prepared to drive them away." He gestured, and the masked figures lined up before the hatchway of the kiva. "Each of you, one at a time, shall walk down this line, then enter the kiva as one who belongs there. Begin now."

Chomoc was in front of the line. Without hesitation he stepped forward. The whistle moaned and the drum shouted as the first whip lashed his back, then again and again as he walked down the line, the whip flicking like a serpent's tongue each time. Chomoc walked bravely, cringing only at the last lash of the whip, then climbed down the ladder to the kiva.

The others followed, trying to show no fear at the monstrous masks and merciless whips, trying not to cry out as rawhide lashed their backs. Acoya was last in line. He did not look at the masks but stared stonily ahead, biting his lips, as seven times a whip struck, leaving a welt each time. He stumbled to the ladder and half climbed, half slid, down into the kiva. Tolonqua was there, wearing the robe of the White Buffalo. He and the other Chiefs stood in silence against the wall.

The boys sat huddled together facing the altar. Some hugged their knees and hid their faces. None spoke.

The drum and the whistle silenced, and one by one the masked figures descended, followed by Two Elk. They lined up before the boys who stared as masks were removed, revealing the Medicine Chief and his priests.

Acoya swallowed. It was hard to believe that these men,

seen every day, trusted and admired, were the fearsome masked gods who bestowed pain.

Two Elk took his usual place of honor by the altar. "You have entered this kiva freed of bad influences," he intoned solemnly. "Now the knowledge you must possess to become a man and a member of the Turquoise Clan will be revealed. You have much to learn. Your first instructor will be the Medicine Chief."

Two Elk sat down and the Medicine Chief rose and regarded each boy with a stern gaze. It seemed to Acoya that the old Chief's gaze lingered on him the longest.

"The first thing you must know is that although you have human parents, your real parents are those who created you—Earthmother, from whose flesh all are born, and Sunfather, who gives life. Therefore, although you are a member of your own family, and will become a member of your clan, you are also part of a great universe that you must honor. First man learned this; you shall, also."

Acoya listened eagerly. What important knowledge would be his as a man?

"You know about the First World. There was only the Creator; all else was endless space. Then the Creator decided to make a place where life would exist. He created a helper, Sotuknang, and said, 'I am your uncle and you are my nephew. Go now and make seven worlds for life to come.' So from endless space the helper Sotuknang gathered what he needed to make land and water. He went to the Creator and asked, 'Does this please you?'

" 'Aye,' the Creator said. 'It is good. Now make the forces of air into peaceful movement.'

"The helper did so, and the Creator said, 'Now life must be created. You must have one to help you as you have helped me.' "

The Medicine Chief paused. "Tell me the name of she who was then created."

"Spider Woman!" Acoya said. Tolonqua had told him of Spider Woman during long evenings around the fire pit at home.

The Chief nodded so that the chickadee nodded also, bobbing its dried-up head.

"Spider Woman took earth, mixed it with saliva from her mouth, and molded it into two people. She covered them with a white garment, which was creative wisdom itself, and sang the Creation Song over them. Then she uncovered them and two people, twins, sat up. They looked around and said, 'Who are we? Why are we here?'

"To one she said, 'You are Poqanghoya. Your duty is to keep the world in order when life is put upon it. Go now and put your hands upon the earth to make solid mountains and soft ground.' To the other she said, 'You are Palonga-whoya. Your duty is to go about all the world and send out sound so that it may be heard throughout all the land. When this is heard you will be known also as Echo, for all sound echoes the Creator.'

"He did as he was told, and all the vibratory centers along the earth's axis from pole to pole responded. The whole earth trembled and was made an instrument of sound carrying messages to the Creator."

The Chief paused again to look at each boy. "Some of you already know this, but it is well to be reminded as you enter manhood." He motioned to Acoya. "Stand beside me here."

Slowly Acoya rose. Was more punishment forthcoming? Hesitantly, he made his way to the altar and stood beside the Chief who turned him around so that his back, with its seven swollen red welts, faced the group.

"Your body and the body of Earthmother are made in the same way. Through each runs an axis." The Chief ran his finger down Acoya's spine and Acoya shivered. "This controls your movements and functions." He pointed to several places on the spine being careful not to touch the swollen welts. "There are vibratory centers here. If something is wrong, they give warning." He pointed to the top of Acoya's head. "When you were born, you had the soft spot, the *kopavi* here, an open door through which you received life from your Creator. With every breath the soft spot moved up and down with a gentle vibration, communicating with your Creator. Then the door hardened and closed and will remain so until you die when it will open again for your spirit to enter Sipapu."

Acoya listened in awe.

The Medicine Chief pointed to Acoya's forehead. "Just below the door is the second center, the brain, that enables you to think about your actions and the work you do on this earth to carry out the plan of your Creator. The third center is the throat that ties together the openings of the eyes and nose and mouth and the vibratory organs here"—he touched Acoya's throat—"that give sound to your breath so you can speak and sing praises to your Creator."

Like singing the Morning Song to Sunfather, Acoya thought.

"The fourth center is your heart," the Medicine Chief said. "It, too, vibrates, pulsing with life itself. The first men felt the good of life and its sacred purpose. They were of One Heart. But there were those who permitted evil feelings to enter and were called Two Hearts. So it is today."

The Chief poked his finger at Acoya's navel. "The last of the important centers dwells inside here, the throne of the Creator himself. From here, the Creator directs all the functions of man." He nodded to Acoya. "You may sit down now."

Acoya did so, proud to have been chosen, and the Chief continued, "The first people knew no sickness; not until evil entered the world did they get sick in body or in the head. The first medicine man, knowing how man was constructed, told them what was wrong by examining these centers, as I do. First, he laid his hands on them." The Chief illustrated, pointing to himself as he continued, "First, the top of the head, the forehead, the throat, the belly." He held up both hands. "These can see, they feel the vibrations from each center and tell where life runs weak or strong. Sometimes the sickness is just from a cold or from uncooked food, but other times it comes from outside, drawn by your own evil thoughts or from those of a Two Heart."

He reached into a small pouch around his neck and removed a crystal as long as his little finger, and held it up for the boys to see. The boys craned for a good look at an object of such sacred power.

"The Creator gave this to the first medicine man. Now every medicine man has one, as I do. You look at it and see nothing but a crystal, but I use this"—he pointed to his forehead—"the vibratory center behind my eyes that every medicine man develops, and I see what you cannot."

Acoya gazed, spellbound. He touched his forehead. Did the center vibrate within? He felt his stomach where the Creator dwelled inside him. Would the Creator help him to become a medicine man, to see with his hands, to see what others could not? Could he endure—did he want to endure— the long years of rigorous training and isolation such training required?

364 **Linda Lay Shuler**

"Tomorrow you shall learn more of the story of creation and the history of our people. . . ."

The Medicine Chief continued to speak but Acoya did not hear him. He listened to a silent voice within himself, the voice of the Creator. Again he saw a figure painted on stone, the holy man with arms upraised.

For a magical moment he was that man.

▲ 41 ▼

Antelope squatted beside the door of her playhouse, a neat square on the ground outlined by twigs. With her were four other girls intent upon the activities of the house's occupants—smooth river stones representing a man, a woman, a grandmother, and two children, all of whom were about to spend the night on leaf sleeping mats.

"The mother goes here." One of the girls laid the mother stone on the leaf in the sleeping room.

"And the children here," another girl said, putting the small stones beside the mother.

"No!" Antelope said. "They are old enough to sleep by themselves." She picked them up and moved them to an adjoining room.

"You always have to change everything! Put them back!" The girl reached for the stones, but Antelope grabbed them first.

"You can't have them in the same room with the mother and father."

"Why not?"

"Because they are making a baby. See?" Antelope laid the father stone on top of the mother. "They like to be by themselves when they do that." She put the children stones back where they were in the other room.

For a moment the girls sat in silence looking at the parent stones and at one another. Finally, the youngest one said, "How do they do that?"

Antelope looked scornfully. "You mean you don't know?"

The girl squirmed under Antelope's withering gaze. "I thought they were playing. You know."

Antelope said, "They play all right. With this." She pointed to herself. "And he pokes his inside of hers."

The girl made a face. "Why?"

"Because they like to."

Another girl said, "They do it all the time. Like this."

She lay on her back, raised her knees, bounced around, and made funny noises.

The girls laughed loudly. One of the older ones had remained silent; now she said, "It feels good."

"How do you know?"

She looked around to see if anybody might overhear, and leaned forward, her round face alight with the joy of telling a secret. "Chomoc showed me."

"Ai-e-e-e!"

Antelope stared. She couldn't believe it. Chomoc was her own special friend who played his flute for her and who called her pet rabbit to come. Why had he not shown *her*?

The girls were agog. "Doesn't it hurt?"

"Yes. At first. But—"

Antelope shouted, "Chomoc did not do that. You are making it up!"

"I am not! He pulled off my undergarment and—"

"That's a lie!" Antelope snatched the father stone and threw it at the girl, hitting her hard.

"Ouch!" The girl jumped up. "I'm going to tell my mother!"

"Tell her! Tell her you made Chomoc take off your undergarment and poke his man part—" She thrust her fist at the girl's groin but she dodged and ran away crying.

The other girls looked at Antelope with shocked expressions.

"You hit her!"

"Yes I did. Chomoc—"

"Who cares about Chomoc with that big nose and funny-colored eyes and—"

"His eyes are not funny!"

"They are, too. And the way he does this"—the girl looked down her nose—"and talks like he is the Creator—"

"He does *not*! I hate you!" Antelope cried. She kicked the playhouse to disarray and ran off, sobbing fiercely.

How could Chomoc do that *to another girl*?

Antelope ran blindly down the path she had taken often to the boulder where the rabbit's home was. Tears ran down her cheeks and dripped from her nose and chin but she didn't care; nobody would see.

She reached the boulder under the cottonwood tree and was disappointed that Chomoc was not there. Often he sat on the boulder, waiting to call the rabbit for her. He must still be in the kiva with the other boys. She would wait for him and hope that Acoya would not be with him again, or that big, stupid dog, Chuka, which scared rabbits away.

She climbed the boulder and lay on her stomach, looking down at the rabbit hole. The stone was warm and the sun felt good on her back. It was quiet but for the breeze in the cottonwood tree and the conversation of squirrels chattering.

Antelope lay there for a long time, watching the hole for her pet to emerge. The rabbit was bigger now, almost grown, and it would not come out if anything frightened it, so Antelope made no sound.

As she lay quietly, Antelope had an odd sensation. It was as though someone she could not see nor hear spoke to her, warning her of danger!

She raised her head and looked around. Nothing. She glanced up into the cottonwood, and froze. A cougar crouched high on a branch. Its blue-gray eyes stared down at her, and its long tail jerked at the tip.

Antelope opened her mouth to scream, but something stopped the sound in her throat and she remained silent and motionless.

Suddenly her rabbit's head poked up from the hole. Its little nose twitched, it glanced about, then jumped out and hopped away under the cottonwood tree.

From a distance came Chuka's booming bark.

Like a hawk the cougar dived at the rabbit, caught it behind the head, and disappeared swiftly into the brush with the rabbit's legs still kicking.

"No!" Antelope cried. "Stop!"

Her rabbit! She slid down from the boulder and stood staring after the cougar. Almost, she ran after it, but again, an inner warning spoke.

Chuka dashed up, followed by Chomoc and Acoya.

Antelope pointed to where the cougar had gone. "My rabbit!" she cried.

Chomoc glanced around. "Where?"

"The cougar took it!"

"What cougar?"

Chuka bumbled about, sniffing excitedly under the cottonwood tree.

Antelope pointed. "It went there. With my rabbit. It was up in the tree. Looking at me. Then my rabbit came out and Chuka barked and the cougar jumped down and grabbed my rabbit—" Tears choked her voice.

The boys looked at each other.

Acoya said, "You were wise not to try to run away. The cougar would run after you. We had better go back and tell Long See. Maybe hunters will want to follow the cougar."

Chomoc nodded. "He is nearby somewhere. I feel him."

"He is eating my rabbit! My poor little rabbit!"

"Come on, let's go back." Acoya glanced around uneasily. "Hurry!"

They ran for home, Chuka loping after them. What things they had to tell!

Antelope's story caused a sensation. It was known that a hungry cougar might attack a child alone in a remote place.

"Antelope is twins; she has powers to protect herself," some said.

"But there are plenty of rabbits and other animals for cougars to eat. It was not hungry. She was in no danger."

"Cougars can kill for the pleasure of killing. Antelope was prey—"

"Her powers protected her."

"Perhaps."

Kwani and Tolonqua sat outside their door, speaking softly so as not to awaken Acoya and Antelope who slept soundly. It was a warm summer night frosted with stars and sweet with breath from the mountain. Somewhere a flute sang love songs; night birds answered.

"I fear for her," Kwani said. "She is too headstrong, too reckless. She was not afraid of that cougar; she almost ran after it. What if—" She shuddered.

"She loved her pet. It's her mother instinct. To protect. Every hunter knows how fierce that instinct can be. There is no fear. Only rage."

"She says an inner voice spoke to her. . . ."

"Of course. She is your daughter."

"And yours."

The flute's sweet song lingered in the air, pleading, caressing. Tolonqua lifted Kwani in his arms and carried her into their dwelling.

Long See, Yatosha, and the hunters and dogs found the cougar and carried the carcass home upside down with its legs tied to a pole. It was a fine specimen with a beautiful coat and there was animated speculation about how it would be used. But Acoya remembered the sleek form drinking in the cove and the blue-gray eyes commanding his. He saw again how gracefully the cougar moved as it climbed the bank and disappeared. Then he thought of his little sister alone with the cougar.

How courageous she is! he told himself, and was proud.

It was several days later and Antelope had waited on the boulder for a long time. There would be no pet peeking from its hole until Chomoc came to call another. But now she wanted no more rabbits as pets. Both had been destroyed before her eyes. Just to look at another rabbit would make her see it all again.

No. What she wanted was Chomoc. That he had chosen another girl to use his man part with still rankled. He had played his flute for her, had called rabbits for her, had taken her side in arguments. Why had he not chosen her?

When he comes, I will make him sorry!

Two jays flew up from a tree, and a squirrel scolded loudly.

He is coming.

Soft footsteps approached, and Chomoc appeared with his flute, as usual.

"I greet you," he said matter-of-factly.

"My heart *does not* rejoice." She slid down from the boulder and confronted him, arms akimbo.

He grinned. "Why not?"

"You chose another girl."

He looked puzzled. "For what?"

She grabbed his breechcloth and tried to yank it off. "For your man part!"

For a long moment he stood looking at her without expression.

"You want me to—"

"You did it to her first!"

"She is old enough."

"But I thought I was your special friend." In spite of herself, her voice quavered.

"You are. That is why I waited."

"For what?"

"For you to be ready."

"I *am* ready." If that other girl was ready, she could be, too. She pulled off her little undergarment and tossed it aside.

"Maybe and maybe not."

He sat down, leaned against the boulder, and lifted the flute to his lips. There was a magical melody to steal into the blood, to warm it, to make yearning surge in the veins.

Antelope loved music. She listened, lips parted, eyes aglow.

"Ah!" she sighed.

He lay the flute aside. Slowly, he removed his breech-cloth.

Antelope was surprised. His man part was different from Acoya's or Tolonqua's; it did not hang limply down but poked up. She reached to feel it. It was stiff inside and soft outside. Odd!

"Do we do it now?"

"Yes."

Gently he laid her down, parted her legs, and looked at her little woman part. "I don't want to hurt you."

"It doesn't matter." If that girl could do it, so could she.

He lay upon her and she felt the penetration. It didn't feel good. Not at all.

"I don't like it! Stop!"

She pushed him away.

Abruptly he withdrew. He snatched his breechcloth and flute and strode away, not looking back.

Antelope was relieved to see him go. She hurt; that girl did not know what she was talking about. She reached for her undergarment and put it back on.

No man part will ever poke inside me again. Not ever!

Chomoc huddled beneath a bush by the riverbank. Both hands covered his mouth, but the bush quivered with his muffled sobs.

He had shamed himself.

Antelope was too young. He should not have . . .

He loved her the most. But now she would never love him.

▲ 42 ▼

"**A**re you ready to purify yourselves, to go alone without food or water to a far, remote place and stay as many days as may be necessary to communicate with the Great Spirit and seek your vision?"

The Medicine Chief faced the boys seated before him in the kiva; his one good eye glanced sharply at each one. "Think well before you decide, then come to me. I will prepare you."

Slowly and with dignity, the Chief bid farewell to the kiva spirits and climbed through the hatchway to this, the Fourth World.

Acoya looked down at his hands, hoping no one noticed his unease. Could he do that—go alone to a distant place and fast until he had a vision, no matter how long it took? Remote places had grizzlies. And what about Querechos? Pawnees could be anywhere. Sounds of a busy city floated down. Acoya gripped both hands. I must remember what has been taught today. I must *remember*.

It had been an important lesson, part of their manhood education. Two Elk had told of Earthmother, and how all living things were made of her flesh. He had said, "Her milk is the grass upon which all animals graze and her corn gives food to mankind. The corn plant is also a living thing with a body like ours in some respects, and we take its flesh into ourselves. Therefore, we also have a Corn Mother, as you know. Each of you has a perfect ear of corn given to you when you were born and which you will keep always—a gift from Corn Mother."

Acoya listened respectfully but he had already learned much from Tolonqua and Kwani of what was being taught. Yesterday he had seen an eagle soaring and it looked down, watching him. It was as though the eagle said, "I know you."

Two Elk's voice rolled on. "You have learned also of the Great Spirit, the Creator whose face appears in Sunfather.

He and Earthmother are your real parents who show their power by giving you human parents in this, the Fourth World.''

''You have been told how the First World was destroyed by fire because people did not honor their Creator. Only a few were saved, those who were grateful and sang joyful praises to their Creator.''

Two Elk's gaze lingered on each boy. ''Tell me how the Second World was destroyed.''

''By ice,'' Chomoc said.

Acoya glanced at him, glad that Chomoc spoke; he had been unusually quiet lately. Something weighed on his friend's mind that he did not want to talk about.

''That is correct,'' Two Elk answered. ''In the First World, people lived simply with the animals. In the Second World, they learned to make things, and to build homes. But each time they thought more about themselves than about their Creator, and only a few people honored him. These were the ones who were saved to enter the next world. Now you will learn of the Third World. Listen carefully.''

Two Elk gestured to the Medicine Chief who stepped forward. Acoya stared respectfully at the turquoise and obsidian eye. How fierce it was!

The old Chief cleared his throat and began.

''Those of the Third World multiplied and built big cities. They used the power of wicked people to make *patuwvotas,* big shields of hide that flew through the air to make war. They flew to a big city, attacked it, and returned so fast no one knew where they came from.''

''Ai-e-e-e-e!'' the boys breathed.

''So Sotuknang—you remember, the Creator's nephew— went to Spider Woman. He said, 'We can't wait this time for the thread to run out. Something must be done before those who sing to their Creator are corrupted and killed, too. You must save them while I destroy this world with water.'

'' 'How shall I save them?' Spider woman asked.

'' 'Find tall plants with hollow stems. Cut them down and put the people inside. Then I will tell you what to do next.''

''So Spider Woman cut down hollow reeds and put the people inside and gave them corn cake for food and water to drink. Then Sotuknang said, 'You get inside and take care of them and I will seal you all up before I destroy the world with water.' ''

The Medicine Chief looked at the boys. "Pretend you are those people inside the reeds. You are crowded together in the dark and you don't know what will happen. Imagine how it felt."

"Ai-e-e-e!"

"That is how they felt when Sotuknang loosed waters upon the earth. Waves higher than mountains rolled over the land." The Chief raised and lowered his arms like waves. "Rains fell and kept falling, and waves kept coming. . . ." The Chief paused, seeing it in his mind. "You, inside the reeds, hear the roar of the waves, the terrible shout of the thunder god, and the sound of rain falling and falling. You feel yourselves tossed high into the air. Then you fall back into the water—"

The boys glanced at one another and hugged their knees.

"At last, it was quiet. Rain stopped falling. Spider Woman unsealed the hollow reeds and pulled the people out. They were on a tiny piece of land that used to be the highest mountain. Everywhere else was water as far as they could see—all that was left of the Third World. They wanted to see farther so they planted a reed that grew high"—the Medicine Chief pointed skyward—"and they climbed up. But all they saw was water. All around, everywhere, nothing but water."

Acoya shivered. He saw himself on that little piece of land, surrounded by endless sea, endless sky.

"Then Sotuknang told Spider Woman to keep traveling. 'Your inner wisdom will guide you. The door at the top of your head is open.' So Spider Woman had the people make rafts of the reeds they had come in. For many days the people floated on the sea, but found no land, no Place of Emergence to the Fourth World.

"Finally land appeared, and the people rejoiced. But Spider Woman said, 'This is not the place. We must keep going.' Again they came to an island with flowers and trees, but Spider Woman said once more, 'This is not the place. You must journey on. Have I not told you the way becomes harder and longer? Walk to the opposite shore and make more rafts and paddles.' "

Acoya was caught up in the drama of the story. He saw himself plodding wearily across an island with flowers and trees, wanting to linger and to rest, but knowing he must find the Place of Emergence to the next world as the Creator planned.

"Spider Woman said, 'Now I have done all I am commanded to do for you. You must go alone to find your own Place of Emergence.'

"They thanked Spider Woman and set out again, paddling hard for many days. At last they saw a great land, a mighty land, rising high above the waters from north to south as far as they could see. 'The Fourth World!' they cried, and tried to land. But as they grew close they saw there was no shore, only steep cliffs. And they were weary.''

The old Chief shifted his weight as though their weariness was in his bones. Acoya raised his hand to speak.

"Speak."

"If their doors were open, why did they not find a landing place?''

"Because they would not let themselves be guided. At least not until they had paddled for many days through high waves, seeking a sheltered shore. Then, not knowing what to do, they stopped paddling, and listened to their inner voice, speaking for the Creator. Almost immediately the water smoothed out''—the Chief gestured with an outstretched arm—''and a gentle current swept them to a sandy shore. They had found their Place of Emergence at last! To this, the Fourth World.''

"Ai-e-e-e!'' the boys sighed.

Chomoc raised his hand. The Chief nodded, and Chomoc said, "You said our doors will not open again until we die. How can we be guided if our doors are closed?''

The Medicine Chief looked down into the amber eyes alight with intelligence. He smiled. "There are different kinds of guiding spirits. The Creator gives you a sacred spirit that departs through the open door when you die. There is also the spirit of your ancestors, the Ancient Ones, born within you. Many grandfathers are in your blood. Their wisdom seeks to guide and protect you, but you must hear their silent voices. You must *listen*.'' He paused again, searching upturned faces. "Maybe sometimes you hear these voices and do not know the Ancients are speaking. Warning you, perhaps.''

The boys gazed up at him with awe.

"When you obey your Creator and seek your manhood vision you will be given another protecting spirit; it will reveal itself to you then.'' The Medicine Chief touched the stuffed chickadee perched on the braid behind his ear. "This bird came to me in my vision and its spirit has protected me all these years. Yours will also do so if you honor your Creator.''

Acoya had watched as the Medicine Chief climbed the ladder to depart. Now the kiva was empty; he would be the last to leave. Still he sat there, head bowed, wondering how best to honor his Creator.

"Acoya!" Chomoc peered down from the hatchway. "Come *on*!"

Acoya glanced about the kiva where shadows lingered. A coal in the fire pit glowed dimly. Spirits were here.

He gestured reverent farewell and climbed the ladder to this, the Fourth World.

Pulatla. Acoya lay on the water in his secret cove and gazed into the awakening sky. It would be a beautiful day, ideal for seeking his vision. He had followed the instructions of the Medicine Chief, purified himself inside and out, and had stopped to bathe here one more time on the way to the sacred mountain.

It was silent but for the lap of the water and the whispering of the trees. The air was cool and fragrant with pine and the sweet breath of the forest. Sunfather's mantle touched the tall stone looming over the cove, illuminating the holy man pictured upon it. Acoya turned from his back to stand neck-deep in the water. He looked up at the holy man and his upraised arms; Acoya had come here so often it seemed that the man recognized him.

"Today I seek my vision," Acoya said.

A bird flew by. Its shadow flicked across the stone and it was as though the holy one gestured.

"Farewell," Acoya said respectfully, and swam through the trailing branches of the willow tree to the opposite shore. He put on his moccasins and breechcloth and looped the strap of the flute case over his shoulder; it was a handsome case Kwani had made of the bobcat skin to protect the flute on his journey.

"Remember the promise to Man Who Runs to play your flute during your vision quest," Tolonqua had reminded him. "He is in Sipapu but his spirit will hear."

Beyond lay the sacred mountain rising to embrace the Cloud People. Acoya followed the course of the river into the valley. Sunfather walked his sky path and Acoya became thirsty, but he could not drink until after his vision. His shadow grew short as Sunfather walked higher. Acoya became hungry, but he could not eat; he must remain purified within.

Foothills rose as the mountain drew near. Acoya climbed

the first hill and gazed up at the awesome dwelling place of mountain gods. Would they welcome him?

What if they did not?

What if no vision appeared?

He touched the flute at his side; the spirit of Man Who Runs would help him.

Clouds soared above the mountain as Acoya reached it and began to climb. He glanced sharply about; there were no trails, no landmarks he knew. He would climb to the mountaintop; visions came best on high places closer to the Above Beings. If it was dangerous, so much the better. The Medicine Chief said that braving danger gave a vision quest more power.

I must not be afraid.

He sat on a fallen log to rest and to allow his spirit to become acquainted with the spirits of the mountain. The sounds, the smells, were different here. Instinctively, he was motionless; only his eyes moved, inspecting the trees, the bushes, the ground, probing the shadows.

What was that track over there behind the berry bush?

Acoya went to see. There was no mistake. It was the new track of a grizzly bear.

Acoya crouched, every nerve straining to sense the bear's presence. Nothing. Carefully, he rose and looked about. A flock of ravens settled in a tree nearby and a squirrel sat on the ground, watching.

No bear was near.

I am protected.

He looked up through the trees to the mountaintop waiting for him. A vision place.

The climb grew steep, and rocky soil made footing difficult. But strong branches of young trees reached low for him to grasp, and bushes lent their sturdy grip on the ground for his feet to push against. Higher he climbed, pausing now and then to gaze over the valley with its shiny thread of a river. Far beyond, where mountains opened their arms to the plains, clouds sailed in majesty, their shadows gliding upon the ground. Overhead, the mountain peak rose in mystic holiness to the Above Beings. Below, two swallows sliced the air in swift curves.

Acoya stood on the steep slope, bracing himself against the root of a chamisa bush. The air was warm and fragrant with pinion and sage. He breathed deeply and felt his inner being opening to the spirits of the mountain gods.

This is a holy place.

He climbed higher to a level spot. A twisted juniper tree was there, and sage and mountain grasses. A hummingbird darted by, messenger to the Above Beings.

He would find his vision here.

Reverently, he gathered sage and made a small altar beside the juniper tree and placed his flute upon it. He removed his breechcloth and sandals so he would stand unadorned before his Creator. It was now late afternoon. He faced west toward Sunfather and raised both arms.

"I come to You who made me, who made the mountains, the sky, the waters, who made all that lives, all that is beautiful. Send me a vision, I pray!"

For a long time he stood with arms upraised until he could hold them up no longer. Sunfather descended behind the mountain and the air grew cool, but Acoya stood motionless until Sunfather's light disappeared like a blanket rolled up and put away.

"I pray for a vision!"

It grew dark. Moonwoman did not come; only campfires of the Ancients flickered in a black sky. Acoya huddled under the juniper tree. The wind passed, speaking to the tree and the grasses. A wolf called in the distance. Night birds answered. Then it was silent. Silent.

Acoya sat leaning his bare back against the scratchy bark of the juniper but he did not feel it. Every pore of his being searched for communication with the Creator. He gazed up through the juniper's scraggly branches to the abode of gods, and it was as though his spirit flew from his body to the stars.

He was floating through darkness . . . floating. . . .

He slept.

A sound woke him. He jerked upright, staring into the darkness. Again the sound came; something was nearby. Acoya did not move; he made his breathing as silent as he could and tried to see what was there. A shadow. A large shadow that moved away.

He watched and listened for a long time, but whatever it was did not return. Acoya found he was trembling.

My flute. I should play it for Man Who Runs.

But he was afraid to move, to make himself known to shadows.

At last Sunfather cast his mantle across the horizon. Slowly, Acoya crawled from beneath the tree and looked about. How beautiful it was in the morning light! He went to the sagebrush altar to remove his flute. Something had disturbed the altar. The sage was in disarray and the flute pushed aside.

He stared. Tracks were all about.

Grizzly!

The bear had come but the altar and the flute sent him away!

With awe and gratitude, Acoya rearranged the altar and faced east where a golden rim arose. He sang the morning chant to Sunfather, standing naked before him. He had no sacred meal to give, but he had his flute. He lifted it to his lips, offering his breath of life through the flute to Sunfather as his fingers danced a sacred dance of their own creation. On and on he played as Sunfather rose in splendor.

At last he could play no more. He raised both arms, chanting praises to his Creator, pleading for a vision.

It was morning of the third day and no vision had appeared.

Again Acoya played his flute to the Creator, but he was weak from having had no food or water, and the flute's song was strange as though it, too, suffered.

The morning passed. Sunfather's breath grew hot and heat waves shimmered in the valley. It seemed to Acoya that the entire world shimmered, quivering in mystical vibration. Colors changed. The world turned red, then green, then blue. Blue faded to sharp white. Through the white, a figure emerged.

"Ah!" Acoya gasped.

It was the White Buffalo. He stood staring at Acoya with eyes of a cougar.

Acoya's flute fell to the ground. "I greet you, Sacred One."

"I have marked you," the White Buffalo said, and his voice was like wind in the canyon. "Because you are a Chosen One, great danger awaits. I give you power—"

The white figure wavered more. It changed, became dark. Cougar's eyes became the eyes of Bear, and a grizzly stood before him. His big head swung low from side to side as he approached. Then he rose, standing on his hind legs, towering over Acoya, his huge forelegs extended and his paws, with long curved claws, inches before Acoya's staring eyes.

"Power!" Bear growled, and his voice was a thunder drum.

Again the light turned red, then blue, and Bear was gone.

Gradually Acoya realized he lay on his back, staring into blue sky. Had he fallen when Bear faded away?

I have been granted a vision!

Exultation welled up in glory. Acoya rose. With both arms overhead he faced Sunfather. A song surged from his heart.

> "It is finished in beauty.
> It is finished in beauty.
> In the house of morning light,
> On the trail of morning light,
> It is finished in beauty."

▲ 43 ▼

"**A**nd then the White Buffalo became Bear! And Bear did this." Acoya stood as Bear had done, with arms extended before him. "He said 'Power!' in a big, deep voice—"

Kwani and Tolonqua looked at each other with pride. How extraordinary and wonderful that *both* Acoya and Antelope were granted special powers!

Tolonqua said to Kwani, "It is because you are their mother. Your powers are in their blood." He put an arm around Acoya who stood beaming. "Yours is a great responsibility. You have a double totem, Bear and the White Buffalo, both strong. Very strong. You will have them on your war shield."

Acoya nodded happily. Now that he had been granted a vision, he could make his war shield, embellishing it with designs of his own creation to give it protective powers.

"We go now to the kiva. The Chiefs and Elders are waiting."

When they had gone, Kwani turned to Antelope who had been listening, brown eyes wide. "Because you are twins you have special powers, also."

"I don't feel any. I can't talk to animals. Chomoc—"

"He is like his father; your powers are different."

She tugged at her ear, a habit she had picked up from old Huzipat who often did that. "I want to talk to animals like Chomoc does."

Kwani looked at her small daughter, like her and yet so different. "You will learn you can do what Chomoc cannot. Come, help me make some water balls. Tolonqua and Acoya will be hungry."

Antelope brightened; she loved to cook. "I want to roll them!"

"You may."

Kwani reveled in the luxury of her cooking place, the finest in Cicuye. Hung on the wall beside the fire pit was an assortment of utensils she had made that were much admired: a sieve basket of coarsely woven yucca; three handsome meal trays, round and flat, of woven reeds, and a smaller flat mat for bread, intricately woven with contrasting colors of yucca fiber; an assortment of gourd and ceramic dippers and wooden stirring spoons, two with handles Tolonqua had carved in fanciful shapes. Pegs held a small pouch of salt and bags of pinon nuts and seeds. Hanging from the wall and rafters were braided cornstalks with ears attached, strings of dried squash, and small bunches of herbs for seasoning and medicinal uses, all of which could be supplemented from the storage room on the first floor. Around the fire pit stood a pitcher, storage bowls for meal and other staples, and six more bowls of different shapes and sizes, some beautifully painted inside so the design could be admired as they sat on the floor. A heavy round cooking pot with four legs to straddle coals was blackened with use, as was the water-boiling pot with a handle on each side and a stone cover.

"Bring some water for boiling," Kwani said.

Antelope lifted a large dipper of water from a tall jar standing in the corner, carried it carefully to the boiling pot, and poured the water in, spilling only a little.

Kwani nodded. "Good!" She set the bowl on coals in the fire pit, added a few sticks of finely splintered pinon wood from a bundle stacked by the fire pit, and poked it with a charred hardwood poker.

"Now we mix the dough. Do you remember what we use?"

"Fine meal and coarse meal and water and—" Antelope paused, pinching a lip in thought. "Something else. I forget."

"Salt."

"Yes. From the prairie dog bag."

Kwani gestured. "Begin now."

She watched as Antelope gravely selected a dipper, scooped out a portion of fine meal, poured it into a bowl, then added coarse meal and a little water. Kwani was pleased to see that the portions were almost right.

"May I get the salt?" Antelope asked. The salt pouch, like Tolonqua's feather pot, was forbidden except by special permission.

Kwani smiled. "You may."

Antelope had to stand on tiptoe to lift the pouch from its peg. It was the tanned skin of a prairie dog adorned with a pretty tassel of braided dog hair and shiny beads of burned and polished juniper seeds; similar beads were at each end of the red cotton drawstring. It was a proper container for something so valuable, and Antelope carried it lovingly in both hands.

"I will hold it while you open it for me," Kwani said.

As she held it, Antelope pulled the top open and peeked inside. "There is not much in there."

"I know. We must be careful. Take out this much." She pinched her thumb and forefinger together.

Antelope's small fingers reached in, took a pinch, and dropped the salt in the mixing bowl. Then she pulled the drawstring closed and returned the pouch to its peg.

"You will make some brave a fine mate," Kwani said.

"I know. I will marry Chomoc."

"I see. Does he know this?"

"*I* know." She watched a moment while Kwani kneaded the dough. "But we won't make babies."

"Why not?"

"I don't like to."

Kwani's hands paused in the dough. She looked at her small daughter. After a moment she said, "Has he tried to?"

"Yes. His man part looks funny. It sticks up."

Kwani resumed kneading and kept her voice casual. "Did he hurt you?"

"Yes. That's why I don't like it."

Kwani leaned back, resting her floured hands on the bowl. Sex play by children was expected, but Chomoc was ten and Antelope was only six. This was different.

"Why do you want to marry him?"

Antelope shrugged indifferently and thrust both hands into the bowl. "Let me knead, too."

"Very well. But tell me why you want to marry Chomoc if he hurts—"

"He does what I tell him, and he calls rabbits, and he makes music—"

Kwani gave Antelope a sharp glance. "He does what you tell him? You mean you told him to?"

"I wanted to know what it was like, so I told him—"

"To do it?"

Antelope looked up from her kneading and scratched her nose with a floured hand, leaving a smear. "It didn't feel good at all. Not like she said."

"Like who said?"

"You know. That girl from the Woodpecker Clan who uses dogs."

Girls of certain clans sometimes used dogs to satisfy themselves, but Turquoise Clan girls knew better. Kwani remembered the older girl who played with Antelope and her friends occasionally. Kwani had resumed her teaching and the girl was one of her students. Always asking questions about sex.

"Chomoc showed her first!" Antelope said in an aggrieved tone.

"And you wanted him to show you," Kwani said flatly.

"He is *my* friend. He—"

"So he did."

"Yes. But—"

"It hurt?"

Antelope nodded. "I made him stop."

"How?"

Antelope pushed back the hair from her forehead, leaving another smear. "I just told him to stop." She looked at Kwani. "He does whatever I tell him," she said smugly.

Kwani kneaded the dough more vigorously than was necessary. How could she guide this twin child? What were Antelope's powers? As she grew to beautiful womanhood how would those powers be used?

The dough was stiff now, so Kwani and Antelope pinched off small pieces to make balls.

"I like to do this," Antelope said, rolling a piece of dough in her hands. She lifted the ball to her nose. "It smells good."

"It will taste good, too. The water is boiling now so we can put the balls in. Use a spoon so you won't splash and get burned."

Instead of disintegrating, the balls became solid as they cooked, yet enough of their substance mingled with the water to thicken it. It would be scooped out with corn cakes and eaten like stew.

"Acoya will want lots of this," Antelope said. "Will you tell him I made it?"

"Indeed I will." Kwani smiled. "He had a special vision and deserves a treat."

Antelope sat on her heels, watching the pot boil. "I wonder where Chomoc went for his vision. I wonder if a vision came."

Kwani wondered other things about Chomoc.

How much would he become like Kokopelli—a lone wanderer, a magical lover? Would he expect his mate to follow him to a far distant place to live a lifetime among a people vastly different from her own?

She watched her small daughter waiting impatiently for the pot to boil. Antelope managed to get about everything she wanted. When she was grown and seeking a mate, what if she chose Chomoc?

Kwani's heart constricted. That must never happen. Antelope would be lost to her forever.

Acoya and Chomoc trotted on a trail, idly kicking a stick before them. They had been in the kiva for a long time discussing visions; tomorrow they would be instructed in the making of war shields. They were glad to be outdoors. It was early afternoon with thunderheads billowing; it would rain soon.

Chomoc kicked the stick down the hill trail and ran after it to kick it again before Acoya reached it, but he stubbed his foot on a stone, stumbled, and sat down hard.

"Wait!" he yelled in his high voice as Acoya reached the stick, gave it a kick, and sent the stick soaring. Acoya raced ahead, and Chomoc flushed in frustration up to his slanted brow. "Wait!" But Acoya was far ahead. Chomoc jumped up and ran after him.

Kicking-the-stick was a favorite game; runners practiced it for agility and endurance. They said the stick helped them to run faster and farther and they took the stick with them on long journeys, kicking it all the way.

Acoya knew he could outrun Chomoc, and since this was merely practice, he slowed down until Chomoc caught up, puffing.

"Look." Acoya pointed upward. "It's going to rain."

First drops fell, big ones. The boys ducked under a tree and sat leaning against the trunk.

Acoya said, "Tell me again about your vision."

"On the second day. I saw an eagle flying." This meant he would have a powerful totem, and Chomoc glanced at Acoya to make sure he was suitably impressed. "He carried a boy in his claws."

"Was it you?"

Chomoc looked down his nose. "Of course. Why else would the eagle show me?"

"Eagle is a strong totem! You will have that on your war shield. Maybe you will fly with the eagle in dreams."

"You have two totems," Chomoc said with more than a

hint of envy. "I never heard of anybody with two before." To have two totems on a war shield was a rare honor, and would give its owner double protection.

Acoya shrugged. "It means I have twice the responsibility. And will have to work twice as hard."

Rain fell, big drops splashing on the ground and through the branches to the boys beneath. It was refreshing after the heat. Acoya removed his moccasins and breechcloth and ran from under the tree, letting the rain splash him all over. Chomoc did the same, and they jumped and danced about, making mud puddles with their bare, muddy feet, shouting and laughing. Soon the rain lessened, became a light shower, and stopped. A brilliant rainbow arched across the sky.

The boys gazed reverently; it was the rain god's path.

Runners practicing for a race from a neighboring village came swooping over the hill. They greeted the boys as they passed, and the boys turned to run after them. For a short distance the boys ran as fast, but soon the racers were far ahead.

"We left the kicking stick back there," Acoya said. It was a special one Huzipat had made for Chomoc. Since Chomoc and Yatosha moved in with him after Tiopi's death, Huzipat regarded them as son and grandson and treated them accordingly. The kicking stick he made for Chomoc was the finest in the city. Concealed inside it was a hair from the big toe of the fastest racer in Cicuye; Huzipat had traded three fine ear ornaments for it to make the stick go far and fast and help Chomoc to become a racer.

The boys put on their wet moccasins and breechcloths and ran back to retrieve it, their figures appearing and disappearing over the hills under the arch of the rainbow.

"Observe," Tolonqua said, holding up a shaggy buffalo hide. "This is from an old bull with battered horns which is best for a war shield because the bull has fought and won many battles; it will give your shield added power."

Acoya watched avidly; to have a war shield was an attribute of manhood. He and other boys were gathered on the ridge and sat in a semicircle before Tolonqua. It was a clear blue day with puffs of white clouds riding the wind. A fire blazed to heat stones piled upon it; a digging stick, a forked stick to carry hot rocks, and several pegs lay nearby. Also nearby were a jar of water and a gourd dipper.

Tolonqua continued, "I shall demonstrate the making of

a war shield. Then each of you are to make your own, keeping in mind that your shield will be one of the most important objects you possess. As Cicuye grows and becomes more powerful, envious enemies will seek to take it. This is inevitable. You will need all the protection you can get, and the more powerful your shield, the greater your protection.''

Tolonqua laid the hide on the ground. ''Now we shall mark the circle to be cut from the hide. It has to be twice as large as the finished shield is to be because hide shrinks when we heat it. The finished shield must cover your body from chin to knee, so we must cut a circle two times as big as the finished shield will be, keeping in mind that you will use this shield when you are grown men. So we shall use myself as a guide for how big the circle should be.''

Taking a length of cord, Tolonqua measured himself from chin to knee, marked the length with a knot, and held it up.

''You can see how long this is. We shall have to cut a circle twice as wide as this is long.'' Tolonqua laid the cord on the hide and marked the double width. ''Who wants to help mark the circle?''

There was a chorus of volunteers. Acoya wanted to help his father, but instead, Tolonqua chose Toho, the smallest and most timid of the group. The boy beamed with pride as Tolonqua handed him a peg and told him to tie it to the cord next to the knot.

When Toho had done so, fumbling in eagerness, Tolonqua said, ''Now we shall decide where the circle will be.'' He laid the cord on the hide, positioning it to best advantage, and told Toho to hold the peg firmly in the center of where the circle would be. Then using the cord as a guide, Tolonqua stretched the cord tight and pulled it around in a circle, marking it with a piece of charcoal.

''Thank you, Toho,'' Tolonqua said. ''Now sit here to hold the hide down while I cut.'' He called another boy to sit opposite Toho, and between the two boys the hide was held firmly down. A sharp flint knife in Tolonqua's experienced hand cut the circle neatly.

''Next, we dig a hole as wide and as deep as from elbow to fingertips.'' He illustrated with his arm. ''Acoya, you have seen me prepare the hole. Will you show how it is done?''

Acoya was surprised. He did not remember watching Tolonqua dig such a hole, but perhaps it happened when he was too young to recall. However, he got to work, pushing the digging stick down with his foot, loosening the soil, then scooping it out with his hands.

Tolonqua said, "Don't forget to make a neat mound of the earth you remove; it will be needed to stretch the hide upon." He motioned to Lapu, a pudgy boy not too popular with his peers. "Help Acoya with the hole; it will be finished more quickly."

Acoya handed the digging stick to Lapu. "You are bigger and can push harder. You dig and I'll scoop out the dirt."

Lapu was pleased to be chosen. He dug with a great show of effort, and Acoya scooped. The hole was finished in no time.

"Measure," Tolonqua ordered.

Acoya thrust his arm into the hole. It reached to his elbow. Pleased, he looked up at Tolonqua expecting approval.

"You forget," Tolonqua said. "Your arm will be longer when you grow more. A war shield is a man's shield." He knelt and reached down into the hole. "See? It must be this much deeper. And wide as it is deep."

Acoya nodded and soon the two boys finished the hole to Tolonqua's satisfaction.

"Good." He handed the forked stick to Toho. "Lift out the hot rocks and put them in the hole."

Toho hesitated. Acoya knew Toho was a bit afraid of those red-hot stones, but he was also proud to be asked. He lifted one and it fell off. He lifted it again, carried it precariously to the hole, and let the rock fall in. Encouraged, he managed to get the rest of the stones in the hole without mishap.

"Well done," Tolonqua said, and Toho flushed with pleasure. It seemed to Acoya that scrawny Toho grew taller right then.

"Acoya, fit the circle of hide over the hole, hair side up. And you, Lapu, fasten it down with these pegs." Tolonqua handed six sharpened pegs to Lapu, and a rock to pound them with. "But leave a place unfastened so it can be lifted up and water poured in."

Chomoc had been squirming with impatience, waiting to be chosen. So Acoya was pleased when Tolonqua said, "Chomoc, you will pour a dipper of water upon the stones, but be careful of the steam."

Chomoc hid his pleasure with a glance down his nose, dipped the gourd into the water, lifted the edge of the hide circle, and poured the water into the hole. Immediately there was a hiss and a billow of steam. Chomoc flipped the hide back down but not before the steam burned his hand.

"Let me see that hand," Tolonqua said.

Chomoc shook his head. "It is nothing."

Acoya said, "I know a plant that will heal—"

Chomoc scowled. "I said it is nothing."

Tolonqua nodded matter-of-factly, and continued, "Water must be added as the steam diminishes. It will take a while for the hide to shrink, but when it does, it will be much smaller. The hair must be scraped off, and then the soft hide will be placed over the mound of soil that was removed from the hole, and pegged down to dry. Who knows why that is necessary?"

When no one else seemed to know, Acoya said, "To make the shield curved so arrows will glance off."

Tolonqua smiled. "That is correct. Then the edge is trimmed all around to make it even. The hide will be wrinkled so it will be pounded with a rock or stone-headed maul to smooth it out. Who knows what comes next?"

Jaywing raised his hand. He was one of the older boys whose family had been in Cicuye for a long time. "My father's war shield has a shoulder loop attached to the back."

"How is it attached?"

"By holes on either side of the shield."

"Exactly."

Tolonqua turned to Toho. "Use the forked stick to lift the flap and see if more water is needed."

Toho glanced at Chomoc's hand that had red splotches. He swallowed, but he took the forked stick and lifted the flap. Only a bit of steam emerged. "Shall I add more water?"

'I am to do that," Chomoc said.

"But—"

Tolonqua said, "If Chomoc wishes to do so, he may. It is his responsibility."

Chomoc filled the dipper with water, took the forked stick, and lifted the flap just enough to pour in the water. He jerked the stick away before steam billowed on his hand.

Tolonqua nodded. "Well done."

Acoya knew that Chomoc was gratified, but his friend was not about to show it. Rather, he sat down casually, crossed his legs, and rested his chin on his burned hand as though it did not hurt at all. Acoya admired that; it was a manly thing to do.

Tolonqua said, "When the hide is shrunk it will be twice as thick. Then we will test it by hanging it on a tree and shooting arrows at it. If the arrows bounce off, the shield is ready to be consecrated and painted. If not, we shall make another.''

Lapu raised a pudgy hand. "How is it consecrated?"

"As I explained, this is a demonstration of how a war shield is made. When you make yours, you will choose who is to help you. Whomever you choose will pray and sing with you to the Above Beings and your guardian spirits to grant your shield protection against enemies. For enemies you will surely encounter during your lifetime, especially if you remain in Cicuye.''

Tolonqua gestured to the hide that was beginning to shrink. "As I said before, when it has shrunk, it will be twice as thick. Notice how the pegs are being pulled inward. Soon they must be removed one at a time and driven in again. Lapu, you will do that.''

Lapu grinned. "I will do it." Acoya knew how happy Tolonqua had made him. Lapu was not very likable; he had few friends. Tolonqua's choosing Lapu gave him prestige.

Acoya looked at his father who sat with his staff beside him. He thought, My father is loved. Was it because he could see into the heart of those who needed his kindness?

"When your shield is ready to be painted, then you will give it the most thought. You will cleanse yourself inside and out and appeal to the gods and to your protective spirits—your totems—for guidance. Finally your prayers will be answered and you will know how your shield should be adorned—with paint and with feathers and whatever other ornamentation is required. Your shield will be like no other, for it will reflect you and your spiritual powers.''

Acoya thought, I already know what figures will be painted on my shield. Bear and the White Buffalo.

He was glad he had a double totem.

He wondered how soon his war shield would be needed.

Acoya and Chomoc stood with five other boys on the roof by a ladder leading down the outside wall, waiting for Long See, Tolonqua, and Yatosha. They were agog with excitement for their war shields were completed and now they could take their next step to manhood. Today they would go on their first eagle hunt! Today they were Eagle Hunters!

They inspected one another's bows and arrows, adjusted their packs, and waited impatiently. The men arrived carrying a cage of woven reeds, lightweight but strong, a coil of heavy fiber rope, bows and arrows, and packs. The boys started to climb down the ladder, but Tolonqua said, "Wait.

There is something more to know about eagles before you
go. Tell them, Long See.''

The Hunting Chief placed his cage on the floor of the
roof so both hands were free to gesture. "As you have been
told, there are three ways to catch eagles." He held up three
fingers. "By luring them with a live rabbit tied to a stake
and grabbing the eagle when it sinks its talons into the rabbit. Once those claws dig in to something, they won't let
go." Long See folded one finger. "Or by hiding in a pit,
covering the pit with sticks, staking a rabbit beside it, and
then reaching up to grab the eagle's legs when it seizes the
rabbit. You jerk the eagle down into the pit and struggle to
subdue it while it fights you." He folded another finger.
"Or you find a nest with young birds just before they are
able to fly, and take them and carry them home in this."
He picked up the cage and passed it around so the boys
could examine it. "Today we shall search for a nest."

Acoya said, "What about the eagle parents? Don't they
fight?"

Long See smiled grimly. "They do. You wait until they
are gone."

"Aye," Yatosha said. "I know where a nest may be. But
to reach it will be dangerous. You come to observe only. Is
that understood?"

Five crestfallen faces regarded him in silence. Finally,
Acoya said, "Chomoc's totem is Eagle. Surely he—"

"Chomoc will watch only. To learn. Like the rest of you.
If that is not to your liking, you may remain here." He took
the cage and descended the outer wall without a backward
glance.

"Go now," Tolonqua told the boys. "Observe carefully.
I shall expect each of you to tell me all you have seen."

Tolonqua watched as Acoya climbed down, followed by
the other boys and Long See. Robbing Eagle's nest was dangerous; foreboding nudged him. He told himself that Acoya
had a double totem and was safe, but anxiety was a lump
in his stomach.

The group headed for the hills. Yatosha walked in front
with the long, easy hunter's stride. The boys followed buoy-
antly in single file with Long See behind.

Tolonqua watched them go while the lump in his stomach
grew heavy.

Would all of them return?

* * *

Shadows grew short as Sunfather rose overhead. The boys had climbed the mountain all morning without stopping, and they were tired and hungry. They had seen tracks of Deer and of Bear, and encountered a badger, and although they scanned the skies constantly, no eagles appeared.

"How much farther is the nesting place?" Acoya asked.

Yatosha pointed. "See the top of that rocky spire beyond the mountain?"

"Yes."

"That is their home."

The boys gazed in awe at the rocky mass thrusting like an arrowhead into the sky.

"Ai-e-e-e!"

"How do we get up there?"

"You do not. You observe from below."

There was disappointed grumbling, but not as much as before. The sight of such an inaccessible place was so-bering.

Long See and Yatosha removed their packs. "We eat now, and rest, and call the eagle spirits."

They sat under an oak tree of a variety Acoya had not seen before, one whose acorns were less bitter than those of home, or so Long See said as he scooped some up and stuffed them in his pack. They ate leisurely of corn cake and jerky and water from the spring at home, and listened to the soft voices of the forest.

Chomoc said, "No eagles are nearby."

"Their nests may be too high up there in the trees for us to see," Acoya said.

"There are none," Chomoc said matter-of-factly, chewing on a big bite of jerky.

Acoya gave him a knowing glance. "Who says so?"

Chomoc pointed at a squirrel watching them from a low branch.

Long See nodded approvingly. "It is true that squirrels do not linger where eagles are."

Acoya and Chomoc looked at each other. Acoya said, "Chomoc knows because the squirrel told him."

"Of course," Long See said absently. He shouldered his pack and picked up the ornate case containing his bow and arrows. "Yatosha and I go now to call the eagle spirits. We shall not be gone for long. You are to remain here."

Yatosha said, "*Here.* Understand?"

"But you said we could observe!" Acoya cried.

"You may do so when we go to find the nest. Now we

go only to call the spirits. You have yet to learn these prayers. Therefore, you cannot be with us.''

"Where will you be?'' a boy asked, glancing around uncertainly.

"Where the spirits tell us to be. We go now.''

The boys watched in silence as Yatosha and Long See disappeared among the trees.

For a time no one spoke. A cool mountain wind blew, rustling leaves and bending the grasses. A magpie called; nothing answered. Silence bore down.

The boys glanced furtively around, concealing unease. Acoya watched Lapu, the biggest boy, wipe his forehead with a pudgy hand; he sweated even when it was cool—a manly trait, as Lapu often pointed out, but which Acoya disliked because Lapu smelled bad.

"If they go only to pray, why do they need their packs and their bows and arrows?'' a boy said. His name was Toho, for Cougar, but he was small and scrawny and had lost two front teeth. "Maybe they go to find the nest and don't want us with them.''

Lapu snorted and shot Toho a withering glance. "Is mama's big brave boy afraid to be alone here?'' he asked in a squeaky little-girl voice, pursing his lips and fluttering pudgy fingers.

Toho blushed painfully. His family was from a poor and distant pueblo whose people had abandoned it and migrated to Cicuye. He was an outsider. He did not answer and tried to squeeze into himself.

"They know we are safe here,'' Acoya said reassuringly. "There are five of us but only two of them, so they must be ready to protect themselves.''

"Aye,'' Jaywing said. He was the quiet one, a member of the Cottonwood Clan. He was ordinary-looking and not outstanding in anything, but his family had been in Cicuye for a long time and was much respected.

Chomoc nodded. "My father is always prepared; we should be also.'' He removed his bow from its case and laid it upon his lap with an arrow beside it.

Acoya regarded his friend with approval. Chomoc needed no bow or arrow here. But he knew what it was to be an outsider and he wanted to make Toho feel better. Besides, Chomoc disliked Lapu as much as Acoya did.

"Chomoc is right.'' Acoya removed his bow and an arrow, also.

Jaywing and Toho did the same. Finally, Lapu did likewise. All had seen the bear tracks.

Time passed. Silence bore down. Yatosha and Long See did not return.

The five boys: Acoya, Chomoc, big Lapu, scrawny Toho and Jaywing sat huddled together under the oak tree, straining to listen, to see, to smell danger.

Silence.

"What was that?" Toho whispered.

"What?"

"I saw something move over there." He pointed to a clump of brush among the trees.

"I didn't see anything," Acoya said. "Did you?" he asked the others.

"No," Jaywing said.

'Toho sees shadows," Lapu snorted.

"Something moved there!" Toho whispered hotly.

Chomoc said nothing.

As the boys watched, a large bush quivered as though an animal moved behind it.

"See? I told you!" Toho hissed, clutching his bow.

"A bear!" Jaywing whispered hoarsely.

"Ha! Squirrels!" Lapu rose. "I'll show you!"

"Wait!" Acoya whispered. "It could be—"

But Lapu was gone, treading silently through the trees. He disappeared behind the bushes.

The boys waited tensely.

"Ah-h-h-!" Lapu screamed. He staggered out, rubbing his face and body with both hands. "Ah-h-h-!"

The boys watched as a little black animal with a white stripe on his back scurried away, flaunting his upright, bushy tail.

"Well done!" Chomoc laughed, waving the skunk farewell.

Acoya gave Chomoc a knowing glance. Toho whooped with laughter, holding his sides, and Jaywing laughed with him, but they all stopped laughing as Lapu approached.

"Stay away!" they shouted, holding their noses.

Long See and Yatosha came running through the trees. "What happened?"

When they were closer, they stopped and clamped their hands to their faces. Lapu stood in wretched uncertainty, trying futilely to wipe the smell from himself, trying not to be sick.

Long See said from behind a hand clamped to his nose, "How did Lapu get sprayed when the rest of you did not?"

There was no answer. Yatosha looked at Chomoc. "You will tell me what happened," he commanded.

Chomoc did not reply.

Toho snickered. "Lapu wanted to scare away the bear."

Yatosha and Long See exchanged glances.

"What bear?"

"Tracks only," Chomoc said calmly.

"I told you to remain here!" Long See said sternly to Lapu.

Lapu nodded miserably.

Long See's young-old face softened. "There is a creek nearby. We will go there. All the smell will not wash off, but some will."

They departed single file, Lapu a good distance behind.

The creek flowed musically over a rocky bed beneath a canopy of cottonwoods, willows, and aspens. All drank from the cool, sweet water; some from cupped hands while others lay on their stomachs and dipped their faces into the stream. The mountain breeze touched them all and made the aspen's leaves quiver.

Acoya thought of his secret cove. This place, too, must be a sacred spot. "It is beautiful here," he said.

Yatosha nodded. "This is an eagle stream. They like to nest near water."

"Are we nearly there?"

"Aye."

Lapu had removed his breechcloth and moccasins and lay in the water downstream, splashing and rubbing himself with sand and pebbles from the creek bed.

Toho giggled. "He will smell only a little worse than usual."

The boys laughed. Yatosha looked at Long See. "Should we leave him here until we return? Nothing attacks a skunk; the smell will keep him safe."

"Eagles don't like skunks, either."

"That is true. Maybe he would be a help in keeping the parent birds away."

Long See shook his head. "Nothing will keep them away if they see us anywhere near their eyrie—"

Yatosha looked at Lapu who was, after all, only a boy. "We should not leave him here. It can do no harm to have him with the others."

"Very well."

It was agreed. Lapu dried himself as best he could with grasses, and the group headed for the butte thrusting against a cobalt sky where two golden eagles soared in majesty, riding the wind. They were so high they were nearly invisible.

"They see us," Long See said.

"From way up there?" Acoya asked, incredulous.

"They can see a mouse from there."

Acoya stared in awe. "How can you rob the nest without them seeing?"

"You can't. You wait until they go elsewhere." He glanced at the butte. "This is an eagle place where eagles return to the same nest every year. Those eagles soaring up there may not be from a nest we find."

"Then again, they may," Yatosha said. "That is why you will remain below when Long See and I climb to the nest."

Chomoc looked at his father. "I want to go with you."

"No."

Acoya gazed at the two men standing there, Hunting Chiefs both, whose protecting spirits would keep them from harm and lead them safely home. Of course.

But what if . . .

"This is the place."

The massive butte, forbidding and rocky, loomed high from a hilly slope at the base. Long See shaded his eyes with his hand and stared up at it for some time. Finally, he pointed.

"Up there. On that ledge."

Yatosha said, "Where?"

"Look from the top of the spire down to that yellowish stripe in the rock formation. There is a ledge just below it where sticks poke out over the edge. See?"

"I think so. Barely."

"That is their eyrie."

Long See turned to the boys who stared up at the ledge. "They build a huge, flat nest of sticks. That is where we go."

Chomoc said again, "I want to go with you, Father."

"You and the others may come as far as there." Yatosha pointed to where the butte soared abruptly from the hilly slope. "That is where you will stay and watch. We will be out of sight when we go around that bulge"—he pointed—"but you will see us when we reach the other side."

"But—"

"I have spoken."

Silently the boys followed Long See and Yatosha as they climbed the rocky soil to the top of the rise. The men set down the eagle cage, laid their bow and arrow cases and backpacks on the ground, reached into the packs, and removed a coil of rope and a net large enough for an eagle. Yatosha lifted the eagle cage to his head and tied it there like a warbonnet.

Long See said, "This is all we will take. You are responsible for the things we leave here."

"We shall take care of them," Jaywing said.

"Aye," the others added.

"Very well. We go now."

"Remain here!" Yatosha said firmly.

The boys nodded.

Acoya watched the men begin their climb up the butte. It was dangerous, and he knew the higher they got the more dangerous it would become.

He glanced at Chomoc who watched his father reaching for handholds and footholds on the butte's stony face. He knew very well that when the men were out of sight around the bulge, Chomoc would follow his father. And he would follow Chomoc.

▲ 44 ▼

"**I** am going up there. My father needs me."

"They told us to stay here!" Toho said nervously. He glanced at Lapu expecting another scornful comment, but Lapu sat at a distance, dejectedly alone. Skunk odor still wafted from him but it was not as overpowering as before.

Jaywing looked up at the men climbing the butte. "Your father has Long See with him. Why does he need you?"

Chomoc did not reply. He placed his bow and arrow case on the ground beside Yatosha's.

"They don't want us with them," Acoya said, knowing that it made no difference to Chomoc. "It's dangerous—"

"That is why I am going. He needs me."

"But why?" Jaywing frowned. "They said—"

"Chomoc can help to keep the parent eagles away." Acoya laid his bow and arrows beside the others on the ground. "I am going to help Chomoc."

Chomoc looked down his nose. "I need no help. My totem is Eagle, remember?"

"Your father thinks he needs no help, but you are going. You think you need no help, but—"

"Then all of us go to help each other? Ha! Only I can help my father. You stay here, Acoya."

"No."

They looked at each other for a long moment.

Chomoc turned and began to climb the steep slope of the butte. Acoya followed. He could not let Chomoc subject himself to danger alone.

"Don't go!" Jaywing cried.

"You will be sorry!" Lapu shouted.

Toho ran after Acoya and grabbed him. "Don't leave us! Stay here like they said to!"

Acoya looked into Toho's frightened eyes. "What will happen to us if Yatosha and Long See are attacked by eagles way up there?"

Toho stared without speaking.

"Chomoc can talk to eagles; he can protect his father and Long See."

"But why must you go with him? You—"

"Chomoc may need my help up there."

"But—"

"You are safe here. Stay until we get back."

Acoya followed Chomoc up the butte. It was not as steep as it looked from below, but finding secure handholds and footholds was not easy; pockets of gravel and loose soil gave way under pressure. Chomoc had climbed cliffs at the Place of the Eagle Clan when he was four years old so this climb was not as difficult for him, but he was slow and careful. Sometimes, loosened dirt and rocks tumbled down and Acoya had to climb to one side to avoid being hit.

The soil became more firm as they climbed; sometimes there was only unyielding stone warmed by the sun. Footing was more secure here, but harder to find. Acoya watched Chomoc and did what he did, but it was scary.

The wind gusted, tugging at Acoya's hair, fingering his hands and feet. Although it was afternoon, the wind was cool. Acoya clutched the rock with both hands, searching with both feet for a grip. He glanced down and his heart lurched; he wished he had stayed below. Instead, he looked up, watching Chomoc, and hoping that Long See and Yatosha would not see them when they appeared from around the bulge on the butte.

The wind gusted again, harder. Pushing. A stone Acoya clung to with one hand gave way and tumbled down. Frantically he reached for another, straining. His fingers found it and clung while he closed his eyes and pressed himself against the surface of the rock. His heart drummed wildly.

I can't do this. I can't.

"You can and you will."

It was as though a silent voice spoke from inside of him. What was it the Medicine Chief had said? *Many grandfathers are in your blood. They seek to guide you. Listen to them!*

Acoya clutched the face of the butte with hands and feet and pressed his face against the stone, willing its strength to enter him, willing himself to listen to an inner voice.

You are a Chosen one, protected by Bear and the White Buffalo. Have no fear.

Slowly the drumming of his heart eased.

"Acoya! Look!"

It was Chomoc smiling down at him from a nearby ledge.

"Come up here and look!"

Strength flowed into Acoya's arms and legs and throughout his body. He reached up for a handhold, found it, and another and another. Chomoc leaned down, took Acoya's hand, and pulled him up to the ledge.

"See?" Chomoc said.

They had climbed around to the side of the butte out of sight of Yatosha and Long See to a spot invisible from below. Here the butte sloped more gently to hills and to mountains beyond. Farther to the side of the butte was another ledge with an eagle's nest sprawled upon it. Three eaglets nestled there.

"Oh!" Acoya exclaimed. "Three!"

"Too young to take now, I think. They still have white spots." He looked at Acoya in triumph. "Ours! Our eagles!"

They laughed excitedly. Three!

From above came a flap of wings. A golden eagle with a rabbit in its talons swooped down to the nest. It dropped the rabbit and turned to the boys with a scream. Great wings spread open and the eagle darted at the boys like a flung spear.

Chomoc faced the eagle. "We are friends," he said.

Acoya cringed as fierce talons reached for him. But the eagle swerved midair and flew to the pinnacle looming above. It perched there, staring down at Chomoc who returned the stare in fierce silence.

Another eagle swooped from the sky, screaming in fury at the intruders. Chomoc watched it with an intense gaze. Acoya could feel the power of Chomoc's effort to communicate. The golden-brown body flung at them, talons extended. Suddenly it swerved and darted away. Again it flew at them, screaming, and again it swerved.

"We are friends," Chomoc said.

The eagle darted upward, flying higher and higher into the sky. It circled there.

Acoya could feel the eagle's gaze, watching them, preparing to attack again.

Long See slid gingerly down to the ledge where a young eagle squawked at him from the nest, a large platform of sticks upon which were bones and debris from years of use. Around Long See's waist was a rope held by Yatosha who clung to a rocky outcrop above. The cage with the net inside sat beside him on the ledge.

"She is the right age." Long See said "she" for all eagles were regarded as female. "Fine brown feathers!" He removed the net from the cage.

"Be quick!" Yatosha called down. "I see an eagle up there!"

Long See saw it, too. Circling.

He flung the net over the eaglet and it flopped about, trying to free itself, screaming.

With an answering scream, the eagle swooped from the sky.

Acoya saw it coming, great wings folding like a hawk darting after a mouse. But it headed toward the other side of the butte!

"Look!" he shouted at Chomoc.

But Chomoc had seen. He stood, staring at the eagle with arm upraised, his face tense with effort, his lips clenched tight.

The eagle disappeared behind the butte.

Frantically Long See grabbed the young eagle and stuffed it into the cage, net and all. As Yatosha yanked on the rope to pull Long See up, the eagle swept down, tore the cage from Long See's grip, and soared away, the cage in its talons.

Never had such a thing happened before! Eagles were known to steal a man's puppy or other small pet, but never had an eagle snatched a cage from the hands of a hunter! The men gawked in stunned astonishment.

"Come back here!" Long See shouted.

The eagle swept over the hills to tall trees near the stream. The men watched helplessly as the eagle dropped the cage and disappeared into the distance.

"Did you see that?" Jaywing pointed. "Over there!"

"Yes! An eagle with the cage!" Toho nearly choked with excitement. "Our cage! It flew that way!" He pointed.

"Where the skunk was!" Lapu said.

The boys looked at one another, then up at small figures high on the butte. Long See and Yatosha were beginning to descend.

"I wonder where Chomoc and Acoya are," Jaywing said.

Lapu stared at trees in the distance. "That cage had an eagle in it."

Again the boys looked at one another.

"We have to get it," Jaywing said.

"But we can't leave here!" Toho pointed to the figures on the butte. "We have to wait until they get back."

"The eagle may come back and carry the cage away before then," Lapu said.

Jaywing nodded. "That's right."

Lapu stood up. "My smell will keep the eagle away, maybe." He blinked, and looked away. "I'll go."

"There were bear tracks!" Toho quavered.

Jaywing shot him a glance. "We have our bows and arrows. If we hurry we can be back before Long See and Yatosha get here."

"Let's go!" Lapu said.

They took their bows and arrows, left everything else, and started down the hill. They scanned the sky often as they went, but saw no eagle. Shadows were long now; soon Sunfather would depart. They hurried on.

At last they reached the stream and stopped to drink.

Toho looked about uneasily. "I wonder where the cage is."

"We will find it," Jaywing said. "I think it's in a tree over that way." He pointed.

Lapu nodded. "I'll go and see." He strode along, looking up into the trees, while the boys followed a distance behind.

Jaywing stopped, staring at the ground. Toho stood with him, mouth agape.

Bear tracks. Fresh ones.

"Let's climb a tree!" Toho cried.

"We can't. We have to find that cage and eagle and get back."

"But bears—"

"Over here!" Lapu shouted pointing up into a tall tree.

Jaywing and Toho ran to see. High up there, on a top branch, the cage perched at a perilous angle with the eaglet and net inside.

"I'll get it!" Lapu shinnied to the lowest branch, swung up, and began to climb.

There was a rustle in the brush and a bear cub emerged. It stopped, looking at them uncertainly.

For a moment the boys froze.

"Quick! Climb!" Jaywing hissed. He gave small Toho a boost and shinnied up after him as a grizzly burst through the bushes and saw them. With a coughing growl it charged, ears laid back, teeth exposed. The boys clawed desperately to reach higher branches as the grizzly was nearly upon them. It stood on hind legs and reached for them, snarling, huge forepaws gashing the bark.

Long See and Yatosha stood at the base of the butte, looking at the things they had left there and at the packs belonging to the boys.

"Where are they?" Long See gritted his teeth. "We told them—"

"Chomoc!" Yatosha called. "Chomoc!"

"Up here!"

The men whirled to see Chomoc and Acoya climbing down the butte.

"What are you doing up there?" Yatosha yelled.

"Fools!" Long See growled.

The men hurried to help the boys down. Neither Acoya nor Chomoc seemed the least concerned about having disobeyed a firm order.

Long See grabbed Acoya by both shoulders and shook him. "You have explaining to do."

Chomoc said, "He wanted to help me."

"Help you do what?"

Chomoc looked at Yatosha and said nothing. His father returned the gaze silently. Finally, he said, "Did you—"

"Yes."

"Chomoc saved you both!" Acoya jerked free of Long See's grasp.

"Leave him be," Yatosha said to Long See.

"They disobeyed—"

"Yes. But—"

"Where are Jaywing and the others?" Acoya cried.

"We thought they were with you."

"No. We told them to stay here—"

"As we told you to do," Long See said bitterly.

"They must have gone after the eagle and the cage," Yatosha said. "Let's find out."

They gathered the packs and bows and arrows.

"Their bows are missing."

Long See nodded. "I hope they don't have to use them."

There was no answer. Each remembered bear tracks.

They found the tracks of the boys and followed swiftly in single file, Long See in front, then Acoya and Chomoc, with Yatosha in the rear. Sunfather had departed to travel underground to his eastern home; soon it would be dark.

Long See stopped abruptly. He leaned to inspect the

ground. The others gathered to look at dark splotches on the soil.

Blood.

Yatosha grunted, pointing at fresh bear tracks nearby.

Instantly bows and arrows were drawn and ready as they walked slowly ahead, scanning every bush, every shadow.

More blood.

There was a rustle, a stirring, as night stalked like a predator.

Long See peered into every tree. "Where are those boys?" he asked as he had a dozen times before.

"Call them," Yatosha said.

"Jaywing, Lapu, Toho!" they shouted.

A flock of ravens flew from a tree, squawking in alarm.

They called again. No answer.

As they stood together, gazing about them, there was a roaring growl. A huge grizzly lurched from behind a bush and charged them, with two arrows quivering in its bleeding flanks.

Instantly four more arrows pierced the shaggy body. The bear rose on its hind legs, clawed the air, shook its big head, and fell to the ground, jerking.

Acoya and Chomoc darted forward, but Yatosha pushed them back.

"Wait. He may not be dead."

For a time they stood there, watching. Long See fitted another arrow in his bow and approached the bear slowly. He stepped behind it and gave it a shove with his foot.

"It is dead."

Long See replaced his bow, removed the arrows, and held them in his hand as he raised both arms, singing the Bear Spirit Chant to ask forgiveness for taking its life and to speed the spirit on its way to be reborn in another bear.

Yatosha joined the chant while the boys followed as best they could. Their voices rose and fell, drifting among the trees.

From a distance came a faint cry.

They stopped, listening. The cry came again.

"That is Jaywing!" Acoya said.

They hurried toward the sound, calling the boys. Answering cries led them to a tall cottonwood with deep gashes in the bark.

"Up here!" Jaywing yelled.

Jaywing and Toho straddled a big branch halfway up the tree. At the top Lapu clung perilously with one hand to a cluster of thin branches, bracing his feet on more branches below. His other hand clutched the cage with the eagle huddled inside.

"Be careful!" Toho cried. "A grizzly—"

"It is dead," Long See said.

Jaywing whooped, "We killed it! We killed it!"

"Almost. We finished it. Come down."

Jaywing and Toho inched down, but when Lapu tried to descend, the thin branches swayed, nearly dislodging him as he held the branches with one hand and the cage with the other.

"I can't!"

Jaywing and Toho jumped to the ground expecting an angry confrontation, but they were ignored. Long See and Yatosha stood gazing up at Lapu.

"Those branches won't hold more weight. Maybe if we can get the eagle cage he will be able to use both hands and climb down."

"If he had our rope he could tie it to the cage and lower it."

"We could try and toss him the rope but how can he grab it? He needs to hang on—"

Acoya said, "I will take the rope to him."

Yatosha flashed him an approving glance, but he said, "You are too heavy."

Instantly all eyes were upon small Toho.

"No!" Toho's voice shook.

"You must," Yatosha said calmly. "You are the only one who can."

Acoya watched Toho peering up into the tree at Lapu who had tormented Toho at every opportunity. He did not want to go up there to help him, and Acoya didn't blame him. But he tried to make his voice convincing as he said, "You will be brave."

"A hero," Chomoc said.

"Aye. A hero," Long See added.

Toho stared again into the treetop where Lapu clung. "I'm scared," he whispered wretchedly, confessing his shame.

Yatosha nodded. "All heroes are scared, but they do what they must anyway. That is why they are heroes." He removed the rope from his pack and offered it to Toho. He said gravely, "You can do what the rest of us cannot."

Toho swallowed. He took the rope and coiled it around his neck. Yatosha boosted him up the tree. Hesitantly, Toho climbed from limb to limb while those below watched tensely, cheering him on.

"You do well!"

"Keep going!"

"Good! Very good!"

Toho climbed higher in the dimming light. Suddenly he slipped and grabbed a small branch. It bent under his weight and swayed back and forth with Toho clinging to it.

"I can't!" Toho cried desperately.

Acoya remembered how he clung to the face of the butte, frozen and terrified, saying "I can't!"

"You can!" Acoya shouted. "You can!"

"What is your totem?" Yatosha called.

"Grasshopper."

"Grasshoppers know trees. Your totem will help you. Let it tell you what to do."

Acoya saw Toho screw his eyes tight shut. For a minute Toho just hung there, trying not to move because it made the branch sway. Then he opened his eyes, reached with one hand to grasp another small branch, pulled it to him, and wrapped his legs around both branches to steady himself.

Above him Lapu watched in tense silence. Then he said, "Try and throw the rope up here."

Very carefully, Toho lifted the rope from around his neck.

Yatosha shouted, "Throw one end only. If it falls you can pull it back up."

Toho uncoiled a lenght of the rope, and threw it. It caught in a branch and dangled there. The branches Toho straddled jerked up and down and he hung on with both hands.

"Try again," Lapu said.

Toho still clung, face frozen.

"You can!" Acoya called. "Do it!"

"Try again!"

Slowly, Toho pulled the dangling rope back down. His hands shook but he threw the rope again.

It nearly missed, but Lapu looped one arm around a branch, reached down and grabbed the rope with the other hand. He swung perilously back and forth, hanging on with his legs until the branches steadied enough for him to tie the rope to the cage.

There were cheers from below.

"You did it!" Acoya yelled.

Lapu said, "Feed me the rope while I lower the cage."

"All right."

Slowly the cage came down, bumping this way and that, until it was low enough for Long See to climb up and take it. He handed the cage down to Yatosha as Lapu and Toho inched their way back down to loud congratulations.

The eaglet huddled in the cage, watching them, its eyes following every move. The boys gathered around the cage, admiring every golden-brown feather.

"A beauty," Long See said.

"We are lucky to have it," Yatosha answered. "I saw no others up there."

Acoya and Chomoc exchanged glances.

▲ 45 ▼

Moonwoman was high; it was the time of the evening fire. Everyone in Cicuye was gathered in the plaza to hear again the story of the eagle hunt. Traders from distant villages had arrived with their packs and dogs, and waited eagerly for news to take home. Songs had been sung, riddles told, old stories repeated. Now there was a buzz of excitement as Yatosha, Long See, and the five boys appeared with a young eagle in a cage and the skin of a large grizzly bear.

Long See raised an arm for silence. When all was quiet, he began the story of what had happened. The people listened raptly, even those who had heard it all before.

"—and then the eagle jerked the cage from my hands and flew away with it!" Long See paused, gesturing.

"Ai-e-e-e!"

Traders stared at one another in disbelief. What a story to take home!

As Long See continued the story, Acoya and Chomoc held up the bearskin with the giant paws still attached.

Long See said, "You can see the size of the grizzly that attacked our boys." He turned the skin around to show the inside. "Here is where their two arrows wounded it. Our arrows pierced it here." He pointed to each place. "We killed it just in time, before it mauled us."

There were murmurs, and people crowded closer to see.

As Long See told of how Lapu retrieved the cage with the help of Toho, both boys stood proudly, basking in the glow of warm approval and admiration. Acoya knew what it meant to Lapu who had few admirers, and to small Toho who had none. The boys stood side by side as friends now. And heroes, both.

"Night came," Long See continued, "so we went back to where the bear was, made camp, and feasted."

Acoya remembered how they devoured juicy hunks of bear meat roasted over a fire. The next day, each carried as much meat home as he could carry, and feasted again. How proud Kwani and Tolonqua were when he brought bear meat to their dwelling!

"So now we have another bearskin for our medicine lodge. And our first eagle. To protect our city and us. One day we shall have others."

"Aye!"

Two Elk strode forward. As he stood there in the firelight wearing authority like a ceremonial robe, Acoya wondered what it must be like to be Chief of Cicuye, responsible for the welfare of all the people. He needed a powerful totem. Acoya wondered what it was.

Two Elk did not raise his hand for silence; it was not necessary. The people knew he had something important to say, and they quieted, waiting.

"I ask Long See, Yatosha, Acoya, Chomoc, Toho, Lapu, and Jaywing to come and stand here with me."

There were curious comments as they all lined up.

Acoya thought, Maybe I and the other boys will be punished for disobeying Long See and Yatosha on the eagle hunt. But he stood up straight and hid his nervousness. Chomoc stood beside him and Acoya guessed Chomoc was nervous, too.

Two Elk said, "Long See and Yatosha and these five boys bravely risked danger to bring us our first eagle. Therefore, I proclaim that from now, this night, they are to be honored as Eagle Hunters of Cicuye, and are to wear the Claw of the Eagle so that all may remember their accomplishment."

He gestured and the bead maker, a recent arrival acclaimed for his artistry, stepped forward. He was short and stocky, but stood tall as he handed Two Elk a deerskin pouch.

Ignoring an impatient buzz, Two Elk took his time opening the pouch. Slowly he extracted a necklace of exquisitely carved bone beads assembled from his treasured bead collection. From each hung a polished eagle claw acquired in costly trade.

"Ah-h-h-h." A collective sigh.

Two Elk gestured to Long See who came to stand before him.

"I name you Chief of the Eagle Hunters," Two Elk said loudly, and placed the necklace around Long See's scrawny neck.

Long See bowed his thanks, beaming.

Again Two Elk reached in the pouch and removed a similar necklace. He gestured to Yatosha who stepped forward.

"I name you Assistant Chief of the Eagle Hunters."

As Two Elk placed the necklace around Yatosha's neck, there were pleased comments from the Anasazis. Their Hunting Chief was being honored by the Chief of the Towa! Yatosha's square face flushed with pleasure.

Acoya held his breath. Would he and the others get necklaces, too? Such an honor would carry enormous prestige. He glanced at White Cloud who met his gaze with a smile that made his heart leap. He had to have an eagle claw!

Two Elk reached into the pouch once more and pulled out five smaller necklaces, but equally as fine, each gleaming with a polished eagle claw. He stepped to where the boys stood together in a row, faces aglow, and draped a necklace around each one.

"I name each of you Eagle Hunter of Cicuye. You are the first to be so honored. May you bring us many more eagles."

"Aye!" the people shouted, applauding.

Acoya and Chomoc exchanged secret smiles. In another moon they would go for their own eagles.

Tolonqua walked alone on the ridge—alone but for Chuka and Mo who dashed about, impatient with Tolonqua's slow gait as he braced himself upon his staff. It seemed to him lately that he needed it more than usual.

It was morning in late summer with white clouds billowing and a breeze hinting of autumn. Harvest and hunting time. Time to go for buffalo. Soon Long See and Yatosha would be with their hunters out on the wide plains. . . .

Tolonqua reached the highest point on the ridge, turned his back to the east where the plains lay, and sat on a big rock to look down at the city he had built. Was still building. More remained to be done until his promise to the Above Beings and to the Morning Star was fulfilled.

He inspected his city critically, as if for the first time. The back walls of each dwelling joined to form a solid wall around the city, accessible only by one guarded door and ladders from the roofs. Each night the ladders were drawn up and bowmen were stationed at strategic points to watch for enemies.

Pawnees.

There were other enemy tribes, of course. Querecho, Apache, wandering tribes from the north, and others. But Pawnees were the greatest danger.

I must make the city stronger. Taller along the outside

walls. And with fortified towers. The bigger and richer Cicuye becomes, the greater the danger of attack.

There is much to be done.

But weariness seeped into his bones and his spirit. Age stalked him.

What if Sipapu calls before my work is finished?

Tolonqua pondered this. Perhaps Acoya was the answer. Soon he would assume a man's responsibilities. He could finish the building if he was willing to do so.

I must talk with him about this, Tolonqua told himself. If he promises to do it, he will.

The thought lightened his spirit and he rose to return to the city. Mo and Chuka had flushed out a rabbit and were chasing it wildly across the ridge. Smoke drifted from morning cooking fires and blew on the wind. Already men were in distant fields preparing for harvest, and women finished with the cooking washed clothes at the river. From kivas came the throb of drums, the heartbeat of Earthmother herself, and chants of supplication for good harvest and good hunting. Children shouted, dogs yapped, and there were intermittent pounding as crossbeams rose on a dwelling. Another clan was on the way, migrating from a distant western pueblo; smoke signals and runners said they would be here before another moon.

I must see that the beams are properly placed, Tolonqua thought. He headed back to the city, bracing himself each step of the way, wondering about the new arrivals and hoping they would be worthy of the city of the Morning Star.

Kwani stirred the piki batter and poured a handful on her baking stone nicely oiled with bear fat. It took much practice to make the thin, delicious cakes and she was proud of her skill. Antelope sat by, watching.

"I want to do that."

"Very well. Try."

Antelope reached into the batter, scooped up a small handful, held it dripping to the baking stone, and let the batter fall. It hardened quickly in a shapeless blob and was ready to turn. Antelope knew how Kwani poked at the edge of a cake with her piki stick, a short, smooth stick with a flattened edge, to lift a corner of the cake, then grasp the loosened edge deftly to flip it over. It looked easy.

"Is it ready to turn now?" Antelope asked.

"Yes. Be careful; the stone is hot."

Antelope jabbed at the blob with the piki stick, tearing

the cake. She jabbed again, trying to lift a corner, tore the cake again, tried again, and finally managed to lift enough to take hold of. She grasped it, tried to turn over the scorched blob, and tore it some more. Exasperated, she yanked at it and burned a finger.

"Ouch!"

She poked her burned finger in her mouth while Kwani scraped charred pieces of piki with the scraping stone. Kwani knew that although Antelope's finger hurt she refused to cry; she was embarrassed and indignant because she could not do what her mother did. Antelope expected to excel at everything, and she was only six.

Kwani sat back on her heels and looked at her daughter; Tolonqua's obsidian eyes looked back. Would those eyes burn when they looked at a man one day? Kwani remembered the first time she saw Tolonqua standing before her, his eyes burning into hers. His presence was overpowering.

Tolonqua.

As Kwani poured more batter upon the baking stone she thought of him, and the thought filled her heart, as always. How much of his strong spirit had he bequeathed this twin child?

As though summoned by Kwani's thoughts, Tolonqua entered, followed by Acoya.

"I greet you," they said in unison.

"My spirit rejoices," Kwani responded, flipping a piki cake. "Come and eat."

Antelope held up her burned finger for Tolonqua to see. "It hurts."

Tolonqua inspected it gravely. "It will be well soon."

"Let me see," Acoya said.

He turned the finger this way and that, looking closely. "I know what to do to make it feel better." He rose. "I will be right back."

When he had gone, Kwani and Tolonqua looked at each other. Kwani said, "How does he know?"

"He spends time in the kiva with the Medicine Society. He asks questions."

Kwani was surprised. She didn't know this, but then women were not allowed in kivas except by special invitation. Boys Acoya's age spent more time in kivas than in their homes. Soon, too soon, he would be grown and a member of one of the men's secret societies that encompassed every aspect of pueblo life. Which would Acoya's society be? Kwani wondered. Okalake, his birth father, was son of the

Sun Chief and would have become Sun Chief himself, but as yet Acoya had indicated no special interest in the constellations. Perhaps that would come later.

Footsteps ran on the walkway and Acoya entered. In his hand was a small piece of juicy green plant that resembled cactus but had no thorns. He squeezed some juice on Antelope's finger and pressed the pulp to it.

"Hold this there and the pain will go away."

Antelope looked at her brother with gratitude and, unabashed admiration. "You will be Medicine Chief when you grow up."

"Yes." Acoya raised both arms overhead like the painting on the stone in his secret hideaway place. "A shaman."

Tolonqua and Kwani looked at each other and at him. He was ten years old. Old enough to know. But a shaman? One who abides more with the spirits than with people? One who undergoes the most rigid and extensive training, sacrificing comfort and personal pleasure for the good of the people?

For a moment Kwani remembered when she held Acoya as a baby and glimpsed the future. She saw him as a shaman then. . . .

Her heart constricted and she put both arms around him and held him close. At least she had him for a little while longer.

"My finger doesn't hurt anymore." Antelope removed the juicy green pulp and showed her finger to Acoya. "See?"

He nodded matter-of-factly. "It will get well." He helped himself to piki from the basket by the fire pit and took a big bite. "Good!"

"Wait," Tolonqua said sharply. "You forgot something."

Acoya stopped midbite. He nodded sheepishly, broke off a bit of piki, and tossed it upon the coals as an offering of thanks to the gods.

The others did likewise, and the four of them sat around the fire pit, eating piki, thin and delicious, a gift from Corn Mother.

Kwani looked at Tolonqua who sat cross-legged, leaning forward as he reached for piki, eating slowly and deliberately, his strong chin moving up and down. Lines creased his face on either side of his nose to his mouth, and two small furrows marked his forehead. His face was thinner than it used to be, so that his proud nose and high cheekbones seemed more prominent.

He grows older. As do I.

He sensed her glance and returned it, his black eyes warming, as always. She responded with a smile. How handsome he was!

Antelope ate greedily, stuffing the piki into her mouth with a brown little hand. her dark hair was pulled back and tied with a bit of red cord, but wisps dangled over her ears and on her forehead that she pushed back impatiently. Soft round cheeks grew rounder with big bites, and pieces of piki clung to her mouth.

"You eat too fast," Acoya said.

Black eyes snapped at him. "I eat the way I want to."

"Acoya is right." Kwani looked at her daughter reprovingly. "The daughter of the Building Chief must have good manners."

Tolonqua regarded Antelope with fond amusement. "The daughter of She Who Remembers is expected to set an example."

Antelope glared at them, swallowed, took two piki cakes, and stuffed them both into her mouth so she could hardly close it as she tried to chew. Her cheeks bulged and some of the piki wet with saliva oozed out the corners of her mouth and dribbled to her chin.

Tolonqua rose, picked up Antelope, and carried her to the door.

"One who eats like a dog should be with dogs."

He pushed her outside, closed the door, and held it shut as she banged against it.

"Let me in!" she yelled.

Tolonqua held the door shut until the banging stopped. Then he opened it, but Antelope was gone.

Kwani said nothing. Tolonqua was right. But her heart ached for her twin child whose path of life would surely be difficult. Tolonqua had, indeed, bequeathed his daughter his strong spirit. Perhaps, being twins-in-one made her own spirit twice as strong, a force that could overwhelm her.

"I wonder where she went," Tolonqua said.

Acoya gave his father a quick glance. "To be with Chomoc. Yatosha and Huzipat are eating now; she will eat with them."

"With better manners, I certainly hope," Kwani said.

"She is different there than she is here. She had good manners there." Acoya shook his head. "I don't understand girls at all."

Tolonqua smiled. "Be assured you never will. That is the seasoning that makes them interesting."

Acoya shrugged; girls were simply odd creatures—girls.

Kwani said, "Someday you will be waiting at the spring." It was true. Acoya was growing up.

"See the new rabbit stick my father made," Chomoc said. It was a smooth, curved stick to be thrown at a running rabbit. "I have to catch something to feed the eagle."

Acoya nodded. The eagle's cage sat on Huzipat's roof, so it was Huzipat's responsibility to see that the eagle was fed. But he was too old to do it, so Yatosha gave Chomoc the responsibility.

"Will you help?" Chomoc asked.

Acoya nodded.

"Where shall we go? Most of the rabbits around here have been taken."

Acoya thought a moment. "We saw rabbits when we were eagle hunting. There should be a lot of mice there, too. Let's go that way."

It was a fine cool morning and the boys walked swiftly over the hills. Each carried his bow and arrow case slung over a shoulder, a pack on his back, and a knife in a pouch at his side in proper hunting fashion. They were Eagle Hunters now.

"Eagles need a lot to eat," Chomoc said.

They walked in silence for a while. Acoya wondered if they were both thinking the same thing—about those three eagles still in the nest. "I wonder if our eagles are big enough."

Chomoc stopped and looked at Acoya. "I was wondering, too. We can go and look."

"But we don't have a net or a cage—"

"No matter. Let's look anyway."

"It's a long way to go. We have to hurry."

"Maybe we will find a rabbit on the way."

They trotted up and down the hills for some time before a rabbit darted from under a bush. It was a big one, fine and fat. Chomoc tried to talk to it and make it stop, but it only ran faster with the boys speeding after it.

"Throw your rabbit stick!" Acoya cried.

Chomoc threw the stick. It flew straight and true but the rabbit leaped to one side, eluding it. By the time Chomoc retrieved the stick the rabbit had disappeared.

"We will see others," Acoya said.

"I will find something. The eagle is hungry."

Ahead, the butte soared skyward, massive and mysterious.

"Let's climb it from behind. The slope is easier there," Acoya said.

They trudged on. As the foothills reached the butte, the boys made their laborious way around to the back and began the climb. It was easier, but still difficult. An eagle soared overhead. Acoya watched it anxiously.

"I wonder if that is a parent to our eagles."

"Maybe," Chomoc mumbled as he reached for the branch of a shrub to pull himself up. A mouse skittered from behind it. Chomoc grabbed it, held it in his hand, looked at it intently for a moment, then twisted its tiny neck.

"You did not ask forgiveness," Acoya said.

"I did. But not your way."

Chomoc dropped the mouse into his pack and continued the climb behind Acoya who ignored danger and climbed as rapidly as he could, struggling to reach the ledge where their eagles awaited. Acoya did not know how they would carry three eagles home, but they would find a way. They would return home with three eagles! Three!

Acoya looked above him, searching for a small ledge with the ragged edge of an eagle's nest protruding. There it was, above and to the right.

"That way!" He pointed.

They scanned the sky for the soaring eagle. It was still up there.

Slowly, carefully, the boys climbed to the ledge. They stared.

The eagles were gone.

Someone else had been there first.

The boys half slid, half climbed back down, ignoring danger in their frustration, disappointment, and anger. Eagle-hunting territories were divided among various tribes and clans; the taker of an eagle from the territory of others had to ask permission to keep the eagle. No such request had been made to Cicuye.

There could be but one answer.

Enemies. Nearby.

They hurried homeward, glancing nervously about.

"What can we tell them?" Acoya asked. "We weren't supposed to be there—"

"We don't tell them. We say we were hunting eagle food, and I have some."

"But enemies—"

"—can be far away by now. Besides, my father knows, the Warrior Chief knows, everybody knows when enemies are near. They hear, they see the signs." He looked down his nose. "Are you scared?"

"Yes, I'm scared. Pawnee—"

Chomoc stopped abruptly to scan shadows among the trees. A chipmunk saw them and made chipmunk remarks.

Chomoc nodded and turned to Acoya. "We are intruders. That means no enemies are near."

They trudged on. At last they neared the river that ran by Cicuye.

Acoya said, "Let's take a swim and cool off."

"Good!"

They peeled off their breechcloths, removed their packs and their bow and arrow cases as they ran. When they reached the river upstream they slipped off their moccasins, tossed everything on the bank, and dived in.

The water felt wonderful. They splashed and swam about, laughing and dunking each other.

"I'll race you to the rock!" Acoya shouted.

They swam downriver toward the big rock that stood in the middle of the stream. As they rounded a bend, they stopped, gawking.

A girl stood there, a newcomer. Sunlight filtered through the trees and illumined her naked, slim body and long, wet hair clinging to her shoulders, and face so beautiful that surely she was unreal, a water spirit.

The girl saw them. Instantly, she crossed her hands over her woman part, concealing it. Flickering sunlight and shadows touched her wet skin, first here, then there, as she stood immobile, vulnerable, and so lovely that both boys gasped.

She gave a small cry, turned, splashed to shore, and disappeared into the forest.

Chomoc sighed loudly. "Ah-h-h! Who is she?"

Acoya could not reply. Never had he seen anyone like her. Never had he felt what he was feeling now. When, at last, he could speak, he said only, "She must be among those who come to Cicuye."

He made his voice casual but his heart was a thunder drum, pounding.

▲ 46 ▼

Tolonqua lay on his sleeping mat. The hour was late but he could not sleep. Beside him, Kwani's breathing was soft and regular. Antelope slept in the adjoining room now since Acoya was old enough to spend his nights in the kiva. Soft darkness enfolded them like a feather blanket.

From somewhere came the ardent voices of young men singing, giving their hearts to the night.

"Hi-yah! Ai! Hi-yah!"

Tolonqua rose quietly and stepped outside to the walkway. It was a moonless night, pulsing with stars. He climbed to a third-story roof and looked down at the plaza. It was empty but for dogs sprawled in sleep around the coals of the community fire. Beyond, the ridge sloped down to the old village and to fields where corn swelled in the husk, ripening.

"Hi-yah! Ai! Hi-yah!"

How beautiful was the night!

He lay on his back, gazing up at campfires of the Ancients burning in the great sky bowl. Which of those belonged to his kin? As Tolonqua searched among them, something hidden deep within him was burned away by those ancient fires. He sighed, sighed again, and drifted into sleep. He dreamed.

His spirit left his body and wandered on the plains. Buffalo were there, a vast herd, grazing. One buffalo turned and looked at him. It walked toward him. As it came close, the shaggy, brown coat faded to white. The White Buffalo!

Tolonqua gestured in homage. "I greet you, Spirit Being."

The White Buffalo grew bigger, and bigger still. It loomed over Tolonqua in overwhelming majesty, its pink eyes commanding his with hypnotic power.

The Spirit Being spoke. "Come. To this place. For one last hunt."

"I cannot!" Tolonqua cried. "My foot—"

"You will come. And hunt again. I demand it!"

"But—"

"Come!" the Spirit Being thundered, then dissolved into white cloud and vanished.

Tolonqua woke and lay for a long time under the spell of the dream.

I must do as the White Buffalo commands.

The sky paled and Sunfather flung his golden mantle; soon he would appear. Tolonqua hurried to his dwelling for the bowl of sacred meal. Kwani was up and the sleeping mat was rolled and put away. She bent at the fire pit, her long hair swinging loose and her necklace swinging with it. She glanced up at him, blue eyes enveloping him.

"I woke but you were gone."

"To the roof. I had a dream." He squatted beside her. He did not want to tell her, but he must. "The White Buffalo commands me to go on one more hunt."

She stared in surprise and glanced at his foot.

"I know." His mouth twisted. "I shall have to be carried. On a litter."

"I rode that way when my leg was broken. The hunters will be proud to have you."

She sat back and brushed her hair from her face with both hands in a gesture of unconscious grace that he knew well. As always, his heart responded; he wanted to hold her close. But Sunfather was ready to leave his eastern house.

Tolonqua took the bowl of sacred meal from the altar and strode outside as Sunfather's rim appeared. Kwani stood beside him and joined him in the Morning Song. Their voices blended and rose with the other voices in Cicuye, offering homage.

Below in the courtyard, Acoya stood with his clan brothers on the kiva roof, singing. His voice soared, high and pure.

> *"Now this day,*
> *My sun father,*
> *Now that you have come out standing in your sacred*
>   *place . . ."*

A flock of birds flew like a puff of smoke across Sunfather's face.

When the song ended, Tolonqua said, "I go to speak with Acoya." He handed the bowl to Kwani and strode into the morning.

Acoya saw him coming. "I greet you, Father."

"My spirit rejoices. Come, there is something you must know."

Acoya followed as Tolonqua left the city and made his limping way along the ridge. They stopped where three boulders squatted together like old women gossiping. Tolonqua sat on one and motioned for Acoya to sit beside him.

"The White Buffalo came to me in a dream."

"Ah!"

"I must go on one last hunt. The White Buffalo says sit."

Acoya's eyes sparkled with excited anticipation. "I shall go with you!"

"No. That is not what I must tell you."

Excitement dissolved to disappointment; Acoya ducked his head in silence.

Tolonqua turned away. How could he say this? He swallowed. "My foot grows weaker, as I do also. This is my last hunt. It may be that—" He stopped, and swallowed again. "It may be that I shall not return."

"But why?" Acoya cried. "Why?"

"No matter. Listen. The Morning Star revealed to me how Cicuye should be built. This you know."

Acoya nodded.

"It is not finished. If Sipapu calls before my work is done, you must finish it for me. Promise me that you will do so."

Acoya was silent for a long moment. "I will."

"You promise?"

"I promise."

Tolonqua looked at his son, Kwani's son, who returned his gaze. For a moment the man inside of the boy looked out from the boy's eyes. Strong and calm as a deep river.

Tolonqua's heart eased; the city, his city, would be finished. His promise to the Morning Star and the Above Beings would be fulfilled. By Acoya, the man.

Tolonqua put his arm around Acoya's shoulders. "Let us discuss what remains to be done."

Acoya sat on the bank of the stream in his hideaway place, and gazed up at the holy man painted on the stone.

"I have to talk to somebody, but you are the only one I can. It's about a girl."

He glanced furtively about to be sure no one overheard such a damaging confession. About a girl! Whose name, it was said, was White Cloud.

"I see her and want to talk to her—sign to her—but she avoids me. She doesn't like me. Why?"

He ducked his head miserably. "She is beautiful."

The holy man remained immobile, arms upraised. But it seemed that he looked at Acoya as though he were listening.

"I don't know what to do. I want to know her, be with her—" There was more, but Acoya could not say it. He wanted to hold her, touch her, the way one held any beautiful thing. And he wanted to kiss her and feel how soft she was.

"I don't know what to do. . . ."

Acoya was mortified to find his voice choked with tears. He waded into the stream to be closer to the holy man. He looked up and raised his arms as the shaman did.

"Help me!"

There was no word, no sound but the sweet voice of the stream. Was the holy man looking at him? Or at the water?

Acoya glanced upstream. Something floated there. It came closer—a small limb fallen from a tree. Upon it a spot of color glowed vividly against the bark. Acoya swam after it.

A feather! A bright red feather!

"Ah!"

Carefully, he lifted the feather and gazed at it. It was long as the palm of his hand, silky and bright. Never had he seen such a feather before! A prize!

He held the feather high out of the water with one hand and swam to the bank. Holding the gift reverently, he retraced his steps to where the holy man looked down from across the stream. He had asked for help and the shaman sent him this!

Acoya held it up for the shaman to see.

"I thank you, Holy One! I thank you!"

For a time Acoya sat on the bank, holding the feather this way and that, gazing at the wonder of its luster and the way each tiny feather grew from the stem to make the perfect whole. How beautiful it was!

Beautiful.

Of course! That is why the shaman sent the feather—to give to someone beautiful. He had asked for help, and here it was! What girl could resist such a magical gift?

He put on his breechcloth and moccasins and ran all the way home, the feather cupped in his hand. He could hardly wait until evening when girls came to the spring with their water jars.

It seemed that Sunfather dragged his feet across the sky;

it took an endless time for him to reach his western house. But when at last it was twilight, Acoya hid among the trees near the stream. He had his flute and the red feather. What he needed now was courage.

Girls began to come. They made their way down the steep path, chattering and laughing, jars on their heads. Immediately young braves appeared, took their jars and filled them, and handed them back, lifting jars to the head of the girls in a way that was an embrace. Then, laughing and whispering, they disappeared into the shadows.

Acoya swallowed. Is that what he was supposed to do?

Others came, filled their jars, and left. Where was White Cloud?

She came at last, stepping down the steep path, her slim body swaying as if to music. He would make some! He lifted the flute to his lips but before he could play, another flute sang out high and sweet, calling her, caressing each movement she made.

Chomoc! Only Chomoc could play like that.

White Cloud paused, listening. She smiled, and continued down the path, enveloped by the flute's sweet song. Chomoc emerged from behind the trees, still playing. He stood beside the spring, waiting for her, his fingers dancing.

For a moment Acoya stood in shock. Chomoc!

What should he do? He could not play his flute; it would be but a feeble echo of Chomoc's.

But he had his feather.

As White Cloud neared the spring, Acoya came silently to stand behind Chomoc who still played and did not see him. Then as White Cloud reached the spring, Acoya stepped forward and offered to take her water jar.

She stared in surprise, and refused.

The flute had ceased abruptly. As White Cloud leaned to the spring, Chomoc came to lean with her, not taking the jar, but helping her fill it. Then he lifted it to her head in a gallant gesture, smiling. She smiled back.

That was too much. Acoya thrust out his hand with the red feather gleaming upon his palm.

"Take it!" he blurted.

She glanced at the feather with surprise, then at him.

He signed. "Take it."

She reached out and her hand touched his as she took the feather. She smiled at them both, turned away, and climbed back up the path, balancing the jar on her head while holding it gracefully with only one hand.

The boys watched her, then turned to look at each other. "She likes my music," Chomoc said.

"She likes my feather." His hand tingled where she touched it.

"Where did you get it?"

Acoya shrugged. He was not about to tell Chomoc, or anyone, about his secret place and the holy man.

Chomoc looked down his nose. "It doesn't matter. No feather can make a girl want you the way my flute can." He laughed. "I'm glad we came to Cicuye. It's going to be fun."

Acoya stared hard at him, and for a moment it was as though he could see behind Chomoc's eyes to a hidden place. Chomoc did not care for White Cloud as he did. For Chomoc it was a game.

"We shall see," Acoya said. That red feather might do more than Chomoc dreamed.

Kwani faced the young girls waiting for a lesson to begin. They were gathered in Kwani's dwelling, known to them as the House of She Who Remembers. They had removed their moccasins and sandals before entering and sat in a semicircle, their upturned faces lifted to her.

Kwani fingered her necklace for inspiration. Some of the girls were newcomers, like that girl from Puname who sat shyly to one side; she was ten or eleven, and beautiful. She did not yet speak Towa well, so Kwani signed as she spoke.

"Because some of you are newcomers, you may not know how Earthmother created the first She Who Remembers. Who would like to tell the story?"

"Me!" Antelope sang out.

None of the others volunteered so Kwani nodded. "You may."

Antelope rose to stand by Kwani and faced the group with the confidence of one who knew the story well. She pushed back her hair with both hands—a gesture Kwani recognized with poignancy as her own—and began, while Kwani signed.

"Earthmother wanted a teacher to teach us. So she planted a grain of corn to make it grow and it grew big." Antelope raised a hand high overhead. "Like this. Then the corn ear turned into a head and the corn silk became hair, like this." She tugged at a wisp. "The leaves turned into arms." She stretched both arms wide. "And the stalk became legs that pulled up from the ground and began to walk. And *that*," Antelope said with satisfaction, "was the very first She Who Remembers. Then Earthmother said for She Who Remembers to wear a special necklace. "See the pretty colors of the stone beads! And the shell with a design." Reverently she touched the shell's turquoise inlay. "It has special powers. Like my mother," she added proudly, and sat down.

Kwani tried not to show how touched she was. "You told that well. Thank you."

The new girl from Puname raised her hand.

"Speak," Kwani signed.

"*Why* did Earthmother create She Who Remembers?"

Kwani smiled. "Because women forgot to remember what Earthmother taught them, so she needed a teacher to teach them again and help them remember." She paused, waiting for more questions. When there were none, she said, "Now, let's see how many remember what I have already taught."

The girls settled down to the question-and-answer period while the new girl watched and listened, large dark eyes intent, as Kwani told once again the story of what happened when women entered the Fourth World and men were bigger and stronger than they.

When the lesson was over, Kwani beckoned the new girl to her.

"What is your name?" she signed.

"White Cloud."

"Who are your parents?"

"They are in Sipapu. Killed by Apaches."

"Ah." Kwani put her arm around the girl who was still too shy to respond. "I understand. My first mate was killed by Apaches. Who brought you here?"

"My uncle, the bead maker. And his family."

Kwani remembered them. A quiet group led by the bead maker, a short, stocky man whose thick hands created beads of exquisite delicacy from bone and stone.

"We welcome you here."

White Cloud smiled, and Kwani wondered if Acoya and Chomoc had seen that smile or looked into those expressive eyes. Come to think of it, Acoya had mentioned the newcomers although he did not mention the girl. Lately, he was acting a bit unlike his usual self. Moody, given to dreaminess. In fact, if he were not so young she would suspect Acoya of being in love.

A thought. Could it be?

She signed, "Have you met my son?" She said, "Acoya."

Long dark lashes swept White Cloud's cheeks. She nodded.

That was it, of course. Acoya was smitten. And no wonder; this was a beautiful girl.

It was true. Acoya was growing up. Soon he would belong to someone else and would be gone. That is how it is supposed to be, Kwani told herself. But poignant sadness lurked in secret places of her heart.

At least she had Antelope. Her twin child. Daughters remained close by always.

The Crier Chief's strong voice floated over the city where smoke already drifted from cooking fires.

"Arise! Be glad! Sunfather comes! Let all rejoice! Tolonqua, our Building Chief and former Hunting Chief, is commanded by his totem, the White Buffalo, to go on a buffalo hunt. Today is the first day of the Buffalo Hunt Ceremonies. Participants will meet in the medicine lodge for final purification before the ceremonies begin. Arise! Sunfather comes!"

Acoya stirred in his blanket on the cold seating ledge of the kiva. He missed the comfortable sleeping mat in his dwelling and the soft sounds of Kwani preparing the morning porridge. But he was a member of the Turquoise Clan now, and an Eagle Hunter; his place was with men in the kiva. Most were young men with no mates, or older men who preferred to sleep in the kiva when they were not with their women.

He sat up. The men had risen and were gone; only one still slept on the ledge. Someone had stirred coals in the fire pit and added a few twigs that smoldered among the coals. Dim light shone through the hatchway; soon it would be pulatla. He would take his morning sun and swim and be back in time to join the song to Sunfather.

He had slept with his sandals and breechcloth on, so he ran out into the cold morning to swim in the icy river. Cold hardened a man's meat.

Chomoc was already there with Jaywing and other boys, shivering in water that flowed from peaks already white with snow. They made a big show of splashing and having fun and could hardly wait to get out.

Jaywing said, "My father will be in the Buffalo Dance."

"Mine, also," Chomoc said.

Acoya was silent.

Chomoc gave him an understanding glance; since the incident at the spring he had been more friendly than usual. He said, "The Building Chief is going on the hunt. His totem, the White Buffalo, told him to in a dream."

Jaywing said, "Can he walk that far? He limps—"

"He will be carried," Acoya said proudly. "In a litter. His feet will not touch the ground unless he chooses."

This made an impression. Only very special persons were carried in litters—unless they were small children or old people or those who were sick, and Tolonqua was none of these.

"I wish I could go for buffalo," a boy said wistfully.

"I, also," Jaywing said.

"I will go," Chomoc announced matter-of-factly.

Acoya said, "They won't allow it. I already asked. We are too young, they said."

"Ha!" Chomoc looked down his nose. "Anybody can follow tracks those hunters and dogs will make."

"You mean you will follow?"

"Of course. Why not?"

"Bears, for one thing."

"Pawnees!" another said.

Acoya took Chomoc's arm and pulled him aside. "You really don't plan to follow the hunters alone, do you?"

"No. You will go with me." He grinned.

"I will not. My father—" He would not embarrass Tolonqua on his last buffalo hunt. And he was not at all sure he wanted to go anywhere with Chomoc. Not after— But Chomoc acted as if nothing had happened. It was just a game.

"He won't know until we have gone too far to return alone. Then, if we promise to stay out of the way and make no trouble, we can remain with them and help in camp. There will be lots of work to do."

Acoya shook his head and the boys waded to shore. They raced up the ridge for their morning run before pulatla.

Chomoc had to run hard to keep up with Acoya. He tagged Acoya's arm and motioned for him to stop.

"What is it?" Acoya said impatiently. Chomoc noticed Acoya was not breathing hard at all in spite of how fast he had been running.

"We will be Buffalo Hunters!" Chomoc said gleefully. "Think about that."

He began to run again and Acoya trotted easily along. In spite of himself, Acoya did think about it. To become a Buffalo Hunter . . . Would it not make him a hero in the eyes of a certain person? A girl? One who looked at him, and then away, even though he gave her the red feather—a prized possession? She wore the feather in her hair, but she would not sit with him at the community fire or walk with him or linger at the spring with him or with Chomoc, either.

He thought, If I were a Buffalo Hunter . . .

▲ 47 ▼

Four days of ceremonies preceded the Buffalo Dances. The kiva throbbed with the deep pulse of the drums. Rattles hissed, eagle-bone whistles wailed, and chants continued hour after hour beseeching the gods for a safe and successful hunt. Sacred intervention was necessary because hunters would invade the jealously guarded hunting territory of the Pawnees.

Tolonqua, in his robe of the White Buffalo, called the buffalo spirits to lure the animals closer. The Great Plains were distant, and meat loads heavy, so bringing home the spoils of the hunt was difficult and dangerous; the closer the animals came, the easier and safer it would be.

For four days Tolonqua chanted. Long See and Yatosha joined him in the sacred songs. Then it was time for the dances, the final persuasion to the spirits of the buffalo to come closer and to allow themselves to be taken.

On the day the dances were to begin, the plaza was cleared and four buffalo skulls, facing the four cardinal directions, were arranged in the center surrounding a tall staff upon which was impaled a buffalo head with feathers plucked from the caged eagle and adorned with claws of Bear and Cougar, predator deities.

Villagers and visitors thronged the roofs and pressed against the walls around the plaza, waiting for dances to begin. Old Tookah, her plump face aquiver, searched avidly for tidbits of gossip with which to enthrall eager listeners in days and nights to come. She noticed there was that new family from Punamé with a girl who some thought was beautiful but who was really quite ordinary, not being Towa. A group of boys sitting nearby kept gawking at her, especially one who should know better—the son of the Building Chief and She Who Remembers. She shook her head. Children these days had no proper upbringing.

There was a great shout from the thunder drum and the crowd hushed in anticipation.

BOOM! BOOM! Boom-boom-boom!

A buffalo's head appeared at the kiva opening, and the dancers emerged, one after the other in time to the beat of the drum. Each dancer wore a buffalo's shaggy head over his own with eagle feathers rising behind the horns, and each carried a hunter's bow and arrows. Upper arms were banded with rattles to which an eagle feather was attached, and more rattles encircled the ankles. Short aprons of buffalo hide hung before and behind with a buffalo tail in back; the tail flipped up and down as the dancers circled the buffalo skulls, stamping feet in time to the drum's beat. Around and around they danced, bending down and up, down and up, rattles hissing.

BOOM! BOOM! Boom-boom-boom!

Now musicians and singers emerged from the kiva with drums of several sizes, whistles, rasps, gourd rattles, and shrill little flutes. They lined up at one side, playing, while singers called the buffalo. The sun rose higher but the dancers never stopped. On and on they danced, feet stomping the ground, shaggy buffalo heads turning this way and that, while singers chanted, drums shouted, and rattles hissed.

BOOM! BOOM! S-s-s-s-s-s.

The best singer was Tolonqua. Kwani heard his voice soaring over the others, as eloquently as if it were for the last time. He stood with the sacred white robe over his shoulders, holding a ceremonial staff adorned with hawk and eagle plumes and bright streamers. His eyes were closed as he sang with the drums and flutes and rattles, calling the unseen.

Kwani remembered how she and Tolonqua called the buffalo at the Place of the Rainbow Flint. No dances, no ceremonies took place, but the hunt was successful. Who could understand the mysteries?

Onlookers watched with absorbed intensity, their eyes shining with hidden, solemn meaning. Some began to chant with the singers and with the drums and flutes and rattles. Others stood, swaying with the beat, responding to an ancient pulsing of the blood. Kwani swayed with them, chanting words she did not know she remembered. Antelope stood with her, chanting made-up words with ecstatic abandon. Others joined and centuries peeled away, one by one.

A buffalo faltered, and collapsed. Immediately another dancer shot him with a blunt arrow. Others mimicked the motions of skinning and cutting up the carcass of the buffalo and he was hauled away.

Shadows grew long and still the buffalo danced, still moccasined feet pounded the ground and singers chanted to the accompaniment of musicians. One buffalo after another was shot and skinned and hauled away to triumphant shouts. When at last only one dancer was left, he removed the tall staff from the ring of buffalo skulls and danced four times around the plaza, holding the staff high, turning it so that the buffalo head on the top, with its adornment of feathers, stared down at all the people gathered there. Then he and the staff disappeared into the kiva. The dances were over; the hunt would begin on the next day.

Acoya and Chomoc omitted their morning swim and run so they would be on hand early in the morning when the hunters prepared to depart. There was the usual excitement and commotion as impatient dogs were fastened to their travois and some were also fitted with saddles to carry supplies for the hunt. Two Elk and the Medicine Chief chanted final prayers, the Warrior Chief strode about giving orders, and Long See, the Hunting Chief, with Yatosha second in command, inspected every travois and each loaded saddle to be certain all was as it should be. Dogs whined, eager to be on the move; women said secret prayers for safety of their men, and hunters now too old to go for buffalo, and boys too young, watched with envious longing.

Tolonqua stood to one side, inspecting the litter; it would have to carry him far. It was made well of two strong, lightweight poles with a buffalo hide fastened between, fur side up. It would be comfortable, and there was room for his bow and arrow case. His shell horn and sharp flint knife hung at his waist; a small pouch on a cord around his neck contained secret objects of medicinal power known only to him. All was ready.

But was he? He looked at Kwani who held the head of one of his dogs between her knees as she adjusted the harness. She sensed his gaze and looked up at him, smiling. Antelope stood beside the dog, talking to it, smoothing the dog's coat; Tolonqua wondered what she said to make the dog so attentive. Acoya was with Chomoc and a group of other boys waiting eagerly for the hunters to leave so they could follow (pretending to be Buffalo Hunters), until they were ordered to return home.

Tolonqua gazed over the crowd with a sudden pang of foreboding. This was his home, his family, his beloved city. Would he return? A foolish thought, but it was not the first time he had thought it.

Of course he would return! He must.

A final boom of the drum and a shout of Long See sent the hunters and dogs on their way. Two strong hunters carried Tolonqua on the litter, and a crowd of excited boys followed, Chomoc and Acoya among them.

Kwani watched them leave. To see Tolonqua going for buffalo while being carried on a litter—Tolonqua, the best Hunting Chief Cicuye ever had, her mate and passionate lover—was a thorn in her heart.

"Mother."

Antelope stood looking after the departing hunters with an odd expression.

"What is it?" Kwani asked.

"I'm afraid."

"Why?"

"I don't know. I just feel . . . funny."

Kwani put her arm around her daughter. She did not tell her that she was afraid, too.

Tolonqua swayed to and fro on the litter. He lay on his back, looking up at the sky of late morning, watching a hawk ride the wind. He thought of Acoya and Chomoc and the other boys who were ordered to return home after they had followed a way, and remembered how reluctant the boys were to leave—all but Acoya and Chomoc who seemed remarkably willing. He wondered about that, remembering how he felt when he was their age, and how desperately he wanted to remain with the hunters. For a moment he had a disturbing thought. He sat up and looked back, but no one followed.

Yatosha strode beside him scanning the hills that opened to the plains beyond, alert to every shadow, every puff of dust or distant motion. Tolonqua watched him approvingly; Yatosha was a good hunter. Since the episode of the boys in the trash pile, and since Acoya gave Chomoc the flute, he and Yatosha had become good friends.

Yatosha sensed his gaze and gave Tolonqua a glance of camaraderie. He pointed. "Look."

It was a small lake, bluer than the sky, where water birds came. Tolonqua remembered a time he was here long ago. When he could walk swiftly all day—and all night—if necessary.

The landscape changed subtly as it flattened and the horizon expanded. Grasses and shrubs were different here. The wind, swooshing over the vastness of the plains, licked moisture from the land; already the grasses were a rich golden-brown with asters and goldenrod blooming among them. As the land flattened and the horizon stretched wide, fewer hiding places were available. Occasional small gullies were about all.

Long See motioned to stop. Instantly every hunter scanned the plain, before and behind them. Tolonqua rose from the litter and went to stand beside Long See. "What is it?"

Long See shaded his eyes with his hand. "Smoke, I think. Over there." He pointed northeast.

"Signal?"

"I am not sure."

As the men watched, a faint puff of smoke, almost invisible against the distant horizon, rose from a different place.

"Signals!" Long See said.

"Aye!"

"Pawnee?"

"Could be Apache."

There was a moment of silence.

A hunter said, "They can't see us from here. And we raise no dust."

Tolonqua pointed overhead where the hawk still circled. "The hawk follows. It waits for prairie dogs or rabbits or other game we send running. Maybe they see the hawk and know it follows us."

"I don't think so," Long See said. "Too far away."

Tolonqua returned to the litter and they continued the march, every man alert. Far ahead, a herd of antelope flashed by, swift as the wind.

Yatosha said, "Maybe that is what they saw."

Long See paused for a brief conference with Yatosha and Tolonqua as to whether they should go for antelope now. The hunters stood by attentively.

Yatosha said, "We are prepared for buffalo. We can hunt antelope closer to home."

"Aye," the hunters said.

No mention was made of the fact that they could not chase antelope with a man on a litter, but Tolonqua was acutely aware of it.

No more smoke was seen. Sunfather approached his western house and descended, trailing banners of pink, purple, and gold in spectacular display. Darkness fell like a blanket thrown, and the hunters huddled around their small fire, listening to the night. The buffalo rutting season was nearly over; there was only an occasional distant bellow carried on the wind. Coyotes sang in jubilant chorus and somewhere a wolf howled at the thin moon.

The men sat in a circle, thinking secret thoughts. Pipes were lit, and smoke carried silent prayers to the gods. Tolonqua sat with legs crossed, elbows on his knees, gazing into darkness. Unease gnawed at his stomach.

Those signal fires were Pawnee.

Acoya and Chomoc huddled in a gully. They had slipped away from the other boys and followed the hunters' tracks, staying out of sight, until darkness. Now they were alone under a sky intimidating in its vastness, and surrounded by a terrible emptiness.

Acoya said, "Do you think they saw us?"

Chomoc shook his head. "I'm hungry. Are you?"

"Yes. Let's eat."

They chewed some jerky, drank from water bags they had refilled at the little lake they passed, and listened to the coyotes and the wolves and the silence.

The silence was the worst. Threatening.

"Play something," Acoya said.

The hunters were too far ahead to hear, so Chomoc took out his flute and played softly. The silence receded and there were only the footsteps of the wind. Chomoc's flute sang the Wind Song, and Acoya joined, singing fear and loneliness away.

> *"Over the windy mountains*
> *The wind comes running to me.*

> *"On its many swift legs*
> *The wind comes running to me.*

> *"Ho ya! Ho ya!*
> *The wind comes."*

Sound carries far at night. Distant listeners heard, glanced at one another, discussed a plan, and agreed.

▲ 48 ▼

For a long time Acoya and Chomoc kept the night at bay with Chomoc's flute and Acoya's singing, but as darkness grew deeper, the boys became silent, gazing up at the stars.

Chomoc said, "I guess the hunters are sleeping now."

"Not all of them. Somebody will watch. They take turns, watching."

"For what? Animals?"

"They are *hunters*; they do not fear animals! They watch for men from other tribes who don't want them there. Who kill—"

"What men?" Chomoc asked sharply.

"My father says that hunters from many tribes come for buffalo. But some of the hunting grounds belong to Apaches and Pawnees—"

Chomoc snorted. "These plains belong only to Earthmother."

"Tell that to their arrows and knives and lances."

Chomoc was silent for a moment. Then he said, "Are you scared?"

"Not really. But—"

"So am I. Let's keep watch. We can take turns."

"All right. I'll watch while you sleep. Then I'll wake you for your turn."

"Very well." Chomoc curled into a ball and closed his eyes. He opened them again. "Can you stay awake?"

"Of course."

Chomoc slept. Acoya stood and walked about, every sense alert. It was easier to stay awake standing up, but after a while he grew tired, and sat down beside Chomoc. He gazed up at the sweep of constellations and wondered if White Cloud was looking at them, too. Did she know he was gone with the hunters, that he was a Buffalo Hunter, too? He visualized his triumphant return with all the travois loaded high. He would march in front with the hunters, signaling triumphantly with a sweep of upraised blanket as they approached the city, and Tolonqua would blow his shell horn and all the musicians in the city would be on hand to welcome them and praise him for his bravery and skill. White Cloud would watch nobody but him and she would be wearing the red feather and tell everybody that Acoya, the Buffalo Hunter, gave it to her. Then she would come to him. . . .

Again Acoya saw her in the river, sun-dappled and radiant, and his heart nearly burst with remembrance.

Time passed. Chomoc slept deeply. I will wait a little longer, then wake him.

Was that a sound? Acoya listened intently.

Nothing.

He lay on his back to study the stars, to see how they moved, how they grouped themselves. But no matter how intently he watched, he could not see them move. They did it so slowly . . . slowly. . . . His eyes closed.

He was in his secret place on the river with the holy man looking down at him. The shaman lowered one upraised arm and pointed it at Acoya.

"Hear the voice of the Ancients!" he commanded, and the air vibrated with the terrible sound of his words. "Danger surrounds you. Danger—"

The arm reached down and grabbed him.

Acoya woke, pulled to his feet with a jerk, his arm griped by a huge fist. Acoya gasped, and stared.

Three men faced him in the light of early morning. They were like none he had ever seen. Terrifying to look at with their huge, muscular bodies painted in red and black and white symbols and designs, and their heads shaved to leave a stubby crest on top of the head reaching all the way to the back of the neck. More hair hung down like a tail in the back, pulled through a bone ornament. They had no eyebrows; fierce eyes glared from within circles of red paint, and red and black stripes zigzagged down each cheek to the chin. Necklaces of bone and stone and turquoise and claws lay thickly on their chests, and ears were heavy with ornaments.

The big fist shook Acoya so that his teeth rattled, and a booming voice spoke in an unknown language. Acoya looked for Chomoc but he was not there.

Acoya tried to sign, but it was difficult in that grip. "I do not speak your language. Where is my friend? What do you want?"

The men looked at one another, speaking in their strange tongue, glancing at him. They argued. The one who gripped Acoya's arm argued the loudest; he released his grip with a shove that sent Acoya sprawling. He signed, "Who are you?"

Acoya struggled to his feet. He signed, "Acoya, Towa of Cicuye."

Again there was heated discussion. Acoya caught the word "berdache." The warrior who had gripped him and who argued the loudest yanked a long knife from a sheath at his waist and grabbed Acoya again. But the other two pulled him away, shouting.

One man with an ornate headband over the shaved portion of his head signed, "For whom do you scout?" The headband had a crow's head perched on top; its beady little obsidian eyes looked alive.

"I am not a scout. My friend and I follow hunters. Where is my friend?"

"What friend? What hunters?"

"My friend Chomoc, son of Kokopelli, now son of Yatosha—"

At the word "Kokopelli" the three men glanced at one another.

The third man, who wore three hawk feathers on the back of his head, glared down at Acoya with hawk's eyes. "What hunters?"

Too late Acoya realized how he had jeopardized the hunters by revealing their presence here. His heart jerked and he did not reply.

Hawk Feathers bent and thrust his face close to Acoya's so that Acoya could smell his fetid breath and the bear grease on his hair. "What hunters?"

Acoya's legs felt weak but he looked the man in the eye and remained silent.

The big man with the big voice reached for his knife again, but Crow's Head stopped him with a command. Big Voice stood sullenly, glaring down at Acoya with hatred like sparks shooting from his eyes.

Crow's Head signed, "Come with us."

"Where is my friend?" Acoya signed again.

They shoved him ahead of them without reply.

Tolonqua stood with the other hunters, gazing into the distance where buffalo spread like a dark blanket over the plain. Exultation flooded his veins in a wild surge. He had thought he would never see such a sight again! And here he stood with other hunters under the great sky bowl, surrounded by an endless circle of horizon, with the plains wind blowing and a strong bow in his hand and courage like fire in his heart.

Long See shaded his eyes with his hand, gazing for a long time. Finally, he said, "I see the one I want."

"Where?" Tolonqua asked.

"Over there." He pointed. "She is a fine fat one."

Yatosha said, "Isn't that a bull nearby?"

They all looked hard, shading their eyes. Ordinarily, bulls and cows grazed in separate herds. The rutting season was nearly over, but an occasional bull might still be around.

"There are plenty of females to keep him occupied," Tolonqua said. "Let's make camp."

Dogs were unloaded and staked down with travois still attached, ready to haul large sections of buffalo meat into camp for butchering. These were buffalo-hunting dogs, trained not to bark in camp. They hated to be staked, and whined protest, but were silenced with sharp words and a whack.

The men sat to eat and to plan strategy. It was agreed that the best thing would be to approach the herd as wolves, since wolves were among them often enough not to cause alarm. The men would cover themselves with wolf skins brought for the purpose, and crawl on hands and knees until they were close enough to aim at the animal each had selected. Meanwhile, a man should remain in camp with the dogs. There were twenty-five dogs, all very valuable, and could not be left unattended. The man staying in camp would prepare for the butchering by building fires and assembling poles brought for racks to hang strips of meat to dry.

During the discussion of who would stay in camp, eyes turned to Tolonqua; it seemed the logical solution. But he shook his head.

"I shall be the lead wolf."

Yatosha broke a surprised silence. "If the herd stays nearby, our hunt may take several days, as you know. We shall take turns. Tomorrow, I will stay in camp; today I go with Tolonqua. Who will stay today?"

Shortfinger raised a hand with half the middle finger gone. "I will. But I hunt tomorrow."

It was agreed. Wolf skins were unpacked, pipes were smoked for prayers to be wafted to the Above Beings, and each man's secret talisman was entreated for safety and hunting success.

It was time to begin. The camp was downwind so the hunters fanned out, bent over with the wolf skins on their backs, and approached the distant herd. As they grew near they dropped to their hands and knees and crawled forward, concealing themselves and their weapons as best they could.

Because Tolonqua was lead wolf, the approach was slow. Yatosha followed immediately behind him and the other hunters kept an equal distance fanned out behind.

Tolonqua's heart beat hard. To be a wolf again, hunting again! He would signal when he was ready; his would be the first arrow. He must choose the target carefully so that when the animal fell it would not alarm the herd. A young cow grazed a short distance from the others; a safe choice.

He signaled. Sped the arrow. The cow fell and a shower of arrows entered the herd. There was a low rumble as the animals stirred and turned to retreat. The hunters stood up and aimed rapidly, running toward the herd. There was a roaring bellow as an enormous bull emerged with an arrow protruding from his throat. He stood higher than a man, with an arm's length between his horns, and his great, shaggy body was long as ten footprints. He saw Yatosha and charged, his huge head low.

Yatosha whipped out another arrow, but a frightened cow bumped him as she ran past, and he slipped and fell. The bull was nearly upon him.

With a yell, Tolonqua waved the wolf skin. Strength surged into him and his weak foot became magically strong. He ran forward, shouting with all the power of his new strength.

"Come! I await you!"

The bull raised his head. Bloodshot eyes found Tolonqua. The huge head lowered. With a gurgling bellow, blood gushing, the bull charged.

Tolonqua faced him with a hunger's savage joy. The buffalo galloped toward him, sod flying, head lowered, horns jutting.

Now he was close enough. Tolonqua threw the wolf skin over the giant head, covering the buffalo's eyes, and darted aside.

But his weak foot betrayed him.

A horn plunged deep into his chest.

* * *

The White Buffalo was there, emerging in the mist. *"You see?"* he said. *"I bring you here to become a totem, a power being as I am. Now you shall save others as you have saved Yatosha."*

"I am at peace," Tolonqua said, *and the mist enveloped him like a sacred robe.*

▲ 49 ▼

Kwani sat in the kiva with the Chiefs and Elders because this was a conference important enough to require the presence of She Who Remembers. Old Huzipat, Chief of the Eagle Clan, was speaking. He stood bracing himself on his staff, dark eyes peering from under shaggy brows streaked with gray.

"It has been said here that Chomoc and Acoya must have followed the hunters. I agree that this is possible, especially since Jaywing told me that Chomoc said he was going to do that. And wherever Chomoc went, Acoya was with him." He paused, tugging at his ear as he did when worry was upon him. "As we know, Pawnees have been reported on the plains two days journey from here. If the boys were following . . ." His voice trailed off.

Kwani clenched the hands resting in her lap. It was inconceivable that Acoya would disregard his father's command to stay. What had got into him? What if . . . She clasped her necklace, refusing to think of what could happen if he were captured by Pawnees. Sacrifice of victims to the Morning Star, and even cannibalism . . . Fear squeezed her heart.

Two Elk said, "Our hunters are well armed, and they have dogs." There was a murmur of agreement. Buffalo dogs could be as savage as buffalo with strangers. "If the boys followed the hunters, they are with them by now."

"Aye," the Sun Chief said. He was young for such responsibility, but his face was weathered from long days spent with Sunfather and nights with Moonwoman. "My calculations tell me this is the time that Pawnees gather for demonstrations of magic. They are not hunting now."

The Sun Chief's expertise was well known and respected. There were comments and sighs of relief.

But Kwani pressed her necklace close; silent voices spoke. *Danger . . . Danger.*

Her heart constricted, but she was silent. What could she
say?

That night she lay sleepless, alone on the mat. All hunters' mates spent nights alone when their men were gone,
and she had done so many times. But this was not the same.
Something was wrong; she felt it.

She appealed to the Ancient Ones.

"I fear for my mate, my son. I fear! Tell me what is
wrong. Tell me what to do."

The answer came immediately.

*"We who are She Who Remembers, of all womankind,
must endure much. Your mate has been chosen by the White
Buffalo. Your son is a Chosen One. Do what you must do."*

"What?" Kwani cried. "Tell me what I must do!" She
pressed the necklace to her more closely. "Tell me!"

"Listen." The voice faded away.

"Don't go! Please!"

Silence.

In the distance an owl called, long and low.

Antelope sat up on her mat. Kwani saw her staring into
the darkness.

"What is it?"

Antelope came and lay down beside Kwani. Her small
body trembled and she huddled close.

Kwani held her tightly. "Did you have a bad dream?"

"I saw—" Her voice choked with tears. "I saw those
men. They have Acoya."

Kwani's heart jerked. "What men?"

"I don't know. Big. No hair except on top and like a tail
in back. Ugly! They will hurt him!" She began to sob.

Kwani tried to control her own trembling. *Acoya captured
by Pawnees!* Could it be?

"Was Chomoc with him?"

Antelope could not speak with sobbing. She shook her
head.

The two boys were inseparable. If, indeed, Pawnees found
one, they would find both. She rocked Antelope in her arms,
crooning, the necklace pressed between them.

"It was just a bad dream."

"No! I saw!"

Abruptly Antelope stopped sobbing. She lay rigid, hardly
breathing. She screamed, a long, terrified cry.

Kwani clutched the writhing body, trying to soothe, to
hush.

"Father!" Antelope gasped. "The buffalo killed Father!" Again she screamed, then collapsed in wild sobbing. *This was no dream.* Kwani fought screams of her own.

Sunfather was directly overhead but the three men did not pause in their swift march eastward. Acoya had to trot to keep pace. If he slowed down, he was shoved. He no longer asked where they were going; he guessed the men were returning to the Pawnee camp. Probably they were scouts on the lookout for enemies.

What would they do with him? Make him a slave? During war raids men were killed but women and children were taken as slaves. However, this was no raid. Or was it?

Acoya's mind struggled like an animal in a trap. What would they do to him? Where was Chomoc? Had they killed him and left his body for those who clean the bones?

The men paused to urinate, so Acoya did the same. Big Voice whipped out his knife, grabbed Acoya's man part, and prepared to chop it off.

"No!" Acoya cried, terrified.

Slowly Big Voice lowered his arm and Acoya felt the knife's sharp point touching his groin, circling his man part as though preparing to butcher.

Acoya was too frozen with fear to make a sound. He stood in stoic silence, face expressionless.

Big Voice gave the knife a small jab, enough to bring a spot of blood. Still there was no sound from Acoya.

Abruptly Big Voice withdrew the knife and guffawed. He pushed Acoya ahead of him and the march continued.

The men jabbered constantly in their foreign tongue. It seemed to Acoya they argued, but then they would laugh and make hooting noises. Finally they stopped to eat, squatting on the grass. They gnawed jerky, ignoring him but for quick sideways glances.

Acoya was hungry and very thirsty. He sat down a little distance away, opened his pack, and removed a packet of corn cake he had taken from Kwani's corn cake storage basket. The men noticed the corn cake and discussed it briefly. The man with a crow's head on his headband strode over, snatched the packet from Acoya's hand, and the three men divided the corn cake among themselves, chewing with relish.

Acoya had eaten only a little and he was still very hungry. He drank from his water pouch; maybe that would make the emptiness in his stomach seem less. But it did not.

He watched the men eating his corn cake and anger surged in him. Hunger obliterated fear. He stood and walked to where the men squatted, pretending not to see him.

He signed, "You ate my corn cake. Now give me jerky."

The men stared at him in mock astonishment. Big Voice scooped up a buffalo chip nearby and tossed it at Acoya. Acoya caught it and tossed it back so that it landed on the last piece of corn cake Big Voice held in his hand on the way to his mouth.

The other two men whooped in laughter. The one with hawk feathers in his crest reached in his pack and pulled out a strip of jerky. He offered it to Acoya who accepted it eagerly. "I thank you," Acoya signed.

Big Voice cast Acoya a searing glance. Why does he hate me? Acoya asked himself. But he ate the jerky and tried not to wonder if Chomoc was eating, too. Tried not to wonder what these Pawnees would do when they reached camp. Tried not to worry about his father and the other hunters whose presence he had betrayed. The men were marching northeast, away from where the hunters were—or had been when he and Chomoc followed—but maybe when they reached camp these men would tell what Acoya had said and a war party would plan an attack.

It is all my fault. Tears stung his eyes but he pretended dust was in them. He swallowed the last of the jerky with effort.

Chomoc stood on the top of a small hill and looked behind him. He scanned the landscape to the horizon. No Pawnees! He sighed in relief and squatted to rest.

Early that morning, while it was still dark, he had left Acoya sleeping and stepped outside their camp to urinate. He thought he heard a rustle and wondered if a skunk or a badger or another creature might be nearby, so he ventured into the fading darkness, using his mind as a beacon to discern who or what might be there. He heard another sound, and crouched behind a low bush, listening.

He saw them! Three men passing in the distance! It was not yet light enough to see who they were, but one of them was the biggest man Chomoc had ever seen, a giant, as tall as seven moccasins!

As though they sensed Chomoc's gaze, the men stopped and turned to look around. Chomoc hunkered behind the bush, trying to squeeze himself into invisibility. He heard them talking in a strange language. They were coming closer! Had they seen him? He held his breath and remained totally motionless, every nerve alert.

Footsteps. Closer. Then passing by! Chomoc raised his head to peer through the bush. Pawnees, striding to where Acoya still slept!

Chomoc watched in terrified silence as the Pawnees confronted Acoya and took him away.

For a long time Chomoc remained crouched behind the bush. A thunderstorm raged in his spirit. Acoya's life was in danger. And so was Yatosha's and Tolonqua's and all the hunters'. Chomoc had read Acoya's signing when Acoya revealed hunters were there.

I must warn them!

He waited until the Pawnees and Acoya disappeared into the distance. It was pulatla now, and getting lighter; he could wait no longer. He ran back to where his pack still lay propped against a rock to protect his flute; the Pawnees had not seen it in the predawn darkness; his flute and bow and arrows were safe.

Chomoc shouldered the pack and faced east as Sunfather rose. He had no sacred meal to offer, but he sang Sunfather's Morning Song, pleading in his heart that his father and the others would forgive him for the disobedience that put them and Acoya in terrible danger. Then he ran for the hunters' camp with his heart pounding hard.

"Antelope told me. She saw a vision! My mate, my son—" Kwani's voice broke.

The Medicine Chief shook his head. "She has lived but six winters. It was a bad dream such as children often have."

"Aye," Two Elk said. He looked at the other Chiefs gathered in the kiva. They sat gazing down at their hands, embarrassed at She Who Remembers's unseemly request for this powwow because a child—a girl child!—had a bad dream.

"Very well," Kwani said, controlling her voice. "Perhaps you can tell me what has happened to Acoya and Chomoc." Her gaze lingered on each man. "I await your revelation."

"They followed the hunters," the War Chief said calmly. "It is not unusual for boys to do that. In fact, I did it myself when I was that age."

"You invaded Pawnee territory?"

"Not Pawnee. Apache."

The men glanced at one another with poorly concealed

amusement. Kwani bit her lips. "So you survived. Therefore, you assume any boy can do the same." She speared the War Chief with a look. "I tell you my daughter received a vision. My son has been captured by Pawnees. And a buffalo killed Tolonqua—"

Again her voice broke. She turned to leave and pulled herself up the ladder with shaking hands. Only when she reached the top did terrible sobs break loose.

The men sat in uneasy silence. The powers of She Who Remembers were well known. But a child, a little girl . . .

"I remind you that Antelope is twins," the Medicine Chief said. "Furthermore, could not the daughter of She Who Remembers be granted her mother's powers?"

More silence.

Finally, the War Chief said, "If it is true that Tolonqua is dead, they will bring him home immediately. Let us wait and see. If the boys are not with them we shall know then what to do."

"Aye."

"Find them!"

It was agreed.

Acoya trudged wearily on. It was late afternoon and they had not stopped since eating. The three men behind him chattered constantly and Acoya wondered if they were discussing what they would do with him. Fear solidified to a hard lump in his stomach.

Suddenly Big Voice gave a whoop, and all the men shouted, looking to their left, waving their arms.

Acoya stared. From behind a ridge in the distance, marching parallel to them, appeared a great crowd of people, men in front and women and children and dogs behind. Big Voice and Hawk Feathers each grabbed one of Acoya's hands and he was half carried, half dragged, as they ran toward the crowd. When they drew near, the men released Acoya and pushed him ahead of them as they approached the leaders of the procession.

Acoya could hardly walk in his astonishment. At the head of the column marched eight men carrying staffs—slender spruce poles like a short lodgepole, wrapped with blue and red and adorned with hawk and eagle feathers. The men had shaved heads with a crest on top, but instead of face or body paint they wore elaborate skin robes, handsomely ornamented and fringed, and much jewelry.

Behind the staff bearers were men who must be Chiefs,

Acoya thought, because of their amazing headdresses. Each wore a wide fur headband to which was attached a long hide triangle, wide as a man's hand and long as from shoulder to elbow. The wide end was fastened over the forehead, and the long, pointed end stuck straight out on the left-hand side, reaching past the shoulder. The entire headdress was covered with beaded and painted designs. One Chief's headdress bore a white handprint directly over the Chief's forehead. Another had the head of a hawk, another a circle within a circle, and so on. At the pointed tip of the triangle thrust out to the left dangled a feather or a braided tassel. On the right-hand side of the headband hung a small white fur tail tipped with black. Ermine? Acoya was not sure, but it was beautiful. Each Chief wore the most elaborate robes, a wide necklace of polished bear claws, and many ear ornaments and bracelets. Acoya gazed in awe.

Behind the Chiefs marched a small group of austere, stern-looking men less elaborately dressed whose crest of hair had a scalp lock greased to stand upright like a horn. The upper part of their heads and faces was painted red so that their eyes peered through a scarlet enclosure. This group was followed by a large company of men, women, and countless naked children, all of whom stared at him, some grinning, some scowling, all jabbering. A huge pack of wolfish dogs brought up the rear, each pulling a loaded travois piled high.

As Acoya stood staring, he was pushed to stand before the Chiefs who returned his stare with expressionless gazes. Finally, one Chief who seemed to be the oldest signed, "For whom do you scout?"

"I am not a scout."

'Why are you on our hunting grounds?"

Acoya did not reply. Instead, he stood straight as he could and returned the Chief's expressionless gaze with one of his own.

The Chiefs glanced at one another and turned to confer with the stern-looking men who, Acoya was certain, were priests. They spoke briefly. The old Chief gestured, and Crow's Head grabbed Acoya's arm and marched him all the way back to where the dogs were. One of the dogs limped. The travois was removed and Crow's Head thrust the harness at Acoya.

"You will pull this."

Acoya hesitated. Crow's Head jerked a knife from a sheath

at his waist and pointed it at Acoya's chest. He signed, "Pull!"

Reluctantly Acoya grasped the two poles joined by a harness that fit over the dog's chest. The load was heavy, but he pulled it—to loud snickers and remarks from those nearby.

The dog was not pleased. This stranger, this foreigner, presumed to pull the load belonging to him! He growled, and nipped at Acoya's legs. A boy about Acoya's age pulled the dog away with sharp commands.

Acoya could not sign and pull at the same time so he said "Thank you," in Towa.

The boy turned away, but not before tossing Acoya an understanding glance.

The noisy march continued. As Acoya dragged the travois over the uneven ground mile after mile, he wondered how dogs did it. He wondered where he was headed, and what would happen to him when he got there. He thought of his father and the other hunters whose presence he had stupidly betrayed. At the moment the march headed north of where the hunters were. Maybe nothing would be done about a small group of Towas on this enormous, undulating plain where there were more buffalo than any number of tribes could use in a lifetime. The thought comforted him.

Acoya watched the children with curiosity. Most of the girls carried puppies and talked to them as if they were babies. Boys shouted and ran about, wrestling, shooting arrows, and playing games. Their elders walked easily along, packs on their backs, chatting, laughing, singing, arguing. Hunters walked together a small distance aside; they carried nothing but bows and arrows. Acoya was impressed with how many there were, at least ten times ten. No wonder the travois were loaded high!

Now and then the crowd paused as the Chiefs conferred with the priests. Acoya wondered what they talked about. Now they paused again, and Acoya took the opportunity to adjust the travois so that he stood between the poles with the harness against his stomach; it would be easier to pull that way. The boy who had called off the dog walked over and nodded approvingly. He signed, "What is your name?"

"Acoya."

"Why were you on our hunting grounds?"

Acoya hesitated. "I search for my friend," he signed. "Who?"

"Chomoc. Have you seen him?"

"No."

"What is your name?"

"Elk Horn."

"Where are we headed?"

"To our home village."

"What will they do with me there?"

Elk Horn shrugged. "You are a slave. You will work. Unless—" He turned away.

"Unless what?"

The march began again and Elk Horn ran to join a game of shooting-arrows-at-the-sky, wagering who could shoot the most arrows before the first one fell to the ground. Arrows, knives, and other objects changed hands as wagers were won and lost.

Acoya wished he could join the game. He wished he knew where Chomoc was. They should have stayed home.

He wished he were with his father.

Acoya plodded on, ignored by everyone, even the dogs. The harness across his stomach was uncomfortable, but it was the humiliation that was hardest to bear. Fear, worry, and weariness gave way to anger. He was son of Tolonqua, Building Chief of Cicuye. He was son of She Who Remembers, an Honored One. How dare they do this to him!

He dropped the travois and stepped out of it, leaving it on the ground. He would go up there and tell those Chiefs and priests who he was!

Suddenly, from behind a small hill, six buffalo appeared. They stood staring, and turned and galloped wildly away. Acoya was astonished to see Big Voice run after them alone, knife in hand. The hunters did not follow; they stood cheering him on with whoops and yells. Acoya gaped; never had he seen a man run as Big Voice did—as fast as the buffalo! On and on they ran, with Big Voice growing closer, until at last he ran side by side with a buffalo. With a mighty thrust, Big Voice plunged the knife into the shaggy body. The buffalo staggered and fell, while the others disappeared into the distance.

The people gave a great shout, cheering and laughing. Big Voice swaggered back, not bothering to so much as skin the animal he had killed. Instead, he gestured at the hunters and two of them trotted to where the buffalo lay.

Acoya listened to the cheering. Big Voice was their hero! He remembered that knife poked at his groin. He thought of that knife plunged into the buffalo. Maybe now was not a good time for a confrontation, no matter who he was. He picked up the travois.

The buffalo was skinned expertly in no time, and the men returned with the hide, leaving the carcass where it fell. The travois had been loaded with as much as the dogs could carry, and all the men and bigger boys carried heavy packs. Women seemed to carry the heaviest packs of all.

Many of the women were beautiful, with long, flowing hair framing round faces with expressive eyes and pretty lips. Their robes, reaching to the ankles, were elaborately ornamented with fringes of elk's teeth, and were tied on the left shoulder, leaving the right shoulder and breast bare. Some wore tattoos like a necklace, and with designs on the right arm from shoulder to wrist. Many carried babies in cradle boards as well as heavy packs.

The shaggy buffalo hide was brought to Big Voice who accepted it with more cheers from the crowd. He stood holding it a moment, obviously trying to decide how it should be transported. Then he handed it to one of the priests who passed it to a young man who trotted all the way back to where Acoya was, dumped the hide on Acoya's travois, and trotted back.

The hide weighed as much as the rest of the load, which made it twice as heavy. Acoya strained to pull it. The procession proceeded with much laughter and talk while Acoya struggled to keep up.

He thought of all that fine meat left behind. Wolves would eat well that night and vultures would feast in the morning.

The march continued for two more miserable days. Acoya ached all over and was hungry most of the time. He was ignored by everyone except Elk Horn who brought him jerky and water at eating times but signed seldom. He said it was forbidden to be friendly with a slave.

Never had Acoya been so weary, so discouraged. Never would he be rescued; nobody knew what had happened to him. Chomoc had disappeared; maybe he was in Sipapu.

I must find a way to escape.

▲ 50 ▼

It was the third day, not yet dusk. Before the Pawnees made camp, the Chiefs conferred as usual with the priests to determine whether or not the site was free of bad influences. After long consultation with one another and with the spirits, the priests decided camp could be made.

Everyone must fear the priests, Acoya thought, since little could be done without consulting them first.

As soon as the decision was reached to camp, piles of buffalo chips were assembled in several places and a hunter with a buffalo horn slung by a buckskin strap over his shoulder was summoned. Acoya was astonished to see him remove a stopper from the wide end of the horn, take out a live coal, and start a fire on one of the piles of buffalo chips. Then all the other fires were lighted from that one.

He signed to Elk Horn, "How does he keep a coal burning all day in that buffalo horn?"

Elk Horn looked surprised. "You mean Towas don't do that?"

"If so I haven't seen it."

"It's easy. You line it with moist, rotten wood, put in a live coal, then fill the horn with punk—dry, crumbly, rotten wood. That feeds the coal. Then you put the stopper on."

"Doesn't the punk burn up?"

"Of course. That's why the Fire Carrier opens it up four times a day and adds more punk."

Acoya thought of all the things he could relate around the evening fire at home. How impressed and amazed White Cloud would be!

Home. White Cloud. Would he ever see them again?

His stomach clamored for food; he was tired and relieved to be free of his burden. Women unpacked the dogs and ordered boys to take them to water. Pawnees knew every water hole, every small stream, and if water was nearby, Acoya would be sent with the other boys to take the dogs to water and get them back to camp. Today, however, Acoya was told to stay and help the women set up their tipis.

This was women's work! More humiliation. Anger seethed in him.

I will escape.

Meanwhile, he would obey orders, do what he was told, and hide his resentment lest they suspect his plans.

The women arranged all baggage, rawhide cases, back-packs, and other belongings in a semicircle, the open side facing east. Acoya was surprised to see that this wall of baggage reached as high as his waist. On the open side, four straight poles were driven into the ground in a row. Each of these had willow rods tied to the top of the pole. Then curved willow poles were inserted into the ground behind the wall of baggage, bent forward, and bound with leather thongs to the willow rods at top of the poles in front of the tipi. A cover of dressed buffalo skins sewed together was fitted over the frame of poles, forming a dome-shaped tipi with the flat side facing east. A door-way in the center of the flat side had a flap that could be raised or pulled aside.

All this was done rapidly and with the ease of much ex-perience. Never had Acoya seen such an odd-looking tipi or one so quickly assembled.

While the women worked, the men rested, talked, smoked, and gambled. Some removed hairs from the face of body with clam shells, a slow and painful process.

One of the Chiefs beckoned to Elk Horn and spoke, giv-ing orders. Elk Horn nodded and turned to Acoya. He signed, "You will come with me."

Elk Horn led Acoya to a tipi; he found himself with Elk Horn's mother and two small sisters.

Elk Horn signed, "My mother likes you. Maybe she will buy you."

Acoya did not reply. Nobody could buy the son of She Who Remembers and Cicuye's Building Chief!

Elk Horn's mother may have been pretty as a girl but she was bent and worn now, with wrinkles encircling her eyes and deep creases on her forehead. She gave Acoya a swift glance and ordered him to find firewood. Elk Horn beck-oned, and Acoya followed.

Now it was twilight. The air smelled fresh and cool and Acoya was relieved to be away from the noise and tensions of camp. He walked behind Elk Horn who seemed to know exactly where he was headed.

Elk Horn strode with the rhythmic gait of a boy growing up on the plains, often walking all day. He wore buffalo-hide moccasins reaching over the ankle, handsomely adorned with dyed porcupine quills, and short apronlike elk-skin flaps before and behind, fastened by a thong around his waist. His black, shoulder-length hair was cut straight across his forehead and fell loosely around his face. A small beaded pouch hung from a cord around his neck. Two pairs of ornaments hung from each ear, and a bracelet of dog teeth and bone beads rattled impressively on his wrist.

Acoya's own moccasins and breechcloth were dirty and worn, and he felt dirty all over. He yearned for the river at home, and the quiet, beautiful pool in his hideaway place. He thought of the holy man. "Danger!" the shaman had warned in the dream.

He would get away. But how? And alone, with no weapons, no food? It was a long, long way home in unfamiliar territory.

Elk Horn stopped and pointed. A dead tree lay in a small ravine; all the wood they could carry was available. Elk Horn slid down into the ravine, and Acoya followed. Now that they were out of sight, Acoya and Elk Horn could converse unobserved.

Acoya signed, "Nobody can see us now. There is something I want to tell you."

Elk Horn nodded, interested.

"I am son of She Who Remembers and Tolonqua, Building Chief of Cicuye. They will not be pleased to learn I have been captured by Pawnees. They will send a war party to get me. Would it not be best for me to be sent home?"

Elk Horn was not impressed. He signed, "They do not know where you are. They think you are dead."

"I told you my mother is She Who Remembers. She has powers. She will know where I am."

Elk Horn looked unconvinced, and Acoya added, "My father has many necklaces, many valuable things. He is a rich man. He will pay you for helping me."

Elk Horn's black eyes sparked. "I will talk to my father. He is a Chief."

"Good."

The boys gathered wood until their arms were full, and returned to camp. Elk Horn went immediately to his mother and talked excitedly. She glanced at Acoya with scorn.

She does not believe me, Acoya thought.

Finally, the woman nodded and Elk Horn gestured for

Acoya to follow him. As they made their way among the tipis, Acoya saw that a shield was placed on a tripod of poles outside each tipi to identify the owner. When they came to one with a Morning Star cross painted on the shield, Elk Horn signed, "This is the Chief Priest's tipi. Wait outside."

The door flap was open so Acoya could see the interior. Against the wall opposite the entrance—the place of honor—sat a man of indeterminate age. His lean face was painted red half-way down, and white with black designs to his chin. His head was not shaved; hair hung loose to his shoulders. He wore a thick fur headband with upright eagle feathers and mysterious objects of medicinal power dangling like fringe. Expressionless black eyes gazed at the Chiefs sitting before him. One spoke while the others listened with eyes downcast respectfully. Behind them the priests sat with arms folded, their eyes in their red enclosures missing nothing.

Elk Horn stood in the doorway until the Chief Priest acknowledged his presence and gestured for him to enter. Elk Horn reached his right foot over the doorsill and then withdrew it three times. On the fourth time he entered, approached the Chief Priest, and bowed. One of the Chiefs came to stand beside Elk Horn as they talked.

That must be Elk Horn's father, Acoya thought. He could not understand what was being said, but the Chief Priest's sharp eyes darted glances at him, and several of the priests turned to look at Acoya as though they had not seen him before.

The discussion grew heated. Elk Horn's father's voice rose, and so did the voices of the priests, arguing back and forth. Meanwhile, the Chief Priest sat in expressionless silence, broken only occasionally by a comment or a question.

Finally, he raised his hand. There was immediate silence. He spoke briefly and with authority. He gestured, and Elk Horn returned to Acoya. He signed, "The Chief Priest wishes to speak with you. Be sure to enter properly and be respectful."

Elk Horn repeated the entering procedure, and Acoya followed, stepping forward and back three times, then entering. As he approached the Chief Priest he bowed, then stood erect and held his head high.

The Chief Priest signed, "It is said that you are son of She Who Remembers and of Tolonqua, Building Chief of Cicuye. What proof?"

"My word is proof enough."

The Chief Priest scowled, and there was a growl of anger from the Chiefs and the other priests.

"Why were you on our hunting grounds?"

"I was searching for my friend, Chomoc, son of Kokopelli."

There were murmurs.

The Chief Priest signed, "Why were you and Chomoc on our hunting grounds?"

"We wish to be hunters. We did not realize we were where we should not be. For that, we apologize."

"The first thing hunters must know is that Pawnees allow no trespassing." He paused, inspecting Acoya with a shrewd and penetrating gaze. "You have no proof of who you are. Therefore, you cannot expect us to believe what you say. A slave you shall remain." He gestured dismissal.

Acoya remained standing, head high. From somewhere deep within himself came a surge of calm assurance.

He signed, "I am a Chosen One of the White Buffalo."

Outraged comments were hushed by the raised hand.

"Proof?" the Chief Priest signed with a sardonic smile.

"Aye."

Acoya sat down and removed the moccasin from his right foot. He lifted his foot for the Chief to see the head of the White Buffalo on the sole. "My totem," he signed. "Given to me by the White Buffalo who came to my mother and told her he would be my protector. Then he went to my father and offered to be taken. That is why my father has the robe of the White Buffalo."

There was a commotion as the Chiefs and priests crowded around Acoya to see the sacred mark. Big Voice spit on it and rubbed it hard with his thumb to learn if it was painted on. He seemed chagrined that it was not.

Finally, Acoya replaced his moccasin and rose. He faced the Chief Priests. "I respectfully request permission to return home."

For a time the Chief sat in silence, face expressionless. Then he gestured, and Elk Horn led Acoya back outside and away.

"The Chief Priest wants a powwow with Standing Bear, the Tribal Chief, at our home village. We shall be there tomorrow."

"Will they keep me as a slave?"

Elk Horn shrugged. "Probably."

Nothing more was said, but Acoya noticed that Big Voice

and others avoided him, turning their faces away when they saw him.

That night Acoya was invited to sleep in Elk Horn's tipi.

He lay on a buffalo robe near the door—the least desirable place, but welcome after having to sleep on the ground near the dogs. He thought about tomorrow, and listened to the night, wondering if a Pawnee camp was ever quiet. Young braves sat together on the outskirts of camp, singing war songs. Children cried. Dogs gathered in packs and howled at the moon.

Two Elk's sisters were asleep. Their mother and father heaved on their sleeping place, making noises. Elk Horn lay quietly nearby; Acoya did not know if he was asleep. Sometimes, Acoya wondered if Elk Horn was chosen to watch him. To prevent an escape?

Acoya stared up at the willow poles arched overhead, thinking of the strong beams of his ceiling at home. Thinking of his mother and her deep eyes looking at him. She must assume he was with Tolonqua and the hunters, so no search would be made for him and Chomoc until the hunters returned. That could be several days, even weeks from now.

Did White Cloud miss him?

What would happen tomorrow?

Acoya sat up and looked at Elk Horn. In the darkness Acoya could not see if his eyes were open, but Acoya sensed that Elk Horn was awake, watching.

Maybe if I go to relieve myself . . .

Acoya rose and slipped out. It was a full moon, and bright. He went a little way to a vacant spot and looked around camp as he urinated. It seemed he could walk away unnoticed until he saw bowmen squatting in open doorways, keeping lookout.

Acoya returned to the tipi and saw that Elk Horn was gone. In a few moments the boy returned and lay down again on his buffalo robe.

Elk Horn is watching me.

Acoya lay quietly, eyes closed, willing himself to sleep and to dream again of his hideaway place and the shaman. He could not sleep, but he saw the painted figure clearly in his mind.

"Tell me what to do!" he prayed silently.

No answer.

He remembered his vision. Again he saw the White Buffalo and Bear, his strong protectors, and he was ashamed.

I have dishonored you in my cowardice. From now on, I shall not be afraid.

As Acoya drifted into sleep and his spirit prepared to leave his body and take him elsewhere in dreams, he remembered the eagle hunt and the time he clung to the cliff. What were the words he seemed to hear then?

Many grandfathers are in your blood. Listen to them!

It was very early in the morning when the Pawnees broke camp. Dogs were harnessed into travois and people shouldered their packs. Acoya was surprised to see that the travois he had been pulling was now harnessed to a dog. However, he was still ignored by all but Elk Horn who marched beside him.

There was no morning meal; they fasted until the noon halt. The land was changing. It was more hilly, with sudden ravines, some deep. Here and there were cairns, small piles of stones to which the priests added others, pausing to recite incantations before the march continued. A cloudless sky arched from horizon to horizon and the wind blew in sporadic gusts.

Sunfather had not yet reached his evening house when the Pawnees' permanent village appeared on a grassy plain. The marchers gave a whoop when they saw it. The women had a special cry, a piercingly loud yodel that could carry for a great distance. They called now, in a clamorous chorus, and women in the village called back. The eight men with staffs leading the group quickened their pace, and the dogs, knowing they were nearly home, whined with impatience and pulled harder in their harnesses.

The dwellings of the village were like none Acoya had ever seen. They were large, domed, earth-covered lodges with a long, tunnellike entrance extending outward, and so numerous they crowded the plain like a herd of buffalo.

As they approached, a small group of men and women came to meet them. Acoya was surprised that there were no more, but since most of the population of the village followed the hunters on their months-long, twice-a-year hunting trips, only those unable to travel would be left behind with some to care for them.

As Acoya stood staring, Elk Horn signed, ''Your home now.''

Acoya did not reply; it was best to remain silent.

There was pandemonium as the marchers entered the village, greeted by the handful of people there and the ecstatic dogs. People rejoicing to be home shouted and laughed as they unloaded the travois, gloating over the piles of dried buffalo meat and hides, enough to last them many moons. Caches, holes lined with stones and adobe, and as wide and deep as a tall man, were stuffed full and covered well to keep out moisture, insects, and predators. The dried meat, plus corn and beans and squash from surrounding fields, would keep starvation at bay another year. Women exclaimed over the hides, planning new winter garments and moccasins and tipi covers and many fine things.

Darkness, and a giant feast followed, with many stories told and retold of events of the hunt. Big Voice held up the hide of the buffalo he had run down and killed, to loud acclaim. Acoya sat with Elk Horn and his family as all of them shared one buffalo-horn spoon for the savory stew and one gourd dipper for the water jar. Acoya noticed a tall, thin man so bent with age he leaned heavily on his staff.

"Who is that?" he asked Elk Horn.

"The Tribal Chief, Standing Bear. He is the one who decides what will be done with you."

"When?"

"At the powwow."

"Tomorrow?"

Elk Horn shrugged. "Maybe." He turned away.

Elk Horn did not like to be questioned, Acoya knew. So he asked no more, but kept his eyes open and his senses alert.

Crow's Head was speaking now. Firelight illuminated the shaved, painted head with the stubby crest and the head-band, and the crow's head and beady black eyes, and the lurid designs on cheeks and chin and body, and the many necklaces and ear ornaments and bracelets that slid up and down his forearms as he gestured. Now and then, people turned to glance at Acoya, especially those who had not been on the hunt.

Acoya thought, He must be talking about me.

Crow's Head gestured, and Elk Horn said, "He wants you to go and stand by him."

"I don't want to."

Elk Horn gave him a sharp jab. He signed, "Trouble!"

Reluctantly, Acoya rose and made his way through the crowd to Crow's Head who grasped him by the hair, announcing something with expansive gestures.

There were loud laughs. Somebody handed up a clam

shell with sharpened edges, and Big Voice shoved his massive frame through the crowd to stand beside Acoya.

Acoya looked across the crowd at Elk Horn and signed, "Tell me what is happening!"

Elk Horn smirked. Big Voice grabbed Acoya's arms and pinned them behind him.

"Stop!" Acoya shouted.

Crow's Head pulled Acoya's hair up tightly, then ran the sharp edge of the clam shell over his head, shaving a swath from front to back.

Acoya struggled. A man's hair was a prideful thing, especially to a Towa; to be shaved was bitter humiliation. He fought, kicking and twisting, but he was no match for Big Voice who held him easily, grinning, while Crow's Head shaved another swath. The people laughed, relishing the entertainment.

Acoya fought harder. Suddenly he stopped. From deep within him a fierce anger, a mysterious power, erupted. He jerked his head loose, lifted his chin high, and from his widestretched mouth a sound emerged, not a cry, not a shout, not a song or chant, but an eerie combination of them all. A sound to stir the blood and awaken the Ancients.

Crow's Head gaped, and the clam shell fell from his hand. Big Voice gripped Acoya's arms even more tightly, and shook him as a dog shakes a rat.

Again came the wild, weird sound, calling the spirits.

A man stood up and waved his arms, shouting something Acoya could not understand.

There was a murmur, a babble of talk, loud voices.

Standing Bear, the Tribal Chief, raised a frail arm for immediate silence. He spoke, and Acoya was abruptly released. Slowly, the aged chief hobbled forward, leaning heavily on his staff as people parted respectfully, making way. He came and stood before Acoya, looking down at him with piercing black eyes nearly hidden in a mass of weathered wrinkles. He signed, "It is said the sound you made has been heard before. It is said to be the voice of She Who Remembers. Are you her son?"

Acoya nodded, too surprised to sign. Never had he made such a sound before, nor even heard it. He was more astonished than anyone. It was as if the sound did not come from him, but from an unknown source.

Standing Bear turned to face the crowd. Again he spoke in a dry, quavering voice. Two priests stepped forward. One signed to Acoya, "You will come with us."

Acoya followed them through the crowd. He passed Elk Horn who glanced at him, then ducked his head. The priests led Acoya to a big lodge, the biggest to be seen. At the doorway, each extended the right foot over the sill three times, then bent to enter the extended tunnel opening, beckoning Acoya to follow. He did so, repeating the entering procedure. The hard earth floor was lower than the exterior so that he had to step down.

It was dark inside, smoky and gloomy. The only light came through a smoke hole in the center of the roof. Through this hole a bar of light entered aslant on the fire pit, a round depression in the center of the floor where coals smoldered.

The priest led him to the rear of the lodge where mats lay before an altar beside which was a willow backrest covered with a buffalo skin. They motioned for Acoya to sit on a mat, and a priest sat cross-legged on each side of him.

They waited in silence, watching the door. Acoya touched the place where his hair had been shaved; it was as wide as two fingers, reaching from his forehead, over his crown, and all the way back to his neck. He burned in humiliation. What would White Cloud think when she saw him again?

If he could escape and go home, that is.

As his eyes became adjusted to the dim light, Acoya saw how large the lodge was—as wide as forty moccasins! Sleeping places along the wall on each side were made with four short poles driven into the floor to form a frame across which were stretched small springy wooden rods laced together with elm bark. A mat of woven rushes lay over this to complete the bed, and was covered with a buffalo robe. The poles supporting the bed extended an arm's length upward to form an arch from which hung a curtain of skins or woven rushes to provide a snug alcove for privacy. Acoya counted the beds. Five on each side! This lodge belonged to a large family.

He signed to one of the priests, "Who lives here?"

The priest did not answer. Rather, he fixed his gaze on the clay altar upon which was a buffalo skull and objects of sacred medicine that Acoya did not recognize. The altar, against the back wall, faced east toward the entrance. Above it hung a medicine bundle heavy with fringe and adorned with shells and bright feathers. Acoya wondered what it contained. He wondered what the priest thought as he gazed at the altar. He wondered why he was brought here.

He felt a prick of fear.

"I will not be afraid."

He did not realize he had spoken aloud until the priests turned to look at him, their eyes expressionless. They glanced at one another and turned away.

Acoya signed, "Who are we waiting for?"

No reply.

Swallowing unease, Acoya studied the room. Shelves held baskets of different sizes and designs. For corn and beans and squash and other things to cook, he decided. Braided stalks of corn ears hung over a shelf, and bunches of dried herbs and grasses. Beside the beds were square storage containers of buffalo hide, some handsomely painted, and fringed and beaded cases for bows and arrows. Pegs held various garments, some of deerskin, very soft and fine. Cooking bowls and implements sat on the floor near the fire pit, but Acoya saw no metate and mano.

How do they grind their corn? he wondered. His glance wandered to a strange object, a pole as long as his leg resting upright on a wooden pestle. The pole was topped by a weight. This must be how they grind their corn, Acoya thought. They sit and pound the pole up and down on the corn. Several bowls and baskets sat beside the mortar. Acoya wondered who worked there.

He thought of White Cloud kneeling at a metate, pushing the mano stone, leaning forward and back, her braids swinging. . . .

Would she do that for him someday?

There was a sound of footsteps. The priests rose.

▲ 51 ▼

When the two priests led Acoya away, Standing Bear, the aged Tribal Chief, stood watching. His bones ached, and cicadas buzzed in his ears, but he could see well enough to beckon the Chief Priest to come forward.

"We must consider this matter," Standing Bear said when the Chief Priest stood before him. "If it is true that the Towa boy is son of She Who Remembers, we must discuss the possibilities, both good and bad. Therefore, we shall adjourn to the medicine lodge with your priests and all the Chiefs."

Standing Bear hobbled slowly through the crowd, followed by several priests who made way for him, beating a small drum while the Chief Priest announced that all Chiefs and priests would assemble immediately in the medicine lodge for powwow.

The medicine lodge was similar to the other lodges except for the altar that was as long as a man to accommodate the bowls and baskets of sacred substances, the pipes, the buffalo skull, and fetishes of Buffalo, Elk, Deer, and Bear. Shelves held masks, drums, rattles, whistles, rasps, flasks of healing substances, jars of special sand for paintings, pigments, surgical instruments; and baskets, jars, and pouches of roots, bark, dried berries, and medicinal leaves. Bunches of herbs hung from pegs on the walls.

All these things provided a scent that no other lodge possessed, and Standing Bear breathed it appreciatively as he entered and made his way slowly to the place of honor against the back wall facing the entrance. He did not sit until all the Chiefs and priests were present. Then, with the help of two priests, he lowered himself painfully to the willow backrest covered with a soft buffalo robe. He regarded the men seated before him, thinking what a fine group they were—the Chiefs with their handsome headdresses and the priests with their shaved heads painted red and sacred designs in face and body paint.

He waited awhile before speaking to allow the men to ponder the seriousness of the occasion. Finally, he cleared his throat and began.

"It is said that our captive Towa boy is son of Tolonqua, former Hunting Chief of Cicuye and who is now their Building Chief. It is also said that his mother is She Who Remembers." He paused. "Tolonqua is known to hunters of the plains; he has friends. She Who Remembers is admired and feared because of her powers. These are the parents of the boy we hold as slave."

Again, he paused and gazed solemnly at each man. "I have summoned you here to determine what we should do with this boy. I await your opinions."

"Keep him as slave, of course," a Chief said.

Another said, "I remind you of the powers of She Who Remembers, she of the blue eyes, who called Masau'u and Motsni for the Eagle Clan, who called the deer for Puname, who called the buffalo at the Place of the Rainbow Flint—"

A Chief interrupted, "So it is said at evening fires when stories are told for entertainment. How do we know the truth of these words?"

"I have seen, others have also seen, the mark of the White Buffalo on the sole of the Towa's foot," the Head Priest said. "His father, Tolonqua, possesses the robe of the White Buffalo. This boy is a Chosen One." He fingered the bear claws of his necklace nervously. "Is it not possible that he can be more valuable to us than as a slave?"

There was silence as the men thought this over. Standing Bear smiled to himself; his Head Priest was shrewd.

"Aye!" one said. "We shall hold him for ransom!"

"Rich ransom!"

"No!" said another. "The powers of She Who Remembers must be considered. For many years it was rumored that she is a witch. Never proven. But what if she is? What will happen to us if she learns we have her son? And demand ransom?"

"One does not have to be a witch to cast spells," a priest pointed out.

"Aye."

Again there was silence. A coal in the fire pit flared. Standing Bear stroked his chin thoughtfully. "Maybe it would be best if the boy's presence among us remains secret."

"I respectfully disagree," the Head Priest said. "Such a

thing cannot be kept secret for long. I remind you that our Great Sleight-of-Hand event will take place soon, with many visitors from distant places. We could take the Towa away and hide him somewhere, but how can we be certain that one of our own people will not tell someone who will tell someone else about our captive? It will become everywhere known.''

"Aye!" a priest said. "The solution is obvious. We give him to the Morning Star."

Standing Bear saw how the men glanced at one another. A sacrifice to their most important deity, the Morning Star, was due, and would be done as it had been for more generations than any man knew. It would satisfy the gods, benefit the tribe, and dispose of a difficult problem simultaneously. An ideal solution.

"Bring the boy to me so he may be consecrated," the Head Priest intoned.

Two men departed.

Acoya stood tensely as footsteps approached. Two priests entered. In the dim light their painted faces were those of evil spirits; eyes in their blood-red hiding places gleamed. They strode to stand before Acoya and the priest on either side, and spoke rapidly in their strange language.

One signed to Acoya, "You are a Chosen One."

Acoya nodded, surprised.

"You are chosen by the Morning Star."

What did that mean? Acoya wondered. He signed, "I am chosen by the White Buffalo."

"Come."

They led him outside. It was dark now, and a community fire burned high and smoke drifted fragrantly from lodges. There was the usual bedlam of noise, and cooking smells, and the sound of flutes and drums, shouting and chanting, shrill women's voices, crying babies, and barking dogs. The priests led Acoya to the fire where Standing Bear sat on a ceremonial mat, a buffalo skin painted with Morning Star designs and illustrations of tribal history. When Standing Bear saw Acoya approaching, he signaled, and two priests helped him rise. When Acoya stood before him, Standing Bear peered down at the boy with an inscrutable gaze, and signed, "I greet you, Chosen One."

"My heart rejoices," Acoya signed automatically, remembering his manners.

Standing Bear nodded. This boy was a suitable sacrifice. Intelligent, perfectly formed, pleasant to look upon, and civilized—for a Towa. He would be treated as royalty—lavishly dressed, fed, and entertained—until the Seven Sisters stars reached their appointed place in the heavens. Then this gift would be presented to the Morning Star deity.

The gods would be pleased, and the boy's death would be quick and merciful. Only after a heavy blow to the head and a sacred arrow in the heart would each priest be allowed to pierce the sacrificial body with arrows dedicated to the Morning Star.

Chomoc trudged in silence beside his father. Yatosha's head was bowed in grief; he had spoken little since Chomoc encountered him and the hunters returning home with Tolonqua wrapped in the skin of the buffalo that killed him. His body lay on the litter, carried by Yatosha and Long See marching in time to the hunters' moaning chant.

When they reached the place where the Pawnees had grabbed Acoya and taken him away, Chomoc stopped and removed the flute from his pack. At the spot where they camped he sat down and began to play. It was the song he and Acoya used to sign when they played roadrunner.

Poi, poi, around the house . . .

It was a happy song with happy memories, but playing it did not make Chomoc happy. Acoya was kidnapped by Pawnees. What terrible things were they doing to him?

Chomoc had to stop playing because tears choked his throat.

It is all my fault!

If he had not insisted on following the hunters, he and Acoya would be safe at home. Now Acoya's father was in Sipapu. What would happen to Kwani? And Antelope? With no men to care for them?

I will do it. I will take Antelope as mate and live in their house and be their protector.

When I am old enough.

But what about now? He had killed Antelope's love for him. She had pushed him away. But maybe when she was older and his flute sang to her, and if he gave her many presents . . . The thought eased his heart. He lifted the flute to his lips and let it assuage his sorrow and guilt and loneliness.

* * *

Kwani stood on the roof of a third story, gazing eastward. It was too soon to expect hunters to return, but foreboding enfolded her like a blanket. Antelope cried too much; she kept insisting that Pawnees had Acoya and that Tolonqua was dead. It could not be, of course.

But . . .

But this daughter of hers—this twin, this blossom and fruit of her body—had powers. That Kwani knew. Could it be that Antelope's revelation was a sign from the Ancient Ones that she was Of The Gods, and should be trained by Kwani as her successor?

If so, it meant that Antelope *was* given a vision, and what she saw in her vision was real.

The thought was too terrible to bear.

She climbed back down to the walkway and went to Anitzal's dwelling; Anitzal's comforting presence would ease her fears. But it was nearly harvesttime and Anitzal and Lumu's girls, Weomah and Imka, were gone. To the fields, probably. Kwani returned to her own dwelling, yearning for someone to talk to. Many kind people lived here, people who honored and admired her, but an invisible curtain separated them. Their spirits and hers did not touch.

She yearned for Tolonqua, his strength and reassuring presence, his lovemaking.

Antelope's light footsteps ran down the walkway and she burst in the door.

"Mother! They come!"

"The hunters?"

"Yes! Yes! Some say they heard father's horn! But—"

"Ah!" Joy enveloped Kwani in a rosy glow. "We must prepare for your father. He will be hungry. Here, take the water jar and go to the spring."

Antelope hesitated, looked away. "But—"

"Go!" Kwani hurried to her cooking place. She would make Tolonqua's favorite blue corn cakes. Acoya and Chomoc would be hungry, too. There was much to be done.

She did not notice the expression on Antelope's face as she left, looking at Kwani over her shoulder, or how she walked away as though wading through water against a current.

Cicuye high on the ridge rose like a beacon in the far distance. The hunters paused in their march to refresh and tidy themselves before returning home. They sat drinking and using the last of the water from their water bags to wipe their faces, smooth their dusty braids, and calm the impatient dogs.

It was midmorning; columns of smoke rose faintly against the shimmering blue sky. Usually there would be talk and laughter and ribald comments about coming reunions, but not today. Tolonqua lay upon his litter, wrapped in the skin of the buffalo he had killed. With him were his pack, his weapons, and the conch-shell horn. Already, an odor rose.

Chomoc squatted beside Yatosha and sensed his grief.

"Shall I play my flute, Father?"

Yatosha gave his son an appreciative glance, but he shook his head.

Chomoc looked at Long See who wiped his too-thick braids with dusty hands, bowing his head to conceal his eyes. Grief enveloped the group like acrid smoke.

Chomoc remembered how he visualized their homecoming while he played his flute and Tolonqua blew the horn. His father did not want the flute, but maybe he would blow the horn for Tolonqua.

"Will you blow Tolonqua's horn to say we come home?"

Again Yatosha shook his head. "I will carry him."

Long See said, "You blow it, Chomoc. You were another son to him."

The hunters nodded. "Aye."

Yatosha loosened the buffalo skin, reached in, and removed the pouch containing the horn. The fine buckskin was stained with dark splotches.

"Tolonqua's blood," Yatosha said in a strained voice. "It will give power to the horn's voice." He handed the horn to his son.

Chomoc removed the great shell from its pouch and held it reverently in both hands. He took a deep breath, and blew. The horn moaned. He blew again harder, and the horn cried out. Again and again Chomoc blew, and the horn bellowed Tolonqua's strong spirit to the gods.

The march continued with Long See and Yatosha in front carrying the litter while Chomoc walked beside them, singing Tolonqua's Death Song with his horn. The hunters followed with the dogs and their loaded travois. They trudged in silence, allowing the horn to lament for them.

As they approached the city, Chomoc's eyes searched greedily for Antelope.

Was that Kwani on a roof with Antelope beside her?

When they were close enough so that the people could see a wrapped bundle on the litter and realized it was Tolonqua, a terrible cry arose. People poured from the city and ran down the path from the ridge to meet them. Six men lifted the litter and carried it overhead as they climbed up the path.

Amid the cries, the babbles, the moaning shouts, Chomoc saw Kwani and Antelope running wildly to meet them. Anitzal stumbled behind, her mouth wide open and shrieking. Kwani reached the litter, and stopped. She glanced at the men carrying the litter and gestured. They lowered the litter to the ground, and stood aside.

Kwani stood looking down at the wrapped bundle, her face a mask. She turned to Yatosha.

"Where is Acoya?" she whispered hoarsely.

Yatosha could not bring himself to tell, and stood with head bowed.

"Pawnees," Chomoc said.

Kwani made a small sound.

Antelope looked up at Kwani, glanced at the bundle on the litter, and drew back. She clutched at Kwani's robe. Her voice squeaked. "Is that father?"

Kwani did not respond. She stood motionless, staring at the litter, her face blank.

Anitzal staggered forward and jerked the buffalo skin aside. There was a stench as Tolonqua lay exposed, the bloody mass upon his chest already squirming with maggots.

Anitzal turned away, vomiting. People held her, murmuring, half carrying her as they led her away.

"Father!" Antelope sobbed, crumpling upon the ground beside him.

Slowly, Kwani leaned down and replaced the buffalo skin. Her face was blank as though she were elsewhere in dreams. She turned to Yatosha.

"Take him home. I will make him ready for burial." Her voice was calm and low. She pulled Antelope to her feet. "Your father enters Sipapu. We must prepare him. Come."

They walked up the path, the woman suddenly old, and the sobbing child clinging to her mother's hand as though she, too, would leave her.

▲ 52 ▼

Kwani and Anitzal stood in silence, looking down at Tolonqua as he lay upon his sleeping mat. They had bathed his body, and the terrible wound was cleansed and covered with a square of cotton cloth. Upon it lay a circular prayer stick, the form most sacred. Kwani wanted to place a cloth upon his face, also, in Anasazi fashion, but Tolonqua was Towa; his face remained uncovered so that he might see as he entered Sipapu dressed in his most splendid ceremonial garments. Notched eagle feathers, indicating his status as Hunting Chief and Building Chief, were thrust in his finest headband.

How handsome he is! both women thought, and forced themselves to swallow their cries; they would allow themselves private grieving when their work was done.

"Should we let Antelope see him now?" Anitzal asked.

"No. Not until we are finished."

"What jewelry will he wear?"

"The best. I will get it."

Kwani descended the inside ladder to the storeroom below. She removed the cover from a cache dug in the center of the floor. Inside was an oblong, lidded box of painted buffalo hide. Kwani lifted it out and set it on the floor beside her. The box was Tolonqua's and contained his most prized jewelry. Kwani placed both hands upon it and bowed her head on her hands; she felt strength draining from her like corn from a torn pouch.

She clutched her necklace. "Help me through this!"

After a time she seemed stronger. She untied the leather thongs holding the cover, and lifted the lid. There were the necklaces, ear ornaments, bracelets, beads—treasures Tolonqua had accumulated during a lifetime. Also, gleaming in the dim light, lay the heavy golden necklace Kokopelli had given Acoya to wear when he became a man.

The sight of that necklace for the son she might never see again was a knife slashing the final bonds of control. She gave a great cry and flung herself to the floor, sobbing, screaming. Terrible sounds tore themselves from her with a power of their own, on and on.

Gentle hands lifted her. Old Anitzal, tears streaming, held Kwani, rocking her.

"Hush, hush. Antelope will hear."

Antelope did hear. She stood upstairs by the ladder, looking down at them, her small face old for her years. She went to kneel beside Tolonqua and inspected him solemnly. She touched his robe.

"You look nice."

The sounds from below continued. Antelope covered her ears. She leaned close to Tolonqua and whispered, "I think Acoya is all right now. But something is wrong. I don't know if I should tell Mother. Won't it make her cry more?"

She sat up and looked at her father as though waiting for a reply. Then she stood, went to the ladder, and climbed down.

Kwani clung to Anitzal, her body still wrenched with sobs. Anitzal saw Antelope descending the ladder.

"Hush! Antelope is here."

Antelope touched Kwani's arm. "Mother."

Kwani struggled to stop crying. Gasping sobs grew quieter.

"Mother, I know about Acoya."

Kwani raised her head. Streaming eyes in a drawn and twisted face looked at her daughter. "What do you know?"

"He is safe. For now."

"For now?"

Antelope nodded. "But I think somebody should go and get him right away."

"Why?" Anitzal asked sharply.

"I'm not sure. The Pawnees wait for something. I'm afraid—"

Kwani looked at Antelope searchingly. She sat up, wiped her face with both hands, and reached for treasures in the buffalo-hide box. She steadied her voice. "Today we bury your father. Then we shall bring Acoya home."

Tolonqua lay in his burial place in the plaza, the first to be so honored. He lay on his side in flexed position in Earthmother's womb as he did in the womb of his birth mother. Beside him were things he would need in the Sipapu world: his fine weapons, an Anasazi mug, and a beautiful bowl that had been broken to release its spirit; the spirit would enter another bowl in the underworld. No newcomer to Sipapu would be more handsomely adorned than he in his ceremonial finery and necklaces of bear claws and turquoise, and shells from the Sunset Sea, his bracelets and ear ornaments, and his shield and sacred pipe.

In the kiva nearby, a discussion was under way. Two Elk stood with Yatosha and Chomoc beside him, facing the Chiefs and Elders as he spoke.

"As we all know, Antelope, the twin child, daughter of She Who Remembers, correctly foretold the death of our Building Chief. She said also that Acoya was captured by Pawnees. You have heard the words of Chomoc telling how he saw the Pawnees capture Acoya and take him away. Now Antelope tells us Acoya is in danger and must be rescued immediately. This you know. It was agreed by all of us here that if both boys did not return with the hunters, we would send a search party to find them."

The War Chief raised his hand for speaking. He was short but powerfully built and his grizzled head was thrust forward like a buffalo's. He stood with legs parted, hands on hips.

"I shall assemble my best warriors for a raiding party. We shall need more lances and many arrows. Let us prepare." He sat down.

There was a moment of silence as the Chiefs and Elders considered this.

Two Elk said to the group. "Is this your opinion?"

Long See shook his head. "It is far to take a raiding party against those much greater in number who know their land better than we do."

"Aye," the Sun Chief said. Deep-set eyes in his young face regarded the War Chief gravely. "This is the time when Pawnees return from hunting to their homes. They are well prepared to repel attack. Furthermore, it is also the time for their great Sleight-of-Hand ceremonies when medicine men of their different clans assemble for demonstrations of their skills. Many visitors will be there, more warriors among them. A raiding party would be at a serious disadvantage."

The Warrior Chief was not pleased. "My warriors are well accustomed to disadvantage. That is no problem. They are warriors."

The Medicine Chief shook his head so that the chickadee bobbed back and forth, and the obsidian eye stared balefully. "They are men who enter Sipapu as all men do. Once there, they can fight no more."

The men glanced at one another, then looked down at their hands.

An Elder spoke. "Let us reason. The son of She Who Remembers is held captive by those whose numbers are much greater than ours. And who are far distant. If our warriors attack, is it not possible that Acoya will be killed by his captives?"

Yatosha and Chomoc had been standing quietly, acutely conscious of the fact that they were neither Elder nor Chief and were guests here. Yatosha raised his hand tentatively.

Two Elk nodded. "Speak."

Yatosha rose. He was tall for Anasazi, wide of shoulder and lean of hip. He still wore his hair in Anasazi fashion in a single braid streaked with white. Tiopi's death had etched new lines in his square face so that he appeared older than his thirty-four winters, but the lines lent him the added authority of age. He spoke quietly.

"Long See speaks truth. The land of the Pawnees is distant, and they know every hill and gully, every mountain trail and tree and bush as intimately as they know their lodges. We hunters travel far but we know the farther our moccasins take us from home, the greater our disadvantage. Let us consider other means of rescuing Acoya."

The Warrior Chief scowled. "Like what?"

An Elder gestured with a hand thin and bony as an eagle's talon. "Pawnees are known for love of booty. Bribe them."

There was silence; this was a new approach!

The Sun Chief smiled sardonically. "Like Talasi's efforts to bribe the Medicine Chiefs?"

"Unsuccessful, I remind you," the Medicine Chief remarked.

Another Elder spoke. "Let us remember with whom we are dealing. Pawnees. A bribe will interest them."

There was long discussion, some in favor of a bribe, and some not. Finally, Two Elk said, "Those not in favor of a bribe have offered no other solution. Therefore, as Cicuye's Chief, I declare that we shall offer Pawnees a bribe to release Acoya."

"And quickly!" Yatosha said.

"The question now is how. Whom do we send?"

There was silence as the distance and danger of travel and confronting Pawnees on their home ground were considered. Eyes lowered as if in deep thought. No one ventured suggestions.

"Send me," Yatosha said.

"And me!" Chomoc piped up. He had remained respect-fully silent up to now, but excitement made him forget his manners. "Acoya is my friend."

Two Elk regarded them both without expression.

Yatosha said, "Acoya's father saved my life. It is proper that I should save the life of his son. I shall do so."

"Alone?"

"No. I shall take Chomoc with me."

"A boy? It is not—"

"A boy and his flute," Yatosha said.

The men considered this. A man and a boy traveling alone would not likely be considered a threat such as a raiding party would be. But it would be dangerous, nonetheless.

Long See said, "Chomoc's flute has Kokopelli's powers. This we know."

The men murmured agreement. Chomoc hid his triumph. He looked down his nose and assumed a manly stance.

Two Elk looked thoughtful. "What should be offered as a bribe?"

Chomoc could barely conceal his joy. Two Elk had not forbidden him to go! Overcome, he blurted, "The shell horn!"

The men glanced at one another in startled surprise. This was an intelligent solution. A man's possession given to rescue his son—and such a treasure as no Pawnee ever pos-sessed!

Two Elk said, "We must obtain permission from She Who Remembers. The horn is hers now but she will give it to rescue her son. Then Yatosha and Chomoc shall go alone to bring Acoya home."

"They must get there in time," added the Medicine Chief.

It was agreed.

Antelope followed her narrow path to the place where Chomoc used to call the rabbit for her. She wanted to sit on the rock and think about things. It was a pretty day in early autumn. Wind Old Woman blew cool from the moun-tain, bringing bright colors to the leaves for ceremonial dress. One by one they fell from the tree and danced all the way down to Earthmother.

Antelope reached the big rock and climbed to the top. There was much to think about. Chomoc, for instance. While he was gone she had missed his flute, missed him. But since he ran away from her . . . that time . . . he had avoided her. Instead, he played his flute for the new girl, White Cloud, who was older. Maybe even nine or ten. Who always wore a red feather in her hair.

Maybe Chomoc loves her now, instead of me.

The thought made her stomach hurt.

I want him to love only me.

She would not think about that anymore.

The stone was warm and smooth and felt good. She lay on her stomach and looked down to where the rabbit hole still was, only no more rabbits were there. It was quiet and peaceful. A lizard paused in the sunlight, did his usual push-ups, and darted away, his tail zigzagging after him. A cloud shadow drifted by, bringing a cool breeze and the taste of autumn.

Antelope closed her eyes so her thoughts could drift like the cloud shadow. Her father was in Sipapu where every-thing was the same as here except reversed. For instance, when it was daylight here, it was night there. Women tied their robes on the left shoulder. Things like that. She won-dered about babies. Did men have the babies in Sipapu? If so, maybe they would not be so eager to use their man parts; it hurt to have babies.

Chomoc. She thought of his man part that stuck up funny and hurt when he tried to push it in.

But he did it because I told him to.

Antelope sat up and hugged her knees. Chomoc was a Buffalo Hunter now. All the girls admired him, even those who used to think he was ugly with his big nose and fore-head that sloped back that way. White Cloud always smiled at him, especially when he played his flute for her.

Antelope felt a twinge of strange emotions. She held her knees tightly and rocked back and forth. Where was Chomoc? He always came here when he knew she was there. He had been in the kiva all morning; maybe he did not know where she was.

I will find him and make him play his flute! For me.

She slid down the boulder and was about to run down the path when Chomoc appeared from behind a tree. He stood looking at her with a strange expression in his amber-colored eyes. His flute in its pouch was slung over his shoulder.

Antelope stared at him. He had been hiding, watching her! She did not like that!

Her black eyes snapped. "Hiding like a scared mouse!"

He flushed scarlet and turned to leave.

"No! Wait!" Antelope cried as he ran down the path.

Chomoc did not stop and Antelope ran after him. She could run as fast as he and soon she caught up with him. She snatched at the thong holding the flute.

He stopped, whirled, and jerked the flute from her grasp. They stood staring at each other.

Antelope flung herself upon him. "I don't want you to love anybody but me!" Her voice wobbled. "Not that other girl!" She sobbed, clinging to him, tugging at his shoulders in angry desperation.

Chomoc's face softened and he patted her back and stroked her hair.

"Here, sit down."

They sat on the leafy ground. Antelope sniffled and wiped her nose on the back of her hand while Chomoc took out his flute. He began to play. It was the sound of water flowing over rocks, of soft birdsong and twilight, a soothing, comforting melody.

For a long time they sat there on golden, crunchy leaves, the boy playing his flute, the girl listening, lips parted, eyes glowing.

Finally, Chomoc lay the flute in his lap and sat looking at Antelope who sat cross-legged, dappled by sunlight through the trees. Like a faun, she was.

He said, "Tomorrow I go with Yatosha to bring Acoya home."

"Ah." She looked away. "What will you bring me?" She wanted a red feather.

"Acoya."

"Behold! A gift from the Morning Star."

It was one of the old women of the Morning Star Society. She stood in the doorway of the lodge where Acoya was confined in lonely luxury, and beckoned to someone behind her.

A girl entered. She was perhaps fourteen, and already a woman with round, firm breasts surrounded with turquoise and shell necklaces. She wore only a little ornate deerskin apron fastened to her waist that hung before and behind and flapped tantalizingly as she approached, smiling, eyes lowered modestly.

"Enjoy your gift," the old woman signed, smirking. She bowed, backed into the tunnel entrance, and left.

"I greet you," Acoya signed politely. He was acutely uncomfortable. He was a prisoner here, confined in luxury, bowed to, his every wish fulfilled except what he wanted most—to go home. He had not asked for this girl. Why was she here?

The girl came and sat beside him on the buffalo robe where he had been stretched out, staring at the ceiling, trying to devise an escape plan. She leaned close so that he could smell her girl smell, and raised her eyes to his.

"My name is Water Bird," she signed, lowering her long lashes.

"I greet you," Acoya signed again. He wanted to be polite but she was too close, and he edged away. "Why did they bring you here? Are you a prisoner, too?"

She laughed. "I am a gift," she signed, and her bracelets of brightly painted bone and seed beads clinked with her feminine gestures. She took his hand and brought it to one round breast. "This." She squeezed his fingers so that he felt the softness. "And this." She moved his hand to the other breast, and pressed it close.

Acoya was embarrassed; he didn't know what he was supposed to do. But he was intrigued. He tried to remove his hand, but not too hard. She giggled and held his hand fast. She slid it down her smooth stomach to the band at her waist that held the little apron in place. She released his hand and lifted the apron so that the little down on her woman part peeked at him. Then she flipped the apron closed and lay beside him on the buffalo robe, her arms stretched overhead, her legs slightly parted, and gazed up at him, her dark eyes shining.

"Enjoy your gift," she signed. She touched a nipple the color of cactus fruit. "Taste." She reached up and pulled his head to her breast.

It tasted funny, but it felt good. He lay down beside her, embarrassed and a bit scared. She drew his head to her other breast and he tasted that nipple, too. He was beginning to have an erection, an exciting feeling!

Water Bird put an arm around him and slid her hand down his back and around to the front. She reached under his breechcloth and he gasped as he felt her fingers enclosing, caressing. When it seemed his man part would burst with power surging within it, she straddled him and used her hand to push it inside of her.

It was delightfully warm and silky soft, and he found himself thrusting against her again and again. When the wonderful explosion came, they both cried out, and Water Bird lay upon him, spent, her soft, black hair falling around his face.

At last she rolled to her side, and lay gazing at him.

She signed, "Is this your first time?"

He did not want to admit it so he did not reply.

She smiled. "A nice gift, was it not?" She sat up. "I shall leave now, but I will come back every day until—"

"Until what?"

She gazed down at him with a look he did not understand. As if she were sorry for him. Then she rose and walked to the doorway, her little apron flipping behind her.

▲ 53 ▼

Yatosha and Chomoc paused on the crest of a small hill and gazed into dim distance where a thin column of smoke arose, barely discernible against a twilight sky.

Chomoc said, "I wonder if that is the Pawnee village."

"I don't think so. Their village is large; there would be more smoke."

"How much farther?"

"Another day. Perhaps two."

They walked on in single file, Yatosha in front. Since Sunfather had gone, the plains wind had grown cooler; soon it would be cold.

"Where shall we make camp?" Chomoc asked.

Yatosha cast him a sardonic glance. "Since you have chosen to become a Buffalo Hunter, you shall select the campsite and make camp."

Chomoc flushed. Yatosha had said nothing before about disobeying orders not to follow the hunters; when Chomoc encountered them, Tolonqua was dead and they were homeward bound. But he knew very well that Yatosha would have much to say about it when he decided it was time to do so.

Chomoc assumed a Buffalo Hunter's erect stance and surveyed the landscape. Low, rolling hills flattened to great stretches of level plain beyond which were more hills and, Chomoc assumed, gullies. Deep, where enemies could hide. To the right, at the foot of a low hill, was a level, grassy spot where a campsite would not be seen from behind and where they would have a good view of the terrain in front. Also, the location would give some protection from the wind that never stopped blowing and that grew cold at night.

Chomoc pointed. "Over there."

Yatosha nodded, but made no comment. When they reached the spot Chomoc had chosen, Yatosha laid his pack on the ground, sat down, and made himself comfortable.

Chomoc cleared a spot of dried grass and saved some of it for tinder. He gathered buffalo chips and used a rock to pound some to add to the tinder; the rest would make a hot fire. From Yatosha's pack he took the wooden fire stick, a round drill split at one end with a hardwood point inserted in the split and lashed tight. This would be twirled in a small hole in a wooden base until heat from the friction ignited the dried grass and the buffalo tinder.

Chomoc had used a fire stick before, but not under such circumstances with his father sitting there watching critically and doing nothing to help.

I'll show him! I don't need his help.

He bent over the drill and twirled it rapidly in his palms, watching for a tiny glow or wisp of smoke from the hole. He twirled it for a long time, but without success.

Frustrated, he sat back on his heels and looked at his father. Yatosha returned his gaze without expression.

"What am I doing wrong?"

Yatosha shrugged. "Buffalo Hunters must make fire, even in the rain. Since you are a Buffalo Hunter now, do it."

Chomoc looked down his nose at Yatosha for some time.

"I will," he said with dignity.

He rearranged the tinder, bent to the drill, and twirled it hard. When it seemed nothing would ever happen, the tiniest spark appeared. He leaned close and blew gently, but the spark died.

Again he twirled the drill. Again, there was a tiny spark and a little curl of smoke. Chomoc blew very gently, again and again, and the tinder ignited at last. He added buffalo chips until a fine, hot fire blazed.

He gave his father a triumphant glance, and Yatosha smiled. "Well done."

Chomoc wished they had fresh meat to roast over the fire, but they had done no hunting and all they had was jerky and pemmican and a bit of corn cake. Some hot water for the pemmican with jerky tossed in and corn cake added for thickener would make a tasty stew.

A rolled-up buffalo paunch to use as a cooking pot was in Yatosha's pack, but no wood was available for poles to suspend the paunch over the fire. A little pit could be dug and the paunch set inside it with hot stones added to boil the water, but there were no stones nearby that were big enough, at least none that he could see, and it was too dark now to search for those stones that would not crack or explode in a fire. He would have to use their one small pot. Chomoc was ravenously hungry and that little pot would not hold enough even for him. He wished he had accumulated some nice big stones before he started the fire. Well, he would make more than one pot full.

Carefully, he poured a little water from his water bag into the pot, added a strip of jerky for more flavoring, and set the pot on the coals. When it boiled he would add the pemmican—a handful would swell to twice its size—and corn cake.

Yatosha had been watching silently or gazing into the darkness. Now, while they waited for the water to boil, he said, "This fire will be seen from far away." He swept his arm from side to side.

Instantly Chomoc remembered the three Pawnees confronting Acoya in early morning. Those same three, or others like them, could be watching now. Maybe he should not have built a fire, but Yatosha had built a fire every night before. However, now they were only a day or two away from the Pawnees' permanent village and scouts were certain to be on guard.

Chomoc stared into the darkness. He didn't know what to do. He looked at Yatosha who returned his glance calmly. The water in the pot simmered; it was time to add the pemmican. Should he finish cooking or should he douse the fire?

His stomach decided. He added a handful of pemmican, crumbled part of the corn cake, and added that. It would be ready in a minute.

"I will smother the fire before we eat."

"No. We want them to know we come."

"But—"

"We bring no dogs. We are not hunters. We are man and boy come to trade. We do not hide."

Chomoc was abashed but he concealed it. He had done the right thing after all! He rummaged in Yatosha's pack for the two forked sticks used to carry hot rocks, and removed the pot from the coals. It smelled wonderful.

There was one wooden spoon that they took turns using. Yatosha did not seem to be very hungry; he let Chomoc have two spoonfuls to his one and the pot was empty in no time. Chomoc filled it again, and while the water heated they sat gazing into the coals.

For a time they sat in companionable silence. Chomoc picked up his flute in the fine case Kwani had made for him. He fingered the fringe and the porcupine quill embroidery, and thought about his flute and how it was said that he played like his birth father.

"Tell me about Kokopelli. People say I look like him, play like him. . . ."

"That you do," Yatosha said flatly. He stared at the coals and his mouth set in a grim line.

Chomoc thought, He remembers something he doesn't want to remember. He said, "What was Kokopelli like?"

Yatosha did not reply.

"Tell me!" Chomoc said.

A look of pain flickered across Yatosha's face like distant lightning. "A buffalo in rutting season."

Chomoc was shocked. "But everyone says—"

Yatosha turned to look at Chomoc, and his square face in dim firelight looked old. "He seduced your mother. Not once, but twice. He diminished me in her eyes." Abruptly he tossed a buffalo chip upon the coals in an angry gesture. "Kokopelli was a trader from Tula, beyond the Great River of the South. He traveled far and took another man's woman in every village." Yatosha propped his arms on his knees and rested his head on his arms. "Kokopelli sang, he danced, he knew magic and had a bright bird that talked to him. Kokopelli played his flute and told stories and riddles and had fine things to trade. He knew how to make women want him." Yatosha's voice was strained. "He made your mother regard me with contempt."

Yatosha raised his head and Chomoc was surprised to see tears in his eyes. Kokopelli had always been Chomoc's secret hero, someone he wanted to be like, but to harm such a man as Yatosha, a good man, master hunter, honorable, a man to make Anasazis proud. . . . No. He, Chomoc, would not be such a man as Kokopelli.

The water boiled and Chomoc made another pot of stew. They ate in silence, taking turns with the spoon, scanning the darkness beyond their camp. Tomorrow or the next day they would be in the Pawnee village where Acoya was. Chomoc tried to visualize what would happen but all he could think about was something Yatosha had said.

He knew how to make women want him.

Antelope. Like a faun she was. But with a burning coal inside.

Can I make her want me? When she is older?

The Morning Star Priest stood looking at the people assembled in the dance plaza. Behind him was the upright wooden rack to hold the Morning Star's gift after the boy's spirit had been released to join that of the deity. Before him the priests stood in a semicircle, holding their bows and arrows. Their faces were freshly painted and gleamed red, black, and white in the morning light. To one side stood the big one with the loud voice; he held his heavy club in readiness. Beside him the aged Tribal Chief stood leaning heavily on his tall ceremonial staff that was adorned with hawk and eagle feathers, small copper bells obtained in trading, and bright streamers. Behind the priests were the Chiefs in their triangular headdresses and elaborate ceremonial garb. Crowding the plaza were people of the village and many visitors. All stood waiting avidly for the Towa boy to be brought for sacrifice.

The Morning Star Priest was disquieted; all was not well. He had experienced disturbing dreams about this son of She Who Remembers, dreams that made him wonder if this sacrifice was wise. He had fasted, purified himself in the sweat lodge, cleansed himself internally, partaken of the sacred sun plant, prayed and sought visions, but no reassuring word from the Morning Star had been forthcoming. Now he stood in his ceremonial buffalo robe with its Morning Star emblem; the robe was draped over one shoulder leaving the other arm and shoulder bare. An eagle-bone necklace with a clam-shell pendant lay upon his chest. The upper part of his face was painted black so that his deep-set dark eyes seemed to reflect light in a black pool. Long dark hair with streaks of gray hung loose, and a cluster of eagle down feathers rose like a crest on top of his head; the feathers stirred in the breeze as if they were alive. One hand grasped a large, round gourd rattle painted with Morning Star insignia; the other held four eagle feathers fastened together at the base. Around the base was wrapped a long cluster of deerskin strips painted blue, the color of Morning Star's dwelling place.

The Seven Sisters stars had reached the appointed spot.

It was time.

He raised the rattle, shaking it for attention. "Bring the gift for the Morning Star."

There was tense silence as people waited for the Towa boy to be brought before them. The Morning Star Priest's head was bowed and his eyes were closed. High cheekbones, jutting from the deep folds of a weathered face, shadowed his cheeks. The somber mouth was clamped shut; if he prayed, it was in spirit only.

* * *

Acoya heard someone entering the corridor of his lodge. He was expecting Water Bird. She had come every day. Sometimes, he lay with her as he had the first time she came. She did not want to do it always, however, so that when she did want to it seemed even better. They played gambling games and laughed and talked, but Water Bird would never tell him why he was there. Or why they treated him as honored Chief but kept him prisoner.

He puzzled over this long nights when he could not sleep. He reminded himself that he was protected by the White Buffalo and by Bear, but . . .

Two priests entered. They did not bow as people usually did when they entered his lodge. Instead, they signed, "Come with us."

"Why?"

They did not answer but stepped forward, grabbed both his arms, pushed him outside and through the noisy throng to where the Morning Star Priest stood waiting.

Acoya shook himself free and stared up at the priest who returned his gaze with aloof inscrutability.

Acoya felt cold fear seeping in his arteries. He turned to search the crowd for Water Bird, but he did not see her. He turned back to the Morning Star Priest who regarded him silently with an unblinking scrutiny that made Acoya feel sliced down the middle and laid open.

The priest's gaze shifted to someone nearby and Acoya glanced to see who it was.

Big Voice! With a stone-headed club in his huge fist! The look in his eyes struck Acoya with terrifying force; Acoya knew what Big Voice was about to do even before he raised the club overhead.

Instinctively, Acoya threw back his head and opened his mouth wide as if to release something within him demanding escape. A terrible singing cry surged forth, a primal call to the unseen.

As if in response, from outside the city came a great shout from a conch-shell horn, a wailing scream to freeze the blood and summon avenging spirits. It swelled, lingering in the air like a curse before fading away.

Big Voice dropped the club and stood staring stupidly. Shouts, babbles, and cries arose, then stopped suddenly as the supernatural sound came again, a sinister voice from the underworld, summoned by Acoya's weird call.

Acoya gasped. It couldn't be, but it was! The conch-shell horn!

There was a bedlam of frightened shouts. Some people ran toward the sound to see what it was; others hurried to hide. Warriors ran for their weapons, and the priests held their bows and arrows in readiness for they knew not what. The aged Tribal Chief could no longer stand; he sank to the ground, still clutching his staff, murmuring inaudible prayers. People gazed at Acoya fearfully. What terrible power did he possess?

Only the Morning Star Priest stood immobile and expressionless, watching and listening to the turmoil. Big Voice leaned to pick up his club.

"Leave it!" the priest said sharply, and beckoned to Acoya to come closer. When Acoya stood before him, the Priest signed, "Do you know from whence comes that sound?"

"Aye."

"What is it?"

"The cry of the conch-shell horn."

The eyes in the black pool gleamed. "Who makes it cry?"

"One who comes to take me home."

There was a growl from Big Voice and muttering from others who crowded to listen.

The Morning Star Priest smiled as one who enjoys an exacting confrontation with equals. He gestured to Big Voice and another priest nearby.

"Return the Towa to his lodge."

"**W**asn't that Acoya's voice?" Chomoc grabbed Yatosha's arm. "It sounded like it!"

"I think so." Yatosha replaced the horn in its pouch, and frowned. "But something is wrong!"

They stood gazing, trying to guess where Acoya might be. The city rose beside a river at the base of rugged hills. Never had Chomoc seen such dwellings! Round, pointed at the top like a woman's breast, and with a long, tunnellike entrance protruding outward. A man would have to bend over to enter, Chomoc thought. Even from far away the clamor of the village had been heard: drums, chanting, shouts, laughter, a babble of talk, and the excited barking of a pack of dogs guarding the city. But as he and Yatosha grew closer to the city, the noise had quieted. Then came Acoya's cry that made Chomoc's hair rise on his neck.

"What are they doing to him?"

"That was not a cry of pain," Yatosha said. "But something *is* wrong."

The sudden quiet was ominous. "What's happening?"

"I don't know. Play your flute now, and don't stop until I tell you to."

What should he play? Chomoc knew that Kokopelli had always played his flute to announce his arrival. But what melody? Chomoc would let the flute tell him. He removed the instrument from its case and closed his eyes for a moment to allow his spirit to communicate with that of the flute. Then his fingers danced with a will of their own and the flute sang, announcing the arrival of important personages—people it would be wise for them to welcome.

Villagers climbed on roofs to watch. Behind a pack of snarling dogs, warriors stood with bows and arrows and lances; more warriors were on the roofs. The quiet grew heavier.

Yatosha stopped. "We shall stand here but keep playing while I sign."

Yatosha raised both hands overhead. Then he signed, "I am Yatosha, Towa of Cicuye. This is my son, Chomoc, birth son of Kokopelli. We come to trade. We ask permission to enter your city."

The warriors conferred; one left. Chomoc continued to play, watching Yatosha for a signal to stop.

Yatosha said, "They send someone to seek permission for us to enter. Keep playing."

The flute changed to another melody, a happy ripple of notes promising delightful events. For a time, there was no reaction. Then a few people smiled and began to speak to one another. Children yelled excitedly from rooftops. Warriors lowered their bows.

Chomoc played on, leaning side to side, prancing. Some listeners began to sway or tap their feet in time to the melody.

The messenger returned and there was more discussion. Finally, a priest appeared. Chomoc recognized him as one of those who had kidnapped Acoya. A crow's head was perched on the band across his shaved head, and feathers were thrust into the crest of hair on top. He gestured to two of the warriors. The three of them approached, the priest in the center and a warrior on either side, bow in hand. Dogs tried to follow but were ordered back.

"Stop playing now," Yatosha said. "And mind your manners."

Chomoc lowered the flute to his side, and stood straight, head high, as the men came to stand before them.

"I greet you," Yatosha signed.

The greeting was acknowledged, but not returned. The priest scrutinized them in silence. Then he signed, "Who made that sound?"

"What sound?"

The priest flushed with annoyance. "That long, loud sound."

"You mean this?"

Yatosha removed the conch shell from its pouch, held it a moment for the priest and the warriors to see, then lifted it to his lips and blew. The men covered their ears with both hands as a terrible wail split the air.

Calmly, Yatosha returned the horn to the pouch at his waist and regarded the priest with a level gaze.

The priest reached out his hand for the horn.

"This is my medicine," Yatosha signed. "It is powerful. You will understand why no one may touch it but me."

Chomoc managed to conceal his surprise. The horn was what they would trade for Acoya. Had Yatosha changed his mind?

The priest scowled and his eyes in their painted red hiding places squinted. He spoke sharply in Pawnee to the warriors and turned away.

A warrior signed, "Follow us."

Yatosha nudged Chomoc. "Play."

With the priest leading the way, they followed in single file: a warrior behind the priest, then Yatosha, then Chomoc, with the other warrior bringing up the rear, all stepping in time to Chomoc's melody.

It was a fine morning with bright sunlight and white clouds sailing. There was tense excitement in the air as those on the roofs looked down at the small procession while bystanders made way. Small children skipped and ran along, crowding around Chomoc as he played. People who had disappeared in hiding came out and joined the crowd, babbling questions.

"Who are they?"

"Traders. From Cicuye."

"Did they make that sound?"

"The man did."

"With something he carries in that pouch at his waist."

"Ah!"

"Look at that boy! How strange he is!"

"Ugly."

"How he plays!"

Chomoc was aware of the reaction to his music, and he glanced around to see if the girls were impressed. They were, so he played even better.

The procession made its way among the round dwellings to the dance plaza. Chomoc looked everywhere for Acoya, but he wasn't there. A cold finger poked Chomoc's heart. It could not be possible, but . . . had these people killed Acoya? But no; Acoya had a powerful totem; he was protected. And surely that was Acoya's voice they had heard.

Chomoc stopped playing abruptly to gaze in astonishment at some of the men gathered there. Their headdresses were massive, triangular, elaborately ornamented structures that stuck way out on one side with things dangling from the point. A very old man, obviously someone important, stood leaning on a tall staff adorned with feathers and bells and streamers.

"Who is that?" Chomoc asked a warrior.

"Standing Bear, our Tribal Chief." He cast Chomoc a scornful glance. "Everyone of importance knows of him."

Chomoc wanted to say, "Everyone of importance knows us, too," but he held his tongue.

Beside Standing Bear stood a man who could be a priest, Chomoc thought, although his head was not shaved. His long hair hung down, ceremonial fashion, and instead of a crest on a shaved head there was a cluster of eagle down feathers. He wore a buffalo robe—the only one there who did—and he stood tall and straight, watching them coming with eyes hidden in black from his hairline down to his nostrils.

Chomoc knew instinctively this man would determine Acoya's fate. If he had not done so already. And he would determine theirs.

The Tribal Chief and the Morning Star Priest exchanged glances as Yatosha and Chomoc stood before them.

The priest signed, "Why are you here?"

"To trade. And to bring the Towa boy home."

Murmurs from bystanders.

Again Standing Bear and the priest glanced at each other. They spoke in Pawnee.

The priest signed, "Do you know who I am?"

"A priest."

"I am Priest of the Morning Star. My duty is to that deity. Who is this boy?"

Yatosha nodded at Chomoc, giving him permission to speak.

"I am Chomoc. Anasazi, born of Kokopelli at the Place of the Eagle Clan." He looked down his nose and unconsciously assumed an arrogant stance. "Now I am son of Yatosha, Towa, of Cicuye. Come to bring Acoya home."

The priest was not pleased at this young *kekelt*, this hawk fledgling, whose manner was offensively presumptuous. Scowling, he shook his big rattle with the Morning Star insignia. "Why are you here?"

"My father wishes it. To bring Acoya home."

The old Tribal Chief raised his bony claw of a hand and gestured for Yatosha and Chomoc to come closer. When they stood before him, he leaned to peer at them with cloudy eyes nearly hidden in shadow under the big headdress. He signed to Yatosha, "You have come far. To Pawnee ground. A long and dangerous trip to find the son of another. Why?"

"He is the son of one who saved my life and is now in Sipapu."

The shadowed glance rested upon Chomoc. "You have come only because of your father's wishes?"

"Acoya is my friend."

The Tribal Chief straightened and turned to the Morning Star Priest. They spoke for some time. The talk grew heated, and Chomoc wondered what they said. Would they take him to Acoya? If Acoya was alive? Again his eyes searched the crowd but Acoya was not there.

The heated discussion ended and the two dignitaries stood looking at Yatosha and Chomoc. Finally, the Morning Star Priest signed, "We go to the medicine lodge. Follow."

Warriors used their lances to wave aside gawking bystanders. A priest beating a small drum led the way for Standing Bear and the Morning Star Priest, followed by Yatosha and Chomac. More warriors brought up the rear.

When they reached the lodge, the man beating the drum stepped aside and the old Tribal Chief prepared to enter. Three times he reached a foot into the tunnel and drew it back. Only on the fourth time did he lower his staff and enter. The Morning Star Priest followed in the same manner.

Chomoc looked at Yatosha. "Should we do that?"

"Yes. And respectfully."

They did so, and entered, followed by the group of priests. The interior was dim and smelled different from any place Chomoc had been before. He gazed at the buffalo skull and other objects on the long altar, and at baskets and bowls and jars and curious things crowding the shelves and hanging from the walls.

Standing Bear hobbled to the willow backrest and used his staff to ease himself into it with the help of two priests. He gestured, and the Morning Star Priest sat beside him.

The Morning Star Priest signed, "Sit," and Yatosha and Chomoc sat on the smooth, hard adobe floor, facing them, with priests behind. Chomoc was hungry and wondered what they would be given to eat. At home, food was offered immediately to anyone entering a dwelling. But this was a medicine lodge; maybe it was different here.

Standing Bear removed the heavy triangular headdress and laid it on the floor beside him. Bony hands pushed his scraggly hair back. Chomoc wondered why some men had shaved heads and others did not. None had eyebrows—they were plucked out—and it made their foreheads look bare and their eyes exposed.

Standing Bear spoke to the Morning Star Priest, then

signed to Yatosha, "You say you come to trade. What have you to offer?"

"It depends upon what you have to offer in return. However—" He removed his pack and placed it on the floor between his legs and removed several splendid necklaces, an elegant little beaded case to hold bone awls made long ago by Tiopi, and a finely made tubular clay and bone pipe, shiny and smooth. He spread the things on the floor before the Tribal Chief. "I offer these."

He paused while Standing Bear picked up the objects, one at a time, to examine them, and handed them to the Morning Star Priest who glanced at them indifferently and lay them aside.

Yatosha signed, "Yours in trade for the Towa boy."

The Chief scowled. "No! He is not for trade. He belongs to the Morning Star."

"He belongs to his people. He is a Chosen One of the White Buffalo."

The priests crowding the lodge murmured, glancing at one another. Standing Bear raised his hand and there was immediate silence. He spoke in Pawnee, and again there was a heated discussion. The Morning Star Priest shook his head, and his eyes in their black pools burned angrily.

Chomoc wondered what the argument was about. And why were these valuable things being offered when they had planned to trade the horn? He leaned close to Yatosha and whispered, "Father—"

"Be silent!"

Chomoc sat, uncomfortably aware of disapproving glances from the priests. He looked down at his folded hands. If trading for Acoya was discussed, Acoya was alive. Nothing must be done to cause his captors to endanger him.

I must not speak until ordered to.

Standing Bear turned to Yatosha. "What you offer is not enough for a gift to the Morning Star."

Yatosha gazed at the Tribal Chief for a long moment. Then he reached again into his pack.

"No!" Standing Bear signed. He pointed at the pouch with the horn. "That."

Yatosha shook his head. "This is my medicine. It has power. It calls to Sipapu and summons protecting spirits. No one may touch it but me."

The Morning Star Priest grunted an order, and four burly priests darted to Yatosha, pinned his arms, yanked the horn from its pouch, and handed it to Standing Bear.

Chomoc hid his amusement as his father made a great show of outraged fury and signed, "You defile a sacred object!"

Standing Bear examined the shell horn carefully, turning it over in his bony hands, stroking its lustrous curves, while the Morning Star Priest watched avidly, waiting his turn to hold it. The other priests craned their necks to see, muttering excitedly.

Standing Bear lifted the horn to his lips and tried to blow, but his old lungs were not strong enough and only a small moan emerged. Embarrassed, he pushed the horn at the Morning Star Priest who accepted it eagerly, inspected it, and blew. A shuddering wail filled the lodge, an eerie voice from the underworld.

Murmurs of awe and fear followed. Yatosha stepped closer to the Tribal Chief and stared into the shadowed eyes. He signed, "My medicine demands justice. Bring the Towa boy to me in trade for the horn."

Standing Bear met Yatosha's steady gaze and held it unblinkingly. He signed, and a priest departed hurriedly.

Chomoc tried not to look as eager and excited as he felt; when trading, one made it a point to appear indifferent. But his heart beat hard. Acoya would be brought here! Chomoc couldn't wait to see him, and hoped Acoya would not be too thin or weak to make the long journey home, or that they had not cut off an ear to mark him as a slave. Or worse, cut off his man part. Chomoc cringed at the thought. Acoya had not experienced the pleasure girls could give; how awful if he could never do so! But no matter what these Pawnees had done to Acoya, he, Chomoc, would be kind to him and be his friend and protector.

Footsteps approached and Chomoc braced himself. Acoya was coming! He turned to watch the entrance; he hoped Acoya did not have to be carried. He hoped these barbarians allowed Acoya to be clothed and had not subjected him to the indignity of being naked in the company of these elaborately dressed dignitaries.

The priest entered, followed by Acoya.

Chomoc stared. Acoya paused in the doorway, looking over the group before he entered. He wore an elk-skin robe, beautifully ornamented with bone beads, fringe, and dyed porcupine quills. A fur headband held his shoulder-length hair in place; ermine tails dangled on each side. A thin strip of hair had been shaved from front to back. Many necklaces and bracelets shone in the dim firelight as Acoya strode confidently into the room. He saw Yatosha and Chomoc and stopped, smiling a surprised, happy welcome. He looked robustly healthy. And different, somehow. As if he were older.

Standing Bear beckoned, and the priests made way as Acoya walked between them to where the aged Tribal Chief reclined against his backrest. Acoya bowed respectfully, and signed, "I greet you, Honored One."

Standing Bear ignored the greeting and signed, "Sit." Acoya immediately sat down and Standing Bear turned to Yatosha. "As you can see, the boy has been treated well. He is better now than when he came. A suitable gift for the Morning Star."

Chomoc wondered what that meant—a gift for the Morning Star. He glanced at Acoya who sat facing Standing Bear with his back to the others gathered there. Chomoc could not see Acoya's face, but the ermine tails on the fur band quivered and his hands were clenched tight.

Yatosha signed, "He is chosen of a Spirit Being, the White Buffalo. Therefore, I offer the beautiful necklaces, the fine beaded case for awls, and the sacred pipe as gifts to the Morning Star instead of the boy."

"No!" the Morning Star Priest signed angrily.

Standing Bear spoke to him in Pawnee, and the Morning Star Priest scowled, shaking his head. Standing Bear held the horn in both hands, his clawlike fingers caressing the smooth curves. He signed, "Only this horn is worthy of the Morning Star, but even it is not enough. The boy shall be given to our deity as promised."

Yatosha watched Standing Bear's bony hands on the shell, how they stroked it, turning it lovingly this way and that. He would take a chance. He hesitated, swallowed, and signed, "Then return my gifts and the horn."

"Wait!" Chomoc said loudly, raising his hand. Facing stern, shocked glances, he signed, "I have one more gift to offer." He removed the flute from its handsome case and lifted it to his lips. Instantly magical sound filled the room, calling memories of childhood, of springtime and summer, of beauty and love and dreams come true. When, at last, the music ceased, there was silence like a collective sigh.

Chomoc rose, and holding the flute in his outstretched hands he offered it to Standing Bear. "In exchange for my friend."

For a long moment the old Tribal Chief regarded Chomoc who continued to stand before him with hands outstretched, holding the most beautiful flute the old Chief had ever seen. His gaze sought the Towa boy who sat transfixed, staring in stunned wonder and gratitude at Chomoc, his eyes shining.

For some time Standing Bear sat in silence with his eyes closed. Finally, he inclined his head. "I accept."

Ignoring outraged comments by the Morning Star Priest and the babble that followed, Standing Bear handed the horn to a priest and reached for the flute. He fingered the fine carving and the bright fringe. He signaled, and was helped to his feet. Still holding the flute, he braced himself upon his staff and faced the group. He spoke in Pawnee, signing simultaneously. "This flute, and the horn, and all the other gifts shall be burned in holy sacrifice to the Morning Star." He gestured. "Return the Towa to his people. I have spoken."

▲ 55 ▼

Antelope stood on the roof of Huzipat's dwelling where the eagle squatted in its cage. Since Chomoc was gone, Jaywing and Lapu and Toho had assumed the responsibility of providing field mice or other small game for the eagle. Since the boys were now Eagle Hunters with the envied eagle-claw necklace, they found themselves held in unaccustomed high esteem, and had become good friends. Sometimes they would allow Antelope to feed the bird, especially if she yelled long and loud enough. Now she squatted beside the cage and peered at the bird who peered back with a gaze that reminded her of Chomoc—not afraid of anything.

"I greet you, Eagle," she said politely. The eagle ruffled what feathers it had left, since many had been pulled for ceremonial uses and adornment. "You look funny. Are you lonesome?"

She decided the eagle was, indeed, lonesome and should be free to fly away to be with other eagles. She reached to untie the thong that held the cage closed. The eagle darted at her finger and bit it hard. Blood oozed and trickled down her arm.

"Now you will stay in there forever!" Antelope shouted.

Her finger hurt, and blood flowed. She ran across the roofs to her dwelling, climbed down, and looked for her mother. Kwani was not there, so Antelope stood on the walkway and yelled down at people in the courtyard.

"The eagle bit me! I'm bleeding. It hur-r-r-rts!" Sob.

There was a small commotion in the courtyard as Kwani was summoned and appeared outside Anitzal's door. "Come here!" she called.

Antelope ran to her mother and held out her bleeding finger. "Look what the eagle did!" More sobs.

Anitzal appeared, making soothing sounds. "Come inside, and let Anitzal fix it."

They sat on Anitzal's immaculate floor while Anitzal

cleansed the finger and applied a healing ointment. Antelope stopped crying and looked about her with interest. She always enjoyed being in Anitzal's house because that's where Weomah and Imka lived since Lumu and the baby died, and there were interesting girl things there—such as the basket that held the juniper-bark stuff they used for when they bled between their legs and had to stay in the women's hut until the bleeding stopped. Antelope had decided a long time ago she would never stay in the women's hut when her moon-flow time came, no matter how much she bled.

Kwani said, "Were you feeding the eagle?"

Antelope shook her head. Her finger felt much better and she showed it to Kwani. "He tried to eat my finger."

"You mean you poked your finger in the cage? Why?"

Antelope glanced at her mother; Kwani's voice was sharp lately—ever since Tolonqua died and Acoya was gone. She looked sad, too.

Black eyes met blue ones. "The eagle is lonesome."

"So?"

"So I was going to let it fly away to find other eagles. And when I—"

"Antelope!" Kwani was shocked. "That eagle belongs to all of us in Cicuye. It helps to keep witches away. And it provides feathers we must have to communicate with the Above Beings. Don't even think about—"

"But I feel sorry for it caged that way, and having its feathers pulled out. That must hurt." Antelope's lips pursed in a firm pout. "Eagles need to fly!"

"And our medicine man and Chiefs need the feathers," Kwani said. "That's what eagles are for."

Sudden shouts in the courtyard sent Antelope running outside. She ran back in, shouting.

"Mother! They're coming! Yatosha and the boys!" She ran back out and down the walkway shouting, "They're coming! They're coming!"

Kwani and Anitzal sat looking at each other. Anitzal beamed. "Acoya comes! Let's go and welcome him!"

Kwani did not respond. She sat frozen.

Pandemonium arose in the courtyard: shouts, laughter, a babble of voices, and Chuka's booming bark of welcome. Someone pounded a drum in staccato beat.

"Come on!" Anitzal said, rising.

"You go. I will come later."

Anitzal cast Kwani a puzzled glance. Kwani was not as she used to be. "What is wrong?"

"I can't do it again."

"Do what?"

"It will be the third time. *The third time, Anitzal!* First it was Okalake, Acoya's birth father of the Eagle Clan. Killed by Apaches and carried home on a litter. Then—" Her voice broke. She could not say Tolonqua's name. "On a litter. Now Acoya comes home. How? *How?*"

"I will go and see. Then I will come and tell you," Anitzal said gently, and left.

Kwani listened to Anitzal's footsteps fading away. She clasped her necklace to her. Since Tolonqua's death and Acoya's kidnapping, her strength faltered like a trapped rabbit's. She closed her eyes, calling to the Ancient Ones.

"Make me strong! Make me strong!" she chanted in a voice no longer her own.

Time rolled away like storm clouds over the mountain. Kwani sensed the invisible presence of those who had gone before. They did not speak but filled the room with peace; it was as though they gave of their strength and powers to revive her own. Then they were gone.

Outside, the happy clamor continued. Kwani rose. For the first time since Tolonqua's death, confidence surged in her. She knew her son was alive. She knew he was safely home.

Anitzal stood in the doorway, smiling. "He is here." She left to leave mother and son alone.

Acoya entered. He stood looking at Kwani a moment before he flung himself in her arms, then pulled away because he was too old for that now. He smiled up at her, aglow.

"I greet you,' he said formally.

"My heart rejoices." She pulled him to her again, hugging him close. "My heart rejoices."

"Mine, too."

She held him at arm's length to look at him. "What happened to your hair?"

"The Pawnees shaved it." He shrugged. "It will grow back."

He seemed taller and had a man's air about him. He wore a most handsome elk-skin robe embroidered with dyed porcupine quills. Some other woman made that for him, and Kwani felt a twinge of jealousy. She fingered the skin; it was expertly tanned.

"Who gave you that?"

"Pawnees. They wanted me to wear it when they gave me to the Morning Star for a sacrifice." He saw her expression, and laughed. "You can see they didn't do that. And they kept all the jewelry and gave me this as part of the trade—"

"Wait a minute," Kwani interrupted. "What made them change their minds about a . . . sacrifice?"

"Chomoc." Acoya glanced toward the door, and leaned close to whisper, "Chomoc is outside, waiting for me to tell you, so when you know you will invite him in." He said, "The horn and all the other fine things Yatosha offered were not enough to trade for me. So Chomoc gave them his flute. Then it was enough."

Kwani's heart swelled. "Where is Chomoc?"

"He is here. Outside the door."

"Chomoc!" she called. "Come!"

Chomoc entered and stood inside the doorway, gazing at Kwani with love in his amber eyes. She held out her arms to him and he ran to her embrace without reservation.

Kwani hugged him, a lump in her throat. "You traded your flute for Acoya."

Chomoc pulled away and looked down his nose at her. "Of course."

The look, the voice, were so much like Kokopelli's that Kwani did not answer; she just stood there looking at him as if the past were present again.

Acoya said, "They thought if they had his flute they could make it play the way he did. They did not know the magic was in Chomoc, not in the flute."

Kwani thought, My boy is a boy no longer; he has a man's wisdom. She said to Chomoc, "You saved Acoya's life. Now you and he are brothers."

"And you are my mother now?"

"Yes."

A flush of pleasure stained Chomoc's high cheekbones and sloping brow, leaving his big nose pale in comparison. He opened his mouth to speak, but closed it again and glanced away.

Acoya said, "Let's go to the other room and see my things."

Chomoc nodded, glad for an opportunity to hide his emotion.

Kwani watched the boys go to the adjoining room. They did not scamper as they used to; they walked. Was it only a few moons ago they raced around this room singing the Roadrunner Song? What happened on that journey, and with the Pawnees, that changed these boys?

From the other room came talk and murmurs and spurts of laughter. Then silence, followed by voices in urgent argument. Kwani wondered about that, but she would not intrude.

More silence.

Then, softly at first, swelling to glorious ecstasy, came the sound of Acoya's flute.

Only Chomoc could play that way. Like Kokopelli.

Kwani tiptoed to the door of the next room and peeked in. Chomoc sat on the floor, legs crossed, eyes closed, playing with such an expression of joy that Kwani swallowed. Acoya sat beside him, smiling.

"See? I told you," Acoya said. "It is you that makes the flute sound beautiful. It is yours now. To keep forever."

Kwani silently withdrew and stood there a moment, her heart full. Then she climbed down to the storeroom and opened Tolonqua's box of treasures. Kokopelli's heavy golden necklace glittered where it lay.

She held it in both hands. How beautiful it was! Large golden balls the size of a young child's fist were graduated in size from the largest, to be worn at the back of the neck, to the smallest, to be worn in front. Where the small ends met, two thick golden chains hung down with golden tassels dangling at the ends.

This was Kokopelli's gift to Acoya to be worn when Acoya became a man.

From the room above came the flute's exultant rejoicing. Now was the time.

Kwani looped the necklace over her arm, returned Tolonqua's box to its special place, and climbed the ladder. She went to the family altar behind the fire pit and laid the necklace beside the sacred objects there.

"Acoya," she called.

The flute silenced and Acoya appeared in the doorway with Chomoc following, flute in hand.

Kwani gestured to the place before the altar. "Stand there."

Acoya did so, staring at the necklace. He had seen it many times, but only in its storage place. As it lay upon the altar it seemed that Sunfather's eye was upon it, making it glow with his own glory.

Kwani turned to Chomoc. "When Acoya was born, your birth father gave this to him as a birthing gift to wear when he became a man."

Chomoc had not seen the necklace before. He reached to touch it. "Ah!"

"Acoya has been accepted into the Turquoise Clan. He has been given his manhood vision. He has become an Eagle Hunter. He was imprisoned by enemies and remained strong, as a man should. He gave you his flute to replace the one you gave for him, a manly gesture. Therefore, Acoya has become a man."

Acoya gazed up at Kwani with a look she had not seen before. As though the man within the boy emerged to stand before her in solemn pride.

"Kneel, Acoya," Kwani said.

Slowly he did so, facing the altar where the necklace lay.

"Chomoc, take the necklace and bestow it upon your brother."

Chomoc lifted the necklace in both hands, gazing at it with awe. He slipped it over Acoya's head and stood looking.

The necklace lay in splendor upon the elk-skin robe. The thick chains hung down to Acoya's stomach where golden tassels swung.

"Thank you, Chomoc," Kwani said. "Now I must speak to your brother alone."

"Where is Antelope?"

"I don't know. Maybe with the bead maker's family."

"Yes," Acoya said. "She and White Cloud greeted me together."

"I shall find her."

Chomoc left, fingers dancing on the flute. The melody lingered behind him, growing fainter as he departed.

Kwani sat beside Acoya and took the family fetish from the altar. It was a small bear, long as a thumb, carved in stone. Around its middle was a thin cord holding a chunk of turquoise on its back. She held it in her cupped hands for a moment, then raised her eyes to her son.

"You are young, but you are a man now. Chomoc is your brother. I shall ask Yatosha to be your uncle; you must honor him."

"I shall."

"You promised your father to finish building his city."

"Yes."

"Yatosha will help you. You have a double totem, Bear and the White Buffalo. A double totem carries double responsibility—to the gods and to your people." She handed the fetish to Acoya. "Promise you will fulfill your responsibilities."

Acoya held the figure reverently. "I promise." He replaced the fetish on the altar.

Mother and son sat looking at each other, smiling.

"Tell me everything that happened," Kwani said eagerly.

Acoya nodded. He would tell her, but not everything. Not about Water Bird.

▲ 56 ▼

Acoya stood beside Two Elk in the kiva facing the Chiefs and others crowding the room. Kwani was also present by special invitation; her son was to be honored here. She looked at him in his elk-skin robe and the golden necklace. How handsome he was, and already a man although he had seen but eleven winters! He stood straight, his dark eyes proud.

Upon the kiva altar lay the robe of the White Buffalo. Kwani's heart constricted as she looked at it.

Two Elk spoke. Kwani noted that Two Elk's hair hung loose in ceremonial fashion. Dark eyes under a jutting brow sought one person and then another as he gestured, rattling his many bracelets. He wore a new deerskin robe ornamented with bear claws and painted symbols of his rank. Kwani wondered which of his two new mates had made it for him. Since his first mate, Aka-ti, had entered Sipapu, Two Elk set to rejuvenate the powers of his aging manhood by acquiring two new young mates, a luxury few men could afford. Speaking, he rambled on for some time before Kwani focused her attention.

"It is known, it has been told, how Acoya, son of our Building Chief and of She Who Remembers, was kidnapped by Pawnees and lived among them in a manner to reflect pride upon us. It is known also that he promised his father to finish building our city according to the plan of the Above Beings and the command of the Morning Star."

Kwani looked at her son standing beside the tall Chief who was made taller with eagle feathers in his headband. Compared to the Chief, Acoya looked small, young, vulnerable, even in his pride. Yet he was assuming a man's responsibility. She had not yet asked Yatosha to be his uncle; she must do so at the first opportunity. She glanced at Yatosha and he returned her gaze as if he had felt it. For a moment Kwani was taken aback; she had not expected that intense glance.

Two Elk continued, "It is known to all that the robe of
the White Buffalo that belonged to Acoya's father now belongs to him and to the Turquoise Clan—and, therefore, to
all of us in Cicuye. But it will be in the keeping of Acoya
and his sons and their sons until the robe of the White Buffalo is no more."

Two Elk lifted the robe from the altar. Chanting, he held
it to the Six Sacred Directions. Still chanting, he draped it
over Acoya's shoulders. It was too large and had to be folded
over at the top so it would not drag on the floor.

Two Elk intoned, "With this robe do you accept the responsibilities the White Buffalo bestows?"

"Aye," Acoya said firmly. He seemed small and defense-
less enveloped in the heavy robe like a papoose in a blanket.
But all knew without question that his responsibilities would,
indeed, be fulfilled.

Kwani sat where she often did on the small boulder overlooking the city, the valley, and the mountains beyond, tier
on tier. She thought again of Tolonqua. She did not know
how much she could miss anyone; her spirit felt ragged and
torn as if chewed by an animal. Here, where they used to
sit together, Tolonqua seemed close. Often she felt his presence, and longed to hold him and be held. But he was not
there and never would be again.

The breath of Wind Old Woman blew cold from the
mountains and heavy, dark clouds hung low. Harvesttime
with all its activity and rousing celebrations had come and
gone. Corn, beans, and squash were stored for the winter.
Kwani had worked with the others, but while Tolonqua was
gone and Acoya missing, part of her was gone, too. She had
worked as if in a dream.

When Antelope told her that Acoya was captured by Pawnees, Kwani knew in her bones it was true.

Antelope. A Chosen One. But . . .

Should she be my successor? Could Antelope bend her
strong will, her fiery spirit, to the will of the Ancient Ones?

I must think about that.

Kwani rose to return to the city.

"Ho!"

It was Yatosha coming, walking with his long stride. He
waved, gesturing for her to wait. She had been planning to
talk with him about being Acoya's uncle. Now would be a
good time. She sat back down and watched his approach.
He had aged since their days at the Place of the Eagle Clan,

and especially since Tiopi's death. She felt a pang of sympathy; losing a beloved one was more painful than anyone knew who had not experienced it.

He stood looking at her for a moment. His eyes were solemn in his round, plain face creased with time and sorrow.

They exchanged greetings and he sat down, making it a point to leave a respectful distance between them. He said, "It is good that Acoya and Chomoc are brothers."

"Yes."

Yatosha sat silently, twisting his hands, gazing into the distance. Finally, he turned to Kwani.

"As you know, it is Anasazi custom for a man to take his brother's wife as mate when his brother has entered Sipapu." He looked away. "Your mate had no brother. . . ." He twisted his hands again and turned to her. "I am Chomoc's father and Acoya is his brother." He blushed painfully and blurted, "I want to be Acoya's father, too."

Kwani was surprised; she did not expect this. She met his earnest gaze.

"You are asking me to be your mate?"

"Yes. I—" He took her hand, looking at it, turning it over in his. "I have long loved you."

She withdrew her hand. "You honor me, Yatosha. But—"

"But you cannot love me. I am not man enough?" His voice was bitter.

Kwani said gently, "You are not Tolonqua."

He turned away and she put her hand on his shoulder. "You are a man any woman would be proud to have as mate. I shall never love another as I loved him who is gone, but—"

He turned to her, eagerness igniting his eyes. "But what?"

"I would be honored if you would be Acoya's uncle."

He rose abruptly and stalked away. He stopped, turned, and looked at her, then came to stand before her.

Kwani gazed at him, into the place behind his eyes where his spirit dwelled. She saw his loneliness, his grieving, his love and need for her.

He squatted before the boulder so that they were face-to-face.

"It is true I am not Tolonqua. It is also true that your only blood relatives here are your children. You are a woman alone, an Anasazi among Towas, with no legal ties, no blood kin."

"But I am She Who Remembers."

"Will that be enough to protect you? Legally, all you own could belong to Tolonqua's sister, Anitzal. Your dwelling, your food, everything."

Kwani knew Yatosha was right. These people had the right to cast her away, leaving her alone in the wilderness as she had been before.

But she was She Who Remembers.

As if summoned, the silent voice of the Old One, who was She Who Remembers before her, whispered in her mind.

We, who are of all womankind, have much to endure. We send you this man to ease your path. Listen to him.

Again Yatosha took her hand and held it in both of his. For a while he did not speak. The wind gusted and a snow-flake drifted down, swirling.

He looked into Kwani's blue eyes and was held by their power. He swallowed. "Allow me to be your mate, your protector. I shall bring you the finest furs, the first corn, the best wood for your fire, and meat in abundance." He paused, and swallowed again. "I will not share your sleeping mat until you wish for me to do so."

He loved her. But she did not, could not, love him. Should she accept his offer, nevertheless?

"I must think about it."

"I shall wait."

More snowflakes fell.

Yatosha pulled Kwani to her feet. "Come."

Together they descended the rocky path back to the city. As Kwani leaned on his strong arm it was as though Tolonqua walked with them.

Kwani stopped, feeling the unseen presence. It was as if Tolonqua wanted to tell her something.

Yatosha looked down at her with concern. "You are tired? Shall I carry you?"

She met his worried gaze through snowflakes drifting. "No. It is just that for a moment, I felt Tolonqua's spirit—"

He nodded. "Aye. I do. Often."

Because Tolonqua saved Yatosha's life, they were brothers. Did Tolonqua want his brother to take Kwani and her children as his own?

Kwani pondered this as they approached the city. Tolonqua's city, strong and beautiful, touched with snow.

She stumbled on a snow-covered rock. Yatosha caught

her and held her to him. Kwani felt the pounding of his heart. Slowly, he released her.

"Kwani . . ." His voice was husky.

She smiled up at him through falling snowflakes and tucked her arm in his.

Antelope and Acoya needed a father. She needed a mate and protector. She knew that was what Tolonqua wanted, what he and the Old One had tried to tell her.

Was it what she wanted?

Or did she want to be a woman with no mate, no protector, no one to comfort her in her sorrowing times? Or to hold her in the night?

Other men would want her, perhaps. But this man shared her past; a bond existed between them. He was second in command to Long See and would become Hunting Chief one day. He was Eagle Hunter. He had been chosen to assume major responsibilities in ceremonials and was consulted frequently on matters of policy regarding newcomers. Respected, admired, he had become an important personage in Cicuye. And he loved her. . . .

As they stood there among the snowflakes, a look in her blue eyes made him catch his breath. He pulled her to him and held her as if he could never let her go.

She said, "I will make your corn cakes."

An exultant laugh rumbled in his chest and Kwani felt the thump of his heart.

"I will plant the corn."

Together they approached Tolonqua's city, strong and beautiful, bequeathed by the Morning Star.

The first snowfall! Acoya wandered alone by the river, watching the flakes fall to dissolve in the stream and be swept away. He had to be alone for a while to think about things. His new responsibilities. And White Cloud. She had been among the crowd welcoming him. He saw her standing there in her white robe embroidered with bone and shell beads. Her luminous eyes met his and Acoya's heart jerked. Then she disappeared and he had not seen her since.

Rounding a corner, he stopped abruptly. A porcupine foraged under a pine tree. In daylight! These were nocturnal creatures; he wondered if it had fallen from the tree. It was a fine specimen with long quills. Acoya had his bow and arrows with him as usual, but he left them in their case and stood watching.

The porcupine glanced up. Little eyes in the blunt,

rounded head saw him, and the fleshy snout twitched. Instantly the animal lifted its quills, stamped its back feet, and waggled its stubby tail from side to side in ludicrous warning.

Acoya laughed. As if insulted, the porcupine whirled around and presented its prickly backside. With tail thrashing it backed up toward Acoya, chattering its teeth as if to say, "Touch me and you will regret it."

The best quills Acoya had ever seen were interspersed with long, fine hairs. Those hairs could be used in weaving, and Kwani would make excellent use of those quills. Acoya removed his bow from the case slung over his shoulder and reached for an arrow.

"No!" A girl's voice.

He whirled. White Cloud stood there.

The porcupine scurried up the pine tree and disappeared among the branches.

Acoya gazed. She was more beautiful than ever in her white, beaded garment reaching her knees, and the beaded moccasins adorning her feet. A red feather in her hair quivered in the wind.

White Cloud glanced up into the pine tree. "He is a friend. I bring him bark and berries sometimes. That's what he was looking for."

Acoya smiled. "Then I am glad he still has his quills."

They stood facing each other. Acoya gazed into her luminous dark eyes, a night sky ablaze with stars, and was swept into infinity. He reached for her hand and heard himself say, "Come. I will show you my secret place."

Hand in hand they followed the stream. When they reached the hidden pool, he led her to the bank and they stood under the winter limbs of the cottonwood tree. The snow had ceased falling. All was still.

White Cloud's lips parted as she stared, enchanted. "Ah!" she sighed.

"Look!" He pointed to the shaman high in his holy place. "He sees us. This is where I come to be alone. And to be with him. Nobody knows but you."

She turned to him. "Why do you bring me here?"

"Because . . ." How could he express it? "Because I want us to be together, to share. . . ."

"I want that, too." She put both arms around him and kissed his cheek.

He held her close, feeling the softness, the warmth of her, and his heart swelled. He would be her protector, her mate, to plant her corn, and bring her meat and furs, and share her sleeping mat. Only White Cloud. Forever.

The shaman's hands were raised in blessing.

Or was it in warning?

PART 4

▲▼▲▼▲▼▲▼▲▼▲▼▲▼▲▼▲▼▲▼▲▼

THE HOUSE OF THE SUN

▲ 57 ▼

Antelope kicked her foot against the wall. "I hate this place!"

White Cloud raised her head in mild surprise. She had finished changing the shredded juniper bark in her moon-flow band and was adjusting it between her legs and around her waist.

"Why?"

"Men send all of us here because they are afraid of us. Of it." She pointed to the red-soaked bark in a basket on the floor. "I don't like staying here until the flow stops. I want to stay in my own home. With Chomoc."

"But—"

"I know. They say nobody can touch us or something bad will happen. We can't touch anyone, not even our mates or their weapons because then they can't hunt; the animals will smell our blood." She flipped a braid disdainfully. "How can they smell blood on a man if no blood touches him, I ask you? If our moonflow blood doesn't harm us, how can it harm someone else? Can you tell me?"

White Cloud shook her head and peeked out the door to see if anyone overheard. "You mustn't say such things!" Her lips quivered nervously.

"Why? Because it's the truth? Chomoc can't drink from my cup or eat my food because it invites evil spirits. Ha! I do not believe it!" She paced the room impatiently. "I want to go and bathe in the river, but I can't, even if I bathe away from them downstream. We have to stay here in this miserable hut behind the city by ourselves for four days—"

"But we are safe here. No man, not even an enemy, would touch us."

"But I want to be touched. By Chomoc." Antelope slid her hands over her bare round breasts. "These want Chomoc, too."

White Cloud nodded. "I know. You want your mate and

I want mine. But it's only a few days.'' She smiled her shy smile. "Acoya will be glad when I return.''

Antelope looked at White Cloud sitting on the floor mending Acoya's moccasin. She had grown to beautiful womanhood; no wonder Acoya wanted her. But there was something odd about her, as though she had not grown inside. She was bent over her work, her long, dark lashes hiding her eyes. Antelope sat beside her.

"What kind of a lover is my brother?''

White Cloud's smooth cheeks flushed a becoming pink. "He makes me—'' She paused, seeking the word.

"Throb?''

"Oh, yes.'' She lay the moccasin in her lap and gave Antelope a questioning glance. "Why did you take Chomoc as mate? You always told me that no man part would ever enter you—''

Antelope laughed. "I know. I know. That was before—''

"Before what?''

"Before I learned what I did not know before.''

White Cloud looked puzzled and bent again to her work.

She doesn't know what I'm talking about half the time, Antelope thought. She stretched out on a sleeping mat and let her mind drift like a leaf on a stream, floating into the past. Outside, a group of young girls ran by, laughing. One of them could have been herself . . . long ago. When she had hurried down to the spring, knowing Chomoc was there, waiting.

He had filled her water jar for her as he always did with an air of manly virtuosity, but instead of lifting it to her head, he had set the jar on the ground and took her hand.

"Come. I will show you something.''

She hesitated. "What?''

Other girls were climbing down the path and Chomoc jerked her hand impatiently. "I don't want anyone else to hear. Come.''

Antelope followed him to a secluded spot among the trees. He sat on a fallen log and pulled her down to sit beside him.

"Look.''

From a pouch at his side Chomoc removed a bracelet of glistening white, a circle sliced from a large shell from the depths of the Sunset Sea. It was a thing of rare beauty and great value, traded from hand to hand over vast distances.

"Ah!'' Antelope sighed, and reached for it.

He jerked it out of reach. "Not now. Tonight. I will be here, playing my flute, telling you to come to me."

"I want it now!"

"No. Tonight."

Antelope stamped her foot. "Now!"

"No."

Antelope jumped up. "I hate you!"

"You love me."

"I do not!" She whirled and ran back to the stream.

His voice followed, "My flute loves you, and so do I."

Antelope pretended not to hear. The girls at the spring whispered to one another, giggling, as Antelope lifted the jar to her head and stomped back up the path.

She had had her first moon flow. She was a woman now. How dare he treat her like a child! Showing her that bracelet and then jerking it away!

I hate him.

That night she lay sleepless. It was spring and Earthmother was in bloom, perfuming the air with subtle seduction. On the highest part of the ridge, young men sang of their longing to Moonwoman. Flute serenaded from the courtyard, but none entreated as sweetly, as provocatively, as Chomoc's, calling from among the whispering trees.

I hate him.

Antelope turned restlessly on her sleeping mat. I cannot hate him. I cannot.

"Come!" the flute called.

Antelope rose and tiptoed to Kwani's door. She and Yatosha were asleep and Acoya was in the kiva. Antelope put on her robe, tied it over her right shoulder, slipped on her moccasins, and crept quietly outside.

Ladders had been pulled up for the night and warriors patrolled the rooftops. They smiled at one another as Antelope pushed a ladder down and disappeared over the wall; they heard Chomoc's flute and remembered their own serenades and secret trysts. A warrior stationed himself near the ladder, guarding; word had come that Apaches were seen eastward on the plains. If an enemy was sighted, the warrior would shout a warning and when all were safe inside the city he would jerk up the ladder.

Moonwoman's silvery glow illuminated the steep path to the spring and the trees beyond. Antelope paused at the spring.

Why am I doing this? she asked herself.

The water reflected Moonwoman's wavering face. Was she smiling?

"Come!" the flute called. The magical sound floated in the air like a fragrance, lingering, enticing.

My flute loves you and so do I.

I shall get the bracelet.

Antelope entered the moonlight-dappled darkness among the trees and followed the flute's call to where Chomoc sat on the fallen log. When he saw her, he jumped up and held out both arms.

Antelope stopped. "I greet you," she said politely, head high.

"My heart cannot rejoice when you are there and I am here." He sat down and patted the log beside him. "You have come. Now sit with me."

Not waiting to see if she would, Chomoc lifted the flute to his lips. Again came the magical sound, enticing, lingering, entwining itself around her heart. Chomoc played with his eyes closed, swaying, compelling the flute to speak for him.

Antelope remembered how he played for her when she was small and they sat on golden leaves beneath the trees. The years rolled away and she felt like a child again, enchanted. She came and sat beside him.

For a while he ignored her and continued to play. Then he lay the flute down, and turned to her.

"Do you know what the flute was saying?"

"Yes."

"Ah. Then . . ." He leaned to kiss her.

His music had made her tremble and her heart beat hard. She turned away abruptly so he would not see. "It said that now I am here you will give me the bracelet."

He chuckled softly. "Of course."

From the pouch at his side he removed the bracelet and held it to the moonlight. It glistened with Moonwoman's own glow.

"Give me your hand."

Antelope held out her hand and he took it in both his own. He held it for a moment, then bent to kiss it as he slipped the bracelet over her wrist and up her forearm, kissing as he went. Antelope pretended to pull her arm away, but he held it fast, and she felt the caress of his lips all the way up to her bare shoulder where the knot of her robe was tied.

She felt his hands untying the knot. She reached to hold

the robe to her, but he pulled it down, exposing her breasts to Moonwoman and to him.

"Beautiful, beautiful!" he crooned deep in his throat, caressing each breast.

This was a Chomoc she had never known. Arousing something within her that had been sleeping all these years. His lips found her breast and she gasped as he caressed each nipple with his tongue, sucking deeply, draining her resistance as a bee absorbs honey.

Antelope felt a surge of exquisite desire. It was overpowering. She gave a small moan.

Chomoc drew her in his arms and held her close.

"My love, my love," he murmured.

Antelope felt his heart thundering and hers matched his, beat for beat. He rose and pulled her up with him. Her robe fell to the ground and she stood before him with only her moccasins and small undergarment shielding her from Moonwoman's revealing glow.

"Beautiful!" Chomoc said again, sliding his hands down her body. His voice had deepened with manhood; it echoed inside her like the song of his flute.

He pushed both hands against her undergarment; it fell to her feet. He pulled her down beside him on the forest floor. As hands and lips made love to her, Antelope felt something inside her opening. Like a cactus flower unfolding its petals among thorns.

"My love, my beautiful love," he whispered, caressing her thighs. As he reached the velvety place moist with desire, Antelope moaned and involuntarily thrust her pelvis upward. Instantly he covered her.

Antelope gasped and cried out as she felt his penetration. He began to withdraw with her cry but she pulled him closer. Deeper.

Above them, the trees swayed as if they, too, heard Chomoc's music.

It was spring.

▲ 58 ▼

More winters, more summers—and trading day again. Kwani stood on the top of the tallest roof, a fifth story recently added, and looked down toward the wide, flat valley east of the ridge where a forest of tipis had risen during the night. Apaches! Come to trade—or so Yatosha had assured her.

"Apaches are good traders," he had said. "We need the tallow and skins and other things they have to trade, just as they need our corn and squash and things we have." He put an arm around her protectively. "Have no fear."

But she did. Apaches killed Acoya's birth father before Acoya was born. Fear and hatred of Apaches would haunt her always.

"I'm ready, Mother. Come!"

Antelope stood below on the walkway outside their door. She balanced a tall basket of corn on her head, holding it with one hand as she looked up at her mother—an Elder now—who had climbed to the highest roof in Cicuye when others her age were content to gather around a fire and gossip.

"Come!" Antelope called again, raising her voice.

"I shall come later. Perhaps."

Antelope flipped her robe with an impatient gesture, and left.

Kwani shook her head. Her twin child had changed little over the years. She was still a passionate firebrand with a tender heart and an indomitable will. Kwani wondered, sometimes, how Antelope and Chomoc got along as well as they did since Chomoc had a dauntless will of his own. Maybe that is why they had no children; their spirits were too strong for a child's to enter.

Kwani sighed, and watched Antelope make her way through the busy city, joined by White Cloud and a crowd of others with baskets and bundles of things to trade. A group of excited, chattering children followed, running and

shouting at one another as they crossed the courtyard. They
raced in circles, jumping up and down with exuberant
whoops. They reminded Kwani of old Chuka, long gone to
whatever Sipapu there was for old dogs.

Friends were gone, too. Dear Anitzal, called by Sipapu
while she slept. Toho, Lapu, and others of Cicuye's boys
were with mates in other villages. Ki-ki-ki and her children
had left with the beadmaker's family, migrating south. Old
Huzipat was gone. And babies, too many babies, gone before their first step. She was thankful both her children lived;
many mothers grieved for small bodies now in Earthmother's arms.

Kwani looked about her at Tolonqua's city. Could he see
how Acoya had kept his promise? Kwani often felt Tolonqua's presence, and sometimes she talked to him. She did
so now.

"Everyone says this is the most beautiful city of all. And
the best planned. Acoya is Building Chief as you were, and
he is still adding stories; this one makes five! He built that
wall all around Cicuye's boundaries, as you told him to.
High as four moccasins."

Kwani's gaze followed the wall reaching the edges of the
ridge. It was tall enough to mark an unmistakable boundary;
breaching it would be an act of war—assuming enemies
could climb the steep slopes where no trees or bushes offered concealment—and enter the city grounds unseen by
sentries or undetected by guard dogs. Also, the wall kept
toddlers and small pets in, and snakes and skunks out.

The single door in the wall opened to a path down the
ridge leading to the camping area. Kwani saw Antelope and
White Cloud walking lightly down the path, balancing baskets of corn on their heads, laughing and talking, ignoring
the wind that whipped their robes like banners.

Kwani watched the steady stream crowding the path. How
Cicuye had grown! Whole villages, besieged by raids, had
migrated to Cicuye, bringing their individual clans, their
skills, their hunters and warriors, to be protected by the size
of the population and by the strength of Cicuye's construction and design. The roof of each story formed a walkway
for the dwellings on the story above. As each story was
added, the dwellings continued to be set back from the
walkway, so that from below the city still looked like a giant
stairway with ladders connecting the steps. One could go
from walkway to walkway by any number of ladders, and
have access to any dwelling without leaving the protection

of the strong exterior city wall—a masterful design executed by Tolonqua and by Acoya with the help of Yatosha as Acoya grew to manhood.

Kwani looked for Acoya and saw him standing near Chomoc who was surrounded by Apaches and piles of trading goods. Chomoc was a master trader, acquiring buffalo hides, tallow, leather goods, and other valuables from people of the eastern Plains, which he traded for turquoise, salt, jars, bowls, and other valuables with pueblos of the west. He was the wealthiest man in Cicuye.

But he was not the easiest to live with. He and Antelope shared her home as was customary, since women owned their dwellings and a man lived in the home belonging to his mate. Chomoc was generous with his wealth and loving attentions to Antelope, but Yatosha chaffed under Chomoc's arrogant assumption that he, rather than Yatosha, was master of the house, an assumption with which Antelope was inclined to agree.

Remembering Chomoc's father, Kokopelli, Kwani sympathized with Antelope's feeling, but all was not well in the relationship between Yatosha and Antelope, and Yatosha and Chomoc.

Kwani sighed. Yatosha was a kind and dutiful mate. If only Tolonqua had lived . . .

No. She must forget.

Drifts of smoke rose from the tipis, and the busy, exciting sounds of trading in full swing wafted with the wind. Kwani wondered what Acoya and Chomoc were acquiring in trade. Acoya had devoted much time to his duties as Building Chief, but he spent many hours with the aged Medicine Chief as an apprentice to take his place when the building of Cicuye was finished and the Chief heeded Sipapu's call. It would not be long; the old man's hearing and one-eyed vision faded and he grew weaker each day.

Kwani knew Acoya would be an excellent Medicine Chief devoted to healing and intercession with the gods. Perhaps that would be a special blessing for his mate, White Cloud. She needed his powers; all was not well with her. It was as if an illness invaded her spirit.

I will not think about that now, Kwani told herself. She threw a blanket over her shoulders and followed the path down to the Apache camp.

She stood uncertainly, hesitating to approach them. They looked harmless enough in their handsome, fringed buckskin robes and beautiful high-topped moccasins. They were not tall people but they were powerfully built, with round faces and deep-set, small eyes under heavy, dark brows. The men wore their hair shoulder length with a band across the forehead and an eagle feather thrust in at an angle; the women had long braids, unadorned. Many wolfish dogs and their travois were attended by the women among a forest of tipis. There was the usual babble of voices, shouts of children, and yapping of dogs. Someone pounded a drum, demonstrating the sound, and rasps and rattles and whistles added their voices. A trading day was in full swing.

Kwani saw Yatosha supervising the bargaining for buffalo hides with one of their many eagles. Since the boys caught the first one years ago, many more had been captured and Cicuye did a brisk trade in eagles and their feathers. Some said it was the intercession of eagles to the Above Beings that had made Cicuye rich and powerful.

As Kwani stood apart, she saw White Cloud bargaining with her basket of corn. She was surrounded by several Apache men, all of whom stared openly at her. She wore a garment of her own creation, a white robe of softest deerskin lavishly embroidered with bone beads dyed in bright colors. Her bead-maker uncle had given her a generous bag of beads before he and his family left to migrate southward, and White Cloud's workmanship was excellent. The robe enhanced her beauty. She seemed unaware of the Apaches' personal interest as she bargained for a fine Apache pack basket.

Kwani watched the men and felt a twinge of alarm. She did not like the way they looked at White Cloud. Swallowing unease, she made her way through the crowd, past the bowls and baskets and blankets and buffalo hides and other objects on display, past the children and dogs and Apache women who watched her with expressionless eyes, and came to stand by White Cloud.

At Kwani's regal approach the men shifted. When she was close enough so they could see the blue of her eyes, they glanced at one another and left, taking the basket.

White Cloud turned to Kwani resentfully. "I wanted that basket! Why did you drive them away?"

"I did nothing to drive them away. They were interested in you, not in your corn."

"I wanted that basket!" White Cloud's lips trembled.

"I know. Let's find another."

They inspected several displays of baskets, but there were none that White Cloud wanted. Then, in the center of the trading area, Kwani saw an Apache man with the basket bargaining in vigorous sign language to Acoya who shook his head.

"Look!" Kwani said. "There's your basket. Go and tell Acoya you would like to have it and let him trade for it.

White Cloud's lovely lips pursed. "But he doesn't like for me to bother him when he is trading."

"He will welcome the corn. And it will please him to trade for something you wish. Go."

White Cloud removed the basket of corn from her head and shoved it at Kwani.

"You go."

"No. It is your corn. You will do it."

"But Acoya doesn't want—"

"If you must have that basket, do as I say. Acoya will get it for you. Go now."

White Cloud lifted the basket to her head and departed reluctantly. Kwani watched her go.

I wish Acoya had chosen another.

But he seemed happy and that was what mattered, after all.

As Kwani stood watching White Cloud carrying her basket of corn to Acoya, Yatosha stepped to her side.

"You brought nothing to trade?" he asked.

"No. I came to watch. I am concerned about White Cloud. Those Apaches—"

"I know. I saw them, also."

Kwani looked up at Yatosha, thinking how the years had marked him. Deep creases lined his cheeks, and many hunting seasons had weathered his square face to a deep bronze.

"Perhaps we should mention it to Acoya."

Yatosha shrugged. "Very well, but really there is no cause for concern."

"White Cloud has her basket now. See?"

White Cloud saw them and hurried over, holding the pack basket triumphantly overhead.

"Look!" she said breathlessly when she was close enough. "I have the basket!" Her face was aglow and her eyes sparkled. "I shall take it home now!" Cradling the basket in both arms, she hurried away, Apache eyes following.

Kwani and Yatosha glanced at each other.

Kwani said, "Let's tell Acoya."

Acoya saw them approaching and smiled broadly. On a

blanket behind him were several buffalo skins. Kwani lifted the corner of one to examine it; it was beautifully tanned.

"White Cloud will make fine things with these," Kwani said. "She is happy with her pack basket."

"I traded some of her corn for it."

Yatosha said, "She tried to trade for it but they were more interested in her than in her corn."

"Too interested," Kwani said. "I don't like the way they looked at her. As if—"

Acoya laughed. "Men always look at her. How could it be otherwise?"

"True," Yatosha said. "She is beautiful. But—"

Two Apaches with buffalo hides swung over their shoulders stopped and signed for trading.

Yatosha took Kwani's arm. "We shall leave our son to his business." He led her away.

Kwani followed him up the path to the city. Unease was a knot in her stomach. Those were not casual glances the Apaches gave White Cloud. They were the looks of men who coveted and intended to acquire.

Danger sounded in her consciousness like the growl of a distant storm.

Evening. Apaches were not allowed inside the city and cooking fires arose from countless tipis in the camp. In the morning, tipis and dogs and people would be gone, leaving refuse behind to be picked over by ravens and field creatures.

Acoya and White Cloud were in Kwani's dwelling for the last meal of the day; they came often to eat because White Cloud did not enjoy cooking and Antelope and Kwani always had something good in the cooking pots. Today it was rabbit and squirrel stew with corn and beans, combined with tasty tubers dug in late spring and stored in a cache in the storage room below.

The family sat in a circle around the cooking pot and savored a delicious aroma while Kwani dipped a wooden ladle into the stew and filled each individual bowl. A basket of corn cakes was passed; each took several and tossed a bit into the fire as an offering of thanks to the gods.

Acoya looked about him at his family—Kwani, Antelope, Yatosha, Chomoc, and beautiful White Cloud with her luminous eyes and sweet body. How the gods had blessed him! He dipped a corn cake into the stew and scooped up a big bite.

Yatosha said, "How did the trading go today, Chomoc?"

"As always." He wiped his mouth with the back of his hand. "I need more macaw feathers and other goods from the south. And turquoise from the west." He scooped a piece of meat from the bowl and chewed with relish. "I want also to cross the plains to the place where men build mountains. It is said many fine things are there. Great cities, different from ours."

Acoya noticed the glance that passed between Kwani and Antelope. Sometimes they communicated without words.

Yatosha said, "You will be leaving on another trading trip then?"

"Of course."

Yatosha frowned. Acoya knew Yatosha resented Chomoc's absences; he felt Chomoc neglected his religious and clan duties to obtain more wealth—a practice certain to bring ill fortune to the clan and to the family. Besides, more wealth was not needed; he had too much already.

Antelope said, "When will you go?"

Chomoc shrugged. "Soon."

"I shall go with you."

There was a thunderclap of silence. Women did not accompany men on trading trips; it was unthinkable.

"No!" Yatosha said. "How can you suggest such a thing? It is not proper."

Antelope's black eyes snapped. "I shall decide what is or is not proper for me to do."

Kwani raised her hand and there was silence. After a moment she said, "Antelope knows I traveled many, many days with Kokopelli, and later with Tolonqua, from the Place of the Eagle Clan to Cicuye—a long journey. Therefore, it is natural that she wishes to travel with Chomoc on his trading journey and sees nothing amiss with it. However—" Kwani paused, looking at Antelope. "It was dangerous, but not so dangerous as now. New tribes from the north are on the plains, and those who come from the mountains of the east for buffalo. They may not be friendly."

Antelope lifted her chin. "I am not afraid. Chomoc will be with me."

"Aye!" Chomoc said.

"I want to go, and I shall!"

Kwani ignored them and continued. "Worse than danger are the discomforts. Stinging insects. Terrible heat and often no water to bathe or to wash garments. Sharp pebbles to puncture the moccasins. Sharp thorns to pierce the body.

Strange people, strange gods, weariness, brutal storms, no shelter. Day after day of terrible solitude, and long nights under a foreign sky. Where darkness closes in . . ." She looked away, remembering.

White Cloud nodded. "I traveled here with my uncle and his family, and it was not far, but it was awful. Don't do it, Antelope!"

Chomoc placed his bowl on the floor and rose. "Acoya, I wish to speak with you." He nodded toward the walkway. "Privately."

Acoya followed Chomoc outside. Moonwoman would not come this night; the only light was from the community fire in the courtyard. Talk and laughter, singing and chanting, children's cries and women's voices mingled with kiva drums and muffled sounds from the Apache camp. No groups of young men sang upon the ridge. Ladders had been drawn up and warriors patrolled the rooftops.

Chomoc led Acoya down the walkway to a quiet spot. He sat and leaned against the wall, and Acoya sat with him. Distant Apache drums throbbed with an eerie, foreboding rhythm.

Acoya and Chomoc sat in silence for a time. Two young boys ran by on the roof overhead, laughing.

Acoya said, "Remember when we fell into the trash pile?"

Chomoc chuckled. "How many years ago?"

"I have lost track."

"Many moons."

"Aye."

Chomoc said, "We have long been friends. We are brothers now. That is why I will tell you . . ." His voice trailed off.

Acoya looked into his friend's face, a pale blur in the starlight. He felt a twinge of concern; reticence was unlike Chomoc. "Tell me, then."

"I want to find my birth father."

Acoya stared in shocked surprise. "Kokopelli? But he returned to his homeland. Everyone says—"

"Maybe they are mistaken. Or maybe he has come back."

"I don't think so. He is a very old man now—if he still lives. Much too old to travel as he did before."

"I must learn for myself."

"How?"

"Follow his footsteps. He is remembered wherever he went. I shall find him."

"If he is there. But—"

"I want to do it, Acoya."

"Why?"

Chomoc looked down his nose. "Have you no intellect? I shall find my father because his blood is my blood. I am he."

"And if he is not there?"

"It will be a fine journey nevertheless. Good trading." He turned to Acoya. "Come with us!"

"Us?' Acoya's voice was sharp. "You will *not* take my sister if that is what you have in mind. And I will not leave White Cloud. Or my responsibilities here. If you go, you go alone."

Chomoc rose. "We shall see." He strode away.

Acoya remained there in the shadows. Foreboding jabbed cold fingers at his spine.

That night, late in star-swept darkness, Acoya lay beside White Cloud, listening to her quiet breathing. They had made passionate love while Apache drums throbbed; now she lay curled up against him, her cheek resting upon her hand.

His heart swelled with love for this exquisite creature— given to him by the Holy Man still standing, arms upraised, in his secret place. That is why White Cloud was not like other women; she was a blessing bestowed by the shaman.

Acoya knew that Kwani and Antelope were troubled by White Cloud's childlike ways, but he found them endearing. He hid his amusement when White Cloud used the shredded cedar bark, reserved for moon-flow times, to feed her endless families of porcupines. At dusk she would leave the city and go into the forest where the porcupines still lived, and wheedle them down from their trees with her soft calls, sprinkling cedar bark upon the ground. They knew her and relished the bark.

Acoya encircled White Cloud with his arm and drifted into sleep.

He woke in the morning to the busy sounds of White Cloud at morning duties, and the aroma of porridge steaming. He had overslept; soon Sunfather would appear. Embarrassed, he said a quick greeting and hurried outside for his morning swim before Sunfather rose. There would be no time for a run.

As he climbed down the outer wall he saw the Apaches were gone. Bits of refuse stirred in the chill morning wind.

Acoya was relieved they had left; now he could shake the feeling of foreboding that had nagged him.

Yatosha climbed out of the river as Acoya arrived.

"You are late!"

"I know. I slept too long."

Acoya dived into the city water and rubbed his body vigorously with both hands. Yatosha climbed up the bank and Acoya admired, as always, the lean, strong body. Yatosha was an old man now, but the years had dealt lightly with him. Only his spirit had aged since Chomoc became part of the household. The old story of a young male challenging the old one for dominance.

Yatosha paused on the bank and stared at the ground. He bent on his hands and knees, looking intently.

"Acoya! Come here!"

Acoya clambered up the bank.

"Look!"

Moccasin prints led to the river.

Footprints were everywhere on the bank where people came to bathe or wash their garments, and children played. Many clans had migrated to Cicuye, and moccasin designs varied. What was unusual about these? Acoya wondered.

"See that narrow heel and how the foot widens at the main joint here, then tapers to a long, pointed toe?"

Realization hit Acoya with a blow. He met Yatosha's gaze. "Apache!"

"Aye. From yesterday."

Acoya bent to study the footprints closely. "But these prints look fresh."

"No. See that tiny line crossing this print here? Mark of a night-crawling insect. The Apache was here before dark. For water, probably." He rose. "Gone now with the others, I'd say."

A great burst of song rose from the city. Acoya and Yatosha had been so intent upon the footprints they had not seen Sunfather's golden rim appear. Now they stood facing him and joined in the singing.

> "Now this day
> My sun father,
> Now that you have come out standing in your sacred
>   place
> From where comes the water of life,
> Prayer meal,
> Here, I give you."

Acoya and Yatosha had no meal with them. They stood naked before Sunfather, offering only themselves.

> *"Your long life,*
> *Your old age,*
> *Your waters,*
> *Your seeds,*
> *Your riches,*
> *Your power,*
> *Your strong spirit,*
> *All these to me may you grant."*

Acoya's song rose high and clear, blending with Yatosha's deep voice as Sunfather rose in majesty.

Neither saw the figure watching in silence among the trees across the river.

▲ 59 ▼

Trading day was over. It was very early the next morning, still dark. Kwani lay alone on her sleeping mat, gazing up at the heavy beams of the ceiling, beams that Tolonqua had smoothed and fashioned with flint tools that Acoya and Yatosha still used. She thought of Tolonqua often even though it was believed one should not remember the dead.

But Yatosha's devotion healed old wounds. Kwani wished for Yatosha's comforting presence when he was in the kiva, as he was now. He spent nights in the kiva frequently, attending to clan business and ceremonies. As Hunting Chief of the Eagle Clan, he was held in high esteem and consulted often by Long See who depended upon Yatosha's experience and wisdom in planning and executing hunts. Also, Yatosha was Chief of the Summer People, those responsible for ceremonial and other events for the entire city during the summer. When the Sun Chief announced autumn solstice, the Winter People would take over; it would be their turn in about two moons. The men's intricate social structure with numerous clans and secret societies kept Cicuye functioning and in harmony with the gods and the universe. But women were excluded; the city's welfare was a masculine domain.

Kwani tossed restlessly. This morning when she woke, the Apaches had gone, but the tension she had felt with their presence lingered.

Automatically, she reached for the scallop shell of her necklace. Usually, the touch of it was consoling, but not now.

Something was wrong.

She pressed the necklace to her, seeking communion with the Ancient Ones once again. She closed her eyes, reaching out with her spirit to those who had gone before. But her spirit was weak; it took long, too long, to reach them.

"Come to me!" she pleaded. "I am troubled."

No reply.

I am losing my powers.

It was time. She must train Antelope to be her successor. Antelope was Of The Gods, and had demonstrated her powers since childhood when she saw Tolonqua's death and Acoya's capture. She was qualified. She had grown up hearing her mother teach; already she knew much. But there was more to learn. Antelope must be trained, and quickly, before she left Cicuye—if that is what she planned to do.

Antelope and Chomoc slept in the adjoining room and Kwani had heard the sounds of their lovemaking. Kwani wondered if Chomoc was like his father in that regard. Listening, she suspected that he was. No wonder Antelope wanted to be with him even on a long and dangerous journey. Kwani remembered how she wanted to be with Kokopelli. . . .

Antelope is of my blood and bone. Of my spirit. But her powers are her own. She has the inner eye.

Far away in the valley a coyote sang to the fading stars. Was it Brother Coyote, her old friend?

She sent her thoughts to him. *I have not seen you for a long time but I greet you, Brother Coyote.*

As if in reply, the coyote's song rose, fell, and died away.

Comforted, Kwani drifted back into sleep, awaiting dawn.

She woke with the song to Sunfather, followed by the Crier Chief's morning announcements:

"The Apaches have gone, and a good trading day was had by all. However, Two Elk and the War Chief remind all people of Cicuye that Apaches have been known to attack a village after trading day. Therefore, all people shall remain inside the city until it is known that Apaches are far enough away so that there is no threat of danger. A party of warriors will accompany women to the spring. All who need water will assemble immediately in the courtyard. This will be the only outside access this day; warriors will stand guard. Warriors will also guard the women's hut for those who must remain there."

A buzz of concerned comment arose. Apaches had come to trade a number of times before and no such restrictions were imposed afterward.

"Why now?" some asked.

"Haven't you heard?"

"Apache footprints by the river."

"But that was when they were here. They are gone now."

"The Warrior Chief is being cautious."

Those who needed water brought their jars to the courtyard. White Cloud was among them, her jar balanced on her head. A group of young warriors led the way down the path, followed by the women, with more warriors in the rear. As they gathered at the spring there was laughter and joking, with references to liaisons formed and intimate events transpiring there.

No one noticed White Cloud slipping away.

As the day passed, men gathered in kivas for weaving, tool making, gambling, and discussions. Some planned a rabbit surround or deer hunt; cold weather would bring deer and elk down from the high elevations to warmer areas. Warriors on rooftops spent long hours knapping arrowheads from chunks of flint as they watched the surrounding area and guarded the ladders. Children and dogs played noisily as always while women attended to their usual chores.

Kwani and Antelope sat at the metate, grinding corn. Women often took their metates to the walkways to visit in groups while they ground their corn, but Kwani had asked Antelope to stay inside with her because there was something important to talk about.

Kwani watched Antelope sit back on her heels and brush her hair back from her forehead with both hands. Antelope ground corn as she did everything else—with zeal—and beads of perspiration dotted her face. They had talked of inconsequential things. Now, while Antelope paused to rest, would be a good time for Kwani to say what was on her mind.

"It is my duty to train a successor, as you know."

Antelope cast her a swift glance. "Isn't that what you have been doing all these years?"

"How?"

"In your teaching. You have always allowed me to be with you in your classes, even when I grew up." She paused, and her eyes sparked. She said hotly, "Why did you do that if it wasn't to train me—"

Kwani regarded her calmly. Sixteen years of coping with Antelope had immunized her to outbursts. "I allowed you that honor because I thought you wished to be there."

"I did. Because I thought that was what *you* wanted."

Kwani was silent for a moment. "Well, perhaps that is so." She bent again to the metate. It was harder than it used to be to push the heavy mano stone to and fro over the corn, but it kept the hands busy while the mind worked.

Antelope sat watching. Finally, she said, "I know what you wish to tell me."

"So?"

"I would be honored to be your successor. But—"

Blue eyes met black ones. "But I have not yet appointed you, have I?"

"You will. The gods wish it."

"How do you know?"

Antelope shrugged. "They tell me."

Kwani regarded her daughter in silence. She felt as if a door had opened. "How?"

"I don't know how to explain it. It's as though they talk to me in my mind. The Ancient Ones."

"Ah."

Kwani felt that she and her twin child had entered the mystical door. They sat looking at each other. Their spirits touched.

Kwani said, "You shall be my successor. Let us begin."

The day passed quickly for Acoya who spent it with the old Medicine Chief in his lodge. They had talked long of the responsibilities Acoya would face when he became Chief.

"You must remember that you have a double totem," the Medicine Chief said. "The White Buffalo for spiritual power, and Bear for healing power. This is a great burden." The Medicine Chief shook his head. "My chickadee totem was demanding enough. But Bear and White Buffalo—"

"I can do it if you will teach me."

The one good eye regarded Acoya with pride and poorly concealed affection. "I shall as best I can. Until Sipapu calls. Come again tomorrow after the morning meal."

Acoya thanked him warmly and bid the spirits farewell. He left the lodge that faced the southwest corner of the courtyard, climbed the ladder to the third story where White Cloud awaited him in the dwelling given to her by the bead maker. As he hurried down the walkway, eager to reach their door, he noticed no enticing cooking smells wafted.

"I am here!" he called as he entered.

There was no reply. White Cloud was not there.

Perhaps she had gone to Kwani's for the evening meal. Acoya glanced around the cooking area for something to take to Kwani as part of the meal. He stopped abruptly. White Cloud's water jar was missing!

Had she taken the jar with her to Kwani's? Then he glanced in the basket where White Cloud kept cedar bark. Some had been left after her last moon flow. Now the basket was empty.

She has gone to feed the porcupines!

Acoya snatched his bow and quiver, ran along the walkway to the ladder and nearly slid down it, then down the ladders to the roof of the first story.

He sped to the back wall where a ladder led down to the outside. The ladder was pulled up and guarded by a grizzled member of the Warrior Society who sat surrounded by flakes of flint knapped from a number of arrowheads arranged in a neat row. Bow and arrows were at his side. He saw Acoya coming and rose.

"I greet you," the warrior said politely in a gruff voice.

"The ladder!" Acoya ordered, lifting one end to shove it over the edge of the wall.

The warrior grabbed it and held it fast. "It is forbidden!"

Acoya hesitated. The warrior was right. And if it was known that White Cloud was out there, a group, maybe a large party, would go after her. She would be frightened. There was probably no danger; the Apaches were gone. White Cloud's gentle, fragile nature needed his protection.

Acoya said, "You speak truly. However"—he glanced around to make certain no one overhead—"I have a special reason to leave." He smiled meaningfully.

The warrior grinned and gave Acoya a knowing glance, but he shook his head. "She will have to wait. I cannot allow—"

"Of course," Acoya said. "I admire your devotion to duty. It should be rewarded." He removed a fine bracelet of turquoise and shell beads and slipped it into the warrior's hand. "It will take but a moment to lower the ladder and you can pull it up immediately. No one will know."

The bracelet gleamed in the warrior's hand, but he hesitated. Orders were orders. On the other hand, this was the son of She Who Remembers and Yatosha, famed and respected hunter and builder, and Chief of the Summer People. He did not care to risk their displeasure. Besides, the bracelet was one no other warrior possessed.

A loud argument arose in the courtyard between a group of older boys over the rules of a game. There were blows, with bystanders joining. Attention was riveted on them—an ideal time to lower the ladder. Acoya helped the warrior slip it over the edge and to the ground. He was down in a flash, racing to the river.

Women had gone for water in the morning; that meant White Cloud had been out all day. Where had she gone?

What was she doing? It would be dark soon, when porcupines feed. Maybe she was there now, near the sacred pool.

He glanced down, and froze. Fresh footprints on the riverbank.

Apache!

Instantly Acoya darted behind a bush and hunkered down. He removed an arrow from his quiver and held his bow in readiness. He crouched motionless, listening.

There was only the sound of the river.

Cautiously, he peered from behind the bush. A flock of ravens settled in a tree nearby. Two wolves appeared like ghosts from the forest, drank at the river, and disappeared among the trees.

No one was near.

Swiftly and silently, Acoya followed the tracks leading to the riverbank. He was nearly at the porcupine tree when something made him stop abruptly. He had an eerie sense of Tolonqua's presence.

"Hide!" a silent voice demanded.

Acoya darted behind a tree, his heart pounding. Nothing like this had happened before. Was it a spirit voice? An omen?

A faint splash!

Acoya gripped his bow as an Apache on the other side of the river swam toward him holding his bow and arrow case overhead. He reached the bank and climbed out.

He was a magnificent specimen, tall and muscular, gleaming wet in the fading light. He gazed intently ahead and padded swiftly up the trail.

Quietly, using every skill Tolonqua and Yatosha had taught him, Acoya followed, staying just out of sight.

His heart jerked. The Apache was heading for the porcupine tree!

Acoya fitted an arrow into his bow. Across the river, a jay flew up, scolding loudly, circling. What disturbed it? Apaches did not travel alone. Was a war party hiding over there? The one who swam across could be a scout.

A shrill scream! *White Cloud's voice!*

Acoya darted from behind the tree and raced up the trail. As he rounded a bend to the porcupine tree, White Cloud screamed again. The Apache slung her over his shoulder like a buffalo robe. She fought fiercely, kicking and clawing. Acoya drew his bow, but could not shoot for fear of hitting White Cloud.

White Cloud saw him "Acoya!" she screamed.

The Apache whirled. He threw White Cloud to the ground and drew his bow in a flash. Too late. He staggered, jerked at Acoya's arrow deep in his chest, and fell, gurgling.

White Cloud ran to Acoya and threw herself at him wildly, still screaming.

"It's all right now," Acoya said, trying to calm her. "We must get back to the city. Fast!"

He grabbed her arm and pulled her after him, running as rapidly as he could. She stumbled after him, sobbing crazily, eyes staring. She stubbed her toe against a rock and fell. Acoya pulled her to her feet.

"Here. Climb on my back."

She did so, her arms clutching his neck. She was bounced up and down as he ran along the trail, but she clung to him, making gasping sounds in his ear.

Acoya scanned the area ahead and on either side as he ran. It was nearly dark; at any moment he expected to encounter Apaches in ambush. When, at last, he reached the path to the city, he set White Cloud down.

"Run home!"

She ran like a deer up the path, her long hair streaming. Acoya followed, glancing behind. As they approached the outer walls, Acoya shouted, "The ladder! The ladder!"

Instantly a ladder was lowered and a crowd gathered. White Cloud scrambled up the ladder, pushed her way through the crowd, and ran to Kwani's dwelling. Kwani was outside and saw her coming; she went to meet her, arms outstretched. White Cloud ran to Kwani and collapsed in her arms, sobbing.

Kwani sat down and held White Cloud to her, rocking. "What happened?"

Acoya hurried to them, followed by a crowd babbling "Apaches!"

Yatosha followed, Chomoc behind him. "An Apache tried to kidnap White Cloud. Acoya killed him."

Acoya lifted White Cloud in his arms. "It's over," he crooned. "It's all right now." Cradling her like a baby, he carried her to their dwelling.

Yatosha and the other Chiefs mingled with the crowd now assembled in the courtyard. A fire blazed and torches were lit. Acoya had told enough of what happened for the basic information to be known. Panic brewed.

The Warrior Chief climbed part way up a ladder and turned to address the people below. He raised one short, muscular arm for silence, his weathered face grim. As he stood facing them on the ladder, feet parted and his grizzled head thrust forward, he reminded Kwani of a mountain ram on a peak.

"Silence!" he roared.

The babble ceased.

"As all know, an Apache tried to kidnap White Cloud, and met Acoya's arrow. The Apache lies where he fell with the arrow in his chest. Other Apaches may have found him by now."

"Ai-e-e-e-e!"

"We must prepare for a siege. Immediately. Women and children will remain in their dwellings and guard them with lances or knives or whatever is available. The Warrior Society and all warriors will assemble here for instruction. Men too old and boys too young to fight will man the roofs as lookouts. Prepare!"

Women grabbed their children and ran to their dwellings.

Yatosha hurried to Kwani. "You and Antelope hide in the storeroom. Underneath the ladder. If an Apache comes down the ladder stab him from behind with this." He unfastened a thong at his waist that held the sheath for his hunting knife, and thrust it at her.

"But you need this!" Kwani cried.

"I have my shield. And arrows and a lance. Another lance is in the storeroom." He pushed the sheath in her hand. "Go!"

Kwani ran to her dwelling, her heart jerking against her ribs.

Apaches!

She flung open the door.

"Antelope!" she called.

There was no answer. Kwani called again, running to the next room. She called down the ladder to the storage room. Antelope was not there.

She must be with Acoya and White Cloud.

Kwani ran frantically to the walkway and climbed the ladders to White Cloud's dwelling. Antelope was there with White Cloud who huddled in a corner, shaking, face blank and eyes wild, as Antelope tried to calm her.

"Mother!" Antelope cried. "I don't know what to do! Help her!"

"I will. But first we must all get to our dwelling and down into the storage room."

"Why?"

"Acoya killed an Apache; they may retaliate with an attack."

For a moment Antelope sat in silence. A faraway look came into her eyes.

"Yes," she said. "They will." She jumped up. "Where is Chomoc?"

"With Yatosha. Hurry! Run to our place!"

Kwani and Antelope scrambled down the ladders, pulling White Cloud after them. They dashed down the walkway to Kwani's door, flung it open, and entered. Smoldering coals in the fire pit cast the only light. Antelope swung down the wooden bolt across the door and climbed down the ladder to the dark storage room.

"Hurry!"

Kwani tried to make White Cloud follow but she collapsed on the floor by the fire pit and clung to the baking stone, babbling. Her eyes dilated with terror. "Apaches!"

Kwani sat close to White Cloud and said softly, "Do not be afraid. I am here."

White Cloud stared blankly, whimpering.

Softly, Kwani began to sing an old song Tolonqua sang to Acoya when he was small.

> *"Lo, the light brown one!*
> *There, in the distant glade*
> *Below, through the opening*
> *In the far, green trees*
> *Wanders the Antelope."*

In the dim light Kwani could see a change in White Cloud; she seemed less frightened.

White Cloud whispered, "Where is she?"

"Who?"

"Antelope."

"Come, we shall find her."

Gently, she pulled White Cloud to her feet and led her to the ladder. "Antelope is down there, waiting for us."

White Cloud hesitated and Kwani gave her a nudge. "Go. I will follow you."

White Cloud climbed down, Kwani after her. Antelope waited at the foot of the ladder and helped them down.

"There's a good place to sit over there."

Antelope led them to a corner where buffalo skins were piled. "Here."

The three of them sat close together in the darkness. The

commotion outside had quieted as women and children hid in their homes and men worked quickly and silently. Dogs had been sent out on the ridge to patrol and warn of intruders.

There were swift footsteps on the walkways and occasional muffled sounds. That was all.

It was quiet.

Too quiet.

▲ 60 ▼

The night was spent in tense preparation. Pipes were smoked, and chants and drums echoed from kivas. More arrows and arrowheads, more lances, and more flint knives were made. War shields were taken from their ornate cases and prayed upon with offerings of corn pollen to the Above Beings. Because it had been a long time since the threat of attack, and since pueblos did not seek war, the shields had not been used for many moons. It was necessary to revitalize their protective powers with offerings and prayers to the gods and to those whose likenesses appeared upon the shields—totems revealed in spirit quests.

As Acoya removed his war shield from its handsome case adorned with shell and turquoise bead embroidery and a luxurious fringe of ermine tails, it was as if he were a boy again beseeching his totems to bestow their protective powers upon the shield he created. Acoya remembered how painstakingly he painted Bear and White Buffalo on his shield, and how he attached his eagle hunter necklace to it so that Eagle would carry Acoya's prayers to the Above Beings for protection and for victory in battle.

For years the shield had slept in its case awaiting the day it would be needed. Now and then Acoya had displayed it on ceremonial occasions, sung over it, and exposed it to Sunfather's holy eye to absorb his powers. But although there had been occasional minor skirmishes with Plains tribes, none had attacked the city. The land was wide, the people few, the game plentiful; room and food enough for all. But now more people migrated through this area where a pass through the mountains led to the vast lands of the west and the buffalo plains of the east. From the north they came, and from beyond the Great River of the South; from the vast plains of the east and the drought-scarred lands of the west, traveling in both directions. Many settled in Cicuye, which had grown wealthy, offering choice booty to any who might conquer it.

From a small village at the base of the ridge Cicuye had grown to a powerful city with three major clans—Turquoise, Eagle, and Cottonwood. All had absorbed immigrants from other clans, combining skills and rituals, increasing strength. Cicuye did not seek war, but it had fine warriors. It would defend itself well.

Acoya fingered the ermine tails of the war shield's case, thinking how their silky softness reminded him of White Cloud. She was with Antelope and Kwani, grinding corn and preparing food for what might be a siege.

Would Apaches attack in revenge for their dead warrior? For booty? No one knew. Guard dogs patrolled the ridge and sentries were on every roof. Watchtowers beside the one gate in the outer wall were manned with warriors and the gate was bolted with a heavy wooden plank. Those women whose moon flow had sent them to the women's hut were herded into the sweat lodge in the hope that the danger of contaminating the city and its people would be lessened if they purified themselves, offered appropriate prayers, and abstained from all contact with others.

Long hours passed. Outside the city all was quiet. Acoya stood on the roof of his third-story home—White Cloud's dwelling—and looked down at the ridge where guard dogs roamed. Nothing seemed amiss. He climbed down to the storage room to check supplies, wondering if he should take some to Kwani since White Cloud would stay with her and Antelope in the event of a siege. He decided upon a basket of corn and a supply of pemmican. Water would be needed, also; he would return for that and for his shield and weapons.

Before leaving, he paused at the family altar to feed his fetish, a smooth stone shaped like a buffalo. He had found it waiting for him beneath a bush near his secret place by the pool, a manifestation of his totem. Also upon the altar was a bear carved from the bone of a grizzly's foreleg, with eyes of obsidian—a rare treasure. Both were adorned with turquoise and shell fastened to their backs with a bit of yucca cord tied around their middles. Reverently, Acoya sprinkled them with corn pollen, chanting prayers of praise and pleas for victory if war came.

War. Would he do honor to Cicuye? To White Cloud? To his Turquoise Clan? He tried to ignore a knot of apprehension in his stomach; he had never faced a siege.

Above the altar, suspended from the ceiling, hung the robe of the White Buffalo in its ornate bundle. He untied the bundle and removed the robe. As he held it before him, he sensed Tolonqua's presence, strong and reassuring. Acoya donned the robe and it was as if his father's arms were around him.

"I shall not be afraid," Acoya said aloud.

Taking the corn and the pemmican, he climbed down to Kwani's dwelling. Yatosha was in the storeroom with Kwani and White Cloud.

Kwani was speaking. "—and I tried to hide from the berdache but he found me and tried to kill me but Tolonqua killed him first. What if—"

Acoya saw his mother tremble. White Cloud was pale, clinging to her.

"There may be no attack. They may not even know their warrior is dead. Whatever happens, I will protect you." Yatosha's voice was calm and certain.

"And I," Acoya said.

Kwani looked at her son standing before them in the robe of the White Buffalo. Her expression softened and she touched her necklace.

"Yes. You will."

White Cloud jumped up and threw herself into Acoya's arms. "I am afraid!"

Acoya comforted her as he would comfort a child. He glanced around the room. "Where is Antelope?"

Yatosha scowled. "Gone somewhere with Chomoc. I told her to stay here!" He shook his head. "She will not listen—"

Kwani said, "She says she knows what will happen. She and Chomoc went to find the Warrior Chief—"

Yatosha and Acoya exchanged glances.

Yatosha said to Kwani and White Cloud, "Remain here. This is the safest place."

Acoya followed Yatosha as he hurried outside. The night was nearly spent; soon it would be pulatla—the time preferred by Apaches for attack.

Acoya, Yatosha, and Chomoc faced the Chiefs and Elders and other men gathered in the courtyard. Antelope stood beside them, the only woman present. Firelight shone dimly on her face as she spoke.

"I have seen, as if in a vision. But it is blurred, like Moonwoman's face in the river. One man comes."

"Apache?" the Warrior Chief asked sharply.

"I do not know. I—" She shook her head. "It is blurred."

There were mumblings and sideways glances at one another. Since Antelope's childhood visions when she saw To-lonqua's death and Acoya's capture it was said that the daughter of She Who Remembers had the inward eye, and Antelope was regarded with awe. But that was many winters past.

"*One man?*" Two Elk asked. "We are to be alarmed by one man who comes? That is what you wish to tell us? Ha!"

There were snickers and murmured remarks. Antelope flushed angrily. "I tell you there is danger!" Her black eyes sparked.

"From one man?" Guffaws.

Chomoc shouted, "You would be wise to listen!"

"Aye!" Acoya said.

Yatosha raised his hand. "Since Antelope warns of danger it would be well for us to look to our war shields. You forget that Antelope is daughter of She Who Remembers."

"A twin child," Acoya said.

"With powers," Chomoc added.

Antelope glared at the Chiefs and Elders with bitter disdain. "It takes no powers to recognize fools!" She strode away, head high.

The day passed without event. Warriors accompanied women to the spring; some made several trips to assure an adequate supply of water. Scouts were sent to search for footprints or other signs, and to bury the dead Apache. They returned saying there were no footprints or other indications that the Apache had been discovered; they buried him in a hidden place in the forest and covered the grave with rocks and leaves.

In the kivas there was discussion.

"Apaches do not travel alone. Why was he there?"

"To kidnap White Cloud, of course."

"Where were the rest of his tribe meanwhile, I ask you?"

"Who knows?"

"Who cares? He is in Sipapu. He—"

"She Who Remembers and Yatosha saw Apaches staring at White Cloud on trading day. One man in particular."

"Ha! All men stare at her. You do, too."

Snickers and ribald comments about White Cloud's charms.

A young warrior recently from the west said wistfully, "I wish one such as she shared my sleeping mat. No wonder the Apache—"

"Dead. Let that be a lesson to you."

Laughter and loud remarks.

Women still remained inside, but children raced up and down the walkways, ready to dart inside for safety if necessary. Boys whooped and shot play arrows, kidnapped girls, were shot by brave heroes, and died with commendable drama.

Antelope sat with Kwani and White Cloud around the fire pit making corn cakes. She flipped one over expertly, let it cook briefly on the baking stone, then placed it in the basket that was nearly full.

White Cloud said, "Did you really see a man coming?"

"Yes."

"Apache?" Her voice quavered.

"I don't know. He was blurred—"

Kwani said, "There is nothing to fear, White Cloud."

"Then why do we have to hide in here? Why are Chomoc and the other men taking out their war shields and getting everything ready—"

"A precaution only."

Antelope raised her head abruptly, gazing toward the door.

"What is it?" Kwani asked.

"He is coming."

"Who?"

"The man."

Antelope hurried out to the walkway, followed by the others. Children ran noisily by, and there were usual sounds from the kivas, but that was all.

Antelope looked up to the sentry on the roof of the top story. He squatted there, knapping flint as usual to pass the time. Now and then he gazed over the landscape, then resumed his work.

"Do you see him?" Antelope shouted.

"Who?"

"A man."

The sentry jumped up, shaded his eyes with his hand, and gazed, turning from side to side. He paused, staring fixedly into the distance. Finally he yelled, "Smoke signals!"

People scrambled to see while the sentry translated for those below.

"A runner comes with news about Apaches! Prepare to receive him."

"Hand up a blanket!" someone shouted.

Immediately, a blanket was handed to the sentry. He swung it overhead and from side to side, signaling "Who are you?"

"Threefingers. Raven Clan."

"Do you come alone?"

"Yes."

By now men had emerged from the kivas and stood watching and listening. Two Elk called, "Allow him to enter."

The sentry signaled reply, and people babbled in excited anticipation.

"News about the Apaches! Now we shall know—"

"Now maybe things can be as they were."

"How foolish! All this preparation for a runner!"

"One man. As Antelope said."

There was a brief silence at this reminder. Finally, a man said, "It is true. She has the inward eye."

"As does her mother."

"Aye."

They turned to look at Antelope who stood immobile, staring into the distance. The smoke signals had ceased, but she remained, gazing.

Kwani went to stand beside her. "What do you see?"

Antelope turned, and Kwani saw her pallor and a faraway look in her eyes. "I am not sure. Danger . . ."

Kwani fingered her necklace. Unease had been with her all morning but she had not mentioned it. Now her uneasiness increased.

There was a shout from the sentry. "He comes!"

"Do not open the city door!" the War Chief ordered. "Let down a ladder."

Kwani watched the runner's approach. He was short and thin, and naked but for a breechcloth and moccasins. He carried no weapons unless they were in his backpack. A ladder was lowered, and as the runner climbed up Kwani saw that the two middle fingers of his right hand were gone.

Two Elk gestured a welcome. "We greet you."

Threefingers bowed in acknowledgment.

"Come to the courtyard so all may hear the news you bring."

As Threefingers turned to follow Two Elk, he confronted Kwani. He glanced into her blue eyes, and froze.

Kwani returned his gaze. His features were small and seemed squeezed together in his narrow face. His shoulder-length hair, sweaty and caked with dust, was held in place by a soiled band across the forehead. He wore no jewelry or feathers, and his breechcloth and worn moccasins were unadorned. Evidently, he was poor—unusual for a runner—and tired and hungry, Kwani knew, and she felt sorry for him until she looked into his eyes.

Animosity looked back.

He knows of me and resents me. Why?

"Come," Two Elk said again, and led Threefingers down the ladders to the courtyard. Kwani and Antelope followed with the others and crowded close as Threefingers stood by Two Elk and the gathered Chiefs, facing the people.

Two Elk said, "Speak now."

Threefingers looked about him, and again his eyes met Kwani's. He looked away.

"I am Threefingers of the Raven Clan," he began in a thin, high voice with an accent; runners sometimes became fluent in foreign tongues. "I bring news from an Apache camp two days' journey eastward. They send greetings and thanks for good trading. They go to hunt buffalo."

A babble of relieved and excited comment was interrupted by Yatosha who stood nearby. He strode forward.

"Did they send you to us to bring this news?"

Threefingers hesitated. He shrugged. "I am a runner." His eyes slid over the crowd. "After I have been given food and water, I shall have more to tell."

Antelope whispered to Kwani, "I do not like this man."

"Nor do I."

But Two Elk gestured grandly. "You shall be my guest." He turned to the crowd. "The Crier Chief will announce when our visitor is refreshed and ready to bring more news."

Two Elk led Threefingers to his dwelling where the Chief's two mates would welcome the runner with choice foods and personal attentions.

The people were reluctant to disperse, so great was the relief that no siege threatened. They gathered in groups, talking.

"If they go for buffalo they will continue east."

"They are four or five days' journey away by now."

"Of course. There is no danger. They are traders and hunters."

"Aye. Women and children are with them."

"Warriors do not take children and women on the warpath."

"Antelope said there was danger. Ha!"

"But she did say one man was coming."

"Runners and travelers come here all the time."

"Aye."

Meaningful glances and snickers behind hands.

Meanwhile, Acoya, Chomoc, and Yatosha were in the medicine lodge for private consultation with the Medicine Chief, the War Chief, and Long See, the Hunting Chief. The door was closed with crossed sticks in front to indicate no admission. Acoya rested his elbows on his knees and listened intently to the discussion. Long See was speaking.

"—and as I said before, he wears Apache moccasins. Raven Clan people do not wear anything Apache."

The War Chief rubbed his chin thoughtfully. "He is a runner. Runners use many moccasins. Maybe he needed more and traded for them."

"But they are badly worn. He has had them for some time."

Yatosha said, "Runners carry extra moccasins in their packs. He may have more. They could be Apache, also."

"That is so," Long See said.

There was a brief silence as they thought this over. If Threefingers carried only Apache moccasins he could have been adopted into an Apache clan and, therefore, be Apache himself.

Chomoc rose. "I shall find out."

"No!" Yatosha said sharply. "You cannot abuse the hospitality of Cicuye nor its Chief by searching a visitor's pack."

Chomoc looked down his nose with poorly concealed disdain. "Certainly not. I shall trade with him; he will disclose the contents of his pack himself."

Chomoc's trading abilities were well known. They pondered this in silence for a time.

Acoya glanced at the Medicine Chief whose head was bowed in thought. The stuffed chickadee, many generations removed from the original, quivered as the Chief raised his head. The turquoise and obsidian eye stared into space as the other eye regarded Acoya.

"Bring to me my crystal."

Acoya rose. It was a great honor to handle the crystal of a Medicine Chief, an honor given only to one long in training. The crystal, in its painted pouch of finest deerskin with beaded turquoise tassels, lay upon the altar. Acoya lifted it reverently and handed it to the Chief.

The old Chief offered the pouch to the Above Beings four times, chanting a prayer. Then he removed the crystal and held it in his cupped hand. It lay in gleaming brilliance, long as his forefinger and polished smooth.

The Chief's lips moved in whispers; his words were for spirit beings and not for others to hear. Acoya knew he called upon the powers of the crystal to reveal mysteries.

Finally, the Medicine Chief lifted his head.

"It is true. I see Apache moccasins."

The men looked at one another. Yatosha said, "He is a spy."

The Warrior Chief frowned. "Maybe not. He could be a decoy. To make us believe something that is not so."

Carefully, the Medicine Chief replaced the crystal in its pouch and handed the pouch to Acoya to be returned to the altar. He said, "Antelope spoke truly. Danger awaits."

The Warrior Chief's stocky frame seemed galvanized with assurance. "We are prepared."

Yatosha shook his head. "We *were* prepared. Now it is believed there is no danger." His square face darkened with concern.

"Already women go to the spring," Acoya said.

"For more than water," Chomoc added.

The Warrior Chief rose. "Sunfather soon departs and the runner will remain in Cicuye this night as is customary. The gate to the city will be closed and barred; ladders will be up and guarded. Every roof will have sentries, and guard dogs will patrol the courtyard as well as the ridge." He placed both hands on his hips and thrust his head forward, face grim. "My warriors will be armed and ready."

"As will I," Yatosha said.

Long See rose. "I, also."

"And I," said Chomoc and Acoya simultaneously.

The Medicine Chief looked at them with his one good eye.

"It is well to be watchful this night."

▲ 61 ▼

The community fire in the courtyard burned low; already people had drifted away to their sleeping mats. Additional news brought by the runner had been disappointing—routine accounts of game sighted and weather reports, but little more about Apaches. Threefingers had told again how the Apaches were headed east, following buffalo. Now was storytelling time, but there was more interest in the unusual number of sentries on rooftops. Few warriors had been at the evening fire; most were in conference with the Warrior Chief.

As the evening drew to a close, Two Elk made the final announcement.

"We are pleased that our guest, the runner Threefingers, has brought us good news of the Apaches. However, as all know, Cicuye must be protected from Pawnees and others. Our vigilant warriors are on duty, as always." He gestured to sentries watching from rooftops. "I thank our guest for his presence and information given us, and invite him to share my dwelling this night. He shall be rewarded with gifts before he departs in the morning. I have spoken."

Acoya and Chomoc stood at the edge of the thinning crowd. Acoya watched Two Elk's grandiloquent posing. The City Chief had grown pompous with age.

Acoya said, "Do you think Two Elk does not realize why more sentries have been added? I can't believe—"

"Maybe he thinks it wise to have Threefingers where he can watch him."

"In his dwelling? With two beautiful mates?"

Chomoc grinned. "A persuasive diversion."

Acoya glanced away. It was not seemly to criticize the City Chief, but Two Elk had become far less interested in spiritual matters than his duties demanded. A dangerous thing for Cicuye and its people who looked to their City Chief to assure divine blessings and protection.

He would speak of something else. "White Cloud will be with Kwani and Antelope tonight. In the storeroom."

"Good. I'll be in the guardhouse by the gate."

Acoya said, "Yatosha and I will patrol the roof of Kwani's dwelling."

Their eyes met. Unspoken affection and trust bound them—friends of a lifetime, brothers now.

The city settled to sleep. Guard dogs lay around the smoldering coals of the evening fire, and soft footsteps of sentries padded up and down walkways. Moonwoman would not be out this night; stars burned brightly in a black sky.

Kwani, White Cloud, and Antelope brought sleeping mats down to the storage room. White Cloud slept, but Kwani lay sleepless with Antelope beside her, listening to footsteps overhead, listening to sounds of the night.

Far away, coyotes sang. A night bird called.

Was it a night bird?

It did not call again. There was silence and footsteps and White Cloud's soft breathing.

Antelope whispered, "I cannot sleep."

"Why?"

"For the same reason as you."

Kwani fingered her necklace, but received no comfort. She heard herself say suddenly, "It is time now for you to become She Who Remembers, my daughter."

She had not planned to say that. Was it the Old Ones speaking?

Antelope sat upright in surprise at the blunt, unexpected announcement. "At last?"

"Yes." Kwani thought, The Old Ones say so. She said, "I shall tell the Chiefs tomorrow. We shall have the ceremony and a feast afterward."

"What made you decide?"

"It is time. Past time," Kwani said.

Yes, Kwani told herself. I grow old, my powers fade. If only I could return to the House of the Sun—

But no, that was impossible. It was her duty to appoint a successor. Antelope was trained and ready; she needed only the blessing of the gods and the Ancient Ones.

And the necklace.

The night deepened. Constellations walked their majestic paths and all was still. Kwani and Antelope slept at last.

Above them, Yatosha and Acoya paced the walkway. Sometimes they paused to speak in whispers.

Yatosha said, "Has anyone seen or heard anything?"

"Not that I know of. There would be an alarm—"

"I know. It is just that—"

"Yes. I feel it, too."

"It is because we are tense that we feel this way."

Acoya nodded. He did not say he knew it was more than that. He felt a mysterious unease, an inner warning. Was it his grandfathers speaking?

Hours dragged by and a cold wind rose, carrying the taste of frost and a change of seasons. Acoya breathed deeply of the clean, sharp air. How good to be alive!

Suddenly, from across the courtyard a whooping yell split the night. A sentry's warning!

Immediately other sentries left their posts to rush to the call. Warriors grabbed their shields and weapons and raced along walkways and across the courtyard. Dogs barked. Women and children staggered from sleep to peer outside and were ordered back. Torches, lit from the smoldering coals, cast weird shadows as men ran by, shouting.

Acoya and Yatosha raced on a walkway encircling the courtyard. The alarm had come from the outer wall facing east, away from the area behind the city where the low wall encircled the ridge and guard dogs prowled. Sentries gathered on the outer wall, talking excitedly.

"What is it?" Yatosha shouted above the babble.

"A ladder. It is gone!"

Men held torches over the wall to illuminate the ground below. It sloped sharply down to where a path led to the trees and the river beyond. No ladder was there.

The Warrior Chief pushed his way through the crowd. He confronted the sentry. "How did this happen? Where were you?"

"I had just been here. The ladder was right there." He pointed. "I continued on my patrol and when I returned, it was gone."

"You were not to leave a ladder from your sight!" the Warrior Chief bellowed.

"But how could—"

"Summon Two Elk!" the Warrior Chief shouted at another sentry. He faced the crowd. "Search the city! See if the ladder has been moved elsewhere! If so, bring it back! At once!"

As people scurried away, Yatosha and Acoya were joined by Long See.

"I don't like this," Long See said. "Somebody has taken that ladder out there so he can sneak back up when he returns. There was no alarm from the dogs. We have either a traitor or a fool in our midst.''

"It could be both," Acoya said grimly.

A piercing scream was followed by shouts. People came running.

"Two Elk is murdered! Two Elk and his mates are dead! Threefingers has gone!''

In the subsequent pandemonium, one name was repeated again and again.

"Threefingers! Find Threefingers!''

Yes, Acoya thought. It was he. The traitor—and a fool if he thinks he can escape punishment as he escaped Cicuye! Acoya gripped his lance, thinking of White Cloud and Kwani and Antelope hiding in the storeroom. Were they safe? He would see.

"Give me your torch," he told Yatosha. "I want to see if our women are safe.''

Yatosha gave him the torch. "Very well, but hurry back!''

Acoya pushed his way through the crowd and ran back to Kwani's dwelling. Sentries and warriors were gathered at the outer wall with the Warrior Chief so none were in the way to hinder his haste. It would be pulatla soon, but now it was still black dark; the torch cast enough light to illuminate the walkway.

He had nearly reached Kwani's door when someone leaped down upon him from the overhang above the doorway. Acoya's lance fell to the walkway, skidded to the rail, and dropped to the courtyard below. He lay on his back on the adobe walkway with the torch still clutched in his hand, struggling fiercely with someone straddling him. A raised knife flashed, but Acoya thrust the torch at the face above him.

Threefingers!

With a snarl, Threefingers jerked back away from the flame and Acoya leaped free. He thrust the torch at him again, but Threefingers kicked it from Acoya's hand. It flew in a burning arc to the walkway behind them and landed by the adobe sill at Kwani's door.

Again, an upraised knife flashed in the torchlight. Acoya leaped upon him, reaching for the knife. The men grappled in deadly struggle, gauging, clawing, growling like animals. Threefingers wrestled Acoya against the rail and in the dim torchlight Acoya saw the snarling mouth, teeth bared with effort.

The knife hovered close. Closer.

Power surged through Acoya in a wild flood. A mighty twist forced Threefingers against the rail. Almost, Acoya had the knife in his hand when, with a loud creak, the rail slumped and Threefingers fell to the floor. In a flash he rolled over and thrust the knife at Acoya's groin.

Acoya darted aside and stomped his foot on the arm holding the knife. As he reached to grab the knife, Threefingers yanked Acoya down to the floor with him.

Grunting, panting, growling, they rolled and wrestled in mortal combat. Hot rage surged in Acoya's blood, bestowing savage strength. This spy dared to invade Cicuye, dared to invade his home and threaten his family, his mate! If it was White Cloud he wanted, Sipapu would have him first!

From behind the city where guard dogs roamed came a sudden commotion, a wild barking, shouts, and Apache war whoops. Bloodcurdling yells.

White Cloud huddled in the storeroom, clinging to Kwani. Antelope crouched under the ladder. She gripped Yatosha's knife in her fist and gazed fiercely up to the hatchway. Sounds of struggle raged.

Then came distant barking, shouts, the terrible war whoops.

"What is happening?" White Cloud cried.

"An Apache attack," Kwani said with calm she did not feel.

Antelope said slowly, "That is Acoya fighting up there."

"How do you know?" Kwani asked. But she knew well.

Antelope gripped the knife in her teeth and used both hands to run up the ladder.

"No!" Kwani cried. "Wait!"

But Antelope disappeared through the opening and Kwani heard her footsteps running toward the door.

Kwani pulled herself from White Cloud's arms. "Stay here! Here, do you understand? Conceal yourself as best you can." She snatched a lance from a corner and headed for the ladder.

"No!" White Cloud sobbed. "Don't leave me!"

"I must. Hide!"

"No! It is dark down here!" White Cloud threw herself upon Kwani. "Don't leave me alone! It's too dark—"

Kwani pulled herself free. "I'll bring you a light. Stay here!"

Kwani reached the door as Antelope lifted the bar that held it closed. They flung open the door to find a burning torch at the adobe sill. Beyond, two men rolled in desperate combat.

Antelope leaped over the torch. "Acoya!" she yelled.

From below came White Cloud's frantic cries. Kwani snatched the torch, propped the lance against the wall, ran to the ladder, and climbed down to the storeroom. White Cloud huddled in a corner, hands over her face, screaming.

Kwani thrust the torch into her hand. "Here!"

White Cloud snatched the torch. "Don't leave me!"

"I must!"

Kwani hurried back outside and grabbed the lance. Antelope was crouched, knife in hand, following the two men as they rolled back and forth on the floor, snarling, clawing, panting in terrible effort. With a shock, Kwani recognized Threefingers. She saw that Antelope waited for Threefingers to get his back in position for her to stab him.

"No!" Kwani yelled. "You might hit Acoya!"

Now the men were on their feet, wrestling for the knife in a grim dance. As they neared the broken rail, Threefingers slashed at Acoya's face. Still clutching the arm that held the knife, Acoya darted aside, but blood on his forehead ran down into his eyes.

Grinning in terrible effort, Threefingers pushed Acoya closer to the broken rail.

Antelope saw her chance. She prepared to pounce.

"Wait!" Kwani cried. "Let me!" She balanced the lance in her hand in the way she had held a heavy spear years ago.

The men fell to the floor at the walkway's edge. Threefingers straddled Acoya, knife in hand. As he raised his arm to thrust the knife, Kwani braced herself, aimed, and threw the lance.

No one noticed a wisp of smoke drifting through the open door.

"We are surrounded!" the War Chief yelled. "To your stations!"

Yatosha raced along the wall toward the back of the city. Apaches fought their way up the steep bank toward the four-foot wall enclosing the ridge. Larger dogs climbed the wall and leaped to attack. Some fell, pierced with arrows. Others downed Apaches, going for the jugular. Those Apaches who made it to the wall were met with more attacks inside. Others, hearing the screams, the growls, the dying cries, retreated down the bank, dogs after them. As Apaches turned to shoot their attackers, more dogs died, writhing.

Apaches who made it inside the low wall met Yatosha's arrows as well as attacking dogs. Two more Towa warriors came running to Yatosha's aid.

"Where is Acoya?" Yatosha shouted above the din.

"We don't know. He may be with Chomoc. Apaches have the ladder at the gate and Chomoc and others are holding them off."

Two Apaches raced by below, dogs after them. One stopped, turned, and aimed an arrow, but Yatosha's arrow found him first. The Apache fell, dogs upon him.

An arrow whipped by Yatosha's ear and lodged in a string of dried squash on the wall behind him. An Apache ducked behind the low wall, then darted up again, drawn bow in hand. A dog and Yatosha's arrow found him simultaneously. Soon, no more Apaches were visible.

"They may have joined others," Yatosha said. "You stay here in case they come back. I'm going to find Acoya."

Yatosha ran down the corner of the walkway to the east side. Arrows whizzed by. He climbed to the second, and then the third story where arrows could not reach, and looked below.

Dead Apaches lay near the gate where the ladder had fallen. Others shot arrows from a distance. Shouts from among the distant trees were echoed by others who stormed the steep banks, met Cicuye's arrows, and were driven back.

Some of Cicuye's warriors lay wounded; others were dead with arrows embedded deep. Warriors shouted, Apaches whooped, dogs barked, women screamed over their dead or peered from windows with terrified children. Enraged women dumped jars of hot ashes down at Apaches below, shouting obscene insults.

Arrows flew everywhere, sometimes falling harmlessly, sometimes penetrating a wall with a *zing*, sometimes plunging into bodies.

The sky paled to dawn. Yatosha searched for Acoya. Where was he? At the gate watchtower with Chomoc? He had gone to see if the women were safe. Could he be with them?

In the growing light Yatosha glimpsed movement beyond the city. An Apache band of perhaps two times ten appeared from behind the trees and ran eastward toward the plains.

Apaches could leave as suddenly as they attacked. Was the battle over? Or was it a ruse?

The wind shifted and Yatosha lifted his head in alarm.

Smoke! Billowing from a door on the first story on the other side of the courtyard!

Terrified shouts. "Whose?"

"Is it mine?"

"Whose?"

"Kwani's! Kwani's dwelling!"

Voices: *"FIRE!"*

Kwani and Antelope stood transfixed, staring, as Three-fingers rose to his feet with the lance quivering in his side. He tried to pull it out, staggered backward against the broken rail, and tumbled to the courtyard below. Instantly dogs were upon him.

Loud cheers followed, mingled with shouts of alarm at the smoke. Women and a few old men had gathered on the roofs above and across the courtyard. They were joined by shouting warriors.

"They're gone! The Apaches have gone!"

"The battle is over!"

There were more cheers and warning cries, but Kwani ignored them. She whirled to see smoke swirling from her door. Her home and everything in it was on fire! With a shock, Kwani remembered White Cloud. She had forgotten White Cloud in her desperation to save Acoya.

She shouted, "White Cloud is down there! In the storeroom!"

Acoya rose unsteadily. His forehead and body oozed red where the knife slashed as they had struggled. "White Cloud—"

"I will get her!" Kwani cried.

"No!" Acoya shouted. With both hands he wiped the blood from his eyes, smearing his face. "I will!"

He disappeared inside. Kwani stumbled after him, choking in the smoke as she followed him down the ladder to the storeroom. The torch lay on a small pile of discarded corncobs, already consumed in flame. Fire had inched greedily toward dried corn stacked against the wall, and the pine posts reaching to the low-beamed ceiling of cedar shakes and rushes topped with adobe. The stack of corn blazed fiercely; already, the room was unbearably hot. Black smoke billowed.

White Cloud crouched beside a sack of pemmican, coughing and choking in the smoke. Her eyes were blank in an empty, eerie stare. When she saw Acoya's bloody mask of a face she jumped up.

"Go away!" She began to scream again, scrambling over sacks to get away, knocking over bowls and baskets, spilling their contents to the floor, coughing in the smoke.

Acoya stumbled after her. Smoke sucked his breath and stung his eyes; tears flooded, blinding him as he tried to see. He fell to his knees where smoke was less and searched frantically for White Cloud. He found her huddled on the floor. He rose, grabbed her, and slung her over his shoulder. She fought like a wild thing, kicking, screaming, clawing. He groped his way through the smoke to the ladder. Kwani followed, trying not to breathe the acrid fumes billowing upward through the hatchway. Her eyes stung and watered; she gasped for breath.

"Hide! Hide!" White Cloud screamed.

Kwani swallowed the terror rising within her and tried to calm White Cloud. "Don't be afraid. It's Acoya."

"Hurry!" voices called from outside. "Come out!"

A loud cracking and hissing sound was followed by a bright flare as the fire reached the cedar shakes and attacked them in a ravenous burst of flame. Choking smoke enveloped Acoya and Kwani as they fought their way up the ladder. Flames licked hungrily at their arms and legs. They stumbled dizzily toward the door.

Kwani tried to see the door through the smoke. Fire leaped up through the hatchway with a roar.

Voices outside called, "Hurry! Hurry!"

Kwani tripped and fell, choking. Acoya was ahead and did not see her. Kwani tried to rise, but smoke had sapped her strength and she fell to the adobe floor that was already hot. She tried to cry out but smoke gagged her. As she lay face down on the creaking floor, she fought to breathe, to rise, and could not.

The necklace pressed against her. Kwani felt it there. She closed her eyes, and with all her strength she called to the Ancient Ones.

"Help me!"

Yatosha's voice. "Kwani! Where are you?"

"Here!"

His figure loomed through the smoke. He scooped her in his arms and staggered, zigzagging, to the door. A babble of exclamations welcomed her as hands reached for her.

Acoya, bloody and haggard, held White Cloud in his arms. She had stopped screaming and her head lay upon his chest like a sleepy child's. He carried her away, murmuring.

People gathered in confusion and panic. There had never been such a fire at Cicuye and they didn't know what to do.

"The whole city will burn!"

"Everything!"

"Gods help us!"

"What can we do?"

The Warrior Chief stepped forward. He gestured commandingly. "Water! Bring water! Cool the adjoining walls!"

Women scurried for their water jars. Above and below, jar after jar of water poured on roofs and walkways, floors and walls of adjoining dwellings.

"Get water down the hatchway!" the Warrior Chief shouted. "Kill the fire!"

Chomoc pushed his way through the crowd. "I will do it. Give me water!"

"No!" Antelope cried. "It is too dangerous!"

He grabbed a jar, crouched low, and disappeared into smoke.

"Come back!" Antelope shouted. She tried to follow but was pulled back.

There was sudden silence as people waited anxiously.

"Chomoc!" Antelope screamed.

A figure appeared through the smoke at the door. He held out an empty jar.

"More water!" he croaked.

"No!" Antelope cried.

Another jar was thrust at Chomoc. He disappeared again.

The Warrior Chief organized a relay, and jars were sent hand-over-hand to prevent the fire's spread. Stone walls helped to keep it at bay.

"Cool the walls!"

The walkway began to tremble.

"Get away!" Yatosha yelled. He backed up, pulling Kwani and Antelope with him. Others scurried out of the way.

"*CHOMOC!*" Antelope screamed.

Chomoc staggered out the door. Yatosha grabbed him. "Get away!" he bellowed.

With a rumbling growl and a great billow of smoke, the adobe floor of Kwani's dwelling collapsed into the storeroom below, partially smothering the fire. A pit of smoking, burning rubble lay where her home used to be.

"Ai-e-e-e-e-e!" the people cried.

Kwani stood silent and numb.

"More water!" the Warrior Chief shouted. He grabbed a

jar and threw water through the door to the pit below. Others did the same.

"Keep water coming!" the Warrior Chief yelled.

Now that the Apaches were gone, people lined the path to the spring, filling jar after jar. Flames died and smoke sullenly diminished as flames licked the last morsels of what had been Kwani's home.

Yatosha enfolded her in both arms. "I shall build you a finer one."

Kwani could not reply. It was as though Tolonqua lay buried in that smoking debris.

Nobody noticed that pulatla had come and gone and Sun-father was already high.

▲ 62 ▼

When it was realized the battle was over and the Apaches were defeated and gone, shouts of triumph mingled with keening cries of women and children who lost sons or mates or fathers.

Burials began immediately. Because the top of the ridge was rock hard, resisting digging sticks, families buried their own as best they could, some under the floor of their dwellings, some beside walls. The only ones given an official ceremony were Two Elk and his mates. All the priests of the Medicine Society joined in digging a grave wide enough for the three of them. Two Elk wore his finest ceremonial robe with his jewelry; with him were his shield, his weapons, and his finest bowl that was broken to release its spirit. His mates were each given a bowl and personal jewelry for their journey to the underworld. As they were enfolded in Earthmother's body, the Medicine Chief chanted the ancient burial prayer songs and wafted them to the Above Beings with smoke from his ceremonial pipe.

Cicuye's City Chief, its principal leader and intercessor with the gods, was no more.

Bodies of Apaches, some mangled by the dogs, were piled and burned. All afternoon the stench blew with the west wind gusting over the ridge. Bones would be discarded on the trash pile.

Acoya stood on a high roof, looking over the city he and his father had built. Sunfather's late light shone on his dark hair, which now hung in two sleek braids. Dark brows hovered like birds soaring over darker eyes; high cheekbones and firm mouth in a round face bespoke his Anasazi ancestors, those ancients within his blood. A slash marked his forehead; several were on his chest and back. The Medicine Chief had applied poultices and the wounds felt better. A cut on his arm still oozed red, but Acoya ignored it. His thoughts were of his city. Tolonqua's city.

It had held under attack.

But Cicuye's leader was dead and now his city was a body without a head. A new City Chief, a strong leader, must be found quickly. Already there was conflict among the clans as to which clan would provide the new City Chief, and who that man might be. Internal conflict could destroy Cicuye as fire destroyed Kwani's dwelling.

Acoya had stared numbly at his childhood home with all its beautiful contents still smoking sullenly. Because the fire had consumed the dwelling and belongings of She Who Remembers, people said it was a bad, dangerous omen. What had she or the members of her family done to enrage the gods? Were they to blame for the Apache attack? There were bitter arguments, especially among newcomers who had been accepted into the Turquoise Clan of which Two Elk was Chief as well as being City Chief. Some gathered in the courtyard, protesting.

Spotted Dog, young Chief of the Eagle Clan, was loud in bitter accusations. "Apaches killed our City Chief because the Warrior Society protected the ladders and left our Chief unprotected!"

"With a murderer—"

"Who knew he was such?" a Cottonwood Clan member shouted. "Except maybe one who has powers to see the unseen."

"Enough!" Spotted Dog hissed, reaching for his skinning knife. "You insult She Who Remembers! You insult my clan!"

Acoya had heard the shouts and arrived just in time to push the two men apart.

"Allow the gods to speak," Acoya said. "This is a matter for the Medicine Chief. Go now to your duties."

The group dispersed with sullen murmurs.

Now, as Acoya stood looking over Cicuye, his heart was heavy. Never before had the city on the ridge been attacked. Some of his people were dead, others wounded. Were the gods punishing Cicuye? If so, why?

People stared in shock at what had been the dwelling of She Who Remembers. A fearful omen! What had so infuriated the gods as to destroy Kwani's home and send Cicuye's brave warriors to Sipapu? Had the Medicine Chief been neglectful of his duties? He was, after all, of an age when Sipapu called. Perhaps he had forgotten important prayers or sacrifices. There were whispers. Maybe it was time for a successor. Had he not been training Acoya?

Trouble brewed, Acoya knew. How could he avert it?

* * *

Kwani thought of Acoya as she sat in the dwelling White Cloud shared with him. Now she, Antelope, Yatosha, and Chomoc would also have to live there until their own place was rebuilt. It would not be an easy time.

It is my fault.

Kwani thought of the smoking rubble that had been her home. She could not bear to linger there, looking. All was gone: Tolonqua's feather bowl and rare feathers, all her treasures, and fine cooking and sewing things, all the corn and squash and pemmican and jerky, all of Antelope's prized belongings, and Chomoc's rich store of valuables—everything gone.

It is all my fault. I gave White Cloud the torch.

They were destitute, dependent upon the people of Cicuye for all their needs. She and Yatosha and Antelope and Chomoc. Once the most wealthy people in Cicuye, now they had nothing.

Humiliation bit deeply. The proudest family in Cicuye was poorest of the poor.

Except for Tolonqua's box of valuables, perhaps? It had been in a stone-lined cache sunk into the floor. Yatosha and Acoya would search for it. Meanwhile, Chomoc would want to be off on another trading journey to begin to rebuild his wealth. Leaving Antelope to wait restlessly for his return.

Did she still want to travel with him? Kwani wondered anxiously. But no. As She Who Remembers, Antelope would remain in Cicuye, of course.

Or would she?

Kwani sat cross-legged beside the fire pit. There were no coals; White Cloud was not there. She wandered aimlessly about the city, her lovely face serene, her eyes blank. Antelope was with her, explaining to the curious and concerned that White Cloud's spirit had summoned her childhood self. Kwani wondered what Acoya thought of White Cloud's strange behavior. Did he love her so blindly that everything she did seemed normal?

Kwani hugged her knees and gazed into the cold fire pit. Her only garments were those she wore, and they had been soiled and torn in the effort to escape the fire. She needed a bath in the river. She needed assurance that the destruction of her home was the mysterious will of the gods and not due solely to her stupidity in giving the torch to White Cloud.

She needed Tolonqua.

Yatosha was a good mate, loving and strong. Kwani cared for him, but no one could fill the emptiness Tolonqua left. When he died, a place in her heart collapsed like her burned dwelling.

Kwani was ashamed to discover tears flowing. This was no time for weakness! Much was to be done. She rose, smoothed her soiled garment, brushed her hair back with both hands, and strode outside, her still-slim figure erect.

Already there was a bustle of activity as rubble from her dwelling was piled in baskets and dumped into the trash pile. But Acoya was not there, nor were any of the Chiefs and Elders. Kwani glanced at the kivas in the courtyard and saw a red banner fastened to the top of the ladder of the Turquoise Clan's kiva. She had been so involved with her own feelings she had overlooked Cicuye's situation. A new Chief must be appointed.

Two of her young girl students approached, heavy baskets of rubble balanced precariously on their heads.

"I greet you, Honored One," they said politely in unison.

"My heart rejoices. I thank you for your help. How is it going?"

"I found something," one girl said. She held the basket on her head with one hand while she reached inside her garment with the other. "Here."

It was the little stone bear fetish from the altar, black with soot but otherwise unharmed.

Kwani took it in both hands. "I thank you," she said with a quaver in her voice. "This is a good omen!"

The girls smiled with pleasure and went on their way, their young bodies swaying under the baskets.

Kwani clasped the fetish in both hands and held it close.

Acoya sat in silence in the kiva with the Chiefs and Elders. They were discussing him and it made him uncomfortable.

"I urge you to consider," the Medicine Chief said earnestly. "Now that our City Chief has entered Sipapu we cannot delay longer to choose another. Meanwhile, I have trained Acoya to be my successor—"

"Exactly," the Crier Chief said. "And a fine one he will make, I am sure. But what we need now is a City Chief, a strong leader—"

"We need one who is strong in his relationship with the

Above Beings," Long See said. "Our Warrior Chief leads our warriors—"

"And you lead us, the hunters," Yatosha added. "As well you know, a City Chief carries crucial responsibilities as head of all Chiefs, all clans, but his greatest duty is to assure our city, our people, blessings of the gods." Yatosha paused, and dark eyes in his square face sought every man. "I remind you that Acoya possesses the robe of the White Buffalo bequeathed to him and to us all by our former Building Chief." He paused to glance at Acoya who sat in silence, head bowed. "He is qualified."

The Sun Chief rose, his long, bony frame unfolding. He stood in dignified silence for a moment, his deep-set eyes lowered in thought. Then he spoke, his resonant voice solemn.

"Our Medicine Chief trains a successor because he knows his call to Sipapu will come as it comes to us all. That is good. We shall need a Medicine Chief when that time comes. Having been trained by a master, Acoya will, indeed, be qualified. But meanwhile, we must consider well the necessity of choosing a City Chief. Keeping in mind that no man can be two people, both City Chief and Medicine Chief. I have spoken."

He sat down to murmurs.

Again Yatosha rose. "We must keep also in mind that Acoya has two totems, White Buffalo for spiritual power, and Bear for healing power. Does this not indicate he is chosen Of the Gods for a special destiny—to be both Medicine Chief and City Chief?"

The Warrior Chief shook his head. "That is too great a responsibility for one man."

"Aye," some said.

"Not for that man," Long See said. "Let us not forget he is son of She Who Remembers. He has powers of his own. Why else did the White Buffalo inscribe his likeness on the sole of Acoya's foot?"

As Acoya sat listening to the discussion that followed he grew increasingly restless. They talked about him as if he were not there. Nobody asked him if he wanted to do what they wanted. It was as if he were a gambling piece to be tossed by first one, then another, to determine his fate and his future.

He raised his hand for silence. Then he rose.

"I am honored to be considered for the duties you may wish to bestow upon me. However—" he swallowed, and continued, "however, as Building Chief and son of She Who Remembers I have an obligation to rebuild my mother's dwelling. Therefore, I respectfully request that any decision involving me be postponed until rebuilding is complete. Also, I must confer with my totems, with the Above Beings, and with my own spirit before I can accept whatever honor you may choose to bestow."

He bowed respectfully, and climbed the ladder to the courtyard.

There was a shocked silence. A man was expected to do what was best for the group, the community, regardless of personal feelings and preferences.

"The gods will punish him," a grizzled Elder intoned.

Heads nodded sagely.

"Let us now discuss who will be new Chief of the Turquoise Clan."

This was a matter for the Turquoise Clan alone. Those of the Cottonwood and Eagle clans rose politely and departed.

It was time for the evening meal. White Cloud followed Antelope and Kwani down to White Cloud's storeroom to inspect the dwindling store of corn. The corn had not been sorted regularly nor spoken to encouragingly and some was unusable.

Kwani picked up a decaying ear and looked at White Cloud who returned her glance with utter serenity. Always, Kwani and Antelope had cared lovingly for their stored corn—gone now, all of it. Not much of White Cloud's store of cedar bark remained either; beside it was the small basket to carry bark to the porcupines. Most of the storage area was taken by Acoya's prized possessions and his trading goods which were not much, but were the only valuables left. His golden necklace, ceremonial objects, and the robe of the White Buffalo were sacrosanct.

Antelope said, "There is cornmeal upstairs. I'll make corn cakes and then we can come down here and save what corn we can."

Kwani nodded. Six people must be fed before the next harvest; they would have to depend upon donations. She cringed at the thought. Maybe she had been too proud and the gods were teaching humility.

Antelope gave her an understanding glance. "Chomoc will trade for whatever we need." She looked away. "But he must have something to trade with. I don't know what. . . ."

"He is son of Kokopelli. He will find a way," Kwani said. She thought of Yatosha. How must he feel to be dependent upon others to replace the fine crop of corn lost in the fire? Or the squash and pemmican and jerky? "Yatosha is a fine hunter. He will go for buffalo, deer, antelope. We shall have much again."

"Of course," Antelope replied, smiling. She turned to speak to White Cloud, but she was not there.

"She took her basket," Kwani said, pointing. "Gone to feed the porcupines."

Antelope frowned. "After what happened last time, I am surprised."

"She does not remember what happened. Her spirit leaves her body as in a dream."

"When will it return?"

"Only the gods know." Unconsciously, Kwani fingered her necklace, seeking wisdom.

Antelope reached out and took the scallop shell in her hand. "When shall I wear this?"

Kwani felt tears sting her eyes. "When once again we have our own altar in our own dwelling. The necklace will be consecrated for you there."

Together, they went upstairs to prepare the evening meal. They worked easily as a unit, each complementing the other.

Kwani said, "Has White Cloud returned?"

"I don't know."

"Maybe she is with Acoya," Kwani said.

For a moment Antelope sat in silence, gazing into the distance. "No!" She jumped up. "I shall find Acoya." She ran out and Kwani heard her footsteps retreating.

Acoya was supervising the last of the cleanup from what had been Kwani's dwelling when Antelope came running. Before she was close enough to speak, Acoya knew something was wrong.

White Cloud! He knew it instinctively.

"What?" he asked when Antelope arrived breathlessly.

"White Cloud has gone to feed the porcupines."

"She always does that."

"This time of day?"

It was morning. Acoya shook his head helplessly. "She doesn't realize—" He gazed at Antelope with unspoken misery. He had not allowed himself to face the truth; he had kept thinking—hoping—that the shock of the fire and Apache attack would wear off and White Cloud would become herself again.

He turned to the men lifting out the last of the black and crumbling beams. "I go to find White Cloud."

"I shall come with you," Antelope said.

"No. I go alone."

Antelope looked at Acoya, searching the secret place behind his eyes. Her gaze softened.

"Go, Brother." She turned abruptly away.

Acoya watched her climbing the ladders to his dwelling on the third story. How much like Kwani she was in form and grace! But none could compare with White Cloud.

Swiftly he followed the trail to the porcupine trees, several now as the porcupine population grew, protected by the Turquoise Clan. It was the time of year when Earthmother adorned her garments with golden leaves. Most had fallen— a time of rabbit drives and hunts for elk and deer. Already Yatosha and Long See had departed with the hunters for game. It was a fine morning of deep blue sky and cold breezes, and Acoya trotted briskly along the trail. At any moment he would meet White Cloud returning.

Or so he kept telling himself.

He reached the porcupine trees. She was not there.

"White Cloud!" he called.

No answer.

He called again, gazing in every direction. What was that speck of dappled brown among the golden leaves on the path ahead? He ran to see.

It was White Cloud's basket, overturned.

Instantly Acoya crouched, searching for footsteps. There were only White Cloud's, heading for his hideaway place ahead.

Like a deer he ran, following the trail, foreboding upon him. At the sacred pool he pushed the trailing branches aside and darted around the boulders beside the stream.

She was there. Floating face down against the opposite bank, her long hair streaming, her body moving gently up and down with the water's motion.

"White Cloud!"

He flung himself into the water and swam, thrashing, to the bank where she lay, her hair caught among exposed tree roots holding her against the tug of the stream. He turned her limp body over. Open, staring eyes gazed lifelessly. A fish had nibbled at her lips.

Acoya clutched her wet body to him. He threw back his head in a shrill, wavering, heartbroken scream.

The shaman looked down with his arms upraised in solemn acknowledgment of the will of the gods.

▲ 63 ▼

Kwani plodded along the path to the city with an arm-load of dead wood. Because much fuel was needed for cooking and heating, everyone who left the city made it a point to gather wood to carry home on the return trip. Even those who were oldest searched among the trees if for no more than a bundle of twigs.

Kwani had been to the porcupine tree to take a bowl of food for White Cloud's grave. Acoya had buried her there, beneath the tree, so that her spirit would enter the tree and be carried by the wind and the birds to the Above Beings. This was not a usual practice and was criticized severely. But Acoya insisted, saying White Cloud was not a usual person. She belonged to the tree and the wind and the birds.

Now Acoya was gone. Where, nobody knew. It was said he had purified himself before leaving. Had he gone to seek a vision?

Yes, Kwani told herself. Her son sought communion with the gods to heal his sorrow. She wondered where he had gone. She wondered if she should seek a vision to assuage her own grieving; it was she who gave White Cloud the torch.

As she neared the city, Kwani heard Chomoc's flute, high and sweet, assuring the people of Cicuye that all was well. "Be happy!" the flute sang. Kwani paused to listen, en-tranced as always, remembering Kokopelli.

How like his father Chomoc had become! He had traded lavishly for this flute before his wealth vanished in smoke. At the time of the fire the flute was with his ceremonial objects in the kiva—all he owned now but for the garments he wore and the shield and weapons he had with him during the attack.

Yet still Chomoc spoke of a distant trading journey.

"What will you have to trade?" Kwani had asked him.

Chomoc assumed the arrogant stance she knew so well. "The gods will provide for the son of Kokopelli."

Now the flute sang its lilting song. Kwani sat to rest on a fallen log; she grew tired too easily these days. She fingered her necklace.

So many winters, so many summers, come and gone.

She had been blessed. But her heart was not at ease. She grieved for Acoya's sorrow, grieved for what she had done to cause it. Fingering the necklace, she sought comfort and reassurance from those who had gone before.

If only she could kneel once more at the House of the Sun . . .

"Ho! Mother!"

Antelope swung down the path. Kwani watched her coming with the wonder she always felt at having given birth to this extraordinary, twin-child creature. Antelope was tall for a woman. She did not walk with modest gait and lowered eyes, but strode like a man, head proudly erect, black eyes challenging. Those eyes, burning like Tolonqua's, could sear the soul. And that body! It seared every man with desire who gazed upon it—as well she knew when she flashed him a glance. If ever a woman was a match for Chomoc, it was Antelope.

"I greet you!" Antelope said, smiling. She sat on the log beside Kwani. "I have news."

"My heart rejoices." As it always did when Antelope smiled that smile. "What news?"

Kwani hoped it was good news about the city. Since the death of Two Elk there were dangerous undercurrents in Cicuye. Some said that the fire was punishment for their City Chief's murder; he should have been protected.

Kwani swallowed and asked again, "What news?"

"Come and see."

Antelope took the bundle of wood from her mother's arms and the two of them followed the path beside the river. It was a cold, cloudy day but children and dogs played noisily in the water while women washed their clothes, slapping them on the rocks, rubbing them with yucca suds. They saw Antelope and Kwani coming and rose in respectful greeting, smiling welcome.

"I greet you," Kwani and Antelope said in unison.

"They wait for you at your dwelling," a woman said.

"Who waits?" Kwani asked.

Antelope shook her head. "Don't tell her! It's a surprise."

The women giggled and returned to their work. Kwani and Antelope made their way up the bank to the city gate, open now as men carried in a heavy beam already smoothed and shaped from a pine log.

"For our dwelling?" Kwani asked.

"You will see."

Women joined them on the path. Some carried water jars, others baskets of clay. A little girl followed her mother, holding a small basket of clay on her head with both hands.

"See?" she said to Kwani. "I am helping, too."

"And so you are," Kwani said.

"I will help to mix it with water," the girl said proudly.

"I know your mother is proud to have such a good helper." Kwani smiled, remembering how Antelope used to enjoy squishing her hands around in clay and water to make whitewash.

When they entered the courtyard Kwani saw Yatosha by her door, supervising busy workers going up and down ladders into what had been the storage room below.

"See?" Antelope said, pointing. "Already they rebuild."

Kwani knew that would be done, so it really was no surprise. But she smiled her pleasure, hurried across the courtyard, and climbed the ladder to the walkway.

Yatosha was helping Spotted Dog, new Chief of the Eagle Clan, and two young men ease a beam through the doorway to another two men inside.

"Back up a bit," he called to the men below reaching for the log. With heaving and grunting the beam was manipulated inside.

"See our new upright beams!" Yatosha said. "Soon our storeroom will have a ceiling, and we shall have an upstairs floor."

He stood there, sweaty and dirty, his tall body still lean muscular as a young man's. Deep creases in his square face arranged themselves in a happy grin. "Come and see!"

He put an arm around her as she stood at the adobe door sill and leaned over to look down. Ashes and debris had been removed, and the final foundation beam was being heaved in place. The blackened walls of stone and mortar would be black no longer; two women busily spread whitewash upon them with both hands. They saw Kwani watching.

"It will be better than before!" one called up to her.

"Aye!" the other said.

Antelope said, "I'll take this wood to Acoya's dwelling, then I'll come and help."

"No! We want only *our* hands upon the walls of She Who Remembers. To give us powers." The woman looked up at Kwani pleadingly. "That is permissible?"

Kwani looked down into the plain face, already wrinkled although she was still young. She was from the north and had been one of Kwani's students years ago. Two missing front teeth were like empty windows, and her hands, smeared with whitewash, were already gnarled. The woman gazed into Kwani's eyes as though to absorb something she saw there.

"Please? Our hands only?"

"If you wish. In the storeroom. Antelope and I shall want to do the walls upstairs." She smiled. "The storeroom is where we keep the food that gives us strength, so perhaps the walls have consumed some of that strength and can bestow it to you." Kwani was not sure she believed that, but something about the woman needed comforting.

"I thank you!"

"And I!" the other woman said happily, dipping both hands into a jar half filled with a gooey, white paste. She slapped handfuls upon the wall and smoothed them with circular motions.

Kwani looked down at the fire-blackened floor to where Tolonqua's box of treasures lay hidden in the stone-lined cache beneath. Yatosha saw her glance. He said, "It is safe. I removed it when no one was looking."

"Where is it?"

"In Acoya's dwelling."

"Was anything burned?"

"I don't think so but I did not open it." He tilted her chin to look down at her. "That is for you to do only."

Kwani met his earnest gaze, and suddenly love overflowed her heart for him in a way never before. He saw the look in her eyes and his own ignited.

"I go to wait for you," she said softly.

"I shall come."

She made her way to the third story, stopping often to acknowledge greetings and expressions of concern for losses in the fire. No mention was made of White Cloud for fear her spirit would return to haunt them, but some asked about Acoya.

"He has gone to seek a vision," Kwani told them.

"Ah. That is good. He will need the help of the Great Spirit and the Above Beings when he becomes City Chief and Medicine Chief," some said.

Kwani did not reply. It was not her place to speak for Acoya, and he had not yet agreed to accept the honor and responsibilities offered. She hid her pride.

As she entered Acoya's dwelling, Kwani saw Antelope seated on a mat of woven reeds in the storeroom. Beside her was Tolonqua's box of treasures. Heat had wrinkled and hardened the lid and the upper part of the box, but it seemed otherwise unharmed.

Kwani unfastened the lock with difficulty; heat had hardened the latch. As she lifted the lid a musty odor rose. Antelope leaned to peer inside. Macaw feathers on top still shone red and green and blue.

Antelope said, "I will get a basket to put them in."

"Look at this!" Kwani lifted out a gleaming necklace of tiny, cone-shaped, iridescent shells from an unknown sea. Each little shell radiated soft rainbow colors.

"Ah!" Antelope sighed, reaching to hold it.

Kwani handed it to her and Antelope held it reverently. "My father traded much for this!"

"And this." Kwani lifted out another necklace, a heavy one of turquoise and obsidian and a dark red stone Antelope had not seen before.

"Ah!"

There was more: a fine ceremonial pipe, beautifully carved; a buckskin pouch of bear claws, bracelets, ear ornaments, a beautiful Anasazi mug of white and black, skinning knives of red and brown and green flint, fine bone awls, notched bone gambling pieces, an elk-horn fleshing knife with a carved and beaded handle, and a small deerskin pouch containing the withered, round sun plant that bestowed visions—the most valuable object of all.

Antelope gazed unbelievingly. She knew her father owned treasures but no one but Kwani had been permitted to see them. She hugged herself in exultation. "Now there are valuables for Chomoc to trade. We are poor no longer!"

Kwani gave her daughter a level glance. "These things belong to me." She began to put everything back in the box.

Antelope flushed, and her black eyes snapped. "But Chomoc needs—"

"We all need. There will be a family meeting to discuss what should be done. Then I shall decide."

"Chomoc is the best trader in Cicuye. He can take one thing and make it bring many things. But he must have something to begin with. Acoya has some trading goods. They are brothers—''

''I know. We shall discuss it in a meeting. If Chomoc says he needs these things—''

Antelope eyes snapped. ''You know Chomoc asks for nothing!''

''I admire that.''

She flushed again and jumped up. ''When he leaves for the trading journey eastward, I shall go with him!''

''You forget. Soon you will be She Who Remembers. You will remain in Cicuye to teach; you are needed here.''

''We shall see. I have waited long and I am not She Who Remembers yet.'' She stomped out.

Kwani sighed, her heart troubled. It was true that Antelope had waited long. But it was more than waiting to be She Who Remembers that made Antelope restless and quick to anger. She longed for a child but none came. Antelope feared she was barren.

The high, sweet notes of Chomoc's flute floated up from the courtyard.

Kwani suspected that Chomoc increased Antelope's stress. She remembered how she had loved Kokopelli when she was Antelope's age. To love such a man was to endure endless uncertainty. He had powers and magical charms; he was admired, desired, and loved by too many other women for his mate not to feel threatened. Especially if she were barren.

How fortunate I was to find Tolonqua. And to have Yatosha now.

As if summoned by her thoughts, Yatosha climbed down the ladder and stood looking at her seated by the closed box.

''I greet you,'' Kwani said.

He smiled. ''You look unhappy. Were the contents of the box damaged?''

''No.''

He sat beside her, his sweaty body bespeaking masculinity. ''Then it is I you are not happy to see?'' He kissed her bare shoulder and slipped his hand under her robe, caressing.

Kwani rose and untied the knot at her shoulder. Her robe fell in a soft heap to the floor. ''You wish to know if I am happy to see you? What does my body say?''

Yatosha's eyes embraced the curves of her, the round breasts still firm and tipped with bloom, the slender waist curving to a lovely swell of hips and the dusky down of her woman part, inviting him. "Beautiful," he said huskily. "Always, always."

She lay down, arms outstretched for him.

"Ho! We are here!" voices called from upstairs.

Yatosha cursed softly. They were supposed to come tomorrow.

"Send them away!" Kwani whispered.

"I cannot. It is a surprise for you."

"Kiss me, then tell them I shall be there."

Yatosha bent and scooped her in his arms. He kissed her mouth, her throat, her breasts.

"Tell them to go away!" Kwani said.

"Ha!" Faces peered down from the hatchway. There were loud giggles.

"Go away!" Yatosha shouted.

"Never mind. Continue. We shall wait." More giggles.

Yatosha cursed again under his breath and set Kwani on her feet. "We must join them. It is a surprise they have long planned. When they have gone—"

"I shall be waiting still."

Yatosha climbed the ladder and Kwani donned her robe, wishing it was presentable. She smoothed her hair as best she could and climbed the ladder, wondering what the surprise was. Yatosha stood by the hatchway. She stood beside him, and stared.

From wall to wall the room was packed with gifts: pemmican, braided strings of corn, dried squash, cooking bowls, mats of woven reeds, baskets, eating bowls, a blanket, a tall water jar—more things, so many that there was no room for people who crowded the door and the walkway, beaming.

"To replace what was lost in the fire," they said.

Kwani was overwhelmed. Tears stung her eyes. "I am grateful." She could say no more.

Yatosha said, "It is because you are She Who Remembers."

Antelope stood in the doorway. She looked at her mother, her eyes eloquent. She came and threw both arms around Kwani as she did when she was a child.

"I am proud to be your daughter," she said.

Wind Old Woman whooshed over the mountain, blowing snow, but Acoya did not feel it. He stood on a high peak of the sacred mountain, gazing into the darkening sky. He wore only sandals. Sometimes, those who came in visions disliked the smell of men so his body was covered with white clay. Nearby, a small fire of spruce needles smoldered, wafting purifying smoke.

For three days Acoya had pleaded for a vision. He ate nothing, drank nothing. He prayed.

"Great Spirit, lean close to this earth you have created and hear me! Sunfather in your holy place, hear me! You, whence comes the Morning Star and the day, hear me! You, Earthmother, merciful to your children, hear me! White Buffalo, Bear, come to me!

"Grant me a vision, I pray! Is it my destiny to be City Chief? Or Medicine Chief? Or both? Grant me wisdom!"

Wind Old Woman whistled and moaned. No vision came.

Darkness fell. It was the evening of the fourth day. In desperation Acoya threw his arms wide and cried from the depths of his heart, "What have I done that you took my mate from me? Tell me so I may make amends. Or take me, also!"

No answer. Even the wind was silent.

Acoya fell to the ground, gazing at the stars.

He slept, and dreamed.

The stars gathered themselves into a radiant cloud and descended, enfolding him in shining mist. A voice—Tolonqua's?— spoke.

"Many grandfathers are in your blood. Listen to their wisdom. Listen . . ." The voice faded away.

"Tolonqua!" Acoya cried. "Appear to me!"

A head emerged from the shining mist. It came close, and closer, staring at Acoya with fierce pink eyes. The White Buffalo!

"I gave you spiritual power!" the Spirit Being roared. "Why are you here, bleating like a calf? My power grants wisdom!"

The pink eyes dissolved in fiery mist, swirling.

The mist turned white. Bear emerged, his great head swinging low. He lumbered majestically to where Acoya lay and gazed down at him. A growl rumbled deep in his throat.

"I bestowed upon you healing power. Heal thyself!"

Acoya woke with a start. He stared up at the stars, remote and indifferent in their vast black dwelling place.

Had he been granted a vision, after all?

As he gazed, a star swooped down across the sky in a swift arc, and vanished.

"Yes!" Acoya shouted. He jumped up, suddenly aware of the cold, of the night, of powers within him. "You came to me!"

Facing east, Acoya sang,

"I thank you, Great Spirit,
I thank you, Holy Beings!
Thank you for powers
To heal, to serve my people.
I shall use these powers
With strength, with honor,
As long as my spirit endures.
City Chief has promised.
Medicine Chief has spoken."

Far below on a flat-topped ridge, the city of Cicuye slept. But one person lay awake thinking secret thoughts. What had She Who Remembers and her family done to enrage the gods? Kwani's burned dwelling and its contents, White Cloud's mysterious drowning, Acoya's attack by Threefingers—surely these were acts of punishment! And what about Antelope, who wanted children and had none?

The Apache attack of the city, with many Cicuye warriors now in Sipapu . . . were She Who Remembers and her family to blame?

Kwani was loved, admired, respected by many—or so it seemed. But perhaps acts known only to the gods merited the punishment.

What could such acts be?

One person lay awake, thinking.

▲ 64 ▼

It was midmorning. A red banner at the hatchway of the kiva still flapped in the breeze; a secret conference was under way and no one but Chiefs and Elders were present.

Because a woven mat covered the hatchway, the interior of the kiva was lit only by flames in the fire pit. Flickering beams illuminated the craggy countenance of the aged Medicine Chief, as he stood facing the men seated before him. Years had taken their toll; the old Chief leaned heavily upon his staff with both hands. His one good eye had grown nearly blind and he thrust his head forward in an unconscious effort to see better. He had been speaking for some time, and continued.

"You have heard our Building Chief declare that the building of Cicuye is completed according to the wishes of the Above Beings and the Morning Star. The rebuilding of the home of She Who Remembers is also finished. However, his duty to the gods may not be complete."

He paused and eased himself on the staff. "It is plain to see I can no longer fulfill my responsibilities as Medicine Chief. But I have trained a successor well. Therefore, I solemnly request that Acoya, son of She Who Remembers, son of Eagle Hunter Yatosha, be accepted in my place. And that he solemnly agrees to assume my sacred duties."

The old Chief eased himself down and Lopat, the Warrior Chief, rose.

"As all know well, our City Chief is in Sipapu. Murdered by Apaches."

Growls of assent.

The Warrior Chief glanced at Acoya who sat cross-legged in silence, head bowed.

"Therefore, a new City Chief must be chosen. You have heard Acoya tell of his vision. Is it not obvious that it is the wish of the Above Beings that Acoya should also assume the responsibility of becoming City Chief? I await your words." He sat down.

For a time no one spoke. The fire popped; sparks drifted upward, dancing.

Finally, an Elder said, "Let the medicine pipe carry our prayers for wisdom."

"Aye."

A pipe was brought from a niche in the kiva wall and handed to the Medicine Chief who accepted it reverently. He offered it to the Above Beings, then held it before him as Acoya, youngest of those present, lit it with a brand from the fire pit. The Chief puffed several times, blew the smoke upward, and handed the pipe to the Warrior Chief sitting beside him who did the same. From hand to hand the pipe went, offering silent prayers each time while the men sat in quiet reverence.

When all had smoked, an Elder spoke. He was thin and bent, and his wrinkled face peered from beneath a worn and ragged hawk-feather bonnet, a prize from long-past warrior days. His thin braids, entwined with hawk feathers, were still black. Vigorous eyebrows, streaked with gray, crouched over eyes alert as a young man's. He squinted at Acoya.

"If you are chosen to be both City Chief and Medicine Chief, are you willing to accept this double responsibility? Think well before you reply."

Acoya gave the Elder a proud and level glance. "I am."

Amid loud murmurs of approval, the Warrior Chief raised his hand. "I shall be honored to serve as Warrior Chief under your guidance."

"And I!" the others said.

The Medicine Chief rose painfully, bracing himself with his staff. He stood looking down at Acoya with unconcealed affection.

"Many moons, many snows have passed since first you came to me as a boy with questions. I answered them all, and you remembered. I knew then, as I know now, you are a Chosen One—to heal, to commune with the Above Beings, to guide our people in ways pleasing to the gods. . . ." Something seemed to be caught in his throat and he paused, turning his head to hide his face. After a moment he continued, "I have prayed long that the gods would grant my wish for you to become my successor. And now—" He gestured to Acoya to come forward.

Acoya rose. He had been listening as though he were someone else, a stranger outside of his body. Could that person, Acoya, do what he was saying he could do—be two Chiefs, the most important Chiefs of all—at once? Now, as he came to face the old Medicine Chief beaming at him with one fading eye, Acoya listened to the drum of his grandfathers in his beating heart.

You can you will you can you will . . .

As he stood before his lifetime friend and teacher, Acoya bowed humbly. "I have come."

"Aye," the old Chief said, his voice trembling. "At last I may give you this."

From within his robe he drew a small pouch of finest white deerskin, painted and fringed with turquoise beads. He offered it to Acoya. "It is yours. Use it wisely."

Acoya accepted it reverently and loosened the drawstring. Inside was a quartz crystal smooth and fine, as long as his little finger. He held it in his hand.

It felt like a thing alive.

"I shall remember the words of my teacher," he said.

Snowflakes fell, clinging like moths to windows and walls. It was afternoon, windy and cold. Acoya sat alone in the medicine lodge, gazing into the fire pit where small flames danced. For a long time he had remained there, seeking to open the mystical place at the top of his head to receive the spirits of the lodge.

Heal thyself.

Around him were all the things the old Medicine Chief had bequeathed to him—bowls and baskets and pouches of herbs and bark; grasses, roots, and berries—each with its own healing powers. But where was the herb to heal sorrow?

Acoya gazed into the empty eyes of the buffalo skull upon the altar. Only dark shadows were there. He looked up at the parafleche suspended above it that contained the robe of the White Buffalo. He needed it now. He removed the parafleche, opened it, and allowed the robe to embrace him.

Kneeling before the altar with the robe around him, Acoya prayed for power to heal himself. He did not know how long he knelt there. Sounds of a busy city swirled outside, but he did not hear; he listened to his inner self, to the silent voices of grandfathers, and to those unseen, the spirits of the lodge. If tears fell, he did not know.

He reached for the small pouch holding the crystal that hung on a cord around his neck. He opened the pouch and held the crystal in his hand. Firelight glinted upon it; it burned with cold fire. He pressed it to his forehead.

"Grant me wisdom!"

He pushed it hard against his heart.

"Heal me!"

Slowly, the pain of sorrow eased. It was bearable now.

Again, he looked about him. The walls, lit by firelight, were a comforting presence. The shelves with their containers of healing substances awaited his touch.

From deep within himself a surge of confidence swelled, a knowledge.

I shall be healed when I heal others.

He rose, the crystal still in his hand.

"I thank you!"

Reverently, he replaced it in its deerskin pouch. Singing a prayer of gratitude, he removed the robe of the White Buffalo, wrapped it in the parafleche, and hung it above the altar.

There was work to be done. He strode outside into the afternoon, eager to meet the day.

Kwani sat with her family around the fire pit in her own dwelling, rebuilt and refurnished better than before. She looked contentedly around her; her own home again! With a beautiful altar where the stone bear reigned. Antelope would kneel there to receive the necklace when she returned from her initiation as She Who Remembers.

Now rabbit stew simmered fragrantly on the coals while Antelope baked piki bread on the baking stone. Acoya was there. When a man no longer lived with a mate he was expected to return to his mother's dwelling. Acoya was glad to do so; White Cloud's dwelling had too many memories for him to endure. He was thinner and the gash across his forehead left a red scar, but he seemed at peace. Already he had assumed his new duties and it was as if he had always done so.

Yatosha said, "There is talk that the Apache attack, and all that happened afterward, is punishment for something we have or have not done. I don't like that."

"There is always talk," Acoya said. "Do not take it seriously." But he was concerned. While Cicuye healed from the attack and the deaths, bad talk festered within the city like pus in a wound.

"Some say it is the eagles. They take revenge because we have not sent any of them home," Chomoc said.

"That sounds like Tookah's talk!" Kwani remembered Tookah's accusations of witchcraft against Tiopi when old

Beaver Paw, Tookah's mate, presumed to carry Tiopi's water jar.

Antelope snorted. "That old busybody gossip is a burr in the sandal. The Apaches attacked because they are Apaches. And they wanted—" Antelope stopped; she should not say White Cloud's name.

"Everyone knows they wanted Acoya's mate," Chomoc said.

Acoya turned away and was silent.

Yatosha scratched his ear thoughtfully. "It is true we have kept all our eagles for their feathers. But it is proper that we should send at least one of them home. It is her right."

Eagles were called "her" because, as everyone knew, they were always female.

"And will allow her to be reborn and lay more eggs and hatch more eagles," Acoya said. He looked at Chomoc. "Shall we do it together?"

Chomoc fingered his eagle-claw necklace. "Of course."

Antelope peeled a thin cake of piki bread from the baking stone and added it to others in a basket. "That won't stop old Tookah. The fire—"

"My fault!" Kwani said sharply. "Everyone knows I gave Acoya's mate the torch."

"Stop blaming yourself!" Yatosha said. "It was not you who started the fire!"

"Let's forget the stupid gossip, and eat. It is ready."

Antelope spread the eating blanket on the floor and set the steaming bowl of stew and the basket of piki bread upon it. When all had honored the gods with a bit of food thrown into the fire, they ate with relish.

When they were finished Kwani said, "As you know, day after tomorrow I shall initiate Antelope as my successor. So it may be well to send an eagle home before the ceremony to carry our prayers to the gods."

"I agree," Acoya said.

Chomoc looked at him. "Let's do it tomorrow. At pu-latla."

"Aye."

Early morning dawned cloudy and cold; soon Earth-mother would sleep under her white blanket. Wind Old Woman blew from snowy peaks and Acoya drew his robe closely around him. Beneath his robe was a prayer stick and a small pouch of cornmeal. Chomoc carried a digging stick, a net, and a strong reed as long as his arm from elbow to fingertips.

They climbed to the highest roof where the eagles were caged. The birds greeted Chomoc and Acoya with anticipation of a field mouse or other delicacy, and were displeased when nothing was forthcoming.

Acoya said, "Tell them they shall be fed well later."

"I already did. But they are hungry now."

Acoya glanced at Chomoc; he was still in awe of Chomoc's ability to communicate with birds and animals. "Offer our apologies."

Chomoc squatted beside a cage and he and an eagle gazed eye to eye. Acoya thought, How like an eagle Chomoc is with that beak nose! And his eagle spirit, wanting to fly free . . .

Chomoc rose. "Our apology is reluctantly accepted."

"Very well. Let us begin."

Acoya opened the cage door. The eagle hesitated, then darted out to be caught by Chomoc's net. Chomoc calmed the bird sufficiently for Acoya to reach through the net and press his thumb hard against the eagle's throat.

"I release your spirit to send it home," Acoya chanted.

The bird struggled for some time before its spirit departed and it was still.

Carefully, Acoya and Chomoc removed the eagle's feathers, one by one, and lay them inside the eagle's cage to be sorted later. Then they carried the naked body—no longer proud and beautiful—down through the city and out to the highest point of the ridge. No snowflakes fell now, but the ridge was sprinkled white.

"This is the place," Acoya said.

Chomoc looked it over. "Do you think we can dig a hole here?"

Acoya pointed. "It looks like it may not be so rocky over there."

They found a place beside a boulder where the digging stick could penetrate. While Chomoc dug a hole, Acoya spoke to the eagle cradled in his arms.

"You are free. Now you shall return to your people in their sky place. They await you."

Chomoc labored, struggling. At last he said, "It is ready."

The hole was not as deep as the old Medicine Chief had taught Acoya it should be, but it would have to do. Gently, he laid the eagle in its rocky grave and placed the prayer stick upon it.

"You are free!" he chanted. "Return to your people. Carry our prayers to the Above Beings to bless our city. Return next year and multiply." Still chanting, he sprinkled cornmeal into the grave. He turned to Chomoc. "Now the reed."

Chomoc nodded. "But first—" He reached into his robe and withdrew a small doll formed of dried grasses and twigs, with a tiny, painted face. He held it over the grave.

"I offer this gift to the Above Beings. Ask them to send Antelope a child."

Acoya watched in silence as Chomoc dropped the doll in the grave and then added the reed, placing it so that it would reach upward and allow the eagle's spirit to climb out and fly home.

Clouds suddenly parted and Sunfather emerged as rocky soil filled the grave. Together, Acoya and Chomoc faced east and greeted Sunfather with the Morning Song.

All that day Kwani and Antelope secluded themselves with Acoya in the medicine lodge, purging mind and body in preparation for the transfer of the sacred powers and responsibilities of She Who Remembers to a successor. Crossed sticks stood at the door; entrance was forbidden.

People lingered as they passed, listening to Acoya's chants to the Above Beings, and to the voices of Kwani and Antelope singing to the Ancient Ones. Acoya's spirit-talker hissed and whispered and cried aloud, and smoke with a strange fragrance drifted through the smoke hole. Never before had such an occasion taken place in Cicuye. Surely, the gods were pleased!

That night Kwani and Antelope disappeared.

"Where did they go?" children asked their parents and aunts and uncles and grandfathers, but no one knew. It was a spirit quest.

Kwani and Antelope stood naked and alone on the highest point of the ridge, alone but for spirits of earth and sky and the sacred mountain outlined against the stars. Silence lay like a benediction over the city below and the valley beyond and beyond. Wind Old Woman's breath was cold but they did not feel it; they drifted with it into a holy presence.

They stood unadorned, opening their pores, their inner selves, to become one with the Ancient Ones.

Kwani gazed into the vast sky bowl. It extended in majesty, dwelling place of the gods. She stretched both arms wide, embracing the unseen. "We are here, Holy Beings!"

"We have come!" Antelope reached high overhead as though to clasp infinity.

"Behold us, Ancient Ones," Kwani cried. "We offer another She Who Remembers into your keeping. Hear us!"

Antelope called, "I am daughter of Kwani, She Who Remembers. Behold her successor! Accept me, I pray!"

Moonwoman had not yet come and the sky pulsed with stars. Silence grew deeper. Wind Old Woman came again and it seemed that mystical music rode with her, and voices sang.

"We welcome you. You are one of us, all who have gone before." The voices soared in splendor, "You are She Who Remembers."

The next day dawned clear and bright with light snow sparkling upon the ridge and adorning the valley. The Crier Chief's rich voice rang out, accompanied by beats on a small cottonwood drum to emphasize the importance of the announcement.

"All people, rejoice! This day Antelope, daughter of She Who Remembers and Yatosha, sister of our City Chief and Medicine Chief, mate of Chomoc, is now She Who Remembers. She will receive the necklace from Kwani in a sacred and private ceremony."

He paused for an impressive drum flurry, and continued.

"After the ceremony, all people, all visitors, will gather in the courtyard for celebration. There will be feasting, singing, dancing, races, contests, and much news and storytelling at the evening fire. Prepare the cooking pots! Don ceremonial garments! Rejoice!"

With a final grand flurry of the drum, the Crier Chief descended to a city already abuzz with activity. Smoke from cooking fires perfumed the air, children shouted with excitement, women called to one another, dogs barked in chorus, and chants and flutes and whistles sounded from kivas as men prepared for ceremonies.

In contrast to the outside commotion, inside Kwani's dwelling there was only the sweet sound of Chomoc's flute as Antelope prepared to receive the necklace of She Who Remembers. Kwani, Yatosha, and Acoya sat behind Antelope as she knelt with her forehead and both hands upon the altar.

Chomoc's flute sang of wonder, of worlds unknown, of mysteries to be revealed. Kwani listened raptly, holding her necklace to her one last time.

"Behold!" the flute sang.

As the scallop shell pressed close, a window seemed to open in Kwani's mind and for a moment she glimpsed something so strange, so terrifying, that she gasped. Animals such as she had never seen, like great dogs, ran like a storm wind, and men in strange, gleaming garments rode their backs! Almost, Kwani cried out, but the window closed and the flute's sweet song soothed her heart.

It was only a daydream.

The music ceased. Antelope raised her head. "I am ready."

Kwani rose to stand beside her daughter. As she looked down into shining black eyes so like Tolonqua's and the face so like her own, she felt she was two people, herself and her daughter—who was also Tolonqua. A sublime mystery.

She said, "Since childhood you have heard me teach young girls what they must know. You have learned. Now, I speak for the Ancient Ones who welcomed you. You have been given a sacred power, to see what is not before your eyes. Use this power wisely. Teach your students well."

Kwani removed her necklace and held it a moment in both hands. It was a part of herself. To be bestowed, now, to another.

"Antelope, herewith is the necklace worn by all who have been She Who Remembers since Earthmother created the first one. Wear it with pride. It is now yours."

Antelope lifted her braids and Kwani slipped the necklace over Antelope's head. The scallop shell with its mystic turquoise inlay found its place between her breasts and rested there.

"I greet you, Honored One," Kwani said. Instinctively, she reached for the shell where it had lain between her own breasts. It was gone.

No longer would she look down into faces like cups waiting to be filled with her wisdom. No longer could she call the Ancient Ones. Never again would she hear the voice of the Old One or the voices of those who had gone before. The necklace was hers no more.

Part of her was gone. Forever.

That night Kwani dreamed. She was back on the mesa at the House of the Sun. She entered the Place of Remembering and the Old One was there, wrapped in her feather blanket, standing by the altar stone. Her eyes, no longer blind, gazed at Kwani with love and infinite wisdom.

"You have learned much," the Old One said, "but one secret remains. Come. I will tell you."

As Kwani approached, the Old One vanished and Kwani stood alone before the altar that glowed with mystical light.

She woke, filled with wonder and a strange longing.

What was the secret?

Yatosha lay on the sleeping mat beside her. Kwani listened to his quiet breathing. Outside, all was still

"One secret remains. Come."

"I shall," she whispered.

Her duties as She Who Remembers were done. Now Antelope had the necklace. For the first time, Kwani felt as if a burden were lifted and she were young again, free of responsibility and care, free to come and go with the wind.

She would return to the House of the Sun.

She would learn the secret.

▲ 65 ▼

Acoya sat in the kiva working at his loom. Weaving was a man's responsibility, and although a City and Medicine Chief was not expected to do such work, Acoya continued to do so because creating something beautiful gave him pleasure and allowed his mind to wander free.

"A fine blanket!" Jaywing said. He had returned to Cicuye from his mate's village after she died in childbirth. Since Two Elk's death he was the new Chief of the Turquoise Clan. Jaywing had acquired dignity and wisdom; he was a good choice, Acoya thought.

"Who will get the blanket?" Because Jaywing and Acoya had both lost beloved mates, there was a bond between them. Such a question was acceptable. A blanket could be a gift for one's bride.

Acoya shrugged. "I don't know yet."

Jaywing fitted an arrow shaft into the groove of an arrow-straightener stone and rubbed the shaft back and forth. For a time both men worked in silence.

Finally, Jaywing spoke. "It is said that since you have become City and Medicine Chief, the gods are pleased and will continue to bestow rich blessings upon Cicuye."

Acoya remained modestly silent, but it was true that all was better in Cicuye than ever before. Rancor and bitterness were gone; people were happy and content. Sacrifices he had made to the Above Beings were acknowledged, and chants and prayers to heal his city had been heard. Of course there was always gossip of one kind or another, and would be as long as people like old Tookah existed, but that was to be expected.

Jaywing continued, "I suppose you know that every girl and woman in Cicuye who has no mate hopes to be chosen by the City and Medicine Chief."

Acoya pushed the shuttle through the bright threads of his loom. "I am not yet ready. Perhaps someday . . ."

"There will never be another as beautiful as she who was your mate."

"No," Acoya answered. In his heart he said "Never!"

"I understand," Jaywing said. "But I am lonely these long nights. I wish for a woman beside me. We are still young, you and I—"

Acoya rose abruptly. "The family waits for me. I must go."

Jaywing watched Acoya climb the ladder and depart. Jaywing shook his head. Acoya was married to Cicuye and to the gods. Little comfort that must be in the night when the blood is on fire.

"I think you should reconsider, Chomoc," Yatosha said. "You can trade your eagle feathers very profitably at the next trading day right here in Cicuye."

"I can get more in the south, along the Great River. There are not as many eagles down there."

"And no snow," Antelope added. "I shall go with you."

"You are She Who Remembers, now." Chomoc glanced at her with pride. "An Honored One. You are needed here and I am not."

"I want to be with you! I—"

"I am needed for trading; I must be where I can trade the best."

"That is so," Yatosha said. "You are the best trader in Cicuye. We are proud you are one of us."

"Aye!" Acoya said.

Kwani looked at her family gathered around her in the cold storeroom. They were down there to take stock of finances, and it was not encouraging. The people of the city had been generous in their gifts, but more was needed, and there was not enough to trade to obtain it all.

Acoya said, "Let us consider what we have to trade. My loom in the kiva has a blanket that is nearly finished. I planned to give this to Kwani, but—"

"You can make another," Kwani said. "Give it to Chomoc."

"I shall give you two blankets when I return," Chomoc said.

Acoya said, "Of course you are to have my share of the eagle feathers."

Chomoc looked down his nose. "I do not take what you need for ceremonies, Brother. Rather, I bring you more."

"A generous thought," Yatosha said. "But let us see

things as they are. A blanket, a few feathers, and what else can be spared will not provide what is needed. The people of Cicuye have been generous. I don't want them to give more. It is—''

"Humiliating. That's what it is!" Antelope's black eyes snapped. "Chomoc will obtain what we need if he has enough to trade with."

Kwani knew this was true. She glanced at the cover of the cache holding Tolonqua's treasures; that would buy everything. But those treasures were all she had left of him. She couldn't bear to part with them—unless it was truly necessary. Perhaps now was the time. Chomoc was a good trader. . . .

She looked at each of them and they returned her glance in silence. They knew what was in the cache and they knew what she was thinking. They waited.

Antelope frowned. "Kwani has said my father's treasures are not for barter. There has to be another way—"

"There is." Acoya reached to remove the lid of the cache.

"No!" Antelope said. "Not my father's—"

"Be quiet for once!" Acoya shot a glance at his sister.

Antelope's black eyes sparked. "I shall speak as I wish."

Kwani shook her head. This brother and sister loved each other; why must they be like two strange dogs snapping at each other?

Acoya ignored Antelope and removed the lid. He lifted out the box and set it before Kwani. "Open it."

Yatosha thrust out his hand. "No, Kwani. Not unless you really want to."

"I do." She undid the latch and lifted the lid. Acoya's golden necklace lay glistening on top.

"I put it back," Acoya said. "Now I shall take it again."

He lifted it out and looped it over his arm. The heavy golden tassels swung majestically as he offered it to Chomoc.

"Trade with this, Brother."

There was stunned silence. The necklace would buy all they needed several times over, but a gift of such rarity and magnificence should remain in the family.

Chomoc looked at Acoya in wordless communication. Finally, he said, "I cannot accept it."

"Why?"

"It is too great a gift."

"You forget."

"What?"

"The flute. You gave your flute for me. Now I give you this to provide for us all."

Chomoc lifted his head in his old arrogant stance, but Kwani glimpsed moisture in his eyes and a look never seen before—humility.

"I accept." Chomoc looped the necklace over his head and let the splendor of it rest upon his chest. "We shall be more wealthy than ever because I, Chomoc, will trade well."

Antelope looked at her brother for some time before she said, "A wise and generous gift, Acoya."

"Aye!" the others said, and it was as if the cold room was cold no more.

Weak sunlight shone without warmth, making the city glisten in its white winter robe. Most people were in their homes or in the kivas, but four old women gathered on the walkway of the third story and sat huddled together in the sun, drinking hot porridge from mugs, warming their hands.

Old Tookah squatted before her door and wagged her head with emphasis at the women seated with her.

"I tell you it is unnatural. All those bad things happening to one family. There has to be a reason." Her flabby face, grooved by wrinkles, assumed a righteous expression. "Of course I do not accuse anyone, especially the family of our City and Medicine Chief, but—"

"Sh-h-h-h!" a woman warned, glancing up the walkway. "She Who Remembers comes!"

Antelope strode toward them, her face a thundercloud.

"I was down there"—she pointed to the second-story walkway directly below—"and I heard you, Tookah."

Tookah blushed. "Then maybe you can tell us why those bad things happened," she blustered.

"Indeed I can."

Antelope stood with legs parted, hands on hips, her eyes searing. "Obviously, we have a witch among us. One who desires to harm me and my family by spreading venomous untruths. While Cicuye tries to heal its wounds from the Apache attack, you try to poison us and our entire city." Antelope loomed over Tookah like an avenging spirit. "This is not the first time your vicious tongue has spread lies, nor the first time you, yourself, have been accused of witchcraft. As I accuse you now!"

"No!" Tookah bleated. "I am not a witch. I am merely an old yaya who—"

"Who lies. Who gossips! I expect an apology to my family and to the entire city at the evening fire this night."

Tookah cringed. "No!" It would be the ultimate humiliation.

"Or you shall leave Cicuye tomorrow and never return. I have spoken." Antelope turned and strode away.

The women looked at Tookah and at one another. Antelope was not like her mother at all.

"You were accused of witchcraft before?" a woman asked Tookah, inching away.

Another nodded. "That was before you came. Tookah said Yatosha's mate—"

"I did not accuse! I never accuse! I have only the welfare of everyone at heart. I—" Tookah's face squeezed into itself. She rose with effort, hobbled into her dwelling, and shut the door.

The three women looked at one another again. She Who Remembers and her family were the most important and revered people in Cicuye. How dare Tookah presume to hint of misdeeds! Everyone said that since Acoya and Chomoc sent the eagle home, and since Acoya had become City and Medicine Chief, the gods favored Cicuye as never before. Like the rest of Cicuye, they had only the greatest love and admiration for these wonderful leaders. They, themselves, had been with Tookah only to warn her against spreading untruths. . . .

As one, they rose to hurry away with the news. By nightfall, everyone in Cicuye knew what had happened and looked forward to evening fire.

Dark closed in. Winter came early to the ridge with its high elevation and no protection from strong winds sweeping across the mountains. The courtyard was the only place where all could be together inside the city for news and entertainment, so even in snowy winter people gathered at the evening fire.

Kwani and Antelope huddled with the others in blankets and buffalo robes, close to the flames, waiting for the Crier Chief to finish his evening announcements.

"Rainfeather, our renowned midwife, announces the birth of three new babies, one boy of the Cottonwood Clan and two girls of the Eagle Clan. Let all rejoice! Chomoc, the trader, will journey south to the Great River; he leaves tomorrow. Long See and Yatosha plan a hunting trip for elk and deer; hunting ceremonies begin at pulatla and will last four days."

There were murmurs of approval. Cold weather brought game down from the high mountains. It should be good hunting; meat and hides were needed. The ceremonies would assure success.

The Crier Chief continued, "All are invited for feasting when our hunters return." He gestured grandly. "Now our esteemed City and Medicine Chief, Acoya, will speak." He cleared his throat respectfully and sat down.

Acoya stood in the firelight with a blanket wrapped around him. Kwani noted with pride the dignity of his stance and the respect in the faces of the people as they looked at him. Since he had become City and Medicine Chief he had changed. He seemed older, more confident, but he was given to silence and introspection and spent too much time alone in the medicine lodge when not busy with duties. Kwani wanted him to take another mate and give her grandchildren, but he showed little interest in the many opportunities to do so. Perhaps that will change with time, Kwani thought. He is young.

He was speaking.

"It is known that one among us has spoken untruthfully of the reason for the Apache attack and subsequent happenings. Antelope, who is now She Who Remembers, discovered the source of these untruths threatening the serenity and welfare of our city."

He paused and looked over the people gathered before him. The wind stirred his blanket and firelight lit his face and the red scar across his forehead. There was total silence as he continued.

"I ask that person to rise."

A small commotion at the edge of the crowd caused people to turn and look. Several old women were pushing another to her feet. "Stand up, Tookah!"

The old yaya stood unsteadily, head bowed, clutching a blanket about her with both hands.

"I have only the welfare of everyone in Cicuye at heart," she quavered. "I meant no harm. If I made mistakes, I am sorry—" Her voice broke. She peered fiercely at Antelope, and pointed a shaking finger. "I am *not* a witch!"

"Then do not behave like one!" Antelope answered.

"Aye!" people shouted.

Tookah retreated into her blanket like a tortoise into its shell. With effort she lowered herself down and pulled the blanket over her head.

Kwani felt a pang of sympathy for the old yaya. Tookah's

mate was long in Sipapu and she had no living kin. Kwani knew well what it meant to be alone. But Tookah's tongue needed taming.

"Festivities will now continue," Acoya announced.

As stories were told and songs sung, Kwani remembered the nights at the Place of the Eagle Clan when Okalake, son of the Sun Chief, sat close beside her whispering endearments. She remembered his embraces as they lay hidden in the secret cave, and his rich voice singing of love at the evening fire. Now Acoya was singing in the same voice.

> *"Your hair is like a rain cloud,*
> *Your lips are berries sweet . . ."*

Are you listening, Okalake? Your son sings.

Closing her eyes, Kwani saw again the beautiful city high in the cliff and the House of the Sun across the ravine. Again, she visualized the Place of Remembering and its sacred altar stone where wonders unfolded.

An overwhelming longing seized Kwani to be there once more, to absorb the stone's mystical powers, to be young again, renewed and reborn, one with all who were She Who Remembers before her.

"Come!" the Old One had said. "Learn the secret."

But it was not to be. The Place of the Eagle Clan was far away; the journey was too long and difficult.

She was the Old One now.

▲ 66 ▼

A moon passed, but Chomoc did not come home. Yatosha and Long See and the hunters had returned in triumph with an elk, three deer, six turkeys, a fat mountain sheep, and enough rabbits and squirrels to make a community stew and three winter robes. There was feasting and many tales of the hunt. Meat was stored, and every part of the animal was utilized including the blood, fat, and sinew. Bones were sorted and those that could not be used for tools or awls or needles or other implements were tossed to the dogs. Turkey feathers were carefully saved to adorn ceremonial objects and to be woven into belts and blankets, and the city resounded with the shrill rejoicing of turkey-bone whistles.

But Chomoc did not return. Kwani sat in her dwelling, making sheepskin winter moccasins for Yatosha and Acoya. Antelope had already made Chomoc's traveling moccasins of buffalo hide that he took with him on his journey. Now Antelope was teaching, and Acoya and Yatosha were busy in the kiva; Kwani sat alone.

Dull light of early winter afternoon shone through the small window opening to the walkway; the door was closed against the cold. Coals smoldered in the fire pit but gave little warmth.

The pieces of sheepskin cut for moccasins lay side by side before her: the foot-shaped soles and the U-shaped pieces for the tops. With the soft, thick fur turned inside, the moccasins would keep the feet warm all winter.

Kwani let her mind wander as her hands worked of their own accord using a bone awl to punch holes for the bone needle and sinew thread to pass through. Because Yatosha's arrow was the first to find the sheep, the skin was his to use as he wished, and he gave it to Kwani. It was a fine one and Kwani shared it with Antelope.

Kwani paused in her work, thinking of her twin child. She had a woman's beauty and a man's strong spirit. Tolonqua's. But she had a woman's heart—which served her well as She Who Remembers and made her an excellent teacher.

It was the man's spirit that caused Kwani concern. Antelope was not like other women, content with a woman's place and a woman's duties. She thirsted to know, to see, to understand; to encounter different people and experience places beyond the plains. But she was She Who Remembers now, and needed here. Loved, respected, admired.

And childless.

Kwani sighed, remembering how she, too, was childless at first. Perhaps later Chomoc's seed would grow and Antelope would give her grandchildren at last. And maybe one day Acoya would have a mate again. . . .

Kwani gazed into the distance, thinking of times past. When she was She Who Remembers and communicated with the Ancient Ones. Now that her powers had faded, Kwani felt an emptiness, a bereavement, a longing more than ever before to be in the Place of Remembering at the House of the Sun, and one with the Ancients again.

As Kwani sat visualizing, there were shouts outside and running footsteps on the walkway. Antelope rushed in, her face radiant.

"Chomoc comes!"

She rushed out again. Kwani wrapped a blanket around herself and followed. What had Acoya's necklace brought? That beautiful necklace of Kokopelli's . . . gone now.

She joined the people who crowded rooftops and babbled excitedly as they gazed into the valley. Chomoc and three other men approached followed by a great pack of dogs with loaded travois. The dogs in the courtyard and within the low wall on the ridge set up a commotion; some jumped the low wall in back and ran to meet the newcomers, followed by Acoya, Yatosha, and others. Antelope stood on the top roof, waving and calling.

"Chomoc! Chomoc!"

Chomoc waved back, circling a blanket overhead, signaling "Success!"

The closer he came, the more astonishing were the loads on the travois, and the more curious people became to learn who Chomoc's companions might be, especially those girls ready for mates. The three men with Chomoc were young, muscular, and had the long, lithe stride of hunters.

The city gate was opened. People on roofs clambered down ladders to the courtyard to shout greetings as Chomoc and the others entered. Dogs with travois were confronted by a frenzy of barks and threats by the dogs of Cicuye. Fights resulted and travois were overturned. The contents of one broke open and objects tumbled to the ground to be scattered by fighting dogs.

In the melee that followed, men brought dogs under control and people rushed to right the overturned travois and retrieve the fallen objects. They inspected them and passed them around for others to see.

"Look at this mug! I have never seen one like it before, have you?"

"Not with such a handle. It has a little frog on top, see?"

"Look at these ear ornaments!"

"Ah!"

"I could use a fleshing tool such as this. Sharp! And a fine handle. See the carving!"

A woman held up a cotton robe. "How fine the weaving!"

The three young men stood by as objects were reluctantly replaced. When at last order was restored, Acoya climbed to a rooftop with the Crier Chief who gave his cottonwood drum a few staccato beats. The crowd quieted.

The Crier Chief announced, "Our City and Medicine Chief wishes to speak."

Acoya faced the people standing below in the courtyard. As Kwani looked at him standing up there with calm authority, she remembered how the White Buffalo approached her in the stream the day before Acoya was born and told her the child would become a great Chief. How true!

The Crier Chief thumped the drum again. Acoya spoke.

"I welcome my brother home. Chomoc, the best trader of Cicuye! The best trader of all pueblos!"

"Aye!" the people shouted.

"I welcome those who came with him." He gestured to the three young men standing quietly aside. "Come up here with me so all may know who you are."

Girls giggled and whispered excitedly as the men made their way to the ladder and climbed to stand self-consciously beside Acoya. He turned to one of the men whose red-brown, muscular arms displayed ornate tattoos from shoulder to wrist. He wore a sleeveless, knee-length deerskin tunic fastened at the waist with an ornate woven belt tipped with long fringe, deerskin leggings, and moccasins badly worn.

"Who are you?" Acoya asked.

Another man stepped forward. "It is forbidden for him to say his own name. I will tell you. It is Fox Tail."

Acoya nodded thanks. "Fox Tail, we welcome you. Tell us your tribe, your clan."

"I am Anasazi. Beaver Clan." He spoke Towa but with an accent.

Anasazi! Kwani was pleased, but surprised. Anasazi did not tattoo in such a fashion, but he was from a clan she did not know.

Acoya gestured the traditional welcome to a member of a different clan. "Where is your pueblo?"

Fox Tail waved a strong arm southward. "Beside the Great River."

Acoya said, "Tell us the names of your companions."

"Gray Hawk and Teal Duck. From my pueblo."

Gray Hawk was short and powerfully built, with a hawk's keen glance. In contrast, Teal Duck was tall and lean with bulging muscles. His long, bony face beamed with good humor. Neither of them were tattooed, at least not where it showed.

Acoya welcomed them and invited them to sleep in his dwelling, although it was obvious other invitations would be forthcoming from girls already offering unspoken enticements.

Travois were emptied and load after load carried into the storeroom of Kwani's dwelling. When the room was too full to hold more, loads were piled in the sleeping room. Kwani and Yatosha stood by unbelievingly. Such wealth!

Acoya remained in the courtyard, but Chomoc and Antelope had disappeared. Kwani wondered what hideaway spot sheltered them.

Feasting followed as mothers outdid themselves in preparing choice dishes for daughters to offer the visitors. Snowflakes fell, swirling in cold wind. Dogs were taken to their shelter behind the city or into the homes of their masters, and the visitors were invited into home after home. Protocol required them to stay first with Kwani and her family, but Kwani sensed their eagerness to accept other invitations. She offered them piki bread, then mentioned that perhaps they should not disappoint others who would also be honored to have them at their fires. Relieved and grateful, Fox Tail, Teal Duck, and Gray Hawk departed with warm thanks.

When they had gone, Acoya said, "Let us see what the necklace provided."

Bundles and sacks and pouches were opened to disclose treasures. There was much food: corn, dried squash, jerky, pemmican, pine nuts, juniper berries—enough to feed the family for two winters if all crops failed and game was scarce. There was a blanket of cotton woven with dog and human hair, and one magically woven of soft feathers and yucca twine.

"Ah!" Kwani exclaimed when she saw it. "It is like the one my mother made."

"Yours, now," Acoya said. He knew of her feather blanket, prized long ago.

There were tools of every kind, some with carved handles of wood or bone. Bundles disclosed three ceremonial pipes with eagle plumes and medicine ornaments, two flutes, tobacco, salt, and six small copper bells from beyond the Great River of the South; bracelets, necklaces, and pouches of shell and turquoise beads. Exotic feathers of red and green and blue and yellow dazzled the eye. There were pigments, medicinal herbs, and strange objects they did not recognize.

"Strong medicine, I think," Acoya said. "Chomoc will know."

There was more. Peyote, the sun plant to bring visions. A magnificent buffalo-horn headdress. And a handsome ceremonial robe for Acoya, embroidered with dyed porcupine quills and intricately beaded.

They sat in awed silence. Finally, Yatosha said, "As valuable as that necklace was, I do not understand how he obtained all this."

Acoya said, "I can guess."

"How?"

"His flute. It persuaded them."

"I believe that," Kwani said.

Yatosha said nothing, remembering too well Kokopelli's flute and Tiopi.

Kwani rose, her blue eyes solemn and intense. "Chomoc returned safely. He restored our wealth—more than we had before. Let us thank the gods."

Raising both arms she threw back her head, closed her eyes, and sang as she had not for a long time. Her voice, high and sweet, soared to the gods.

> *"We thank you, Above Beings.*
> *You returned Chomoc to us,*
> *you restored our possessions,*
> *more than we had before.*

Thank you for your generosity.
Thank you for your great kindness.
We shall honor you each day
as Sunfather rises from his eastern house,
as Moonwoman abides in your holy place,
And stars walk your celestial paths."

Acoya looked at his mother standing there, transported, beautiful, surrounded with an aura of mystery—a priestess from an ancient time. His heart swelled, and he sang,

"I thank you, Above Beings.
Hear my song, hear my prayer.
Grant my mother long life,
Strong spirit,
And fulfillment of her heart's desire.
Hear her prayers!"

Outside, an eagle cried.

The prayers were heard.

Involuntarily, Kwani reached for the necklace, and it was as if it were still there. She knew in her innermost self where wisdom dwelled that her heart's desire would be fulfilled.

She would return to the House of the Sun.

She would learn the secret.

▲ 67 ▼

Chomoc and Antelope lay beneath a willow tree, concealed by trailing green branches encircling them. Nearby, the river sang its seductive song and Wind Old Woman whispered.

Chomoc lay on his side and looked down at Antelope naked upon the mossy ground. She lay with arms overhead, stretched out in beautiful abandon, returning his gaze with eyes that burned dark fire. This mate of his continued to amaze him. From a hesitant young girl she had matured into a woman of passions that equaled, even surpassed, his own. Demanding, unsatiable, challenging—and infinitely satisfying. Chomoc had lain with women in other villages, and even with some in Cicuye, but as compared to Antelope, other women were but sparks to Antelope's fire that blazed and smoldered and blazed again. How he had missed her while he was away!

He bent to kiss her stomach and tease her with his tongue. They had mated several times already, but he wanted to again. With a sound low in her throat, Antelope wrapped both legs around him and pulled him close. She purred like a cougar as he caressed her.

"Give me a child!"

He flung himself upon her and together they lay as one upon the moss and grasses beneath the trailing branches of the willow tree.

Kwani and her family had finished the evening meal. Now they nibbled on pine nuts and basked in the warmth of family and home. All that was missing was children, Kwani thought. Would she never hold a grandchild?

They were gathered around the fire pit in Kwani's dwelling, all of them—Yatosha, Chomoc, Antelope, Acoya, and Kwani—listening again to Chomoc's exciting tales of his travels to the villages along the Great River of the South. Fox Tail, Teal Duck, and Gray Hawk were absent—being feasted by families with daughters seeking mates. The three young men already were welcomed as citizens of Cicuye and were expected to contribute their skills, to enhance evening fires with new stories of which they had many, and to add to Cicuye's population with fine new babies—all of which they seemed more than willing to do, especially in regard to the population.

"—and they eat fish from the river!" Chomoc said. "Imagine!"

They stared at one another in shocked surprise. Everyone knew that fish had been people at one time, and to eat them was devouring one's own kind.

"Then they throw the bones back into the river to become fish again," Chomoc added.

"Were the women beautiful?" Antelope asked.

"Yes." Chomoc took another pine nut, cracked the tiny shell with his teeth, and spit the shell into the fire. "But not as beautiful as you, my love."

"I shall accompany you on your next trip and see for myself."

There were chuckles but Kwani did not laugh; she knew Antelope meant what she said. She gave her daughter a sharp glance. "Will you take all the young girls, your students, with you?"

"Of course not. I shall leave them with you."

"I am She Who Remembers no longer. To teach is not my duty. It is yours."

Antelope flipped her dark braids. "Cicuye had no She Who Remembers before you came and it can do without while I am away."

Yatosha frowned. "It is well that Acoya and others with important responsibilities do not regard their obligations as lightly. The gods will not be pleased."

"I fear that is so," Acoya said.

Chomoc said, "Antelope is a twin, and a Chosen One, as you know. If she chooses to follow me, perhaps it is because that is what the gods desire. Who knows their ways?"

Kwani said, "That is for Acoya to determine. Meanwhile, winter approaches; mountain passes will be blocked with snow. You have traded well, Chomoc, and no more trips will be necessary until snows are gone." She leaned against her backrest and smiled. "It has been long since we heard your flute. Play for us now."

"Aye," Acoya said.

"I shall get your flute for you." Antelope went into the sleeping room and returned with the flute. "Play Kokopelli's song."

Kwani started to object, but did not. Why should she? After all, Kokopelli was Chomoc's birth father. It was just that the song brought memories . . .

> *"Does one live forever on earth?*
> *Not forever on earth, only a short while here."*

Antelope's voice, so like Kwani's, soared with the sweet song of the flute. She smiled as she sang; she loved singing.

> *"My melodies shall not die, nor my songs perish.*
> *They spread, they scatter."*

Chomoc continued to play. The flute told of mysteries, of wonders to be discovered, of magical lands far away. No one but Kwani visualized the sacred temple on the mesa, the House of the Sun. Only Kwani saw the Place of Remembering and the altar stone, waiting.

She told no one of her decision to return.

She would bide her time.

Winter closed in. Sunfather walked his sky path from his house in the east to his house in the west and descended to the underworld to travel again to his eastern home. Earthmother slept under her white blanket. Days passed.

For Kwani it was a time of waiting for winter to end and first flowers to bloom; only then could the journey be made across rugged mountains and vast, rocky canyons to the House of the Sun. Kwani knew she could not walk that distance again; she would have to be carried. But that did not matter. A way would be found.

Winter was when Cicuye's most sacred and demanding ceremonies took place: Wuwuchim, Soyal, and Powamu. Wuwuchim celebrated man's emergence from the underworld. For sixteen days intricate rituals in procedure, dance, and prayer would supplicate for germination of all forms of life on earth. Wuwuchim, meticulously observed, assured rebirth.

Soyal was when Sunfather reached his southernmost place in the sky at the time of winter solstice. For many days the Sun Chief would watch Sunfather's progress to the point at the mountain's rim beyond which he could not go or the earth would be doomed forever to winter. When that point was reached, Soyal would begin. Twenty days of complex ceremonies with prayers, sacrifices, and secret rituals were required for the Sun Chief to turn Sunfather back to his northern home, bringing ever-lengthening days of light, warmth, and life for all living things.

One moon later was Powamu, a sixteen-day ceremony celebrating the Planting of the Beans and the final phase of creation. During the first four days, men chosen by Acoya would each be given a prayer stick—a paho—with instructions to gather soil from a sacred spot, plant the paho with prayers that beans planted in that soil would grow quickly and well as an omen of an abundant harvest. After gathering the soil, the men would return to their kivas and plant the beans in earthen pots and trays.

Day and night fires in the fire pits would be stoked, and the beans carefully watered, ritually smoked over, and sprinkled with sacred meal. On the eighth day young plants would appear—a green-leafed miracle in the dead of winter, symbolizing the plants bestowed to mankind at the time of Creation. As the many bean plants sprouted, Powamu dancers wearing squash-blossom flowers made of corn husks would visit the kivas, dancing to help the bean plants to grow.

For twelve more days the ceremonies would continue, during which young boys would be initiated into the Powamu Society and learn from Acoya the Creation mysteries.

During the time of these three all-important ceremonies, Kwani saw Acoya seldom, but his influence was profound. Never before had the people of Cicuye been as confident that the gods were pleased and all was well and would continue to be so. The aged Medicine Chief hobbled painfully about, peered with his one fading eye at all he met, remarked joyfully on Acoya's achievements, and modestly accepted the praises due him for training his successor well.

For Kwani, the ceremonies passed as in a dream. When days came and were gone, while Moonwoman appeared in all her changing forms and constellations circled in splendor, Kwani waited for spring.

It came at last with thunderous announcement. Wind Old Woman beat against the walls, snows melted, and the river ran wildly, clawing the banks. Rain gushed from roofs, splashed on the walkways, inched at doorways, and flooded the courtyard. The hatchway covers of the kivas were soaked, and rain dripped down to the inside to be caught in a bowl and saved for ceremonial corn planting, a gift from the gods. Much rain meant good crops this year!

Rain stopped, clouds ran with the wind, and Sunfather appeared. Kwani stood on the walkway outside her door and looked up at the washed sky. Soon snow would be gone from the passes and first flowers would bloom. She hugged herself in exultation.

Tonight, after the evening meal, she would announce her plans.

The day passed quickly. Families responsible for irrigation ditches worked busily on repairs. Women swept their dwellings, draped sleeping mats on walkway rails to sun, and gathered in groups to speak of new pots and jars and mugs to be made and whitewashing of walls to be done. There was speculation about which girls would mate with which young men.

"They all want Fox Tail," one said.

"I don't know. Teal Duck—"

"Gray Hawk will make the best babies. I took my night jar to empty and saw him urinating in the trash pile." She rolled her eyes. "Such a baby-maker he has!"

They giggled like girls.

"When our mates go to their farming plots, perhaps we might invite him for piki."

"More babies you want?"

"No. Only the baby-maker."

"Ha!"

"Look. There goes Kwani."

"To the ridge again. She likes to sit where those boulders are. She goes there often."

"I wonder why?"

"She is the senior yaya. Maybe she likes to think about when she was young."

There was silence as they watched Kwani make her way slowly through the courtyard greeted by exuberant children and yapping dogs. People called to her from rooftops and walkways and she answered, smiling and waving.

"She does not seem old."

"I know. Look how she carries herself. Like a Chief."

"Like She Who Remembers."

"Aye."

Kwani climbed the ladder to the passageway leading to the ridge behind the city. Another ladder took her down to the rocky ridge still damp from the rain. She walked slowly, acutely conscious of protests in the bones and meagerness of breath as she climbed to where the small boulders sat among the bushes.

The stone was warm from the sun and felt good as she sat on it. She gazed across the valley and to the mountains beyond, and as always, her spirit flew free. Mountaintops still wore winter robes and their whiteness slashed into vivid blue of the sky. From all around came the fragrance of Earthmother's breath as she prepared to give birth.

Soon, first flowers would bloom.

Exultation filled Kwani again. "I shall tell them tonight," she said aloud.

For a long time Kwani sat there, remembering Tolonqua.

The evening meal was not yet over when Chomoc said, "I have news."

"And I," Antelope added.

"Then tell us!"

"When I was at the Great River of the South I spoke with an Elder who has seen the great city of the east where Kokopelli is said to have gone. He told me of the riches there, of the dwellings on hills, mountains they make themselves."

"And they ride on the river!" Antelope added. "They sit in long—" She paused. "I forget the name."

"Boats."

"And push themselves through the water with poles wide at one end—"

"Yes. Many people come from distant places, riding on the river. They bring wonderful things, riches—"

"Chomoc is going there and I am going with him." Her face was pink and her black eyes sparkled.

Kwani interrupted a babble of talk. "You cannot go," she said calmly.

Chomoc lifted his chin with an arrogant glance. "Indeed she can."

Yatosha said, "You are She Who Remembers, Antelope. Consider that."

"I do. My mother will be She—"

"I will not," Kwani said firmly. "Because I shall not be here. I wish to return to the House of the Sun."

There was stunned silence.

Acoya looked at Kwani and she felt the penetration of his wise and compassionate glance. "Tell us why."

"Because the Ancients call me to come. There is something they wish to tell me there—"

"But you cannot!" Antelope cried. "You are too old, Mother. It is far!"

"And dangerous," Yatosha said. He came to sit beside her and take her hand. "Have you forgotten—"

"I shall go. Because you will take me."

"No! You cannot walk so far!" Antelope said.

"Of course not. I shall be carried. On a litter."

Again there was silence.

Antelope stared grimly at Kwani. "Who will carry you? Chomoc cannot; he takes me to the great city of the east."

Blue eyes met black ones in a steady gaze. "Chomoc is a trader; his duties do not tie him here. I am She Who Remembers no longer; my responsibilities are now yours. You must stay."

"I will go."

Tension filled the room like black smoke.

Acoya gazed at Antelope. "My city needs one who is She Who Remembers. Can you not train a successor before you go?"

"I leave with the next moon," Chomoc said.

"And I go with him. The girls will wait for my return. I shall teach them then. Better than before."

"You will not return," Kwani said quietly.

Antelope paled. "Why not?"

"You will not want to." Kwani stared into the distance. "It is a different world there. I see—" She stopped. "You will not return."

"But I will. There is something you do not know." Antelope met Kwani's questioning gaze triumphantly. "I am pregnant!"

"Ah!" Kwani's face glowed. "Then you will stay until after the child is born."

"No. I shall go with Chomoc. We will return with the seventh moon."

Kwani leaned forward. "You cannot go on a long journey through unknown lands with a child growing within you."

"You did."

"I was forced to. Driven away. You are loved, respected, needed here—"

"I shall return, Mother. Chomoc will give our son his birthing ceremony here in Cicuye."

Kwani gazed at Antelope in silence. Again she looked away into the distance, as if seeing the unseen. Finally, she said, "It is a girl. And she will be born far away from home. I shall never see her, never hold her—" Kwani's voice broke.

Yatosha said, "You know this?"

"Yes."

"Then you still have your powers. There is no need to—"

"The Ancients call me. I must go."

"And I must go. At the next moon when snows are gone," Chomoc said. "And I assure you we shall return. Our child, my son, will be born here. I have promised. That promise I shall keep."

Antelope looked at her mother. She said faintly, "You are sure it is a girl?"

"Yes."

"I felt it was, but I want—Chomoc wants—a boy and I thought if I wanted it enough, and prayed enough—"

Mother and daughter gazed at each other with unspoken understanding.

Chomoc shook his head. "How do you know it is a girl?"

Kwani and Antelope looked at him without reply, for none was necessary. Chomoc knew; he did not want to accept it.

Acoya put his head in his hands. "I do not want either of you to go. I need you. Cicuye needs you. Stay."

Antelope shook her head. "I cannot stay. Something in me calls to follow the trails, to see beyond the mountain and the next, to learn, experience, discover—"

"The man twin," Kwani said.

"Whatever it is, I shall go. Acoya thinks he needs me here, but he does not. All is well here, better than ever before. Cicuye can do very well without me until I return."

Yatosha said to Chomoc, "Your mate, and mine, are not like other women. They will go where their spirits call."

"Yes," Antelope said. She turned to Kwani. "Who will carry you?"

"I will," Yatosha said.

"But—"

"Yes, I am old. But I shall take her. Fox Tail, Teal Duck, and Gray Hawk will go with us."

"You have asked them?"

"No. They are Anasazi. They will want to see the cave cities and the House of the Sun."

"As I want to see where Kokopelli went," Chomoc said.

They glanced at one another and sat in silence.

A decision had been made that would change the lives of all of them forever.

▲ 68 ▼

Cicuye was agog with the news. Both Kwani and Antelope were leaving on long journeys! With the next moon! And in opposite directions!

Heads wagged and dire predictions were whispered. It was unheard of. Unnatural. Dangerous, suspicious, unseemly. For She Who Remembers to desert her people, even temporarily, was unthinkable, and for Kwani to undertake such a journey—at her age!—was impossible to believe. Furthermore, Yatosha, Teal Duck, Fox Tail, and Gray Hawk as well as Chomoc would be gone during the planting season when they were needed most.

There were mutterings.

"Why does not Acoya forbid them to go?"

"Kwani and Antelope do as they please. Where is their respect for our city and Medicine Chief, I ask you?"

"Maybe he knows something we do not. Maybe he thinks they should go."

"Why?"

"Who knows?"

One morning when Kwani was bent at the metate, Yatosha entered, smiling.

"It is here."

He extended his palm upon which was a rosy pink mallow, the first flower. A bit of sunset in his hand.

Kwani took the flower and held it to her nose, savoring the freshness. She looked up into Yatosha's weathered, wrinkled face. "Thank you!"

Now it was truly spring.

Birds who brought summer began to arrive, a few at a time, and the air was alive with their chattering and songs. Kwani and Antelope and the men busied themselves with preparation for departure. Travois were made, dogs selected; food, clothing, and other supplies were assembled and packed in readiness for the next moon.

As time drew near for Kwani to leave, she struggled with

mixed feelings. She longed to be at the House of the Sun but it was heartbreaking to leave her children, her home, Tolonqua's city. Here she was protected, revered, with cherished possessions to comfort her, and friends to attend to all her needs. The journey would be long and dangerous for Yatosha and the others as well as for herself. Was she doing the right thing?

Could she make the long journey back?

Teal Duck, Fox Tail, and Gray Hawk were eager to go, much to the displeasure of their new mates who insisted they should stay for the planting. But the men expected good trading on the way and the women were promised treasures. Yatosha did not mention the vast, empty canyons where no people lived, or the meager villages they would encounter.

He, too, had mixed feelings. He wanted to fulfill Kwani's heart's desire, but how could he face his past in the Place of the Eagle Clan? Could he bear to see again Tiopi's red handprints over their door, one for each moon until Kokopelli's son was born? Could he bear to remember?

For Antelope there was nothing but excited anticipation. She rejoiced at the prospect of adventure, discovery, and acquisition of new riches. The fact that the gods had listened to Chomoc's prayer for a child—the prayer carried by the eagle sent home—was proof the Above Beings were pleased and all was well. She would return with many wonderful tales to tell around the evening fire, many fine things to display! And a baby to be born. Happiness shone from her like an inner light glowing.

At last, Moonwoman was round and full. It was time.

The evening fire was over, good-byes and well wishes were spoken, tears shed. The men were in the kiva beseeching the gods for a safe journey. Now Kwani and Antelope sat alone in their dwelling, wanting to say much to each other, but their hearts were too full to speak.

Coals in the fire pit smoldered dimly and shadows grew closer, enfolding mother and daughter as if in final embrace. Finally, Antelope said, "I shall name her Kwani."

"I shall be her guardian."

They looked at each other.

Kwani said, "I remember the words of the Old One at the House of the Sun. She told me that we who are She Who Remembers are not of one clan, one people, but of all womankind. You shall be needed wherever you go." She paused and continued, her voice trembling. "I shall be with you."

"And I with you."

Antelope removed her necklace and held it in her hands a moment, fingering the smooth stone beads of bright colors. She untied the fastening cord and slid off four beads. "These are for you. To keep us together when we are apart."

Kwani cupped the beads in her hand. She looked at her daughter, her twin child, thanking her without words.

Antelope rose and went to the shelf where a reed basket held a supply of twine. She removed a short length and brought it to Kwani.

"Now you shall have a necklace, also."

Kwani strung the four beads on the twine, tied it, and looped it over her head. The beads lay where the scallop shell had been, belonging there.

Kwani pressed the beads to her, smiling at Antelope through tears. "Until we meet again."

"Yes." Antelope enfolded Kwani in her arms and they clung to each other.

Each knew they would never see the other again.

▲ 69 ▼

Kwani lay awake in the tipi listening to Yatosha's rhythmic breathing; they had traveled swiftly for many days and he was tired. Fox Tail, Gray Hawk, and Teal Duck, half his age, eagerly devoured distance and gave little thought to the rigors of a fast pace. They hungered for the next place, the next village. The trading was meager but the thrill of adventure sped them on.

If Yatosha doesn't tell them to slow down, I will, Kwani thought.

She lay sleepless beside Yatosha in the darkness. The three young men slept in another tipi, and the two dogs, who hauled the tipis on their travois, were tethered nearby. From time to time the dogs roused themselves and listened to the sounds of the night, alert to the strangeness of the canyon. Not far away, a wolf howled, another answered, and the dogs stirred restlessly.

Kwani thought of Antelope and Chomoc. Where were they now? They had departed in a flurry of excited farewells with dogs and a small party of warriors thirsting for adventure, but Kwani knew the trepidation her daughter hid in her heart. Antelope was torn between eagerness for discovery and concern for the safety of the child within her.

As I was.

Time is a great circle. . . .

Kwani touched the necklace of four beads. No scallop shell was there but each bead was infused with the necklace's essence. Kwani felt close to her twin child.

She thought of Acoya when he came to say good-bye. It was a solemn, important occasion so he wore the robe of the White Buffalo. As he stood before her in their dwelling with the robe around him, Kwani remembered the boy in the kiva who assumed Tolonqua's responsibilities as the robe enveloped him. When Acoya took her in his arms one last time, Kwani felt for a moment Tolonqua's embrace.

"My spirit will be with you at the House of the Sun," Acoya said, and Kwani knew it would be so.

Now, as she lay awake and sleepless, Kwani remembered the words of the Old One. *"You have learned much, but one secret remains. Come."*

"I am coming," she whispered. But the journey was difficult. Many winters had passed since she had come this way with Kokopelli. The vast canyon, with its soaring, rocky spires and forbidding emptiness, was unchanged—swept by sudden storms, gouged by flash floods, seared with heat and cold, and haunted by strange spirits.

Kwani huddled closer to Yatosha and drifted into sleep, dreaming strange dreams she could not remember afterward.

Days passed, more and more. Kwani lay on the litter with Yatosha walking beside her, Gray Hawk at her head and Fox Tail at her feet. Teal Duck walked beside Yatosha. All carried heavy packs and were armed. Trotting with them were the dogs and their travois. After weeks of traveling, her body felt molded to the litter, absorbing every jolt as if the rough poles were her own bones already dry and bleached white. As if Sipapu had called and she was now a skeleton at one with the wild mesa.

Occasionally they saw distant hunting parties out for jackrabbits and antelope. One day they encountered such a party at a meager water hole. There were five men with lances, arrows, and rabbit sticks. They saw Kwani and the men approaching and rose to face them, bows in hand.

Yatosha said, "They are Querechos. I know their people and I speak their tongue. I will talk. Hold the dogs."

Gray Hawk and Fox Tail placed the litter on the ground and Kwani sat up to watch. These were the fearsome Querechos she remembered; her heart thumped. They were short, dark, and powerfully built, with long hair on one side of the head and short hair on the other. The long hair was looped and tied with colored cords; many ear ornaments covered the ear exposed, and bone and claw necklaces lay upon naked chests. They regarded Kwani and the others with dark, expressionless faces.

Yatosha laid down his pack and weapons and made the sign for "friend." Fox Tail, Teal Duck, and Gray Hawk held bows in hand as Yatosha approached the group. He spoke in Querecho so Kwani did not understand the words, but she saw their effect. The Querechos jabbered at one another and at Yatosha who replied calmly. Finally, he returned.

"They know of She Who Remembers and want to see her blue eyes to be certain it is she before they allow us in their hunting territory." He held out a hand to Kwani. "Come."

Kwani rose. She swallowed her unease and followed Yatosha to the water hole where the men stood in stoic silence, watching. Yatosha signed so Kwani would know what he said.

"This is my mate, She Who Remembers, who journeys to the House of the Sun on a spiritual quest."

Kwani stood regally, returning the men's dark gazes with a face as expressionless as their own.

The Querechos glanced at one another. One spoke to Yatosha who took Kwani's arm. "They say we may go but we cannot hunt."

The Querechos left, looking back at Kwani over their shoulders. Kwani's unease increased at the veiled hostility in those dark faces.

She had lived long, endured much, come far. Would these barbarians cut her down before she learned the Old One's last secret?

No! She pressed the four beads tightly to her, willing herself to survive until she was once again at the altar in the House of the Sun. She commanded her spirit to find the Old One.

"I come," she said. "Wait for me."

There was no reply, but Kwani knew the Old One listened.

Yatosha and the young men filled their buffalo-skin water bags while the dogs drank deeply. Kwani returned to the litter and soon they were on their way. She lay on her back, watching the ever-changing sky with its billowing clouds and hawks soaring. It seemed to her as they made this journey to the House of the Sun that she was also making a journey back in time to be again as she was when Kokopelli took her to the Place of the Eagle Clan, the stone city high in the cliff. She felt enveloped in unreality as if in a dream.

As days and nights followed one another, as storms brought rain in the mountains and flash floods in the canyon, to Kwani it was a vision of the past. She huddled in the tipi, sometimes with Yatosha to comfort her, sometimes alone. Always in the back of her mind were the words of the Old One. *"One secret remains."*

When it seemed that the journey would never end and

that Sipapu would call before she saw once more the great temple on the mesa, there it was! The House of the Sun stood in majesty facing the Place of the Eagle Clan across the ravine.

"We are here!" Yatosha cried. "Look, Kwani!"

Kwani tried to rise from the litter, but the journey had stolen her strength and she could not until Yatosha took her hands and pulled her to her feet.

The sharp light of midafternoon made the stone walls gleam. The temple had no roof so that Sunfather's holy eye would sanctify each room. It was totally silent but for wind in the grasses. Kwani gazed, her heart overflowing. She was here. At last. Where her spirit longed to be.

Yatosha and the other men stood gazing across the ravine at the Place of the Eagle Clan. Walls had crumbled and windows stared with empty eyes. It was silent. No voices, no flute, no thunder drum. Nothing.

The entire area was deserted.

Kwani saw only the House of the Sun. She tried to climb the rocky rise where the temple stood, but could not. "Carry me there."

Teal Duck cast a quick glance at Yatosha who had grown thin with exertion of the journey and was pale with exhaustion. "I shall be honored to carry her, with your permission."

Yatosha nodded, and Teal Duck scooped Kwani in his long arms deeply bronzed by weeks of sun. "Tell me where to go."

Kwani pointed, and the others followed with the dogs as Teal Duck carried her.

She shook her head. "No. Only Yatosha."

Fox Tail and Gray Hawk held the dogs as Kwani was carried to the House of the Sun. When they reached the courtyard entrance, Kwani said, "I thank you. Please put me down now, and return to the others. Only Yatosha is to be with me."

Teal Duck glanced at Yatosha, who nodded. He set Kwani on her feet and backed away, his face solemn.

As Kwani entered the courtyard, she sensed a spirit presence. She touched the four beads at her breast. "I am here," she whispered. She turned to Yatosha. "Now I must enter the Place of Remembering alone. Will you wait for me here?"

"Aye." He sat and slumped wearily against a wall. "I shall wait."

Kwani crossed the courtyard to the room facing east. She stood in the doorway looking at the knee-high altar stone at the back of the room. Wind Old Woman had blown leaves upon it and upon the floor. Dust, turned to mud by rains, had dried and caked; it lay thickly everywhere. Leaves rustled as Wind Old Woman stirred them with her breath; a field mouse scurried among them.

An unseen Presence was there.

"I greet you, Sacred One," Kwani whispered.

"Enter," a silent voice said.

Kwani approached the altar stone. She brushed the leaves and dust from the altar, knelt before it, and laid both arms across its smooth top. She pressed her cheek against the stone warmed by Sunfather's holy eye.

"I have come."

There was no response. With all her strength, Kwani sought to absorb the stone's mystical power, to feel it rising from within the depths of the stone to enter her.

She did not know how long she knelt there. Overhead, a bird flew by, calling, and a cloud covered Sunfather's face.

"Speak to me!" Kwani whispered.

The cloud passed, and again Sunfather's radiance embraced her. Slowly, like water rising from the depths of a sacred pool, Kwani felt the stone's power flowing into her. It seemed suddenly that Acoya and Antelope knelt beside her, and Tolonqua put both arms around her, and the Old One spoke.

"You have come to learn the secret. Behold!"

Kwani stood alone on the mesa. There was a sound like water pounding the banks in floodtime and great animals appeared, running wildly across the mesa, long tails streaming behind them. Some beasts were white, some black, some spotted, others brown. All had flowing hair along the top of their necks; the hair rippled in the wind as they ran.

Kwani gasped. A god rode the back of each animal! Glittering garments clothed the gods from head to foot. Beneath the covering on their heads, dark, bushy hair concealed their faces from nose to neck. Mouths opened, shouting fiercely in a foreign tongue.

The vision faded and Kwani knelt alone at the altar, trembling.

The voice of the Old One spoke again. "They will come. Terrible beings from across the Sunrise Sea. Our people will suffer, become slaves, die."

"No!" Kwani cried.

"But one man will save us. One whose ancestor you are. He alone will unite us and drive the foreigners from our homeland. The blood of She Who Remembers will be renowned forever. . . ."

The voice faded and was gone.

"Stay with me!" Kwani cried.

But all was still.

As Kwani knelt at the altar stone she felt power leaving it like water receding from a spring. She was alone in an empty room with leaves whispering.

A terrible loneliness flooded her. She had come far, endured much. She belonged with the Ancient Ones now.

Kwani pressed the four beads to her.

"Come to me!" she cried, her voice pierced with longing. "Come, I plead! Take me with you!"

They came. Like a soft breeze, like the first spring rain, like autumn leaves falling, they came.

Yatosha stirred, and woke. He had slept. For how long? He stood and looked about. Where was Kwani? He stepped outside the courtyard, searching. The three young men and the dogs still waited; they saw him and called impatiently.

He shook his head. Kwani must still be inside the Place of Remembering. He glanced at the sun; the hour was late. Unease poked a cold finger at his heart.

Something has happened to Kwani.

He tiptoed to the Place of Remembering and looked in the door. Kwani lay motionless among the leaves at the base of the altar stone.

With a cry, Yatosha ran to her. He knelt beside her, cradling her head in his arms. Her face was serene and she seemed, somehow, to be young again.

"Kwani!" he cried brokenly, rocking back and forth. "Kwani!"

After a time, he laid her back down among the leaves. He strode outside and called the men. They tethered the dogs to nearby trees and approached uneasily; Yatosha motioned them inside.

They stood in the doorway of the Place of Remembering, staring in awe at the figure lying motionless beside an altar stone. She lay curled like a child in sleep, one hand upon the necklace of four beads. Her long hair, still dark and lustrous, shone among leaves that whispered as Wind Old Woman lingered, and passed. To the men who stood gazing, it seemed the quiet figure was surrounded with an unseen aura, a mystical power that filled the room with her presence.

When Yatosha could speak, he said, "We shall bury her there, beside the stone."

"Aye."

Gently, they lifted the fragile body and laid it aside. They brushed the leaves away and removed the paving stones, one by one. When Earthmother's body lay exposed, digging sticks made a place for Kwani at the base of the altar stone.

Yatosha knelt beside her grave, singing the only Burial Song he knew.

> *"You who dwell in Sipapu,*
> *Receive this spirit.*
> *You who dwell above the Turquoise Mountain,*
> *Receive this spirit.*
> *You, Holy Beings,*
> *Accept this spirit,*
> *Receive it in your sacred place. . . ."*

His voice broke and he could sing no more.

Slowly, gently, they lowered Kwani into Earthmother's arms, hands crossed upon her breast where the necklace lay.

It seemed to Yatosha that Kwani smiled as Earthmother embraced her.

▲ Epilogue ▼

Moonwoman waxed and waned before Yatosha and the others reached home. Yatosha had to force himself to leave the House of the Sun where Kwani lay entombed. Grief aged him more; there were shocked whispers when the people of Cicuye first saw him.

When they learned of Kwani's death, the city echoed with heartbroken cries and ashes covered heads in mourning.

Acoya isolated himself in his medicine lodge for four days. When at last he emerged, anguish seamed his face but his voice was serene.

"She Who Remembers is at peace. She asks that we grieve no more."

But the heart holds its secret sorrow.

Two moon's journey toward the rising sun, in what would one day be known as eastern Oklahoma on the Arkansas border, a great ceremonial center rose in splendor. Manmade mountains thrust high surrounding a great plaza. Upon such a mountain the *caddí*, a ruler known as the Great Sun, stood upon the terrace of his royal dwelling and gazed into the distance.

He frowned. Runners had brought word of an approaching party. This was not unusual; the city was a great trading center as well as a ceremonial complex. But these who came were not the usual traders. One was said to be son of Kokopelli! Others whispered that he was Kokopelli reincarnated! With him was a woman, a beautiful woman who claimed to be daughter of She Who Remembers! *It was said she had dangerous powers*.

A scowl creased the Great Sun's tattooed brow. He gestured, and a slave immediately knelt before him, face down and hands extended.

"Summon the priests."

He watched the slave run down the stairway embedded in the mountain's sloping flank; then the Great Sun climbed more stairs above his dwelling to where the temple stood atop the mountain. He entered the sacred place and faced the hallowed bones of those who had been Great Suns before him.

"Those come who will challenge us," he said.

He knew in his innermost being that nothing would be as it had been. These newcomers would change his world.

Forever.

Chomoc and Antelope and their party paused to gaze in wonder at the vast city spreading before them with mounds and mountains, and a great throng of busy people in odd garments. Strange scents and sounds drifted with many plumes of smoke from cooking fires.

Antelope swallowed with excitement. A great, wonderful city! New people, new discoveries! She removed the cradle board from her back and held the tiny baby in her arms—her blue-eyed daughter born a moon ago.

"See your new home!" she crooned. She touched the scallop shell of her necklace and spoke to Those Gone Before. "Thank you for a safe journey!" She began a wordless song of joy, gazing at the city and all it promised. Dreams come true! She pressed the necklace to her, singing her gratitude.

Chomoc smiled and raised his flute, fingers dancing. Melody announced their coming as they approached the city and the magical future awaiting them.

Time turns with the constellations. Neither Antelope nor Chomoc could know that one day Kwani's vision would come true. Strange men on terrible beings would, indeed, bring disaster. But Kwani's descendent—and Antelope's—would defeat them, save his people, and become renowned forever.

History would know him as Popé.

Time is a great circle;
there is no beginning, no end.
All returns again and again
forever.

▲ Bibliography ▼

Ambler, J. Richard. *The Anasazi*. Flagstaff, Ariz.: Museum of Northern Arizona, 1977.

Ambler, J. Richard, and Mark O. Sutton. "The Anasazi Abandonment of the San Juan Drainage and the Numic Expansion." *North American Archaeologist*, Vol. 10(1), 1989, pp. 39–53.

Bahti, Tom. *Southwestern Indian Ceremonials*. Las Vegas: KC Publications, 1979.

Bandelier, Adolph F. *Papers of the Archaeological Institute of America*. American Series III, Part I. Cambridge, Eng.: John Wilson and Son, University Press, 1890.

Brandt, Rich B. *Hopi Ethics*. Chicago: University of Chicago Press, 1954.

Catlin, George. *North American Indians*, Vol. II. London: David Bogue, 1844.

Courlander, Harold. *Hopi Voices*. Albuquerque: University of New Mexico Press, 1982.

Cronyn, George W., ed. *American Indian Poetry*. New York: Ballantine Books, Inc., 1972.

Cushing, Frank Hamilton. *Zuñi*. Lincoln: University of Nebraska Press, 1979.

Dennis, Wayne. *The Hopi Child*. New York: D. Appleton-Century Co. for the University of Virginia Institute for Research in the Social Sciences, 1940.

Densmore, Frances. *How Indians Use Wild Plants for Food, Medicine, and Crafts*. New York: Dover Publications, 1974.

Dozier, Edward P. *The Pueblo Indians of North America*. New York: Holt, Rinehart and Winston, Inc., 1970.

Eddy, Frank W. *Metates and Manos*. Popular Series Pamphlet No. 1. Santa Fe: Museum of New Mexico Press, 1964.

Erdoes, Richard, and Alfonso Ortiz. *American Indian Myths and Legends*. New York: Pantheon Books, 1984.

Grinnell, George Bird. *Pawnee, Blackfoot and Cheyenne.* New York: Charles Scribner's Sons, 1961.

Hayes, Joe. *Coyote.* Santa Fe: Mariposa Publishing, 1983.

Hewett, Edgar L., and Bertha P. Dutton. *The Pueblo Indian World.* Albuquerque: University of New Mexico and the School of American Research, 1945.

Hultkrantz, Ake. *Religion of the American Indians.* Berkeley: University of California Press, 1979.

Hyde, George E. *The Pawnee Indians.* Norman: University of Oklahoma Press, 1974.

Jackson, Donald, ed. *Letters of the Lewis and Clark Expedition,* 2d ed. Champaign: University of Illinois Press, 1978.

Josephy, Alvin M., Jr. *The Indian Heritage of America.* New York: Alfred A. Knopf, 1971.

Kidder, Alfred Vincent. *An Introduction to the Study of Southwestern Archaeology.* New Haven: Yale University Press, 1962.

Kidder, Alfred Vincent. *Pecos, New Mexico: Archaeological Notes.* Papers of the Robert S. Peabody Foundation for Archaeology. Andover, Mass.: Phillips Academy, 1958.

Kidder, Alfred Vincent. *The Story of the Pueblo of Pecos.* Papers of the School of American Research, No. 44, 1951.

Krupp, E. C. *Echoes of the Ancient Skies: The Astronomy of Lost Civilizations.* New York: Harper and Row, 1983.

Lowie, Robert H. *Indians of the Plains.* New York: Published for the American Museum of Natural History by McGraw-Hill Book Company, Inc., 1954.

Lummis, Charles F. *The Land of Poco Tiempo.* New York: Charles Scribner's Sons, 1928.

Lummis, Charles F. *Pueblo Indian Folk Stories.* New York: The Century Company, 1910.

McHugh, Tom. *The Time of the Buffalo.* Lincoln: University of Nebraska Press, 1972.

Mails, Thomas E. *The Mystic Warriors of the Plains.* New York: Doubleday and Company, 1972.

Mails, Thomas E. *Secret Native American Pathways.* Tulsa, Okla.: Council Oak Books, 1988.

Marriott, Alice. *The Ten Grandmothers.* Norman: University of Oklahoma Press, 1945.

Maxwell, James A., ed. *America's Fascinating Indian Heritage.* Pleasantville, N.Y.: The Reader's Digest Association, Inc., 1978.

Moorehead, Warren King. *Archaeology of the Arkansas*

River Valley. New Haven: Published for the Department of Archaeology by Yale University Press, 1931.

Mora, Joseph. *Year of the Hopi*. New York: Rizzoli, with the Smithsonian Institution, 1979.

National Geographic Society. *The World of the American Indian*. Washington, D.C.: 1974.

Newcomb, W. W., Jr. *The Indians of Texas*. Austin: University of Texas Press, 1961.

Noble, David Grant. *Ancient Ruins of the Southwest*. Flagstaff, Ariz.: Northland Press, 1981.

Ortiz, Alfonso. *Handbook of North American Indians*, Vol. 5. Washington, D.C.: Smithsonian Institution, 1979.

Reichard, Gladys A. *Navaho Religion: A Study of Symbolism*. New York: Pantheon Books, 1963.

Sando, Joe S. *The Pueblo Indians*. San Francisco: The Indian Historian Press, 1976.

Scully, Vincent. *Pueblo Mountain, Village, Dance*. New York: Viking, 1972.

Silverberg, Robert. *Mound Builders of Ancient America*. New York: New York Graphic Society, Ltd., 1968.

Simmons, Leo W., ed. *Sun Chief*. New Haven: Yale University Press, 1942.

Southwest Parks and Monuments Association. *Pecos, Gateway to Pueblos and Plains*. Tucson: 1988.

Spielmann, Katherine Ann. "Inter-Societal Food Acquisition Among Egalitarian Societies: an Ecological Study of the Plains/Pueblo Interaction in the American Southwest." A dissertation for degree of Doctor of Philosophy in Anthropology, University of Michigan, 1982.

Stuart, Gene S. *America's Ancient Cities*. Washington, D.C.: National Geographic Society, 1988.

Studer, Floyd V. "Archaeology of the Texan Panhandle." *Panhandle-Plains Historical Review*, Vol. 28, 1955.

Tanner, Clara Lee. *Prehistoric Southwestern Craft Arts*. Tucson: University of Arizona Press, 1976.

Terrell, John Upton. *American Indian Almanac*. New York: World Publishing Co., 1971.

Tyler, Hamilton A. *Pueblo Animals and Myths*. Norman: University of Oklahoma Press, 1975.

Tyler, Hamilton A. *Pueblo Birds and Myths*. Norman: University of Oklahoma Press, 1979.

Tyler, Hamilton A. *Pueblo Gods and Myths*. Norman: University of Oklahoma Press, 1964.

Underhill, Ruth. *Workaday Life of the Pueblos: Indian Life and Customs.* Washington, D.C.: U.S. Department of the Interior, Bureau of Indian Affairs, 1954.

Waldo, Anna Lee. *Sacajawea.* New York: Avon Books, 1978.

Waters, Frank. *The Book of the Hopi.* New York: Penguin Books, 1963.